THE
EMPTY
SHIELD

First published in 2020
by Eyewear Publishing Ltd
Suite 333, 19-21 Crawford Street
London, WIH IPJ
United Kingdom

Cover design and typeset by Edwin Smet
Printed in England by TJ International Ltd, Padstow, Cornwall

Seth Benardete, excerpts from 'Two Notes on Aeschylus' Septem' from *Sacred Transgressions: A Reading of Sophocles' Antigone*. Originally published in *Wiener Studien* 80 (1967) and 81 (1968). Reprinted with the permission of St. Augustine's Press.

Eihei Dogen, excerpts from *Moon in a Dewdrop: Writings of Master Dogen,* edited by Kazuaki Tanahashi. Copyright © 1985 by the San Francisco Zen Center. Reprinted by permission of North Point Press, a division of Farrar, Straus & Giroux, LLC.

Douglas Linder, excerpts from 'An Introduction to the My Lai Courts-Martial' (1999). Reprinted with the permission of the author.

Ezra Pound, excerpts from Canto I and Canto CXIII from *The Cantos*. Copyright 1934, © 1969 by Ezra Pound. Excerpts from 'Homage to Sextus Propertius' from *Selected Poems of Ezra Pound*. Copyright 1926 by Ezra Pound. Reprinted by permission of Faber & Faber, Ltd. and New Directions Publishing Corp.

From *Zen Mind, Beginner's Mind,* by Shunryu Suzuki. Protected under the terms of the International Copyright Union. Reprinted by arrangement with The Permissions Company, LLC, on behalf of Shambhala Publications Inc., Boulder, Colorado, www.shambhala.com.

We have made every effort to contact The Fugs to obtain permission for the use of copyright material. To no avail. In any event, the author wishes to thank Edward Sanders and the late Tuli Kupferberg, who is at the heart and soul of this book.

ISBN 978-1-912477-92-0

WWW.EYEWEARPUBLISHING.COM

THE EMPTY SHIELD

A DECISION

POLITICAL AUTOBIOGRAPHY

GIACOMO DONIS

 **EYEWEAR** PUBLISHING

in memory of Wolfango Intelisano
6 October 1942 – 15 December 2012

friend, true brother,
genius of political art,
even dead you breathed life
into this Empty Shield

An Enemy of the People

a grilling

Friday, 13 June, 2014: I go to Milan in peace, with a light heart. Joyful.

I had written to the Consul:

Pardon me, but I would like to say this, and correct me if I'm wrong: I think that being a citizen of a free country entails being able to freely relinquish this citizenship, just as it means being able to freely leave the country. Isn't this one of the things that has always distinguished the United States as a free country from certain unfree countries around the world?

And the Section Chief, Mr. W., actually responded! and gave me the appointment for renunciation of my almost 64-year-old US citizenship that had been denied me for four months.

So here I am.

The Consulate itself is a menacing little skyscraper right in the center of Milan. US soil. A medieval fortress with a modern face. An invisible moat around it, full of piranhas, or probably worse. 2 p.m., a blazing sun, I stand outside the door with 4 or 5 other visitors. We sweat. We wait. Security. One person admitted at a time, to the first chamber.

'Take off your jacket, take off your belt, take off your shoes, NO SUNGLASSES, KEEP YOUR HANDS IN PLAIN SIGHT AT ALL TIMES'—Hey, hey, USA! And you keep asking, 'Why do they hate us?!' Second door opens. Empty chamber. Third door, opens. Long empty corridor. Elevator, goes exclusively to the

7th floor. Up I go. 7th floor: more 'security'—armed to the teeth.

Feeling a little less joyful. Tired. I get to meet Signor S.! the 'nameless' clerk ('no, I'm not allowed to tell you my name') I'd been phoning nearly once a week, whatever the day, at 2 p.m. sharp, since last March, a kind, friendly, patient man. News of my appointment? 'I'm between a rock and a hard place,' he told me one day. And yesterday at 2 p.m. *he* phoned *me!* Told me his name! Spoke Italian. (He is Italian.) Wanted to have all my papers filled out and ready for me. '*Stia tranquillo*, take it easy, you'll just be signing these papers, swearing the oath of renunciation, won't take you long at all.' Last address in the US: 1972, 137 Rivington Street, NY NY. Want my phone number too? I joked: 777-1056, it's so catchy I can't forget it. 'Where's this Rivington Street?' he asked me. Lower East Side. Puerto Rican then—violent, cheap—gentrified now. We chatted about his trip to New York, to Harlem in particular.

Now, in Milan, I see Signor S. beaming at me, a white-haired man in his (late?) fifties, from his side of the bullet-proof glass separating us—just a little hole to speak through. Without thinking, I put out my hand (IN PLAIN SIGHT) to shake hands with this kind, formerly nameless man—an awkward gesture! The security guard flinched.

Through the small slot I give Signor S. my US passport, for good, and my Italian Identity Card and name-change (James to Giacomo) document to be photocopied. I go to another hole in the glass and pay the $450 'renunciation fee.' Then I wait to meet the Consul—actually Section Chief. Sitting down, I hope. Nope. Standing in front of another hole in the glass.

'Hi, I'm Patrick.' Throws me for a loop. I don't even remember that Mr. W.'s first name is Patrick, I try to glance at the copy of his email I have, in plain sight, among the papers in my hand, to check the name. Yes, Patrick. Very friendly! Good! I see Signor S. standing, deferentially (Patrick was the only one sitting down), behind him, to his right. I say, I really want to thank you for responding to my appeal and facilitating this procedure [after 4 months of agony], and I want to thank Signor S. too, for his patience. [Sure, I'm trying to be friendly, but I'm also perfectly sincere.]

Now, Patrick says: 'This is a very very sad day for me.' [Ye gods, I wonder, what's wrong?! I hope his cat didn't die this morning.] 'This is the one part of my job that makes me feel very very sad.' [Yes, he said 'very very sad' twice in a row.] I see Signor S. stop beaming. I feel a Euripidean black cloud descending, and I'm not wrong.

'US citizenship is the most valuable thing in the world. It is the most precious thing anyone can have and there can be no good reason for giving it up. You are going to have to tell me *exactly* why you want to renounce it.' My tongue is suddenly heavy as lead. Billy Budd flashes through my mind, killing the Master-at-arms because of his 'convulsed tongue-tie.' 'Speak, man!' said Captain Vere. 'Speak! defend yourself.' But Billy could not speak—'his right arm shot out and Claggart dropped to the deck.' I tell myself: relax, there's bullet-proof glass. *Stai tranquillo.* Ride out the storm.

'Do you feel animosity towards the United States?' 'Not at all,' I say. [So much for sincerity, but I realize I'm about to be grilled like a sausage in a skillet.] 'I hope we can part as friends.' But this is not Patrick's intention. Not in the least. 'You have to tell me the *real reason* why you want to give up this citizenship.' For a long quarter of an hour he tries *relentlessly* to heat things up, and I to cool them down. Not easy! And I'm really tired now, it has already been a very long day for me, getting up early, the trip from Venice, the heat.

So, I go through the—completely sincere—reasons I'd already stated at the Venice consular office last week. Knowing all along that Patrick has read the report and is—clearly, and to my complete surprise— not happy with it in the least! In short:

9

I've been living in Italy for over 40 years; in the past 20 years I have been in the US for exactly one week; due to ill health I cannot travel at all—and certainly cannot cross oceans—not now and, in all likelihood, not ever. When I became an Italian citizen in 1999 I had no intention whatsoever of retaining my US citizenship, and the Embassy in Rome informed me of how *simple* it was to renounce it. But my mother *pleaded* with me, please, why can't you keep both citizenships?! [Other reason, *unmentionable*: my cousin's hare-brained idea that with dual citizenship 'you can get Social Security' (ha ha!) plus 'you have everything to gain and nothing to lose' (ha ha ha ha!).] But my mother has changed her mind over the years, we have talked about it a lot. About the fact that citizenship means *owing allegiance* to a country, not just having—benefitting from—its passport, and I owe all my allegiance to Italy and none at all to the United States. Which does not mean Italy is perfect or that I love every single thing it does or that happens here ——
Patrick interrupts me: 'Yes, yes, that's all fine and good, but none of this is a *reason* for renouncing US citizenship. With all the trouble you're going through, waiting so long [thanks!], coming to Milan despite your health, paying the fee—No! this is *not a reason* for renouncing your being a citizen of the United States!'
'But I've been living in Italy since I was 21, for 42 years, practically my whole adult life.'
'But you lived the first 21 years in America, what about that?!'
'Well, what about it?' I stammer. 'My allegiance is to Italy, not to America. I do not consider myself an American, I do not feel American, isn't that a reason?'
No, that's not your real reason, Patrick says.
I feel like I'm trying to break a hole in the prison wall with my bare hands.
'I also stated that I oppose dual citizenship *on principle*. For so many people—rich people especially, football players—a

passport is just a convenience, a tool, there is no *identity* involved, no political obligation whatsoever.'

Patrick liked the word 'political'—he'd been waiting for it and he pounced on it.

'OK, you left the US in 1972 and have never lived there since. Why did you leave at that time, and why didn't you ever go back?'

SirYesSir! Vietnam. Patrick knew where he wanted to get me. 'Yes, I was very strongly opposed to the Vietnam war. [but I want to avoid this! this is a consulate, not my draft board! if the US is a free country why can't I just stop being a US citizen and be the Italian citizen I am?? why do I have to submit to all this? how can I be forced to accept the premise (most precious thing anyone can have!)? why do I have to *give reasons* at all? why? I come in peace, damn you all!] [be calm! cool and calm!] Yes, very much opposed. When I finished college I decided I did not want to go on living in a country that made a war like that, and I left, and never went back.'

'So, you opposed the foreign policy, correct?' 'Yes.' [*do not say*: I opposed it then, I have opposed it from Hiroshima to Korea, to Afghanistan and Iraq, and everything in between, and everything still to come!!!] 'You were against the Vietnam war. So were a lot of other people. But they didn't renounce their citizenship [great for them!]. And that was 1972. *You are not telling me the reason why you are renouncing your citizenship right now.'*

'Speak, man!' said Captain Vere. 'Speak! defend yourself.' But Billy could not speak. 'Just ease these darbies at the wrist./ And roll me over fair./ I am sleepy, and the oozy weeds about me twist.' Ah, Billy! Ah, humanity!

'OK, opposition to US foreign policy.'

'Is that your statement? Is that what you want me to write: "opposes US foreign policy"?'

'Yes, is that OK? Not animosity towards the US. If my mother makes it to 100—she's 95—and my health miraculously improves, I can always ask you for a two-week visa as an Italian, to go to her party, can't I?'

'You can certainly ASK,' Patrick says, very clearly meaning: Ask away! You'll never get it in a million years.

I imagine all the Italians lined up outside the fortress, summer heat, winter cold, begging for visas to visit the Big Fortress. And US citizens can travel anywhere in 'Old Europe' without any visa at all. And they wonder, Why oh why do they hate us, and knock down our Towers?

Patrick looks more dissatisfied than ever—yes! he looks *very very sad*. But, OK, he's gotten as far as he can with me. He asks me if I still intend to go ahead with the renunciation. Light at the end of the tunnel. 'Yes,' I say. He says some pretty stale things about the great advantages I am giving up, and the possible grave consequences [such as? who knows!].

At last, I read out the long 'oath of renunciation'—slowly, clearly—then I sign the documents, Mr. Patrick W. signs them. *In some cases* the State Department can take a full year to approve this, he says, menacingly. A new limbo. Less than half an hour earlier Signor S. very kindly explained that State Department approval is a formality, it takes a month or two. I glance at S., he looks away, a dark cloud covering his face.

I leave, passing through the corridors and chambers of illusory emptiness leading out of this fortress. Out into the blazing sun. All this took 45 minutes.

All my life, in moments of crisis, I remember my brother, Joseph K., his Trial, and his End: *Wie ein Hund!* the knife thrust deep into his heart. Have I been *defeated* at the US Consulate in Milan, on 13 June 2014? To be born under tyranny means to die under tyranny? 'I raise my hands and spread out all my fingers.'

My *real* reason for relinquishing US citizenship—the one Patrick seemingly thirsted for so avidly? Well, I could [not!] have simply said, Patrick, *my* real reason is precisely *your* reason for asking me for it. ['Asking' is far too weak a term here, but 'waterboarding' would be an exaggeration.] Some old Pilgrim 400 years ago called America 'a City upon a Hill, the eyes of all people upon us' and you still take this dead seriously. US citizenship the most precious thing anyone can have—you are dead wrong. The US is less cruel and vicious than some other countries, in some ways, and more cruel and vicious than others, in many ways. There are plenty of good, and plenty of bad, countries to live in in this world. Freedom means recognizing the freedom of others, otherwise it is tyranny. I sincerely wanted to part as friends, and instead you ended up pronouncing me an enemy of the people.

Malcolm X took a lot of heat after the Kennedy assassination for saying: 'President Kennedy never foresaw that the chickens would come home to roost so soon.' In an interview, he made his meaning very clear: 'by "chickens coming home to roost" I meant it was the *result* of something, the *result* of a climate of hate.' Later, he explained: 'It was, as I saw it, a case of "the chickens coming home to roost." I said that the hate in white men had not stopped with the killing of defenseless black people, but that hate, allowed to spread unchecked, had finally struck down this country's Chief Magistrate.'
I oppose US foreign policy, from Hiroshima to today, and to tomorrow. I oppose its climate of hate and its claim to *moral* superiority (a.k.a. *exceptionalism*). This is what my grilling yesterday—and, alas, its future consequences—is all about.

Venice, 14 June 2014

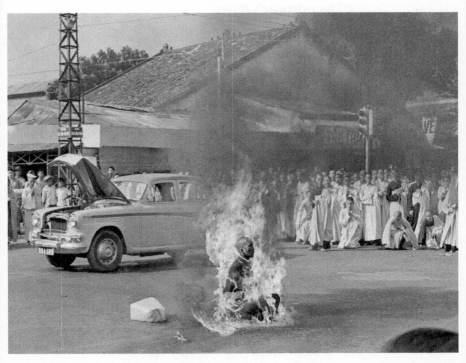

The self-immolation of Buddhist monk Thich Quang Duc, Saigon, 11 June 1963. AP photo Malcolm W. Browne.

The prisoner's deed.

With that alone we have to do.

— Herman Melville, *Billy Budd*

The Empty Shield

PROLOGUE

I just dreamed I'd never finished high school when in fact
here I am, graduating from NYU in a few months. It's the
end of March, 1972, and it's been a long winter, with lots of
snow. OK, it was nothing compared to the blizzard of '69, the
famous 'Lindsay Snowstorm,' as if Hiz Honor, John Vliet Lindsay,
had conjured it up all by himself. Our mayor has sure had a
rough time—in '68 for example, with all those strikes, real
or threatened: teachers, policemen, firemen. All the schools
closed. The garbagemen! Mountains of garbage all over the
city. The man is cursed. I mean, he was hit by a transit strike
the very day he took office. No subway, no busses for almost
two weeks, in the dead of winter, and what did he do? Why,
he walked his four miles, right on down to City Hall, cheerfully
quipping, 'I still think it's a fun city.' Fun City! The (mis)nomer
seems to have caught on. What eloquence. Like that time at a
parade when he infamously quipped, 'It's a parade. A parade is
a parade is a parade.'[1]

---

1 See the film *Loin de Vietnam* [*Far From Vietnam*], 1967. The parade in question
was a Veterans Day Parade on 29 April 1967. Lindsay was flustered by the pro-war
vehemence of the participants, screaming VICTORY! and SUPPORT OUR BOYS
IN VIETNAM! Two days later, on May 1st, on Wall Street, anti-war demonstrators
('Stop the war in Vietnam!' 'Bring the troops home!') were ferociously assaulted and
battered by the (patriotic) chant: BOMB HANOI! BOMB HANOI! BOMB HANOI!

17

But, eloquence aside, for me this winter has been small fry compared to last year. My Long Winter of 1971, from January to June. A Long March is not a stroll. I took a stand. I came to grips with my life and with the Vietnam War. I made my decision and carried it through. To an unexpected happy end. It was during my trip to Europe the previous summer that I figured my life out, made up my mind. Especially during my month in Greece—Athens, Thebes, Argos, Delphi, up to the peak of Mount Olympus. In Fascist Greece, the Greece of the Colonels. The silence. The people. The frightened forced compliance. All those jeeps rolling through the streets all the time, day and night. The 'special' police. This is what it's like to live under Tyranny. Under Fascism, in the 'Cradle of Democracy.' A great lesson for me. A political education. When I got back to New York I knew I was going to stand up to the Tyranny in my own country, as best I could, on my own, and in my own way. I'd known this all along, but now—it was now or never.

There is a long story here, but I'm going to keep it real short. Basically, it goes back to the Bay of Pigs. April 1961. JFK, the Great White Hope, in office for three months. Even a child— even the ten-year-old I was—could understand—as I did—that Batista in Cuba was the tyrant, and Castro the liberator. But the government—the President—of my country had other ideas. I still don't get it. Castro the tyrant, to be overthrown, throttled, butchered? Come on now. The defense of freedom? Something was—is—deeply wrong here. It's the world turned upside down.

Why does my country do what it does? I fear I'll be asking myself this question for as long as I live. But, last year, I gave a straight answer to the question 'What will I do?', as far as the Vietnam War is concerned. My understanding, my position, has been clear all along: we are fighting on the wrong side. I am no pacifist. In the struggle between freedom and tyranny it is fine to take sides, but in Vietnam we have been fighting on the side of tyranny. The Vietnamese people have been struggling against foreign conquest for over two thousand years. Against the Chinese in particular, then, more recently, against the French, the Japanese, the French again, and now us. Why do we fight them? Well, for more or less the same reason we fight Castro, I guess. To keep the communist hordes away from our shores. To preserve our sacred freedom in the face of terrible enemies. Vietnam. If those dominoes start falling they'll come crashing down on the shores of California. San Francisco will turn red. Hollywood will be forced to make commie flicks. The Mid-West will be flooded with gook creeps. In no time, the monsters will be eating children right here in New York. Communism! Misery, terror, and death.[2]

But I am a student. At NYU, Washington Square. A good student, a top student. I can't understand why I dreamed just now, just before waking up at 11 a.m. sharp, that I never finished high school. I did finish that miserable high school. I've almost finished college. I study hard, I study all night long, I'm graduating in June. I study Ancient Greek, Greek philosophy, Greek tragedy, Kierkegaard, Hegel, plus anything political I can find the time for. I was just reading the Vietnam Declaration of Independence.[3] Ho Chi Minh wrote it, and read it out to a huge crowd in Hanoi on the first Sunday in September, 1945. The first lines may sound familiar:

'All men are created equal. They are endowed by their Creator with certain inalienable rights; among these are Life, Liberty, and the pursuit of Happiness.'
This immortal statement was made in the Declaration of Independence of the United States of America in 1776. In a broader sense this means: All the peoples on the earth are

---

2 Just for the record, the expression is Silvio Berlusconi's, referred to Italian communists and all communists ('miseria, terrore, e morte': April 2005).
3 See *Vietnam and America*, edited by M. Gettleman, J. Franklin, M. Young, and B. Franklin, New York: Grove Press, 1995, pp. 26–28.

equal from birth, all the peoples have the right to live, to be happy and free.

The Declaration of the French Revolution made in 1791 on the Rights of Man and the Citizen also states: 'All men are born free and with equal rights, and must always remain free and have equal rights.'

These are undeniable truths.

Nevertheless, for more than eighty years, the French imperialists, abusing the standard of Liberty, Equality, and Fraternity, have violated our fatherland and oppressed our fellow-citizens. They have acted contrary to the ideals of humanity and justice.

....

They have built more prisons than schools. They have mercilessly slain our patriots; they have drowned our uprisings in rivers of blood.

Believe me, I'd love to quote the whole Declaration for you, it's not that long. I'll settle for the ending:

For these reasons, we, members of the provisional Government of the Democratic Republic of Vietnam, solemnly declare to the world that Vietnam has the right to be a free and independent country—and in fact is so already. The entire Vietnamese people are determined to mobilize all their physical and mental strength, to sacrifice their lives and property in order to safeguard their independence and liberty.

When I got back from my trip to Europe two summers ago I knew it was time to mobilize all my physical and mental strength and take my stand. Yes, I was a student. I had a student deferment and two more years at the university. Yes, I had been a big winner—i.e. loser—in the Tricky Dicky Draft

Lottery: number 27, without the deferment I'd be drafted in a minute.[4] But I did something that, alas, no one has ever understood. I wrote a letter to my draft board stating: I am a student and a good one, in my third year of college, but I hereby renounce my student deferment. Why did I do this? There is a long story here. My political autobiography. But, like Captain Vere in *Billy Budd*, I'm going to stick to the deed and drop the motivation. Let's just say, it was all those jeeps rolling through the streets all the time, day and night. Well, here's what I did. I went almost entirely without food for five full months. Three times a week I had a high-nutrition little 'meatball' my doctor cooked up for me, and an apple a day. I went up to the university for my classes, I studied every night until dawn. My normal life. Apart from the hunger. It's true that one winter night I did try to chew on the little wooden leg of my kitchen cabinet. But Knut Hamsun, in *Hunger*, regularly munched on woodchips, on shavings, on stones, on slivers, chewed on a pocket of his coat, and finally bit his own finger. After two days without his sandwiches he was ravaged by 'fiercely raging pain.' The hunger! Long Winter of 1971. The Chicago Seven had already happened, Nixon's invasion of Cambodia, My Lai, Kent State, already happened. I went from

4 The first Draft Lottery was held on December 1, 1969, to determine the order of call to military service in Vietnam for men born from 1944 to 1950. (SirYesSir! 1950.) It worked like this. The days of the year (including February 29) were represented by the numbers 1 through 366 written on slips of paper, which were placed in separate plastic capsules that were mixed in a shoebox and then dumped into a deep glass jar. As practically everybody in the country watched on TV, the capsules were drawn from the jar one at a time. The first number drawn was 258 (September 14), so all registrants with that happy birthday were assigned lottery number 1. The second number drawn corresponded to April 24, and so forth. (My best friend from high school got 365, I got 27.) As it turned out, and just about as predicted, the first 195 numbers got drafted, 196 to 366, no. A lottery. All this was a Nixon ploy—and a pretty successful one—to get about half the potential SirYesSirs off his back immediately, since they knew they'd never be 'called to serve.' The Lottery was repeated for later draftees in 1971 and 1972. During the 1968 presidential campaign Nixon had promised to end the draft, and he did it! On June 30, 1973: an all-voluntary military. No more draft, no more Vietnam War, and pretty soon—thanks to Watergate—no more Nixon.

my slim 120 down to 86 pounds. My draft physical had been scheduled for June. At that weight I was fit for Dachau, Bergen-Belsen, Auschwitz, but not for the United States Army. ARBEIT MACHT FREI. I could not be drafted—for the time being. But that was only half the story. I wanted a hearing. I *needed* a hearing. I have something to say! 'I raise my hands and spread out all my fingers.'[5] I got a hearing. A board of military psychiatrists. I was ready—for prison, for the madhouse, for whatever. I said: I gave up my deferment because student deferments are wrong. What justice is there in sending the poor and the blacks to fight while we white students wallow in universities? Now *you must send me to Vietnam. I must go to Vietnam. To tell my fellow soldiers, my brothers, that we are fighting on the wrong side. We are fighting for tyranny and against freedom.*

OK, what happened wasn't as calm as I make it sound now. Not by a long shot. You'll just have to use your imagination. After the hearing I walked back uptown from Whitehall Street, through Chinatown, headed east, up to Grand, to Broome, on up to Delancey. I strolled all the way through the Essex Street market, its stalls stretching the whole long block from Delancey to Rivington. Just as my grandfather, Harry Donishevsky, had done so often, seventy years before, though in his day the stalls were outdoors, not inside one very long building as they are now. I thought about the fact that maybe I'd better start eating again. I stopped at Larry's stall and bought a dozen coffee yogurts, like I used to do. I hadn't seen Larry all winter—this short man, a chunk of muscle, his forearms like smoked hams, the death camp numbers glaring as he passed me the food. He once told me he could still hear the SS guards screeching at him, at night, when he couldn't sleep. I came out of the market, strolled along Rivington Street, crossed Norfolk, and stopped a while in front of my building, looking long and hard at Streit's matzo factory on the far corner.

---

5 Joseph K., on the last page of Kafka's *The Trial*.

Two days later I got a letter from my draft board with my new classification: 4-F. Not qualified for military service *under any circumstances*. *Ever*. Normally you had to be missing an arm or a leg or both, at the least, to get a 4-F. I guess they were riled up. Or just didn't want to have anything to do with me anymore. Ever?

So, what did I do next? I'll tell you: I bought a copy of *Moby Dick*. And read it. Call me Ishmael. 'Because the Lord hath heard thy affliction.' 'Whenever I find myself growing grim about the mouth; whenever it is a damp, drizzly November in my soul; whenever I find myself involuntarily pausing before coffin warehouses, and bringing up the rear of every funeral I meet; and especially whenever my hypos get such an upper hand of me, that it requires a strong moral principle to prevent me from deliberately stepping into the street, and methodically knocking people's hats off—then, I account it high time to get to sea as soon as I can. This is my substitute for pistol and ball. With a philosophical flourish Cato throws himself upon his sword; I quietly take to the ship.' Now, I bring this up for a number of reasons. For one: hell yes, I do get *riled up* from time to time, but Captain Ahab was an *evil* motherfucker. I mean, personally, I don't *like* Nixon at all, but Ahab *really had it in* for that whale. But my main reason is this: I like the way the book starts with Ismael's decision. Especially since my latest story—this one—is about a decision. What a decision is and what making a decision means. I've noticed that Melville's greatest works—*Moby Dick*, *Pierre*, *Billy Budd*—are basically about decisions. About actually making them—the 'direct reverse' (as Melville liked to put it) of *Hamlet*, which is about *not* making them.

Then again, at the same time, as I see it, what I did during last year's Long Winter was more a question of tactics than of *decision* in the proper sense. I mean, I *had* to do something.

Ishmael had to do something, and he found a way. *I had to act according to my political principles.* (Or is 'political principles' a contradiction in terms?) The only question was: How? By falling on my sword? Well, after studying all night I used to go out just before dawn and run across the Williamsburg Bridge (I've given that up now, the Long Winter sapped my strength) and think about the Vietnam War, and what I was going to do about it. So, I 'decided' to do what I did: I quietly took to the ship, as Ismael put it. Because Ishmael is Ishmael, Ahab is Ahab (or is he? Is Ahab Ahab?), I am who I am. I wrote to my draft board, and the rest of the voyage just took its course. Naturally. By nature. Necessarily.

> And then went down to the ship,
> Set keel to breakers, forth on the godly sea, and
> We set up mast and sail on that swart ship,
> Bore sheep aboard her, and our bodies also
> Heavy with weeping[6]

But last summer, apart from reading *Moby Dick,* I did something else—something big. I stopped jogging and started meditating. Zen. Zazen. Sitting meditation. It happened by chance. Serendipity. I was strolling down Chrystie Street one sunny afternoon—in June, just after my 4-F—my still-emaciated body—heavy with weeping—when I saw a little hand-printed sign in a window: ZEN MEDITATION EVERY DAY 6 P.M. Well, check it out. I went home and came back at 6. The door was open, a few people were going in. An empty room, a stack of round black cushions in one corner. A Japanese lady. We each took a cushion—six of us in all—and sat in a circle, facing the walls. Smoke rising from an incense burner in the center. The other people were not too young—in their forties, I'd say, or even older. Fifties, maybe. We all sat in the lotus position, it was easy. The lady tapped a tiny gong with a

6 Ezra Pound, Canto I.

miniscule hammer and we all sat there with eyes half-closed, looking at nothing, until she rang it again (30 minutes later). Meditation. Then we got up and walked in a circle around the room, extremely slowly and precisely: walking meditation (it's called kinhin). Then, zazen again. After that, we sat facing the incense in the center of the circle and one of the men read for half an hour from a book called *Zen Mind, Beginner's Mind*. Then, everyone got up and left. I went back every day for about a week. The people were nice, though not very sociable. It was as if I'd always been there. I stopped going because I couldn't stand the incense—what a horror. It burned my eyes and my nose. Terrible. Zen mind. Buddha mind. No-mind. The Dharma Eye. 'When you're hungry, eat; when you're tired, sleep.' Satori: direct experience. The gate of emptiness. Now I meditate on my own, here in my railroad flat on Rivington Street. Meditate, and study, I bought a bunch of great books, Alan Watts, but especially the two Suzukis: *The Zen Doctrine of No-mind* by the great Zen scholar D.T. Suzuki, who wrote a hundred books, and *Zen Mind, Beginner's Mind* by the Zen master Shunryu Suzuki, the Roshi who created the Zen community in San Francisco. He died last December and this is his only book, but I think it's the most important book in the world,[7] a book to be read ten thousand times. Roshi didn't actually *write* this book, it's made up of 'informal talks' he gave after meditation sessions, recorded and transcribed.[8] The first talk is titled 'Posture':

> Now I would like to talk about our zazen posture. When you sit in the full lotus position, your left foot is on your right

7 Over forty years later I think so more than ever. Shunryu Suzuki, *Zen Mind, Beginner's Mind*, New York: Weatherhill, 1970. But this one's important too: D.T. Suzuki, *The Zen Doctrine of No-mind*, York Beach, Maine: Samuel Weisner, Inc., 1972.
8 A second book of the Roshi's talks was published many years later, and since this is actually 2014 (I'm 64 now) [first stab at this Empty Shield] I'll refer to this one too: *Not Always So*, New York: HarperCollins, 2002.

thigh, and your right foot is on your left thigh. When we cross our legs like this, even though we have a right leg and a left leg, they have become one. The position expresses the oneness of duality: not two, and not one. This is the most important teaching: not two, and not one. Our body and mind are not two and not one. If you think your body and mind are two, that is wrong; if you think they are one, that is also wrong. Our body and mind are both two *and* one. We usually think that if something is not one, it is more than one; if it is not singular, it is plural. But in actual experience, our life is not only plural, but also singular. Each one of us is both dependent and independent.

When I first read this it reminded me, a little, of that great quip by Kierkegaard's nephew. Kierkegaard, philosopher and militant radical Christian, saw himself as a man of *decision*, an 'either/ or' man. He spent half his life relentlessly (*outrageously*) blasting the blasphemous Hegelian 'both/and'—the cop out. The non-decision. In his opinion. His nephew—son of a Hegelian bishop—confined to a madhouse, quipped, tellingly: 'My uncle was Either/Or, my father is Both/And, and I am Neither/ Nor.' OK, this is neither here nor there, the Roshi's point is *no dualism*. 'You and I, this and that, good and bad. But actually these discriminations are themselves the awareness of the universal existence.' Big mind. In his talk titled 'Bowing'—after zazen we bow to the floor nine times, I forgot to mention that— he tells the story of Rikyu, the Tea Master, who committed hara-kiri in 1591 at the order of his lord, Hideyoshi. 'Just before Rikyu took his own life he said, "When I have this sword there is no Buddha and no Patriarchs." He meant that when we have the sword of big mind [Zen mind, Buddha mind], there is no dualistic world. The only thing that exists is this spirit. This kind of imperturbable spirit was always present in Rikyu's tea ceremony. He never did anything in just a dualistic way; he was ready to die in each moment. In ceremony after ceremony he died, and he renewed himself. This is the spirit of the tea ceremony. This is how we bow.'

A few weeks ago I came across a new Zen book, *The Empty Mirror: Experiences in a Japanese Zen Monastery*,[9] which I took home and devoured in a single night. A fun book. The author is a young Dutchman named Jan, a heavy smoker, big-time beer drinker, motorbike rider, and 'alarmed soul' (as he puts it) who went off to Kyoto and spent two years in a Zen monastery. 'Looking for truth—why it has all started, and what's the good of it.' He had a good time in Japan, and did find something, if not everything. But the book has one absolutely stunning chapter—the 'empty mirror' story. I can't get it out of my head—and don't want to, there's something important going on here. Important for me personally. For my decision. What is it? As Jan's friend says at the end, 'The empty mirror. If you could really understand that, there would be nothing left here for you to look for.' I keep telling myself this story, which was told, somewhat unwillingly, by a monk in Kyoto. 'By listening to stories you don't deepen yourself much,' said the monk. 'Unless, of course, the story comes at exactly the right moment.' This is the story. A court lady, in China, long ago, was attracted to the 'new' and mysterious Zen teachings, and wished to be enlightened by a 'real master,' if such a one exists. She set off for a deserted part of the country in search of 'an uncouth old man,' a hermit, a Zen master who lived in a ruin. She found him, 'a man of few words, and unkind words at that,' who tried to send her away. 'I don't teach. I pass my days in dreams and usually I sit and stare.' But the court lady was rich, and extremely tenacious. In the end, the hermit-master reluctantly agreed to let her restore his ruined

---

9 By Janwillem van de Wetering, New York: Ballantine Books, 1973. OK, I confess, I actually read it a few years later. I do take some liberties with my chronologies— poetic license—but not with my politics. The 'story of the mirrors' is Chapter 15, 'A court lady discourteously treated.'

temple; her only request was that he let her come back later and spend a week listening to him. When the temple had been repaired the lady returned, and instead of a week stayed three months. 'She meditated, she learned the fire ceremony, and sometimes the master spoke a few words. She did her utmost, but when it was time to return she had to admit that she had learned nothing, and that the mysteries she had tried to comprehend were as veiled as ever. She blamed the failure on herself and didn't complain, but said goodbye politely to the master and thanked him for his trouble.' The master was a little upset. 'Have you got a large room in the palace?' he asked her. She nodded. 'Good. See if you can gather together about fifty mirrors.' About a month later the 'old bald-pated bum' (as the master described himself) came to the palace. 'He placed the mirrors in such a way that they reflected into each other. Then he asked the lady to sit down in the middle of the room and to look around her and describe what she saw.' She sat in the lotus position and remained quiet for a long time. 'I see that everything that happens is reflected in everything else.' 'Anything else?' 'I see that every action of anyone has its result in everyone else, and in all beings, and in all spheres.' 'Anything else?' 'Everything is connected with everything.' In the end, the master grunted. 'It isn't much, but it is something.' After that he left. When she wanted to visit him again later he had died. So, what's the point? Suzuki-roshi would get it right away. Jan got something, right away: *Those mirrors are empty, there is nothing. Nothing reflects, nothing can be reflected.*' OK, I need to meditate on this. The empty mirror. 'Nothing left here for you to look for.'

I happened upon Zen by chance, last summer. Now, ten months later, my life is different. 4-F is forever, but now is now. No more tactics. Now I have a 'real' decision to make. In the 'proper' sense. Now, as Frank Zappa put it, I'm 'absolutely

28

free.' To decide. When I finish writing this great paper on 'The Division of the Soul in Ancient Greek Religion and in the Ashanti Religion of West Africa' and get my degree at NYU—what then? In other words, *what will I do to put my political principles into practice?* Now that I don't have the draft to fight with anymore. Well, as I see it, like Oedipus in the myth I am coming to the fork where three roads cross. (Where Oedipus—cursed, fated, doomed—killed his father, but that's another story.) I see three paths I can take. The easiest: become a GAM—a Great Academic Marxist. Like my mother's cousin at the New School— the one she calls 'the jackass' (quite rightly, though not particularly because he is a GAM). I can have a brilliant PhD by the time I'm 25, and my 'Marxist credentials' are impeccable. I'm sure I'd make a great professor, and have a lot of fun.

But—is that my path? I have a different one in mind, the hardest of the three. I would really like to blow up the Williamsburg Bridge. *A political statement.* I think I can actually do it. I have studied *The Anarchist Cookbook*[10] and I have a good plan. Of course, I know the Williamsburg Bridge like the palm of my hand. Especially at dawn. Very few cars and little subway traffic (the J, M, and Z Trains) at that hour, and no one jogging back and forth since I stopped. With proper timing I ought to be able to avoid killing anyone. The 'Fertilizer Bomb' in the *Cookbook* is pretty crude, but I can refine it somewhat.

How to make a fertilizer bomb by Jolly Roger
Ingredients:
- Newspaper
- Fertilizer (the chemical kind, GREEN THUMB or ORCHO)
- Cotton
- Diesel fuel
Make a pouch out of the newspaper and put some fertilizer in it. Then put cotton on top. Soak the cotton with fuel.

---

10 1971, you'll find it on the Internet, I left my copy in New York.

Then light and run like you have never run before! This blows up 500 square feet so don't do it in an alley!!
— Jolly Roger —

That's the general idea. I'm thinking, if I rent a little van, put a big container in the back with a lot of fertilizer, hook up a remote-controlled detonator, park the van exactly half-way across the bridge (i.e. half way to Brooklyn)—I mean, if all goes well the whole middle of the bridge ought to drop right down into the East River. Of course, I don't think I can *get away* with this, but *getting away* is not my intention. No, my intention, after my hearing with the military psychiatrists, is to earn myself a true and proper TRIAL. Shit, there may be fewer soldiers in Vietnam right now but *there are more and more bombs*. Right now. And there will be *more and more.* What justice shall quench the tears of blood? I ask not, Who will speak out? No, I ask, Shall I speak out? And *what* will I say?

I realize that Ishmael is not enthusiastic about this possible decision, and I'm far from convinced myself. Ahab, of course, is overwhelmingly in favor, but Ahab is a *mean* motherfucker.

The third path has a famous name, but who knows where it leads. Its famous name is LOVE IT OR LEAVE IT, also known as 'exile.' Not forced but voluntary exile. Not escaping to Canada or Sweden—that is escape, it has nothing whatsoever to do with exile. 'Exile' is a very complex term, and state of being. Or mind. Being and/or mind. Something like Hegel's vanishing of vanishing (on the heels of 'being is nothing'). Exile is something like the escaping of escaping. Escaping escape, possibly. Escaping escaping actually. In Aeschylus' *Seven Against Thebes* Polyneices has been 'forced' into exile but also *went* into exile. Greek exiles have one totalizing *raison d'être*—namely, to *come back*. But if I decide to LEAVE IT does that mean I also decide to come back? If I leave *decisively* (to go where? by the way), WHAT am I actually deciding? WHY leave? A HEARING—yes, that's what it's all about. Political responsibility. A way to make myself HEARD. A real hearing, a *true* hearing, not just an overdrafted military-psychiatric hearing. An uncontaminated hearing that people—MANY people—actually HEAR. I raise my hands and spread out all my fingers. A fork. Exile? What would it lead to? An abyss, possibly. End of the line. Last stop, an abyss of dreams. My head is spinning. What do I want? WHAT is a decision? What does it all mean?

Then again—could there be a 'soft' version of this third path? A 'third way' that somehow skirts the first two paths? 'A way of living outside the jurisdiction of the Court,' as Joseph K. put it. I was reading an article about 'internal refugees'—I'd call them 'internal exiles,' it's more dramatic.[11] Such people are de facto political refugees even though they are still living in their home country. They live in a country—in some cases may even love that country—but feel completely alienated from its politics and political system. They may vote in elections and march in protest, but realize that what they want in the way of policy—for example, an end to the permanent war system—hasn't the remotest chance of realization. But, then, what's the point? Howard Zinn said that dissent is the highest form of patriotism. Does this make any sense? Doesn't it just mean that to be born under tyranny is to die under tyranny? What if you DO NOT LOVE IT? What about the Bay of Pigs? Or Hiroshima. Wasn't that mass murder? Blowing up a bridge—a crime of fact—may have a statute of limitations, but a crime of ideology is infinite. I mean, the jurisdiction of *what* Court? If the whole government is above the law, what use are laws at all? How can you ever 'return' from internal exile? Kafka wrote in his *Diaries:*

> It is indeed a kind of Wandering in the Wilderness in reverse
> that I am undergoing. I think that I am continually skirting

11 *Z Magazine*, December 2011, Edward S. Herman, 'Internal Refugees and the War System,' pp. 7–8.

the wilderness and am full of childish hopes... that 'perhaps I shall keep in Canaan after all'—when all the while I am decades in the wilderness and these hopes are merely mirages born of despair, especially at those times when I am the wretchedest of creatures in the desert too, and Canaan is perforce my only Promised Land, for no third place exists for mankind.[12]

I mean, some day—'when I'm sixty-four' maybe, as the Beatles put it—if I look back on decades of internal exile, 'will you still need me, will you still feed me'? OK, enough is enough. Now I've totally confused myself, and you. Why did I dream I'd never finished high school? Why dream? Enough! It's time to DECIDE.

There's a thing I do sometimes, when I need to 'get away from it all' and get my head together. Just as Ishmael takes to the ship, I take to the subway. Usually with my mini-volume *Selected Poems of Ezra Pound*: 'And then went down to the ship.' — 'When, when, and whenever death closes our eyelids,/ Moving naked over Acheron.' 'The waters of Styx poured over the wound.'[13] I mosey on over to the Delancey Street station: along Rivington Street to Norfolk, another short block to Essex, then a long block down Essex (possibly going through the Essex Street Market, especially in case of rain), and here I am. I go down the steps, whip out my token—30 red cents now, just a year ago it was 20—go through the turnstile, then down to the platform. Some people may not know that on the New York City subway with one single little token—if you know what you're doing, watch out for tricky turnstiles, and avoid dead ends—you can ride for the rest of your natural lives. Every day twenty-four hours a day until you drop. Unless, of course, the

---

12 Franz Kafka, *Diaries 1914-1923*, New York: Schocken Books, 1965, pp. 213–214.
13 Ezra Pound, Canto I and *Homage to Sextus Propertius*.

subway goes on strike, or ceases to exist.

That's the system now, at any rate. Maybe some day they'll decide to plug up all the cracks and make it 'one token, one way,' but right now this city has far bigger fish to fry. It's almost bankrupt and the murder rate—I read it in the *Post*—is up to 2,000 per year. Crime, drugs—dealers and addicts and both together, knives and guns on Rivington Street. Bums sleeping on the streets, drunks puking, hookers galore, heaps of garbage, more rats and cockroaches than people. 'Whores, skunk pussies, buggers, queens, fairies, dopers and junkies,' that sums it up pretty well.[14] Shit, I got my hack license so easily a few summers ago because three cabbies had been murdered in the previous three months. 'Have a cigar!' my new boss spouted, when I said I wanted to drive at night. But the subway is my way. It's a world all its own—nether, but world. It has all its own places where you can eat, drink, piss, and shit, no problem at all. At the Times Square station, for example, you can get your hair cut, find a hooker, and possibly meet the Ghost of Christmas Past. I know it doesn't work like this in most, or all, other cities, but New York is FUN CITY. There's no *dernier métro* in New York. One little token and off you go, forever.

One other singularity on the New York subway is the incredible ear-shattering mind-scrambling *screech* every single train makes every single time it stops at a station. It's indescribable, you have to hear it to believe it. I wonder whether full-fledged permanent subway riders hear it so often they don't notice it anymore. I'd find that hard to believe. It has occurred to me that this *screech* is a fact but not a *necessary fact*. I mean, it's possible that other subways in other cities, somewhere in the world, *do not screech*. They might have less screechy wheels, or tracks, or both together. They might even be *very quiet*. I don't know. In New York the

---

14 The reference is before its time, it's Robert De Niro/Travis Bickle in the film *Taxi Driver,* 1976.

stops screech the drums right out of your ears. That's for sure.

So, down to the ship. I go right down to the platform and hop on the first F Train that comes along. The F is about the only train I ever take, unless I have something special to do. I normally walk to school—up to Houston, past Katz's Delicatessen ('send a salami to your boy in the army'), over to the Bowery and then on up to Washington Square, it only takes me about half an hour. But if it's raining hard I take the F Train to West 4th. The car will be absolutely packed, which I don't like, and from West 4th to the Classics Department on Waverly Place I get plenty wet anyway, but, what the hell, I guess I'd get even wetter if I walked the whole way. (I am not completely sure about this.) In any event I'm not talking about that, I'm talking about my occasional 'getting my head together' excursions. Now, riding the F Train may not seem to be an ideal way to 'get away from it all,' but the fact is—I avoid the rush hours. As a matter of fact, I usually make the trip around three in the morning.

Hold on! I just reminded myself of an incredibly great story I read the other day, by Chuang Tsu, a fourth century B.C. Chinese Taoist. Listen to this, it's called 'three in the morning.'

When you wrack your brain trying to unify things without knowing that they are already one, it is called 'three in the morning.' What do I mean by 'three in the morning'? A man who kept monkeys said to them, 'You get three acorns in the morning and four in the evening.' This made them all very angry. So he said, 'How about four in the morning and three in the evening?'—and the monkeys were happy. The number of acorns was the same, but the different arrangement resulted in anger or pleasure. This is what I am talking about. Therefore, the sage harmonizes right with wrong and rests in the balance of nature. This is called taking both sides at once.[15]

---

15 *Chuang Tsu: Inner Chapters*, translated by Gia-fu Feng and Jane English, New

Ye gods, there's food for thought here. Take 'which side are you on?' and 'both sides at once' *at once*, and who knows what you'll get.

Now, by a 'trip on the F Train' I mean this: first of all, hopping onto the first train that comes along and riding it to the end of the line. This means: either to 179th in Jamaica, in the outermost boondocks of Queens, or, in the other direction, to Coney Island, in Brooklyn. (But will I ever actually *see* Coney Island and, perchance, *eat* a famous hot dog? *Not* likely.) The 'three in the morning' I call the 'short' head-getting-together trip: either Delancey to Jamaica to Coney Island and back to Delancey or, vice versa, Delancey to Coney Island to Jamaica and back to Delancey. Whichever train comes first. Either way, it takes about three hours all told—'three in the morning.' But I also take less Taoist trips. If my head is full to exploding when I get back from NYU, I might have an early dinner, mosey out at 9 or 10, and ride the F hither and yon—Delancey-Jamaica-Delancey-Coney Island-Delancey or, so to speak, vice versa, again and again—till dawn. I might take some Greek with me to study, if studying was what I needed to 'get my head together' about. Or I might concentrate on Vietnam—take Howard Zinn's *Vietnam. The Logic of Withdrawal*, or Robert Scheer's *How the United States Got Involved in Vietnam*, or the latest issue of *Ramparts*. Or I might just set out Naked in the Naked City,[16] traveling the road of the 'original emptiness of the mind,' as Suzuki-roshi taught me. 'If your mind is empty, it is always ready for anything; it is open to everything.' Satori:

'To empty' water from a cup does not mean to drink it up. 'To empty' means to have direct, pure experience. Our experience is 'empty' of our preconceived ideas, our idea of

---

York: Vintage Books, 1974, p. 30.
16 Police drama TV series (1958–63), famous for its closing narration: 'There are eight million stories in the Naked City. This has been one of them.'

being, our idea of big or small, round or square. Round or square, big or small don't belong to reality but are simply ideas.[17]

The finite, said Hegel, is 'ideal.' F Train. 'Flashings into the vast phenomenal world.'

101 ZEN STORIES
56. The True Path
Just before Ninakawa passed away the Zen master Ikkyu visited him. 'Shall I lead you on?' Ikkyu asked.
Ninakawa replied: 'I came here alone and I go alone. What help could you be to me?'
Ikkyu answered: 'If you think you really come and go, that is your delusion. Let me show you the path on which there is no coming and no going.'
With his words, Ikkyu had revealed the path so clearly that Ninakawa smiled and passed away.[18]

Now—my journeys on the F Train. Let's say the first train that comes along is the Brooklyn train. After just one stop in Manhattan—East Broadway—it goes right over to Brooklyn through a tunnel called the Rutgers Tube. Of course, since you're underground anyway you hardly notice you're in a tunnel under the East River, never mind its being named the Rutgers Tube. (For some reason someone knows, but I don't.)[19]

---

17 *Not Always So*, p. 36.
18 *Zen Flesh, Zen Bones,* compiled by Paul Reps, Pelican Books, 1971, p. 58.
19 OK, for the record, the proper name is the Rutgers Street Tunnel, since it's from Rutgers Street in Manhattan to who-knows-what street in Brooklyn. It's always the Manhattanites who give the names, to everything, as I shall note. A question of power. Amazing but true, Henry Rutgers, a Revolutionary War hero, has *two* streets named after him on the Lower East Side. First name and last. Henry Street and Rutgers Street. By the way, Rivington Street, my street, is named after James Rivington, a Brit-born American journalist. What a story! He published a *loyalist*, i.e. pro-Brit, newspaper in New York right up to the Revolution, when they kicked his ass, burned his house down, and kicked him out of town. At which point he went

If you don't happen to know where you are, you won't notice it at all. Other trains go to Brooklyn *on* the Williamsburg Bridge, and others *on* the Manhattan Bridge, but the F has the Rutgers Tube all to itself. Now that I'm in Brooklyn I hardly notice it of course, I'm under the ground. York Street, Jay, Bergen, Carroll Streets—but then something big happens: I see Brooklyn. A breathtaking view. It's just for a couple of minutes, but the train has to go *over* the Gowanus Canal, and it has to go *high*. The canal is so deep it was impossible to build a tunnel under it. Then back to the netherworld for a while, as far as Church Avenue. *But then we come up again.* Between Church and Ditmas. And we stay up all the way to the end, to Coney Island. A miracle. A Wonder of the World. All the trains in this part of Brooklyn are elevated. They should put up signs saying 'You are now leaving the SUBway.' We aren't under the ground anymore. What an experience. As if Achilles actually did come up from Hades into the dear light of day. Just for a while. Better a slave on earth than lord over all 'the sunless dead and this joyless region.' Like Elpenor, my friend, unwept, unburied, '*A man of no fortune and with a name to come.*'[20] Then, since my journey is 'endless' (i.e. until I decide to end it) (at Delancey Street, of course), I hop on a new F and head right back through the shimmering Brooklyn night, on the long trip to Jamaica, Queens. The Brooklyn night. Then, after Ditmas, heading back to Manhattan, underground again, infinitely, in the Hadean night. Apart from that fleeting moment high above the Gowanus Canal. As William Blake put it, 'Some are born to sweet delight,/ Some are born to endless night.'[21] A darkness

---

back to England, but soon came back, to live in disgrace and poverty, beaten up by the Liberty Boys, until his merciful death in 1802. What a story. Long and strange. Worthy of *Mad* magazine. It wasn't until the 1950s that they discovered, officially, that he was a *spy* for the *Revolutionaries* and furnished George Washington with important information. How, in the meantime, did he manage to get my street named after him? I have no idea.

20 Ezra Pound, Canto I.

21 William Blake, *Auguries of Innocence*; doubly immortalized in Jim Jarmusch's film *Dead Man*.

pierced by screeches, again and again and again. And again to infinity. Back to Manhattan now—East Broadway... Delancey... 2nd Avenue... Broadway-Lafayette... West 4th... 14th... 23rd... 34th... 42nd... Rockefeller Center... 57th... 63rd. And then, somehow, I'm in Queens. Not that I really notice it. Actually, I'm *under* Queens, of course. SUBway. I know about as much about Queens as I do about Timbuktu. Roosevelt Avenue... Woodhaven Boulevard... Union Turnpike... Parsons Boulevard... 179th Street/Jamaica. All just screeches to me. Then, a new F and I head back. To Delancey. Three-hour journey. Three in the morning.

Or, as I said, I might double the trip, or triple it—9 p.m. till dawn.

But today is different. The Challengers are taking their positions at the Seven Gates, menacing, brandishing their shields. How shall I Defend the City? The enemy is camped outside the walls of Thebes. Why? Why are they here? What am I to do? Who has decided that I—I of all people—have been chosen to decide the fate of my City?

Extreme situations demand extreme measures.

'Extremism in the defense of liberty is no vice! And moderation in the pursuit of justice is no virtue!' Go Barry Go![22]

Pardon me. A Strangelove moment. It won't happen again. I promise.

Extreme measures: I'm taking to the subway *indefinitely*. Not the 'short' head-getting-together trip, doubled or tripled, against the Tao. No, the life-and-death subway struggle. To the bitter end. Really? No, not really. No, let's just say 'indefinitely.' This damn *fork*. I know it's there. I eat my spaghetti with it every day, so to speak. But, at every meal, I think about the spaghetti and not the fork. GAM, bomb, exile: there's a prong

---

22 Barry Goldwater's speech at the 1964 Republican Convention.

in the offing. Just like the beginning of *Heart of Darkness:*
'The *Nellie*, a cruising yawl, swung to her anchor without a
flutter of the sails, and was at rest... The only thing for it was
to come to and wait for the turn of the tide... The sea-reach
of the Thames stretched before us like the beginning of an
interminable waterway. In the offing the sea and the sky were
welded together without a joint, and in the luminous space the
tanned sails of the barges drifting up with the tide seemed to
stand still in red clusters of canvas sharply peaked, with gleams
of varnished spirits.' There was plenty of time for Marlow to tell
the story of Kurtz in the 'heart of darkness'—the story of his
'horror.' The brutes. What is to come will come. What is there
to decide? Didn't I decide, last year, what to do about the draft,
about 'my body... heavy with weeping'? Now, why not let the
future take care of itself?

Damn good question. But, something stinks, like fish gone
bad. Or moldy cheese. Even spaghetti can go bad. A fork—no,
a fork cannot go bad. But a life can go bad. When I finish NYU
in June—what? What will come will come? Makes no sense.
Shall I turn to stone? I don't feel like stone. Decide? Enough of
Rivington Street. When my grandfather had had enough, he got
married and moved to Scranton. Me—Delancey, and what's my
next stop? *Screech.* Shit. Stuff happens. Fucking fork, what do
I know. Decide. Make up your *mind*. What mind? Monkey mind?
The restless, capricious, *indecisive* mind the Buddha described
as filled with drunken monkeys, jumping around, *screeching*,
chattering. *What* mind? Since when do 'political principles'—if
they exist—have mind? Just fork your spaghetti down, things
will work out. Decide? About a fork? What did Oedipus decide?
What?

DEPARTURE

Right now. End of March, 1972. Today is Friday. I get up at 11
a.m. as I always do, have a coffee yogurt—today, two coffee
yogurts. I'm a little worried about this dream that I never
finished high school. So be it. Right now. It's just after noon
and I'm moseying on over to the Delancey Street station. No
school today. I'm taking the subway indefinitely. I put Hegel's
Logic in my book bag, along with *Billy Budd and other Tales*...
Selected Poems of Ezra Pound... *Zen Mind, Beginner's Mind*...
Heart of Darkness... *The Zen Doctrine of No-mind*... *Seven
Against Thebes*... and, in particular, these two articles—*Two
Notes on Aeschylus' Septem*—by Seth Benardete, my Greek
Political Theory professor. Except for the Hegel, all the books
are real small. I also toss the four apples I happen to have
in the house into the bag, along with a piece of (non-moldy)
cheese I come across in the refrigerator. I fill up a plastic bottle
with water, I don't drink much. Don't talk much and don't drink
much. 'Indefinitely'—but I can pick up all the food I want, here
and there in Hades. Or, not eat at all. My grandfather, on his
long walk to Vilnius around 1895 to find his uncle after both
his parents died, told me that all the food he had was some
very hard bread and some onions. 'Be strong as an onion,' he
always tells me. I eat lots of onions. Cooked onions—sautéed,

fried, baked. But raw onions on the subway—no, not a good idea. I'll skip the onions. My grandfather came to New York from Lithuania around 1898, and lived on Rivington Street just one block from where I live now, on the block between Suffolk and Clinton, where Streit's Matzos stands today. On Orchard Street a couple of years ago I paid a dime for a battered *Guide to New York City* published in 1908, which claims—I quote—'Rivington Street on the Lower East Side has the highest population density of anyplace in the world today.' It even beat Calcutta (Black Hole excepted). An apartment like mine must have been packed like the subway at rush hour. Just imagine, my grandparents met at the inauguration of the Williamsburg Bridge in 1903. It was the longest suspension bridge on earth at that time. There was a big celebration—fireworks and all— and hordes of people walking to Brooklyn and back, and that's how they met, got married, moved to Scranton, and had eight children.

I go down the steps, and here's the F Train, bound for Queens. I sit down and look around. Not many people in the car. A few. I sit here and look around. 'Facing the sunless dead and this joyless region.' OK, I have a *decision* to make. *Screech*. 2nd Avenue. *Screech*. Broadway-Lafayette. *Screech*. West 4th: NYU will carry on without me today. I'm heading uptown. The car is filling up, by 42nd Street it'll be pretty full. Dark is dark, under the ground is under the ground, but it feels different at noon than it does at three in the morning. Doesn't matter. Should I start rummaging around in my books right away, or maybe wait until I'm on my way back from Jamaica? OK, let's wait until I get to Queens. *Screech screech screech*... Queens Plaza. Hooray I'm in Queens. I think I'll rummage around in Hegel for a while.[23] The *Science of Logic*. There is

---

23 [Third stab.] From 1971 until this year, 2016, my rummaging was always in my hardcover first edition copy of *Hegel's Science of Logic*, translated by A.V. Miller, London: George Allen & Unwin, 1969. All my quotes in the first two stabs at The Empty Shield were from Miller, whose prose is often quite beautiful, and which I know by heart. However, Miller is also quite often seriously inaccurate and, over the

plenty of rummaging to be done here. As usual, '*Being, pure being*... is pure indeterminateness and emptiness.... Being, the indeterminate immediate, is in fact *nothing*, and neither more nor less than *nothing*.' 'The system of logic is the realm of shadows, the world of simple essentialities freed from all sensuous concreteness.' 'The proposition that the finite is ideal constitutes idealism.' But I'm thinking in particular about something my professor said the other day, that the real beginning of Hegel's Logic is 'the *decision* to consider *thinking as such*.'²⁴ Watch out for this one. It's in the innocent looking little chapter, 'With What Must the Science Begin?'. The logic 'begins with *pure being*,' with 'mere *immediacy* itself... an *absolute*... an *abstract* beginning... that *presupposes nothing*.' *The pure blankness of being*, 'completely empty being.' 'This emptiness is simply as such the beginning of philosophy.' OK, but how shall we *make* this beginning. 'If no presupposition is to be made and the beginning itself is taken *immediately*, then its only determination is that it is to be the beginning of logic, of *thinking as such*. All we have is the *decision*, which may also be regarded as arbitrary, to consider *thinking as such*.' The *decision*. Ye gods. Let's go down to the ship. Let's take to the subway. Call me Ishmael. I mean, isn't *deciding* to consider

years, his translation of key terms has been rejected by almost everyone (including Miller himself). Hence I've always modified Miller's Hegel at will, also since over the years I've learned (just barely) enough German to read (and translate) Hegel's own Hegel on my own (more or less). But, this year, the plot has thickened, grievously: I got myself a copy of the *new* translation, by George Di Giovanni, Cambridge: Cambridge University Press, published in 2010. Di Giovanni is much more, and at times *much* much more faithful to Hegel's text, even if his prose is perhaps less beautiful than Miller's—Miller, whom I, and forty years of Hegel readers in English, know by heart. So, now, at my third (and last) [alas no, I've been stabbed again, and now I'm stabbing again, May 2017] stab, I'm doing what (as you shall see) I did with *Seven Against Thebes*: I take liberties. I mix the translations up and modify them all at will, based on my own modest opinion, and/or what fits best on an empty shield.
24 OK, I confess: Hegel's word is *Entschluß* (not *Entscheidung*), and *both* Miller *and* Di Giovanni translate it, correctly, as 'resolve.' But it *also* means 'decision': a pondered rather than a snap ('Chinese-menu') decision. (Never mind pondering over a Chinese menu.) *In any event*, 'decision' is the word that makes my point, i.e., the point I'm making. Forks! Prongs. Menus. Even if Hegel really meant 'resolve' I know he forgives me. He knows how much I love him.

43

thinking as such a little like 'deciding' to kill your father at the fork where three roads cross when you don't even know who your father is, and don't even know you're coming to a fork? Wisdom? *Sophia*. What a *screech.* No, I don't think it's Hegel's Owl of Minerva.

In any event—OK, pure being is pure *thought*—in other words, thinking that is not a*bout* anything. Specifically, not about any of the categories of the 'old logic'—anything that is already 'out there.' This reminds me, somewhat, of the Roshi's distinction between noise and sound—the *peep-peep-peep* of blue jays on the roof during zazen. If we think about the birds singing 'out there,' that's noise, and we are disturbed. But Buddhists understand everything, every noise, as a sound that *we* make. The sound is *in* our practice. Everything is in our mind. In Zen mind. At-home-with-itself, as Hegel liked to say. If a bird stays at some place—at some lake, for instance—its home is not only the lake but also the whole world. This is how birds fly and live in their world. Pure being is pure thought. For Hegel, *pure* thinking is the life of what he calls the 'concept'— its free play and self-realization. Logical motion. Now—we decide to begin with an empty screen. With a screen, but with nothing on it. But this is not so simple. Hegel refers to this *'decision'* to consider *thinking as such* as 'willful'—a product of will—but not as 'free.' He even uses the word 'arbitrary.' Perhaps because, in some sense, it is the *subject matter* that 'decides,' not the subject. But doesn't a *decision* involve *freedom?* What does Hegel mean by freedom? Is 'being is nothing' an expression of freedom? I don't think so. There *is* freedom in being is nothing, but it's the bare minimum, the degree zero. Ground zero. Construction site. Deep hole. Up up up. A freedom not built to last. Ends, beginnings, everything ends, nothing ends. Ends end. End ends. 'I decide to brush my teeth' is an expression of my freedom. But not of what Hegel means by freedom. OK, I am mixing up logic and practice here, but—I'm thinking about Woody Allen's film *Bananas*, where the Castro-lookalike Caribbean dictator willfully *decides*: From this day forth the official language of this Banana Republic will be Swedish. Now *that*, in terms of logic, is the freedom of 'being is nothing.' And it's *not* what Hegel means by freedom, or by a free decision. What *does* he mean? Well, this will take some serious rummaging, luckily I have all the time in the world. But now... *screech*... 179th Street/Jamaica. I am *under* the boondocks of Queens. It's the middle of a late March afternoon, 'up there' but also 'down here.' It's time to stretch my legs and wait for a new F. This one has come to the end of its line.

Good, I'm on the new one, heading for Coney Island. The car is completely empty. I have to tell you—recently I've been reading again and again, and again, the very last pages of the *Science of Logic*, the last pages of the last chapter, 'The Absolute Idea.' My professor, William Barrett—I'm doing one year of independent study—'Hegel'—with him in the Philosophy Department—suggested I do it: 'Stop reading "being is nothing" all the time,' he suggested. 'Realm of shadows, et cetera. The Logic of Being is just the First Part of the book, then there's the Logic of Essence—seeming, semblance, relation, and so forth—and, finally, the Logic of the Concept: Subjectivity, Objectivity, The Idea.' So, I skipped from Determinate Being and Infinity—the true versus the bad concept of infinity—straight to the last chapter of The Idea. Straight to The Absolute Idea. These last pages are hard going, but I'm starting to get the hang of it—in particular, starting to get an idea of what Hegel means by freedom, necessity, and *decision*. It's far from obvious at the beginning, and it's hard to get a grip on at the end. But I'm getting there, I think. I hope. Slowly. Very slowly. As my professor pointed out,[25] the curious thing here is that, after *beginning* his Logic with a decision Hegel decides to *end* it with a decision too. At the *end* of the Logic, another decision. Let's

---

25 To be perfectly honest, it was a couple of Italian professors a couple of years ago. Both translate *Entschluß* as decision [*decisione*], both times, beginning and end.

see. Hegel gathers up the threads of his 'method'—his science of logic—and tells us that 'the science presents itself as a *circle* that winds around itself, where the mediation winds the end back to that beginning which is the simple ground; the circle is thus *a circle of circles*, for each single member ensouled by the method is reflected into itself, so that in returning to the beginning it is at the same time the beginning of a new member.' Now, these 'members' are the individual sciences—of logic, nature, and spirit.

There is so much happening on these last pages. *Screech*. I may already be back in Manhattan, I don't know where I am. On the F Train, definitely. Traveling indefinitely. My rummaging is going wild. But I just want to say this. In my extremely limited experience as an NYU (undergraduate) student, if I want to know what freedom, necessity, and *decision* mean for Hegel, I'd better keep on reading these last pages of the Logic. At the very end, he says things like: 'this idea is still logical, it is shut up in pure thought, the science only of the divine *concept*'—absolutely, the one thing this book is really about is the 'concept.' No, not *about* the concept—it is the self-expression, the self-realization, *of the concept itself*. 'We' have decided to break with all the old forms of logic and to consider *thinking as such*. Hegel calls the 'pure idea' that *ends* the science of logic 'an absolute *liberation*'—this *'freedom* in which no transition takes place. The simple being to which the idea determines itself remains perfectly transparent to it: it is the concept that in its determination abides with itself.' Keeps to itself. Stays at home with itself. *Bei sich*, so to speak. *Chez soi*, as the French put it. At this point—and we are just fifteen lines from the end of the whole book, the end of the Science of Logic—Hegel suddenly 'decides' to sum up his *entire* 'system of totality,' his *tangle* of logic, nature, and spirit. His *idea*. If you like extreme sports, this page is for you. How shall we get from the 'realm of shadows' to the 'externality of space and time'—

from logic to nature. From the subway to Washington Square Park. Not exactly, but, as it were. From shadows to substance, so to speak.[26] Behold! The passage is *absolutely free.* 'The idea *freely releases* itself, absolutely certain of itself and internally at rest. Thanks to this freedom, the *form of its determinateness* is just as absolutely free—the *externality of space and time* absolutely existing for itself without subjectivity.' Nature. *Hegel's* nature. But what about *spirit.* Believe you me, this logic-nature-spirit relationship is so complex that I could rummage from here to eternity and not get to the bottom of it. But Hegel is writing the very last lines of his longest book, and he is in a good mood. To get from a Frank Zappa 'absolutely free' nature[27] (but 'we're only in it for the money'—long live the 1960s![28] apart from the war against Vietnam) to the rich but strenuous experience of spirit, behold! *another decision.* I kid you not! The Science of Logic *begins* and *ends* with a decision.

Screech. Not only am I back in Manhattan already—time flies—but this screech is Rockefeller Center, a major screech, a VIS—Very Important Screech—tons of people are pouring into the car, a weekday, mid-afternoon, this stop is hipping and hopping like Hegel's concept. The joint is jumping. I'd better stop rummaging around in Hegel and *look* around, there are some weird people in the car. But, I think they're tourists, so it doesn't matter. Let me just read this one more time. *In the idea* (the end of the Logic) the *externality of space and time* (i.e., nature, barely) remains in and for itself the totality of the concept. But, the transition from nature to spirit? A

26 Actually, by 'the externality of space and time' Hegel doesn't mean Washington Square Park. He's not referring to 'substance' either. I'll get back to this, I hope, at the end of this book.

27 OK, to be precise, his second official album (he cut ninety-nine) was *Absolutely Free* (1966) and his fourth was *We're Only in it for the Money* (1968), both of which I bought, and listened to, often. For the record, the first was *Freak Out!* and the third, *Lumpy Gravy.*

28 As Tuli Kupferberg of the Fugs, immortal author of 'Kill For Peace,' said: 'Nobody who lived through the '50s thought the '60s could have existed. So there's always hope.'

decision. Arbitrary, possibly, like the first one.[29] (Hegel is an elephant, he sure as hell remembers 'the *decision* to consider *thinking as such*.') Free, necessary, whatever. Responsible, irresponsible, who knows. I'd better just read this, fast. Weird people. 'But what is posited *by this next decision* of the pure idea to determine itself as external idea is only the mediation[30] out of which the concept, as free concrete existence that from externality has come to itself, raises itself up, completes this self-liberation *in the science of spirit*, and in the science of logic finds the highest concept of itself, the pure concept conceptually comprehending itself.'[31]

Beautiful. Makes me want to take a walk in the park, on a sunny spring day. But I have a decision to make, and the *sub*way is *my* way. *Screech*. 34th Street. I'm right under 6th Avenue, also known as Avenue of the Americas. From Rockefeller Center (a *long* station, from 47th to 50th Streets) down to West 4th I'm under 6th Avenue all the way, then a little turn to the east—Delancey—then the Rutgers Tube, then Brooklyn. Under 6th Avenue business is brisk, a lot of people getting on and off, many of them tourists, not commuters. I put Hegel back into my bag, for now. Look around. Nothing special. People coming and going. Sitting, a few standing. Ever since I read *Moby Dick* last summer, after my military-psychiatric draft hearing, I never stop thinking about Melville. I'd like to know more about his life. I think he had a hard time. I know his books never sold—not during his lifetime. I know he wrote *Moby Dick* when he was living up in the Berkshires— beautiful country, they say, but he went broke and moved back to Manhattan. Hard times. I think he was a really good person. I imagine him very quiet and very passionate. He finally got a job as an inspector at the New York Customs House. Held it for

---

29 Actually, since the idea is now, at the end of the Logic, the *supremely free*, this time the decision may *not* be regarded as arbitrary.

30 Not to be confused with *meditation*. An interesting idea, though.

31 This is pure Di Giovanni, he's wiped Miller out here, not only more faithful but the prose is absolutely beautiful.

twenty years, earned just enough to scrape by. When he retired he started working on this little book, *Billy Budd*—it wasn't quite finished when he died in 1891, and wasn't published until 1924. I've read it three times since last summer. It's short. It's an incredible story. An abyss: you can look into it forever and never see the bottom. *Screech*. Where are we? I've been daydreaming. Look! The world! We're going over the Gowanus Canal. It's still mid-afternoon, Friday afternoon. Down again, under the ground. 'A wide landscape of snows'—just a flash. In the 'Whiteness of the Whale' chapter in *Moby Dick* Melville writes: 'a dumb blankness, full of meaning, in a wide landscape of snows.' I take *Billy Budd* out of my book bag. Yes, I'm going to read it again. It's short, and I'm traveling indefinitely. On a sea of time.

This book ('novella' is the proper term) is not exactly an action story. Then again, in Proust much less happens, in a hundred times more pages. (Not that I've read Proust, but I've heard about him.) *Billy Budd* is very short. A few years ago I just happened to pick up this 'Magnum Easy Eye Books' edition, with large type and wide spacing—great for underlining passages and making notes. And, who knows, 'when I'm sixty-four' it might be really great for my own Eye. Less than 140 pages. But in a Normal Eye edition I bet it'd be 70 pages—a long short story. Now, OK, since I've read it three times recently I'll sum up what happens, in advance. The action. The bare episodes.

Everyone adores Billy Budd, the 'welkin-eyed,' twenty-one-year-old, 'Handsome Sailor.' Innocence personified. A foundling: no past (and no future). They adored him—their *peacemaker*—on the merchant ship happily named the *Rights-of-Man,* after the book by Thomas Paine. (He of the 'times that try men's souls.') The year is 1797. The British Royal Navy is at war with Revolutionary France—a war that culminated happily (for the Brits) in 1805 off Cape Trafalgar, where Nelson triumphed (and died), earning his statue in Trafalgar Square. But 1797 was the year of the Great Mutiny—a lesser one at Spithead (near Portsmouth), then the Great one at the Nore (in the Thames Estuary). These were not violent insurrections, they were more like strikes against the miserable pay and despicable working conditions in the British Navy. But the Admiralty got *extremely riled up* about it all and at the Nore 29 of the leaders were hanged, to say nothing of the floggings, imprisonments, and transportations to Australia. And all this just two months before Melville's tale. Which begins with Billy impressed into service on the warship *Bellipotent* ('power of war': in the first version Melville called it the *Indomitable*), cheerfully bidding adieu to his old shipmates, and then to the ship itself with his innocent quip, 'And good-bye to you too, old *Rights-of-Man!*'

Now, the action. In a nutshell. Billy—now the 'fighting peacemaker'—is happy as a lark and gets on fine with his new shipmates. But, for unexplained reasons, he arouses the enmity of the ship's master-at-arms, John Claggart, who goes to the Captain—Edward Fairfax 'Starry' Vere—and accuses the Handsome Sailor of conspiracy to mutiny. A serious charge, and a bloody bad time to level it. At poor absolutely innocent Billy. Captain Vere summons the antagonists to his cabin for a showdown. Claggart repeats his accusation. And Billy is unable to respond, due to his 'tragic flaw'—the 'little card' slipped in by that devil of a Serpent, the 'envious marplot of Eden': when emotionally challenged—'under sudden provocation of strong heart-feeling'—Billy falls prey to an *extreme stutter*. Unable to speak, 'his right arm shot out and Claggart dropped to the deck.' Dead. Captain Vere *immediately* convenes a drumhead court-martial. He is fully convinced that Claggart's charge was false and Billy is morally innocent, but *this is war* and in war it is the *deed alone* that counts. The capital crime. Motivation or circumstance count for nothing. As Vere puts it: 'Struck dead by an angel of God! Yet the angel must hang!' So, at the court-martial Vere lords it over the three (unconvinced) officers he himself appointed, will brook no contradiction, and sees to it that Billy indeed be hanged. 'Quick action': from death blow to death sentence 'less than an hour and a half had elapsed.' The 'slumbering embers of the Nore' must not be awakened—this is Vere's sole concern. The Letter of the Law, i.e. the Mutiny Act and the Articles of War. Vere loves Billy like a son. As dawn breaks, in the presence of the crew, Billy is hanged from the yardarm. His last words are 'God bless Captain Vere!'

That's the story. And all this in the broad daylight of Brooklyn, and here I am at Coney Island. Time flies when you're telling stories. Will I ever eat a Coney Island hot dog? Probably not but, anyway, I have to say that this is one of the greatest stations in the entire subway (as far as I know). Its full name is Stilwell Avenue/Coney Island, and it has a special charm that Penn and Grand Central can only dream about. Maybe because it's quieter way out here. Wow, the Atlantic Ocean is a stone's throw from where I'm standing right now. And I love these eight tracks lined up side-by-side—8 tracks, 4 island platforms, 2 tracks for each platform, supremely geometric. To get my new F I just have to cross over to the other side of the platform. What's more, there are platforms right here where I can also get the D Train and the B Train, two trains that definitely interest me. No, I never changed trains on my 'three in the morning' or less Taoist head-getting-together jaunts, but this time I've embarked on an 'indefinite' figuring-out-how-to-make-a-decision venture. This time I've taken to the subway *indefinitely*. (I could also take the N, the Broadway Local, it goes to Astoria, but I already have Queens covered.) The D would take me quite a ways up in the Bronx, and I already know the train pretty well from the many times I've taken it to Yankee Stadium to see the Yanks. (Never the Giants, of course, you need an impossible-to-get season ticket for that.) And the B takes you way up in Manhattan,[32] to Washington Heights. I've been up there several times, to the Cloisters, to see the fabulous beautiful Unicorn Tapestries. My favorite is 'The Unicorn in Captivity' where the poor thing is chained to a pomegranate tree and penned in by a miniscule fence. Since I'm traveling 'indefinitely' now, later on maybe I should give the D and the B a try. Of course, it would mean losing touch with Delancey Street. So be it. Also—I can switch from F to D or to B at West 4th, 34th Street, 42nd Street, or Rockefeller Center, in case I want to make a snap decision, to keep myself alert, create some randomness. But here at Coney Island—well bless my soul, the randomness has been here all along, I just never thought about it. 'Three in the morning' or at any time at all. Change trains! When I'm here I can ponder and then decide, or do a Zen 'no-mind,' the sudden way. Or both together. But—for the moment I'm sticking with the F. By the time I get back to Manhattan it will be *rush hour on a Friday afternoon*. We shall see what poor Billy has to say about that. So, here I go. Back on the F.

Now, why am I about to read *Billy Budd* for the fourth time since last summer? I already said why. Because it's about decisions, like *Moby Dick* and *Pierre*. (*Pierre* is really an *extreme*—possibly pathological—case of a book about decisions, I'd better not start talking about *Pierre*, if I do I'll never stop.) *Billy Budd* is as short as *Moby Dick* is long, there isn't much action, the narration is relaxed, avuncular, not intense (and not dreamy like Ishmael's), but—as I said, the book is an abyss. It is bottomless. It is semantically unfathomable—I mean, it doesn't have just one right interpretation. In terms of 'what it all means' it is what is known as 'undecidable.' Which is *not* to say that Melville decided not to *mean anything*. No: 'some certain significance lurks in all things, else all things are little worth, and the

---

32 But not exactly to the Cloisters (for that you need the A to 190th Street). Shoot me. Poetic license. Anyway, it's just a (pretty) short stroll in a lovely neighborhood.

round world itself but an empty cipher,' as Ahab notes while contemplating The Doubloon. (One of my favorite lines in *Moby Dick*, it's in Chapter 99.) No, let me say two things about *Billy Budd*, as I gaze from the F Train at the Brooklyn twilight— look! a last trace of this winter's snow, soiled by the coming of spring. 'White jumper and white duck trousers, each more or less soiled, dimly glimmered in the obscure light of the bay *like a patch of discolored snow in early April* lingering at some upland cave's black mouth,' Melville wrote, about Billy, 'already in his shroud.' Waiting for his hanging. At dawn. And here he is now, not far from Coney Island.

Two things. First, Melville's story continuously rewrites itself, working itself into and out of a tangle. For two reasons: because Melville was a genius, but also because he kept rewriting it. He was undecided. And the story is about decision—one who decides, and two who are 'decided for.' He decided to have three characters—Billy, Claggart, then Vere— but kept changing his mind about which one would ultimately be the focus of the book. What's more, while the characters of Billy and Claggart are well defined—innocence and iniquity, let's say—Melville may have dramatically changed his mind in midstream about Vere—from an Abraham with his Isaac to a pedantic pawn of war. With the muffled voice of an old and tired man Melville *rails* against war—'the abrogation of everything but force'—in the last chapters of the book, and against the 'God of War' (Mars, in Greek Ares). Let me not forget that I myself am writing an 'anti-war' story here; that I have to decide to make a decision that will be decisive for the rest of my life *because of a war*—the U.S. war against Vietnam; and that what really spurred me on to 'take to the subway *indefinitely*' were these *Two Notes on Aeschylus' Septem* by Seth Benardete, my Greek Political Theory professor. (*Septem*, short for *Seven Against Thebes*.) The second Note is on Eteocles' 'decision,' but the first is about Ares, God of War, and about who [what] this god is and, more specifically, about why Aeschylus himself (according to Aristophanes) claimed he had 'made the Septem *full of Ares.*' My feeling is that—against his original intention—Melville made *Billy Budd* 'full of Ares.' And, what's more, that his *real* questions turn out to be: What/Who is Ares? *Who decides? What* is a decision?

Second thing. Melville dramatically—decisively—titles this novella *Billy Budd, Sailor (An inside narrative).* Prima facie, 'inside narrative' signifies the symbolic projection of a personal crisis (in this case, of Melville's) and its resolution. But Melville himself defines it from the start as 'the inner life of one particular ship and the career of an individual sailor.' But at that moment the story's focus was Billy, and Claggart's antagonism, with Vere simply 'presiding over' this (one-sided) antagonism. Then the story lost its clear outline. A question: if Billy and Claggart are clearly antagonists, who is Vere's antagonist? I think his antagonist is Admiral Horatio Nelson. Melville tacked on a whole chapter 'beckoned by the genius of Nelson'—'the greatest sailor since the world began,' as Tennyson put it. For me personally, this is what the story is all about. What/Who is Ares? Answer that first, then you can say: what/who *decides*. One note here: Melville's declared 'inside narrative' is in fact one of the greatest 'outside narratives' of all time—right up there with Dalton Trumbo's *Johnny Got His Gun.* (Which I was very careful *not* to take with me on this trip, which is *not* intended to be 'from here to eternity.') And, here, by 'outside narrative' I mean—for once—something truly plain and simple. I mean: a *political* narrative.

There's a lot going on right now here on the F Train. For starters, it's FULL of people, what are they all doing here? I've always been a night-journeyer down here among the 'sunless dead,' I'm not used to these crowds. We haven't even come as far as the Gowanus Canal, it's not even five o'clock. Isn't the *rush hour* supposed to mean Brooklynites rushing *back to* Brooklyn from Manhattan after work? Or not. I'm no expert. What do I know about Brooklyn? Just the subway stops, the Coney Island station, the few minutes towering over the Gowanus Canal (in its depths, they say, it's one of the murkiest places on earth), and the *landscape* I can see from the F Train between Coney Island and Ditmas Avenue. This is the first time I've ever been here in the daytime, at 'three in the morning' the 'obscure light' of Brooklyn is a dim glimmer. A hazy dream. 'A wide landscape of snows.' Billy in his shroud, *like a patch of discolored snow in early April*. What do I know. I myself am in the subway indefinitely, studying my decision. Are these people rushing *around* Brooklyn, putting in their 30 red cents to go ye gods know where in Brooklyn itself? Or are they headed for Manhattan, at this hour, to do what? Beats me. They are definitely not tourists, they all look like Brooklynites— Flatbushers, Borough Parkers, Park Slopers, Sheepshead Bayers, Williamsburgers, Brooklyn Heightsers, or whatevers. I read a little article—it's called a 'filler'—in the *Post* a while back, titled 'How the Dodgers got their Name' (a nostalgia piece)—I mean the Brooklyn Dodgers baseball team, long since decamped to Los Angeles after a mere 73 years (1884-1957) in Brooklyn, with the baseball Giants hot on their heels, bound for San Francisco. Like bats out of hell. Go West, young man! (Is Vietnam east or west? A tricky question. It's in the East, but to get there fast Go West, young man! Go West! It's Manifest Destiny. But watch out for falling dominoes, falling east, *screaming* 'California here we come!'.) We still have the football Giants of course (to say nothing of the Mets and Jets), but you need an impossible-to-get season ticket to see them. Anyway— shit, the car is packed like sardines, the Gowanus Canal will have to look after itself, I won't even get a glimpse of it this time. Now, the 'Brooklyn Trolley Dodgers'—this is the story. It's about trolleys, trolley cars—what in Europe they call trams. No, nothing to do with draft dodgers, the draft didn't exist in 1884, it only dates back to 1917. Woodrow Wilson. Peace in our time—no, sorry, that was Neville Chamberlain, 1938, 'peace for our time.' 'Make the world safe for democracy,' that's Wilson, and the draft. 1917. This means war! Anyway, the story is this. (A fat lady is threatening to sit on my lap. What fat lady? Ye gods know. All I know is that it ain't over till the fat lady sings. God Bless America.[33]) Trolley Dodgers, I read it in the *Post*, the story is this. Once upon a time, in the late 19th and early 20th century, Brooklyn was criss-crossed by trolley cars weaving their way through the borough, a veritable streetcar labyrinth, every way you turned—Watch out! A streetcar! Wild animals. Surviving took real skill here in Brooklyn. And the Manhattanites disparagingly termed the Brooklynites 'trolley dodgers.' Because in Manhattan they had a lot more money, to dig their metropolitan Hades? Today most City Transit is *under* the ground, only sight-seers and old ladies take the bus. Down here you *get there fast*. The subway is our way here in Fun City. Hiz Honor was right. A parade is a parade is a parade.

But what are all these people *doing* down here. I can't even see the name of the stations, I wonder if I'm back to Manhattan yet. Will I even *see* Delancey? How am I going to read *Billy Budd* with all this going on. So—in Manhattan, disparagingly, they called them 'trolley dodgers,' but they called their team the Dodgers anyway. I think because they were proud of their skill at dodging the trolleys, even though in baseball itself it's a question of pitching, batting, running, throwing, and catching, not of dodging. In 1895 when they first gave the team its name—Brooklyn Trolley Dodgers—the trolley cars in Brooklyn had just been switched from horse-power to electricity. A lot faster, and a lot more dangerous. A maze, a veritable jungle of speedy streetcars. So I guess skill at dodging them was something to be proud of. A skill. A sport.

---

33 The expression refers, possibly, to Brünnhilde in Richard Wagner's *Götterdämmerung*, but I prefer (no patriotism intended) the (possibly questionable) version in which it's Kate Smith, singing 'God Bless America.'

Have I ever been in the subway during the rush hour before? Not that I recall. If it's raining and I decide to take the subway to or from NYU, (debatably) to get less wet, Delancey to West 4th or vice versa—well, I go to school just before noon and usually come home around 7 or 8, and neither way is rush hour, even though the car is crowded because of the rain. As far as I can recall I've always avoided the rush hour. I don't like crowds. 'Three in the morning' is one thing, crowds are another. Speaking of the Dodgers, whenever I go up to the Bronx to see the Yankees I always sit way out there in the Bleachers (the ticket went up recently from 75 cents to a dollar), lots of room out there, a real relaxed atmosphere, great view of the game, even if almost all the action is half a mile away. No crowds, unless it happens to be the World Series, and we haven't had one of those for quite a while. Back to the subway. I've definitely never been in the *morning* rush hour because I sleep in the morning, until 11. The afternoon—well, the peak is from 4 to 6 I'd say, though I guess things are busy from as early as 3 to as late as 7. Of course, this takes no account of the tourists in Manhattan (the *action* tourists, getting from sight to sight *fast*, seeing nothing but subway in between), or of rainy days. And weekends have no rush hours—thank goodness. In this God-fearing city in this God-fearing country good God-fearing people don't work on weekends. Tomorrow is Saturday. I just hope it doesn't rain.

I wonder if that *screech* was Delancey. With all these people practically on top of me—of course, at least, *I am sitting down*—I can't see a thing. It's funny, when there are just a *few* people in the car you can actually *see* the people; when there are quite a few, you still get a feeling for who the people are and what they're like; but when it's *packed*—zero. They might as well all be green with two heads, five arms, and three legs. Lots of people are a lot like no people at all. Being is nothing. The empty mirror. This is going to be one

hell of a long trip to 179th Street/Jamaica, I'll just have to ride
it out. Maybe I'll have an apple. No, too complicated. A piece
of cheese. Maybe my grandfather was right, a nice raw onion
would hit the spot right about now. Earn me a little elbow-
room. I'll nibble the cheese slowly, just a small piece of it, like
a mouse. 34th Street—a *lot* of people get off, I can breathe for
about 30 seconds, then a *lot* of people get back on. I nibble.
42nd Street—same deal: lots off, lots on. Sooner or later we'll
make it to Queens, then through Queens, but the car will be
packed all the way. Enough cheese for now, it was just to pass
the time. *Billy Budd, Sailor (An inside narrative)*. I'm definitely
somewhere under Queens by now, traveling indefinitely,
because I have to make a decision. I'll reread *Billy Budd*
properly a little later on when things quiet down. Meanwhile,
a snippet here and there, thinking about the subject that
interests me most right now—the *inside* narrative, which is
all about 'inside' *decision*. Sure, the 'outside' narrative—the
political narrative—interests me too, and one hell of a lot. And
it interested Melville too, and one hell of a lot. But—political
decision? Isn't a 'political decision' a contradiction in terms?
Politicians 'function,' necessarily. It's the military-industrial
complex. (Not all that different from the Oedipus complex.)
Basically, what they do is like taking a shit. Necessary. Just
do it. (Ask Captain Vere, with his instant drumhead court.)
If politicians 'decide' something it means they're not really
politicians. War is hell, and politics is worse. Decisions smack
of ethics, free will, responsibility. Stuff for suckers. Just ask
Richard Nixon.

Let me say something about the three characters—Billy,
Claggart, Vere. They are—as Ahab so graphically put it—like
'pasteboard masks.' Melville makes them all surface and
absolutely no depth. This is not *Moby Dick* (or *Pierre* either).
'If man will strike'—shrieks Ahab—'strike through the mask!
How can the prisoner reach outside except by thrusting through

the wall?' No, this time it is the masks themselves that strike, and with no intention to 'reach outside.' On the contrary, this is an *inside* narrative. Claggart strikes Billy (iniquitously). Billy strikes Claggart dead (unintentionally). Vere strikes Billy dead, in the name of the King and the Articles of War. All *inside* the Captain's cabin. No harpoons here. Melville draws us three *inseparable* masks (no character can exist without the others), and then *violently separates them.* The novella is a masterpiece of abstraction. It reminds me of Mark Rothko's great works with the three rectangles—inseparable, but most definitely separated. To see *what is there* you have to look at *the whole picture*. Step back and look closely.

I must be somewhere under Queens, where else could I possibly be. This is the F Train. *Screech.* Bless my soul, there's a little space between the sardines. Roosevelt Avenue. I wonder what Queens is like. How many of these people are genuine Jamaicans, headed for the end of the line, like me. Headed home on a Friday afternoon at the end of March, after a long winter. Why should a neighborhood in Queens have the same name as an island south of Cuba? Beats me. Maybe the first inhabitants were actually from the Jamaica south of Cuba. Maybe the first inhabitants of the Jamaica south of Cuba were actually from Queens. (A long shot.) In any event, Melville paints his masks in contrasting colors. The contrast between Billy and Claggart couldn't be sharper. Billy is 'a young Adam before the fall,' 'an angel of God,' and Claggart 'the direct reverse of a saint.' But Melville has incredibly little to say about Billy, his hero. A nature that—as Claggart puts it—'had in its simplicity never willed malice or experienced the reactionary bite of that serpent.' If it hadn't been for his *extreme stutter* at the worst possible time, he would have been an insignificant character in his own novella. A mere 'welkin-eyed' foil for the other masks. By contrast, Melville has a lot to say about Claggart. Not about the role he *plays* in the story, his

personage—he is a pasteboard mask, and there is no striking
through him—but about his 'hidden nature' and the 'mysteries
of iniquity' that lurk there. Not in the depths but on the surface.
I think we're coming to the Jamaica screech, a few moments of
relative peace. Stretch my legs, take it easy before I get back
on the next F. I'm curious to see whether there will be a wild
bunch of Jamaicans rushing *out* of Jamaica in the rush hour.
Going to Manhattan to do *what?* We'll see. I have my *Billy Budd*
in my hand now, full of my notes and underlined passages.
There are some things I want to take a good look at.

    Melville devotes three whole chapters to Claggart's
'mysterious' nature—ten times, a hundred times as much as
he does to Billy's, which was, we might say, the 'direct reverse'
of mysterious. Welkin-eyed. A clear blue sky. 'What was the
matter with the master-at arms?' Melville's narrator asks. (By
the way, he defines master-at-arms as a 'maritime Chief of
Police.') To answer the question—incredibly—he quotes Plato.
'Natural Depravity: a depravity according to nature.' This is
Claggart's problem. (And, consequently, Billy's.) In Claggart
this 'mania of an evil nature' was 'born with him and innate.'
But Melville says some remarkable things here. I'll get back
to this when I contrast Claggart with Captain Vere. 'The thing
which in eminent instances signalizes so exceptional a nature is
this: though the man's even temper and discreet bearing would
seem to intimate *a mind particularly subject to the law of
reason*, not the less in the soul's recesses he would seem to *riot
in complete exemption from that law*, having apparently little
to do with reason further than to employ it as an ambidexter
implement for effecting the irrational. [I think this is one hell of
a mouthful.] That is to say: towards the accomplishment of an
aim which in wantonness of malignity would seem to partake of
the insane, he will direct a cool judgment sagacious and sound.
These men are true madmen...' As we shall see, Claggart and
Vere may seem the 'direct reverse' of one another, but when

it comes to madness I'm not so sure. (Basically, the only thing you can be *sure* of in this story is that Billy gets an *extreme stutter* when he's 'under sudden provocation of strong heart-feeling.') In these true madmen 'the method and outward proceeding is always perfectly rational.' 'With no power to annul the elemental evil in himself, though readily enough he could hide it; apprehending the good, but powerless to be it; a nature like Claggart's, surcharged with energy as such natures almost invariably are, what recourse is left to it but to recoil upon itself and like the scorpion for which the Creator alone is responsible, act out to the end the part allotted it.'

All this, yet in the *story* the man is purely and simply a pasteboard mask. In a few words, a few lines, he toys with Billy a little, then falsely accuses him, and then gets himself killed *because of Billy's extreme stutter*. Period. Exit the master-at-arms. 'Could I have used my tongue I would not have struck him,' Billy notes. 'In the jugglery of circumstances—Melville's narrator observes—innocence and guilt changed places.' But this is not the *real story*, this is not what *Billy Budd* is really about. I'm going to reread it again tonight, it won't take me too long. I'm back on the F Train—*screech*—it's metal on metal, these metal wheels on the metal tracks, and the way they brake *fast* down here under Fun City. Why can't they use rubber wheels like on cars? I guess with this fast braking ten-thousand times a day the rubber wouldn't last long. I wonder how long the metal lasts, for that matter. *Screech*—the screech is the same during the rush hour or at 'three in the morning,' screeching right into the marrow of my mind. Do I notice it less when the car is packed or when it's practically empty? I'm not sure, it's a good question. *Screech*—I'm already back to Roosevelt Avenue. There weren't that many Jamaicans, good for them. But I'll be back in midtown Manhattan before long. Shiver my timbers and batten down the hatches. At least I have a seat. When I get to Coney Island I'm going to jog up and down the eight platforms for a while, if they're not too crowded.

Now, before I get caught in traffic again, I want to say something about 'being and seeming'—a big issue Professor Benardete raises in his Notes on the *Seven Against Thebes*, and one of the main things I am traveling indefinitely here in Hades to think about. Along with 'decision' and with 'war' and who's 'responsible' for it. (I mean, is only the President, the government, responsible, or is an NYU student in a $55 a month apartment on Rivington Street also responsible? A draft DODGER? Hell no. A 4-F war veteran. An enemy of our war against Vietnam, looking for a *proper* hearing.) This is what I'm down here in 'this joyless region' to think about, since, as we now know, I have to make my *own decision*. About the fork, so to speak: GAM, bomb, exile. 'Being and seeming.' 'Claggart, the monomania in the man... covered over by his self-contained and rational demeanor.' But this is not play-acting, it is 'depravity according to nature' (says Melville, says Plato). OK, fair enough. But just wait until I take a good look at *Captain Vere*—'the monomania in the man... covered over by his self-contained and rational demeanor.' Claggart and Vere—now *this* is a lesson in abstraction. Separate, but unseparated. Self-contradiction. 'Separation of the inseparable'—this is what Hegel means by 'abstraction.' But—*screech*, the car is packed, and I think we're still in Queens—listen to this one: Claggart gives Vere a lesson on the dangers of confusing being and seeming. He should know, we might say. But Vere, the upright downright rational military intellectual, what does *he* know? That's what I want to know. Anyway, in a nutshell, Claggart, in his false accusation, *warns* his Captain: 'You have but noted his fair cheek. A mantrap may be under his fine ruddy-tipped daisies.' In other words: watch out for your *Handsome Sailor*, your picture of innocence, plotting a new—and *very ugly*—Great Mutiny right here on your very own peaceful power-of-war *Bellipotent*. Being and seeming *are not the same*. Sure, 'appearances can be deceptive' is a platitude, but—this is 'natural depravity' addressing martial law. The plot, as they say, thickens.

As does this madding horde. Shit, here's a really cute really young woman, possibly a girl (how old? 18? 16? 21? 19? I'm not good at ages) barely hovering over me in a position that I'm sure is included somewhere in the Kama Sutra. Strap-hangers may take dozens of such positions, every day, twice a day, at their pleasure, I guess. Be my guest. My other great NYU professor, Dave Leahy, who is also my friend, once said something confusing and ambiguous, in his course on Kierkegaard. He said: on the one hand, the majority of 'love stories' in New York start up in the subway during rush hour (or, perhaps, when it's raining hard); and, on the other, do not confuse 'love' with that chick splayed all over you in the sardine-packed car. Don't confuse love with commuter-contact sports, is what he means. A crude and subtle notion. Not a 'three in the morning' issue. We're not talking about 'chance encounters' in the (relative) emptiness of the middle-of-the-night subway—in New York the subway is never empty. No, it's a question of extreme close-contact sports. Action. Compulsory physical education. 'Eight million stories in the Naked City.' Edward Fairfax 'Starry' Vere, captain of the *Bellipotent*—a pasteboard mask, but intricately drawn. Ambiguously drawn— more ambiguous than intricate. We believe he truly loves Billy— real fatherly affection, not 'subway love.' We're in Manhattan. Rockefeller Center. Coitus interruptus: the girl got off. Maybe she's going ice-skating. New sardines, just as packed as before. A guy in a suit just stepped on my foot. I think it's going to be like this all the way to Coney Island. Every train on the whole 'city transit system'—IND, IRT, BMT, from A to Z, from 1 to 9—every single one is packed right now. It wasn't like this in Melville's day. My traveling companions, green with two heads, five arms, and three legs. Going home to Brooklyn? Whatever. Naked City. Eight million stories, plus tourists. *Billy Budd, Sailor*. Captain Vere 'had a marked leaning towards everything intellectual. He loved books, never going to sea without a newly replenished library.' Billy 'could not read, but he could sing.' There's 'a queer streak of the pedantic' in Vere. 'Sturdy qualities, without any brilliant ones.' 'A resolute nature.' 'The most undemonstrative of men.' Still, his 'knowledge and ability' made him a pretty good Captain. Despite 'a certain dreaminess of mood. Standing alone on the weather-side of the greater deck... he would absently gaze off at the black sea.' At the moment of our crisis—Billy with his 'convulsed tongue-tie' followed by Claggart's 'lasting tongue-tie' of the dead—we find Vere 'apparently in one of his absent fits, gazing out from a sashed port-hole to windward upon the monotonous blank of the twilight sea.' How I wish I could write like that. But, I'm only 21. Still just an NYU student.

Ye gods, West 4th already. Maybe you do notice the screeches less when the car is packed with people. Wow, another cute woman/girl, with a book bag, hanging Kama-Sutra-like from a strap right in front of me. Come to think of it, she looks like a possible fellow NYUer, so to speak. Though I've never seen her in the Classics Department. Then again, our department is the smallest in the whole university. We're four cats, *quattro gatti*, as the Italians put it. (I'm also studying Italian. PCI. Gramsci. Eurocommunism. Enrico Berlinguer.) Few and far between. Book bag. Cute. Zen Mind. Samurai. 'Hi,' I say, courageously. (Chatting up chicks is not easy for me.) 'What're you reading?' she asks, smiling, I think. '*Billy Budd*.' 'Heavy!' she says. 'I love it.' 'No kidding'—I say—'I read it all the time.' *Screech*. Now I hear the screeches. 'But I love *Michael Kohlhass* even more,' she says.[34] *Screech* again. Who

---

34 Kleist's novella about a man with an *extremely exaggerated* sense of justice. Kafka's favorite story. See *Selected Prose of Heinrich von Kleist*, Brooklyn! Archipelago Books, 2010, magnificently translated by Peter Wortsman, p. 235 and p. 165. Too bad Kafka never got a chance to read Melville.

cares. Kama Sutra. 'You can make me mount the scaffold, but I can get you where it hurts.' Taken aback, I note: 'He sure has a great sense of justice.' 'Better to be a dog than a man, if I'm to be kicked around!' she quips, still quoting. 'Are you from Brooklyn?' I ask, an extremely dumb question at this point in the conversation. 'Yeah, York Street. It's near the Navy Yard.' 'Nice place,' I say, absurdly. 'First stop after the Rutgers Tube,' I add, eruditely. *Screech*—it's Delancey, my stop. 'My stop's Delancey.' 'But you're not getting off?' 'No'—I'd better not get into a traveling-indefinitely decision-making rap with this nice girl, getting off in just a few minutes—East Broadway, then York, if she lived in Coney Island I might have given it a shot— 'No, I'm going to visit my Greek Tragedy professor in Borough Park.' *Screech* again. 'What do you think about Captain Vere?' she asks me. Wow. 'I think about him all the time,' I say. I say, 'I think *he's* the true madman, not Claggart.' She says, 'I think he's an abyss: you can look into him forever and never see the bottom.' *Screech*. York Street, and off she goes. Vanished. And I wanted to say: An abyss! But he's a pasteboard mask, like the other two. What does this girl know anyway. The car is still packed, but I think it's going to thin out bit by bit, these are all people going home, not fun-seekers yearning for a Coney Island hot dog. An abyss. No, not Vere, no, the *whole story* is an abyss, there's no getting to the bottom of it. But it's time for the heart of the matter—decision! decision! *This* is what it's all about, and this is why I'm thinking about *Billy Budd* and am about to reread it *again* while traveling *indefinitely*, and before rereading *Seven Against Thebes* and Benardete's two Notes on it. That chick was cute and pretty smart, I think. Ye gods, prefers Kleist to Melville. What a chick. I think I'll just chill out until I get to Coney Island. Now, the nether darkness. Soon, the obscure light of Brooklyn, even though the last dim glimmer has already faded. The rush hour is fading. It's night. Night, the mother of counsel. Another platitude. The Mothers of Invention. Uncle Meat. Zappa. Necessity. Absolutely Free. No doubt about it: being is nothing. Logic. 'The *decision* to consider *thinking as such*.'

'Which may also be regarded as arbitrary.' Coney Island. Gazing off at the black sea. In my mind, since I can't actually see it from here inside the station. The monotonous blank. The whiteness of the sea. The empty screen. I'm glad the station is not too crowded. End of March, no tourists around. The Coney Islanders happy at home, looking forward to the weekend. My legs are stiff. Time for exercise. *Fast* walking up and down and back on all four island platforms, there's no law against it. Walking. A good half hour. Walking walking. I feel better. Ready for the F Train. Here it is. Almost no one on it. Should I have an apple? *Screech* already, *screech* again—Neptune Avenue, sounds nice—the name, I mean, not the *screech*. No, I'm not hungry. It's barely past 7 and I never have my daily meal until 11 o'clock, before studying all night. Coffee yogurt in the morning, and I had two of them today. At school, possibly an apple, cut into pieces. I ought to have the cheese before it goes bad. Later. A sip of water. This is no gourmet tour, the rest of my life depends on what I decide on this journey. Shit, last year I went almost entirely without food for five full months. A few days down here fasting with the sunless dead won't kill me. My grandfather could have gotten halfway across Europe with the four apples I have here in my bag, as long as he also had some onions. Billy, Claggart, Vere. Billy and Claggart decide nothing, both of them are *decided for*. By what? In the first place, by *nature*. (For Billy, in the second place by his God-Bless-You Captain Vere. Believe me, I'm coming to that.) Did Billy *decide* to be the Handsome Sailor? Did he *decide* to have an *extreme stutter* when 'under sudden provocation of strong heart-feeling'? (Never mind his not *deciding* to get impressed by the Royal Navy, or his not *deciding* to arouse Claggart's enmity.) *Nature*. If Claggart's is *Natural Depravity* (as Plato apparently put it), then our master-at-arms is well and truly *decided for*. A 'true madman' precisely in the sense that he *decides nothing*. (In contemporary criminology—'diminished responsibility'—this is open to considerable debate, but I'm talking about *Melville's story* here.) Billy is tongue-tied by nature, and Claggart is *doubly* tongue-tied (to death) by nature—by Billy's nature, and by his own. Decided *for*. They, *themselves*, decide nothing.

But *Captain* Vere's tongue *and especially his hands* are not tied. O Captain! Vere is a 'complex' of *decisions*—Oedipus complex, military-industrial complex, the more the merrier. The 'heart and soul' (so to speak) of the novella is all in the three decisions Vere makes in the span of a very few minutes. Vere is no Hamlet. This is 'quick action' Vere—'Sudden Vere,' as a Zen master would put it. This is the *sudden way*. *Billy Budd*, prima facie, is not a complex work. But in these few pages Melville yawns an abyss. No, sweet chick, the abyss is not Vere, but the 'system of totality' (as Hegel might put it) we have here. The 'inside narrative' (Vere, Claggart, poor Billy). Absolutely. But it is inseparable, *and separated*, from the 'outside'—political—narrative. Watch out! My brisk walk in the Coney Island station has got the blood racing in my brain. Vere is, as usual, 'absorbed in his reflections,' promenading on the quarter-deck. Claggart 'deferentially stood awaiting his notice.' Claggart quietly drops his bombshell of false accusations. Vere's immediate reaction is 'of strong suspicion clogged by strange dubieties'—in short, he doesn't believe him. But what is to be *done*. *'We must do'*—this is Sudden Vere. On the high seas, in the year of the Great Mutiny. Think, Vere, think! His first thought, *his first decision*: secrecy, secrecy at all costs. Keep the matter from 'getting abroad.' No one must know—not his lieutenants, and especially not the crew. Keep the 'inside' narrative as far 'inside' as possible. This will be this Captain's prime concern, from the very beginning to the bitter end, when Billy's body, after his hanging, is disposed of in the sea—this ceremony, at least, in the presence of the crew. The 'burial spot'—the ship has left it astern, but 'sea-fowl... flew screaming to the spot... circling it low down with the unmoving shadow of their outstretched wings and the cracked requiem of their cries.' Silence! Vere shifts the scene to his cabin, he summons Billy. 'Shut the door there, sentry.' 'Speak, man!'— the extreme stutter, 'his right arm shot out.' 'Fated boy... What have you done?' 'What was best not only now at once to be done, but also in the sequel?' First and last, 'guard as much as possible against publicity'—a policy, Melville's narrator notes, worthy of 'Peter the Barbarian [a.k.a Peter the Great], great chiefly by his crimes.' Shades of Vietnam, of LBJ, of Kissinger, of Nixon![35] We get a queasy feeling that Melville is not too happy with his Captain. But the *second decision* is the key to this pasteboard mask, and the key to the *whole story*. Vere stands over the master-at-arms, dead for less than a minute, 'thick black blood oozing from mouth and ear.' He covers his face (his own face, not Claggart's) with one hand, 'absorbed in taking all the bearings of the event.' This is how Melville describes his second decision:

> Slowly he uncovered his face; forthwith the effect was *as if the moon, emerging from eclipse,* should reappear with quite another aspect than that which had gone into hiding. The father in him, manifested towards Billy thus far in the scene, was replaced by the military disciplinarian.

War is hell but war is war, LOVE IT OR LEAVE IT. This is what Vere 'decides.' The moment is absolutely *decisive*, but is it a decision or is Vere decided *for*, like Billy and Claggart? Doesn't decision mean freedom and responsibility? What freedom, what responsibility, and, for that matter, *what necessity* does

---

35 Nixon! Nixon! Your Watergate! 'Publicity,' as Melville puts it. You just couldn't keep a secret.

the moon have, 'emerging from eclipse'? An abyss. Not Vere himself, but *Billy Budd* itself. I can barely hear the screeches. I'm under the ground. The 'obscure light' of Brooklyn has long since been eclipsed by the deep subway night. People come into the car, people go out of the car. I'm not that far from Delancey again. York Street, where that nice looking girl— probable fellow NYUer—will be home having dinner. Sudden Vere *immediately* makes his third decision—'quick action': 'I shall presently call a drumhead court.' Now *this* is a decision, no doubt about it. No one and nothing decided *for* him this time. 'Was Captain Vere suddenly affected in his mind?' A drumhead court—why? It's bloody murder. What ever happened to justice? WHAT JUSTICE is there in turning this tangle of tongue-ties into tied tongues? Why not a *proper hearing!* A fair trial. (Martial, but fair.) The immediate reaction of the ship's surgeon, summoned to certify Claggart's death, is: A drumhead court—is the Captain 'unhinged'? Why not 'place Billy Budd in confinement, and in a way dictated by usage, and postpone further action in so extraordinary a case to such time as they should again join the squadron, and then transfer it to the Admiral.' Hell yes. Submit the matter to the judgment of the Admiral. Hell no. Not Vere. A drumhead court, and *in the utmost secrecy*, in his own *cabin*. Worthy of Peter the Great at his worst.[36] A *proper* drumhead court, however brutal (basically, it's halfway between a trial and a lynching), is, at least and essentially, *public*. On a ship, the drumhead is *on the deck, not in the captain's cabin*. Summary justice while the ship is still at sea. But it's a sort of *show* trial, the 'direct reverse' of Vere's shrouded 'privacy.' Watch out, this is the heart of darkness. 'Mistah Kurtz—he dead.' (A penny for the Old Guy?)[37] During the 'ceremony' Vere remarks, acutely: 'War looks but to the frontage, the appearance. And the Mutiny Act, War's

---

36 Nixon! Nixon! Already in your shroud.
37 Hip readers know this one, of course: *Heart of Darkness*, Guy Fawkes—twin epigraphs to T.S. Eliot's poem *The Hollow Men*.

child, takes after the father.' The 'direct reverse' of Claggart's discourse on being and seeming. But what 'frontage' can you expect from a Captain who is nothing but War's puppet, a pasteboard mask. Who will strike *through* him? A white whale, perhaps?

Now—Vere's second decision was one thing, it was perhaps a nondecision, the aftermath of an eclipse. But the third, the drumhead court—Quick! Quick! 'The angel must hang!'—this is another matter. We might call it an 'arbitrary' (Hegel's word) decision stemming from a (non)decision. It struck Melville— putting it politely—as 'impolitic.' How much freedom and how much compulsion is there in this—unnecessary—decision? Did Vere 'need' to decide this, just as Claggart 'needed' to be naturally depraved, and Billy 'needed' to kill him because of his *extreme stutter*. I don't think this analogy holds water, but I'm not sure. Sudden Vere—*Whoosh*. The samurai. No hesitation. Just do it. The zendo. The sword. No-mind: decision and action are simultaneous. If the samurai thinks *about* what he's doing, he's dead. The sword of Zen mind: although it was a matter of surviving on the battlefield, the samurai fought his fight in the zendo. But Vere strikes me as the 'direct reverse' of a samurai. A military academy is no zendo. No, this third decision reeks of being is nothing, like 'I decide to brush my teeth' or 'from this day forth the official language of this Banana Republic will be Swedish.' I think Vere *decides to decide*, just as our 'sturdy' and 'resolute' (and none too 'brilliant') generals in Vietnam *decide* to decide to destroy a village, *in order to save it.* What justice! Decisive action. This is war. Falling dominoes—this is exactly what's on Vere's mind. Dominoes. From Billy right on to another Great Mutiny. Does this make any sense? Commie gook creeps on the shores of California. *Freak Out! Lumpy Gravy*. Frank Zappa is *not* mad, but *this* is madness. These are not samurai, they are madmen. True madmen *decide nothing*. Logic? Being is nothing. Ground zero. Your delusion. 'Let me show you the path on which there is no coming and no going.'

This F is right smack in midtown Manhattan—42nd Street station, right under 42nd and 6th Avenue, a block from Times Square. Watch the ball drop. Happy New Year. It's pretty crowded but I barely notice, I'm a little bit riled up. I barely remember I'm on the subway, traveling indefinitely until I make my decisive decision that will decide the rest of my life, be it long or short. Ecstatic or miserable. Or both. Fucking generals, fucking Vere. I have no doubt that Melville, at first, intended to compose an 'inside narrative'—basically, I'd say, a twist on the 'corruption of innocence' and its consequences. But the tiger got out of the bag. It is the complexity of the relation between 'inside' and 'outside' narrative that makes the story 'undecidable.' An abyss. The 'drama' here is closed up *inside* the 'outside narrative' *inside* Vere's cabin. Long live the Mutiny Act and the Articles of War. Vere 'elects' the First Lieutenant, the Captain of Marines, and the Sailing Master to be the members of his farce of a court, and then eloquently bullies them, since not one of the three believes Billy deserves to be hanged. In a few hours. At dawn. 'The cracked requiem of their cries.' 'They exchanged looks of troubled indecision, yet feeling that decide they must, and without long delay.' These men are sailors—good ones, probably, and they have a conscience. The horror. Vere hammers them: 'Tell me whether or not, occupying the position we do, private conscience should not yield to the imperial one formulated in the code [i.e. in the Articles of War] under which alone we officially proceed?' But Vere is a Captain, an *intellectual* (for Hegel 'intellect'—the understanding—*isolates thoughts without bringing them together*, no, it is *reason* that brings the thoughts together), and, in the end, an 'impolitic' politician. (Though Hegel also calls the understanding 'the most astonishing and mightiest of powers, or rather the absolute power'[38]—precisely because it is the power to *separate*. It is

---

38 *Hegel's Phenomenology of Spirit*, translated by A.V. Miller, Oxford: Oxford University Press, 1977, pp. 18–19.

the power of 'the negative'—the power of *death*.) ('Death is a democrat,' Melville wrote—in *Pierre*, I know it by heart: 'There, beneath the sublime tester of the infinite sky, like emperors and kings, sleep, in grand state, the beggars and paupers of the earth! I joy that Death is this Democrat.'[39]) Vere expresses himself beautifully (so to speak)—secreted in his own cabin, he is eloquent. 'But your scruples! Do they move as in a dusk? Challenge them. Make them advance and declare themselves.' Here is the heart of his speech to the miserably cowed members of his court. It really does ring like *Johnny Got his Gun* in the year of the Great Mutiny:

> Now can we adjudge to summary and shameful death a fellow-creature innocent before God, and whom we feel to be so?—Well, I, too, feel that, the full force of that. *It is Nature*. But do these buttons that we wear attest that our allegiance is to Nature? *No, to the King*. Though the ocean, which is inviolate Nature primeval, though this be the element where we move and have our being as sailors, yet as the King's officers lies our duty in a sphere correspondingly natural? So little is that true, that in receiving our commissions we in the most important regards *ceased to be natural free-agents*. When war is declared, are we the commissioned fighters previously consulted? *We fight at command*. If our judgments approve the war, that is but coincidence. So in other particulars. So now, would it be so much we ourselves that would condemn as it would be martial law operating through us? For that law and the rigor of it, *we are not responsible*. [But then again, who is?[40]] Our vowed responsibility is in this: That however pitilessly that law may operate, we nevertheless adhere to it and administer it.

---

39 *Pierre*, Book XX, Chap I.
40 See the end of *Blade Runner* (director's cut): 'Too bad she won't live. But then again, who does?'

Shades of Adolf Eichmann, without the banality? Does this sound like an 'inside narrative,' 'restricted to the inner life of one particular ship and the career of an individual sailor'? Personally, I'm sick of Starry Vere, his deciding to decide. But not of Melville, a true genius. I want to reread the novella again, here in the subway, tonight. 'I strive against scruples that may tend to enervate decision.' WE MUST DO, the good Captain tells us. In the obscure light of the bay like a patch of discolored snow in early April. Already in his shroud. We destroy the village in order to save it. The pitiless law. The dominoes. And, God bless Captain Vere.

THE FIRST GATE

Screech. Roosevelt Avenue again, halfway through Queens. Halfway to Jamaica. Night. The end of March, 1972. Traveling indefinitely. A decision. Everything pretty quiet on the F Train. Night. Pretty quiet. Evening. Sure, a reasonable number of freaks. A decent number of fun seekers. Fun City. Naked City. Five boroughs. (Do they have as much fun on Staten Island?) Eight million stories. People always moving around. I wonder how Melville got home from the Customs House. Long walk? Horse-powered trolley? Cold winters, hot summers. Who knows.

What justice? *Seven Against Thebes*. Jamaica, also an island south of Cuba. Thebes, of the Seven Gates. Greece. Also an even more ancient city in Egypt. Names. Just names. I don't even know what time it is, I'm not wearing my watch. (When I go to NYU I have to wear it.) Ought to be around 8:30. One thing I like—maybe *the* one thing I like—about the subway is that it doesn't live by the clock, like almost everything else in a city, or town. (Farmers, possibly, live by the sun, and the seasons.) Trains, planes, schools, offices, doctors, lawyers—all by the clock. Factories. The clock. Port Authority Bus Terminal, Grand Central Station—all one big clock, all clockwork. Airports. I don't know if the subway even has schedules. It might, but

I don't know. Do people say, I go to work on the 8:13 F Train at Delancey? Beats me. People definitely do say, Shit! I just missed the F. But it's because they see it pulling out right in front of them. Satori, sudden enlightenment, immediate experience. Not a question of clocks.

Jamaica. End of the line. Time for a new F Train. First, I decide to take a piss. Nice quiet toilets out here in this boondocks station. At 42nd Street the toilets are an amusement park gone berserk. Action. GENTS: buggers, queens, fairies, dopers and junkies. LADIES: whores, skunk pussies, queens, dopers and junkies. Fun City. Back on the F now, heading for Coney Island, other end of the line. Fucking Vere. At some point Melville decided to make him the 'hero'— anti-hero, I'd say—instead of Billy, transforming a possibly banal morality play into a work of genius. A tangle. Fucking Vere. Make love not war. Smart chick, would you call General Westmoreland an abyss? Do abysses spout pearls of wisdom such as: 'War is fear cloaked in courage.' (One of his deepest.) 'The military don't start wars. Politicians start wars.' (The stuff of pasteboard masks.) 'As the senior commander in Vietnam, I was aware of the potency of public opinion—and I worried about it.' (Here's to you, Starry Vere.) 'Vietnam was the first war ever fought without any censorship. Without censorship, things can get terribly confused in the public mind.' (Goddam 'outside narrative.') 'I don't think I have been loved by my troops, but I think I have been respected.' (Do abysses say things like this?) 'Never has a nation employed its military power with such restraint.' (An inside joke?) Then again, this one is truly deep (and dark): 'As the philosophy of the Orient expresses it, life is not important.'[41] And this last one is actually pretty abyssal, Vere never spouted anything like this: 'I was participating in my own lynching, but the problem was I didn't know what I was being lynched for.' God bless you, General Westmoreland. God bless America.

---

41 You can see this quote for yourselves in the 1974 documentary *Hearts and Minds*.

It ain't over until the fat lady sings. Fucking Vere. In Melville's mind, I think, in his first version Vere was practically his alter ego, and *Billy Budd* Melville's own 'testament of acceptance': innocence is defeated in this world, good intentions count for nothing, we lose what we love best. This is the 'inside narrative.' Melville never intended his Captain to be a superhero, certainly not 'the greatest sailor since the world began,' but, yes, a decent man—flawed, like Melville himself, but decent. Not brilliant but sturdy. Resolute. I believe Vere was a troubled man, as Melville most certainly was. But Melville also wrote a chapter 'beckoned by the genius of Nelson.' He probably wrote it in one of his first stabs at the Handsome Sailor. He kept writing and rewriting this story, stab after stab, for five years, on into the last year of his life. I read that he kept this chapter in a separate folder, out of the manuscript. But then he *decided* to include it (it is Chapter 4)—because he changed his mind about Captain Vere? We lose what we love best, and what Melville lost was not the innocent sailor but the intellectual Captain. 'Decided'—'changed'—'lost': 'the moon, emerging from eclipse.' *We fight at command.* This is Vere, not Melville. 'The military don't start wars. Politicians start wars.' Soldiers and sailors fight them, while Generals and Captains decide to decide. Am I too hard on Vere? Does Melville condemn him outright? I don't know. This is the abyss of *Billy Budd, Sailor*. Not 'war is hell' but 'What/Who is Ares?'. Melville greatly loved ships, and sailors, and he greatly admired the *genius* of Horatio Nelson. 'In the year of the Great Mutiny.' *Why not* 'postpone further action in so extraordinary a case to such time as they should again join the squadron, and then transfer it to the Admiral'? Those cocksucking dominoes. Great Mutiny. 'Slumbering embers of the Nore.' *Screech*. Roosevelt Avenue again, heading for Manhattan. Friday evening, end of March. Who decided to fight this war against Vietnam, the Generals or the Intellectuals? Curtis LeMay and William Westmoreland, or

Kennedy, McNamara, and now Kissinger? Sturdy Vere and his allegiance to the King. Maybe I get riled up too easily. Maybe Vere reminds me somehow of the Great Academic Marxist I may yet decide to decide to become. Do I hate authority? But a ship *needs* a Captain—*this* Melville knows. (How about Ahab!) But Captain! My Captain! Richard Nixon is not Abraham Lincoln. Poor Billy, his inside narrative, lost in the shuffle. 'The effect was as if the moon, emerging from eclipse, should reappear with quite another aspect.' Ares, full of Ares. Starry Vere, full of Ares. But Nelson was *overflowing* with Ares. 'This reckless declarer of his person in fight.' In the end, I think Melville's war is between intellect and genius. Geniuses don't grow on trees but intellectuals do, in bunches, like bananas, which, moreover, grow upside down. (A purely naturalistic observation.) Hegel would say, the distinction between intellect and genius *is itself intellectual*. The understanding is what separates but doesn't bring its thoughts together. I think we may be under the East River at this very moment. Under the East River. That's pretty far down. The 'Indians' who sold the island for trinkets could never have imagined *this*. Not many people in the car, but in Manhattan things will get lively fast. Manhattanites—and tourists—on a Friday evening, I expect a bunch of fun seekers. All of a sudden I feel a little hungry. I'm going to eat this piece of cheese, before it gets moldy.

Why did Vere have to decide to decide what he did? He decided to murder Billy Budd, to lynch him. Bloody murder. A terrible precedent. Dominoes, really? Goddamit, dominoes seem to be the only game in town. What about chess, checkers, gin rummy? Monopoly. Badminton. What would Nelson have done? A drumhead court—not in a million years. If he was truly a genius—a military genius, in the year of the Great Mutiny—I think he could have pardoned Billy on the spot and then *publicly* told the crew the reason why, winning them to his command, hearts and minds.[42] But this is not the story

---

42 See Hershel Parker's *Herman Melville. A Biography. Volume 2, 1851–1891*,

Melville tells. *Screech*. Rockefeller Center, you guessed right, a lot of people getting on. Wow ye gods what's this. HOLY SHIT, IT'S A GUY IN A WHEELCHAIR. All by himself. He must be damn good at maneuvering that chair, down here in the subway. All those stairs! A young fellow, nice looking, seems to be around my age (I'm 21), or not much older. A short, well-trimmed beard, like me. White t-shirt, wearing a cap. (I never wear caps.) Holding something in front of his chest, a poster—no, it's a sign, a placard, hanging from his neck by a string. And he has no legs! No legs at all, just two stumps. This fine looking young man, *mon semblable,—mon frère!*[43] (pardon my French). *Hypocrite lecteur!* My fellow human being. But take a look at this placard, it is *a work of art*. Two exquisitely drawn legs—or, to be more precise, lower legs, below the knee, with feet. They don't look real, of course, but they are exquisitely depicted. And at the top of the placard, the words: I GAVE MY LEGS FOR MY COUNTRY. This must be a Vietnam veteran. In a wheelchair in the subway. I wonder if he's a veteran for or against the war. He doesn't say a word, just looks around. He sure is agile with that chair. When I was a kid I used to go to the annual wheelchair basketball game in the high-school gym, it was a big event, those wheelchair players were just amazing. I remember, they were like gladiators, blood and guts, smashing into each other, getting knocked out of their chairs onto the floor, the referees picking them right up again. Wild games. Amazing people. Gladiators. Blood and guts. I have a neighbor on Rivington Street who lost both legs completely. 'Call me Stumpy. I don't *have* stumps, I *am* a stump.' Third floor, on the back of the building, two railroad flats, me on the left, Stumpy and his brother Frank on the right. Parallel flats. Mirror images. Stumpy and Frank are great conversationalists. Amazing neighbors. Stumpy stepped on a mine—a goddam Bouncing Betty—on the beach in Normandy. The Germans

Baltimore: Johns Hopkins, 2002, p. 886.
43 Charles Baudelaire, *Fleurs du mal*, 'Au Lecteur.'

produced *two million* of them during World War II. Bounding mines. Bad fucking news. But this man right here—*mon frère!*—doesn't say a word. With incredible agility he maneuvers his chair through the car, from one end to the other, holding out his cap. 'The beggars and paupers of the earth!' The fellow will not speak, and he is begging. A penny for the Old Guy. Some people in the car actually give him a dollar bill, or a quarter, or a dime. I give him a quarter myself. A Vietnam veteran. My fellow human being. *Screech*. 42nd Street. He deftly turns his chair, goes out of the car, I can see him on the platform, people make way for him, he wheels himself into the next car down. I wonder how many cars there are on the F Train. MANY cars. And MANY F Trains. And MANY MANY other trains with MANY MANY MANY MANY other cars. I wonder if he is an F Train specialist, or whether he changes trains every day, or even changes, for example, from the F to the B or the D on the same day, as I myself may well do, in the course of this indefinite journey. Why would he even bother to do that? Just for the variety? Do you think that, if he takes exactly the same train every day, he may have his 'regulars'—regular benefactors, people who get to know him? (But he doesn't speak.) Regulars—would that be an advantage for him, or a disadvantage? Just think of HOW MANY CARS there are on the entire New York subway—like the stars in the sky. Do you think he makes his journey every day, and from morning till night? I don't think he can maneuver during the rush hour. I've dazzled myself with so many questions. Maybe he just comes out in the evenings, for a few hours. Maybe only on weekends. Friday night, start of the weekend. Saturday, Sunday, no rush hours. I wonder if he makes A LOT of money. It's possible. A man in a hurry. I'm really sorry I didn't have the chance to speak with him a little. I'm sure he stepped on a mine, in Vietnam. He gave his legs for his country. A veteran. Disabled. Not a basketball player. I know a lot about mines, I talk about them with my neighbors all the time. Landmines have killed or maimed more people than have been killed by nuclear, biological, and chemical weapons combined. Yes, I'm a mine expert. 'Antipersonnel' mines—two general types: blast mines, and fragmentation mines (such as the Bouncing Betty). Blast mines are the kind you step on and they may well not kill you, but they sure as hell will blow your leg, or legs, off. Fragmentation mines spring up into the air before exploding and are usually set off by a trip-wire. They *totally wipe out* the person who tripped over them, but also project shrapnel in all directions, tearing bodies to shreds up to a hundred yards away. Basically, we are talking about individual-destroyers versus group-destroyers. In Vietnam one of our favorite mines has been the high-tech M14 blast type known, euphemistically, as the 'toe-popper.' Another great favorite is the gravel mine, a.k.a 'button mine'—smaller and less lethal but very popular because we can drop whole clouds of them from airplanes. Then, of course, the Vietnamese have lots and lots of mines of their own. They have a very popular 'M14 lite' called 'dap loi' or 'step-mine.' This mine is a booby trap made from an empty .50 caliber machine gun shell filled with gunpowder and scrap metal. The casing is sealed in wax and placed in a bamboo cylinder with a nail in the bottom, which is then buried in the ground so only the wax on top is showing. When one of our soldiers steps on the wax top the casing is pressed into the nail, which then blows scrap metal into his foot. A dap loi is rarely fatal but is sure to blow a toe off and, 'with luck,' a big piece of the leg. Our own 'toe-poppers,' however, are rarely limited to toes. Our mines are no-joke mines. I wonder whether *mon frère!*—does he change cars at every stop? he has *so* many cars to choose from—stepped on a home-brewed dap loi, or—yes yes yes, his *two* stumps, maybe he stepped on one of our very own, highly superior M14 poppers. Yes, it looks like a case of friendly fire. A genuine American blast, never mind bamboo cylinders. Stepped on a bit of 'unexploded ordnance'—I mean, a mine, or possibly an unexploded bomb, that no Vietnamese soldier, or woman, or child has had a chance to set foot on yet.[44] Friendly fire, so-called. A fucking shame. I read this interview with General Gray, a Marine Corps commandant, who said he'd seen more Americans killed by our own landmines than enemy forces killed by U.S. mines. Holy shit, we're mining ourselves. They say it's the anti-war creeps here at home who are *undermining* the war effort, but over there they are mining themselves into holy hell. Freak Out! Lumpy Gravy. Shit, you say, a mine is a mine is a mine. Shit my ass. Whose mine. And whose legs is it blowing to smithereens. Mining and bombing, bombing and mining, and especially bombing, for that matter. Not only anti-personnel mines, we also have anti-personnel bombs, each one containing thousands of flesh-shredding darts. I read—maybe it was in *Ramparts*—some purloined report from the Defense Department (or was it the State Department?) stating that a major objective of our bombing raids on North Vietnam is *not to kill the population but to maim them*. Serious injury is more disruptive than death, since people have to be employed to look after the injured, while they only have to bury the dead. *Mon frère!* What did you step on? Maybe you don't even know. Are you a Vietnam veteran for or against the war? Why won't you speak with me? With me, who neither beg nor fear your favors nor your hate.[45]

I don't know what to make of this. A veteran in a wheelchair, on the F Train, without legs, with a placard hanging from his neck, his cap in his hand, begging. An image on the

44 In a recent report (ca. 2010) the Vietnamese government estimated that about 14 million tons of ordnance was dropped on Vietnam between 1959 and 1975 (nearly three times the amount used by the Allies in World War II), and that between 10% and 30% of it failed to detonate. Today 15% of the total surface area of the country is contaminated by buried bombs and mines, which claimed around 105,000 civilian victims between 1975 and 2007. The government predicts the 'cleanup' work may go on for the next 100 years.
45 *Macbeth*, Act I, scene iii.

placard of the legs he gave for his country. *Screech*. Already down to West 4th. Maybe I should hop out and change trains. Will I ever see that man again, a fellow about my own age? I don't hop out, the doors close. Does he always take the F Train or does he take all the trains? What did he step on? Will I ever see him again? I'm going to read *Billy Budd* now, for the fourth time since last summer. I'm going to Coney Island. I just realized—he may well still be in one of the cars of this very train. Should I chase after him? No, I shouldn't. I won't. I have to make my own decision, no one here in the subway is going to help me, and certainly not this veteran, be he for or against the war. Ten months ago I got my 4-F draft classification, it sure as hell wasn't easy. I'm not going to Vietnam myself. The war itself is 'winding down,' they say. More bombs, fewer troops.[46] Nixon, Kissinger. Military genius. Political genius. Diplomatic genius. Whatever. A load of shit. A big big big load. Should I blow up the Williamsburg Bridge? At times I see it so clearly, it's the right thing to do, the only thing. Most of the time I just think it's a tale told by an idiot. Signifying what? Nothing. Nothing. Being is nothing. Logic. '*Being, pure being*... is pure indeterminateness and emptiness.... Being, the indeterminate immediate, is in fact *nothing*, and neither more nor less than *nothing*.' Totally blank. An empty screen. Pure being, pure nothing. Pure white, pure black, pure black, pure white. The whiteness of the whale is the blackness of the whale. The system of logic is the realm of shadows. The zendo. Zazen. Zen mind. The Roshi said that our everyday life is like a movie playing on a screen: most people are interested in the picture without realizing there is a screen.[47] In zazen practice we stop all our activities and make our screen pure, plain white. Blank. Mind. No-mind. In this blankness, however

---

46 The 1972 'Christmas Bombings' (Operation Linebacker II, to be exact) was the largest heavy bomber strike launched by the U.S. Air Force since the end of World War II. In 1973, according to the official statistics, there were 50 (FIVE–O) American troops in Vietnam.
47 *Not Always So*, pp. 50–52.

fleetingly, we have direct experience of the original emptiness of our mind. The movie plays, full of color, sound, and fury. But the screen is always there, and in itself it is *empty*. We just screeched into the Delancey Street station. I'm going to Brooklyn, Coney Island (station). Realm of shadows. First, reread *Billy Budd*. Then, reread Benardete's 'Two Notes' and reread *Seven Against Thebes*, and think about Eteocles' decision, not to mention Polyneices' decision, to say nothing of Oedipus. Travel indefinitely. Figure something out. The fork. A decision. 'Signifying nothing.' Vere *decides to decide*. Does that count as a decision twice over or as half a decision, a half-assed decision? Is a bad decision better than none at all? No! It's not a question of good or bad, it's a question of *what a decision is*. Freedom, necessity, responsibility. Who/what decides? It's a question of looking back forty years from now and asking, Who/what decided? Who/what is responsible for my being where I am now and doing what I'm doing now? A question of asking, and of not being able to answer. Of having to say, How in the world did I get here? I don't remember deciding anything. It just happened. End of March, 1972. York Street. I'm in Brooklyn again. Asking and not being able to answer. 'When I'm sixty-four.' No no no no. I'm traveling indefinitely, subway, realm of shadows, 'facing the sunless dead and this joyless region.' A decision. A decision I can, and will, be responsible for. Hopefully. I'm taking a stab at it right now.

I'm reading now. (An inside narrative.) 'In the time before steamships, or then more frequently than now, a stroller along the docks of any considerable seaport would occasionally have his attention arrested by a group of bronzed marines....' There are some Brooklynites moving around Brooklyn on the subway on this Friday evening, but not many. The subway is never empty. Above ground, in the streets, at night there's always something going on. A lot going on, generally. In quality—often bad quality—if not in quantity. A couple of years ago I drove a taxi all night. All summer every night, then only on weekends. In midtown Manhattan after 3 in the morning things got pretty quiet, but if you drove fast and smart and knew where to go there was *plenty* going on. It depended on the territory and the driver. The subway is all one territory and has no driver. Night on the subway is a good time to do some serious thinking. Peaceful reading. The 'Handsome Sailor.' The screeches. The night. Ditmas Avenue, the F rises from the eternal subway darkness into the Brooklyn night. Coney Island, the 8 tracks side-by-side. I take a nice stroll. A new F, bound for Jamaica. Practically no one else on the train. Chapter 4: Concerning 'The greatest sailor since the world began.' The Brooklyn night, like 'the regular wash of the sea against the hull.' The train a long hum punctuated by screeches. The *Bellipotent*, power of war. 'Life in the foretop well agreed with Billy Budd.' Delancey, my stop. Must be around 11, my dinner time. 'What was the matter with the master-at-arms?' 42nd Street, right under 6th Avenue. Plato! Natural Depravity. True madmen. There happen to be a few freaks in the car, but I barely notice. *Screech*. Rockefeller Center—the whole complex, some 19 buildings, including an ice-skating rink, built by John D. Rockefeller Jr. in the 1930s. A little later he bought the land for the United Nations headquarters too, out of his own pocket, but his son Nelson just couldn't quite get himself elected president, despite Kissinger's strenuous efforts, time and again. God Bless America, land of the free. Nixon was too tricky for him. Back to Queens now. I bet the Jamaica station will be hopping round midnight, like a Thelonious Monk quartet. With John Coltrane. Melville! Melville! His humanity, his genius. Claggart, who are you really? Welkin-eyed Billy, eyes blue as the cloudless sky. Vere's eyes are gray. But Claggart? 'Upon an abrupt unforeseen encounter, a red light would flash forth from his eye, like a spark from an anvil in a dusk smithy. That quick, fierce light was a strange one, darted from orbs which in repose were

of a color nearest approaching a deeper violet, the softest of
shades.' True madmen. Jamaica. I'll have to wait a while for the
new F, they don't run so often at this hour. I guess the trains
must have a schedule, it's just that nobody knows it. A little
like the sound of one hand clapping. But one hand *is* sound.
When you're hungry, eat; when you're tired, sleep. That's Zen.
Fork. Decision. No-mind. What? What, me worry? A decision?
Is 'traveling indefinitely on the subway' a crazy idea? 'A dumb
blankness, full of meaning.' Who knows. I had to try something.

I'm on my way back through Queens. Concentrate on my
reading. Claggart's accusation. 'Speak, man!' The whole story
concentrated in these few pages, Vere's decisions. Sudden
Vere. Waxing eloquent. His poor flunkies. This joyless region.
'I strive against scruples that may tend to enervate decision.'
What in the world is the man saying. A dumb blankness.
What decision? Who decides? I feel a little depressed. 'Behold
Billy Budd under sentry lying prone in irons.' Already in his
shroud. 42nd Street. I wish something would happen, like,
some freak freaking out, screaming, smashing something,
some genuine all-American Fun-City molestation. Shit, on my
street, Rivington Street, we have action all the time, the whole
neighborhood is Puerto Rican. I pay $55 a month for a more-
than-decent two-room-plus-kitchen-plus-bath railroad flat. But,
the neighborhood is hard as a motherfucking nail. Especially at
night. During the day, lively. The urban poor, the 'underclass'—
that's what the sociologists call us. The Marxists, Franz
Fanon, use the term 'lumpenproletariat.' Here in New York
it's all about money. Silk stockings and gutter rats. If you're
rich, Park Avenue, or some such. If you're a rich, or at least
a subsidized, NYU student, the East or even West Village, to
say nothing of the *great* dormitories, if you can get in. *Lots* of
sociality. *Otherwise*, there's always the Lower East Side. Always
has been. Down here, in 1900 it was full of Jews without
money; now it's full of Puerto Ricans without money. No other

NYU students that I know of. C'est la vida. Have no fear, on Rivington Street we have absolutely no lack of tiny little knives, gigantic knives, clubs, cleavers, bats (out of hell), guns, shotguns, muggings, break-ins, break-outs, junkies, small-time pushers, intergalactic drug dealers, and general all-around mayhem. Mostly after dark, or on rainy days. Mostly. The subway is quiet. The car is pretty full, it's well after midnight, they're all half asleep. Not a single fun seeker. I wish that guy in the wheelchair, who gave his legs for his country, would show up again, and talk with me this time. Have an apple with me. *Screech. Screech.* West 4th—some Village people. But, not very lively. The ship's Chaplain, who 'kissed on the fair cheek his fellow man.' 'The cracked requiem of their cries.' Billy's burial at sea. That's the story. I'm in Brooklyn again, under the ground. Reading the last three chapters. A surprise! The death of Captain Vere. 'On the return passage to the full English fleet from the detached cruise during which occurred the events already recorded, the *Bellipotent* fell in with the *Athéiste*.' Formerly the *St. Louis*: those French Revolutionists pulled no punches when it came to names, they re-christened all the saints. 'The aptest name ever given to a war-ship,' Melville remarks. Vere is hit by a musket-ball. 'More than disabled... he lingered for some days, but the end came.' Even in death Vere is outrageously upstaged by his *real antagonist*. Nelson's was the epitome of heroic death, the stuff of epic poetry. Melville depicts Vere's as somehow pedantic, shabby, petty. Dime-a-dozen intellectual captains. Geniuses don't grow on trees.

I look out the window at the calm Brooklyn night, the dim glimmer, I see Billy, already in his shroud, *a patch of discolored snow in early April*. His story ends with what Melville refers to as an 'artless' ballad, a 'rude utterance from another foretopman, one of his own watch.' Billy is waiting for the dawning of his last day. His hanging. I think it is truly great poetry. Melville wrote it *before* he wrote *Billy Budd*. It is the seed. The abyss. The beginning, and the end. '—*but aren't it all sham?/ A blur's in my eyes, it is dreaming that I am.*' An abyss of dreams. Melville shifted the focus from Billy to Vere? Yes and no. The story, after all, is Billy's. *Screech.* Neptune Avenue, such a nice name. I read the ballad again. Again. Shivers up and down my spine. Pulling into Coney Island in the dead of night. 'Emerging from eclipse.' Has *Billy Budd* helped me answer the question: What does it mean to decide? I don't know. Maybe. Maybe. I'm traveling indefinitely. I need to think about it. Maybe something will happen.

The Coney Island station is very very quiet. The whole ocean is a stone's throw from here. The next F won't be leaving for quite a while. I walk up and down the platform. I think about Vietnam. I think about the curse of Oedipus—of Oedipus cursed, and cursing. A decision. Why has my country gotten into the habit of fighting on the side of tyranny? I made my own personal decision about Vietnam, I would have gone to jail if I had to. I am not responsible for the Vietnam War, but *I am responsible for what I myself do about it.* So I decided, and I *did do something.* Do it. I did. But now? Now, at times, I feel as if I've lost my identity. The Roshi says *good,* you never really had one. The fundamental truth is that everything changes. There is no abiding self, no permanent identity. But, now, I mean *political identity.* This is a little different, a different kettle of fish—no, not the whole kettle, it's just one fish that is different. The water is always the same. 'In order to see a fish, you must watch the water.' When I got the 4-F the battle line shifted—not the scene, but the line. Shifted from personal responsibility to political responsibility. More exactly, the *focus* shifted from the personal: No, I will not go, to the political: What is my responsibility as a citizen of this country? I realized *immediately* that for 99 percent of my fellow citizens this question is a joke. A 'real madman' question. From those who cut and run to those who don't give a damn, I hear

America screaming: Who are you kidding? Whose leg do you think you're pulling? You're absolutely free, you're out of the draft, you're graduating from NYU—what the fuck more do you want? To be a hero? Wow, what shit. They're pulling out all the troops, the war is ending. But even the few people I know who *do* give a damn say: What the FUCK is this 'responsibility as a citizen of this country' shit? This is a democracy. Vote against Nixon. Go to grad school. It's a free country. You never went to the demonstrations anyway [true: I don't like crowds], and now you're worried about 'responsibility.' Political responsibility. Get your head together. What the fuck *is it* that you want?

I don't like the fork I'm at. In the film *Loin du Vietnam* there's an interview with Norman Morrison's wife, in 1967. In 1965 Norman Morrison doused himself in kerosene and set himself on fire below McNamara's office at the Pentagon. His wife says: 'At meal time, we talked about the incongruity of our health and prosperity, our three healthy loving children, contrasting this with the suffering of the people in Vietnam and how difficult it was to know that we were in some way responsible for this—how difficult it was to live with this.' She says, Norman wanted to tell people 'this is how it feels to be burned, as we are burning people—men, women, civilians— every day. Individual lives have been changed by this. I think it has been worth it,' Norman Morrison's wife says. I think a lot about these people, Morrison and his wife. *To know that we were in some way responsible*. Grad school. Blow up the Williamsburg Bridge. Being is nothing. Why not set myself on fire while I'm at it? *Good* question, but, *Why* set myself on fire? What's the point? *Changing individual lives?* But Norman Morrison's death really did change some individual lives. Probably not many, but some. A few. But right now, me, end of March, 1972, what is the fucking point? What's wrong with becoming a Great Academic Marxist? Why do I smell a rat? Just because the GAMs I happen to know are such assholes? No, it has to do with *knowing that we are in some way responsible*. This is why I'm traveling in the subway, indefinitely. Why? I want to decide my own future. Politically. Responsibly. Freely. Like Lady Liberty? And not be 'decided for,' like everybody else seems to be. A 'true madman'? A decision. The fact is, I do *not* like the fork I'm at.

I'm back on the F Train, it must be around 2 o'clock. There doesn't happen to be anyone else in the car, but there are quite a few cars, and there will be many screeches. Time to rummage around in my book bag. The apples! Four of them. OK, I'm going to watch the dim night glimmer for this short while and have an apple, why the hell not. Just take it easy, enjoy being above ground. Let's see, apart from *Billy Budd*, Ezra Pound, Hegel, Zen Mind, No-mind, 101 Zen Stories, *Heart of Darkness*, Benardete's two Notes, and two translations of *Seven Against Thebes*, one by David Grene and one by Philip Vellacott,[48] I have a few odds and ends at the bottom of the bag. A small notebook with my translations from Aeschylus and Euripides. The issue of *Ramparts* with Che's diaries, stuffed with a bunch of clippings on Vietnam. A small envelope with my collection of 'filler' clippings. I often find copies of the *Post* just lying around, on a bench, wherever, and I like to read these tiny curiosity pieces. I collect them. (*Post* readers read fast and drop the paper any old where, not like *Times* readers, they chew the paper up and spit it out of their windows, dirtying the plebes.) Let's see—I love this one, the camel lady, I love camels, my favorite animals are hamsters, cats, and camels.

---

48 The first dates from 1956, my edition is Washington Square Press (original edition University of Chicago Press), edited by David Grene and Richard Lattimore; the second is from 1961, Penguin, with an interesting introduction and notes by Vellacott. Translations in my story are by Grene, or Vellacott, or Benardete (from his Notes), or my own(!), or, most of the time, all four of us mixed (up) together.

Woman arrested naked behind the wheel: she thought she was a camel

LOS ANGELES — The police arrested a woman who was stark naked behind the wheel of a car involved in an accident. The woman, aged 35, told the officers she thought she was a camel in Morocco. She explained she was convinced of this because of the palms lining the streets of Oxnard in California. Charged with reckless driving, the woman was handed over to the health services for a psychiatric examination.

Here's another good one, also involving animals.

Lioness kills credulous man

A man shouting that God would keep him safe was mauled to death by a lioness in the Kiev zoo after he crept into the animal's enclosure, a zoo official said. The man shouted, 'God will save me, if he exists,' as he lowered himself by a rope into the enclosure, where he was promptly killed.

See what I mean, fact is more incredible than fiction, as Van Gogh put it, I think.[49]

---

49 OK, it was Antonin Artaud in his essay *Van Gogh. The Man Suicided by Society*: 'Because reality is terribly superior to all history, to all fable, to all divinity, to all surreality. All that is needed is the genius to interpret it.' See *Antonin Artaud Anthology*, San Francisco: City Lights Books, 1965, p. 143.

THE SECOND GATE

I've learned a lot at NYU these past four years. I had intended
to major in philosophy or political science, but when I took
Dave Leahy's Greek Tragedy course my first semester I got
hooked on the Classics Department. A stroke of serendipity.
I have a lot of good professors—Bluma Trell, who taught me
Greek, a monument, her wrinkles as ancient as her Greek.
But Dave Leahy[50] and Seth Benardete—true greatness. They

50 Dave Leahy died on August 7th of this year, 2014, ten days after I *FINALLY* started
writing this story. (I learned of his death today, by chance, September 25th.) Born,
in Brooklyn, in 1937, he was just 31 years old when I took his Greek Tragedy course,
and now I'm 64 myself.
Dave—D.G. Leahy—resigned his NYU professorship the month I graduated.
Serendipity? We both made our life-changing decisions at the same time (and
place). Dave was quietly *furious* about the lack of 'academic integrity' (as he put it,
mildly, but he also put it a lot less mildly). In general, not just at NYU. The academic
BROTHEL, he said—let me call it a GAB, a Great Academic Brothel, in his honor.
Academic *responsibility* for Dave meant the responsibility of teachers, students, and
the institution itself. He was not happy with any of the three. In particular, he said
that the university was becoming/had become *a business like any other*. That it was
no longer a place of teaching and learning.
In my own way, in these pages, in my 'decision,' in my musing on freedom/
necessity/responsibility, I give voice to Dave's fury. In the end (to paraphrase Plato)
he 'founded a university in himself.' Literally. A very real ideal university, truly
a place of teaching and learning, which he christened The New York Philosophy
Corporation. He also wrote a series of amazing books, beginning with *Novitas
Mundi. Perception of the History of Being* in 1980. Dave, I guess, can best be
described as a radical theologian, but he was much more than that. He was unique.
You may wish to look at his immense website, dgleahy.com, which includes a four-
and-a-half-hour Video Interview dated March 19, 2014. No blackboard, no chalk;

have taught me *what it CAN mean to be a professor*, and in diametrically different ways. Dave Leahy can *roar* through the whole history of Western philosophy in two semesters, from the Pre-Socratics to Sartre. He looks at Kierkegaard from every possible, and impossible, angle. Intensity. When he teaches he's practically in a trance, and at the end of the class so are his students, or some of us anyway. A trance. Absolutely. Before each class he walks up and down the corridor talking to himself, babbling softly, incoherently. Then he enters the classroom and all these ideas gush out. In class he almost always faces the blackboard, scribbling one word at a time, two words at a time, maybe erasing one (sometimes with his fingers), then scribbling again, one at a time, two at a time, until he ends up with ten, twenty, a hundred, the blackness of the board overflowing with chalk-white chaos. It reminds me of Queequeg in *Moby Dick* (Ishmael's cannibal friend, the harpooner) with his infinite tangle of tattoos, 'in his own person a riddle to unfold; a wondrous work in one volume; but whose mysteries not even himself could read, though his own

---

Dave always the same, always different. His laugh is exactly the same, after 45 years.

For me, he was a very special friend. In the 1970s, '80s, up to the mid-'90s, when I visited New York we always got together for dinner, usually at the Cedar Tavern, and our conversations were as wild as his university lectures had been. The last time I was in New York was nearly twenty years ago, he had sold his big house in Brooklyn and moved to the Poconos, but he drove into the city to see me. We always kept in touch. A couple of years ago we had a long talk, on the phone, about the subway—he was the expert. About what I needed to know for this story. In 'real life' I only took the subway to Brooklyn one single time, in the winter of 1986 or '87, to visit Dave at his home. A raging fire in the fireplace. We had even more than usual to talk about that time. I'd been talking to him about *The Empty Shield* since the 1970s. This story, inspired by Benardete's Notes. I'd been talking with Seth Benardete too. Chasing images. A decision. But the 'seed' of the story in the form I've been trying to give it for the past thirty years—the placard-men in the 'realm of shadows'—was that trip on the subway to see Dave, coming right after my afternoon meeting at NYU with Seth Benardete. The dead of winter, the dim glimmering of the Brooklyn night. Billy already in his shroud.

My friends. Gianfranco died, Wolfango died, now Dave. *Abyss of Dreams*—the unfinished prequel to this tail—is dedicated to Gianfranco. *Empty Shield* to Wolfango, *mon frère*. But *Empty Shield* is Dave's gift, for me and from me.

live heart beat against them.'[51] Dave's mind, indelible: 'Out of emptiness, wondrous being.' Then, emptiness again: he erases it all (with a very chalky eraser) and starts over, filling the blackness with his whiteness two, three, four times in a single class, depending on how steamed up he is. The blackboard, Dave's skin—an ephemeral mappa mundi. Believe me it's an incredible experience. Unforgettable. The biggest classrooms, and always packed. The students somehow understand that this man *is not bullshitting them*, that teaching what he is teaching is a serious matter—no, a *life-and-death* matter. Absolutely a matter of life and death. Aeschylus Sophocles Euripides—Aristotle Augustine Aquinas—Descartes Hegel Heidegger—all a life-and-death struggle. The struggle *to learn something important*, something that will change your life, a lot, a little. 'Individual lives have been changed by this,' said Norman Morrison's wife. This is not the 'intellect' Hegel criticized, the mighty power that isolates thoughts without bringing them together. But it's not just reason either. It is reason wed with passion. The word is *commitment*. Total commitment. Dave's great passion is Kierkegaard, who makes his appearance, one way or another, in every single class (and conversation). Even in Euripides. I wrote a paper last year for Sidney Hook's course 'The Philosophy [sic] of Karl Marx' on 'Marx and Kierkegaard'—Dave loved it, Hook *really* hated it. Kierkegaard is faith, paradox, the passion of inwardness—*crisis, decision, and an extreme sense of responsibility*. Dave lives and breathes Kierkegaard, Kierkegaard is his *abyss*. Every single time he says something about Kierkegaard he says something different, even if it's about the very same line of text. Monk, Coltrane. The Grateful Dead. Same scores, same concerts, always different. Never the same twice, or thrice, or ten thousand times. As the case may be. This is Dave's genius. He teaches the 'same' Greek Tragedy course every single year—I wish I had the chance to take it another two,

---

51 Chapter 110.

three, ten times, I know it will always be completely different. St. Paul says, we now see *per speculum in aenigmate*, 'in an enigma by means of a mirror.'[52] I think Dave sees in a shattered mirror with its ten thousand facets, so that the same work is always different. This is a hard way of seeing. The epigraph to Kierkegaard's *Stages on Life's Way* is a quote from Georg Christoph Lichtenberg: 'Such works are mirrors: when a monkey peers into them, no Apostle can be seen looking out.' Total commitment can itself be an enigma. We were reading St. Augustine's *Confessions* in class one day, Dave quoted this line: 'In order to search for God, one must have found Him already.' I looked at the text, raised my hand—'That's not the same as the text.' 'Sure, sure, it's the same,' Dave said. He's absolutely right. The same. A 'gloss'? A shattered mirror. A continuous shattering. Dave is a very joyful man, always, but also troubled. It is *hard*, living and breathing Kierkegaard the way he does—I mean, taking Kierkegaard *absolutely seriously*. This year I have discovered Hegel—actually, it was last year, Dave told me, I think you're reading Kierkegaard too much (in fact I have *roared* through *all* his books), try reading Hegel. *Take him seriously*. That's what I'm doing now. Independent Study in the Philosophy Department. Dave and Bluma sent me, to Professor Barrett. He wrote an interesting book, *Irrational Man*, which I read. Interesting curriculum, for my 'Hegel' study, in general. The *Science of Logic*. It's another world. I think Hegel is as joyful (like Dave) as Kierkegaard is gloomy. (Kierkegaard only *claimed* to be joyful.) But Hegel is also *totally committed*— like Dave. Of course, Kierkegaard speaks daggers when it comes to Hegel, but Kierkegaard has his own ax to grind. A few months ago Dave lent me his copy of a recently published book, *The Last Years: The Kierkegaard Journals 1853-1855*. It's an expensive hard-cover edition, he said, don't buy it, I'll

---

52 The usual translation is 'through a glass darkly'; I follow Jorge Luis Borges, who translates it, he says, 'literally': see 'The Mirror of Enigmas,' in *Labyrinths*, Penguin, 1970.

lend you mine. I devoured it immediately, of course. (Dave and I *feast* on books, like wild animals devouring their prey.) Dave is deeply troubled by this book. By Kierkegaard's references, in the last two years of his life, to 'darkness,' 'pitch blackness,' 'extraordinary blackness.' It is a deeply troubling book. All Denmark is a prison. Worried Man Blues. As Woody Guthrie sang it, It takes a worried man to sing a worried song. The train I ride is twenty-one coaches long; and the gal I love is on that train and gone.

So many *screeches*, all across Brooklyn, absolutely no one else in the car. Eerie. On my 'three in the morning' journeys I've never been alone like this. The screeches are definitely louder when you're alone, in the middle of the night. But—I think I notice them less. They have no meaning. They lose all meaning. When the car is packed you hear them less but notice them more—their dumb blankness, *full* of meaning. They tell you where you are. On this night journey—where am I? A fork, a decision, traveling indefinitely. Thinking about my professors. Dave Leahy is also my friend. Forever, no matter what. But I must also say that even if I live to be a hundred I'll never forget Professor Benardete. Smallest classrooms, and few students, and he is the most 'illustrious' member of the Department. The only one who has his own office—which is as big as a broom closet, and may actually have *been* a broom closet before he took it over. In this miniscule office he always takes his shoes off and smokes his pipe, relentlessly. Last year I took his two-semester 'Greek Political Theory' course. Half the students disappeared after a few weeks. He sits behind his desk on the dais with no notes of any kind (but Dave Leahy never has the shadow of a note either), with one, or at most two books in front of him, and stands up maybe three or four times (it depends) to write a word on the blackboard. He writes it very gingerly, and usually twice—once in Greek and once transliterated. The course is not a Greek-language course, but the book or two on his desk are always only in Greek, no translations. He translates on the spot. We *did* Aeschylus' *Persians* and *Septem* (*Seven Against Thebes*, he always says the *Septem*), Plato's *Republic*, and Aristotle's *Politics*. *Did!* Hold your horses. We only *did* the lines of text that Benardete decided to discuss. *The lines of the text*. Nothing general, no background, no foreground. (But in all Dave's *roaring* there is nothing *general* either, believe you me. No 'general ideas' or 'overall picture.' He is just as 'specific' as Benardete, but in a different way.) I think we *did* about a hundred verses of the *Persians*, and maybe three hundred of the *Septem*. Last May—a year ago, when my 86 pounds were getting ready for their military-psychiatric hearing—we *did* about a hundred lines from Aristotle's *Politics*. In between—say, about two thirds of the course—we *did* most (but 'most' would be an exaggeration) of the *first* of the ten books of Plato's *Republic*. He often spent the whole two hours on a couple of sentences. How did he do it? Magic. I venture, courageously, to say that his point was this: as scholars, and students, all we have are words on a page. Dead letters. All just names. And all the more so in the case of Ancient Greece, a long-gone civilization and a 'dead' language. If we just accept these ancient words *uncritically*, we will never know what their authors are actually saying. So, start from a word, or a phrase, and travel with it, follow its circuitous route, its twists and turns, its stops and starts, see if you can get back to where you started from, and take stock of what you've learned along the way. Come to think of it, it's something like this train I'm riding. Except that Benardete doesn't travel 'indefinitely'—or does he? He keeps getting somewhere, but never stops—I mean, his 'train' stops (as does mine, the F—is there any sense in changing trains?), but only to start again. There is no end to the journey. Aeschylus, for example, says 'Ares'—the war god—but *what Ares?* We discover that there is more than one. Which one does he mean *here? Who* is Ares?

Dikê, goddess of Justice—but *what* Justice and, even more radically, *what is Justice?* If it means one thing to Eteocles and another to Polyneices, then what is it? Who can decide? What does it mean? What if 'justice' has meant something different to every man, woman, child, animal, and insect who has ever lived since the world began? That would be *bad* news for *logos*, whether you translate it as logic, discourse, reason, or what have you. But the title of this course was 'Ancient Political Theory,' so the question of the year was: What does *political* mean? One hell of a question. What does it mean to Aeschylus, to Plato, to Aristotle? (To Lyndon Johnson, to Richard Nixon, to Ho Chi Minh?) 'Political' comes from the word 'polis'—fantastic. 'Polis' is one hell of a word. Originally it referred to the fortress of a city, the citadel, as distinguished from the city itself; then, to the city itself (or town: Thebes, as I saw for myself two summers ago, is a town, not a city); then to a whole country, or state; and finally to the citizenry, the citizens who form the state—hence a free state, a republic. Is that clear? No, it isn't, it can mean a zillion things. And on this murky foundation we build our conception of 'the political'—to say nothing of *politics*. Take Plato's *Republic*: justice is of the essence, but it's hard to come by, and even harder to define. So Plato ends up by 'inventing' an ideal City, 'which has its being in words,' in the hope that some student of his may 'see it' and '*found a city in himself.*' I love this line: to found a city in yourself. But this is at the end of Book IX, and we only *did* 'most' of Book I. *In all justice* to Professor Benardete, he told us at the beginning of the course that we were expected to read the whole *Republic* 'two or three times during the year, possibly in different translations.' (He gave us an interesting 'background' reading list too, while he himself only spoke about tiny pieces of the texts themselves.) His *gran finale* was Aristotle's *zoon politikon*—the 'political animal.' Ye gods an abyss. An abyss! Such an innocent-looking little expression. Strangely enough, from their two sides of a yawning abyss these two professors present their students with exams that are very similar. Dave: 'Discuss pity and fear in Greek tragedy.' Benardete: 'What does *political* mean in Aristotle's *political animal?*' (At least he didn't ask what *animal* means!) That's the exam. Such easy questions. Write about *this* for two hours. These men are killers. The Classics Department is a deadly place. No 'multiple choice' here. If I live for ten thousand years I'll never forget Benardete's course. An absolutely incredible experience. Satori: direct experience of what is right here. Let me put it this way: we live and breathe in generalizations, in hand-waving. (Most of the time, in bullshitting.) (Never mind *flag*-waving.) When do we listen to *what we are actually saying?* When do we look at what is *right here?* Benardete made me a Zen Buddhist. (My serendipity on Chrystie Street only confirmed it.) No, I didn't tell him *that.* At the end of the course, I just told him—privately, I went to see him in his broom closet—Professor, this course has been one of the greatest experiences of my life. He glanced at me, puffed on his pipe, I could see he'd taken his shoes off, and gave me this copy of *Two Notes on Aeschylus' Septem*, which he'd published a couple of years before.[53]

'We' screeched through Delancey a while back, we're under the Village now, West 4th, and suddenly the car is half full of moderately lively people. The Village lives! Gays, straights, and whatevers. *Screech screech*, 34th, 42nd—almost three in the morning. Quite a few people coming and going. Times Square by night. Fun City! Muggers galore. Parades. Fun seeking tourists who can't afford taxis. This will perk me up a little, not that these people—the car, empty or full—makes much difference. It's the netherworld itself that makes a difference, the 'subworld,' the train, the stops and starts, the screeches.

53 Published in *Wiener Studien* [the text is in English], Graz—Wien—Köln: Hermann Böhlaus Nachf., Neue Folge—Band 1 (80. Band) and Neue Folge—Band 2 (81. Band), 1967 and 1968. I'm afraid you'll need one hell of a good library to find this. [I've discovered that the Notes were republished recently in: Seth Benardete, *Sacred Transgressions*, South Bend, Indiana: St. Augustine's Press, 2015, pp. 144–162.]

The darkness. The light in the car, day and night, does not erase the indelible darkness of the Hades outside. Moving on towards Queens, towards Jamaica, the end of the line. 'The fire is in the minds of men, not on the roofs of houses.' Dostoevsky, somewhere in *Demons*, a.k.a *The Possessed*, a.k.a *The Devils*.[54] Anarchists. Revolutionaries. Solitary students. *Nihilists*. Burning villages. Whatever light there is *down here* is the light *in my mind*. A decision. Traveling indefinitely. A fire *in the minds of men*. Mind. No-mind. Original emptiness.

Time, at last, for the *Seven Against Thebes*. (Or the *Septem*, as Benardete likes to call it.) Time to mull over the plot. The action. Guess what! If the plot of *Billy Budd* fits into a nutshell, I have to say that the 'plot' of the *Septem* would fit on the head of a pin. Practically nothing happens. This play is not recommended for Clint Eastwood fans. (I take that back, I'm a Clint Eastwood fan myself. The Spaghetti Westerns.) Actually the play is *full of war and blood,* but it's all *in the mind*. The movie screen is blank. Let's stick to the actual action. Eteocles speaks to the Thebans. The city is about to be attacked by an army led by his brother. (Here and there in the play there are extremely terse, and enigmatic, hints at the reason for this: as usual, the problem is Oedipus, their cursed and cursing father, along with grandpa Laius, the *real culprit*.) The Chorus of Theban women are scared out of their wits, they pant, rant, moan, and wail. (And dance, presumably.) Eteocles tries to calm them down. They get a *little* calmer. The messenger/soldier/spy[55] goes to the seven gates in turn, coming back after spying on each one to tell Eteocles the names of the enemy attackers/challengers/kings/champions and describing the devices on their shields. Eteocles chooses a defender/champion (with shield, with device) for each attacker. The

---

54 Unbelievably, George W. Bush quotes this—'untamed fire of freedom,' *'a fire in the minds of men'*—in his 2005 Second Inaugural Address. I'm sure he was not aware of the sort of books his speechwriters had been reading. For the record, the quote is from the chapter 'The End of the Fête.'

55 Translation by Grene, Vellacott, Benardete, in that order.

seventh attacker is his brother, Polyneices, and Eteocles, most unwisely, to say the least—*tragically*, is the word—*decides* to go to the seventh gate *himself*. This decision *really* upsets the Chorus. This coming/going/describing, and then deciding, takes up about two thirds of the play. The messenger/soldier/spy (I think I'll stick with 'spy,' Benardete's word) reappears to announce that the Thebans have successfully defended the first six gates, but at the seventh the brothers killed each other. (Hegel called it 'reciprocal suicide.') The body of the princes are carried in, escorted by their sisters, Antigone and Ismene. Aeschylus' play probably ended right here, with the sisters mourning over their brothers. The current, rather wordy, ending is probably spurious, tacked on fifty years later, after the blockbuster success of Sophocles' *Antigone*. That's the story. On the head of a pin. But, guess what. We have another abyss. This time, on the head of a pin. An abyss and a decision. Big time. Not that *Billy Budd* is small time, but the *Septem* is a white whale of an abyss. A genuine Moby Dick. The remarkable thing is that only Benardete, in his second Note, seems to have noticed it. I've read a number of commentaries, and they all say, ye gods, two thirds of the play is a recital of the blazonry on the shields, what's on old Aeschylus' mind. Then they talk about the historical background—or foreground: a play, set, in Thebes, sometime before the siege of Troy, about the successful defense of a strongly walled city—referred to contemporary Athens. It was produced in 467 B.C., twelve years after the Persians had run roughshod over an Athens without walls. Athens needed, and needs, *walls*[56]—that's what Aeschylus is saying, they say. And in fact, within a year or two after the production of the *Septem* the fortification of the Acropolis was begun in earnest. Walls! *Defend the City!* One hand clapping. You can't have *gates* without *walls*.

Meanwhile, in my mulling over this pinhead I've long since come to the end of the line. Jamaica again, and not the one

---

56 Ye gods, shades of Donald Trump (May 2017). Pardon my palimpsest.

south of Cuba. All the way through Queens there were only a
couple of other people in the car, and now the Jamaica station
is—well, let's say very very quiet. On my occasional 'three in
the morning' trips things seemed a lot less desolate, but maybe
it was the novelty of the thing, the fact that I was concentrated
on journeying *under the ground*, and the fact that it was just
one round trip, Delancey-Jamaica-Coney Island-Delancey or
vice versa, with its many stops and screeches. How many times
have I been up here in Jamaica today? I've lost count. I don't
have the slightest idea. I couldn't tell you how many if my
life depended on it. Strange. Time blurs in this netherworld.
Who's counting. I'll probably have to wait quite a while for
the next F, it must be around four in the morning. (No Taoist
story here, monkeys and acorns.) To Coney Island—it seems
to me now that Coney Island is on the other side of the world,
when in fact it's only about an hour and a half on the F Train.
Rush hour, dead of night, different trips, same time, I muse.
SUBway. Grateful Dead. Never the same, always the same.
Dead. Rush. Setting sail for Coney Island—it's like Columbus
setting sail on his trip to discover America. (Wasn't one end
of his line somewhere around Jamaica?) Cristóbal Colón, a
Man of the World. King Ferdinand's Dominican advisors, the
Dogs of God. Motherfuckers. The Inquisition. Torquemada.
Torture in Spain. Holocaust in America. 1492, God's will be
done: Spain cleansed of Moors, and Jews (Edict of Expulsion),
purified, a beacon to the world. In the New World they used
to hang thirteen (heathen) natives at a time in honor of Christ
Our Savior and the twelve Apostles—hang them all day from
a gibbet with their toes just barely touching the ground, and
then burn them alive. Anyway, I'm not alone. In the car I may
turn out to be alone, but looking up and down the platform
there *are* a number of people, waiting. One thing for sure: I
said something pretty damn stupid a while ago when I said to
myself, I don't know if the subway even has a schedule. Shit,

during the rush hour there are Fs rushing right through every station every five or ten minutes, I'd say. And at this hour, who knows. All just by chance? Random, like dots on a page. Absolutely unscheduled? A no-mind mass transit system? Still, maybe I was right when I said that no one *knows* the schedule—I may actually be right about that. But it doesn't mean that a schedule doesn't exist. Ignorance of the law is no excuse, even if there are *many* laws, I think, that absolutely no one knows. Not even lawyers. Or judges. Strolling up and down the platform here in Jamaica sometime around four in the morning. OK, now I'm on the F again, it's moving. Strangely enough, I notice a few fellow human beings in the car. *Mes semblables!* Very few, but a few. Did we all unconsciously bunch together when the cars opened their doors? The herd instinct, like cattle? Or something in our 'humanity genes.' Genes, jeans, Levi Strauss, Lévi-Strauss, blue, anthropologist, all just names. Chasing images. It looks like a long trip. Not that there's any actual socializing, or even *wondering* ('wonder,' said Aristotle, is the origin of philosophy) what anyone else is doing here at this sunless-dead netherworld hour, going where to do what? But there has been a little bit of smiling here and there, just a little, but in a natural way. A *decision*. Defend the City! It's not *walls* that are on Aeschylus' mind in this Tragedy. No, he's wondering about Eteocles' *decision*. *What in the world is Eteocles thinking?* Why does he decide to go *himself* to the Seventh Gate, to slay and be slain by *his own brother*, when he could have sent some other defender in his place, or changed the order of his defenders and gone himself to some other gate? Slay and be slain by his own brother. A blood-curdling transgression in Greek religion and the Greek 'polis.' *Bloodguilt.* Pollution of the City. Why did he *decide* on this reciprocal suicide, this *bad* ending, this *ugly end* to the curse on his House? Do you call this 'Defending the City'? *This* is what's on Aeschylus' mind. Why did he decide *this?* Or, much more precisely: How did he *come to decide* this? What was *on his mind?* No, *not on the roof of his House*, we know what's on the roof of his House. It is in this sense that Eteocles is my 'brother.' Not a *real* brother, like Joseph K., but a brother in circumstance. A brother in a dilemma that *we just can't quite bring into focus*. What does it mean to decide? Freedom, necessity, responsibility—what *about* them? Deciding and being decided for. When I read Benardete's second Note it was satori, sudden enlightenment: *'to decide' is extremely complex*, it is 'the direct reverse' of simple. A dilemma is innately complex, a complexity 'according to nature.' A 'fork' is simple only if it's to twirl your spaghetti on. Oedipus had a *bad time* at/with his fork. I have a good time when I twirl spaghetti, but I'm having a *very bad time* with this GAM-bomb-exile fork. I'm in trouble with this fork, that's for sure, but my 'brother in circumstance' is in big big big trouble with his dilemma—the Seventh Gate— because he *loses sight of* or *refuses to look at* the origin of the trouble. Namely, the series of CURSES on his House. BIG trouble. His father, Oedipus, blew his fate at the fork, where he unwittingly killed his father, but he was *serially* cursed and a *serial* curser, and this spelled *deep shit* for the whole family: wife/mother (not to mention father, whom he killed), sons, and daughters. Believe me, one hell of a yarn. A complex. What is my little fork compared to this. Nothing. But the comparison— thanks to the *Septem*, and Benardete's second Note—is there. It's *right here*, on this indefinite journey. *Indefinite*. Shit, suddenly I'm riled up, in this goddam almost-empty car on the F Train somewhere in Queens at somewhere around four in the morning. I swear I will *never leave* this joyless region of the sunless dead until I figure out what Aeschylus, and Benardete, are trying to tell me about the freedom and the necessity in Eteocles' decision. My brother in circumstance. Like Elpenor, my friend, unwept, unburied, *A man of no fortune and with a name to come*. Ezra Pound's great friend. 'Defend the City!'

This is what it's all about. In fact, we're in Manhattan already. Fun seekers? At this hour? No, but New Yorkers have things to do. Everywhere in the world, I think, the subway *slams its gates shut* around midnight (in Paris, for example, they have *le dernier métro*), but Fun City never sleeps. ACTION. Boots on the ground, sneakers underground. Sandals. Clogs. Spike heels. Whatever.

The *Septem*: the *action* (it *seems*) is simple, but the background—the curse—is *complex*. This has nothing to do with Freud's Oedipus Complex but everything to do with Complex Oedipus—I mean, his outrageous complexity. Cursed and cursing, riddled and riddling. *In aenigmate*—shit, Oedipus combs his hair and brushes his teeth through a glass darkly. Freud or no Freud, this is deep shit. Let me say this. Ancient Greek *myth*, or *history*, or whatever in the world it is, is an outrageous uproarious tangle—both because there are tangled versions ('sources') of the same events, and because the events themselves are wildly tangled. *In any event*, in my mind I need to untangle the story of Laius, and his son Oedipus, to say nothing of Jocasta, their famous wife-mother-wife, and *in particular* of Oedipus' sons Eteocles and Polyneices, who kill each other at the Seventh Gate in the *Septem*—to say nothing of his daughters Antigone and Ismene, thrown in for good measure. (Antigone! A star is born.) I've worked through this tangle many times already in my 21 years on this earth, but it's like the Hydra—so many heads to begin with, and if you cut *one* off she grows *two* more. This Lernaean Hydra, by the way, was a local monster: her lair was in the neighborhood of Argos. She had *countless* heads and *extremely bad breath*. A deadly combination. Fortunately Heracles—it was his Second Labor—found a way to decapitate the monster *in toto*. No small feat. In our minds she remains a menace forever. With her *infinite* proliferation of heads, and her *bad* breath, she may have been the inspiration for what Hegel called the 'bad infinite.' *In any case*, do I think I can untangle all this by the time I get to Coney Island? I doubt it. *Screech*. Rockefeller Center, the whole complex, some 19 buildings, ice-skating rink—no, wait, forget that, I already said that. Anyway, the F is pretty lively, Friday night, Saturday night, even at this hour, midtown, good nights for taxi drivers. But there are lots of people here in Hades too. Obviously, they can't afford taxis. Shit, I drove a taxi myself one year, on Fridays and Saturdays I drove until 5 or 6 in the morning, the garage was in Hell's Kitchen, West 48th Street, how did I get home? Took a taxi? Hell no. Who are you kidding. No, I took the C or the E, whichever came first, at 50th Street under 8th Avenue, then changed at West 4th for the F, to Delancey. A token for the turnstile, a token dime in my pocket. Not a red cent. Ground zero. I taught the Rivington Street muggers a lesson we'll never forget. Don't waste your time and talent mugging *me*. All that blood from my neck for a tiny token dime! Tangle with some other motherfucker. With bills. Greenbacks. Now—in Brooklyn and Queens people move around less in the middle of the night, but in midtown— ACTION. Not much, but all the time. Oedipus, cursed and cursing. What a tangle. A tangled tangle. In multiple versions, depending on the 'sources': Homer, Hesiod, Pindar, Aeschylus, Euripides, the more the merrier, each 'source' with his own spin. Sophocles, of course, is the King of this particular Curse Saga, he owes his immense fortune to it: his trilogy *Oedipus the King, Oedipus at Colonus, Antigone* has been a blockbuster for 2,500 years. But his version is just one of many. Aeschylus wrote his own trilogy—*Laius, Oedipus* (both lost), and our *Seven Against Thebes*—before Sophocles wrote his. Euripides wrote *his* own trilogy, *The Phoenician Women* (the version we have is a patchwork), *Chrysippus,* and *Oedipus*—alas, lost. What a loss! I think this curse was made to order for Euripides. But let me say this: In any event *this particular curse* (there are others) all begins with Laius, he started it all. Who started our war against Vietnam, in the defense of tyranny? Defend the City! This war that we call the Vietnam War, and that the Vietnamese, quite rightly, call the American War. Who started it, this war in the defense of tyranny? Ike maybe? Was it JFK? LBJ? The newfangled ATM? McNamara and his band? John Foster Dulles? Allen Dulles and his CIA? Or perhaps it was Lee Harvey Oswald? Or Raul Castro's sister? Or maybe Richard Nixon's dog? It's hard to get to the bottom of it all, hard to say *this is the one who started it all*. But for the curse that concerns me now there is no doubt whosoever that Laius *started it all*. In quite a scabrous way. Watch out, this is a racy story. *Screech*, West 4th. It warms my heart to see so many fun seekers under the Village at this hour, heading back to Brooklyn tired but happy. Now—I need to *begin at the beginning*, with Laius. Alas, we have a tangle of 'soft' and 'hard' versions of his, so to speak, transgression. *Screech. Wait a second:* Delancey Street. Untangle all this by the time I get to Coney Island? Whose leg was I *pulling*. It would take a full week on the *Titanic* to work all this through. *Who* is Laius, the *beginning* of *this* curse? I'm sorry to say this, but Laius is the great-grandson of Cadmus, the founder of Thebes, who had his *own* curse. And you just cannot understand Aeschylus' *Septem*—who are these 'sown-men' for example, that Eteocles sends off to the Gates?—if you don't know the story about the founding of Thebes. Another *very long story*, these myths go on forever. Yarns. Tangles. This one involves, first, a special cow, with a white, full-moon-shaped spot on either flank, and then a water-dragon, the Ismenian Dragon, a son of Ares himself (and cousin of our bad-breathed friend the Lernaean Hydra) and sacred guardian of the Ismenian Spring, just outside what is now (i.e. ever since Cadmus founded it) Thebes. Cadmus sent his men to the spring to get water and, alas, the dragon devoured them. Stuff happens.[57] Cadmus was *furious*, and forgetting that the dragon was the son of Ares, he

---

57 As Donald Rumsfeld put it.

managed to slay it somehow. (Another long story.) Shades of
Curtis LeMay. *Screech*. York Street, Brooklyn, that Billy-Budd-
Michael-Kohlhass reading chick, I wonder whether she's getting
up soon or going to bed soon. Doesn't matter. I have other fish
to fry. Eight million stories in the Naked City, a shame she isn't
one of mine. Shit, I can't talk to myself about the *Septem*
without talking about Cadmus. Another curse. If I wanted to do
this right, there would be an inflation of curses here that would
make the Big Bang look like a popgun. So, since he'd lost all his
men to the dragon, he needed more. Athena, who had helped
with the slaying, advised him to plant the dragon's *teeth.*
(Other version: plant half the teeth and give the other half to
Athena, for her own delight, such as it may be.) (Put them
under her pillow? No, the Tooth Fairy hasn't been invented yet.)
From the teeth emerged fully armed warriors of Ares, ready to
make mincemeat of Cadmus, but he (tactics! let this be a
lesson to all present-day politicians) threw stones at them,
making it appear that they were attacking one another. So
Ares' men forgot about Cadmus and fought with each other
until only five worn-out warriors survived. These five, 'whom
Ares spared,' came to be known as the *Spartoi*, 'the sown men,'
who then helped Cadmus found Thebes. Eteocles—Defend the
City!—counted heavily on their offspring to Defend the City
against the army led by his own brother. But, just a moment.
What about Cadmus himself? Did he come out of all this
unscathed, smelling like the proverbial rose? Did Ares forgive
Cadmus for slaying his Dragon? Not on your life. To atone for
his crime Cadmus slaved for the War God for eight years; then
married his daughter, Harmonia, at a lavish wedding attended
by all the gods.[58] Happy ending? No way. First, Zeus turned
Cadmus and Harmonia into serpents (see the unhappy ending
of Euripides' *The Bacchae*), incinerated their daughter Semele

---

58 Forgive me this intrusion on myself, it is October 2nd, 2014, and we Venetians
have just survived the lavishness (15 million dollars worth, they say) of George
Clooney's Hollywood-Venetian nuptials, IN OUR FACE. Thanks a bunch. Fuck you
George.

(mother of Dionysus) and their palace, and banished them from Thebes. Agave, their other daughter, is the mother of Pentheus, ripped to pieces by the Bacchae, led by Agave herself. And this is just the beginning. Ares, or possibly Hera, or possibly even Artemis, have it in for this family. Cadmus, the serpent, slithers away with his wife, leaving the kingship to their son Polydorus, father of Labdacus, father of Laius. Laius, in person. What was his problem? Look, Brooklyn! I've been above ground for some time now. The dim glimmer of dawn. Billy hanging from the yardarm. 'The vapory fleece hanging low in the East was shot through with a soft glory as of the fleece of the Lamb of God seen in mystical vision; and simultaneously therewith, watched by the wedged mass of upturned faces, Billy ascended; and ascending, took the full rose of the dawn.'

And I, less dramatically, hop off the F Train at Coney Island. I'm thinking about changing trains. I'm not sure. A decision. *A decision.* Am I getting anywhere with my fork? Am I getting a glimmer of *what a decision is?* I'm strolling up and down the 4 platforms, contemplating the 8 tracks. I'm thinking about something I read in the *Post* a few days ago. A decision. 'I read the news today, oh boy,' as Sgt. Pepper put it. A 14-year-old boy who died stopping a suicide bomber at his school in Pakistan.[59] The boy, named Aitazaz, was late for school. His two thousand schoolmates had gathered in the yard for their morning assembly. Just outside the main gate, along with some other students he saw an older boy acting suspiciously. They realized almost immediately that he was wearing an explosive vest. The other students backed off, but Aitazaz challenged the bomber and tried to catch him. During the scuffle the bomber panicked and detonated his bomb, killing himself and Aitazaz. His father said, 'My son has made his mother cry, but thanks to him hundreds of other mothers are not crying for their children.' His brother said, 'I'd never thought Aitazaz

---

59 I totally renounce all chronology here. The incident is true and took place on 9 January 2014. The boy's name is Aitazaz Hassan Bangash.

would choose such a glorious death.' Quite a story. All this probably took place in less than five minutes. *Choose* such a glorious death. A decision? Absolutely. Aitazaz *decided*, made a decision. But, oh boy, is this what we mean by 'deciding'? I see a child step down off the curb with a truck bearing right down on him and I *immediately* snatch him out of the way. Without thinking. No thinking, no deciding. I think. No-mind? Zendo, Samurai, what do I know. But while Aitazaz's companions ran away he stood his ground and confronted the danger. He didn't have much time to think about what he was doing but I guess he had some, a few seconds. He did think, I think. This story was on the front page of the *Post*, and not only of the *Post*. I'm thinking of Hegel's '*decision* to consider *thinking as such*.' The decision that he refers to as 'willful' but not as 'free' because, I think, in some sense it is the subject matter that decides, not the subject. *But doesn't a decision involve freedom?* It must. But does this mean that *it excludes necessity?* I don't think Hegel thinks so. I called 'I decide to brush my teeth' a 'being-is-nothing' decision, the 'ground zero' of freedom. But Aitazaz does not make a being-is-nothing decision, he does something very different. Has he been 'decided for'? By what? Sure, if he hadn't encountered a suicide bomber right in front of his school, ready to blow his schoolmates sky-high, he could never have decided/chosen to challenge him, and get himself blown sky-high in the process. But if we take 'decided for' to mean 'whatever the circumstances happen to be,' we empty it of all meaning. In this circumstance all his companions decided to run away. I admire Aitazaz, the whole world does. I wish he could help me with my *decision*, but—believe me, I'm no Hamlet. At the age of 21 I've already made some very important decisions in my life. I'm not an *undecided* sort of person. This damn fork. My problem is that, this time, before I decide I have to figure out *what a decision is*, in my own specific circumstance. I have a fork. If I suddenly encounter a suicide bomber in the subway I may well throw myself on him, but that isn't my specific circumstance right now. Not my problem right now. What have I done? I have *chained* a general, and presumably philosophical, question—possibly a question of *logic*, no less—to a specific, practical question. To one specific fork. The logic of a fork, of *this* fork. Who gave me this fork, where did I get it? Wise cats chase their tails, they learn a lot from it and it keeps them out of trouble. Suddenly *I hop onto the B Train*. No-mind. Without thinking about it. A decision? A being-is-nothing decision? No decision? I've been strolling up and down these platforms, oblivious to everything, thinking about Aitazaz. Ishmael, 'growing grim about the mouth.' 'I quietly take to the ship.' Brooklyn is glimmering. In the east I see the orb of a pallid sun. A new train, a new line, a new day. Early April. Patch of discolored snow. In his shroud. Already. Decided for. Poor Aitazaz. The glorious death he chose. He had no fork. No time for it. No time for logic?

Ye gods I'm on the B Train. Traveling blind—blind as Oedipus, cursed and cursing, riddled and riddling, after he blinded himself, as we shall see. Like a new life, after all that time on the F. 'New' screeches. B screeches. *Screech*, Bay 50th Street. Sounds exactly like the F screech, but what the dickens sort of name is 'Bay 50th Street'? So be it. *Screech,* 25th Avenue, wow, Brooklyn has a lot of avenues, puts Manhattan to shame. What counts is that I'm *above ground*, a.k.a *elevated*, like on the F, and now I'm seeing the western part of Brooklyn—in fact, this stretch is called the West End Line. I happen to know quite a bit about the subway—OK, a true confession, I am a *student* of the New York subway, an avid subway-map reader, even though I rarely go anywhere, except on the F for 'three in the morning' or, possibly, to get to or from NYU if it's raining hard. Dave Leahy is my *practical* subway expert, I only have a little subway theory, he was born in Brooklyn and lives there and has taken the subway *a lot. In any event*, while traveling blind (I've never *seen* any of this before) I do have some idea of what to expect. Bensonhurst, Sunset Park (I told you we were in the *west*), elevated until 36th Street—then, Hades again. No more Gowanus Canal, towering briefly over infinite murk, but something MUCH BETTER. SirYesSir, the Manhattan Bridge! Forget about the Rutgers Tube under the river, the B Train (and the D) goes right over it. I've never done this in all my life, and I expect something at least as exciting as a trip to the Grand Canyon. After my view from the bridge, Manhattan will take care of itself. I'm going all the way up to 168th Street/Washington Heights—the Cloisters, the fabulous beautiful Unicorn Tapestries. Manhattan is very narrow way up there, you can throw a stone (possibly, if you're Sandy Koufax) from the Harlem River to the Hudson. And between here and there we shall enjoy—from beneath, of course, in its 'sunless dead' version—Central Park West from start to finish, 59th to 110th, a.k.a. Columbus Circle to Cathedral Parkway. Maybe Lindsay is right, it's a fun city. A parade is a parade is a parade. What a glimmer in Bensonhurst at this hour, looking towards the east. Sunset Park at sunset may be too beautiful to bear. Cursed and cursing. *Screech*, 20th Avenue—I'm enjoying the view. 18th Avenue—79th Street—the B makes a lot of stops, very scenic. 71st, 62nd, 55th, 50th, Fort Hamilton Parkway, 9th Avenue, before entering the netherworld—but then it heads like a bat out of Hades straight for the Manhattan Bridge. Oedipus, the curse, cursed, cursing his sons, Eteocles and Polyneices—it all begins with Laius, his old man. But watch out, we are coming to a crossroads of curses that would make a bald man's hair stand on end.

Now, what is Laius' problem? We have two *quite* different versions—one 'tame' and one 'racy.' Let's start with the tame one. In a nutshell. Laius is King of Thebes and he is married to Jocasta, daughter of a descendent of the *Spartoi*. Problem: they have been married for quite a while and haven't had any kids. So Laius journeys to Delphi to consult the Oracle of Apollo, who gives him *most unwelcome* news: namely, any kid he has will grow up to kill him and marry Jocasta, so he'd better not have any. But then, one night, Laius is drunk—alas, such things happen—and the result is little Oedipus. Variation (another 'source'): they have just had their first child (Oedipus), and Laius goes to the Oracle in search of future knowledge, in general, to broaden his mind, I suppose, only to hear that his newborn son will grow up to kill his father and marry his mother. In either event, they have a servant 'expose' poor little Oedipus on a nearby mountain to die, but the servant saves him, and he goes to Corinth where the childless King and Queen of Corinth adopt him. Young Oedipus is convinced he is their real son until a drunk calls him a 'bastard,' saying he has no idea who his father is. His Corinthian parents deny this, Oedipus is perplexed, so off he goes to Delphi, and guess what, the Oracle tells him he's destined to murder his father and marry his mother. So Oedipus does not return to Corinth, where his real father and mother are *not*, but heads for Thebes, where of course they *are*. *Screech*. Fort Hamilton Parkway, we cross right over it. On his way to Thebes he comes to a fork where three roads cross. Here he encounters a chariot driven by Laius, who claims he has the right of way, they fight, Oedipus kills him. Continuing his journey to Thebes, Oedipus encounters a Sphinx (no, we're not in Egypt), a terrible monster who has been terrorizing Thebes (in Greece) *with her riddle*. (Thebes, Thebes, here, there, everywhere. All just names.) Whoever wants to get to Thebes is subjected to this riddle: What has four legs in the morning, two in the afternoon, and three in the evening? Reminds me of Chuang Tsu's story about the man who kept monkeys. When the traveler fails to answer, the Sphinx devours him. Thebes is effectively cut off from the outside world. Then along comes Oedipus, who has just killed his (real) father. With his 'three in the morning' spirit he promptly gives the correct answer: Man! Anthropus! The baby crawls on all fours, the grown man has two legs, and the old man walks with a cane. The Sphinx is astounded, horrified, terrified, and throws herself off a cliff into the sea. *Screech*. 9th Avenue. Great view of Sunset Park. End (beginning, actually—or end? or beginning?) of the West End Line. So, naturally, Oedipus goes on to Thebes, where, as the slayer of the Sphinx—a hero!—he weds the freshly-widowed Jocasta and, of course, the new king and old queen have four lovely children and live happily ever after, or for many years anyway, until—but, hold your horses, I'll get back to this. We need the 'racy' version now, which concerns this first part of the story—which concerns *Laius*. A question: *Why* is this horrible Sphinx stationed there on the road to Thebes, devouring everyone with her riddle? A good question. Just by chance? Just for a laugh? She fell out of the sky and landed right there, riddle and all? Euripides has an answer. What a tragedy that so many of his tragedies have been lost completely, or reduced to fragments. His *Chrysippus* may have been too racy even for the Greeks. Just think, in Euripides' version (which became quite popular with Christian era sources) the Sphinx has been sent by the gods to terrorize Thebes as punishment because *Laius raped the prince* [sic] *of a neighboring kingdom*. What a story. I have to admit, there are at least a dozen variations on it, which, of course, I won't go into. In any case Euripides didn't just make this version up, there are extant vases from before his time that show the lecherous Laius as he abducts his victim. *Screech*. 36th Street, and under the ground we go, bye bye glimmering light of Brooklyn. A long netherworld stretch now, an express stretch, only one stop, Pacific Street. (The Pacific, in Brooklyn?) Anyway, when Laius was a young man the throne of Thebes, to which he was heir, was violently usurped. Some Thebans managed to smuggle young Laius off to Pisa (no, not in Tuscany, no Leaning Tower), in the Peloponnesus, 'island of Pelops,' where he is welcomed—be my guest!—by King Pelops in person. A fine upstanding gentleman, who gave his name to the entire Peloponnesus, even if there are a few gray areas here, which I cannot entirely ignore. Pelops has many sons, but his favorite is Chrysippus, a 'bastard' he had either with the nymph Axioche or with Danais, as the case may be. Anyway, Chrysippus is sharp as a tack and Pelops intends to have him inherit the kingdom. But two of Pelops' non-bastard sons, Atreus and Thyestes, later kill Chrysippus—this is a *long* story, the story of the other Big Curse in Greek Tragedy, where, on a pinhead, we have the *Oedipus* Curse and the *Orestes* Curse, Aeschylus' other Curse, his blockbuster Curse, the *Oresteia*, whereas the Oedipus Curse was Sophocles' blockbuster. (Euripides' Oedipus Curse Trilogy was too racy, I think, and they lost it.) The Orestes Curse is just the last act of what, to be precise, is the Pelops Curse (ye gods, even more complex than the Laius/Oedipus Curse, which concludes with the 'reciprocal suicide' I am so desperately committed to)—this curse on Pelops' children, grandchildren, and great-grandchildren, including Atreus, Thyestes, Agamemnon, Aegisthus, Menelaus, and—the more the merrier, last but not least—finally Orestes. (To say nothing of Electra, his sister. Mourning became her.) But, now, Chrysippus. Poor fellow. *Screech*. Pacific Street. From sea to shining sea. A genuinely gifted young man. His first misfortune (before being murdered by his half-brothers, in one version; in the 'racy' version, after being raped by Laius he slit his own throat out of shame) is that Pelops entrusts him to the 'care' of poor exiled Laius, another promising young man, who becomes his official 'tutor.' Now, 'tutor' can be a big or a small word: in America no big deal, in Britain pretty big, in Ancient Greece *really* big. Huge. Who knows what was on Laius' mind (or body), but, as the story (which story? I've lost count) goes, Laius is escorting Chrysippus to the Nemean Games where the unlucky lad is to compete (sharp as a tack! body and mind) when, alas, tragically, he kidnaps him and carries him off to Thebes in order to rape him. Which he did, and repeatedly. No, it was not just a passing fancy. What a great tutor. My ass. Deep shit. But, what the fuck. Chrysippus lives on, to be murdered by his half-brothers. No harm done. (Or, in the other version, slits his throat out of shame.) Laius somehow or other becomes the rightful King of Thebes, and weds the comely Jocasta. Sic semper tyrannis. What's the problem?

What's the problem? If we don't have enough problems here, how many do we need? But ye ye gods look at this, we're on the Manhattan Bridge. On the south side, I can see the Brooklyn Bridge just a little way downtown. OK, the East River is not quite the Grand Canyon, but seeing it from inside a subway car is a whole new experience for me. I know a great Chinese restaurant right near the entrance to the Manhattan Bridge, they fish live shrimp right out of the tanks in the window and sweet-and-sour them for you on the spot.[60] And it's cheap. Better not think about it now, I didn't have dinner last night. Of course I'm an expert on the Williamsburg Bridge, there it is! Quite a way uptown from here, it's five minutes from my house, I used to jog across it at dawn, but I never crossed it on the subway (J, M, or Z). Manhattan Bridge. And now, Manhattan. I'm under the ground again, and I'll be down here for a long long time, all the way to 168th Street/ Washington Heights and back. 168 streets uptown, plus these unnumbered streets as far as Houston, of course. Who's counting. Anyway, getting back to Laius. On the bright side, despite the many problems we also have one solution: we can say that the Sphinx was sent to Thebes by the gods to avenge Laius' buggery. I mean, in all places at all times being a tutor is a more or less serious business. It's no joke. Tutorial responsibility or some such. Young Laius is the *tutor* of the

---

60 For the record, I discovered this restaurant around 1990, how I miss it! Who knows if it's still there.

(bastard) son of a *king*, what's more he is a *guest* (another *big* word in Greece, no, nothing like the 'guest-worker' Turks in Germany today) in the king's house, and what does he do, he kidnaps and *rapes* the unlucky lad. An act as unpopular with the Greek gods as it would be with whatever gods we have today—possibly more so. Sending the Sphinx to terrorize Thebes was the least they could do. We have a reference to Laius' sex life in the *Septem*—pithy, but absolutely crucial if we are to understand the tragedy. Let me see—ye gods, we're at Grand Street, one of my favorite streets, a ten-minute stroll from Rivington, where I live—I need to find this line from the *Septem*, line 750. This doesn't refer to his raping poor Chrysippus but, rather, to his big night with Jocasta. Aeschylus subscribes to the Laius-drunk-defying-the-Oracle variation. This is the climax of the play. Eteocles has just—most unwisely—*decided* to go to the Seventh Gate *himself* to fight his brother. The Theban women of the Chorus are, to say the least, distraught, and they say (or sing, or wail):

> Old is the tale of sin I tell but swift in retribution: to the third generation it abides. Three times in Pythian prophecies given at the Navel of the Earth Apollo had directed King Laius all issueless to die and save his city. But he was mastered by loving folly and begot for himself a doom, father-murdering Oedipus, who sowed his mother's sacred womb, whence he had sprung himself, with bloody root, to his heartbreak. Madness was the coupler of this distracted pair.

This (more or less) is David Grene's translation, the one Dave Leahy uses in his course. We note that these upstanding Theban ladies express themselves with extreme delicacy, and on such a crucial matter. 'Distracted,' for example. Pretty dainty. 'Mastered by loving folly'—namely, getting drunk and having sex with your wife when Apollo has told you, three times over, 'live and die childless'—'die without issue and save the city.' 'Mastered by the rashness of love,' Vellacott translates it. The Greek could be rendered as 'ill-advised in love,' no less. Laius did something 'rash,' 'ill-advised.' To put it mildly. A little later (line 842), confronted with news of the 'reciprocal suicide,' the ladies express themselves more bluntly: 'Laius' disobedience was the cause of it all.' (Vellacott); '*The decisions of Laius*, wanting in faith, have had effect until now.' (Grene). In whatever version or variation we choose, Laius never hesitated when there was a (bad) decision to be made. My lesson from this, to help me on my indefinite journey? Bad decisions are quick and easy, but also very costly. Fast and loose. Decide now, pay later. Watch out for forks. This really doesn't help me much. I'm not at a Chinese restaurant here, about to decide on 1 from group A and 2 from group B. Pork- or shrimp-fried-rice? No, it is *Eteocles'* decision that has to teach me something, if anything will. Defend the City! Benardete's second Note. The Curse. From Laius to Oedipus to Eteocles/Polyneices. The Curse of Oedipus. In what we've seen thus far (but this is Part One, Oedipus Cursed; stay tuned for Part Two, Oedipus Cursing!) Oedipus is, relatively speaking, the most innocent/least guilty of the lot. Sure, killing your elders at forks in the road is nothing to be especially proud of but, it seems, it was Laius who picked the fight, as usual. What's wrong with wedding the comely Queen of Thebes. Raising such a fine family, two boys and two girls. Sounds good. *Screech*, where in the world am I? Well bless my soul, it's West 4th. What day is it? Saturday. What time is it? I don't know, for me everything up to 11 is 'early morning.' It must be around 7:30, breakfast of champions. I *did* finish high school, even if I dreamed I didn't. I'm not hungry. If I *wanted to* I could even switch back to the F—to Jamaica, or even back to Coney Island. Or Delancey. Why in the world should I? I could *suddenly* get off the B and take a D, to the Bronx. Why? These are not the decisions that trouble me. Right now I'm on the B Train. For now. Definitely indefinitely.

Part Two: Oedipus Cursing. This facet of the Complex is less well known, by far, compared to the 'Sophoclean' (so to speak) Oedipus Cursed (but *we all know* that Oedipus was cursed). What a shame. I still have to finish Part One, even if everyone knows it already. I need to prepare my mind fully for the sequel. Too many people just *leap* straight into this Complex unconsciously (so to speak) without understanding the full complex of curses, damn them all. In a nutshell. Many years after the (happy) marriage of Oedipus and Jocasta suddenly a *plague of infertility* (of all things) strikes Thebes. Crops no longer grow in the fields and women no longer bear children. Even the livestock no longer reproduce. Oedipus swears he will end the pestilence. He sends Creon, Jocasta's brother and his uncle/brother-in-law, *to the Oracle at Delphi* (of all places), seeking guidance. Creon tells him that the Oracle told him that the murderer of Laius must be brought to justice. Oedipus responds by *cursing* his wife's late husband's murderer, pronouncing the eminently memorable (Sophoclean) command: Find the slayer! At this point all hell breaks loose, the blind-prophet Tiresias gets into the act—ON A PINHEAD, but, really, on a pinhead (I want to get to Part Two, which is what really interests me), the truth will out! 'Find the slayer!' cries Oedipus, the parricide. A cry of shadow, terrible and perfectly ambiguous, meaningless and 'full of meaning.' Less philosophically, I limit myself to just two versions, of many. When Jocasta 'finds the slayer' she goes into the palace and hangs herself ('a patch of discolored snow in early April'); Oedipus, using the pin from his mother/wife's brooch, stabs his own eyes out. 'Already in his shroud.' Euripides' less 'humane' version: Jocasta does *not* (even) kill herself, and Oedipus is blinded by one of Laius' servants. It's always Laius. The *real*

120

beginning of all this, as I said quite a while ago. Absolutely. The *beginning* of *this* curse. In either event, Oedipus is blinded, and up shit creek. Without, or possible with, a paddle. We'll see.

Now I can finally get to Part Two, which is what interests me. Here, again, we have curses and riddles, and to the second degree. It's not my fault. Now—bless my soul, Rockefeller Center. Who's in the car with me, I'm not even noticing what's going on. 34th, 42nd, all I'm thinking about is Oedipus. Rockefeller Center, John D. Rockefeller Jr., 19 buildings, ice-skating rink—forget all that, let's stick to the point—is a subway fork: F to Jamaica, D up into the Bronx, B to Washington Heights, the Cloisters, the fabulous beautiful Unicorn Tapestries. I don't give a shit about this fork. I'm on the B Train, with Oedipus on my mind. No Memphis Blues, not now, not again. What becomes of him? Without, or with, a paddle. Sophocles says, famously, that with the loving guidance of his wonderful daughter Antigone after considerable wandering he settles down in Colonus, a posh suburb of a wonderful Athens splendidly ruled by Theseus, where, the epitome of ancient (blind) wisdom, he marvelously vanishes from this earth. But other versions are considerably less hunky-dory. In the version Aeschylus follows the blind Oedipus, after all the revelations and Jocasta's death, continues to rule Thebes. No rhinoceros has ever had thicker skin. However, since—I suppose—he is old (possibly, but his 'age it means less') and blind (definitely), he makes a proposal worthy of Henry Kissinger. The gist: OK, it's time for my two sons to rule, to Defend the City! of the Seven Gates. It seemed like a good idea at the time, like, they can give me a succulent office in some wing of the White House where I'll have nothing to do (or to see, since I'm blind), while they take turns in the Oval Office, one year each at a time. Sounds good. But, what happened? In all the versions and variants I know, it's not really clear. What's that! A strange screech. No, not Hegel's Owl of Minerva, which begins its flight

121

only at dusk, it's barely 8 in the morning, possibly. (And I don't mean eight acorns.) No, I am now under the western edge of CENTRAL PARK. Upper West Side screeches are so *refined*, so *tip-top*, somehow. They sound different. They sound more refined, more tip-top. Could it be the effect of being under a refined/tip-top edge of Central Park? Under the eastern edge— 5th Avenue—*there are no subways* to disturb the aristocratic surface, no, only demure and proper busses, the subways are under Lexington. So, what's the problem now? Oedipus is *not happy*. Not happy with his sons. Riled up. Furious. Pissed off. Enraged. Why? Well, once again it depends on your sources. In all versions, basically, he's furious about the way they've treated him since his blinding. But we have, among others, a 'bland' and a 'juicy' (so to speak) version. Aeschylus follows a bland version, which, of course, is what counts for the *Septem*. But the 'juicy' version, wow! It's from the *Thebaid*, an ancient epic poem of uncertain authorship (possibly Homer, of uncertain authorship himself) about the war between Eteocles and Polyneices. We only have a few fragments, but one of them gives us a very explicit account of what pissed Oedipus off. As he saw it, his sons were disrespectful to him not just once but on two occasions. First, when they served him using the silver table of Cadmus and a golden cup, which he had forbidden. Then, after *that*, when they sent him the haunch of a sacrificed animal instead of the shoulder, which he richly deserved. Ye gods. The horror. The haunch instead of the shoulder. To their own father. But Aeschylus—wisely, I think—does not join this fray. In the *Septem* Oedipus is upset about their attitude, generally. He's angry that they don't love him enough to take proper care of him. They show no concern for their poor blinded father—who, after all, is leaving them his kingdom out of the goodness of his heart (possibly). The Chorus in the *Septem* speaks (sings, wails) about their 'cruel tendance' of him (Grene), their 'grudging him his place at home' (Vellacott).

No culinary reference to haunches or shoulders. But the *point*
is that—bland, spicy, juicy—Oedipus *does not take it lying
down*. What does he do? Take a guess. *He curses them.* As
if we didn't have more than enough curses already. And how
does he do it? *With a riddle.* As the chorus puts it, 'A stranger
coming from the sea, born of fire, will prove a harsh divider
of his inheritance.' This riddle isn't as tricky as the Sphinx's,
we are given some hints in the course of the *Septem* about a
'Scythian colonist,' and then the solution: not 'man' this time
but 'iron'—iron, steel, *the sword*. 'The stranger apportioning
their inheritance, a Chalyb, Scythian colonist, a bitter divider of
possessions, is cruel-hearted steel.' Quite right, the 'stranger'
here is iron, a metal recently imported from Pontus (*pontus* is
a Greek word for 'sea'), then forged and sharpened into the
sword, 'hammered steel of Scythia.' 'An iron sword was the
image of Ares among the Scythians,' as Benardete notes in
one of his Notes. Oedipus' riddled/riddling curse on his sons is
that they divide his kingdom by the sword. This curse, a direct
result of Laius' 'loving folly'—it all begins with Laius, dammit
all—is what spurs the *Septem* on, from Polyneices' rebellion to
Eteocles' *decision*. But my point here—if, possibly, I have one—
is that Oedipus *Cursed* is Oedipus *Cursing*, Oedipus *Riddled* is
Oedipus *Riddling*. A tragic flaw—

A tip-top screech, 86th Street, under Central Park West,
AND WHAT DO I SEE. What's this. I can't believe my eyes.
Another young man with a placard. Hanging from his neck by
a string. No wheelchair, he's standing on his own two legs. A
penny for the Old Guy. Again. He sure got up early. But the car
is pretty full, people going uptown. Let's see what he has to
say for himself, so to speak. That nice-looking I GAVE MY LEGS
FOR MY COUNTRY fellow yesterday didn't say a single word.
Didn't need to, I guess. The image on the placard and the
reality on the wheelchair—this physical presence of my legless
fellow man, *mon frère!*—spoke all the volumes (and, possibly,

123

daggers) he meant to speak. Still, I wish he had spoken with me, told me his story. What's on this placard? Ye gods, what a tale. A magnificently painted image of a soldier in full dress uniform saluting the American flag, his right hand on his heart. Bless my soul, it's the Pledge of Allegiance. (Until World War II the pledge began with the hand over the heart, but after reciting 'to the Flag' the arm was extended towards the Flag, palm-down. The extended arm was eliminated because it looked too much like the Nazi salute.) There are two captions: above the image, SUPPORT THE TROOPS, and below, GOD IS ON OUR SIDE. Great, a Bob Dylan fan. Memphis blues, again. You never ask questions. As St. Paul told the Romans, if God is for us, who can be against us? Another young fellow, quite like the legless one. My age or a little older. No beard, very clean cut, very short hair, military style. Wearing a green t-shirt and green pants. With a cap, in his hand. He's asking for pennies (or whatever), moving slowly through the car, here he comes, his placard really is stunning, a work of art. The man is not dressed as a soldier but the image on his placard sure is. His cap is in his hand (with quite a few coins in it, but no bills), 'Vietnam veteran' he says, that's all. I'm feeling ironic. I give him one red cent. 'A penny, for the Old Guy,' I say, 'old Guy Fawkes, who tried to blow up the House of Lords.' The veteran is unfazed. Totally unimpressed, actually. A blank. *Screech.* (Tip-top.) He isn't making as much money as my legless friend but he's doing very well. 96th Street, and out he goes, and right back onto the next car down. I wonder if shouting *Ho Ho Ho Chi Minh* would have gotten a rise out of him. Maybe. Probably not. Probably the other passengers in the car would have been pretty ticked off. Well, let me say this. *Having* to recite the Pledge of Allegiance all the way through school, from kindergarten (or first grade maybe) to the end of high school, every blessed morning, sure as hell ticked *me* off.

I pledge allegiance to the Flag of the United States of
America and to the Republic for which it stands, one nation
under God, indivisible, with liberty and justice for all.

It's short but it's a mouthful. At least in college we don't recite
it. Do children in schools all over the world have to swear
similar oaths? I don't actually know, but I don't think so.
In Albania, maybe. Do the Brits sing 'God Save the Queen'
in school every bloody morning? Anyway, I know the whole
history of this Pledge, which I won't go into except to say that
the phrase 'under God' was only added in 1954, by a Joint
Resolution of Congress—a kick in the balls for those Godless
commies. What ever happened to the separation of Church
and State? That's been a joke for two hundred years. Ironically
enough, it was the devoutest of the devout, the Jehovah's
Witnesses, who most heatedly objected to the pledge because
their beliefs preclude swearing loyalty to any power other
than God. Atheists, of course, are fucking commies, so they
have no rights and are better off keeping their mouths shut.
Fucking creeps. We red-blooded Americans have God on our
side. We have liberty and justice for all. For all Americans.
For the 'strange fruit' of the blacks lynched in the South[61] and
oppressed in the ghettos. For the poor and the homeless. We
even have it for people everywhere on this planet. Long live the
Shah of Iran. Long live tyrants everywhere. I really should have
shouted *Ho Ho Ho Chi Minh.* Too late now. Maybe I should dash
out at the next stop and chase after this guy—he'll only be two
cars down—and ask for my penny back, and definitely shout
Ho Ho Ho Chi Minh. And not only that. I should shout SUPPORT
THE TROOPS, BRING THEM HOME NOW. What the fuck, at their
parades these fuckers scream BOMB HANOI! BOMB HANOI!

---

61 Billie Holiday, 1939: 'Southern trees bear strange fruit/ Blood on the leaves
and blood at the root/ Black bodies swinging in the southern breeze/ Strange fruit
hanging from the poplar trees.' 'I was participating in my own lynching, but the
problem was I didn't know what I was being lynched for,' sez Westmoreland. That's
his problem.

BOMB HANOI! With liberty and justice for all. Or am I being unjust? *Can you support the troops, and the veterans, without supporting the war?* Is that a good question? No, I think it's a bad question. What is it the troops are doing, except fighting this war? How can you support troops who defend tyrants. Who kill babies. Murderers. The soldiers who should be supported are the ones who are resisting the war, or looking for a way to resist it. *What honor* is there in dropping napalm on civilians, shooting children in a ditch, and raping women in their villages? You, anti-war activist, how can you accept the logic of 'supporting the troops' without being pulled into supporting the war they are waging. With liberty and justice for all. A penny for this Old Guy. A penny? This individual man, a former soldier, a veteran, is not dressed as a soldier, but *the image he carries* is of a man dressed as a soldier. What's happening to me here? *Am I pissed off at the man or at the image?* Or at the Pledge of Allegiance itself, which the image put in my face?

Still, I have to say this about the Pledge. Despite its rabid in-your-face way of doing it, I think it expresses something important and true. Being a citizen of a country means owing allegiance to that country. Otherwise, neither 'citizen' nor 'country' have any meaning, you might as well call them 'apple' and 'cheese.' I still have three apples, but I'm not hungry. Being a citizen of a country involves *political responsibility*. Try explaining *that* to a first-grader, who's already reciting the pledge some two hundred times a year. What do five-year-olds understand about 'political allegiance'? Or fifteen-year-olds? Or fifty-year-olds? Does it mean saluting the flag and waving flags at parades? In the last few years a million young men got a quick and surefire lesson in 'political allegiance': they got drafted and shipped to Vietnam. For them, 'owing allegiance' means fighting in Vietnam in the defense of tyranny. But what about all the rest of us? Does 'owing allegiance' mean *supporting* the war in Vietnam? Apparently not. Not necessarily.

A lot of people oppose the war. It's a free country. We have free elections. If you don't like the war, I guess you can vote against Nixon in November. Or, you could have voted *for* Nixon in 1968, he had a whole pile of peace plans, and Humphrey was the 'LBJ's war' candidate. (I would have voted for Eldridge Cleaver, Peace and Freedom Party, but I was 18 at the time—old enough to fight, too young to vote. No peace, no freedom.) *Screech.* 110th Street. Time almost stood still for a moment. But here we are, at the border between tip and top. The northern edge of Central Park. I've been here before, at this very stop, I have a friend on 110th Street, and I've been up to Columbia, and to Harlem too. There's a lively neighborhood here, above ground, which I haven't visited for quite some time. And won't be visiting now either. A decision. Traveling indefinitely, 'the sunless dead and this joyless region.' 'The system of logic is the realm of shadows.' I decide to think about the *logic* of pledging and owing allegiance—to a country, I mean. To a *cause*—this would be far easier to explain and understand, *logically* speaking. A cause is by definition something you owe allegiance to. If it's *your* cause, of course. You choose it freely and necessarily owe it allegiance. Freedom and necessity stand (or fall) together. Your decision. And you are responsible for and to it. But with a country, logically speaking—no, it's not clear to me. You are born in a country, therefore you are a citizen of that country, therefore you owe it allegiance. I guess this is what they're telling you every morning at school. A syllogism? No, I think this is *fact*, not logic. I mean, it is most definitely a fact. But the logic? Well, you might say, Logic has nothing to do with it, and who can prove you wrong. 'Logic has nothing to do with it': a powerful answer. What more can I say. But—what if you don't feel you *belong* in and to the country. What if you *really* don't like the wars the country fights and the way it treats its own people. Don't like it *at all*. *Screech.* 125th Street. A soul screech. What do you do? Go to Vietnam anyway. Pay your taxes to fund the war anyway. Vote. Protest like hell. Raise hell. Get an education. Read. Become a doctor, a plumber, a lawyer, an electrician. You don't have to recite the Pledge every morning anymore, so, as for 'owing allegiance,' you can put it out of your mind, let it drop into your 'unconscious,' into your abyss. Have children. Send them off to school, where—OK, let *them* pledge. That's the system. It's not the system of logic, no, but somehow it is The System. Not to be confused with The Establishment, which is far more limited. No, The System is a *totality,* and 'totality' is something Hegel has understood better than anyone else, ever. But it's a *political*, not a logical totality. It's not a system of logic. So why the hell am I traveling indefinitely under the ground in a realm of shadows. I know why. Vaguely, but I know it. 135th Street. But it's hard to explain. I resent the fact that I *had* to pledge allegiance to the flag in school every morning. I always have this feeling that I don't belong in/to this country. Is this feeling free or necessary? For example, there are homosexuals—I like the new word 'gays'—who feel very deeply that they are women born in male bodies or vice versa. Do they owe allegiance to those bodies anyway? Why should they. It's not so easy to change your sexual identity, but it's possible. But what about your country? I'd like to blow up the Williamsburg Bridge. Why? Purely and simply to be able to say: I'm not passively accepting what my country is doing. I take responsibility for what I do *and* for what my country does. *There is logic in this.* The problem is, this logic does *not* tell me to blow up the Williamsburg Bridge. What it *does* tell me is: I have to make a decision, and to make it I have to understand *what making a decision means*. Facts are not enough. This is why *Billy Budd* fascinates me so much: 'The prisoner's deed. With that alone we have to do.' Captain Vere reminds me of my pledging allegiance to the flag every damn morning. Facts. I can leave the country. If I feel that *I have to change the country* AND if I'm convinced *I can't change it from inside the country*, then I'd better leave the country and try to change it from outside. But, I wonder, how am I going to change it from outside? I think about this *a lot*. Plus, a lot of people ask me: Are you really convinced you can't change it from inside? Why in the world are you convinced of this? Look at all these great Marxist professors here and there, writing books, their classes full of students. The academic world is a FUN world. You say you're not convinced that these GAMs [as I put it] will actually change the country in the least, but, how do you know? They might. Why not give yourself a chance? Give it a shot. Take a stab at it. What have you got to lose? What's worrying you so goddam much? Questions questions. What, me worry? as Alfred E. Neuman put it, definitely. The train I ride is twenty-one coaches long; and the gal I love is on that train and gone.

The B Train has come to the end of its line. 168th Street/Washington Heights. I've had so much *screeching* inside my head that I've hardly noticed the *screeches* outside. Here, above ground, at the Cloisters, the Seven Unicorn Tapestries, created 500 years ago by an unknown artist for unknown royalty in Western Europe, probably in Holland. I know the whole story. I've seen them a number of times—not as many times as I've been to Yankee Stadium, but quite a few. I have a reproduction of 'The Unicorn in Captivity' hanging on the wall in front of my desk, along with Leonardo's 'Saint Jerome,' which I'd seen when I was in Rome two summers ago. Too bad I won't be seeing the Seven Unicorns again today, but, some other time, I hope. It must be around 8:30 in the morning, I'm taking a stroll around the station waiting for the next B back downtown, and all the way back to Coney Island. Cheer up. The Manhattan Bridge. There are quite a few people waiting for the trains, you can also get the C Train here but I don't even want to think about that, I have my hands full with the B. Later on I think I'll take the D, or get back on the F—or, next the F

and then the D, or next the D and then the F. Later. Maybe the
B again, after that. I notice that the people are not wet or
carrying umbrellas or even wearing particularly heavy coats.
It's the end of March, I think it may well be a nice spring day.
I'll find out for sure when I'm elevated in Brooklyn on the West
End Line. I have a lot on my mind now. Sure, the academic
world is a fun world, and New York is a fun city, and a parade is
a parade is a parade. Become a professor, like Dave, or
Benardete, who are not Marxists but are truly radical, each in
his own way. Become a radical professor of philosophy, of Hegel
and his critics, Feuerbach, Kierkegaard, Marx. Or, if worst
comes to worst, of 'political science.' But 'Marxist'—I mean, in
the sense of professing the absolute need for *systemic change*
in this country. Capitalism! Profit! Military. Industrial. Defend
the City! Find the Slayer! Sic semper tyrannis. Cursed and
cursing. Riddled and riddling. Profess political freedom for the
people of this country and of all countries. Freedom, and
necessity. Logic. A *human* society. What? The B is on its way
back downtown now, 163rd Street, *screech*, 155th. Have fun.
Earn money. Pay taxes, to finance wars in the defense of
tyranny. Political freedom, but what about political
responsibility? Norman Morrison. What is the *political role*—and
political *responsibility*—of universities in this country? I have
two questions eating away at me. First question: What and
whom are these universities working *for?* Do our universities
decide anything, or are they completely *decided for?* This is a
big question in my mind. What is the university's real purpose?
Does it work for the cultural, intellectual—and 'civil'—
development of its students? In short, is its purpose to teach
students something in a 'wide landscape' of fields? So-called
'liberal arts.' If possible, even to teach them *to think*—or, at
least, to teach them that *the ability to think* is both possible
and valuable. That the alternative is passive acceptance. Follow
the leader. Intellectual flag waving. Loyalty. Eichmann in

Jerusalem. Isn't the university supposed to be a place of teaching and learning? Take my university, NYU, for example. The official seal sports a silver ceremonial 'torch of learning' looming over a group of four running figures symbolizing effort or striving in the 'pursuit of learning.' The motto is in Latin: 'Perstare et Praestare'—very catchy. It means 'To Persevere and to Excel.' Wonderful. But is that what it's really all about? *Screech*. 145th Street, a biggish station, you can also get the D Train here, but I'm not thinking about that. Take Columbia, just a few stops down. In the spring of 1968 the students—SDS, Students for a Democratic Society—protested in a big way. I'll skip the gruesome details. Why? Because they discovered that Columbia University was/is working with/for the IDA: Institute for Defense Analyses. What's the IDA? I have it right here, documents, stuffed into this issue of *Ramparts*. It's a weapons-research 'think tank' (I love this expression, it clearly refers to Hegel's *'decision* to consider *thinking as such'* combined with Bodhidharma's 'in order to see a fish you must watch the water')[62] affiliated with the Department of Defense. What does it do? It 'brings scientific and technical *as well as operational* military expertise to bear in evaluating weapons systems, employing advanced techniques of scientific analysis and operations research.' Defend the City! (What City?) An effort in the pursuit of learning? Hell no. The war effort. The Vietnam War—the Vietnamese call it the American War—in the defense of tyranny. The IDA has been working with twelve universities. Caltech, Case Western Reserve, MIT, Stanford, and Tulane since 1956, and California, Chicago, Illinois, Michigan, Pennsylvania, Princeton, and Columbia since 1964. And at Columbia the students found out about it and really raised hell, until the police stormed them and bashed their heads in. 125th Street, soul screech, Harlem. But—is this what the university is supposed to be about? Take MIT, another place of higher learning, not here in Fun City but in the tip-top city of Boston.

---

62 *Zen Mind,* p. 134. Bodhidharma was the First Patriarch of Zen Buddhism in China.

(Sorry, of Cambridge, but who's counting.) In 1968 students *and teachers* protested 'the militarization of university research' at the MIT *Institute* for International Studies, and in 1969 all hell broke loose at the MIT *Center* for International Studies, the CIS. Guess why. A few headlines, I still have the clippings, here in my mixed bag, just a second: 'CIS IS CIA'; 'MIT Admits Work for CIA'; 'MIT To Drop Research Contracts With CIA'—drop them, only because SDS found out about them and raised holy hell. How about Harvard. A bomb exploded in Harvard's Center for International Affairs (CFIA) in October, 1970. Why oh why? At Harvard, the highest learning we've got! The true Academic Torch. Who oh who did such a horrible thing? *Screech*. 116th Street, Hi Columbia, greetings from the realm of shadows. Who? Revolutionary women! Here's their statement: 'Tonight the Proud Eagle Tribe, a group of revolutionary women, bombed the Center for International Affairs at Harvard. The Center figures out new ways for the Pig Nixon to try to destroy people's wars in Asia, Latin America, and the Middle East, and grooms toads like Henry Kissinger, who left the Center to join Nixon's death machine.' A little more softly, an SDS spokesman said in 1971: 'The CFIA helps develop the military strength of reactionary governments to contain popular uprisings and *paves the way for foreign investment.*' (He's got a good point there.) So that's what it's all about. Meanwhile, Kissinger didn't resign from Harvard until January, 1971, when he'd already been Nixon's National Security Adviser for two full years. *Screech*. 110th Street, tip to top and bottoms up, we're coming back under Central Park West, B Train, lots of people in the car. A place of teaching and learning. I'm not finished. The Midwest demands, and deserves, equal time. After all, it has God on its side. Right on, Bob! The land you live in.[63] They're singing your song in Madison, Wisconsin. Sterling Hall bombing, August,

---

63 A third-stab purely historical note (a touch of context, I'm re-visioning the two previous stabs): yesterday, 13 October 2016, Dario Fo died and Dylan won the Nobel Prize.

1970. Army Mathematics Research Center, at the *University* of Wisconsin-Madison. A 'think tank' consisting of about 45 mathematicians funded by the U.S. Army. By contract, all the mathematicians had to spend at least half their time on U.S. Army research. Any time that happened to be left over was for teaching students. 'Perstare et Praestare.' Pure math, mathematical logic, number theory, and ballistics. The Madison students were *extremely riled up* in general, and this 'Army Math' Center was too much to bear. Their slogan was 'Smash Army Math,' and they did, they blew up the building. But the Madison students also persisted and excelled in the campaign against Dow Chemical. Their action in 1967 really sparked the national protests against these *unimaginable war criminals* at Dow Chemical. I don't take part in many demonstrations myself—*screech*, 96th Street—but for Dow Chemical I make an exception. This company produces *the napalm and the Agent Orange that is devastating Vietnam and its people*. All this *HORROR*. Napalm in flamethrowers and napalm bombs dropped by B-52s, burning people's skin off, they die after ten minutes of excruciating pain. Agent Orange raining down from the skies, fifty times more powerful than any herbicide ever made before, destroying the land and poisoning the people. *All this in our name.* We—we Americans, me, I'm American—are responsible. Sure, I'd say Dow Chemical is even more responsible, and I bet they got the ideas for all this *HORROR* in some military funded *university* 'think tank.' And they have the gall to recruit students on university campuses all over the country. When they did it in Madison they crossed the line, the students went wild. Teaching and learning. But what about Dave Leahy. What about Eugene Genovese.

THE THIRD GATE

Screech. Tip-top, 86th Street again, this time heading downtown. Serendipity? ANOTHER VETERAN. I presume. A placard. Hanging from his neck by a string. Spitting image of the GOD ON OUR SIDE guy. Might even be his brother. My age or a little older. No beard, very clean cut, very short hair, military style. But instead of a green t-shirt and green pants he's wearing green army fatigues. The man's dressed as a soldier. Actually, lots of young people wear some variety of fatigues these days, they're in style, khaki-brown or green. I wonder what he thinks of our university system. The car is fairly full, some people standing, but he's slithering his way through with ease, everyone makes way for him. After all, he's a Vietnam veteran. Cap in his hand, and filling up with coins. Of course I'm sitting down, I'm an end-of-the-line man, I always have a seat. I'm sitting close to one end of the car, as usual, and he came in at the other end. Here he comes. Let's see the placard. A simple drawing, not as artistic as the other two— the legs, and the flag salute. I wonder if this fellow will be a little more loquacious. I doubt it. The image is of one solitary G.I. approaching a village: the G.I., a path through roughly sketched vegetation on both sides, and a village of huts. That's it. Presumably in Vietnam, but the drawing is so stereotyped that the village, the huts, could just as well be in Africa, or in Tahiti for all I know. Haiti. Jamaica, south of Cuba. Not much artistic merit. His caption, at the top of the placard, reads: THE DEFENSE OF FREEDOM. 'Vietnam veteran' he says, that's all. Exactly like the second man. The first, the legless fellow, didn't say a single word. I look up at *him*, not at his cap, and spout: 'How about the G.I. Bill? College. Higher education.' He stares back at me with horror, shock, and awe. Reminds me of the Sphinx when Oedipus solved the riddle. *Screech*. 81st Street, Museum of Natural History. He slithers right out of the car.

Ye gods, man, *mon frère,* my ass. *Mon semblable*, my dick. What's going on here. 'The sunless dead and this joyless region.' His shroud, cracked requiem, who are all these placard-men? What are they up to? I hesitate to call them beggars, though, basically, that's what they are. *But why down here in the subway?* What are they doing down here in Hades, with me? With me. It's neither logical nor practical. I'm traveling indefinitely because I have to make a decision and to make the decision *properly*—logically, practically, responsibly—I have to figure out what *making a decision* is. What it means. That's what I'm doing down here. But what are *they* doing. *Down here.* If begging's really their game, why not stand (or sit) *up there* in the street, Central Park West, Fifth Avenue, Washington Square, wherever they please, shit, they're clean-cut young Vietnam veterans, no one will bother them, lots and lots of people will give them money. Why hassle down here among the sunless dead? What's the point? The fellow in the wheelchair, *mon frère!* I actually gave him a quarter, and I'd have given him one of my apples too, if he'd given me a chance. All this incredible hassle down here in the subway when he could have stationed himself comfortably somewhere around Rockefeller Center—why? Why is he *down here? Why are they down here?* Maybe it's a strategic question, higher mathematics that I can't even imagine, 'Army Math.' Shit, if they hadn't blown up Sterling Hall maybe someone at the Army Mathematics Research Center could have helped me out here. Mathematical logic, number theory, ballistics, what do I know. *How many of these placard-men are there down here?* Dozens? Thousands? Millions? Ten thousand? Or just these three? Tip-top *screech*, 72nd Street. If I get out of the car, get out of the subway, and never ever come down here again, would it mean that I'll never ever see a Vietnam veteran placard-man beggar ever again? Adios Beggars Banquet. Gathers no moss. I can walk to NYU even if it's raining hard, I don't really need the F Train. Vice versa, if I continue this subway travel of mine not indefinitely but definitely for the rest of my life, is it possible that I'll never see another Vietnam veteran placard-man beggar anyway, never ever? Another placard-man or, possibly, one of these three, maybe these three are the only ones in the entire totality of the transit system. Never see one again, even if I travel definitely for the rest of my life. What time is it? It must be around nine in the morning, and I don't mean acorns or Taoist monkeys. I sleep in the mornings, for five hours, from 6 to 11. Like a log. Sink like a stone. Not today. I'm definitely traveling indefinitely. A decision. But have these beggars been sent to help me or to throw me into complete and definitive confusion? Are they a curse or a blessing? THE DEFENSE OF FREEDOM. We'll see about that. Defend the City! Fun City! Anyway, I've gone from an image of the legs of a legless man, to the image of a man *dressed* as a soldier, to the image of a *real* soldier on the placard of a man *dressed* as a soldier, but who is not now a soldier. Is that correct? This third guy is dressed as a soldier but the image, not the man, is the soldier. Or, might I say that, comparing the third with the second *image*, the individual not only *seems* (his dress) but *is* (his reality, his circumstance) a soldier, a real individual soldier. Is this correct? The second image is of seeming and the third is of being. Quite possibly, I'm not making any sense. A blessing or a curse. WHAT FREEDOM? WHOSE FREEDOM? *Screech*. 59th Street, Columbus Circle. Lower left-hand corner of Central Park. Upper right-hand corner if you're standing on your head. In any event, if one of these veterans stationed himself *up there* for a week he'd probably become a millionaire. I don't get it. Then again, why am I traveling indefinitely *on the subway* myself, instead of spending a couple of days and nights sitting in my solitary railroad-flat zendo or pacing back and forth on the Williamsburg Bridge? Kinhin. Walking meditation. No, what a stupid question. I can hear the beggars laughing at me for this one. Will I ever see one of them again? Are there others? Are there ten thousand others? On the subway. Traveling indefinitely. Like me.

But what about teaching and learning. The university. Is that what it's really all about? I was posing two questions, and the second question is just as big or even bigger than the first, in its own way. Now—the first question: What and whom are universities in this country working for? For the Department of Defense? For Dow Chemical? For Henry Kissinger? (But, until January of last year, wasn't Kissinger supposedly working *for* the university?) So I get to thinking about Eugene Genovese. A remarkable man. Same age as Benardete, born in 1930. Born in Brooklyn, like Benardete and Dave Leahy. But Genovese is a Marxist—SirYesSir, a Great Academic Marxist.[64] And not a jackass, like my mother's cousin at the New School. Genovese is a historian, and his specific field is the American South and American slavery. He has brought a Marxist perspective to the study of power, class, and relations between planters and slaves in the South. I read his book, *The World the Slaveholders Made*. Pioneering research, important issues. *This* is what it's about. But Genovese became very important in my

---

64 In the 1990s Genovese took a sharp turn to the right, to traditionalist conservatism, to the point of supporting conservative Republicans like Pat Buchanan. He also re-embraced the Catholicism in which he had been raised (before becoming a Marxist). In a 1996 interview he said: 'I never gave a damn what people thought of me. And I still don't.' He died in 2012.

life for the stand he took against the Vietnam War when he was teaching at Rutgers back in 1965. It was the same year that Norman Morrison doused himself in kerosene and set himself on fire, right below McNamara's office at the Pentagon. I was fifteen years old, it was an important year in my life. At a teach-in at Rutgers, on April 23rd, 1965, Genovese stated:

> Those of you who know me know that I am a Marxist and a Socialist. Therefore, unlike most of my distinguished colleagues here this morning, I do not fear or regret the impending Viet Cong victory in Vietnam. I welcome it.

Of course, all hell broke loose. Of course. Amazingly, no one put him in prison. Shit, isn't this treason? And this was 1965, not 1968, not 1970, not this year. *Screech.* 42nd Street. Great, the car is crammed. Rutgers did not even fire him. No. He did move to Canada to teach two years later, but of his own volition, and now he's back in the USA, at the University of Rochester. In 1968 he signed a pledge (no, not of allegiance to the flag), vowing to refuse to pay his U.S. taxes in protest against the Vietnam War (a.k.a. the American War). GAM, bomb, exile. A fork. If I could believe that *genuine* GAMs like Eugene Genovese will actually be possible in the future, in this country, maybe I could twirl spaghetti on my fork and fuck this indefinite subway journey. But. But, even today, to survive, a Genovese had better speak softly. At least about certain things. But the Vietnam War is practically over, just another zillion tons of bombs and we can call it a day. No more boots on the ground. Combat fatigues only on the streets (and subways) of Fun City. But tomorrow? Are we about to enjoy a Pax Romana? So to speak. HELL NO. These gook creeps will have hell to pay, and we'll fuck payment out of their motherfucking asses on every square inch of this earth. Fucking commie creeps. Until someone stops us, and that will not be soon. Defend the City! SPQR, the Senate and the People of Rome. No laughing matter. Teaching and learning. Hiroshima, what a great day. Korea, fucking mire. Vietnam, fucking quagmire. We *are* losing the war. But—Kissinger professes—*we're teaching them a good lesson anyway*. The future is ours. Speak softly, Genovese. Watch your back. The future is not *ours*. Defend the City! FIGHT to defend tyranny. The tyranny not just of capital over labor, but of capital over *people*. Of the 'means of production' (but in unimaginable senses) over human being, human life. However much I admire Genovese, how can even the greatest of GAMs fight this? We welcome a VIETNAMESE victory, in Vietnam, which will come. But, who's next? A Kissinger will always know how to celebrate a defeat as a victory,[65] just imagine how he'll celebrate future (real and/or imagined) victories. Holy shit, what can the greatest of GAMs do? Speak to me, Genovese. The teach-ins are over. I myself am graduating in a couple of months. Let me say something a little more pessimistic, why the hell not, I may not get another chance (or even this chance). Let me say this. Political crimes by big countries, horrific war crimes against small countries—who gives a shit. A few ripples wash

---

65 See (on the Internet) *Lessons of Vietnam* by Secretary of State Henry Kissinger, ca. May 12, 1975 (two weeks after the *liberation* of Saigon, as the Vietnamese put it): 'I believe we can honorably avoid self-flagellation and that we should not characterize our role in the conflict as a disgraceful disaster. I believe our efforts, militarily, diplomatically and politically, were not in vain. We paid a high price but we gained ten years of time and we changed what then appeared to be an overwhelming momentum. I do not believe our soldiers or our people need to be ashamed.' We stopped Communism in its fucking tracks, goddamit. From now on we'll pick our targets more carefully, but, cheer up! after Vietnam everything will be a lot easier.
On the other side of the 'defeat as victory' coin we have Noam Chomsky, *What Uncle Sam Really Wants*, 1992 (excerpted, on the Internet, as 'Inoculating Southeast Asia'). 'Contrary to what virtually everyone—left or right—says, the United States achieved its major objectives in Indochina. Vietnam was demolished. There's no danger that successful development there will provide a model for other nations in the region. [No dominoes.] Of course, it wasn't a total victory for the U.S. Our larger goal was to reincorporate Indochina into the U.S.-dominated global system, and that has not yet been achieved.' Not yet, in 1992, but, cheer up! Uncle Sam is making progress, as usual.

them away like images in sand. But ideological crimes of free individuals—in 'free countries'—(GAMs, for example, but not only GAMs) are *indelible*. No ocean can wash them away. A tsunami can barely blur them. This is why I'm here among the sunless dead. My country is THE world power, and getting worse. I need to decide what to do about this. I put that badly. Rather, I need to decide what to do *about myself*. This is why I'm here. I mentioned that I have two questions, about the university, 'place of teaching and of learning,' and that the second question is just as big or even bigger than the first, in its own way. OK, this is what I'm here for, *on the subway*, indefinitely, so if I don't say it now, here, in the netherworld, when in the world will I? Hereafter? The afterworld comes a long time after, infinitely after—*never* after. Here's the second question. If 'political responsibility' means *working for real political change*—systemic change—*can you do this from within the university system?* In this country. THIS is what it's all about. Can the Academic Torch *burn* real political systemic change into 'the minds of men'? Can it? Here? In *this* university system? In the United States of America, and to the Republic for which it stands. Now is the time for *a decision*, not for wishful thinking. Dostoevsky is absolutely right: if there is fire, it is in the minds of men. *Just ask Norman Morrison.* And his wife. 34th Street, crowds getting off, coming on. How about blowing up the Williamsburg Bridge. My fork is in my hand. LOVE IT OR LEAVE IT. A free and responsible decision, such a thing must exist. I'm not down here traveling indefinitely *just to take my pick*. 1 from group A, 2 from group B, pork or shrimp. A Chinese menu of the mind. 'Take my pick'—believe me, I don't need this indefinite journey to do that. I know what the university is. *I know that the exile's life is a slave's life.* A bombing, self-immolation—I know that the fire is in my mind, in my *burning need* not to accept this System passively. To change the whole System. To change even a few individual lives. To change myself? The fork? The fork wasn't part of the prophecy, Oedipus just happened to meet Laius there, and kill him. A fire. I *know* that the fork is *in my mind*.

THE DEFENSE OF FREEDOM. This third guy is dressed as a soldier but the image, not the man, is the soldier. I think I should just sit here for a while and chill out. Enjoy the ride, so to speak. I feel a little tired, and I also feel I'm not making much progress. If any. Well, I'm traveling indefinitely. A decision. The whole idea was to reread the *Septem* and Benardete's two Notes, and I haven't even started yet. I still feel that, in the tragedy, Eteocles has a *direct experience* of what a decision is, and I want to learn from his experience. (His satori maybe. Possibly post mortem.) Shit, this is why I took this trip. Call me Ishmael. 'Because the Lord hath heard thy affliction.' B Train. End of March, 1972. Saturday morning, must be a little after 9. West 4th. Broadway-Lafayette. Grand Street—there's no Delancey, this is the B. Just chilling out. No-mind. Saturday morning, what do I know about Saturday mornings, what do I know about mornings in general, I don't know shit about mornings. I sleep in the morning. Morning in the subway. Morning in Hades. Quite a few people going to Brooklyn. Why? *Here we go.* I'm on the Manhattan Bridge, and in fact it looks like a beautiful spring day, sunny, warm, not a winter day. Sunny, warm. A Coney Island day, at the end of March? Maybe I should ask the man next to me, 'Sir, are you going to Coney Island, to have some fun?' No, I'm too shy. Just down the river I see the Brooklyn Bridge gleaming in the morning sunlight. And now night falls. Two stops on this stretch of night. Pacific Street. 36th Street. And up we go. West End Line. Up into the light of a Brooklyn morning. What a funny feeling, thinking about nothing for a little while, it felt (I guess) like riding the rollercoaster in Coney Island. I didn't even notice the screeches. I heard the silence that gives birth to the screech. *Screech.* 9th Avenue. Now I hear it.

The West End Line has a screech a minute, there must be at least a dozen from here to the end of the line. Chill out. Look around Brooklyn. *Screech screech screech*. A dozen screeches. Here I am. Coney Island station. Time for a little stroll, on the four platforms. Eight tracks. Four different trains: B, D, F, N. Strolling. I see a clock. It's way down there, in the direction of the ocean (I presume). I never noticed it before. It's 10 o'clock. What—Me Worry? I'm definitely taking another B. This first round-trip has been a thrill. Two Vietnam veteran placard-men. Plus my legless brother on the F. Will I meet them again? Are there any more? Are there ten thousand more? OK, I'm back on the B, West End Line, a dozen screeches. A real man dressed as a soldier who is not now a soldier with the image of one actual individual soldier approaching a village in Vietnam. Why is the soldier approaching the village? Is he just stopping by to say something like 'I wish y'all gook women and children a good morning, how'r y'all doin' today?' Possible, but not likely. Let's not forget the caption: THE DEFENSE OF FREEDOM. The plot thickens. What's the connection? Between this solitary G.I. approaching a Vietnamese village along a path with vegetation on both sides, evidently not yet sprayed with Agent Orange, and his motto, THE DEFENSE OF FREEDOM. Now I get it. Defend the City! Thebes of the Seven Gates. Fun City. Perhaps Plato's Ideal City, which the soldier wants to found in himself. Why the hell not. Found a City in himself. A great idea. Perhaps this is why we've sent a million soldiers to Vietnam over the years, so that each one can found a City in himself. Win his own inner freedom, and then defend it. Fraternize with this great gook culture, *learn* from the fucking gooks, they've had their villages, their civilization, for over two thousand years. Teaching and learning. Shit, two thousand years ago George Washington, the Father of our City, hadn't even cut down his cherry tree. Thomas Jefferson had not yet penned those immortal words about 'Life, Liberty, and the pursuit of Happiness.' Why ask WHOSE FREEDOM? or WHAT FREEDOM? It's obvious. Everyone's freedom. Freedom is freedom. Defend the City! With liberty and justice for all. Isn't this what the Vietnam War is all about? What's the problem? Are we perplexed about the fact that two or three million of these gooks are dying in this DEFENSE OF FREEDOM of ours, not to mention our own dead soldiers? Well, freedom isn't free, as the saying goes. Profit has a price. Are we perplexed about this *incredible generosity* of ours, that we send our boys *to the other side of the world* to fight IN THE DEFENSE OF FREEDOM. I mean, why can't these gooks fight their own battle IN THE DEFENSE OF FREEDOM. Shit, haven't they already pledged to do just that, penned it like regular Thomas Jeffersons: 'The entire Vietnamese people are determined to mobilize all their physical and mental strength, to sacrifice their lives and property in order to safeguard their independence and freedom.' So why do we have to send our boys *to the other side of the world* to help them. Or stop them. As the case may be. Defend the City! What about defending our Fun Cities right here. Every American city is a Fun City, and needs to be defended.

OK, I'm pulling my own leg. The West End Line is extremely picturesque, but a dozen *screeches* one after the other has slightly jarred my slightly tired brain. After all, the third placard-man is a Vietnam veteran and deserves my respect. Deserves to be taken seriously. Then again, even a child can see that *it's the Vietnamese* (apart from *our* Vietnamese) who are fighting tyranny, in the defense of freedom. Fighting *our* tyranny. The Viet Cong. Ho Ho Ho Chi Minh. But a lot of people sincerely and fervently believe we are fighting *them* in Vietnam in the defense of freedom. Gook commie creeps. Freedom in Vietnam, freedom here at home, freedom all over the world. *Practically none of these people happen to be G.I.s*, but, what does that matter. The third placard-man—a *former* G.I., for that matter—is the exception that proves the rule. *Many* Americans sincerely believe that it is this country's *responsibility* to defend freedom everywhere. Wherever it may be threatened. Wherever we may threaten it. After all, we did a great service to humanity by defeating the Nazis and the Japs. No question. So let's keep up the good work. People are happy that we are creating a permanent war system. Never mind those hippie freaks, their geese are already cooked. A smattering of GAMs can do no harm. But why are so many people so happy about our permanent war system? Nostalgia for Genghis Khan? Perhaps because the *military-industrial complex* guarantees prosperity and fun for all? No, no, there are deeper reasons. Sure, the blacks in the ghettos, and in the South, *and in the army*, are not all that happy. The American Indians are definitely not overjoyed, or do you think the 19-month occupation of Alcatraz was a fun fest. The homeless are not delighted. Shit, you can't please everyone. How about 'the tired, the poor'—are they jumping for joy? Maybe, maybe not, but I think that quite a few of them—immigrants of the first, second, third generation (my grandfather, my father, me)—are strenuously waving flags. Not all of them. But many. Strenuously. Happily. They *believe* in this country, founded by the Pilgrim Fathers, 1620, the Plymouth Colony—Brits who first moved to Holland, and then on to the New World. What was on their minds? Ye gods, a bright and shining city. I'm on the Manhattan Bridge already. What a beautiful spring-like day. When I drove a taxi when I was nineteen, the older—much older—drivers always told me, 'Be careful, hacking gets into your blood.' This was not banal, these guys knew what they were saying, they knew what they wanted to tell me. Here I am, less than 24 hours on the subway, with this strange feeling that this is the world, that it's in my blood, that I've always been here and will always be here. On the subway. My home, the House of Hades. The sunless dead. Am I losing sight of *my* City? My traveling 'indefinitely' to discover what making a decision is and means. A voyage of discovery? Traveling indefinitely *on the subway*, but the point is not supposed to be *the subway*. No! The means are threatening to become the ends. But my travels are far from over. The *Septem*, Eteocles, Benardete's Notes. Hegel. I have not yet begun to quote![66] Ye Pilgrims, Defend the City! That's what so much of this is about. Defend the City! Thebes of the Seven Gates. At the seventh, ruler-brother-foe against ruler-brother-foe, that goddam curse. Laius. His 'loving folly'—'mastered by the rashness of love'—'ill-advised in love.' Whatever. Find the Slayer! Defend the City! *What* City? Here I go again. John Winthrop, that goddam Puritan. 1630, still on the ship, and preaching away to his future Massachusetts Bay colonists that 'we shall be as a City upon a Hill. The eyes of all people are upon us.' A *Shining* City upon a Hill. John Fitzgerald Kennedy, President-Elect, January 9th, 1961: 'I have been guided by the standard John Winthrop[67] set before his shipmates on the flagship Arbella three hundred and thirty-one years ago, as they, too, faced the task of building a new government on a perilous frontier.' Ye gods a *perilous frontier*, goddamit—those fucking Indians, ignorant, uncivilized, just hanging around in America doing nothing for some 70,000 years. We showed them what civilization means. And now, goddamit, we'll show these perilous gook commie creeps. When will it ever end! Dammit all. The eyes of all people. Defend the City! Damn

66 John Paul Jones, revolutionary hero, 'Father of the United States Navy'—his famous reply to the Brits: 'Surrender, HELL, I have not yet begun to fight!'.
67 Ronald Reagan had an orgasm—let's say, a 'fire in the mind'—whenever he thought of that goddam Puritan, with his goddam Pilgrim's progress. 11 January 1989, his farewell speech to the nation: 'I've spoken of the shining city all my political life, but I don't know if I ever quite communicated what I saw when I did. But *in my mind* it was a tall proud city built on rocks stronger than oceans, wind-swept, God-blessed, and *teeming with people of all kinds living in harmony and peace*, a city with free ports that hummed with commerce and creativity, and if there had to be walls, the walls had doors and the doors were open to anyone with the will and the heart to get there. That's how I saw it and still see it.' BOMB HANOI! BOMB HANOI! BOMB HANOI!

straight goddamit, but what City and what people? The people in Havana? In Hanoi? What City? Dammit all, this is not Plato's Republic. Goddamit, is this the City I want to found in myself? Shit, 'We are setting out upon a voyage in 1961 no less hazardous than that undertaken by the Arbella in 1630. We are committing ourselves to tasks of statecraft no less fantastic than that of governing the Massachusetts Bay Colony, beset as it was then by terror within and disorder without.' Ye gods, *terror within and disorder without.* The horror. Fucking redskins, how dare they. Terrorists! Disorderly savages. Poor JFK, tormented by terrifying disorderly gook commies on the other side of the world. Mistah Kurtz—he dead. The horror! A penny for the Old Guy. THE DEFENSE OF FREEDOM. Leader of the Free World. Goddam this fork. I wish I could stab a Pilgrim or a Puritan with it. Roast him like a Thanksgiving turkey and then STAB HIM WITH THIS FORK. This fork that wasn't part of the prophecy, Oedipus just happened to meet Laius there, where three roads cross, and kill him. Stuff happens. The point here is this: I detest Thanksgiving. The horror. Why do I hate it! This Great American Holiday. Those delicious turkeys. Those fabulous parades, just ask our mayor. A parade! is a parade. Is a parade. What's my problem? *Screech.* Grand Street. The netherworld. Headed for Washington Heights. And back. The prisoner's deed. A long stretch in the House of Hades.

My problem with Thanksgiving is a very serious problem. The problem is this: Holocausts need to be commemorated, not celebrated.[68] Not even a turkey believes that the Brits in Massachusetts or Virginia settled in an empty land. Christopher Columbus. The Spaniards. Cuba, Hispaniola, the New World, from Mexico to Peru—an empty land? The best estimate for, say, 1492, gives 145 *million* natives in the hemisphere as a whole, with 18 million of them in the area north of Mexico. But we palefaces emptied the land fast. Cleaned it right up.

---

68 See David E. Stannard's great work, *American Holocaust. The Conquest of the New World,* Oxford: Oxford University Press, 1992.

'Holocaust' is an absolutely appropriate word for it. I'll settle for the example of Hispaniola: eight million inhabitants in 1492, less than a hundred thousand by 1508. Sure, the poor Spaniards were disappointed because they expected to find a lot of gold and, instead, there wasn't much, so the poor soldiers passed the time killing the natives for fun. There were famines and disease. It was no picnic. In any event, by 1535 the native population of Hispaniola was *extinct*. It's true that the Spaniards were unequaled exterminators in numerical terms but, it seems, they had their logic. The extermination of entire communities[69] and cultures, though commonplace, was rarely their declared goal, since to do so meant a large expenditure of energy with no financial return. Their mammoth destruction of whole societies was generally the by-product of conquest and native enslavement, a genocidal means to an economic end, not an end in itself. Here lies the central difference between the genocide committed by the Spaniards and that of the Anglo-Americans. In British America extermination *was* the primary goal, precisely because *it made economic sense*. In a nutshell. The Spaniards met resistance. What's more, they *needed* slave labor, to devour. But for the Brits in America the natives were simply in the way. *Pests*. Defend the City! Shining City on a Hill. Now, in all fairness, famine and disease are terrible things in themselves. But how about when they are deliberately provoked—I mean, used as instruments of war. It wasn't our fault that millions and millions of Indians dropped like flies from European diseases—*screech*, West 4th, lots of fun seekers in the Village. Smallpox, typhus, measles, influenza, bubonic plague, cholera, malaria, tuberculosis, mumps, yellow fever, whooping cough—diseases that were chronic in Europe but totally unknown in the New World until we brought them. After all, *they* gave *us* redskin

---

69 What follows is a direct quote from Stannard, p. 221. For the numbers—years, population—see p. 11 and p. 261. On the extermination of the native population of Hispaniola see pp. 62–75.

syphilis (when we raped their women). But how about the smallpox-infested blankets the Brits gave them as 'gifts,' to help matters along. All's fair, when it comes to 'Extirpating this Execrable Race.' 'We gave them two Blankets and an Handkerchief out of the Small Pox Hospital. I hope it will have the desired effect.'[70] How about that? It was a holocaust. It started with the English plagues and ended with the sword and musket. No, the recent Native American occupation of Alcatraz was not a fun fest, by any means. These people are riled up—in fact, on the West Coast they now celebrate *Unthanksgiving Day*. In New England on Thanksgiving Day in 1970 they painted Plymouth Rock red in protest and organized the first annual National Day of Mourning. Mourning the 'extirpation' of a great civilization, which loved the Earth and lived in harmony with all living beings. Totally unlike us. People with so much to teach us, and we just blew them away. A turkey, a family gathering, a parade. There's a lot of confusion, myth, and falsehood about the origin of Thanksgiving, I think it's important to clear it up. In a nutshell. Every red-blooded God-loving American man, woman, child, and pet knows the story. Squanto, the good Indian. When the Pilgrims arrived at Plymouth in 1620—'tired, poor' and ready to starve and freeze to death—within two days the local Wampanoag Indian tribe came to help them. Squanto taught them how to plant corn, catch eel, hunt. In exchange, as soon as the Pilgrims had gotten settled in they busied themselves with stealing the Indians' stored corn and bean supplies, digging up their graves for dishes and pots, and selling them as slaves for 220 shillings each. All this in the first year, and according to the Pilgrims' own written account. Then, as the story goes, the following year, 1621, after the harvest, they decided to have a little get-together to celebrate their survival and, by the way, thank those friendly Indians for helping them. This is where the Thanksgiving myth really begins. Now, in all fairness, it must be said that the Pilgrims

---

70 See, on the Internet, *Jeffrey Amherst and Smallpox Blankets*.

were, traditionally, big thankers. No, they weren't exactly fun seekers like we are today. They preferred thanking. Even back in Europe they were thanking every chance they got—thanking God, thanking anyone who came along. Religiously. Actually, what is generally referred to as the 'first Thanksgiving' was, originally, a three-day celebration among the Pilgrims after their first harvest. Then—*screech*, 34th Street already. Right under Herald Square. Fun seekers galore. I was saying—after their first harvest. Indian corn, I presume. So, someone figured, why not invite Massasoit, our local Indian chief, to thank him just a little. Life is short. Maybe he'll bring some Wild Turkey. Much to the Pilgrims' chagrin the chief turned up with ninety of his men, rearing for a feast. Then again, the redskins did go out and kill five deer for the shindig. Two years later the Brits invited a number of tribes to a feast 'symbolizing eternal friendship.' They offered them plenty of food and drink this time, and two hundred Indians dropped dead from unknown poison. Stuff happens. In fact, it may well have been the stuffing. But all these goings-on in Plymouth were not yet officially what we now call Thanksgiving. No, the first official 'Day of Thanksgiving' was in 1637 and was proclaimed by— guess who—our dear John Winthrop, that goddam Puritan. Our old friend who just seven years earlier, still on the ship, was preaching away to his future Massachusetts Bay colonists that 'we shall be as a City upon a Hill. The eyes of all people are upon us.' A *Shining* City upon a Hill. Well let me tell you about this *shining*. The subway car is packed now, end of March, 1972, Saturday, around 11 in the morning, I think it's a very nice day, I think I'm going to have a whole lot of company, 42nd Street, Columbus Circle, all the way up Central Park West. I think the Park will be full of people today, if it doesn't rain. I'm going to start reading the *Septem* along with Benardete's first Note soon. It's the second Note that really interests me, it's complicated, I'll read it later on, when things have quieted down. I'm also thinking about a thing or two in Hegel. It gets dark early at the end of March, the Park quiets down considerably, at night the fun seekers pass the torch to the muggers. I wonder how many of my traveling companions here on the B Train know the real history of Thanksgiving. Not a single one I bet. They'd choke on their turkey. It would rain cats and dogs on their parade. I wish these people could read my mind right now, they'd learn something important. And choke *me*. But, they have other things on their minds. Besides, Thanksgiving isn't until November, but that has nothing to do with it. Anyway, I'm telling myself the real story. I can't remember why. How in the world did I get onto this subject. Doesn't matter. Let me finish the story. No doubt about it, a *Shining* City upon a Hill. Traveling indefinitely. In the House of Hades. A decision. That goddam Puritan. The *Pequot. Captain Ahab's ill-fated ship.*[71] The name gave Ismael the shivers, and with good reason. *Screech*, 42nd Street, under Bryant Park, a block east of Times Square. In the 1630s the Pequot were a tribe in the Connecticut River Valley. They were fighting with their traditional enemies, the Mohegan. (Or Mahican, or Mohican: 1637, and we'll need James Fenimore Cooper to see the Last of them, in 1757.) But then the Dutch and the English, from Europe, along with the Puritans from Massachusetts Bay and the Pilgrims from Plymouth, all leaped into the fray. Imperialism, Manifest Destiny, Go West, call it what you like. One day you're starving and the next, you're invading. 'Expanding.' Or call it 'building a new government on a perilous frontier.' This particular 'expansion' is referred to as the Pequot War. Winthrop, the goddam Puritan, was the spearhead (so to speak). Shining City on a Hill. The Indians were good fighters, but European-style warfare—'total war'—was totally new to them. New, and bad news. Now, in a nutshell, after a bunch of skirmishes the 'Colonists' decided to take the bull by the horns.

---

71 Melville 'fictionalized' the name to *Pequod,* but we know what he was referring to.

May, 1637, they raised a serious militia, a coalition, commanded by Captain John Mason, who wrote a graphic and gruesome account of his expedition, as we shall see. It seems that many of those goddam Puritans had a way with words. On a pinhead: the Pequot were holed up in a village (fort, enclosure) called Mystic. Mason tricked them into believing he and his men had gone back to Boston. All the Pequot warriors came out of Mystic to check out the countryside, leaving 700 Pequot women, children, and older men behind. Mason attacked Mystic by surprise. He ordered that the enclosure be set on fire. Later, trampling on the ashes, he declared that the attack was the act of a God[72] who 'laughed his Enemies and the Enemies of his People to scorn making [the Pequot] as a fiery Oven.... Thus did the Lord judge among the Heathen, filling [Mystic] with dead Bodies.' Mason insisted that any Pequot attempting to escape the flames be killed. Of the estimated 600 to 700 Enemies of the People at Mystic that day, only seven survived to be taken prisoner, while another seven escaped to the woods. *Screech*, 59th Street, under Columbus Circle. It's clear why Ismael got the shivers when he saw the name of the ship. But the point of the story is this: Governor John Winthrop proclaimed the first official 'Day of Thanksgiving' in 1637 *to celebrate the return of the men that had gone to Mystic*. More precisely: to celebrate the Mystic massacre. *Shining* City on a Hill. 'Beset by terror within and disorder without.' The *Pequot*. Moby Dick sucked it down into the abyss. 'And I only am escaped alone to tell thee.'[73] Call me Ishmael. The few Pequot who survived the war and the massacre at Mystic offered themselves as slaves in exchange for life. Colonists appropriated Pequot lands under claims of a 'just war.'[74] Speaking the name of the Pequot people was prohibited. The

---

72 See, on the Internet, Wikipedia, *Pequot War*. I quote directly from the Wikipedia account here.

73 'Epilogue' to *Moby Dick*.

74 Again I quote directly from the Wikipedia article, which is concise and extremely well written.

Pequot were declared to be extinct.[75] This, of course, was just the beginning of the Holocaust in North America. (The Spaniards to the south had been furiously killing away since 1492.) But the extermination of the Pequot remains memorable and emblematic, and our first Thanksgiving celebrated it. A good thing to think about next time you carve your turkey.

---

75 Rejoice rejoice, the tribe has made a remarkable comeback, quite recently. The total population in 1910 was 66 and falling. But today, in Connecticut, the Eastern Pequot number 1,130, and the Western or Mashantucket Pequot over 800. Rags to riches, the enterprising Mashantucket have emerged as 'the most financially powerful Indian tribe in the nation' (as Peter Nabokov tells us, in *Native American Testimony*, Penguin, 1999, p. 446). They opened a bingo operation in 1986, followed by the Foxwoods Resort Casino. Revenues from the casino financed the absolutely magnificent and amazing Mashantucket Pequot Museum & Research Center, which opened in 1998. Just think, back in 1637 *even speaking their name was prohibited.*

THE FOURTH GATE

The fork a fire in my mind. A decision. Traveling indefinitely
in the House of Hades. A labyrinth of stops, and starts.
Screeches. What making a decision is and means. Why did I
dive headlong into my problem about Thanksgiving? I wish I
knew. What does it have to do with what making a decision is
and means. With traveling indefinitely. To get beyond the fork.
But there is nothing beyond the fork. Each screech is the last.
The first and the last. Monkey mind and no-mind. The Gate and
the Gateless Gate. I'm under Columbus Circle right now, 59th
Street, lower-left corner of Central Park. An individual soldier,
approaching a village, in Vietnam, on the placard of a Vietnam
veteran, dressed as a soldier. But why do the brass call these
villages 'hamlets'? Are these generals all Shakespearians? In
any event, the soldier in the image is, possibly, approaching
the village just to say 'I wish y'all gook women and children
a good morning, how'r y'all doin' today?' Possibly. But I think
the soldier in the image has something else in mind. I think
he's *thinking about war*. The war against Vietnam, against
its right to self-determination, which, ludicrously, he refers
to as THE DEFENSE OF FREEDOM. Well, so be it. This soldier
on the placard is a humble servant of the War God. What's
on *my* mind now is Eteocles, his decision, *what a decision is*.

The *Septem*, 'full of Ares'—which means *War*. Benardete's first
Note. Fun seekers. The car is really full, I'm sure the whole
B Train is really full—not rush-hour *packed* but fun-seeker
full. Not people going to work but people out to have a good
time. It must be a nice day. Saturday morning, end of March.
Strolling in the Park. The Museum of Natural History. There's a
bunch of kids in the car, with their parents—mothers, fathers,
mothers *and* fathers possibly. The Cloisters. The Unicorns
will be having plenty of company today. What are all these
people thinking about—*screech*, 72nd Street, tip-top—what's
on their minds? Are they thinking about the Vietnam War? Are
they thinking about war in general? Hell no. How about the
Pequot War, and their Thanksgiving turkeys? Absolutely! I'm
sure that every man, woman, and child on the B Train, and
on every other Train, at this very moment, Saturday morning,
end of March, 1972, is thinking about the Pequot, about
how even speaking their name was prohibited, about family
get-togethers, turkeys, and parades to give thanks for their
extinction. Beset by terror within and disorder without. *This
means war.* THE DEFENSE OF FREEDOM. So it's true, they're all
thinking about war. Like hell they are. In Hanoi, in Saigon, in
the White House, at the Pentagon, they're thinking about war
every minute, about the Vietnam War, or the American War, as
the case may be. East-West River. On some Indian Reservation,
possibly, they're thinking about some old Indian War. *Eteocles*
is thinking about war—shit, he has it right at his seven gates.
An 'outlandish' and 'savage' (according to some sources) army
of Argives that his own brother has raised. Defend the City!
Screech, 81st Street, see what I mean. Half the people are
getting off the train—wait, more than half. Museum of Natural
History. What's more, this stop is an ideal starting point for
strolls in the Park. Some people are getting on, going uptown—
getting off, getting on, next stop, getting off, getting on, I'm
sure there's a logic to all this, it's just that I don't happen to

156

know it, I sleep in the mornings. I take the subway as rarely as possible. Only if necessary. In fact, *generally speaking,* I don't have much fun. Mostly I just study (for another two months anyhow), think, and think about the Vietnam War. I wonder if anyone from the Weather Underground happens to be in this car right now—after all, the B Train is underground, apart from the Manhattan Bridge and the West End Line. No, not likely, not likely at all. Mark Rudd[76] taking an underground stroll under his old university. Guess not. No, these fun seekers are not thinking about war in general or the Vietnam War in particular, unless, of course, they have, or had, a son or brother or husband or father over there, approaching villages. They may, or may not, be thinking something like KILL A GOOK FOR GOD, just for the hell of it. Just for a change from thinking about fun—or, come to think of it, maybe because KILL A GOOK FOR GOD is a real fun thought. For them. But the Vietnam War is almost over now, Nixon has taken care of it, practically no more G.I.s, just another zillion tons of bombs, not even worth thinking about. Why do I think about it all the time? *Screech*—86th Street, let's see! let's see! No, no placard-man this time. Twice in a row was a coincidence, three times would be a plot. I'm kidding. A penny for the Old Guy. The people in the Weather Underground, wherever they are, whatever they're doing, every minute, are thinking about the war in Vietnam. I'm not the only one who hates this war. I have a big problem with my fork, I don't like this fork I'm at, but I cherish my hate for the war[77] against Vietnam, in the defense of tyranny. The Weather Underground have taken *responsibility* for a lot of bombings—with no casualties, in fact, apart from

---

76 Head of Columbia SDS during the 1968 occupation-cum-bloodbath, he joined Weatherman in 1969, which renamed itself Weather Underground in 1970. Tired of life as a fugitive, he turned himself in to the authorities in 1977. Curiously enough, when he turned himself in he was living underground (no, not in the subway) in Brooklyn.
77 A striking expression of Bernadine Dohrn's in the film *The Weather Underground* by Sam Green and Bill Siegel.

the townhouse explosion on West 11th Street exactly two years ago, when three of their own members accidentally blew themselves up. Senseless violence? 'Bring the war home.' Their watchword is that doing nothing about the war is violence— doing nothing, that's the true violence. The war is *in our name* and we have to do whatever we have to do to stop it. Sure, Nixon bullshits us about 'the same thugs and hoodlums who have always plagued the good people.' With the oceans of blood he has on his hands. My fork. My problem with blowing up the Williamsburg Bridge. I call it a *political* statement, but what if it's just a *personal* statement. What 'individual lives' would it change? Other than my own.

Serious questions. Violence. Whose violence, and against whom, and why. A question for Henry Kissinger, hell yes, he's got the answers. Let's call napalm and B-52s 'pacification.' Why the hell not. What ever happened to *Seven Against Thebes* and Benardete's two Notes. Just look at these happy people in the car. Laughing and having fun, and still down here in Hades. Where are we, what's this—116th Street already. Where are they all going? To Harlem? To the Cloisters? Where's my copy of the *Septem?* I want to read the first lines of the play. Vellacott's translation. Eteocles addresses a crowd of Thebans:

> Citizens, sons of Cadmus! The man who holds the helm of State, and from the bridge pilots with sleepless eyes his country's fortunes, must speak what the hour demands. If things go well, the thanks are due to Heaven; but if—which Heaven forbid!—there is disaster, throughout the town, with threats and wailings a multitudinous swelling prelude cries on one name: 'Eteocles'! From all this, may Zeus the Protector now protect the city Cadmus founded!

Sleepless eyes, this Great Helmsman. If all goes well, thank the God. If not, they'll make *him* take the blame. Make mincemeat of him, literally. Throw him to the dogs. *Screech*, 125th Street, Harlem. Quite a few people get off, but I still have a number of companions. This 'outlandish' and 'savage' army of Argives encamped on the dusty Theban plain is no laughing matter. The time is just before dawn. The Seven Gates. The attack will be at dawn. No time for filibusters. Eteocles. Straight to the point. But—does this mean that most of the people still in the car are going to the Cloisters? Apart from the unicorns, Fort Tryon Park is a beautiful place for strolling. Better than Central Park, in my modest uninformed opinion. This gives me food for thought. I've been traveling for nearly twenty-four hours now—in fact, I wonder what time it is, not that it matters— and I have really paid very little attention to my *many* fellow travelers. Practically no attention. Apart from the rush hour yesterday, but that was *force majeure*, as the French put it. I did pay attention to the Kleist-reading chick, you can bet your ass on that. But, after all, I'm not on a pleasure trip, a tourist excursion. A little jaunt around Hades. No. I'm graduating from NYU in two months. I'm 4-F. I'm master of my fate, so to speak. I have a fork. A decision. But what is a decision, what does it mean to make a decision? Am I tired? No. Hungry? No. Getting anywhere? I plead the fifth. Come to think of it, I can't help but notice this young woman sitting right next to me. Where did she come from? Did she sprout right out of the earth like the *Spartoi*, the sown men whom Ares spared? A sown woman? Not a girl, no, I think she must be thirty or even older. What's more, she's gorgeous. Dark hair and beautiful dark eyes. A Latin type. Possibly Puerto Rican. Probably. I wonder if she reads Aeschylus. Going to see the unicorns, possibly. What should I do? A decision. Let's see if she gets off at 145th Street, that's a big stop. No, she's still here. Sure I'd like to talk to her but what's the point. Ask her what she thinks about Eteocles' decision to go *himself* to the Seventh Gate. Tell her about my love for unicorns. *Screech*, 155th Street. Suddenly,

turning towards her, I plead, softly: 'Have you got the time?'
She smiles, she's friendly, she says: 'Eleven thirty.' Fun city!
Screech, 163rd Street, she gets off. No Cloisters no Unicorn no
Park. The plot thickens? Yeah, sure, the plot. What plot. The
Gunpowder Plot? The Old Guy? His plot is already as thick as
it'll ever get.

OK, end of the line. At least I know what time it is, and who
gives a shit. I'm waiting for a new B back downtown. Maybe
I am tired. Losing my focus. Sunless dead. Joyless region.
Traveling indefinitely—whose idea was this? Richard Nixon's?
Dien Bien Phu's? It's time to take the *Septem* seriously, and
Benardete's two Notes even more seriously. *Very* seriously.
But I *do take* them seriously, I *have taken* them seriously.
Absolutely. But I took to the subway *indefinitely* to take them
seriously seriously. To learn from Eteocles' *experience* of
deciding something of (more or less) *decisive* importance for
my own decision. And what have I learned so far, and when
will I ever learn, if I do nothing but beat around a thousand
bushes—*trample* ten thousand bushes. When will they ever
learn? Where have all the flowers gone? Latin-type gorgeous
women indifferent to unicorns. Billy Budd—I've learned many
things from Melville. Absolutely. A decision is, by definition, a
tangle. A complex. Possibly, a complex tangle or, vice versa, a
tangled complex of diverse decisions. I'm on the B Train again,
bound for Harlem, Central Park West, West 4th, the Manhattan
Bridge, the West End Line, Coney Island. *Hades*. It really is all
in the mind. Never mind. Zen mind. Here's Benardete's *first*
Note. No! not yet. First—what, exactly, is Eteocles' problem?
I thought *deeply* a little while ago about Oedipus cursed and
cursing—the cursed and the cursing are, of course, inseparable.
But, now, let's focus on the cursing. *Screech*, 163rd Street. I
wonder if she lives here or if she's just visiting. Maybe she's
meeting a friend, and *then* they'll go to the Cloisters. Who
knows. A stroll. Oedipus cursing and *riddling*: 'A stranger

coming from the sea, born of fire, will prove a harsh divider of his inheritance,' as the Chorus in the *Septem* puts it. He's furious with his sons, and curses them with this riddle, which means: they will divide his kingdom with the sword. Reciprocal suicide, as Hegel put it. An unhappy ending. Thebes! Defend the City! Oedipus had that Kissingeresque idea: I'm old (relatively) (how old?), tired, blind, I think it'd be fun to play the Sage Elder Statesman, à la Mao Tse-tung, and leave it up to my boys to Defend the City! One year at a time, taking turns. It seemed like a pretty good idea. Well, alas, there were a couple of snags. I already mentioned the first one a while back: he got royally pissed off at both of them, Eteocles and Polyneices, because, more or less, they didn't take proper care of him, didn't love him enough. Never mind the haunch and the shoulder, that's another version. Suffice it to say: cruel tendance. Hence, his riddling curse. Exit Oedipus, riddling and cursing. What in the world happened to him? Well, famously, according to Sophocles, he wandered off to an Athens suburb with his daughter Antigone. What does Aeschylus think? The *Septem* was the third play of a trilogy, *Laius, Oedipus, Septem*, and since the first two were lost, well, we'll never know. In any event he's left the scene, leaving his curse behind him. 145th Street. A family tradition, of course, since all this begins with Laius, may he rot in hell. Sure, Laius was cursed—he *richly* deserved it—but Oedipus was cursed *and* cursing. This 'Scythian colonist' dividing his inheritance is no laughing matter. Basically, *this curse is the soul of the play*. No, the *Septem* is not a Spaghetti Western, it's not *The Longest Day*, it's not *The Wild Bunch*. There are Seven possibly 'outlandish' and 'savage' Attackers at the Seven Gates, but it's not *The Magnificent Seven* either. It's not *Seven Samurai*. It's 'full of Ares,' it's a war play, absolutely, an 'outside narrative,' but it's the curse that counts, dammit all. All this rigmarole about devices on shields. That's the play. But what's the point?

The point is Eteocles, his decision, *and the curse*. But that's not the whole story. What's the *point* of the point? The *point* of the point is the question: How much freedom and how much necessity is there in Eteocles' *decision* to go *himself* to the Seventh Gate? What does he actually experience? Responsibility? Is he himself responsible for his decision? Is he *decided for* by the curse, i.e., fated, doomed to go *himself* to the Seventh Gate? That's all she wrote? Dear John, Dear Eteocles.[78] Responsibility? Irresponsibility? Or does he make his 'decision' to go *himself* to the Seventh Gate *freely?* Freely? How freely? Absolutely freely? Partially freely? A smidgen freely? Bless my soul, I've finally come to the point. It's taken me a while, but what's the hurry. I mean, where's the fire. *In my mind.* No, not on the roofs of houses. No? *Not in the napalm? Not in the war in Vietnam in the defense of tyranny?* In my mind? Eteocles doesn't seem especially fiery—no, but he sure gets fired up by those devices on the shields. No, his brother Polyneices is the fiery one, but exiles often are, they're blatantly 'decided for' as a rule, and that often fires them up. It's quite true, *the exiled* are extremely riled up, as a rule. Polyneices sure as hell is. Sure, both brothers were cursed together and, what's more, in fact, they will be *done in* by the curse together. Suicided together. No small matter. 'Reciprocal suicide.' If Eteocles had decided *not* to go to the Seventh Gate *himself* when he *knew* his brother was there, both brothers could have been *done in* anyway, one way or another, but not *done in together by the curse*. Polluting the City. Spitting in the face of Zeus, 'whoever Zeus may be' (as Aeschylus liked to put it). But the *Septem* isn't about Polyneices, it's about Eteocles, and his decision, that's the point. The curse. And the *point* of the point is: How free is Eteocles' decision? How much compulsion? Absolutely free? Basically unfree? But this

---

78 OK, I'll help you younger readers out. The famous 'Dear John' letter. The expression 'that's all she wrote' goes back to World War II, the sad serviceman overseas who receives a letter from his sweetheart back home, 'Dear John'—and 'that's all she wrote.' Aeschylus wrote a lot more.

point of the point is more *complex* than that. Aeschylus is asking—according to Benardete, and I agree with him—*what is a decision? What does it mean to make a decision?* This is what Benardete's *second* Note is all about.

Ye gods! Where in Hades am I. Coming to the point, and to the *point* of the point, *in my mind*, for a moment, temporarily, I left Hades behind. We've screeched all the way down to Cathedral Parkway, a.k.a. West 110th Street, the north-west tip of Central Park, albeit not tip-top Central Park West, which is further downtown, West 72nd and on down, with its famous 'residences'—The Dakota, or The Majestic for example, where serious professional gangsters like Meyer Lansky, Lucky Luciano, and Frank Costello used to live. Tip top. Absolutely. I'm sure they never took the subway. It must be around noon now, a little after noon. Saturday afternoon, and I think it's a nice day. The car is quite full and these are not tourists but New Yorkers not working today because it's Saturday. Enough speculation! logic! syllogism! *They* know where they're going, or if they don't I'll let *them* figure it out, I need to concentrate on Eteocles. On his 'decision' to go *himself* to the Seventh Gate. 'Dear Eteocles': Is that really all she wrote? But first I have to back up, because this was his *second* crucial decision. As I learned from Starry Vere, big decisions often come in little bunches. Like bananas. This *second* crucial decision is the one that really concerns me, and is the *true plot* of the *Septem*. 'Concerns me': now that's an understatement for you. It's why I'm here, in Hades, the *raison d'être* of this journey. Eteocles made his decision and, Benardete says, in his second Note, Eteocles' 'decision making' can help me with my own. 'This fire is not on the roofs of houses,' Dostoevsky said. Is Eteocles' 'decision' absolutely *in his mind?* No. There's the curse, and he *knows* it. There's his brother, with his Seven Against Thebes. The Vietnam War is my curse—it has been since I was 14, 15 years old—and I know it. It's *in* my mind and *out* of my mind.

Just like Eteocles, and not temporarily like Achilles, as Dylan put it, but permanently. Just like Eteocles, I feel *both* free *and* 'decided for.' *Screech*, 86th Street. ANOTHER VIETNAM VETERAN PLACARD-MAN. Absolutely not. No sign of placard-men, past, present, or future. The legless man, the pledge-of-allegiance man, the 'hamlet'-approaching man—will I ever see them again? Who knows. Fun seekers, that's all I see, no sign of the Weather Underground. Manhattanites mostly, but in midtown, possibly, mostly tourists. Many tourists. I'll be able to tell the locals from the tourists, possibly, if I look closely. Which I probably won't, because I absolutely have to start *thinking seriously* about Eteocles. I keep talking about his *second* decision, to go *himself* to the Seventh Gate, but, as the saying goes, I'm putting the cart before the horse. The Roshi very rightly says, If the cart won't go which do you whip, the cart or the horse? But, come to think of it, that's beside the point here. So be it. No, nevertheless, the second decision makes no sense without the first. 72nd Street. Just imagine those tip-top mobsters living up there at The Majestic, right across the street from The Dakota. Just think, in 1957 Vincent 'The Chin' Gigante (a Sicilian name straight out of Greek myth) shot Frank Costello in the lobby but he botched the job. Mobsters die hard. Costello took it from The Chin but didn't go down for the count. But what concerns me is Eteocles dammit all. Eteocles and his second decision. But, first, his first decision. I notice that the car is not too full, but, I *predict*—now here's something new for me—I *predict* that after Columbus Circle it will be practically *packed*. Tourists and locals together, Saturday afternoon, end of March, and a nice day to boot. Now—Oedipus' Kissingeresque idea seemed pretty good, Defend the City! one year at a time, taking turns. After all, they're good boys. Then, the first snag: cruel tendance—haunch, shoulder, whatever—hence the riddling curse. What next? We don't actually have the details on this, so I have to settle for a rough idea. What's more, as

usual we have various 'sources' with their various versions.
In one version—apparently curseless—Eteocles simply (but
how simply? how did he do it?) expels Polyneices by force and
keeps the throne of Thebes—the inheritance—for himself. But
in the version Aeschylus subscribes to the brothers agree to
divide the kingship between them, switching each year. I guess
they figured, we're already cursed, at least let's try to live in
peace and possibly avoid killing one another (if possible). They
decided/agreed that Eteocles would rule first—flipped a coin
maybe? I wish I knew, this is quite a good question actually,
but the 'sources' don't go into it, as far as I know. (Which is
not that far, I'm just a 21-year-old NYU student.) Maybe if
Polyneices had ruled first things would have been different.
Maybe even worse, if possible. (What could possibly be worse!)
After all, 'Polyneices' means 'much strife' while 'Eteocles' mean
'true glory'—but, what's in a name. In fact it was Eteocles
who provoked 'much strife' with his *first* decision. Here we
are at last. And I don't just mean 59th street, the hordes are
coming, a wild bunch, outlandish, the car is practically packed.
I keep thinking about his *second* decision, to go *himself* to the
Seventh Gate *knowing full well* that his own brother is there,
but, that's the cart (a *big* one), first we have the horse. The
second snag: Eteocles *decides* to refuse to give up the throne
when his year is up. Ye gods, he *decides* he just won't give
his brother the throne. I wonder what Kissinger thinks about
this. What in the world came over him. Who knows. No one
ever talks about this. Stuff happens. Does he think his 'much
strife' brother is going to take this lying down. This in-your-face
FUCK YOU. His own brother. *Screech*, Rockefeller Center. This
fiery son of Oedipus, that old buzzard who didn't even take the
haunch instead of the shoulder lying down. Eteocles! Wake up.
Get your act together. The apple doesn't fall far from the tree.
Now, it's true that Polyneices has had a pretty nice year. No,
he hasn't been hanging around Thebes watching his brother be

king—no, he's been traveling. Travel broadens the mind. Just think, he thought he was a traveler and he turned out to be an exile. External, not internal. But, in the meantime, he had a *fine* time in Athens with king Theseus, the Minotaur slayer, and then he went to Argos to pay king Adrastus a visit. In Argos he had a *great* time. What a great town. Just a few miles from the sea surrounded by a beautiful fertile plain, while Thebes is inland and very dusty. While he was at it he married Argea, the king's daughter, *after he raped her*. After all, he's Laius' grandson. As I said, the apple doesn't fall far from the tree. (At least he didn't rape the king's *son*.) A pretty nice year, and then the snag: his brother's FUCK YOU. Well, Polyneices is sure as hell no Billy Budd, hell no, justice is justice and injustice is injustice, absolutely no *extreme stutter.* That smart chick on York Street, near the Navy Yard, loved Michael Kohlhass—his exaggerated sense of justice—more than Billy Budd, despite her abyssal esteem for Starry Vere. 'You can make me mount the scaffold, but I can get you where it hurts.' But, at the moment, we're in Ancient Greece, no one takes anything lying down. Come to think of it, Clint Eastwood would have felt right at home. Polyneices' reaction is truly the stuff of Spaghetti Westerns. No holds barred. He tells his father-in-law Adrastus, hey, shit, are we going to take this lying down. Argea and I with our bags all packed, ready to spend a year as king and queen of the dusty but *massively walled* town of Thebes. *Screech*, 42nd Street, what a wild bunch. And my brother says FUCK YOU. Come on, Adrastus, just give me a fucking *army*. If *this* doesn't mean war, what does!

In my mind, I see Adrastus not terribly enthusiastic. My men, the Argives, certainly don't lack fighting spirit, he muses, they more than held their own at Troy. But, do we have to fight all the time? Can't we enjoy the beautiful fertile plain for once, take a little stroll down to the harbor with our ladies for a dip in the sea? What's more, I have this fantastic local prophet,

Amphiaraus, a great guy and an anti-war activist. A 'winter soldier,' as one day someone will put it. He'll take *considerable* convincing, and I'm not all that convinced myself. Ares Ares Ares, with all our gods and goddesses it's always Ares. How about a dollop of equal time for his wife, Aphrodite. What's more, those two—Ares and *Aphrodite*, luscious sea foam—are the divine begetters of Thebes. Their daughter, Harmonia, was the wife of Cadmus, founder of the city, along with the *Spartoi* whom Ares spared. Ares may not be thrilled if I give Polyneices an army to attack his city. My prophet says Ares will see to it that we get our asses whipped and our balls cut off and I think he's probably right. Aphrodite will be pissed off too, and that is *not good*. Not in the least. JUSTICE, shrieks Polyneices, strike through the mask! Justice Justice Justice, it's a goddam *screech*. 34th Street. Jam packed. Fun seekers. I think most of them will be getting off by West 4th, I don't think they're going to Brooklyn, of course I may be wrong. Tourists, 'like a patch of discolored snow in early April.' They need the Statue of Liberty, not Coney Island. Nonetheless, Polyneices convinces Adrastus—I think, because the whole Argolid is full of 'outlandish' and 'savage' 'champions' with absolutely nothing to do and itching for a fight. An unemployed Wild Bunch. 'Make war not love' is their watchword, what can Adrastus do. At this point the prophet Amphiaraus is forced, unwillingly, to go along for the ride. Because that's the sort of prophet he is. An abyss and, in the end, an abyss abyssed.[79] No 'summer

79 As one of the stories goes, according to one of the sources, in keeping with his own prophecy (Benardete: 'Amphiaraus will soon predict his own conversion into a Theban oracle'), after the defeat of the Challengers at the gates and the 'reciprocal suicide' of the Kings, Amphiaraus took flight, Zeus threw his thunderbolt, and the earth opened to swallow him together with his chariot. At the site of this abyss, near Thebes, he was propitiated and consulted as a chthonic hero. We have, however, another major source, which neither coincides with nor blatantly contradicts the first. Here, again, Amphiaraus is an oracle, a chthonic hero, swallowed by the earth, our Mother. But this time his abyss—pardón, sanctuary—is rather farther from Thebes, at Oropos, about 25 miles northeast of Athens, a magnificent spot overlooking the channel that separates Attica from Evia. I visited the Amphiareion of Oropos in the summer of 1970. This story/tale/book originated then and there.

soldier and sunshine patriot' he. Myth has it that he went
because Polyneices enticed his wife Eriphyle with the cursed
necklace of Harmonia but, for me, that's neither here not there.
Amphiaraus took being a prophet seriously. Curses were not his
bag. Time for Benardete's first Note at last. The second Note—
Eteocles' 'reading' of the shields—is more complicated, more
important, and—even if very complicated—easier to follow than
this first one. I've read these *Two Notes on Aeschylus' Septem*
(that's the title) half a dozen times since Benardete gave them
to me last May. But just look at them. Each one is a sort of
tiny pamphlet, the reprint of an article from *Wiener Studien.*
Zeitschrift für Klassische Philologie und Patristik. The first, from
1967, is exactly eight pages long; the longer one, from 1968,
is twelve pages. Small pages, large print. So be it. I have to
treat them gently, they're already falling apart.[80] If I want to
be able to read them forty years from now, I'd better treat
them *very* gently. Well, we'll be getting to West 4th soon. Shit,
a middle-aged man *and* woman, each with binoculars. What
in the world's on their minds. Bird watchers? Frankly I don't
give a shit. This is getting to be a long trip, must be around
24 hours already. Time. What is this thing called time? as the
fantastic beautiful Nina Simone sang it. Who knows where the
time goes. I have this eerie feeling that when I finally start
reading these Notes *something* is going to wake me *wide up*.
I still think I'm going to get *somewhere*, with my fork. No, the
point is not really the fork. I *will* make a decision, today, in
the next few months, in any event, and it will be decisive for
the rest of my life. But what *really* concerns me is not *what*
I decide but *how* I decide it—my understanding of what a
decision is and means. Who am I kidding, *it's the fork*. Blow
up the bridge, become a GAM, go into exile—this is the point.
I *have* a fork. HAVE. I'll decide. Who gives a flying fuck about
what a decision is and means. Just do it. The prisoner's *deed*.
Am I contradicting myself? Constantly. Sure. A little quote from

---

80 You should see them now!

168

Hegel's *Aesthetics*, I know it by heart. 'Yet whoever claims that nothing exists that carries in itself a contradiction in the form of an identity of opposites is at the same time requiring that nothing living shall exist. For the power of life, and still more the might of the spirit, consists precisely in positing contradiction in itself, enduring it, and overcoming it.'[81] Right *now*, something living exists. 'When I'm sixty-four'—shit, I may not even make it to twenty-four. Who knows. I have this feeling that what I need to know isn't *where I am* now but *what I'm doing* now. Am I decided *for* and done *for*, or do I still have a decision to *make*. No no no, not '*Why* am I doing this?' No, 'The prisoner's deed. With that alone we have to do.' Doing, making. What is the decision that decides the deed? What is a decision? What does it mean to *make* a decision? *This* is the point. The might of the spirit.

West 4th Street. When it rains hard, OK, I take the F, and walk ten minutes instead of half an hour, and get less wet— possibly. I still consider this an open question. The Roshi says: Walking in the fog is a strange thing. You end up completely drenched, but you're not aware of it on the way. I was right, the car is a lot quieter now, a lot of people got off, going to the Village, or heading on downtown on the A, C, or E. Chinatown, ye gods it's time for lunch. Little Italy, hero sandwiches. Or on down to the brand new 'World Trade Center,' these in-your-face Towers destined to make the Empire State Building passé. A thing of the past. They just 'topped-off' the second Tower last summer. New Wonder of the New World. They razed a great neighborhood to the ground, dug a Hole deeper than Hell for the foundations, then up up up went the Towers. Quick as a wink. In your face. Seeing is believing. The Lighthouse of Lower Manhattan. World Trade. A Shining City. So be it. Wonders. The New World. Cristóbal Colón, a Man of the World. A Man on

---

81 An old friend of mine, a philosopher born in Arkansas, his window looking down onto the Mississippi River, scribbled this quote for me by hand, years ago. I still have the scrap of paper, but there's no page number. It was a friendly, not a scholarly, exchange.

the Moon, step, leap, whatever. What's next in Fun City? The Great Wall of Chinatown or the Hanging Gardens of Houston Street? How about the Colossus of Washington Square. Defend the City! In any event, apart from the screeches I'm looking forward to a peaceful trip to Coney Island, and back, reading this first Note. The Note has a title: 'I. The Parodos and First Stasimon.' It begins: 'The Chorus sings twice about the Argive attack, first before and then after Eteocles has rebuked them.' This, in theory, is the subject, which, however, in practice, is a lot more complicated. Basically, Benardete tackles three questions: first, the rebuked Chorus; second, the threefold meaning of Ares and its relation to the Curse; third, the dual origin of the City—sexual (divine and human) and non-sexual (serpent's tooth)—and its relation to Eteocles' decision. That's putting it very roughly. In any event, the title of the second Note is 'II. Eteocles' Interpretations of the Shields' and that's exactly what it's about, whereas the first Note is a labyrinth. *Screech*, Broadway-Lafayette. Now, the parodos—the first ode sung by the Chorus, lines 75–180—is, as Eteocles puts it in his rebuke, full of 'wild panting and moaning' or, as Benardete himself puts it, of 'vain and wild snortings.' It must be said that Eteocles pants and snorts quite a bit himself, these women get on his nerves, which, of course, are already considerably frayed. The Argive hordes, led by his brother, encamped on the Theban plain, have been besieging the City for a 'long time' (days, weeks, months?) and now they're about to attack the Gates. In the first stasimon (287–367)—the strophe sung from east to west, then the antistrophe from west to east—the women, of all ages, referred to at times as 'virgins' and at times as 'women,' rebuked, wail less. But I'd better take this one step at a time, otherwise I'll confuse myself. Back to the beginning, Eteocles' first speech to the Citizens, his famous last words: 'Never fear this horde of foreigners! God will give victory.' This is before the 'women' get into the act. Then the messenger/soldier/spy (I like 'spy') enters, to tell Eteocles what he has just seen:

> There were seven men, fierce leaders of armies, who cut bulls' throats into an iron-rimmed shield, and dipped their fingers in the bull's gore, taking their oaths by Ares and Enyo, by the bloodthirsty God of Battle Rout, either to raze your city to the ground or by their death to make a bloody paste of our soil.

No question about it, Clint Eastwood would have been right at home. The spy assures Eteocles he'll keep him posted with his 'clear reports.' Eteocles' immediate reaction: 'O Zeus, and Earth! Ye gods who guard this City! *O Curse of Oedipus my father*, mighty evil spirit, do not deliver this City to her enemies.' Defend the City! But it's a mouthful: Zeus, Earth, and Curse. And this is just the beginning. *Screech*, Grand Street. Absolutely, one of my favorite streets, I get my longish hair cut on Grand Street, and my short beard trimmed, it's like a rolling stone's throw from Rivington. Grand Street, where the bricks lay. Falling perfectly. So well timed.[82] Absolutely. One of Dylan's favorite streets too. Very soon, Manhattan Bridge Again. Now we have the parodos, and the Note. Regarding the Chorus, I have to say that Benardete's point is uncharacteristically simple, it's his second and third points that are not so simple. As a result of Eteocles' rebuke—his reasonably tame snorting about their wild snortings, as it were—'the movement seems to be from fear outside to fear inside the heart, and this turning inward characterizes the entire stasimon.' 'The main reason for this difference lies in the shift in the object of the Chorus' imaginings. They shift from imagining the enemy to imagining the imminent condition of themselves and other citizens.' Manhattan Bridge Again, now the F Train is 'my' train, as it were, but, take your pick, Tube or Bridge, no contest.

---

82 It's 'Memphis Blues Again.'

It is one hell of a nice day. Sunny and I bet it's pretty warm. What a great day for Hades. No doubt about it, Hades *will have its day*. No complaints. I've come this far, and as far as Eteocles is concerned I'm finally coming to the point. Tomorrow is another day. Today, what really concerns me is 'Eteocles' Interpretations of the Shields'—his decision, and *what making a decision is and means*. What splendor, the East River. I see the Williamsburg Bridge, which I may yet bomb, gleaming in the distance, the early-afternoon end-of-March sun. The fork. 'Some are born to sweet delight,/ Some are born to endless night.' Being born and dying, the separation of the inseparable. Back, back under the ground. Now, the parodos, 'imagining the enemy.' From the 'clatter of hoofs' the women, in a disorderly panic, imagine they see 'a cloud of dust, sky high' (the plain of Thebes is dusty, I saw it myself two summers ago) and immediately wail: 'Death rushes upon us!' This is exactly the sort of pessimism that gets on Eteocles' nerves. On the stage some primitive images of gods stand on pedestals. 'Who will protect us? Who will be our champion of gods or goddesses? Shall I kneel at the images of the gods? O Blessed Ones, throned in peace, *it is time to cling to your images*.' The women go to the images and sit clasping them, wailing dubious things like 'I see the sound!' and 'Look upon us, a band of virgins!' (The Chorus represents all the Theban women, of all ages—all virgins?) They make their snorting prayers to the gods and goddesses, beginning—quite rightly—with Ares: 'Ancient lord of our land, Ares, will you betray your own land?' Then, Zeus, Athena, Poseidon, Ares again, his wife Aphrodite, Apollo, Artemis, and Hera—as Benardete notes in the third part of this first Note, four gods and four goddesses. On the face of it this prayer doesn't seem so bad, though they might have done well to skip the references to 'stones showering on our parapet!' and the 'rattle of bronze-bound shields at our gates!' and concentrate on their praying. *Screech*, Pacific Street, this long stretch without stops. But it's their constant screaming that really irks Eteocles: 'You intolerable creatures! I ask you, is this the way to save us? Will this encourage our fighters on the walls—to fling yourselves at the images of our guardian gods and howl and shriek, to every sane person's disgust?' Still, he cuts a poor figure with his wild tirade against women in general, which begins 'Neither in evils nor in fair good luck may I share a dwelling with the tribe of women!' and then gets even worse. I'll come back to this, but Benardete's point, on a pinhead, is that Ares is also the *husband* of Aphrodite—a fact that Eteocles conspicuously ignores. In fact, in the whole play he refers only to *virgin* goddesses—Artemis, Athena, Dikê (pronounced *dee*-kay, the goddess of Justice, no reference to lesbians). Meanwhile, Eteocles offers his own prayer as a model for the women's. In fact, it's quite a respectable Defend the City! prayer—'May the gods stand our allies!'—designed 'to inspire our men and make them fearless in the field.' No 'vain wild panting and moaning.' Eteocles seems to have calmed down. He exits, to round up 'six men, myself to make a seventh, to guard our seven gates.' Now comes the first stasimon, which begins: 'I heed him but through fear, my spirit knows no sleep, and neighbors to my heart, anxieties, kindle terror of the host that beleaguers us.' It's true, there is a shift from fear outside to fear inside the heart. *Screech*, 36th Street, I'll be seeing the Brooklyn afternoon in a few minutes. I want to follow Benardete's analysis of the stasimon closely. He notes: 'The parodos and stasimon equally contain prayers to the gods, but they are entirely different in kind. In the stasimon no god is invoked by name, in the parodos eight gods are thus invoked. This anonymity of the gods seems to be occasioned by the Chorus' leaving their statues at Eteocles' behest, for the gods they first invoked by name were clearly present as statues before them. *Eteocles' ridicule of their reverence for images* apparently *compels* them to avoid mentioning specific deities.'

Eteocles ridicules images *now*, but just wait until the spy starts describing the devices on the shields. From compelling to compelled. Magnificent. I was right, it really is a beautiful spring-like day. Sunset Park, early afternoon. Daylight. The B Train. Pulling into the 9th Avenue station. A dozen screech screech screeches in the offing on the way to Coney Island. Screech away. Car about half full but I don't even notice, I'm concentrating on the Note. Meanwhile, the women do seem calmer, but their hearts are full of dread. They no longer cling to the images but, now, as Benardete puts it, 'the gods are no longer loving gods.' The gods have become citizens: 'Fellow-citizen gods, grant me not to be a slave.' Benardete: 'Whatever loss of vividness the absence of statues and divine names entails would seem to be compensated for in the gods' more intimate enrollment in the city's defense. [I translate the Greek in the Note: 'O children of Zeus, ye gods, I pray you—protect the city and the army, the Cadmus born.'] But the Chorus' prayer is short-lived, and they dwell more on the disasters that await women and children if the city is captured than on the gods' confounding their enemies. The gods are not now assumed to see and hear as they were in the parodos.' But this 'anonymity of the gods' has two related consequences: first, 'the stasimon could almost apply to any city under attack, the parodos can only refer to Thebes'; second, 'Ares in the parodos is the Theban Ares and in the stasimon the god of war.'

Benardete is about to say something extremely important—his *point*, actually. His two-pronged point: the Curse, and Ares. Shit, his *second* Note is so linear, but this one is a labyrinth. The Note itself is 'full of Ares'—skirmishes, coming and going, cropping up here and there, again and again. I'd like to do my own more linear analysis of 'Ares' in the *Septem*, but for now I'm following Benardete. With *Billy Budd* I did the analysis all by myself—that business about the inside and the outside narrative, I made it up myself, right here among the sunless dead. The abyss. Well, I think the *Septem* is *even more* of an abyss (whatever that means), with its own abyssal inside and outside narratives: inside, the Curse/Decision; outside, Ares, in his [its] *many* senses. Theban Ares, war god, and—bluntly—just plain WAR. War is hell. Make love not war! Fuck war! Bring the war home! I said a little while ago that the curse is the soul of the play. Well, Ares is its heart. OK, I have to back up in the Note. I *wanted* to make my analysis of the Note a linear one-two-three: rebuked Chorus—threefold meaning of Ares—dual origin of the City. But it's impossible, they're all tangled up together. *Screech away*, just let me know when we get to Coney Island. Extremely important. OK, let's jump around. 'Ares, who is invoked at first as the founder of Thebes, shows himself second as the frenzy of war. Even when Ares appears as war's personification in the parodos, the context is the animated inanimate or rather the fusion of the animate and the inanimate. He is not the madness-breathing Ares who pollutes piety [as he is in the stasimon]. When Aristophanes has Aeschylus claim that he made the *Septem* full of Ares, the claim raises a question that lies at the heart of the drama. Which Ares? The Ares to whom Eteocles refers when he says that Melanippus descended from the sown men whom Ares spared, or the Ares of two lines later, who seems to be simply the fortunes of war. [412–414: 'From the sown men whom Ares spared his root springs—very native is Melanippus to this land. His deeds shall Ares with his dice determine.'] This ambiguity, I believe, points to *the* question of the *Septem*: *tí estin Áres;* [what is Ares?].' Now, jumping back ahead to the Chorus: 'Two traits, then, distinguish the stasimon from the parodos. It is more "psychological" in tone and more general in content. [There are no more *images* to cling to.] Could there be a connection between these two aspects? Does the Chorus' turning inward effect a corresponding loss of distinctness? *Does the anonymity of the gods point to an area where the gods*

have less and human beings more control over their destiny?'
Pardon my brackets, and my italics. Does this seem like an
innocent little question to you? To me it seems like the 'direct
reverse' of an innocent little question. To me, it seems *exactly
what this journey in Hades is about*. A decision. *'An area where
the gods'*—sure, it's hard to say what this means, to me, to
us, here and now. No, not on the roofs of houses. *In my mind*,
it's Hegel's realm of shadows, his system of logic. A decision.
What is a decision, what does it mean to make a decision? In
the end, I think only Hegel can help me. If I ever make it to the
end. If there *is an end*. There must be. Will be. The might of
the spirit. Identity of opposites. Everything ends. The end ends.
No question.

Meanwhile, Coney Island. End of the line again. Quick, a
new B, screeching back up the West End Line, I need to get on
with the Note. I've never been to Coney Island. I really wonder
what it's like. No, I think I'll take a long walk in the station
instead, 8 tracks, 4 island platforms, 2 tracks for each platform,
systematically, up and down the platforms one after the other.
Now unsystematically, take the platforms in no order at all. No-
mind. Not so easy. As the Roshi said, putting dots on a page
randomly is not so easy, you always end up imposing some
order on them. The clock. Down there, in the direction of the
ocean, in the other part of the station, I might as well check it
out. 5 to 2. I've been walking for a while. A toilet, OK, I'll take
a piss, and refill my water bottle. How many apples do I have?
Still three apples, I've only had one apple all this time. I'm not
hungry. I know very well, from experience, that if I don't eat at
all I can not get hungry if I put my mind to it. It's *eating* that
makes you hungry. Somewhere along the line, the Hades line,
I decided not to eat anything—decided? See what I mean! No,
I didn't *decide* anything of the sort. It just happened. Freely.
How freely? Am I sticking with the B Train. Guess so. Why not.
Hades is Hades. A screech is a screech. I like the B. All one

Hades, all one screech. But many stops. Many trains.

On the B Train. A lot of fellow travelers here in Brooklyn? Not that many, actually. Well, it's not really my business, I have my seat, and I travel. Placard-men in Coney Island? Maybe in the summer. Anyway, that's their business. Maybe the three I've seen are all there are, three raindrops on the ocean. Vietnam veterans. OK, the Note. In the parodos the Chorus pants 'What is happening to our city? What will become of it? What is the end that god ordains?' But in the stasimon it only asks 'What will become of me?' 'The gods' purpose is lost from view.' Benardete asks whether this reflects 'a turning inward and a less certain reliance on the gods.' Suddenly, he hits us with the soul and the heart of the play, the Curse/Decision and Ares. 'It is plain, I think, that to answer this question would help answer *the question that has exercised so much recent scholarship.* Does Eteocles decide his own fate, or is his fate determined by the curse of Oedipus? The possibilities are not as clear-cut as they would seem, but as intertwined as Ares in his dual aspect. Only if one could show that the Ares in "the sown men whom Ares spared" is utterly distinct from the Ares of "his deeds shall Ares with his dice determine," and only typographical consistency endows the second with a capital letter, would one be justified in positing that alternative; for between these two Ares lies a third, the Ares the spy ascribes to Hippomedon: "*full* of Ares, he revels in violence like a Bacchant." [The Greek word is *entheos*: the god is 'in' him, has entered into—possessed—him. A quirky translation: 'enthused by Ares.'] The way in which this triad is understood ultimately determines the way in which Eteocles' decision can be understood. Ares as 1) a willing, acting, anthropomorphic god, 2) a personification of war, and 3) a certain state of the soul, presents in himself the difficulty of understanding Eteocles.' Now if this isn't a mouthful, what is! Shit, this is Benardete. He's a master of mouthfuls. Mine are less than tidbits compared to his. And he even managed a one-two-three, the old buzzard. *Screech away*, B Train. We're still in broad daylight, Hades by day. Too bad it won't last but, then again, what does. In this direction, Sunset Park is sunset indeed, the Gate to the Night Journey. Benardete has stunned me again with this Note—the *first* Note—and I'm only halfway through it. I still have the 'sexy' part, the sexual (divine and human) and non-sexual (serpent's tooth) origin of the City that Eteocles is trying to defend, as best he can. Defend the City! 18th Avenue—how can they possibly have so many avenues in Brooklyn? It puts Manhattan to shame. A *threefold* Ares, or are the folds even more than three? I mean, take the 'Vietnam Ares': JFK folded it one way, McNamara another, LBJ yet another, 'bomb them back to the Stone Age' Curtis LeMay one hell of another, Nixon yet others, and Kissinger several dozen others all at once. Willing/ acting—personification—state of the soul, or heart, or liver, or whatever. Roll all the folds up into a ball and you've got a *state of mind*, that's what I think. A state of mind. What is my state of mind? What is Eteocles' state of mind? Fuck Polyneices and *his* state of mind. As far as I'm concerned, we three are the Good, the Bad, and the Ugly, but I'm just kidding. The fact is, Eteocles has a City to defend, and so do I. And it's not a City on a Hill, that's the one Nixon is currently 'defending' with his extreme unction in the defense of tyranny. No, alas, extreme unction no, it's the celebration of a Defense that's just getting revved up. Defend the City on a Hill! Is this *my* City? I don't really care *what* City Eteocles is defending, no, in any case, the apple doesn't fall far from the tree. No, I care about *what I can learn from him about making a decision*. Screech, screech, screeching, I'm underground again. 9th Avenue, Brooklyn. Not Hell's Kitchen but Hades by night.

The last time I read the *Septem* (as Benardete always calls it)—two or three nights ago, I've lost count—I decided to make a note of every time I saw the name 'Ares' (or, possibly, 'war').

Take some initiative, I thought, why leave it all up to Benardete. I've got one hell of a list, makes my head spin, I have it right here. *Screech*, 36th Street. But, after all this, I think I'd better start with Benardete's note on page 5 of the (first) Note. 'How much the problem of the threefold Ares is connected with that of Eteocles is shown by considering together'—and here we have two passages quoted in Greek, like everything else in the Notes, which I have to work out, based on Grene's and Vellacott's translations, along with my own death-defying deciphering. Benardete: '.... by considering together 709–711 [Eteocles: 'This rage was kindled by the curse of Oedipus. How true a prophet is that figure of my dreams who comes each night to apportion our inheritance!'] and 944–946 [Chorus: 'A bitter and cruel divider of possessions, Ares, who made their father's curse come true.']' Heart and soul, soul and heart, Curse and Ares, separate and inseparable, like reciprocally suicided rulers-brothers-foes. Benardete adds: '(cf. 907–910)'. The Chorus wailing in lamentation for the reciprocally suicided. In Grene's translation: 'In bitterness of heart they shared their possessions in equality: no blame from friends has their arbiter, Ares, impartial to both sides.' What/Who is Ares? One hell of a question. *The* question of the *Septem*, Benardete says. Let's see if I can get through this 'Ares list' of mine quickly, before we get to the Bridge— god, war, state of mind. Benardete jumps around so much, I want to follow the order of the play. I think I'll follow Grene's translation, for the most part. No, maybe not. Equal time for the translators. Line 45: 'taking their oaths by Ares and Enyo, by the bloodthirsty God of Battle Rout.' God of War. 54: 'Their spirits were hard as iron and ablaze breathed courage: Ares looked through their lion-eyes.' War or the War God? Or in-between? Pacific Street already. And the car is really filling up, Brooklynites going to Manhattan for the afternoon. 62: 'You, like the skillful captain of a ship, barricade your city before the blast of Ares strikes it in storm.' War. 105: 'I dread the clanging; that rattle is of ten thousand spears. Ares, what will you do? Will you forsake this land, your own from the beginning?' Good god. 115: 'A surge of soldiers with waving plumes seethes around our city; the breath of Ares drives them on.' War, the War God, or in-between? 135: 'And you, Ares, Ares, guard the city Cadmus named, with your bright presence protect us.' A bright god. 245: 'murdered men are Ares' nourishment' or 'men's blood is Ares' diet.' A bloodthirsty god. 345: 'The madness of Ares masters men in masses, and breathes defilement over all reverent feeling.' God, war, 'madness-breathing' in-between. 412: 'From the sown men whom Ares spared his root springs.' God. 414: 'His deeds shall Ares with his dice determine.' War. 470: 'Ares himself shall not cast me from the tower.' This is the caption on the device of the shield of the third attacker, defying the god, the Protector of Thebes. 497, the fourth attacker: 'Ares has entered into him'— 'full of Ares'—inspired, possessed, 'enthused' by Ares. Benardete's 'state of the soul,' the in-between. This long screechless stretch of Hades, we're close to the Manhattan Bridge. Bring the war home. Ares. All in the mind. Here we are. Yes, it's a beautiful afternoon. Just up the river, the Williamsburg Bridge is gleaming in the sunlight. Almost four years living on Rivington Street and I can't remember seeing it gleam like this. After studying all night I used to go out before dawn and jog across it, thinking about the Vietnam War; not any more, the Long Winter sapped my strength. In any event, I didn't see it gleam. Too early in the morning I guess, and now I also think you have to see a bridge from the distance to see a gleam. The B Train (or the D) on the Manhattan Bridge at almost-mid-afternoon on such a nice day is the perfect place to see it. When I have time, on weekends, especially in the summer, in the late afternoon, I often stroll down to Grand Street, to Broome Street too, they have the most beautiful buildings I've ever seen anywhere in New York—in Manhattan I mean, I've seen practically nothing of the rest of the city—and when the light is just right and the time is just right they have a gleam like nothing else in the world. The Grand Canyon will have its gleam, the Great Pyramid of Giza will have its gleam, but so does Grand Street. A gleam all its own. Come to think of it, it's more a glimmer than a gleam—I'd say, a gleaming glimmer. I can't describe it, the buildings, the street itself, seem to be throbbing gently. Memphis Blues Again: Bob Dylan really is a poet. Grand Street, where the neon madmen climb. Throbbing gently. Underground again. Hades. The nether darkness. *Screech*. Grand Street. I wish I lived on Grand, or Broome, rather than Rivington but, you know, an apartment in Manhattan when you don't have money—shit, you take what you can get if you can get it. Ask my grandfather. In any case, he lives in Atlantic City now. He's over 90 years old. The car is fairly full, after all that thinking about Ares I need to look around for a few minutes, before I tackle the second part of Benardete's first Note, which, I think, is *the most complicated part* of the two Notes. *Screech*, Broadway-Lafayette. So many screeches and all the same screech. Ares' diet. The War God's nourishment. Being is nothing. Zero degree of freedom. Am I getting anywhere? The screech and the subway, separate and inseparable. Hegel. Bad infinity. The Lernaean Hydra with her countless heads and extremely bad breath. The B Train, this extremely long stretch of darkness, to Washington Heights, and back, back to the Manhattan Bridge, the gleam of day. F Train B Train D Train. But there are many—many—*long long* Trains on the subway *that never see the light of day*. Ever. At all. I couldn't stand that. *Screech*, West 4th. *Holy shit! Holy shit!* A PLACARD-MAN, HERE HE IS, RIGHT IN FRONT OF ME. But *holy shit look at this placard*. This time, the *placard,* not the *man*. Forget about the legs, the flag salute, the crudely drawn solitary G.I. approaching the village. Ye gods, this is a piece of the Sistine Chapel ceiling. Michelangelo had a hand in this. But, let me take a good look. This placard-man is *yelling* 'Vietnam veteran' like a hot dog vendor at Yankee Stadium. He's waving his hat in people's faces, the car is jam-packed, a horde got on at West 4th, and it's a long way to Herald Square. Have you got a beer, Mr. Placard-Man? Baseball and Ballantine. Purity, body, and flavor. Out there in the Bleachers with my shirt off. Will I have afternoons like that after the fork? Holy shit, did this Vietnam-veteran placard-man paint/draw all this himself? Is the man a Michelangelo! A Vietnam-veteran placard-man Michelangelo? Waving his hat in my face. This blazonry on his shield—it's painted, not drawn—is almost too much to take in. Vietnam veteran—I wonder what he *did* in Vietnam. I bet he wasn't a clerk on the base at Da Nang like the fellow in my Ancient Greek class used to be—Ancient Greek on the G.I. Bill—no, this guy SAW ACTION, as the saying goes. He definitely *saw action*, so to speak. Absolutely. Get a piece of *this* action, all packed into his placard. On the upper left, an army helicopter breathing smoke and fire—Typhon, the Father of all Monsters. In the center, further down, not just one crudely drawn solitary G.I. approaching a village but a *wild bunch of individual G.I.s*—tiny but so vividly depicted, each one with his own body, his own face, the hand of a real artist. Incredible. I can see it in their eyes that they are *storming* the village, not 'approaching' it. On the upper right, a Vietnamese village—wow. Take a good look. Stereotyped? THIS IS VIETNAM, right here on the B Train. Not 'huts' but beautifully built little houses with thatched roofs and the lushest greenery in the world all around them, and the placard-artist shows us all this. Amazing, in a nutshell, a real Vietnamese village. I can imagine the children, the women, the old and infirm, huddled in corners in these homes, terrified. This placard-man has seen this. The image. The caption, at the bottom, tops it off: WE DESTROY THE VILLAGE IN ORDER TO SAVE IT. B Train, between the West

4th and the 34th Street stops. The car is packed and the passengers are excited. The placard-man maneuvers slowly, gingerly, through the car, with his masterpiece, like an eel in slime, slithering for daylight. We are all stunned. Have my fellow passengers ever seen a Vietnam-veteran placard-man before? A *great* question, I wish I could poll them, I have no idea, I wish I knew. This is my fourth in about twenty-four hours, but this one has changed the tune. I've barely even noticed *him*, so overpowering is his image. I don't have the slightest idea whether he's been getting lots of dimes, quarters, or bills in his cap. Do the passengers approve or are they angry? I'm not sure. In any event, I have the feeling that THIS placard-man doesn't give a shit. 'Speak then to me, who neither beg nor fear your favors nor your hate.' He may be a murderer, but not a mercenary. He is on an *extremely obscure* mission. What mission? I don't have the slightest idea. 'Trick or treat' definitely not. Pennies for the Old Guy, forget it. *Hypocrite lecteur!* Possibly, but debatable. Possibly, a Vietnam-veteran placard-man approaching an abyss. What abyss? Does 'abyss' even have a plural? Is 'abysses' nonsense, does the word even exist? Is 'abyss' like 'screech'—actually only one, the same and always different? Or is there *one and only one abyss?* DESTROY THE VILLAGE IN ORDER TO SAVE IT: Is this a name for the only abyss there is? He has changed the tune, where in hell is he? He's maneuvering, militarily, through the packed subway car. He knows what he's doing. This man is WAR-hardened. Ares, the war god, the fortunes of war, or *in-between?* Is this a placard-man with an image or an image with a placard-man? I see him now, a dozen feet down the car, maneuvering, screaming 'Baseball and Ballantine'—no, sorry, screaming 'Vietnam veteran.' *Mon hypocrite lecteur*, not for the pennies, but for the *image*. THIS, AT LAST, IS WAR. Here we are. The man—and the answer to the riddle was 'man'—*anthropus*—he's right here on the B Train—'on the scene,' as the Greeks, and we, put it. Theater of War. I think he is in fact older than I am, older than the other three placard-men, but not much older. Three, four, five years older. But I barely saw him. With an image like this, who looks at the man. I see him down there now—military crew cut, green combat fatigues. Dressed like a soldier. But this man is no longer a soldier. What's more, there's something in the scene that tells me he will never again be a soldier, not in a million years. Not in a million years a soldier again, but not in a zillion will he ever be a *war reporter*. This is just my own personal interpretation of the shield, but I have the feeling that this placard-man is pissing in the mouth of one 'war reporter' in particular, named Peter Arnett. Shitting on his head, possibly in anger, I think. This is my feeling. I read recently that the only thing you can be sure of about 'war reporters' is that they 'stink'[83]—literally. I mean, the best of them, so they say, are always in the field. They never get the chance to take a bath. But also figuratively. News *makers*, not reporters, in bed with the War God. Screeeeech, 34th Street. An abyss of dreams. The image and its man have vanished. I sit here stunned. Hordes pour out, hordes pour in. A midafternoon Hades dream, end of March, 1972, a nice day, definitely. Me. Traveling indefinitely. Fun city. DESTROY THE VILLAGE IN ORDER TO SAVE IT. I want to say something about Peter Arnett, I've heard a lot about him and his 'unvarnished truth.' But here's his varnish on the placard. Aren't Nixon and Kissinger enough, without his 'reports' and 'counter-reports'? I remember this very well. In February 1968 Arnett published a story about the provincial capital Bén Tre. Get a load of *this*. "'It became necessary to destroy the town *to save it*," a United States major said today. He was talking about the decision by allied commanders to bomb and shell the town regardless of civilian casualties, to rout the Vietcong.' One hell of a load. It *seems* that—to Arnett's *great and undying*

---

83 I actually did read this about Christiane Amanpour, some years ago, but I'm sure it was pure slander.

chagrin—the quote was then distorted, ending up as 'We had to destroy the village in order to save it.' I have *no doubt* that this placard-man never had a chance to peruse the original story, or the 'distorted' one either, he had other things on his mind. So be it. But we all know this quote, all of us. Veterans, non-veterans, and in-betweens. I read that the accuracy of the original quotation and its source have often been called into question. Arnett never revealed his source, except to say that it was one of four officers he interviewed that day. U.S. Army Major Phil Canella suggested that the quotation 'might have been a distortion' of something he said to Arnett. Ye fucking gods. WE DESTROY THE VILLAGE IN ORDER TO SAVE IT—a *grievous distortion* of 'it became necessary to destroy the town to save it.' Ye gods, a distortion! Fuck distortions, *this is the War God*—god, war, or in-between. Fuck all your gods, ye reporters. An image like this, worthy of Michelangelo, and I get myself bogged down in the caption, and in Peter Arnett. Shit, he has a glorious future ahead of him, he's not even 40, he can take care of himself. He'll be bullshitting for all he's worth when Nixon is long gone. But, *holy* shit, where has the image gone, and the man? *Screeeeeeech*. 42nd Street.

Suddenly I storm out of the car. I'm so riled up I can barely see. It's darker here on the platform than it was on the train. Two cars down I see the placard and the man getting out of one car and right into the next. This darkness! What am I doing here? Chasing after him? What for. No point. I have seen what I have seen. What is happening to my traveling indefinitely to make a decision. *What a decision is and what making a decision means.* Never mind the caption, Peter Arnett, just words, stupid words for a *bad war*. 'Evil and abominable,' Martin Luther King called it. But the image! the image! By the hand of a Vietnam-veteran placard-man Michelangelo. I need to get my head together here. Now! Where am I? The crowd. I see the B Train vanish into the heart of darkness, placard,

man, and all. Now. What. I need a new train. An F? No, a D,
a D to Yankee Stadium. Drink beer, sit in the Bleachers with
my shirt off. I'm stumbling around, in the crowd. I make it to
the 'D' platform. Uptown. I stand here. *Screeeech*, it's even
louder here on the platform than it is in the car. I stumble in,
it's packed, I make it to a pole to hold onto—a pole is much
better than a strap. The train is moving. I'm heading for the
Bronx. Holding onto the pole. The helicopter breathing smoke
and fire—the wild bunch of G.I.s about to storm the village—
the children, the women, the old and infirm, huddled in corners
of their homes, terrified. Vivid colors, figures that seem alive.
Get a grip on yourself. The helicopter—it must be a Cobra,
a HueyCobra attack helicopter, the Chinook transport copter
must have unloaded the soldiers and taken off. The helicopter
immediately reminded me of Typhon, in the *Septem*, on the
fourth shield. An image of terror. I'll reread the description later
on, when I get a seat. I remember Benardete's description in
the second Note, 'breathing soot-laden fire through his mouth.'
Graphic words, a terrifying image. A terrifying reality. 'The
first image of a god on the shields.' I hold on tight to my book
bag, clinging to it. Rockefeller Center, people get off, people
get on. 7th Avenue/53rd Street is next, in just a couple of
minutes, then 59th, I'm sure I'll get a seat when we stop at
59th, Columbus Circle, a big stop. I may even just sit there
for a while and eat an apple, suddenly I feel hungry, I still
have three of them. Maybe have one, maybe not. Maybe my
stomach is better, calmer, just as it is. Babe Ruth used to get
big bellyaches from eating a huge number of hot dogs—Yankee
Stadium hot dogs of course, not Coney Island hot dogs. I have
the same problem he did, if I eat one hot dog my stomach
suddenly screams, Give me another five. Another ten! Plenty
of mustard. I know the D Train pretty well from my trips up to
the Bronx to see the Yanks. The D has a special thing about it
the B and F don't have, that a friend of mine and I call 'Route

66': incredibly, it makes no stops from 59th Street to 125th Street. Count 'em, that's 66 blocks. No stops. It follows the same route as the B as far as 145th Street, but on Route 66 the D never stops and the B stops all the time. I haven't been on the D as often as I used to lately, especially since Mickey Mantle retired a few years ago, and I've had less free time. 7th Avenue/53rd Street. Clinging to my book bag, and to the pole. I'll never forget the first time I went to Yankee Stadium, also because it was very very special. The World Series, 1960, Game 3, and we won 10–0! (Alas we lost the Series, to Pittsburgh in seven games.) I was only ten years old. My father got two tickets but he wasn't interested himself so I went with a neighbor, a great guy, he must have been eighteen or so. What a great day. I didn't mind the crowds that day. *Screech*, 59th Street, three quarters of the people get off, next stop Harlem. Who's going to the Bronx at this time of day? Anyway, Opening Day is still a couple of weeks off, the Yankees are still in Florida for spring training. I pick a good seat, a few people get on, the car is barely half full. Chill out. *'It is time to cling to your images,'* wail the women of the city Cadmus founded, with the help of the sown men whom Ares spared. Primitive images of the gods, on pedestals. Nothing like the image I saw just a few minutes ago. Hades, 66 blocks, not a screech. Time to take stock. 'Kill a gook for God.' I wonder how many people know where the word 'gook' comes from. It's a good red-blooded American word with an (infamous) history going back to the early 1900s: from low prostitute (harlot), to tramp, to fool, to any *slimy* thing or person (creep), and from there to an Oriental, and now, more specifically, a Vietnamese. Isn't that great. Of course racism is as American as apple pie, but—and I'm afraid that this is true—many soldiers see the 'gooks' we are killing in this war as less than human—as *slimy* sub-humans, barely even animals. Insects. Slime. I remember reading—it was testimony at the Winter Soldier investigation last year—one former soldier saying 'my mind was so psyched out into killing gooks that I never even paid attention to look around and see where I was. I just saw gooks and I wanted to kill them.' *Yelling* 'Vietnam veteran' like a hot dog vendor. The attack helicopter, the wild bunch of soldiers about to storm the village, the people huddled in terror. This train seems to go faster and faster, roaring through Hades like a rocket. The placard-man *Michelangelo*. To paint with such genius *he has seen the action he depicts*. He has been there. Done that. 'Full of war,' he has been possessed, inspired, 'enthused.' Now, here in Hades, he *glories* in the image. Or, does he? Who knows. Maybe he's tormented by it. Who knows. I see *his* image of the War God—god, war, state of mind—but I have *my own image* of the event. I have it right here in my bag. Only an image can respond to this image. Two images, two sides of the same image, a war of images, or *an image at war with itself*.

I have a very recent article[84] in my bag, it's stuffed into the copy of *Ramparts* with Che's Bolivia diaries. Wait—here it is, right on top of the article on Vietnam War helicopters with their 'redskin' names. The title is 'An Introduction to the My Lai Courts-Martial' and the author is—no, not Peter Arnett. The author's name is Doug Linder. This text is as beautifully written as the fourth placard is painted. It's the best and fullest account of the My Lai atrocity that I know of. The 'story' hit the media some eighteen months after the event, with cover stories in *Time* and *Newsweek* in November 1969. But that was journalism, this is real writing by someone who has really thought things through. The text is nine pages long, the second half is on the cover-up, I want to concentrate on the first part— the image that responds to the placard-man Michelangelo. I just want to quote to myself my underlined passages, without

---

84 OK, never mind *Taxi Driver*, 1976, this time my reference is *way* before its time. My poetic license. The article was written in 1999 and is very famous, and rightly so. It's all over the Internet. By all means, read it. Doug Linder is the creator of the *Famous Trials* website, which is itself famous and richly deserves its fame.

comment, just the text, the image. On this long stretch without screeches.

Two tragedies took place in 1968 in Viet Nam. One was the massacre by United States soldiers of as many as 500 unarmed civilians—old men, women, children—in My Lai on the morning of March 16. The other was the cover-up of that massacre.

......

Charlie Company came to Viet Nam in December, 1967.... Its commanding officer was Ernest Medina, a thirty-three-year-old Mexican American from New Mexico who was popular with the soldiers. One of his platoon leaders was twenty-four-year-old William Calley. Charlie Company soldiers expressed amazement that Calley was thought by anyone to be officer material. One described Calley as 'a kid trying to play war.'

......

Medina told the soldiers that the VC's crack 48th Battalion was in the vicinity of a hamlet known as My Lai 4, which would be the target of a large-scale assault by the company. The soldiers' mission would be to engage the 48th Battalion and to destroy the village of My Lai. By 7 a.m., Medina said, the women and children would be out of the hamlet and all they could expect to encounter would be the enemy. The soldiers were to explode brick homes, set fire to thatch homes, shoot livestock, poison wells, and destroy the enemy. The seventy-five or so American soldiers would be supported in their assault by gunship pilots.

......

At 7:22 a.m. on March 16, nine helicopters lifted off for the flight to My Lai 4. By the time the helicopters carrying members of Charlie Company landed in a rice paddy about 140 yards south of My Lai, the area had been peppered with small arms fire from assault helicopters. Whatever Viet Cong might have been in the vicinity of My Lai had most likely left by the time the first soldiers climbed out of their helicopters.

......

My Lai village had about 700 residents.

......

By 8 a.m., Calley's platoon had crossed the plaza on the town's southern edge and entered the village. They encountered families cooking rice in front of their homes. The men began their usual search-and-destroy task of pulling people from homes, interrogating them, and searching for VC. Soon the killing began. The first victim was a man stabbed in the back with a bayonet. Then a middle-aged man was picked up, thrown down a well, and a grenade lobbed in after him. A group of fifteen to twenty mostly older women were gathered around a temple, kneeling and praying. They were all executed with shots to the back of their heads. Eighty or so villagers were taken from their homes and herded to the plaza area. As many cried 'No VC! No VC!', Calley told soldier Paul Meadlo, 'You know what I want you to do with them.' When Calley returned ten minutes later and found the Vietnamese still gathered in the plaza he reportedly said to Meadlo, 'Haven't you got rid of them yet? I want them dead. Waste them.' Meadlo and Calley began firing into the group from a distance of ten to fifteen feet. The few that survived did so because they were covered by the bodies of those less fortunate.

......

Meanwhile, the rampage below continued. Calley was at the draining ditch on the eastern edge of the village, where about seventy to eighty old men, women, and children not killed on the spot had been brought. Calley ordered the dozen or so platoon members there to push the people into the ditch, and three or four GIs did. Calley ordered his men to shoot into the ditch. Some refused, others obeyed. One who followed Calley's order was Paul Meadlo, who estimated that he killed about twenty-five civilians. (Later, Meadlo was seen, head in hands, crying.) Calley joined in the massacre. At one point, a two-year-old child who somehow survived the gunfire began running towards the hamlet. Calley grabbed the child, threw him back in the ditch, then shot him.

......

By 11 a.m., when Medina called for a lunch break, the killing was nearly over. By noon, 'My Lai was no more': its buildings were destroyed and its people dead or dying. Soldiers later said they didn't remember seeing 'one military-age male in the entire place.' By night, the VC had returned to bury the dead. What few villagers survived and weren't already communists, became communists. Twenty months later army investigators would discover three mass graves containing the bodies of about 500 villagers.

An image at war with itself. *All this in our name*, as the Weather Underground 'terrorists' have noted. In the name of this City on a Hill. In *my* name. MY NAME. '(Later, Meadlo was seen, head in hands, crying.)' This is how I would like to remember my fourth Vietnam-veteran placard-man. WHO KNOWS. With his Peter Arnett caption. To shit on his head? Or not? In any event, *this* is what Arnett—his source—whoever—calls 'saving the village.' The one thing I have definitely learned on this, my traveling indefinitely in Hades, is that the transit system is huge, gigantic, enormous. But not endless. I presume that the placard-man Michelangelo is parallel to me at this moment, screeching up Central Park West on the B Train, just as I roar through the darkness on this D. If I happened to meet the *man* on the street—if I met him sitting on the stoop of my building at 137 Rivington Street—I would not recognize him. His *image* is indelible, I have met it before, I met it just now, I'll meet it forever. Forever. I am grateful to Mr. Doug Linder for responding to it, perfectly. Life goes on. I feel bad, and bewildered. In the very bowels of Hades, WHAT? What am I 'figuring out'? What am I doing here. I feel like going home. Does the F Train stop at 125th Street? Hell no, from Rockefeller Center it heads for Queens. Never mind. The D, the B, go back down to Grand Street, the madmen, the neon. Just a stroll, such a nice day. They all fall there so perfectly. It all seems so well timed. A decision. What making a decision is and means. What American has not been 'decided for' by the Vietnam War? Which is not just the My Lai atrocity but is *one unremitting atrocity from the first to the last day*. From the very first day until the day our tyranny is defeated. An atrocity. But how many Americans give a shit? The Vietnam veterans do, along with their parents, siblings, wives, children. The placard-men definitely do. That's why they're here. Why are they here? It would be miserable but probably true to say, simply, because they 'give a shit.' A decision? Suddenly, it occurs to me that the placard-men may be the *negation* of decision. Not the undecided, hell no. I mean, the definitively *decided for*. The big losers in a war of images.

125th Street, soul screech. The end of this magnificent screechlessness. It is all one screech, the Screech of the War God, always the same, always different. And now? 'Forward! into the slave's life.'[85] The night journey that ends in shadow. Day, night. Dave Leahy told me about this Greek image of the Sun's 'night journey' through darkness. Day and night *together*, separated and inseparable. A journey through *endless* darkness, but the journey, too, is endless. Everything ends. End ends. The might of the spirit. 'Out of dark, thou, Father

---

85 Last lines of Euripides' *The Trojan Women*, Richard Lattimore's translation.

Helios, leadest,/ but the mind as Ixion, unstill, ever turning.'[86] A fire in the mind. What a beautiful afternoon, up there, in the other world. What other world? Up, down, saved, damned, it's all one, the purgatory is broken. Shattered. Continuous shattering. Heading on up to 145th Street. Headed for the Bronx. In the second part of his article Doug Linder tells the sordid tale of the cover-up that 'began almost as soon as the killing ended,' but that's another story. I have enough on my mind with the massacre, and the placard. The two images, and the placard-*man*. I don't know what to think about this fourth placard-man, except that he's a great painter and has definitely *lived* what he's painted. But what does he think about it? *Yelling* 'Vietnam veteran' is no clue. He could be yelling in pride or in shame, in delight or in anger. Who knows. Some are born to sweet delight, some are born to endless night, as William Blake put it. All I have is his image, my image of his image, and the reality of My Lai somewhere in between. The nightmare of My Lai. What curse was on these people? Did they have a grandfather like Laius, 'ill-advised in love,' or a father like Oedipus, furious about a haunch? I happen to know quite a lot about our Vietnam War helicopters, I study these things. Our military has one hell of a collection, nineteen different types on this list I have here. The 'usual suspects' have made a fortune producing them—Bell, Boeing-Vertol, Kaman, Piasecki, Sikorsky. Lockheed made an abortive attempt with its infamous Cheyenne gunship helicopter. Transport helicopters for troops and equipment, and 'attack helicopters' for machine-gunning and fire-spitting. I'm sure the one on the placard is a HueyCobra ('Huey' is the name of the series, produced by Bell), a sister-Huey is used for spraying Agent Orange. What ugly birds. This flock is called the 'air cavalry'—a curious moniker, since most of them have Indian names. Screech again, 145th Street. The B Train heads for the Cloisters, two more stops, then it comes to the end of its line, but we are going to the

86 Ezra Pound, Canto CXIII.

Bronx. Some of our helicopters do have good red-blooded U.S.-military names like Cobra, Sea Knight, Raven, Huskie, Seasprite, Hound, and Jolly Green Giant, but what about these others, they're all Indian tribes. A perilous frontier. Let me see—Chinook, Cheyenne, Sioux, Kiowa, Iroquois, Cayuse, Shawnee, Mojave, Chickasaw, Choctaw. U.S. helicopters in the Vietnam War. Air cavalry. Our military can't even tell the cowboys from the Indians! And not a single helicopter named after the Pequot, to give thanks for their extinction. I guess because even speaking their name is prohibited, apart from Ahab's ship. Just think of the poetic justice: a Pequot attack helicopter spewing smoke and fire down onto the village of My Lai, contributing to the massacre. Magnificent. A new extinction in the name of an extinct people. Even speaking their name is prohibited. *Screech*, 155th Street, last stop in Manhattan before the D goes under the Harlem River to the Bronx. A historic stop, the Polo Grounds where the New York Giants played until they moved to San Francisco in 1958—played baseball of course, not polo. What a funny name. There's a story here, which I happen to know. There were three different stadiums in Upper Manhattan called the Polo Grounds—no, not all at the same time. It's like with Madison Square Garden, they tear one down and build another one a few blocks away, all with the same name. What's in a name. Now, the original Polo Grounds was built in 1876 for the sport of polo, as the name does in fact suggest. The last was torn down in 1964. When will I ever see daylight again. Manhattan Bridge. Again. Well timed. What time is it? Afternoon. There aren't many people in the car. *Screech*. Cheer up. First stop in the Bronx, 161st Street/Yankee Stadium. The House that Ruth built, they'll never tear this one down.[87] So many great memories. No game today. Mickey

---

87 Torn down in 2009. Yankee Stadium redux was built one block north. Everything ends. Identity of opposites. By the way, they say the new one is the most expensive stadium ever built (Babe Ruth was happy with hot dogs), and with the highest ticket prices. Gentrification. Five star hotels and superchic eateries on Rivington Street, ye ye ye ye gods, I kid you not (as Jack Paar put it, long ago). Stab stab stab. Fun City. A parade. A far cry from the old Bleachers—infinitely-long wooden benches, no

Mantle retired four years ago. Hot dogs. Take your shirt off in the sun. Chill out. I'll never forget that image on the placard, it was *alive*. It hit me right in the face—Typhon on the shield. The fourth shield, the fourth gate, Hippomedon, the fourth challenger—wait, I like Vellacott's translation, but, also Grene's. The spy's clear report to Eteocles: 'The fourth... takes his station with a shout, Hippomedon's vast frame and giant form. Believe me, when I saw his great round threshing-floor of a shield, and watched him spin it, I shook. It was no shoddy workman who bestowed such craftsmanship upon his shield. The emblem shows Typhon, *his mouth with fiery breath belching black smoke that glitters, almost flame....*' Literally, 'black smoke that glitters, *brother of fire*'—Grene has 'hurling from his fiery mouth black smoke, the flickering sister of fire.' This is the most vivid *image* in the entire *Septem*. It may be untranslatable, but it is definitely inescapable. I know that the people of My Lai didn't think of this Typhon-image when they saw the Cobra attack helicopter spewing smoke mixed with fire, and I doubt whether the placard-man thought of these lines from Aeschylus when he painted his image—but, who knows. I'll never know. But I did, I thought immediately about these lines from the *Septem*. *Screech*, 167th Street. Six blocks and a new screech. This is unknown territory for me, post-Yankee-Stadium Bronx, I feel like a pioneer, where's my covered wagon. This Hadean darkness is so deep I can't see my hand in front of my face, as it were. Apart from Yankee Stadium I don't know shit about the Bronx. Apart from the Bronx Zoo, I went a few times, with my parents, a long time ago. I *love* zoos and this is a great one. But that's it. From my subway studies I know that the D goes to 205th Street—if I'm not mistaken, the IRT has trains all the way up to 241st Street. The Bronx is a big place. *Screech*, 170th Street. These 'Bronxites' must be kidding. (What in the world are they called? I think I just made

---

numbered seats, the ticket cost about as much as the round-trip subway fare, and you could chat with the relief pitchers in the bullpens.

this up, maybe not, anyway I've never heard of the word 'Bronxite' but, what do I know.) Subway stops every three blocks, shit, can't these people walk. This may turn out to be a screecher paradise. Cries of the War God, ye gods I hope not. How am I supposed to read the *Septem* and the Notes and figure out what it means to make a decision with a screech every two minutes. It's true, there are a lot on the West End Line, but at least those screeches are 'elevated'—I mean, in the light of day (or night). *Screech*, 174th Street. The Bronxites are toying with me. Now, wait—the heart/soul of Benardete's *second* Note is his noting that this vivid, this *living* image of Typhon on the fourth shield is the heart/soul of the entire *Septem*. The crucial moment. The tipping point. In a *very complicated way*, which I am traveling indefinitely to *see*, it is what 'decides' Eteocles' fate, when he chooses a champion with the *image of Zeus* on his shield to Defend the City! against Hippomedon and *his* shield with the *image of Typhon*. ('Seals' his fate, we say, but I want to say 'decides' his fate. Never mind trained seals.) Believe you me, I'll come back to this. Typhon, the Father of All Monsters. To say nothing of his wife, Echidna (what an improbable name), the Mother of All Monsters. Wait, I mean Monsters in the ambit of Ancient Greece, we've had ten thousand Monsters since, and I doubt whether Typhon and Echidna (what a name!) were their parents. Now—*screech*, Tremont Avenue, OK, I see you, but you can't be more than three or four blocks from 174th Street. Are they all cripples in the Bronx? I never imagined such a thing when I went up to Yankee Stadium. Why do they need a station every four blocks? Are they *long* blocks? But they screech every two minutes. OK, I'll get used to it, I'm still shaken by the placard-man Michelangelo. And his image. I know a lot about Typhon, I've studied him because he's so important in the *Septem*, as Benardete notes, and as I can see for myself. His name comes from the Greek verb 'to make smoke, fume, singe, burn slowly.' One 'source' describes him as the largest and most fearsome of all creatures. His human upper half reaches as high as the stars, and his hands reach the Far East and Far West. From Mao Tse-tung to John Wayne. He has a hundred dragon heads—though other 'sources' say he has a human head, with dragon heads for his fingers. *Screech* ye gods, it's 182nd Street. His bottom half consists of gigantic viper coils that constantly make a hissing noise but, at any rate, not a screech. His whole body is covered in wings and his eyes flash terrible fire. To say nothing of his mouth, or, possibly, hundred mouths. Shit, that's heavy fire. With his incredibly-named wife, Echidna, Mother of All Monsters, he fathered a big and monstrous family. *Screech*, Fordham Road. Two minutes. Many of his children are famous. If they were around today they'd all have their own TV shows. Just to name a few of these monsters—*the Sphinx*, in person. Flesh and blood riddles. The Nemean Lion, no joke of a feline. Heracles had quite a time with him. And Cerberus, the three-headed dog, guarding the way to Hades. (No, he was *not* a three-headed turnstile.) Knightsbridge Road, never mind the *screech*. The Lernaean Hydra with her bad infinity of bad breaths was his daughter. His last child was his daughter Chimera—as good as gold, no contradiction intended. Believe you me, she was the 'direct reverse' of a chimera. A fire-breathing lioness with a goat's head emerging from the middle of her back and a snake for a tail, bringing destruction and bad omens. *Screech*, Bedford Park Boulevard, but it's only two minutes from Knightsbridge Road. Where have all the flowers gone. When will it ever end. Where's the zoo! My fate for a seal! But, wife and children aside (and, I wonder, is his black smoke the brother or the sister of fire?), what's crucially important for the *Septem* is his famous, earthshaking, sky-splitting battle with Zeus. Now, for a change, we have a variety of versions—a number of 'sources.' *Screeeeech*, 205th Street. Stop. End of the

197

line. These screeches have been drilling holes in my brain. All one screech, but, so many, coming at me so fast. In the dark. Let me out of this cage, I'm rattled. Not much of a station here. Just another D on the other track waiting for me with open arms, ready to *screech* away again. Look! a Subway Map. Let me see—quite right, an outrageous number of stations in such a short stretch. Wait, what's this? 'Grand Concourse'—I've heard of this, I've just been under the Grand Concourse. I wonder what it's like, I don't have the slightest idea. A majestic name. It might be the Bronx equivalent of Central Park West without a Park, or 5th Avenue. That could be why it has so many stations, even more than Central Park West. But not many people on the train on this beautiful spring-like Saturday afternoon, end of March, 1972. Maybe because there's no Park up there. Maybe because the Bronxites have gone to the Zoo, or to the famous Botanical Gardens, or taken the IRT to Van Courtland Park, a huge park, right next to Woodlawn Cemetery, I've heard of it, it's huge. Might be a nice afternoon for visiting a tomb, with a stroll down the Grand Concourse later. What do I know. The downtown D ready for takeoff. The car I'm in is *empty*. First time in my life in an empty car. Off we go. The D— what a strange train. In the Bronx a stop every four blocks under the Grand Concourse, and then not a single stop from 125th to 59th, downtownwards-speaking. What a contradiction. Ends end. End ends. The might of the spirit. OK, I'm going to try to *ignore* the screeches until I get to Yankee Stadium. Totally ignore them. Concentrate on this very important battle between Typhon and Zeus. Just imagine a placard-man on the D under the Grand Concourse or getting on the D at 125th heading downtown or at 59th heading up. Extreme sports, no! unstopping stops, stopless stops, no! these men like to keep moving, in, out, in, out, a Penny for the Old Guy or some such. Keep the extremes together—this is the placard-man. Hegel made the point of this point, when he said, as I recall it: 'I am the struggle between the extremes of finitude and infinity. I am not one of the fighters locked in battle, but both, and I am the struggle itself. I am fire and water.' In the mind. Spirit. But, after the My Lai placard-man Michelangelo I have the feeling that I've seen the last of the placard-men. Michelangelo is a hard act to follow. Then again, in the history of art Michelangelo was an end, but he was also a beginning.

THE FIFTH GATE

Pseudo-Apollodorus, in his version,[88] relates how Typhon attempts to destroy Zeus at the will of Gaia, because Zeus imprisoned the Titans. Typhon overcomes Zeus in their first battle and tears out his sinews, which Hermes recovers and restores to Zeus, who then finally gets the better of Typhon, trapping him underneath Mount Etna, in Sicily, near Catania, not too far from Taormina. In another version, Typhon is destroying cities and hurling mountains in a fit of rage. The Father of all Monsters. *Screech*. Apart from Zeus, Dionysus, and Athena, all the gods of Olympus flee to Egypt, where they hide by taking the forms of various animals. When Athena accuses Zeus of cowardice he regains his courage and attacks the monster. A furious battle. Ferocious. No-holds-barred. Unimaginably furious. Which ends when Zeus hurls *one hundred lightning bolts* (just imagine) on top of Typhon, trapping him. What fury! What a battle. But then we have Hesiod's version, and Hesiod was a heavyweight in the Greek world, the hardest hitter after Homer. He describes Typhon as a vast grisly monster with a hundred serpent heads 'with dark flickering tongues' flashing fire from their eyes and a din of voices and a hundred serpents for legs. Terrifying. Then again, for the people of My Lai a HueyCobra was no joke. His struggle

---

88 My own source for these descriptions is the Wikipedia entry *Typhon*.

with Zeus creates earthquakes and tsunami. But, in the end, Typhon is no match for the thunderbolts of the God of all the gods, who casts him into Tartarus, the prison of Titans, the Abyss. *Screech*. Tartarus is *as far below Hades as the earth is below the heavens.* Ye gods, that's deep. He'd have been far better off under Mount Etna, or in the Hole under the World Trade Center. Now, what's my point here? Well, I've been thinking a great deal about the Greek gods these past few months, and about so-called 'pagan' gods in general. In spite of the mythology, many people consider the Greek gods to be simpletons. Crude. Boorish. Unsophisticated. Ignorant. Uncouth. Banal. Ye gods, banal! Or, at best, 'primal forces' (more or less like 'primal screams') with names but no faces. In short: pasteboard masks! Well, just tell Typhon he's a pasteboard mask. Look Zeus in the face and say: Pasteboard mask. It's a free country. But what a pack of lies. No no no, these are *gods*, each with his—or her—own face and character, body and soul, struggle and personality, strength and weakness. They are *gods* because they are absolutely *specific*, not 'forces of nature' in some general sense. *Screech*. The great—the immortal—Walter Otto, in his book *Dionysus. Myth and Cult*, wrote—I quote this from memory—that the road to the gods never starts from 'powers,' whether we call them 'magical' or dress them up in theological terminology.[89] No life proceeds from a concept. 'The gods are there'—Otto's polemic with Wilamowitz—means that they are *living beings*, not capabilities or powers. I've been talking about all this lately with my Greek professors, driving some of them crazy. With Dave Leahy, of course, with Benardete (who doesn't have much to say on the subject), but most of all with Bluma Trell, her wrinkles as ancient as her Greek. She and her husband Max believe in the Greek gods or, at any rate, take them very seriously. Let's say, they have *experienced* them. Her husband

---

89 *Dionysus. Myth and Cult,* Bloomington: Indiana University Press, 1965, pp. 12–16. An immortal book. I still have—and read—my NYU copy.

wrote a novel about them last year, *The Small Gods & Mr. Barnum*, in which they are small but extremely vivid and very much alive. Bluma is a renowned expert on ancient coins. Numismatics. In her long and very active life she's spent a lot of time in Greece, and in Turkey at the Temple of Artemis at Ephesus. I've only been to Greece once in my short life, two summers ago, and the first god I experienced, immediately, was Ares. *Screech*. The air full of a new, a contemporary Ares. The Colonels, the Fascists, all those jeeps rolling through the streets all the time, day and night, the 'special' police. A fire in the mind. In Athens, in Argos, in the dusty town of Thebes. The Silence. The Tyranny. Still, Bluma was right, Greece was full of gods. I looked very closely at the things she suggested I look *closely* at. Long and hard. The Sky, the Sea, the Earth. She says that if you look closely, long and hard, at the Greek sea, the *póntos,* the *thálassa*, you will see Poseidon. You will see him. *Him*, personally, not just a primal force, a power, a concept. You may have to look for quite a while, she told me, but the Ancient Greeks had all the time in the world, *it was their time*. I hiked up Mount Olympus that summer, I looked at the sky—the *ouranós*—clear, pure, blue as Billy's 'welkin eyes.' Unbounded, infinite—Zeus, God of all the gods. *Screech*. Look! The world as the *will* of Zeus. I imagined a thunderstorm (it was August and very dry)—rain, lightning, thunder, lashing the earth, lashing Zeus' temple at Olympia, lashing the Acropolis in Athens, *crash, clap, bam*. I see the thunderbolts flashing out of the sky. Then, on Olympus, I looked at the sky again, long and hard, from dawn to dusk—the cloudless sky, bright, blue, pure, limpid, *absolutely empty*, and *here it is*—Zeus! Zeus! The will of Zeus! The lightning flashes down out of nowhere. The bolt. *Screech*. Zeus! Zeus! I see you depicted with the thunderbolt in your hand, but no one has ever seen you hurl it. Now it is in your hand, now it is flashing across your sky. *Now*, not later, *now* it strikes the Greek earth, *gaîa*, Gaia, the Great Mother, who gave birth to the Earth and to all the Universe. Myth. This is serious business. People have actually experienced this. The Native Americans had an immense experience that we—alas—fail to dream of and will never have ourselves, and we exterminated them. Miserable pagan redskins. What's my point? *I have one*, I'm getting there. Typhon and Zeus, Eteocles' decision, what a decision is and what making a decision means. *Screech*. The *Septem* and—watch out—'the realm of shadows,' I still have Hegel in my bag and he's coming out again soon, before I give up the ghost and get off the train forever. The last dance. The Indian Ghost Dance. Chief Seattle, wow, he gives me the shivers, why don't people in this country read his speech instead of carving turkeys.[90] 'When the green hills are covered with talking wires and the wolves no longer sing, what good will the money you paid for our land be then.' 'Man did not weave the web of life, he is merely a strand in it. Whatever he does to the web, he does to himself.' Meanwhile, I still have two months to finish this big paper I'm writing—Bluma, Dave, help me, encourage me. It's an ambitious, complex paper. The title is: 'The Division of the Soul in Ancient Greek Religion and in the Ashanti Religion of West Africa.' My mouthful. I took an anthropology course, and read a bunch of books on the Ashanti. What an incredible culture. And people know practically nothing, or less than nothing, about it—far less than they know about Native American culture, which is next to nothing. In the paper I show how the 'soul' is composed of three parts in both religions, but never mind that now. The point is, I've been thinking about the question, What is a Greek god? Be he Zeus or Typhon. *Screech*. Believe it or not, the car is filling up, where are we—167th Street already. I've been ignoring the screeches for once, I set my mind to ignoring

90 The many 'versions' of the Chief's speech (or possibly letter) in Seattle in 1854 (the city of Seattle was later named after him) reminds me of the many Greek 'sources' I refer to in the text. My favorite version is *Brother Eagle, Sister Sky*, with paintings by Susan Jeffers. Since the end of March, 1972, a lot of people have in fact been reading this marvelous document.

them and I've been ignoring them. If I hadn't ignored them I couldn't have gotten a word in edgewise. But where have these people come from? Where are they going? Never you mind. I don't have the slightest idea what time it is, I'm totally losing track, the placard-man Michelangelo and the My Lai image kicked time right out of me, not that it ever mattered, no, I'm traveling *indefinitely*. I'm on Hades time, period. Anyway, it must still be afternoon, Saturday afternoon, *end of March, 1972*—I keep repeating this to myself, like a soldier missing in action clinging to what he's missed. I guess I'm a little like Zuikan the Zen master in that story the Roshi likes to tell.[91] He always used to call out his own name. 'Zuikan?' he would call. And then he would answer. 'Yes!' Zuikan? Yes! Of course he was living all alone in his small zendo, and of course he knew who he was, but sometimes he lost himself. And whenever he lost himself, he would address himself. Zuikan? Yes! It's a famous *koan*. Now, Zeus, god of the *will* and of the *thunderbolt*—out of a clear blue sky. Just do it. Bluma told me, before my trip to Greece, look closely, long and hard, at the *Greek* sea, *you*—meaning *me*—will see Poseidon. She has a lot of faith in me, but it's not entirely misplaced. *Screech*—Hello again Yankee Stadium. First, AND LAST, stop in the Bronx, depending, of course, on whether you're coming or going (from or to Manhattan). After this gauntlet of screeches under the Grand Concourse I'm ready to *dive right into* the Harlem River. Baseball and Ballantine. Purity, body, and flavor. I have to tell you, Yankee Stadium, I don't know whether I'll be seeing you again today. From you to the end of your line, and back, I'm sorry to say that there's an *unbearable inferno of screeches*. Grand Concourse, whatever it may be. I know a lot more abut Zeus than I do about the Grand Concourse. OK, Hades is Hades—the sunless dead, this joyless region, as Ezra Pound put it, but this stretch under the Grand Concourse is what they call 'cruel and unusual punishment.' Even an NYU student

91 *Zen Mind*, p. 81.

graduating in two months, traveling indefinitely, asking what a decision is, what making a decision means and, at this point—possibly—actually *making a decision*, has rights. I raise my hands and spread out all my fingers! as Joseph K. put it. (At THE BITTER END of his trial, when it was definitely too late.) No, not 'possibly'—'necessarily.' Freely? How free? Absolutely necessarily free? I suppose I'm under the Harlem River right now. So much the better. Strangely enough, quite a few people got onto the train—into the car—under Yankee Stadium. The car is pretty full. What time is it—is it still afternoon—what do I know. Logic tells me that these are not tourists but Bronxites headed for Manhattan for a fun evening. It's Saturday, if I remember correctly. Great day for taxi drivers. Or, vice versa, Manhattanites headed home after a fun afternoon in the Bronx? At the zoo? At the cemetery? Place your bets on Brooklynites in the Bronx going home to Brooklyn, a genuine long shot. Get rich quick. What a far cry from what this D Train is like after a Yankees game. Can you imagine. What a crowd. How do they do it? OK, 'special trains.' (NO reference here to Nazi Germany or to the Greek 'special police' and their jeeps.) But there are lots—and I mean LOTS—of people headed downtown after a game and, after all, even the 'special trains' are just more of the same old Ds. People headed, for example, to the Port Authority Bus Terminal, Jerseyites, who came by bus through the Lincoln Tunnel with the note penciled on their arms, 'A to 59th Street, D to Yankee Stadium.' *Screech* again, 155th Street. And vice versa. In 1960, third game of the World Series, 'official attendance' (unrelated to Oedipus' 'cruel tendance') 70,001 spectators, my friend and neighbor, when I see him, always tells me, 'you were the 1.' We won 10–0 but lost the Series in 7 games, fucking Pirates. Spoilsports. Anyway, I'm back under Manhattan. This Grand Concourse screechiness has been a strange, and distracting, experience. I should have focused more on the placard-man Michelangelo, with his fantastic overwhelming image, but this journey is relentless, the subway never stops. Never starts, as it were, and never stops. A zillion stops. Never stops. Did the *subway itself* ever start? It must have. On X day of X year, the *very first* subway trip. Wright Brothers, Kitty Hawk. Or did it actually start with 'being is nothing'—with the *decision* to consider thinking as such. Quite possibly. Unlikely. Likely. Freely? Being is nothing, it's the logic of being is nothing. Ends end, where shadows end. I wonder how many placard-men there are— hundreds, thousands, zillions? But, I will be stopping pretty soon. The end ends. Everything ends. Perhaps only the four I've seen, that's what I think. In any event, traveling indefinitely doesn't mean traveling *forever*, not on your life. Not on my life. I am here for a reason, I have a fucking *raison d'être*, as the French put it, pardon my French. Whether I will, in the end, be fucked by my *raison d'être* is another matter, who knows, *screech*, 145th Street. What do the placard-men have to do with it. To do with my *raison d'être*. Something? Nothing? All I intended was to spend a day or two on the subway, to think *seriously* about my decision, a decision, what 'decision' means, HEGEL, decisions in *Billy Budd*, Eteocles' decision, Benardete's Notes on Eteocles' decision, and the more the merrier. God bless you all. (A miniscule inside-narrative joke.) Inshallah. No joke about Absolute Power is a joke, not in the fucking least. God Bless America. Ask the redskins, ask the gooks. I wonder how the Ashanti are doing. Watch out. 'I wish y'all nigger women and children a good morning, how'r y'all doin' today?' HueyCobra. Soul screech, 125th Street, God bless you all. Eat shit, motherfuckers. Give me a break. I'm tired. A monumental screechless stretch. Did I have an apple lately or not? Now *this* is a question. Which I cannot answer, I have to look. I still have three apples, hallelujah, in no sense of the word. I haven't been eating shit. I need a serious statistician. IF I remember correctly, I started out with four apples, and a piece of cheese (which I did eat, eventually). I did actually eat one apple, possibly in Brooklyn. (Possibly. We enter the realm of possibility.) I now—actually, definitely, unquestionably, factually—have three apples. I am screechless for 66 blocks. I am going to eat an apple. Not because I'm hungry. Not at all to appease my hunger—fuck and forget Knut Hamsun, who regularly munched on woodchips, on shavings, on stones, on slivers, chewed on a pocket of his coat, and finally bit his own finger. Who after two days without his sandwiches was ravaged by 'fiercely raging pain.' No, my friends, this is Fun City, we don't get that hungry so easily. Hell no. I'm not hungry at all. I am willing to risk *awakening* my hunger by munching on this apple, slowly, screechlessly, from 125th Street to 59th Street. I shall calmly munch. The will of Zeus. Not a screech. Tiny bites. Munch munch. Thinking about Dogen-zenji, Suzuki-roshi's true master.[92] The Dharma Eye, which sees the reality of Buddha—reality as emptiness, free from any dualistic frame of mind. The Dharma Eye not only *penetrates* the true reality of all things but also *discriminates* all things. Hunger. Dogen-zenji once recited this little poem, about 700 years ago:

When hunger comes, have rice.
When fatigue comes, sleep.
Furnace and bellows, each covers the entire sky.

---

92 Eihei Dogen (1200–1253), born in Kyoto, after traveling in China founded the Soto school of Zen in Japan. An incredible person and an absolute genius—monk, philosopher, poet—he wrote an enormous book in ninety-five fascicles, *Shobogenzo*, translated as *Treasury of the True Dharma Eye*. The 'hunger' quote is from the marvelous book *Moon in a Dewdrop: Writings of Master Dogen*, multiple translators, edited by Kazuaki Tanahashi, New York: North Point Press, 1985, p. 126. Dogen uses the image of a dewdrop reflecting moonlight to describe the state of meditation: just as the entire moon is reflected in a dewdrop, a complete awakening of truth can be experienced by the individual human being. Most importantly, Dogen teaches that zazen is not a method by which one *attains* enlightenment, but *is itself* enlightenment. Suzuki-roshi emphasizes, repeatedly, that 'our practice should be without gaining ideas, without any expectations. [...] When you do something, just to do it should be your purpose.' (*Zen Mind*, pp. 41 and 43). I am making a big effort not to talk too much about Dogen in this book: believe me, if I start I'll never stop.

208

I know his commentary by heart:

> 'When hunger comes' is the vital activity of a person who
> has had rice. A person who has not had rice cannot have
> hunger. Since this is so, a person who gets hungry every
> day is someone who has had rice. You should understand
> this completely.

Dogen, the Roshi's Zenji. Thinking about the Ashanti. This
year I've been reading fantastic things about them. I found a
whole book of Ashanti proverbs, written in the 1920s by Robert
Sutherland Rattray. My great favorite is 'no one shows a child
the sky.' (Commentary: because they see it for themselves.)
But this is extraordinary. It says everything all at once—
everything about religion, culture, *human* reality, the reality
of all sentient beings. I do not like monotheistic religions, in
the least. Judaism, Christianity, Islam—not in the least. Full
of showing, telling, power, command, authority. Showing you
the sky all the time. I like 'no one shows a child the sky.' I
like Zen Buddhism, absolutely. I like the Greeks, the Native
Americans, the Ashanti, because they know—what? That we
create the gods, that we are the gods? No, that *we see the
gods*—or, more exactly, that *the gods are what we see, if we
look*. Which *we power people* never do. 'To see a fish you must
watch the water.' Just ask our own natives, ask the Pequot. I
read about an Ashanti 'religious ceremony' that you won't find
in any synagogue, church, or mosque. They do it when there's
a violent thunderstorm approaching their village—no, this has
nothing to do with the solitary G.I. on the placard, approaching
the village, the 'I wish y'all gook women and children a good
morning' G.I. No. At the first sign of the storm all the people of
the village go to the top of a high hill or mountain. A number
of them—five I think—have big drums, and each time thunder
claps and rumbles in the distance they *respond* with a clapping

rumbling beat on their drums. Zeus! Zeus! No, no name at all, *but the god is there.* 'Watch the water.' The anthropologist who witnessed this wrote that the effect is incredibly spiritual, awe-inspiring, *sublime.* This is their religious practice and experience. Pretty simple? Primitive savages? Worshipping precisely the 'primal forces' I spoke out *against* a moment ago? Raw power? Well, 'power' cuts two ways, it's a double-edged sword. The Ashanti also have an exquisitely articulated conception of a three-part soul, similar in some ways to the Greek conception. But the more I think about it I find the Ashanti soul more immediate, less contrived, and more profound. Less 'intellectual,' Hegel would say, but by no means less complex. If this soul is their exquisitely painted placard, we'd have to say that, like the placard-man Michelangelo, they have truly *lived* the image. I'm working on this paper now, it's very complicated. Traveling indefinitely. A decision. *The gods are there.* They love, hate, shake the earth, get drunk. They fight. Zeus and Typhon. Out of the blue—the bright, pure, absolutely empty sky—Zeus with his thunderbolt defeated the Father of All Monsters, whose upper half reaches as high as the stars. It wasn't easy. Myth. Junk religion. The pagans that all the monotheists, from Moses to Muhammad, have railed against. But they have so much to teach us. Look! A bolt from the blue can slay the greatest of monsters. 'No one shows a child the sky.'

   Screeeech after long silence. 59th Street/Columbus Circle. I cling to my book bag and leap out of the car. No-mind. Just do it. D Train, *finito.* Apart from Yankee Stadium I don't think I could ever come to love this Train. Exaggeration, contradiction, nonsense. Too many screeches in the Bronx and too few in Manhattan. And then there's Brooklyn. I asked Dave Leahy about this because the D is his train—Newkirk Avenue to West 4th and vice versa.[93] The D does strange complicated things

93 OK, sue me, I've twisted myself into a tangle with these subway lines—the history of the F, D, B *over the past 45 years.* The ever-changing history. It's all change. The

in Brooklyn. It's not beautifully elevated like the F and the B, it's only elevated on the very last stretch—Sheepshead Bay, Brighton Beach, Coney Island. From Prospect Park to south of Newkirk Avenue the line is 'open cut,' which means below ground but open to the air. Goddam scenic. After that, as far as Sheepshead Bay, it is 'embanked,' as in 'embankment,' whatever that means in this case. Well, do you know what I think? I think, Who needs this shit. I'm going back to the B, and the F, and I intend to stick with them until the end of this indefinite traveling. It's a free country, a free city, Fun City! Defend the City! Bring the war home. So, here I am under Columbus Circle, which is *thronged*. So be it. I think it's getting late in the afternoon. Saturday afternoon. Never fear. I'm heading for the B. I may not get a seat, but, I wasn't born yesterday. When it rains I get the F at West 4th and the train is *packed*, I only have to go three stops, but I have developed my technique for *trying* to get a seat anyway. I don't always succeed, but, I'm a good sport about it. Anyway, if I don't get a seat at West 4th you can bet your life that I won't get one at Broadway-Lafayette or 2nd Avenue. No one's getting off there, they're all going to Brooklyn. BUT a lot of people get OFF at West 4th—a lot off and a lot on. Off and on. 59th is similar. Here I am, I'm waiting for the next B, what a crowd. The first thing is to wriggle myself through—very innocently—to the edge of the platform. Now, *I'm ready. Most* everyone else is just daydreaming, especially the tourists, thinking about what they're going to be doing in midtown, in the Village. But I am totally focused and concentrated. If I don't make it, if I don't get a seat, fuck it, no big deal, but I'm going to give it the old college try. After all, I'm still an NYU student. Here comes the B. Technique. Concentration. The doors open

---

lines shift, twist, tangle. When I asked Dave *not so long ago*—but, an eternity ago—about his stop, where did I stop to see him back in 1986 or '87, he told me East 18th Street, Midwood Park. Good, take the D to Newkirk Avenue. The D? Sounds good, if I got it straight; and today it is, perhaps, the B. Or the F? No, that's 18th *Avenue*, not East 18th *Street.* Never mind. The Transit System.

and a *zillion* people get off, colliding with the people waiting
to get on, now, wriggle wriggle—and I was lucky, the door
opened *right in front of me*, an overwhelming advantage in this
sport—off—ON, I'm on and I dash—innocently—to a vacant
seat. Great. I did it. Life is beautiful. Now I can get back to
Benardete's *first* Note. I take it out of my bag. I couldn't do
this hanging from a strap or clinging to a pole. The car is *jam*-
packed, no, no placard-man could possibly slither into it, with
his *placard*. But I don't think there are any more placard-men
anyway, and the chance of one of those four turning up again
is infinitesimal. The transit system is gigantic. The screeches
are badly infinite, as Hegel would put it, and I only take one
screech at a time, out of zillions. What time is it? Hades time.
When I get to the Manhattan Bridge I'll see for myself. What
about all these people? Well, what about them. That's their
business. Fun seekers. Now's the time: if Benardete's two
Notes on the *Septem*, and the *Septem* itself, and Eteocles'
decision itself, don't help me figure out what a decision is,
what making a decision means, and, what's more, doesn't help
me *actually make a decision*, then my goose will be cooked.
Then again, luckily I still have Hegel in my bag. I don't want
to say 'as a last resort'—no, I practically 'went down to the
ship' with Hegel, the realm of shadows, the *decision* to begin
with *thinking as such*. Shit, Hegel knows a lot more than
Eteocles. A lot more than Benardete, for that matter. It's these
placard-men that distracted me, but I think I've seen the last
of them now. Rockefeller Center, hordes off, hordes on, have
fun. But I definitely haven't seen the last of Hegel, after all,
I have all the time in the world. So to speak. A sea of time,
putting it poetically. Traveling indefinitely, but not *forever*.
Then again, let's give Eteocles, Benardete, and the *Septem*
a fighting chance. This has been my idea all along, and I'm
sticking to it. I hope no strap-hanger loses his or her grip
and falls on me and messes up this Note. Well, I'll take my

chances. If worst comes to worst, better a 'her' than a 'his.'
In any event, as Dave Leahy said, don't confuse 'love' with
that chick splayed all over you in the subway. Now—I want to
finish reading Benardete's *first* Note, the *second* part of the
first Note, on the dual origin of the city. No, no more placard-
men. Who could possibly top the image of the Michelangelo
My Lai man. These placard-men—especially the last of them—
have thrown me completely off track, they've led me by the
nose into the wilderness. With *Billy Budd* I felt I was getting
somewhere in this *strenuous effort* to make a decision, to
discover what a decision is and what making a decision *means*,
because it *definitely means something*. It has to. I have to
get somewhere. Or—show me the path on which there is no
coming and no going. No, not get *somewhere*, just *get it*. Ye
gods, deliver me from all being-is-nothing *Bananas* decisions.
All these screeches, just to discover that from this day forth the
official language of this Banana Republic really will be Swedish.
It's all been *decided for*. No. I can't give up now. Or—just a
second, where's my *Zen Mind*—what about taking both sides at
once. Wait—page 47: 'When you give up, when you no longer
want something, or when you do not try to do anything special,
then you do something. When there is no gaining idea in what
you do, then you do something.' Times Square, have fun.
Benardete! Where was I.

I have to admit it, reading the second part of the first Note
in this jam-packed fun-seeker environment is not going to be
all that easy. Late afternoon, end of March, 1972. Saturday
afternoon. I'll do my best. After West 4th things will quiet
down, relatively, these people don't look to me like they're
going to Brooklyn. Let's see, 'I. The Parodos and the First
Stasimon.' In a nutshell, Benardete tackles three separate
questions, which he manages to *mix up together* in a sort
of philological soup. Which he stirringly stirs. Questions: the
rebuked Chorus; the threefold meaning of Ares and its relation

213

to the Curse; the dual origin of the City—sexual (divine and human) and non-sexual (serpent's tooth)—and its relation to Eteocles' decision. Now, I've pretty much gone to town on the first two questions, I'm ready for the tricky part. Benardete himself, all too innocently, slithers (like a placard-man) into the third question, the second part of the first Note, with this monumentally innocent sentence: 'Something else marks the difference between the parodos and the stasimon, but its import is not easy to discern.' Not easy, but we'll do our darnedest. Herald Square, What—Me Worry? This is the B, not a screech now until West 4th. I'll get back to the F later on. I have to admit it, I like the West End Line and the Cloisters, with its unicorns. (From now on, Yankee Stadium for Yankee games only.) I'm sure that Jamaica end-of-the-line Queens cuts a poor figure compared to Jamaica south of Cuba. Let's get serious. Let's try to see how—as Benardete notes—the 'dual origin of the city' has direct bearing on *what* Eteocles decides and *how* he comes to decide it. Benardete: 'In the parodos but not in the stasimon goddesses are thrice distinguished from gods. Sexual differentiation disappears in the stasimon along with the names of the gods. What prompts the disappearance of sex among the gods might be Eteocles' outburst against women, which is so violent that he divides his subjects into male, female, and the in-between [!]—as though the very walls of the city must obey him, but whose effect is to minimize the differences in gender and embrace everything in the city under a neutral term (something like "the citizen body").' In the first part of the note we saw how the women (possibly virgins) get on Eteocles' nerves (to say the least) with their constant wailing, howling, and flinging themselves at images, until Eteocles wails back, violently, with his 'intolerable creatures' tirade. But now the plot thickens. Let us not forget that Eteocles is not just any old woman-hater. No. He—thanks to his decision to screw his *brother*—is the

King of Thebes. He is about to make a *decisive* decision, which again concerns his *brother*, at the Seventh Gate. He *and* his *brother* have been cursed by their *father*. Who, of course, was fucked—figuratively—by *his father*, and who fucked—literally—*his mother*. Now—this is an inkling of Benardete's point—these are all *family matters*, there's no getting around it. And family matters are *sexual* matters, there's no getting around that either. Generation. Human sexual generation. In the family way, so to speak. And what does Eteocles do? Eteocles *King of Thebes*. He tries to get around it. *Screech*, West 4th. You see! A lot of people getting off and not that many getting on. This isn't the time to go to Brooklyn, hell no, it's not the rush hour, this is Saturday, it's time for fun in the Village or in midtown. Eteocles tries to get around it. Sad but true. He wishes that women, family matters, and sexual matters would *all just go away*. Now, let me say this, since I'm right under the West Village. Gay Pride. The gay liberation movement came into its own after the riots at the Stonewall Inn, on Christopher Street, in the summer of 1969. (I was driving a taxi that summer.) It's quite true that if I go to the Stonewall Inn and mention that 'family matters' involve women, the men there might take umbrage. If I mention to a crowd of lesbians that 'family matters' involve men, I think they'll get riled up. *Quite* rightly. But, I'm talking here about sexual *generation*, which, until science finds an alternative, involves *something* male and *something* female— in the case of the founding of Thebes, a male and a female *god*. *Screech*, Broadway-Lafayette. The expression may be old-fashioned, but what I mean is 'getting in the family way.' Laius knows what I mean. So does Oedipus. Everybody knows. Eteocles knows. Birds, bees, even educated fleas know. But, as Benardete notes, he wants to ignore it, to get around it. Why? A damn good question. A story of straight misogyny would make for a pretty poor tragedy. No, Aeschylus was no hack, not by a long shot. A point is being made here, in the *Septem*.

Let's not jump the gun. Benardete: 'Eteocles does not mention the names of major gods in the prayer that he wishes the Chorus to copy, but he subordinates their separate existence to their collective function, the city-protecting gods [Defend the City!] who preside over field and market-place; whereas before the entrance of the Chorus he had appealed to Zeus, Earth, and his father's Curse as well as to the city-protecting gods. Eteocles seems to have suppressed the sexuality of the gods in revulsion against the Chorus' excessive femininity.' If you can call wailing, shrieking, screaming, howling, and flinging themselves at images 'excessive femininity.' So be it. *Screech*, Grand Street. I'm close to the Manhattan Bridge. Sweet delight. Is it day or night? This time my 'night journey' seems endless. A lifetime in Hadean darkness. The light of day. *Now* I understand Achilles' words in the *Odyssey*: Better a slave on earth than lord over all 'the sunless dead and this joyless region.' The light of day. A decision—what a decision is and what it means to make it. I have a decision to make, and I don't want it to be 'arbitrary.' Is Eteocles' decision to go *himself* to the Seventh Gate *arbitrary?* I have to figure this out *now*, at last. Hegel said that the *decision* to consider *thinking as such*— the beginning of his Logic—'may also be regarded as arbitrary.' A no-mind Zen 'decision' is not arbitrary, it is Zen Mind that 'freely releases itself' (Hegel, the end of the Logic) after a 'lifetime' (a minute, a day, a century) of Zen practice. Satori: direct experience. Emptiness. The original emptiness of the mind. The Roshi says: 'What appears from emptiness is true existence. We have to go through the gate of emptiness.'[94] The gateless gate. How does one pass through this gateless gate? Eteocles *did not know*, but perhaps Aeschylus did. Captain Vere didn't, perhaps Melville did. I don't. Do I? The empty mirror. The Dharma Eye penetrates the true reality of all things but

94 *Zen Mind*, p. 110. See also p. 128: 'To have a firm conviction in the original emptiness of your mind is the most important thing in your practice.' And p. 137: 'The purpose of [Zen] practice is to have direct experience of the Buddha nature that everyone has [is].'

also *discriminates* all things. Decides. Get *somewhere?* Just *get it.* No coming and no going. Here. Right now.

The Manhattan Bridge. *Carpe diem.* 'Had we but world enough, and time.' Why in the world should I think of such a line. Andrew Marvell, *To His Coy Mistress.* Definitely not one of Eteocles' favorites. Or mine. What splendor. The light! The river! On Hades time, and such splendor. The dear light. What a beautiful time of day. I can't see the face of Father Helios, hidden by Manhattan, but his light is gleaming. And not for too much longer. These are not the short short days of December, but at the end of March, 1972, Saturday evening, the days are not long. 'A patch of discolored snow in early April lingering at some upland cave's black mouth.' But I see everything. The river. To my right the Brooklyn Bridge. To my left, uptown, the Williamsburg Bridge already more a glimmer than a gleam. The subway has vanished. I look outwards and totally forget where I am. What I am. Inside narrative, outside narrative. A decision to be made, traveling indefinitely. The B Train, already on the very last iota of the Manhattan Bridge, over the East River. But in Brooklyn they should call it the *West* River. West of Brooklyn and Queens. See what I mean. 'To go east one mile is to go west one mile,' Dogen-zenji said. It's a serious matter. You go to Washington Heights, end of the line, and start again— downtown. Why downtown? Because it's north to south? Bull shit. Just look at the East/West River, or look at the Manhattan/ Brooklyn Bridge[s]—just names. As arbitrary as they come. As I noted quite a while ago, Is Vietnam east or west of here? Uptown/downtown is, definitely, a question of arbitrary will. But I think it's preeminently a question of *power*—of someone-who-is-no-one *deciding* DOWNtown/UPtown. Somebody/nobody, I think, in a Shining City on a Hill. A question of our being *decided for.* Power. Authority. I don't know what Eteocles-cum-Benardete will give me, but Melville was definitely not a waste of time, on this indefinite journey. It's the placard-men who have created so much confusion. Hades, darkness again, sweet delight, it's OK, I know the score now. A long stretch to Pacific Street—that Billy-Budd-Michael-Kohlhass-reading chick. Near the Navy Yard. Nice place. No, that was York Street, on the F, I'm getting confused. Then another long stretch to 36th Street. *Then*, the West End Line. Elevated, but, before too long, enveloped in night. But elevated. A night journey *in*, not *under*, the night. I will be finishing Benardete's first Note and reading the second: 'II. Eteocles' Interpretations of the Shields.' What more can I do. Hegel. Or, just fuck it and get off the train. Go home. At least we don't have placard-men on Rivington Street. We have PLENTY on Rivington Street, but no placard-men. Now, Benardete, revulsion against the Chorus' excessive femininity. But the women are not so dumb. Later on, at *the* crucial moment, when the spy reports that his *brother*, Polyneices, is at the Seventh Gate, they give Eteocles good advice. They tell him: Do not go *yourself* to the Seventh Gate, send someone else, change the order of the defenders, you can go to some other gate. The *women* know what *bloodguilt* is, what *Pollution of the City* means. They speak out. Virgins or (very possibly) not, they know what sex is—they know what sexual *generation* is and means. But Eteocles doesn't listen, he caves in to the Curse. Fuck the family. As Benardete notes, 'By disregarding women at the beginning, Eteocles cannot listen to them at the end. The Chorus, whom he had addressed as "intolerable creatures," are addressed after his death as "mother's darlings."' *Screech*, Pacific Street. Benardete: 'If we now go back to examine the gods the Chorus names in the parodos, we find that there are as many female as male: Athena, Aphrodite, Artemis, and Hera; Zeus, Poseidon, Ares, and Apollo. Aphrodite and Ares are the parents of Harmonia, who as Cadmus' wife founded with him the present generation of Thebans. But Aphrodite and Ares are only one source, the serpent's teeth that Cadmus sowed are another. Thebes, then, has a sexual (divine and human) and a non-sexual (sub-human) root, and according to Eteocles it is the latter in which the city must especially put its trust. The first and third Theban defenders are Spartoi, and of the first Eteocles says that "consanguine justice" impels him to defend the "mother who gave him birth." Every able Theban is to aid "mother earth, their dearest nurse," who nurtured the inhabitants to be reliable soldiers in time of need. Eteocles presents the earth as the sole progenitor of the Thebans, regardless of whether their ancestry warrants it or not; for in listing what has to be defended—city, altars of native gods, children, and earth—he does not mention human parents.' I'm elevated again, the West End Line. I was so engrossed in my reading I screeched right through 36th Street without even noticing it. Sunset Park. Aptly named. Absolutely. Now I see you, Father Helios, almost ready to set, sitting there in the sky just above New Jersey. This is south-west Brooklyn, Manhattan is way off to the north, from this spot you look west right out over Upper Bay. A magnificent view. With super eyesight you can even make out the Statue of Liberty. So, the time is twilight—Hades time, twilight. Luckily not yet its last gleaming, what so proudly we hailed, whose broad stripes and bright stars, et cetera. No, it's still a bright gleam. *Screech*, 9th Avenue—it's true, there are *more* screeches on the West End Line than under the Grand Concourse, but the feeling is completely different. The atmosphere is different, the 'quality'—as Hegel, being-and-nothingly, put it—is different. Here *I see the sound*. Where have I heard this before? The Chorus. One of the dubious things they wail in the parodos. They really aren't so dumb. Seeing the sound is much better than just hearing it. Sound is not noise, as the Roshi explains. The *peep-peep-peep* of blue jays on the roof during zazen. Virgins or not, they pray to female gods—no, they don't disdain Aphrodite in their prayers—and know about sexual generation, which Eteocles has adamantly decided to ignore. A bad, a possibly fatal decision. Serious business. He does not even *mention* human parents. Ye gods, just try to imagine a red-blooded apple-pied American politician who doesn't mention the family—God and Family, the American Way. Deadly serious. Eteocles' 'silence about women and human ancestors,' as Benardete puts it. Mother's Day. Apple pie. Turkeys. But let me enjoy the sun sitting over the Jersey horizon, in a second it'll be sitting on Staten Island. With a view like this I don't mind the screeches, the D is good for Yankee Stadium, period. Bathed in the gleam. Too bad it won't last. But then again, what does? Everything ends, ends end, the end ends. Logic. The vanishing of vanishing. Escaping escaping. Still, I think it may gleam as far as Coney Island. Then, on the new B, it will be a gleaming glimmer, and then a glimmer, and finally a dim glimmer. Already in his shroud. 'White jumper and white duck trousers, each more or less soiled, dimly glimmered in the obscure light of the bay.' By the time I get back to the Bridge, I wonder if it will be too dim to be a glimmer at all. And then the 'night journey' twice over—night below and night above. In flashes. The broken purgatory. A continuous shattering. Benardete's first Note, bathed in the light of the dying day. Now—where was I. Silence about women and human ancestors. Benardete: 'Such a silence implies, I think, *an unqualified devotion to the country*... The devotion can remain unqualified because Eteocles has made the "fatherland" into a literal mother, who needs no help in generation from the family. Eteocles understands, in short, the Ares who spared the Spartoi but not the Ares who married Aphrodite... He tries to ignore the family and regard it as a sub-political (and hence insignificant) element in the city; as though he did not know that Laius' sexual passion—his "loving folly" as the Chorus delicately puts it—was the ultimate cause of the present war. Apollo had told Laius to "die without issue and save the city" and Eteocles, in extending autochthony to include all Thebans, glosses over the fatal doubleness of sexual and non-sexual generation with a single origin. In obedience to Apollo, as it were, he tries to save the city "without issue." A patriotism, whether genuine or assumed, blots out that fatal doubleness in the city that he and his family particularly reveal (cf. 753–756).' Benardete refers to these lines, which I myself mentioned earlier: 'But he [Laius] was mastered by loving folly and begot for himself a doom, father-murdering Oedipus, who sowed his mother's sacred womb, whence he had sprung himself, with bloody root, to his heartbreak. Madness was the coupler of this distracted pair.' You bet, a distracted pair, Oedipus and his mother-wife. In short, the Curse—Laius rightly cursed, Oedipus, cursed, and cursing his sons. 'A sin sown long ago,' as the Chorus puts it, and 'now it abides to the third generation.' But it's time to try to get to what Benardete is getting at, if possible before I get to Coney Island. He has a grand strategy in a very short note. Benardete knows Aeschylus better than Aeschylus knows himself. Why does *Aeschylus* give us *this Eteocles*? Who rebukes the Chorus, goes wild on the subject of 'excessive femininity,' rejects the very existence of sexual generation in favor of unqualified serpent-tooth generation, and all this in a tragedy 'full of Ares' in which '*the* question' is 'what is Ares?'— 'Ares in his *dual* aspect,' writes Benardete, who then immediately turns around and lists his *three* aspects. And all this intertwined with THE '*the* question'—namely, the question of freedom and necessity (never mind responsibility) in Eteocles' decision to go *himself* to the Seventh Gate: 'Does Eteocles decide his own fate, or is his fate determined by the curse of Oedipus?' OK, let me put this very very bluntly. My curse is the Vietnam War, which has decisively convinced me that my country is fighting in the defense of tyranny, from the Halls of Montezuma to the shores of Tripoli. So to speak. I mean, not just in Vietnam, not just now, but everywhere,

yesterday, today, and *tomorrow*. 'A sin sown long ago.'
Cristóbal Colón, a Man of the World, Father of all Holocausts.
The Pequot. Hiroshima. My Lai. And *tomorrow*. A decision:
What am I *myself* going to do? Today. Here. Now. A question:
*Am I going to decide my own fate, or am I going to be decided
for by the curse of Vietnam?* THE question. A decision: What is
it? What does it mean to make it? A problem: the two horns of
my dilemma are separate and inseparable, 'as intertwined as
Ares in his dual aspect'—which isn't even 'dual' but is triple.
One hell of a tangle. Eteocles is, in some way, in some sense,
in a similar situation, which is why I am here, in Hades. With
these Notes, and the *Septem*. I've already screeched halfway
down the West End Line—down, up, it's all one, all one Line.
The way up is the way down, as Heraclitus, the 'weeping
philosopher,' put it. I could use a good cry myself. The
purgatory is broken, there's nothing left but the journey. Sweet
delight. In flashes. Now—what's Benardete getting at? I think
he's getting at the question: Why does *Aeschylus* give us *THIS
Eteocles?* This Eteocles—King of Thebes—obsessed with his
Curse while ignoring—rejecting—its origin. Spitting in its face.
'Unqualified devotion to the country' while blotting out the half
of its origin that is the origin of his Curse. Eteocles the blind
patriot—this is what Aeschylus gives us. Self-blinded, just like
his cursed and cursing old man. This women-rebuking Eteocles
with his City 'full of Ares' who willfully ignores Ares *the husband*
of Aphrodite. This is a one-hundred-percent pure-grain serpent-
tooth Eteocles—unqualified devotion, *no duality*, and fatally
entangled in his own self-contradiction. Isn't it a little strange
that Aeschylus gives us an Eteocles totally unconcerned with
his own blatant injustice? He broke his pact with his own
brother. It is Polyneices, at the Seventh Gate, who shrieks
about Justice, putting the goddess Dikê on his shield. I don't
think Eteocles gives a good goddam about Justice—no! Defend
the City! That's what he gives a good goddam about. And yet—

and yet—in some way he is my brother. No, not like Joseph K., truly my brother. No, let's say my half-half-half-brother, because we do have something vitally important in common. Joseph K. is the definitively decided for par excellence. Eteocles and I—let's say, we're still on the field of battle, we're still standing, worms that we are. Cursed. Somewhere *between* freedom and necessity—but, *logically speaking*, there is *nowhere* between them—*we still pretend we're about to make a decision.* This, for me, is the Eteocles that Aeschylus gives us: just the Curse, period, and fuck the 'loving folly,' the haunch, and the injustice. We are the King of Thebes *now*. For me, the *Septem* is about a decision. Right *now*, it's about my own decision. Right *now*, Hades time.

I have to admit it, I'm thinking these things in the middle of the Coney Island station. I got carried away. I ignored the screeches, ignored the people, just sat there in the place I 'innocently' conquered under 59th Street. The glimmering gleam, my delight, my friend. Flashes. Perhaps I just got an inkling of why I am here. Again, again, a new Train—a new B, I'm sticking with the B, let me get it now, before the coming of night, let me back onto the West End Line. The glimmer, then, a dim glimmer, 'dimly glimmered in the obscure light of the bay.' In his shroud. *This* Eteocles. Benardete's point does not fit into a nutshell. For one thing, I am convinced that Benardete is convinced that the *Septem* is *not* about the successful defense of a strongly walled city, twelve years after the Persians had run roughshod over an Athens without walls. The complexity of the play belies this. To be precise, the complexity *Benardete* sees in the play, and which he expresses in the Notes: more obviously, the complexity in Eteocles' interpretation of the shields; much less obviously, the complexity of his 'patriotism'—his unqualified devotion to the City while *willfully blinding himself* to its real origin. Alas, blinding runs in his family. The duality in its origin. *This*

is the Eteocles that Aeschylus writes the *Septem* to give us.
He's making a strong political point. A crucial political point.
Let me make a bold analogy, between the origin of Thebes
and Eteocles' attitude to it and the origin of the United States
of America and 'our' attitude to it. This is bold, but, at this
point, what've I got to lose. Go for broke. Here I go again! The
goddam Puritans, the City on a Hill, the perilous frontier, the
redskins. The Pequot goddamit. For example. But I'll put this
in an infinitesimal nutshell. West End Line, the twilight's last
gleam. We Americans see the origin of our country as a Shining
City on a Hill and willfully blind ourselves to its origin in the
massacre of millions of Native Americans. A Shining City whose
foundations float on an ocean of blood, to which we willfully
blind ourselves. Complete devotion to the City. Dual origin of
the City. Thanksgiving. For once, I won't belabor the point.
Ares—human and divine—serpent's teeth. A tangle. My analogy
may not be exact—among other things it turns Eteocles upside
down, his City on a Hill is under the ground, where Cadmus
sowed it—but I don't think it's far-fetched either. Benardete
considers Aeschylus, among other things, a *political* genius.
Aeschylus has a reason for giving us *this* Eteocles, who rebukes
the Chorus, ignores the sexual (divine and human) root of
his City 'full of Ares' and, in the end, caves in to the Curse
and makes the decision he has been decided for. As far as I,
traveling indefinitely, am concerned, my point is: What can
I learn from my half-half-half brother? About the power of a
Curse. About a 'citizen body' that willfully blinds itself to the
'dual origin' of its City. A 'citizen body' of which I am a member.
Here. Now.

I think the car will be full by the time we get to the
Manhattan Bridge. Plenty of Brooklynites going to Manhattan
for the evening. It really was a magnificent day today,
Saturday, end of March, 1972. I'm not referring to the
Hadean day of course, in Hades there is no day, no rain,

no shine. How long have I been here now? No idea. This 'elevated' stretch of Hades with its illusory glimmer. Let's read Benardete's conclusion. 'Both the Chorus, then, as maidens [Benardete's word, circumventing the distinction between 'virgins' and 'women'] and the goddesses they revere show up the weakness in Eteocles' apparently complete devotion to the city. Although Eteocles might insist on and obtain the Chorus' silence, and though he might stop all mention of the gods as sexual beings—he himself later refers only to the virgin goddesses Artemis, Athena, and Dikê—he cannot at all affect the principle for which they stand. His wish to live apart from the female race is indeed only a wish, and Antigone survives him to split the city exactly where he boldly assumed that it was whole (1069–1071).' Let me quote these lines, at the very end of the play. The Chorus divides in two, one half mourning Polyneices, the other half, Eteocles: 'This grief is common to the race, but now one way and now another the City approves the path of Justice.' No question about it, this is *the* question: WHAT JUSTICE? Benardete concludes: 'Not only perhaps does Eteocles disregard the later pleading of the Chorus to abstain from challenging Polyneices because they are women, but also because he has so equated his own concern with the city's that he has ceased to be aware of his own family. Who else is more just, he asks himself, to stand against Polyneices: "I will go and face him—I myself. Who has more right than I? King against king, and brother against brother, foe against foe we'll fight." The specious symmetry of ruler-brother-foe against ruler-brother-foe blinds him to the difference between ruler and brother, brother and foe. It is a blindness to which the Chorus, in the presence of male and female images of the gods who form the family of Zeus, could never wholly succumb.' The dim glimmer has vanished, I am under the ground again. We just screeched through 36th Street, a long stretch now—Pacific Street, then the Bridge. Dave Leahy will always be 'my' professor and my friend, for life, and when he decides to start writing he's going to write the most incredible books anyone has ever seen. He's going to burst right out of the Classics Department and rattle ALL the cages. Then again, it's no secret that I consider Benardete a genius. It's also no secret that I would love to be a professor—a GAM, a Great Academic Marxist. Teach students and write books. Hegel, and his critics—Feuerbach, Kierkegaard, Marx. Great. Like Eugene Genovese, but more philosophical. Then again, is 'Academic Marxist' an outrageous contradiction in terms? Yes and no, I think. Marx himself spent most of his life in libraries—*not in universities*—studying and writing, but that's not my point. I use 'Academic Marxist' in a derogatory sense, because I don't like the GAMs I've met. In fact I apologize to Genovese, whom I'd call a Marxist professor, historian, author, not a GAM. I insist on the term 'Marxist,' but I use it in a very broad sense. To put it bluntly, a Marxist knows that the capitalist *system* is rotten *to the core*. A Marxist knows that *capitalism* will produce nothing but misery, terror, and death. Is being a Marxist professor contradictory? This is a good question. *Screech*, Pacific Street, it's true, the screeches are harder to take when I can't *see* them. For me, being a *Marxist* professor means not just producing theory but *creating practice*. In the case of *this* City, on a Hill, the USA, it means *doing* something that turns the defense of tyranny into an attack on tyranny. It means 'bringing the war home.' It means *working* for systemic change. Working *in a university* for systemic change. Do I think this is possible *in this City*? Do I? Do all the GAMs in this City *in toto* have the impact of one Norman Morrison? To put it mildly: I have my doubts. How can I live *responsibly* in *this* City. Frankly, the question is too big for me, a twenty-one-year-old NYU student with the decision of a lifetime to make. Touring Hades indefinitely, in the hope that, forty years from now, when I look back at my decision, I can say *at least I knew what making a decision meant.* It may not necessarily have been the right decision, but I made it responsibly. Freely? WHAT freedom? The freedom of being is nothing? Eteocles' *totally wrong* decision is *not* a being-is-nothing decision, it is far more complex. That's why it interests me.

Manhattan Bridge Again. So well timed. Night glimmer. Lights glimmering on the other two bridges, dimly. The river is dark. Benardete's first Note leads straight into the second, and the *second* Note—the interpretation of the shields—is what concerns me. It's what this indefinite journey is definitely all about. The night glimmer, let me ponder it while it lasts. Eteocles' decision, then mine. Climb, neon, climb. What making a decision is and means. Under Manhattan, B Train to Washington Heights. The car is full but not jam-packed, but—what time is it? Hades time—Saturday evening, time for a crowd. Absolutely. I'm ready for the second Note, which is why I'm here. For *this* Note, and to think about the relation between freedom and necessity in Hegel's Logic—*here*, in the realm of shadows. This is why I'm *here*, traveling indefinitely. Curses, fates, deciding, being decided-for, being-is-nothing decision, right-wrong decision, figuring out what a decision is and what making a decision means. *Screech*, Grand Street. Absolutely, sweet Marie. Where are you tonight. In flashes. Flashes in the Underworld, joyless region, sunless dead, realm of shadows. 'Flashings into the vast phenomenal world.' Quite a few people got off at Grand. So patiently. To see how the bricks lay. To go through all this twice? *Pazienza*. Absolutely. Got off to go to Chinatown, to Little Italy, a lot of people have dinner early. I normally have dinner at 11 p.m., then I study all night, listening to my Well-Tempered Clavier records, my Pablo Casals cello suites, or to Monk, Coltrane, Albert Ayler, or to Harry Fleetwood on the radio, WNCN after midnight, or maybe WBAI, it depends on what I'm studying, and what Fleetwood is playing. WBAI for special news reports or on special occasions—birthdays and deaths. Anti-war demonstrations. Dylan's thirtieth birthday last year, twenty-four hours of Dylan music. The deaths of Jimi Hendrix, Janis Joplin, Jim Morrison, all in the past two years. Twenty-seven years old. A curse? A blessing? Both? Neither? Hendrix put it this way:

> People still mourn when people die. That's self-sympathy. All human beings are selfish to a certain extent, and that's why people get so sad when someone dies. They haven't finished using him. The person who is dead ain't crying. Sadness is for when a baby is born into this heavy world, and joy should be exhibited at someone's death because they are going on to something more permanent and infinitely better. I tell you, when I die I'm going to have a jam session. I want people to go wild and freak out. And knowing me, I'll probably get busted at my own funeral. The music will be played loud and it will be our music.
>
> ....
>
> It's funny the way people love the dead. You have to die before they think you are worth anything. Once you are dead, you are made for life.
>
> When I die, just keep on playing the records.[95]

Most of the time I listen to 'The Well-Tempered Clavier,' played, for six hours, by João Carlos Martins, a bargain set of seven records I bought on 8th Street. I used to go out before dawn and run across the Williamsburg Bridge, but I don't feel up to it anymore. No, now I meditate. Zazen. On my own. Shit, I'm sitting here like an idiot thinking about Bach and Bob Dylan, still clutching Benardete's first Note. It's time to put it back in my bag and take out the second Note. The people around me look happy, not at all like 'sunless dead.' Then again, they are definitely not traveling *indefinitely* like I am, and for such an

---

95 I quote this from the recent book, *Jimi Hendrix. Starting At Zero. His Own Story*, London/New York: Bloomsbury, 2013, p. 250.

indefinitely definite reason. Almost all of them are young, like me, or youngish, and definitely know where they're going and it definitely won't take them an *indefinite* time to get there. Shit, it might take them less than ten minutes, two stops, to West 4th. In twenty minutes or so they can be in Times Square, in less than twenty-five at Rockefeller Center, always a fun place. There's LOTS to do on the Upper West Side—visit friends, great neighborhoods, go out to dinner—and it definitely won't take them all that long to get there. Even Washington Heights is not that far, but I don't think many people are going up there right now, unless they happen to live there. The unicorns are already fast asleep. Should I rummage around in my bag a little—read a little Ezra Pound. More *Zen Mind*. Some *No-mind*, I haven't read that at all yet. Hegel. I definitely intend to read some more Hegel, that's for sure. But, now, or later? Why did I bring *Heart of Darkness?* I guess, just in case. I always have *Heart of Darkness* in my bag. The issue of *Ramparts* with Che's diaries, stuffed with a bunch of clippings on Vietnam. *Screech*, Broadway-Lafayette. Wait a second, my collection of 'filler' clippings. I think I'll read my absolute favorite filler—it's really the filler of all fillers, the full and absolute fulfillment of the filler as such, *and* it has to do with freedom and necessity, with *a decision*, with Eteocles' decision, my decision, his 'reciprocal suicide,' as Hegel put it. This will perk the daylights out of me. I found this in the *Post*, of course. No, you can't beat this one.

Offer of Beer Cools Off Prospective Suicide Here
After threatening for two hours to jump from the top of a 10-story building, a man was lured to safety Friday with a can of cold beer.
The man, tentatively identified by the police as Ulysses Allen, 28 years old, had walked on tiptoe around the edge of the roof in 90-degree sunshine, complaining, 'I don't have any freedom.'

He had foiled a series of police moves to lure him to safety, but yielded to the beer offered by a casual acquaintance. He was taken to a hospital for examination.

Lured to safety. You can't possibly *invent* a story like this, nobody would ever believe you. Purity, body, and flavor. Baseball and Ballantine. In, not under, Yankee Stadium, sitting out there in the Bleachers with my shirt off. *Screech*, West 4th, let's see what's up under the West Village. FREAK ME OUT, A PLACARD. HELL NO HELL NO HELL NO. ANOTHER ONE. Definitely not one of the four I've seen. Wait—HELL NO. FUCK THIS MOTHERFUCKER. UP AGAINST THE WALL. What MANIAC SCUMBAG would dare put this MANIAC SCUMBAG IMAGE on a placard and parade it around the subway. In New York City—Fun City!—at the end of March, 1972, Saturday evening. Right under the Village, *the* place for peaceful freak outs, free love, and gay pride. Among other things. My university, for example. A parade is a parade. Turkeys. This time the people in the car are going wild—more in sorrow than in anger, more in anger than in sorrow, or—the people are definitely riled up, but, it seems, more in *wild enthusiasm* than in sorrow or anger. I see some of these young or youngish people *throwing coins* at the placard-man. At his image. And by coins I don't mean pennies, for the Old Guy or for any old guy—now they're shoving bills right down the back of his pants as he goes by. Filling his asshole to the brim. Dollar, five-dollar, ten-dollar bills, FUCK YOU ALL. Am I riled up myself? You bet. I'D LIKE TO BLOW THIS PLACARD-MAN AWAY. Motherfucker. Up against the wall. How dare you. The image is *graphic*, extremely well drawn, the work of a born draftsman. Vivid black on white. *A B-52 BOMBER* seen from below, like a huge bat with outstretched wings, filling the entire breadth of the placard. A B-52 mass murderer, the Hiroshima mass murderer's worthy heir. Never in my life have I seen such a *menacing* image. This heart of darkness. This horror. The image is so simple, so elementary, so *immediate*, that I can't describe it in words. Not a Michelangelo-Sistine-Chapel but a genuine Clint-Eastwood-Spaghetti-Western image. Not in your face, like the new Twin Towers, but a fire exploding *in your mind*. On the roofs of houses *and* in the mind. Indescribable, because it's too *immediate* to be described. Lord and Master of the Sky, domineering the full breadth of the placard. Wide. It makes me think of a bat—its *blackness*—but the image has a supreme immobility, and bats are mobility mobilized. Then again, the familiar supersonic super-zigzagging bats are microbats with a 6-inch wingspan (I happen to be a bat expert), while the largest of the megabats, *pteropus vampyrus*, familiarly know as the *flying fox* (its face looks just like a fox's), has a 6-*foot* wingspan and hovers like a vulture. This B-52 is A BAT OUT OF HELL, its wings stretching to the bitter ends of the world, all-embracing and all-*menacing*. Disquieting. Unnerving. Devastating. Terrifying. Overwhelming. The 'direct reverse' (as Melville put it) of Dante's image in the last Canto of *Paradiso* where Neptune, from the depths of the sea, looks up, in wonder and delight, at the 'shadow of the Argo' plowing the waves far above him. Flashes. A strange but *extremely vivid* image just came into my mind, something I once saw, on a white wall somewhere—perhaps in Greece, two summers ago—I can't get it out of my head. A mosquito, absolutely immobile, apart from its own immanent quiver—like the quiver of this B-52 on the placard—in bright light, *there* on a white wall. Menacing. The infinite intricacy of its form expressing the end of the line of complexity. Its indefinable but *overly*-defined body, a *mise en abyme* of the universe. An image that expresses what the matter of the entire universe 'boils down to' without losing the most infinitesimal detail of its form. *The horror*. This mosquito—'exquisite,' blacker than midnight in hell. *Vivid*, alive, the finest details of its body expressed with a graphic immediacy that no artist can even imagine, let alone express. But this motherfucker placard-man does a damn good job, with his B-52 image. The image of this mosquito torments me—OK, Ill say it: its *evil*. Its exquisite evil. Its heart of darkness, its horror. The greatest artist in the history of the world can't *capture* this image, but—no one shows a child the sky. You can't miss it, the infinite infinitesimal horror. This B-52 on the placard is this mosquito writ large. Writ huge. A 'mere' image. A 'less than mere' placard-man. Who in this cocksucking world are these placard-men. I really thought I'd seen the last of them. The leg-lost, the allegiance-pledged, the village-approached (how'r y'all doing), the village-destroyed (to save it), and now, what? Is this even a Vietnam veteran? My fellow passengers here on the B Train are going wild. *Vox populi*. Bread and circuses. 'Unqualified devotion' and B-52s. My fellow travelers in the realm of shadows, showering the image and the man with their adoration, as if he were one of the Magi. Well fuck you too, motherfuckers. Make love not war. Gave my legs, God on our side, defense of freedom, 'saved' the village—OK, but holy shit, this B-52. True love. And this placard-man has a double caption on his maniac-scumbag placard. At the top, above the bat out of hell: KILL FOR PEACE. At the bottom, below the bat: WELCOME FELLOW B-52 ENTHUSIAST![96] Shit, I've heard about this—people actually form *clubs* to revere and cherish this mass murderer. Then these 'patriots' go to anti-war demonstrations and scream BOMB HANOI! BOMB HANOI!

---

96 OK, some Internet-speak, on 29 November 2014. Internet references have been very useful and important in the composition of this story—Wikipedia really is excellent, and I've used it a lot—but they sure as hell have their limits. The B-52 pages in *The Empty Shield* are directly inspired by an Internet site—titled *Welcome fellow B-52 Enthusiast!*—which I accessed and printed out *quite* a number of years ago—in 2007, to be precise. The site opens with a 'very plain' black-and-white image of a B-52 seen from below, as I describe it in the text. Today it seems you need a special 'login'—I am the direct reverse of an expert on these things—to access it. DO try for yourself, if you like. This extremely 'simple' black-and-white image of a B-52 seen from below has made such an indelible impression on my mind that, along with Aeschylus, and Benardete's Aeschylus, it has become a 'co-source' of this political autobiography. I hope you manage to see it for yourselves.

BOMB HANOI! Quite right. A parade is a parade is a parade, as Hiz Honor put it. This love fest will be going on all the way to 34th Street. This 'Group Grope' AS THE FUGS PUT IT—'Kill for Peace' is THEIR FUCKING SONG. *The* anti-war anti-mass-murder song of all time. The 'sunless dead' are going out of their minds. Some of them are *screaming* Kill for Peace. An unrebuked Chorus, worshipping this MANIAC SCUMBAG image. This ABSOLUTE AND TOTAL IMAGE, to which no other can correspond or respond. SUPREME IMAGE, which no other image can *survive*. Zeus! Zeus! God of all the gods! YOUR thunderbolt, YOUR welkin-eyed sky. Already in his shroud. Zeus, who defeated Typhon, Father of All Monsters, WHAT IS THIS? This IMAGE, this unqualified devotion. This cracked requiem. My skin is crawling, my mind on fire. Flashes. Their cries. Why was the serpent a sacred animal for the Greeks? Two reasons. First, because its bite kills *instantly*, the soul leaves the body without the slightest hesitation. No suffering, no 'process,' pure release, absolute immediacy. The thunderbolt. Pure. Out of the blue. Second, because it changes its skin. Leaves its old skin behind. Rebirth. Immortality. Group Grope. The Fugs are my absolute favorite rock band, the first *underground* rock band of all time. First and last. Ends end. Escaping escaping. *Political* rock. I'm glad Tuli Kupferberg isn't here in the car to see this, he's such a sensitive person. As for me, I wish I could *crawl out of my skin*. What a decision is and what making a decision means. All this time, in the Underworld, traveling, screech after screech and all one screech. The placard-man keeps going up and back in the car, the passengers make way for him like the Red Sea parting for Moses. Kill for Peace. B-52 enthusiasts. Group Grope. All this going on and I can't say a single word about the placard-*man* himself. I don't think I've even seen him. Too much confusion. Young, old, joker, thief,[97] dressed as a soldier, as a pilot, as a stockbroker, as a madman, I don't know. I can't get no relief. I

---

97 It's Dylan, bro. 'All Along the Watchtower.'

don't know why but I don't see his face, he has been effaced by the image. The B-52, the *Great Effacer*, the image of Utter Effacement. He doesn't even speak, shit, it's my fellow passengers who are chanting Kill for Peace. SCREECH SCREECH WHERE ARE YOU? Where have all the screeches gone. When will it ever end. The flowers. My light come shinin'. Shall I be released.[98] Ye gods, don't let them start chanting BOMB HANOI! Joseph K! Order in the Court. I raise my hands and spread out all my fingers. 'Screech': I barely heard it. 34th Street. The scumbag-maniac placard-man is getting off, ready to get on the next car. Or, like Moses, will he be leading my fellow travelers out with him? Where? Out onto the platform to prolong this 'unqualified' Group Grope? Out into the Wilderness? Out of Hades, up into Herald Square? Great, 'Give my regards to Broadway/ Remember me to Herald Square.' Will I be left completely alone in the car, under Herald Square, midtown Manhattan, Saturday night, end of March, 1972, to fend for myself? 'Fend for myself' in what sense? I don't have the slightest idea. Fend for myself. What a decision is and *what making a decision means*. Bob Dylan. Eteocles. The Fugs. In flashes. The empty mirror. A continuous shattering.

After all this, some got off, some got on, the car is packed, I sit here. What now? I have been trying to pose a serious question. To pose it not just for the hell of it, not because I have nothing better to do. No, to pose it to answer it, somehow. To try to come up with some sort of answer, as if my life depended on it, which, in a sense, in several senses, it sure as hell does. Hades. Hegel's Logic. Realm of Shadows. Zen mind. The Dharma Eye. A decision. Billy Budd. The *Septem*, Benardete's two Notes. This was the idea. It's the placard-men who have fucked it all up. Did I say 'distracted' me? I also said—quite rightly—they've thrown me completely off track, they've led me by the nose into the wilderness. And that was before this fifth and faceless placard-man, effaced

98 Dig Dylan on The Band's album *Last Waltz*.

by the image—I don't even say 'his' image, even though
I presume he did draw it himself, what do I know. Maybe
some 'fellow enthusiast' drew it and he just carries it. Fuck
them all in any case. The depicter of this BAT did a fine job,
but in this case the image BLOWS the imagery away. Blows
it fucking away. Overwhelmingly overshadows the imagery
and the imaginer. What now. Here I sit so patiently. Madmen.
Neon. Patch. Discolored. Snow. Cracked. Requiem. I think
the effaced placard-man put 'Kill for Peace' on his placard
because 'exterminate all the brutes'[99] would have cut a poor
figure in the subway. Or, incredibly, he's never read *Heart
of Darkness*. 'Mistah Kurtz—he dead.' A penny for the Old
Guy—no. The effaced placard-man is no Gunpowder Plotter,
he's as *mainstream* as they come. He's just one of the boys,
a red-blooded, dyed-in-the-wool, good old guy. 'One of us,'
as Conrad put it. Sardonically. *Screech,* 42nd Street, have
fun. Have lots and lots of fun. A good old guy with a good old
image. A good-old scumbag-maniac image. A B-52. A good
red-blooded B-52 ENTHUSIAST, touring the subway to group
grope with fellow enthusiasts. Fun City! Maybe he only comes
out on Saturday nights. Is he a Vietnam veteran? Possibly.
Possibly not. I don't have the slightest idea. Who knows. How
should I know. Who cares. With an IMAGE like this, who needs
qualifications, who needs words. I didn't even see his face,
but I saw his pants chock-full of bills in the back, his asshole
full of bills, and I don't mean electric bills or phone bills but
good red-blooded DOLLAR bills. Perhaps he takes to the
subway, possibly only on Saturday nights, to become a budding
capitalist. Maybe he doesn't give a shit, he just loves B-52s,

---

99 Mistah Kurtz, 'a kind of note at the foot of the last page' of his 'pamphlet'—'it
blazed at you, luminous and terrifying, *like a flash of lightning in a serene sky.*' He
dead: 'The vision seemed to enter the house with me—the stretcher, the phantom-
bearers, the wild crowd of obedient worshippers, the gloom of the forests, the glitter
of the reach between the murky bends, the beat of the drum, regular and muffled
like the beating of a heart—the heart of a conquering darkness. It was a moment of
triumph for the wilderness....'

WHAT DO I KNOW. What now. Has he ever even *heard* of The Fugs? Can it possibly be *sheer coincidence* that the caption to his B-52 MASS MURDERER happens to be the title of The Fugs greatest *anti-war anti-mass-murder* hit. Do I think my fellow passengers were all Fugs fans? No, I don't. I think they are all FUCKING B-52 ENTHUSIASTS. What now. Not only is the placard-man *effaced* but his IMAGE *effaces* ZEUS, God of all the gods. *Screech,* Rockefeller Center. Have fun. It is a FUCK YOU ZEUS image. Zeus, father of Ares, who spared the Spartoi. Zeus will Defend the City! Against the Attacker with *Typhon* on his shield Eteocles sends a Defender with *Zeus* on his shield. It's a war of images he's sure he can't lose: the reality will reduplicate the image. Hunky-dory, Typhon and Zeus. And now a B-52 challenges Zeus. Now what. Zeus, YOUR thunderbolt, YOUR clear blue sky, Zeus! Defender of the City. Ye gods, God of all the gods, you are a MOSQUITO about to be DEVOURED by this terrible BAT OUT OF HELL. Bats *never sleep* (possibly), and can eat as much as two-thirds of their own weight in bugs *every night*, including mosquitoes, grasshoppers, locusts—and GOOKS. (I'm an expert on bats.) Just ask the effaced placard-man and his fellow enthusiasts. Kill a gook for God. Kill for peace. Fuck you Fugs, you commie creeps. The *effaced* placard-man and his *utterly effacing* image. What am I doing here? What's next. What will become of my traveling indefinitely. Goddam placard-men. The wailing rebuked Chorus. Zeus! Your sky up in flames. Your earth reduced to cinders. Thebes of the Seven Gates. *Screeeech*, the War God. How many heads on the Hydra of War. How many tears of blood. Every screech a horde at the Gate. A sky studded with bombs. The Fucking Fourth of July. 'The bombs bursting in air.' 'Proof through the night.' I can't take these screeches anymore. Maybe I should take the D at 59th, just to go screechless into this good night, as far as 125th, and then get back on the B. I'll never get a seat, it's Saturday night in Fun City. I need to get my head back together, fast. At times like this I take to the subway for a 'three in the morning,' a head-getting-together trip, but I'm *already* in the cocksucking subway. I can't 'take to it' if I'm already here.

'The sage harmonizes right with wrong and rests in the balance of nature. This is called taking both sides at once.' Joni Mitchell. Wailing rebuked Chorus. 'It is time to cling to your images.' Get your head together. Fuck the screeches. Just go on up to the Cloisters, where the captive unicorn dreams. Where the green ant dreams. Where the neon madman climbs. Let me *think* about these placard-men—that's what Hegel would do. What's going on? Both sides now. Taking both sides at once. Peace. Love. Easy does it. What both sides? One side is the B-52 image. Let's say the other is the B-52 reality. Seeming and being. A thought experiment. An infinitesimal think tank. 'Watch the water.' Now—the effaced-and-effacing placard-man presents us—graphically—with the Triumph of the Image. *I have no Image with which to challenge this Image.* But, taking both sides at once, I do have reality. Facts. Boots on the ground, so to speak. We're under 59th Street already, that's their problem, I'm going to think all this through. This B-52 so many are so enthusiastic about. Not me. Reality. A taste of reality. Where's my *Ramparts* Che's Bolivia diaries issue with the clippings. Right here in my bag. Do you think I only have articles about our ugly-bird helicopters, hell no. Look: Everything you always wanted to know about B-52s but were afraid to ask. Facts. Boots in the air. Look! Facts. Official name (rarely used): B-52 Stratofortress. Nicknames: Whispering Death, Rolling Thunder, and (the troops' favorite) BUFF—Big Ugly Fat Fucker, a.k.a Big Ugly Flying Fuck. Designed and built: by Boeing. (I presume the 'B' in B-52 stands for Boeing.) Date of birth: in active service, 1955. Cause of birth: carry nuclear weapons for Cold War-era deterrence missions. Psychiatric problem (B-52 Complex): shit! born too late for Hiroshima, goddamit. The B-52 has been trying to 'compensate' for this ever since.[100] Population: 742 B-52s built between 1954 and 1963; about 200 of them have been dropping bombs on Vietnam. Call them birds, bats, or mosquitoes, that's one hell of a lot of bombers. Bombs: external racks under the wings for 24 bombs, 750 pounds each; 'Big Belly' modifications in 1965 to beef the internal payload up to 84 bombs, for a total capacity of 60,000 pounds in 108 bombs per Flying Fuck. One HELL of a lot of bombs.[101] Range and altitude: they can fly for more than 10,000 miles—10 to 12 hours with aerial refueling—and at altitudes up to 50,000 feet. Whispering Death, so high in the sky. The lightning flashes down out of nowhere. Zeus! With the thunderbolt in your hand, but no one has ever seen you hurl it. A high flyin' bird. Way up in the sky. Does she look down as she goes on by, wonders Richie Havens, though he definitely isn't thinking about a B-52. No, 'Whispering Death' is what the Vietnamese themselves call it:[102] they are constantly

---

100 They're still trying to this day, December 2014. These bats are restless. By now they have been equipped to drop *every bomb in the book*—gravity bombs, cluster bombs, precision guided missiles, 'joint direct attack munitions' (whatever that means). But they were born for Big Fucking Nukes, goddamit. Vanished cities. These are *frustrated* bats. Poor fucking things, will they ever manage to do what they were born for. Where there's life (and death), there's hope. Current engineering analyses show their life span to extend beyond the year 2045. You may still encounter their Image in the subway, writ super-huge.

101 B-52s flew 126,615 combat sorties over Vietnam. All told, in the course of the war the United States dropped some 8 million tons of bombs. During World War II, the Allies dropped about 2 million tons.

102 Speaking of 'whispering,' I just read a review of the book *Kill Chain: The Rise of the High-Tech Assassins* by Andrew Cockburn. (*Z Magazine*, September 2015, review by Jeremy Kuzmarov.) [second stab revision of first stab]. Cockburn 'traces the roots of today's drone warfare to Robert S. McNamara's concept of the electronic battlefield in Vietnam in which infra-red censors ringed along the Ho Chi Minh Trail were hooked to computers that relayed target information to bomber pilots.' Alas, the system was not as effective as the drones we have today. 'The Vietnamese got around the censors by erecting fake decoys and bridges, by sending herds of cattle to simulate troop movement, and by dumping human and animal urine to confuse.' Goddam wily gooks. 'A symbol of American futility was the failure to destroy the Thanh Hoa Bridge along the Ho Chi Minh Trail in 871 bombing missions where 104 pilots were downed.' But I was speaking of 'whispering.' The missiles fired by the drones in the Global War on Terror (in Afghanistan, Palestine, et cetera, while the 'pilots' sit at computers in Nevada) *don't even whisper*. 'From the ground it is

caught off guard since they hear no plane, then all of a sudden the ground starts to erupt all around them, apocalyptically. Methodology, route, and *raison d'être*: the Fuckers work in threes (called 'cells') and their attacks are called 'Arc Lights'; these famously super-long-range birds fly out of Andersen Air Force Base on Guam[103] and, more recently, also out of U-Tapao Base in Thailand; their mission, basically, is to 'clear the jungle.' We do 'carpet bombing' and 'saturation bombing,' but the B-52s also do special 'B-52-bombing,' pulverizing whole 'boxes' of territory, killing everything that moves in multi-square-mile rectangles. Particularly in SOUTH Vietnam. Fucking gook Viet Cong. FELLOW B-52 SCUMBAG ENTHUSIASTS, it's mass murder pure and simple. And for years you've been dreaming and screaming BOMB HANOI! BOMB HANOI! BOMB HANOI![104] A parade is a parade is a parade. And yet, with all these bombs—to say nothing of 'approach the village' search and destroy missions, and ye gods know what else—we are not winning and will not win this war in the defense of tyranny. Napalm, Agent Orange,[105] B-52s, to warn the Vietnamese,

---

impossible to determine who or what they are tracking as they circle overhead. The buzz of a distant propeller is a constant reminder of imminent death. Drones fire missiles that travel faster than the speed of sound. A drone's victim never hears the missile that kills him.'

103 The base is still full of B-52s today.

104 Of course one cannot do justice to the B-52 performance in Vietnam without mentioning their crowning achievement, Operation Linebacker II, the 'maximum-effort' Christmas Bombings of Hanoi and Haiphong in 1972, nine months after the end of my tale. Eleven days and nights, 100,000 bombs. Fantastic. The ultimate paroxysm of slaughter. But, what the hell, in South Vietnam alone the BUFFs left TEN MILLION bomb craters after the war. Combatants, noncombatants, cats, dogs, fuck them all. TEN MILLION. What would the Pequot say about that. The 'Christmas Bombing' was the heaviest bombing by the U.S. Air Force since the end of World War II. Why such fury? Because peace was at hand. The U.S.—Kissinger the mind, Nixon the 'heart' (so to speak)—ceased operations a month later. A savage act of mere revenge? Let us not be so cynical. The Paris Peace Talks, the Nobel Peace Prize. May I be so bold—in honor of The Fugs—as to call the Christmas Bombing the *Kill for Peace Bombing*.

105 The United States dropped some 400,000 tons of napalm (versus 14,000 tons in World War II and 32,000 tons in Korea) and sprayed 11.2 million gallons of Agent Orange on South Vietnam.

North and South, of the perils of self-determination. We're
only trying to help. THE DEFENSE OF FREEDOM. And ye gods
we aren't winning. People—a few people—in this country were
shocked by Curtis LeMay's suggestion, back in 1965, that we
'bomb them back into the Stone Age.' But with all these BATS
OUT OF HELL what is it we've been doing! Perchance dropping
millions of tons of care packages from the sky? Whispering
Death, Rolling Thunder, Big Ugly Fat Fuckers, 60,000 pounds,
108 bombs, multiplied by three, at every 'Arc Light'—and guess
what. General Harold K. 'Johnny' Johnson, Army Chief of Staff
from 1964 to 1968, observed recently: 'If there's a lesson to be
learned from Vietnam it's that *air power can't do the job*.'[106] Sez
who! Some fucking general! Go on, maniac scumbags, give it
the old college try. Go right ahead. Be my guest.

Boots in the air. Reality, part two. SAM. And I don't mean
Uncle Sam. Screech away, I'm under 72nd Street, car full,
people happy, heading for a nice evening on the Upper West
Side. The Dakota, The Majestic, well, fuck Lucky Luciano,
long gone, he's done his damage, in New York, in Cuba, in
Italy, he died of a heart attack at the Naples Airport in 1962.
Motherfucker. Frank Costello, Cosa Nostra 'Prime Minister'—
Vincent 'The Chin' Gigante shot him in the head in the lobby
of The Majestic in 1957 but, alas, he mercilessly survived and
is still fucking the world from his Waldorf Astoria penthouse.
Have no fear, today there's no lack of maniac scumbag
killers—Mafiosi, patriots, groupies, idiot freaks. I see that John
Lennon moved into The Dakota last year, he'd better keep
his head down, it's a tough neighborhood, a tough world.
Just ask the gook creeps in Vietnam. Ask the B-52 Flying
Fuck pilots. No, not Uncle Sam. I mean SAMs, Surface-to-Air
Missiles. A Very Important Player in our war against Vietnam,
which the Vietnamese call the American War.[107] SAM, the

---

106 Sorry, I twisted the quote a little, since he said it after the end of the war. Exact
quote: 'If anything came out of Vietnam it was that air power couldn't do the job.'
Pardon my grievous distortion.
107 By the way, April 30, 1975: we call it the Fall of Saigon, they call it the Liberation
of Saigon.

enemy. B-52, 'image and reality.' SAMs have no images, they are pre-eminently self-effacing, but are very much there. B-52s and SAMs are a couple, they go together, like insects and insecticide, mosquitoes and mosquito repellent, birds and bird watchers—no, that's different. BUFFs and SAMs, a happy couple, like love and marriage, soup and a sandwich. As Frank Sinatra sings it, 'This I tell ya, brother, you can't have one without the other.' The Vietnamese SAMs are, as it were, the *dap loi* 'step-mine' booby traps writ very large. And internationalized—not as indigenous as the *dap loi*. A Reality versus Reality affair. Hold on, I'm getting my SAM article out of my bag. Let's see—our bombers over Vietnam, since 1965. The Soviets sent 17,000 missile technicians and instructors to North Vietnam in 1965 to install their System SA-2, and eventually supplied 7,658 SAMs to North Vietnam. The first SAMs were fired on 24 July 1965, and three days later we were already strafing and bombing the installations. As a result, SAM batteries have to change launching sites after every firing. A big job. It takes all night. Everything packed up, carried thirty to forty kilometers, then set up again. And camouflaged. *Self-*effacing. And effacing? Well, it's not easy to shoot a bomber down with a SAM. The old college try, fuck you all. Technology, great. But it takes training, skill, patience. It's something like shooting at a mosquito, or a microbat, with a slingshot. Difficult, but not impossible. High in the sky, but not pie in the sky. What's more, paradoxically, since *high*-flying birds are 'easier' (in a manner of speaking) for a SAM to bring down than *low*-flying birds, our Air Force hurled the low-flying F-111, TSR-2, and Panavia Tornado into the fray. Napalm and Agent Orange are guaranteed SAM-proof, their birds fly by just above the ground. Then again, if you want to drop 3 times 60,000 pounds of 108 bombs at every Arc Light, you need to fly HIGH, Fat Fuckers. Facts. Reality. In the beginning the Fuckers' problem wasn't the SAMs, no, it was the fact that they were *fucking* *themselves.* Very first mission, 18 June 1965, 30 B-52s, striking a 'communist stronghold' near the Ben Cat District in South Vietnam. The first wave of bombers arrived too early at a designated rendezvous point, and while maneuvering to maintain station, two B-52s collided, resulting in the loss of both planes and eight crewmen.[108] The other Flying Fucks made it back, more or less, to the Andersen base on the beautiful island of Guam. Post-strike assessment found evidence that the Viet Cong *had left the area before the raid*—the usual scenario in all these years to come. Strike an area chock-full of Viet Cong, who are not there, and after the strike whoever was not a fucking commie gook creep before the strike sure as hell is one now. Long live the Pentagon. Motherfuckers. I wish there were a stronger, more insulting word. Maybe 'war criminal'—no, it's too reductive. No, motherfucker is better, *le mot juste*. Eldridge Cleaver pronounced it better than anyone. I went to a Peace and Freedom Party rally before the 1968 elections, Cleaver was running for president, I'd have voted for him but I was too young, only eighteen. Too young to vote, not too young to be drafted, SirYesSir! He gave a speech of course, and a pretty long one, here's the full text: 'NIXON IS A MOTHERFUCKER, HUMPHREY IS A MOTHERFUCKER' repeated over and over again, it reminded me of the 'Ode To Joy' in Beethoven's Ninth Symphony. *Le mot juste*. Definitely. I've survived five placard-men without losing my sense of humor, how do I do it? Zazen? Ever since I read *Moby Dick* last summer, after my military-psychiatric draft hearing, Melville has really been helping me. Ishmael never loses his cool, never lets Ahab or the Whale get him down. It's not easy for me to get my head together after this fifth-placard man with his carload of fellow B-52 enthusiasts. This *effaced* and *effacing* placard-man. I need a SAM—*the* pre-eminently *self-effacing* weapon—just for him, and Melville never lets me down. 'The

---

108 Much of this account and my statistics are from the Wikipedia article *Boeing B-52 Stratofortress*.

sage harmonizes right with wrong and rests in the balance of nature. This is called taking both sides at once.' For Ahab there is *one* Captain—'Fate's lieutenant'—and *one* God. But Ishmael sees both sides. Just like Joni Mitchell. Looks at life from both sides now. For him Moby Dick is not an Angry God but the simple 'unsourced' fluidity of divine mindless power—'ubiquitous' and 'immortal' ('ubiquity in time'). The Whale is *effaced*, 'has no face,' just a brow 'pleated with riddles' of Deity.[109] The breaching of the Whale—for Ahab his 'act of defiance'—is, for Ishmael, 'the grand god revealing himself.' Both sides at once. Absolutely. 110th Street, upper edge of Central Park, I like this stop. It's dark in the Park now but there's lots of light on 110th Street. Car still pretty full. Upper West Side. 'Pleated with riddles'—what an incredible writer Melville is. How I admire him, just as I admire the Vietnamese people fighting for their freedom. Shooting at bats 50,000 feet in the air, with slingshots. OK, it's taking them a while to get the hang of it, but they're definitely getting there. They haven't quite brought a Fat Fucker down these past seven years but, as I mentioned, from the very beginning the poor Fuckers have been fucking themselves. Wait, I have the whole list here, a fully up-dated 'Summary of USAF B-52 Losses in the Vietnam War': twelve so far, including the two in the first mission. Fucking themselves. Check this out. 'Cause of loss': 'mid-air collision en route to target' (2 down); 'same' (2 down); 'engine failure, crashed on takeoff'; 'insufficient speed, crashed on takeoff'; 'accidental ground fire while preparing for Arc Light mission'; 'crashed in the Pacific Ocean en route to target, cause unknown'; 'nose gear failed, crashed on takeoff'; 'structure failure, starboard, crashed on takeoff'; 'mechanical failure, crashed en route to target'; 'struck by lightning, crashed en route to target.'[110] Ye gods, struck by lightning. It

---

109 *Moby Dick*, Chapter 79.
110 The list is from the Wikipedia *Boeing B-52 Stratofortress* article. The last two losses I mention were three months after March 1972, sorry, I couldn't resist including them.

wasn't their fault. But, alas, the war is not over, even though our Fearless Leaders assure us it's 'winding down.' Alas! our Fearless Leaders are also our LEADING B-52 ENTHUSIASTS. 116th Street, Columbia University, great neighborhood, lots of good restaurants. Students. What ever happened to the BOMB HANOI! BOMB HANOI! BOMB HANOI! that so many unqualified patriots are counting on? Isn't a parade a parade a parade, I muse. Are we going to let this war just peter out and slither away. I doubt it, seriously. Reality. Taking both sides at once. 'Three in the morning.' The Vietnamese have been working night and day, soul and body, installing SAMs around Hanoi. They've created the most concentrated, complicated, and camouflaged anti-air defense in the world. BOMB HANOI! Be my guest, what can I do about it. But it may not be the picnic the enthusiasts are expecting.[111]

Boots in the air, boots on the ground. Reality, part three. The Fugs. BAT B-52, Supreme Image that owns the sky and overshadows the earth. Poor Zeus, God of all the gods, can't hold a candle to it. I don't have an IMAGE that can correspond to, respond to, and *survive* this maniac-scumbag effaced-and-effacing placard-man's IMAGE but I WANT THE FUGS BACK and, fuck you placard-man, I'M TAKING THEM BACK. You can't have them. Not that you even want them. No, who knows, but I bet you are NOT a habitué of the East Village, of Tomkins Square Park, no, I think they would fuck you and then eat you alive in Tomkins Square Park, you and your Flying Fuck B-52. In a manner of speaking, of course. The East Village is the most peaceful neighborhood in Manhattan, how I wish I lived there instead of on Rivington Street, but the rents are

---

111 Operation Linebacker II, the Christmas Bombing, a.k.a. the 'Kill for Peace' Bombing. The SAMs got their act together. The full list shows 18 B-52s lost 'hit by SAM'—4 in the month of November, followed by another 13 during the Christmas/'Kill for Peace' Bombing between December 18th and December 27th, followed by a last SAM-hit on January 3rd. The list ends on 13 January 1973 with this anticlimactic 'cause of loss' (after 18 straight 'hit by SAM'): 'battle damage, emergency landing, scrapped.'
A total of 31 B-52s were lost—in various ways, fucked or fucking—during the Vietnam War.

double or triple. (And for the West Village, double or triple THAT.) 125th Street, Harlem, soul screech. Musical. The Fugs give a free annual performance in Tomkins Square Park, in the summer. I went for the first time in 1967, I was only 17 but I was already hip to The Fugs. Sure, to Uncle Meat Frank Zappa too, but Tuli—Tuli Kupferberg—he's beyond words. WAY beyond words. Say what you want about the great Frank Zappa, his genius, his music, his wit. But Tuli is WAY BEYOND WORDS. Way beyond. Neon. Madmen. Climb. No words for the man. Allen Ginsberg tried to 'capture' him (like the unicorn) in *Howl* as the person 'who jumped off the Brooklyn Bridge and walked away unknown and forgotten into the ghostly daze of Chinatown.' Tuli, however, later said that it was not the Brooklyn but the Manhattan Bridge, that he jumped because he had 'lost the ability to love,' and that 'nothing happened. I landed in the water, & I wasn't dead. So I swam ashore, & went home, & took a bath, & went to bed. Nobody even noticed.'[112] Beyond words. One night, with my taxi—summer of 1969, a few days after the first man hopped around on the Moon, on my nineteenth birthday, it was round midnight—one night, cruising with my taxi I picked up Abbie Hoffman, he was going to Chinatown for dinner with some friends and he invited me to come along. Wow! I *adore* Abbie Hoffman. A good person. A Mensch if ever there was one. Yippie political theater. Still, there are no words for Tuli. No words. He wrote 'Kill for Peace' and the maniac-scumbag effaced-and-effacing placard-man can't have it, or him. Fuck him he can't have Tuli, or any other Fug, or The Fugs as a whole either. No way. Not that he wants them, I'm sure. A one-in-a-zillion coincidence that he came up with the title of Tuli's song as the caption for his UNSPEAKABLE IMAGE. A PURE stroke of cocksucking motherfucking fortuitousness. An absolute BRAINSTORM.

---

112 This is reported in the prose poem *Memorial Day 1971* by Ted Berrigan and Anne Waldman. See the Wikipedia article *Tuli Kupferberg*. The actual fact was less poetic: Tuli did jump from the Manhattan Bridge in 1944, and broke his back. He was picked up by a passing tugboat and ended up in a body cast.

A bona fide SHITSTORM in the scumbag's brain. Or, maybe maybe he happened to read about The Fugs—a concert, the titles of their songs—in some copy of *The East Village Other*— or, possibly, *The Village Voice*—that he picked up on a bench or picked out of the trash. I doubt it, but what the fug do I know. Now—Tuli is beyond words but we can speak of The Fugs. Perhaps I should hazard—hazard's the word!—an *extremely long discussion* of Hegel's 'power of the negative' at this point, to say nothing of negation-of the-negation, but I don't feel like it right now. How long have I been traveling, who knows, it's Hadean time. I'm barely noticing the stops, and the screeches not at all, just whispers. Whispering Death, 300 bombs all at once, out of nowhere. I see the sound. I'm on the B Train. Naturally, The Fugs say 'Kill for Peace' in a 'negative' sense, Hegelianly speaking, whereas the MANIAC SCUMBAG with his B-52 IMAGE uses it in a 'positive' (for *him*) sense. A POSITIVE maniac-scumbag sense. Hegel, among quite a few other things, wrote: 'The proposition that the finite is ideal constitutes idealism.' Negativity. A 'negative' sense. Logical moments. Let's let it lie for now. Lie low for the moment. Let's just say—in a pathetically and dramatically *impoverished* sense—that Tuli says 'Kill for Peace' in a 'politically sarcastic' sense or, possibly, in a 'sarcastic/satirical self-satirizing' sense (Hegel: a 'negative-which-is-positive and positive-which-is-negative' sense), whereas on the placard it has a 'merely positive' 'abstract understanding' sense, precisely, of KILLING FOR PEACE. Let's talk about art versus life? No, no, not now anyway. Let's just say that the 'enthusiasts' take it *literally*—let's say, in a PAX AMERICANA sense of a whole wide world without commies, because they have all been killed, for peace. 145th Street, 'change for the D,' no thanks. I discovered The Fugs—and a lot of other things—during our Summer of Love of 1967.[113] The

---

113 The 'official' Summer of Love, 1967, was in San Francisco. Haight-Ashbury. Big-time organized hippydom. But in New York we had our own Summer. We had Zappa! Our peerless leader, Uncle Meat, doing wild things on Bleecker Street. Absolutely free. Frank! Frank! I'll miss you forever.

'direct reverse' of last year's Long Winter. ('Fug'—by the way—was Norman Mailer's euphemism for 'fuck' in *The Naked and the Dead*.) My last summer of high school I got into an NYU special summer program in computer programming—FORTRAN, statistics, really, a load of shit, as far as I'm concerned. And the whole next year I went to NYU night school way downtown at Trinity Place to learn BAL—Basic Assembly Language—bytes, bits, and *the pits*. As a matter of fact they were busy down there digging the Abyss for the Twin Towers. The Hole. Why did I subject myself to such a thing? I figured, quite rightly, that with a BAL diploma I could get a well-paid job at the age of 18 and tell my father to go fug himself. But, in the end, I was better off studying Greek and driving a taxi. *C'est la vie*, as the French put it. (Not to mention the draft—selective service, so to speak. Pre-lottery. In a jiffy, from a well-paid job at 2 Broadway to computer programming in Saigon. *Uniformed* computer programming.) So be it. NYU, Washington Square, the too-short summer of 1967, the classes really sucked, but what a summer. For starters, one of my computer professors was a *Fugs fanatic*. I swear on my hamster's ashes—Omar! dead on my 21st birthday—a genuine *Fugs fanatic*. That's how I first heard about them. Ye gods, the end of the line. All this reminiscing, I'd forgotten that the B Train isn't infinite. May Hegel forgive me. The stops, the screeches, are—if anything—the *bad* infinity, not the genuine concept of infinity. In any event, I'm under 168th Street/Washington Heights, the end of the line. The unicorns are fast asleep, closeted in the Cloisters, closed up tight. What time is it, I muse. Evening up there, Hades down here. Night. Yes. 'Some are born to sweet delight,/ Some are born to endless night.'

At least I'm out of that subway car, which reeks of B-52s, maniac-scumbags with an assful of dollars, and 'fellow B-52 enthusiasts.' Cries. Cracked requiem. I understand now that there is no end to the placard-men. After the destroy-the-village man I was convinced I'd seen the last of them, but now I'm convinced they're endless. It's just a matter of traveling forever. If I keep going I'll keep meeting placard-men. Endlessly. But I am not traveling forever, here, in this particular Hades. I need to think about Hegel, about the bad infinity. About what a decision is and what making a decision means— which means, in particular, the relations between freedom, necessity, and responsibility. What would the scumbag-maniac fifth placard-man have to say about that. I muse. He'd have SHIT to say about that. Motherfucker. Up against the wall. Sure. I'm still riled up. Parading the image of a B-52 around the subway. A KILL FOR PEACE B-52. The car reeked but now even the platform reeks. 'Stinks,' if you prefer. Stench. There isn't much of a station here, Washington Heights. On the other side of the platform a new B Train awaits me. It just coughed a little. Might have a sore throat. I could use a good stroll—a BRISK walk—but this isn't the place. Wrong end of the line. I'll have to wait for Coney Island, then I'll take a real, long, serious, BRISK WALK, the 4 platforms, 8 tracks, plus the station itself. The ocean. Just for the hell of it I may even look at the clock, set at 'Ocean Time.' It seems like a thousand years since I've been to Coney Island. I can't deny it, the fifth placard-man kicked the shit out of me. What ever happened to Benardete's *second* Note? Blown away. 324 bombs per Arc Light. The *raison d'être* of this journey. Billy already in his shroud. I could use some air. Darkness, artificial light, but what air? Come up for air. No, a long way still to go. To the end of the endless subway. Sweet delight. The Fugs. OK, I'm on the B for Coney Island, come what may. Placards, birds, B-52s. The car is practically empty right now, here at the end of the line, but it's Saturday night, so, what can I say? Pretty soon I'll be saying 'I wish y'all "fellow B-52 enthusiasts" a good evening, how'r y'all assholes doin' this evening? Where's your friend the fifth placard-man, the scumbag maniac?' Motherfuckers. Reality, part three. The Fugs. What an old man Tuli Kupferberg is, he's nearly 50.[114] He's a 'counterculture poet' and 'pacifist anarchist.' I sing his song 'Dirty Old Man' every morning in the shower. The lyrics are out of sight. Just ask Hegel. The negative-which-is-positive, et cetera.

Hangin' out by the schoolyard gate,
Lookin' up every dress I can,
Suckin' wind through my upper plate,
I'm a dirty old man, dirty old man, dirty old man.

Tuli got the band on the road (in the East Village) back in 1963, along with Ed Sanders, 'the intellectual of the group,' much younger than Tuli (then again, who isn't?), sharp as a tack, a good poet too. Just think, Ed got a degree in Ancient Greek in 1964 in my very own NYU Classics Department. Shit, I'll be graduating in June. He made quite a splash, my professors— Dave, Bluma Trell—OK, Benardete isn't a great story-teller— like to tell little stores about him. Proud of Ed Sanders. And I am too, my fellow Ancient Greek enthusiast. Meanwhile, my computer professor in the summer of 1967 was a Fugs fanatic. He invited the students (we were maybe twenty in all) to his apartment for a buffet, *played us Fugs records,* and talked a lot about his friend Ed Sanders, who, however, did *not* study so-called 'computer science' as I did, for a short time. 'Suckin' wind through my upper plate'—Ed wrote it in fact, about Tuli, Hegelianly, along with 'Group Grope.' Tuli wrote 'Kill for Peace,' and 'Morning, Morning,' the beautiful song that Richie Havens has made famous. MEANWHILE, *soul screech,* 125th Street, musical, time flies here on the B Train when I remember The Fugs and forget the B-52s. The car is still only half full, I'm a terrible singer—maybe if I sing it *real softly*—but I can't

114 He was born in 1923 and died in 2010, at the age of 86. In one of his last interviews he said: 'Nobody who lived through the '50s thought the '60s could've existed. So there's always hope.' The reader of this tale will have noted my 'unqualified admiration' for Tuli Kupferberg, whom I haven't seen since the end of the '60s. A man beyond words.

resist, I just have to sing this song and this is one of the best
stretches of subway to do it, 125th, 116th, 110th. Farther
down—Central Park West—tip top—they might get riled up.
Hold on. Here goes.

> Kill, kill, kill for peace/ Kill, kill, kill for peace
> Near or middle or very far east
> Far or near or very middle east
> Kill, kill, kill for peace/ Kill, kill, kill for peace
> If you don't like the people or the way they talk
> If you don't like their manners or the way they walk
> Kill, kill, kill for peace/ Kill, kill, kill for peace
> If you don't kill them then the Chinese will
> If you don't want America to play second fiddle
> Kill, kill, kill for peace/ Kill, kill, kill for peace
> If you let them live they may subvert the Prussians
> If you let them live they might love the Russians
> Kill, kill, kill for peace/ Kill, kill, kill for peace
> [Kill 'em, kill 'em, strafe those gook creeps!]
> The only gook an American can trust
> Is a gook that's got his yellow head bust
> Kill, kill, kill for peace/ Kill, kill, kill for peace
> Kill, Kill, it'll/ feel so good,
> Like my captain said it should
> Kill, kill, kill for peace/ Kill, kill, kill for peace
> Kill it will give you a mental ease
> Kill it will give you a big release
> Kill, kill, kill for peace/ Kill, kill, kill for peace
> Kill, kill, kill for peace/ Kill, kill, kill for peace

Holy shit I feel so much better. I sang real soft, no one in
the car freaked out. A decision! Singing 'Kill for Peace' from
125th to 110th Street is the first decision I've *actually made*
since I went down to the ship, indefinitely, definitely, but

there's much more. It gave me an inkling of *what making a decision is and means*. Something's happening. Slow down. Time to mull. The B Train goes on by itself. Not on the roofs of houses—or, there too. Dostoyevsky, who died in 1881, a few weeks after my grandfather Harry Donishevsky was born, not too far away. 'I am a sick man... I am an angry man. I am an unattractive man. I think there is something wrong with my liver.' The Underground Man. 'At that time I was no more than twenty-four years old. Even then my life was gloomy, untidy, and barbarously solitary.' *Notes from Underground*. Rivington Street. What a decision is and what making a decision means. Forty years from now, if I'm still alive, I'm going to be able to say: right decision, wrong decision, fuck it, that's not the point. No—I *actually had an inkling* of what a decision is and what making a decision means. *That's* the point. That's what I desperately wanted, and that's what I got. Melville helped me, the *Septem* helped me, Benardete's Notes—especially the *second* Note, which I SHALL NOW READ—helped me. The decision to take to the subway indefinitely definitely helped me. Before I get to the *absolute end of the line* Hegel is going to help me, indefinitely, definitely, beyond all definitions and indefinitions. But holy shit, The Fugs have helped me. Have they simply UNDONE what the fifth placard-man DID? No, that can't be. For one thing, the placard-men are infinite. Today—end of March, 1972—'New York City Transit'—a.k.a. The Subway—IS the placard-men. Synonymous with—no, IS. The subway IS the placard-men. Being is nothing. Any day now, any *way* now, I shall be released. A patch of discolored snow in early April. The maniac scumbag hits me with a B-52 IMAGE, and with a Fugs WHAT? And I hit you back with the REAL Fugs, motherfucker. Satori—I suddenly realize that we have gone beyond the war of images. What's more, as for the war of realities, any insect repellant on the market will take care of that. We are now approaching the war of decisions. A curious war, a looking-glass war. Reflections, apparitions, fires.

Whispering Death. A war not of deciding *this or that*, but of *seeing* what a decision is, and what making a decision means. The Dharma Eye. Satori and shadow. The night journey that ends in shadow. I thought the fifth placard-man had fucked me badly—fucked my mission. But this is no mission, no gaining idea. This is zazen. This is traveling indefinitely. This is a life-time. Here. Right now. 'No gaining ideas.' 72nd Street again, who in the world was Vincent 'The Chin' Gigante and who cares. As things turned out, not even Frank Costello cares, motherfucker, still fucking the world from his Waldorf Astoria penthouse. What—You Worry? Well, fuck you too. What—Me Worry? Alfred E. Neuman will outlive the Mad universe, satirically self-satirizing. Before I get to Columbus Circle—and Long Live Cristóbal Colón, Father of all Holocausts—I'd like to sing one last song. Killing me VERY softly.[115] It's Saturday night now, the car is full. 'I raise my head. The offing is barred by a black bank of clouds, and the tranquil waterway leading to the uttermost ends of the earth flows somber under an overcast sky—seems to lead into the heart of an immense darkness.'[116] The too-short summer of 1967, when the computer classes really sucked, but the ABSOLUTELY FREE concerts set a *fraction* of the new generation—my generation—on the road to wherever the hell we're going. The pouring rain. The Chambers Brothers in St. Mark's Place singing, infinitely, 'Time Is Come Today,' with naked girls throwing flowers—literally—from the roofs (into our minds, figuratively?), fucking the 'gloomy, untidy, and barbarously solitary.' The Fugs. What a fugging downpour. You really have to be 17 to rejoice under the rain like that, but it was summer, it was warm, it was beautiful. Tomkins Square Park, they ended the concert with their *absolute* (as Hegel would put it) classic. The 'official title' is 'Wide, Wide River' but fug that. It's 'River of Shit,' and I

115 Just to internationalize the songfest, I refer to the Demis Roussos version of 'Killing Me Softly With His Song,' which they played *incessantly* in Greece in the summer of 1973 (the second summer of my 'exile').
116 The last lines of Conrad's *Heart of Darkness*, verb tenses modified.

dedicate it to the fifth placard-man, scumbag maniac, fearless leader of 'fellow B-52 enthusiasts.' Am I singing it? This is a chic stretch of B Train, bordering on unadulterated midtown Fun Seeking. Well, fug it. They sang this song that summer in Tomkins Square Park—a fugging deluge—me, just turned 17— fug them all, we were all naked and happy. Not like the people of Vietnam, with their clothes—and their skin—burnt off by napalm. Zeus! Zeus! Immortal Fugs! Just do it. The thunderbolt in your hand, but no one has ever seen you hurl it.

   River of shit/ River of shit
   Flow on, flow on, river of shit
   Right from my toes
   On up to my nose
   Flow on, flow on, river of shit
   I've been swimming
   In this river of shit
   More than 20 years
   And I'm getting tired of it
   Don't like swimming
   Hope it'll run dry
   Got to go on swimming
   Cause I don't want to die.

   Oh I can feel another 1000 years
   Of the flapjacks of sorrow! Unless!
   Unless we make 2000 A.D.! 2000 A.D.
   Our glorious deadline
   A glorious deadline to make the
   World a better place!
   Or else the flapjacks of sorrow
   Are going to slide down our throats
   For another millennium
   Of pain and war and oppression

And all our children's children's children's
Children's children's children
Shall have to wade and swim
In the same grim river
In which we now swim
Sing along with us
Sing sing sing sing sing sing sing sing!
River of shit/ River of shit
Flow on, flow on, river of shit.

This year they put it in their album *It Crawled into My Hand, Honest.* But it's not the album, it's the immediacy, the *now,* the *here.* The pouring rain in Tomkins Square Park. The jeeps rolling through the streets day and night. In the mind. Emptiness. Not an oceanic crowd. Just a group of people. Mostly young or very young. The crossing. The river of shit. Endless. Infinite. Always now. Always here. Everywhere. A whole world. Fellow B-52 enthusiast. God bless you, Captain Vere.

THE SIXTH GATE

Columbus Circle. Cristóbal Colón, a Man of the World. Genoa,
Lisbon, the meandering monarchs of Spain. Dogs of God. 1492.
The Jews, the Moors. Hispaniola. The New World. A Discoverer.
Father of all Holocausts. The Pequot. End of March, 1972.
Saturday evening. Wide, wide river. What a decision is and
what making a decision means. Hades. Traveling indefinitely.
Cracked requiem. Art and life. FUGs, GAMs, IMAGEs. Off,
on, B Train packed. Midtown Manhattan, the beating heart of
Fun City. Queequeg, 'in his own person a riddle to unfold; a
wondrous work in one volume; but whose mysteries not even
himself could read, though his own live heart beat against
them.' His infinite tangle of tattoos—try to put THAT on a
placard, ye placard-men. I think I'll *never* see the last of you.
I decided to sing two Fugs songs on the B Train. 'River of
Shit' under Central Park West, wow. Sure, I sang them *real*
softly, but sing them I did. Actually, the only songs I like to
sing are Fugs songs. 'Dirty Old Man.' 'Morning, Morning.' 'River
of Shit,' what a great tune. I sing it to myself if I can't fall
asleep. *Screech*, 7th Avenue. Political songs—'Where Have All
the Flowers Gone' is one of my favorites. Pete Seeger, Woody
Guthrie. Dylan. Today we have lots and lots of protest songs,
of all kinds. Country Joe and the Fish. What in the world are

we fighting for? Don't ask me. Pearly gates. Don't give a
damn. Next stop, Vietnam! Fine music. A 'rag,' they call it,
as in 'ragtime.' Political music, political theater, political art—
that's fine. But, there's one thing that bothers me. Possibly
the same thing that bothers me about politics itself. I mean,
the way politicians always speak to the people of their *own*
party, just as political rockers always sing for their *own* fans.
Shit, this train is really JAM-PACKED right now, I wonder if
it's going to be like this in Brooklyn too. Saturday night fever,
in Brooklyn too. Possibly. Maybe more on the way *back* from
Brooklyn, fun-seeking Brooklynites heading for Manhattan.
Or maybe they have more fun in Brooklyn, what do I know.
How am I going to read Benardete's second Note.[117] What
if a bunch of strap-hangers lose their grip and *smash it to
a pulp.* Deep shit. *Screech*, Rockefeller Center, what a mob
scene. I bet there's lots of people ice-skating up there. Was I
making a point. Yes, I was. Politics, political art. What bothers
me about political art—and about politics, though everything
about politics bothers me, especially the fact that it's made by
politicians—is the way it speaks to people who already agree
with it. SirNoSir, this is not my idea of politics. Politics is—ought
to be—the art of speaking to *other* people, of doing something
to convince the people who *don't* see things the way you do.
Or, simply, who have never looked. Who is Country Joe out to
convince. Absolutely no one. Politics? He doesn't do shit. No!
Politics—political art—means *changing* minds, but this is all one
big self-celebration. Soliloquy politics, the politics of talking
to yourself and your friends. Yes, I *do* have a point, but—OK,
take Jimi Hendrix, he's one of the few these days (too bad he's
dead) — *screech*, 42nd Street, what a wild bunch, I'm *thinking
more slowly* right now, more musing than thinking, this mob
is crowding my mind — one of the few whose songs aren't

117 I note that my question marks have given up the ghost, little by little. After such
a long time in the subway my 'straight' questions have become reflections. Musings.
Musings are not questions, hence no question marks.

political at all. Jimi. Let's see if I can hum this, I can't even see who's right on top of me, ye gods, a PURPLE HAZE. Help! IS IT TOMORROW OR JUST THE END OF TIME? No, nothing political here. How about ROOM FULL OF MIRRORS, just like in the story of the Zen master who lived in a ruin, the uncouth old hermit. The empty mirror. Somewhat just like it. I take my spirit and crash my mirrors—can you call that political? No. Or—maybe this is exactly what I *mean* by political: *crash the mirrors.* Let's do it. What about the GAMs, the Great Academic Marxists. What about them. My fork. My spaghetti. Who are they talking to. I have this sick feeling that their students are *already* Marxists, more or less—which, in itself, is hunky-dory, but, then, what's the point. There's a contradiction here. Where in the world will *systemic change* ever come from if Marxists only talk to one another. Or to themselves. Sure, the vanguard—I mean, Lenin was talking to practically no one, he was freezing to death in Zurich, but he brought *big-time systemic change* to Russia. Big time. Then again, he sure as hell wasn't a GAM. My mind is being crushed by this mob. *Screech*, off, on, 34th Street, Remember me to Herald Square. Now, thirty screechless blocks until West 4th. Plus, I won't be seeing any placard-men anytime soon, unless they are SARDINE-placard-men. Take Eugene Genovese, though I'd call him a Marxist professor, historian, author, not a GAM. A Marxist intellectual. When he said, at that teach-in—I don't fear or regret the impending Viet Cong victory in Vietnam. I welcome it.—who was he talking to? Was he trying to convince anyone who didn't agree with him? No, not exactly. No, not at all, possibly. I was 15 at the time and I was already as riled up as I could ever get about this motherfucking war in the defense of tyranny. Ho Chi Minh, the Geneva Accords, free elections, that cocksucker Ngo Dinh Diem—the Bay of Pigs, the CIA, shit, I knew what was going on. Genovese helped me, he made me feel less alone. But, did he *convince* me. Be my guest, convince a fish it can swim. 'Watch the water.' The Dharma Eye. The Fugs, shit, they aren't out to convince anybody and they make no bones about it. I would call The Fugs 'acute observers of and commentators on the current socio-political scene' but no, I don't mean like Walter Cronkite, Huntley and Brinkley, or even the exceptionally ironic Roger Grimsby on Eyewitness News. The Fugs are fugging artists. Yes, no, yes, *political* artists. They wouldn't 'convince' a mosquito not to bite you. No compulsion. No. None. Plant seeds. Transit. Free release. SATORI. Direct experience that cuts through the layers and layers of your preconceived ideas and lets you experience WHAT IS RIGHT HERE RIGHT NOW. A River of Shit. A Kill for Peace. A sudden enlightenment.

Speaking of IMAGEs, when I started NYU in the fall of 1968 I wanted to study theater and write *political theater*, it was a pretty vague project, but then I took Dave Leahy's Greek Tragedy course and I don't regret it. I saw the Living Theater and they really gave me the shits. *Marat/Sade*, much better. Grotowski, not bad. But—but—*political* theater. I'll take Aeschylus any day, he spoke to the *whole polis*, which included *lots* of people who didn't agree with him. MEANWHILE—Pigasus for President! THIS is political theater. Abbie Hoffman, the Yippies—Youth International Party—the Democratic Convention in Chicago—political theater at its tip top. The Yippies nominated a pig named Pigasus for President of this Great Nation. On the Democratic Party ticket. The Lernaean Hydra, with her badly infinite heads and extremely bad breath, was out of the question—the very antithesis of what the American voter wants. And a female to boot, and her siblings were no better. Sphinx, Chimera, Nemean Lion—who in this Great Land would vote for Cerberus, a three-headed dog guarding the way to Hades. No! Typhon and Echidna (what a name) have spawned no viable candidates for President. No, Abbie, bless his soul, found a far more appealing figure from Greek myth, a regular Pat-Boone type, someone every God-fearing bread-and-butter milk-and-honey stars-and-stripes apple-pie American Mother could love and vote for: Pegasus, the winged horse. Pure white, a winged divine stallion, sired by Poseidon, from sea to shining sea. PIGasus, of course, was not a horse (winged or otherwise) but a 100% dyed-in-the-wool PIG that the folk-protest-singer and fellow Yippie Phil Ochs bought from a farmer in the countryside not far from Chicago. A red-blooded mid-Western American PIG, with a name inspired in some sense, and to a certain extent, by a Pat-Boone figure of Greek mythology, combined with the expression 'when pigs fly,' which means 'when something highly improbable occurs.' Which I find inappropriate, because a pig president, or a motherfucker president (as Eldridge Cleaver put it), is the direct reverse of improbable. An exception? Who are you kidding! Pig presidents have been the rule in the history of this Great Land, and not only recently, Dickhead! In any event, in the course of this contemporary historical political-theater event (Brecht's approach was different, too didactic for my tastes), a number of things occurred. The candidacy was announced in Chicago, and the Yippies demanded that Pigasus be treated as a legitimate candidate, with secret service protection and White House briefings. Instead, just when his 'acceptance speech' was being read Pigasus was arrested by the Chicago police and taken to the Chicago Anti-Cruelty Society. Never mind the napalmed Vietnamese. Seven Yippies were also arrested, and PUT ON TRIAL. *It Crawled into My Hand, Honest*. ON TRIAL, charged with 'disorderly conduct, disturbing the peace, and bringing a pig to Chicago.' The police claimed that the pig squealed on them. THIS is political theater. Both sides now. The Yippies survived this trial, and others. And Pigasus? It's rumored that a police officer ate him. Image, reality, all's fair. All of it. Politics. Defend the City!

'And then went down to the ship.' *Screech,* West 4th Street.

WHERE'S THE B-52! THE MY LAI MASSACRE! Where have all
the flowers gone. West 4th, 86th Street, prime placard-man
territory, and I know I haven't seen the last of them. WHERE'S
THE B-52! Maybe in the next car down. Maybe it changed to
the F, or maybe the D, it might be launching an 'Arc Light' this
very minute—three times 108 bombs—against Yankee Stadium
from below. Whispering Death. Or is it wending its way through
the transit system getting ready to attack MY CAR again. Sing
sing sing sing sing sing sing! Sing a political song. A battle
hymn, an anthem, a song of resistance or of rebellion. I think
I'll hum my way into Brooklyn with some all-time political-
song hits. In this mob I can't read the second Note anyway.
'II. Eteocles' Interpretations of the Shields.' Saturday night.
Let's listen closely to the words, some of these anthems are
actually pretty gruesome. 'The rockets' red glare, the bombs
bursting in air,' no, that's perfectly tame: after all, the Brits—
the Royal Navy, the HMS *Erebus* and the HMS *Meteor*—were
attacking our fort in Baltimore during the War of 1812, we had
every right to be riled up. Even if there's a certain irony in the
fact that Francis Scott Key's lyrics were set to the tune of a
popular British song written for a men's social club in London,
the Anacreontic Society. Long live Anacreon! the Ancient Greek
lyric poet who sang of love and wine. 'Our flag was still there,'
thank goodness. Proof through the night. But—OUR flag—well,
some of the bros, and not just the Panthers, are *riled up* about
this line. Ours? they ask. Whose? In this Great Land three and
a half million Blacks were slaves in 1812, and the half million
'free' Blacks couldn't vote, and that was the least of it.[118]
Meanwhile, the third stanza—absolutely justified—is a pretty
gruesome blast at the Brits:

---

118 OK, I confess, I added this to the second stab at the third stab, October 2016.
The stabs are all tangled up. Black athletes—Black Power! years after Tommy Smith
and John Carlos—refusing to stand for/during the National Anthem. Right on! Colin
Kaepernick, with his Afro hairdo, a pretty wild name for a bro. To be precise, these
bros are protesting racist police violence, not 'our flag' as such.

And where is that band who so vauntingly swore
That the havoc of war and the battle's confusion,
A home and a country should leave us no more!
Their blood has washed out their foul footsteps' pollution.
No refuge could save the hireling and slave
From the terror of flight, or the gloom of the grave.

Screech, Broadway-Lafayette—the Marquis de Lafayette, a
Frenchman who fought on our side during our Revolution. The
star-spangled banner in triumph doth wave, it's a catchy tune.
'La Marseillaise,' of course, is, musically speaking, far superior.
It's downright inspiring. Gripping. Stirring. Thrilling. Musically.
The lyrics pull no punches. 1792, French Revolution (Lafayette
in the thick of it again), France invaded by reactionary armies
(Prussia and Austria), 'Against us tyranny's bloody banner is
raised.' Absolutely. No question. The rockets' red glare. Fucking
foreign reactionaries. A revolutionary song. An anthem to
freedom. It became the French national anthem on Bastille Day
1795, but has had a checkered history. Napoleon 'dethroned'
it, and later it was banned outright, like the Pequot—even
speaking their name was prohibited. Banished. Giving thanks
for their extinction. 'La Marseillaise' made its comeback not
nationally but *internationally*—this is a *marching* song, and I
think the fact that many European workers and revolutionaries
didn't know French helped a lot. Musically it really is superb —
screech, Grand Street, it all seems so well timed, Chinatown
for dinner, *bon appétit* — and it came to be the anthem of the
international revolutionary movement. Marx hummed it all
the time, during the Paris Commune in 1871 they sang it for
all they were worth, and in 1879 it was restored as France's
national anthem. *Avanti popolo!* But some of the lyrics really
are gruesome, and the song has a lot to gain if you don't
understand them, or just don't think about them too much. OK,

'the roar of these ferocious soldiers, coming right into our arms to cut the throats of our sons, our women!'—this is perfectly legitimate. But this world-famous refrain, repeated about a ZILLION times—

> *Aux armes, citoyens,*
> *Formez vos bataillons,*
> *Marchons, marchons!*
> *Qu'un sang impur*
> *Abreuve nos sillons!*

—this is a wee bit graphic. 'Let an impure blood/ Water our furrows!' Great music. Stirring. Still, I prefer 'Where have all the flowers gone.' It's poetic, and it makes its point.

Bless my soul, the Manhattan Bridge. The real night, after so much Hadean night. The Night Journey. Night, the blackness of death. *Qu'un sang impur/ Abreuve nos sillons!* Fellow B-52 enthusiasts! As Hesiod noted, 'Night gave birth by herself to Death,' notes Benardete, in his second Note, which I am about to read, soon. Meanwhile, Dylan, *himself*, notes: Any day now, I shall be released. The glitter of these bridges. Night. The B Train a little less jam-packed. Headed for Coney Island, it seems like a million years since I've been there. The *reek* of that B-52, from West 4th all the way to Washington Heights, and back, a new B, but the reek still *in my mind*. Political songs. River of Shit. Sing sing sing sing sing sing sing! I feel like having a Coney Island hot dog (I've never had one and almost definitely never will) and then, post-haste, diving into the ocean and sinking like a stone. End of March, 1972. Saturday evening. Like a rolling stone. Neon madmen climbing. It's a long way to Tipperary. Am I losing it. I'm musing. How long have I been screeching along like this. Since noon yesterday. Not so long. What a decision is and what making a decision means. A B-52 on the B Train. Have the placard-men succeeded in leading me by the nose into the wilderness. Is that a question or an answer. A beautiful clear night—the *real* night—the black sky studded with stars. Stripes. The rockets' red glare. 'Our flag.' Fun City. Sing sing sing, as the Fugs put it. Under the ground already, under Brooklyn ground, long stretch to Pacific Street, then 36th Street, and then the West End Line, elevated and screechful, Sunset Park by night. I don't think many of these people are going to Coney Island, it's not the season, I think, what do I know, Christmas in Coney Island, the Fourth of July. I think the West End Line will be relatively peaceful, perhaps. Many screeches, but they are systemic, so to speak. Sing sing sing. I know a couple of Italian political songs, I'd better practice them, I may end up with Italy at the end of my fork. At least in Italy you can be a communist without having someone yell 'misery, terror, and death' at you.[119] These two songs are not gruesome at all, they're short, the lyrics are simple, the songs are highly singable, Italians love to sing. Sing sing. 'Bandiera Rossa' is the revolutionary song of the Italian workers. The workers themselves. The Party Secretary may sing it, but it belongs to the workers. They belt it out for all they're worth, every chance they get, and they get one often: '*Avanti o popolo, alla riscossa,/ Bandiera rossa, bandiera rossa.*' HIGHLY singable. Liberation! Avanti! Wave the red flag! A few of the stanzas are a little more complicated — 'From the fields to the sea, to the mine/ To the workshop, those who suffer and hope/ Be ready, it's the hour of vengeance/ Red flag will triumph.' — No, the *song* is lost in translation:

Dai campi al mare, alla miniera
All'officina, chi soffre e spera
Sia pronto è l'ora della riscossa
Bandiera rossa trionferà.

---

119 Until Berlusconi came along.

Sing sing sing sing. Forget about watering our furrows with an impure blood, here half the song is just *Bandiera rossa trionferà/ Bandiera rossa trionferà/ Bandiera rossa trionferà/ Evviva il comunismo e la libertà.* Sing sing sing sing! Some sing *Evviva il socialismo e la libertà* instead of *Evviva il comunismo e la libertà* but, never mind, that's not the point, the point is SING. *Canta che ti passa.* Sing, it will give you a mental ease. Sing, it will give you a big release. Canta canta canta canta. *Screech*, Pacific Street. OK, I'll be pacific, I'll refrain from singing Italian political songs on the B Train because I can't just hum them softly, like I can with 'Kill for Peace' or 'River of Shit,' hell no, you have to belt them out.

Una mattina mi son svegliato
o bella ciao, bella ciao, bella ciao, ciao, ciao,
una mattina mi son svegliato
e ho trovato l'invasor.

This is more or less the whole song, just sing it! Whatever your native tongue, from the Beltway to the Great Wall, *bella ciao, bella ciao, bella ciao, ciao, ciao!* Belt it out. Sing sing sing sing sing sing sing, as the Fugs put it (a 'sing' or two more or less). This happens to be the song of the Italian *partigiani*—the partisans, the freedom fighters of the anti-fascist resistance movement between 1943 and 1945. The *invasor* 'they found when they woke up one morning' *bella ciao, bella ciao, bella ciao, ciao, ciao!* refers not to Mussolini and the Italian Fascists, which would, in a manner of speaking, qualify the *partigiani* as 'internal exiles' invaded by their own local tyrants. No, they mean the Germans, namely the Nazis. The author of the lyrics—such as they are, and definitely not gruesome—is unknown, and the lyrics themselves are not what you could call all that 'stirring' 'gripping' 'inspiring' 'thrilling' or whatever. *Bella ciao.* The music is based on a folk song sung by the riceweeders along the Po river, who got up early in the morning — *una mattina mi son svegliato* — to work in their paddies. Now, politically-musically speaking, *Bella ciao* is not even a 'tune' but the rhythm is as catchy as they come (please, let's not compare it to a TV jingle), which is why this song has been, and WILL be, possibly the greatest political-music hit of all time.[120] If Defend the City! is your bag this is the song for you, from Rome to Paris to Istanbul! Peking Nairobi Baghdad, Hoboken Calcutta Kabul, Lima Phoenix Timbuktu, *bella ciao, bella ciao, bella ciao, ciao, ciao!* Sing sing sing sing sing. *Screeech*, wow, THIS one was well timed. The B Train singing *Bella ciao*. 36th Street, in just a second the West End Line, the *real* Brooklyn night. Elevated. The sky studded with stars. 'Our flag' still there.

'Night gave birth by herself to Death.' Where has Benardete gone. I hope to meet him in Coney Island. The car is not jam-packed now, just half-packed. Time for my favorite political song, the epitome of political song, actually, political song, political theater, political history all in one. A hymn to freedom. Incomparably beautiful. A call to battle. To revolt. 'Pote tha Kanei Xasterià.' I first heard it in Greece two summers ago, and I'm absolutely sure I haven't heard the last of it.[121] Today it's the song of resistance to the regime of the military junta

120 For the record (as of August 2015, my second stab), people have been singing 'Bella ciao' recently, and somewhat more or less stirringly, during the 2010 student demonstrations against tuition fees, in London; the 2011 Occupy Wall Street movement in New York City; the 2013-14 Taksim Gezi Park protests in Istanbul; the funeral of two victims of the Charlie Hebdo shooting in Paris (January 2015); the 2015 political campaign of SYRIZA in Greece; and in Syria by the Kurds. Recently. *Bella ciao, ciao, ciao.*

121 The three-day student uprising at the Athens Polytechnic that culminated on 17 November 1973 marked the beginning of the end of the CIA-Greek military junta, which collapsed the following June. The jeeps had turned into tanks—ten of them, in the center of Athens, firing on the students, dead and wounded, one tank crashed through the gates of the Polytechnic itself. In the most stirring moment in recent history that I know of, the students responded by singing 'Xasterià.' Words fail me here. The courage of these young Greeks who put their lives on the line, coupled with the haunting beauty of the song itself. A testament to political resistance and to political song.

that seized power in 1967, the Colonels. Tyrants. Fascists, with their jeeps rolling through my mind day and night. The *invasor*. This time we could speak of a whole population of 'internal exiles,' invaded by their own countrymen. *Screech*, 9th Avenue. Screech for screech the West End Line may be the screechiest stretch of the entire transit system, even more than the last stretch of the D under the Grand Concourse, but here in Brooklyn *we are elevated* and that makes all the difference. The screechiness is mitigated *by the outside world*. I should count them. How many screeches on the West End Line. About a screech a minute. *Screech*, Fort Hamilton Parkway. See what I mean. No, I'll just try to ignore them for now. *Xasterià*, what a word. Greek is the greatest language on earth, of the languages I know, barely. 'Astéria' means stars, like the Latin *astra*, as in 'astrology' or 'per aspera ad astra'—'through hardships to the stars.' Put an 'x' on it, and you have the sky studded with stars, *xasterià*. This is also, I think, the most untranslatable song of all time, I've been studying the words, and the history. The first lines, translated literally: 'When it's *xasterià* [as in: when it's cold, when it's hot—'when it's sky-studded-with-stars'], when it Februaries [February as a verb, 'to February'], I'll get my gun, my beautiful mistress.' When the season of starry night comes again. When the night-skies clear. The song was written in Crete in 1770 during one of the many revolts against the Ottoman Turks. Crete has always been full of freedom fighters, they don't take things lying down in Crete. But 'Xasterià' is unique, it really is 'both sides now': hauntingly beautiful and *really* gruesome. 'I'll get my gun, my beautiful mistress, to make mothers without children, wives without husbands,' and that's just for starters. 'Let an impure blood water our furrows!' is no joke but in Crete, believe me, they pull no punches. No, don't mess with us Cretans, you fucking Turks. When the cold February sky is clear and the night is studded with stars I'll come down from the mountains and nail your asses to the rocks, right through your fucking assholes. I'll fuck you till you fart on my balls, as the saying goes. Fucking Turks. Invading my country again. Ye Cretans! Ye Greeks! Get your heads together and, above all, get your guns. Wipe the assholes out. Nail their asses to the rocks. Fight the Tyranny! Defend the City! The Labyrinth of Knossos. Thebes of the Seven Gates. Musically, as you like, depending on the circumstances, the song can be as ethereal and tender as Joan Baez or as hoarse as Joe Cocker. You can sing it solo or en masse. In Greece they've been singing it for two hundred years now, they've been invaded one hell of a lot, from outside and from inside the country, by 'friend' and foe alike. Since the star-spangled Colonels took over they've been singing it again, and believe you me, we haven't heard the last of it. Absolutely not. Right now a popular singer and *resistance fighter* named Nikos Xilouris,[122] known as Psaronikos, also know as The Archangel of Crete, has got the Greeks singing 'Xasterià' again, *in earnest and with a vengeance. Screech screech screech*, the West End Line. Getting into Coney Island soon. I need a good brisk walk. Desperately. I need to take stock. Political songs— whatever happened to what a decision is and what making a decision means. I can't sing 'Xasterià,' it's much too beautiful for me, and the lyrics are too complicated. Anyway, I really can't sing. 'Dirty Old Man' in the shower, that's my top speed. 'Xasterià'—I can't even hum it, no, for me it's not on the roofs of houses, it's *in my mind. Screech*, let's see, 20th Avenue. Let me tell myself a little story, related to Psaronikos, who has two younger brothers, also great Cretan musicians, Antonis and Yiannis, known as Psarantonis and Psaroyiannis. This is a fish story—*psari* in Greek means *fish*. Watch the water. Their grandfather, Antonis, was known as Psarantonis (the Elder). He was part of a little band (no, not musicians) that stole whatever they could from the Turks, these fucking invaders. Since he was

122 He played an important role—musically and militantly—in the Athens Polytechnic uprising.

the fastest runner in the band, when they encountered Turks he ran so fast he caught them all as if they were fish, hence his nickname Psarotourkos, 'Fishturk,' and then Psarantonis, which was nicer, and since then all his male family members have had nicknames like his—Fishantonis, Fishnikos, Fishgiorgos, Fishyiannis, the more the merrier, a magnificent platter. Wow, I'm hungry. What ever happened to 'when you're hungry, eat.' 'When hunger comes, have rice.' But this is Hades. This is definitely traveling indefinitely, a fork but no spaghetti, a decision. What a decision is and what making a decision means. In his shroud. Already.

The prisoner's deed. Coney Island, famous for its hot dogs. But they must have fish. No question. To paraphrase Dogen-zenji, 'When hunger comes' is the vital activity of a person who has had fish. A person who has not had fish cannot have hunger. Since this is so, a person who gets hungry every day is someone who has had fish. Babe Ruth used to get big bellyaches from eating a huge number of hot dogs, and when I go to Yankee Stadium I eat a few too many myself. I definitely need to take stock. They've led me by the nose into the wilderness, with their B-52s on the subway. Why did I devote so much of my Hadean time to political songs. I have an inkling, it has to do with 'II. Eteocles' interpretations of the shields,' a.k.a. Benardete's second Note. With chasing images. My own images. Serendipity. Zazen. We'll see. The Dharma Eye. What time is it anyway. Where's that clock. I'm wandering around, dazed, in the Coney Island station. Dazzled by my own indefinite, possibly endless journey. Endless perhaps, pointless no. I hope. Everything ends. The end ends. Ends end. End of March, 1972. Quite a crowd here after all. Saturday night. The clock—it's way down there towards the ocean, possibly, let me mosey on over. 9:10 p.m. What are the practical consequences of this. The logical consequences. The logico-practical or practico-logical consequences. Zero on all counts, 'the round world itself but an empty cipher.' Nothing lurking. No loomings. IS IT TOMORROW OR JUST THE END OF TIME? No more time. Fuck it. Shall I have an apple. No answer. Zuikan? Yes! Just musing. Some water, yes! and I'll refill my bottle, my throat's dry from all this singing. May as well take a piss. Now an extremely brisk walk—wait, behold a subway map. OK, screeches of the West End Line, let's see, starting at the End (which one is the End), OK, *this* is the End, my only friend, The End, as The Doors put it, Jim Morrison came to The End in Paris last July, 27 years old, and The Doors with him, but not their name, their quote from William Blake, *The Marriage of Heaven and Hell*, 'If the doors of perception were cleansed every thing would appear to man as it is, infinite.' Food for thought. From *this* end, Bay 50th Street, 25th Avenue, Bay Parkway, 20th Avenue, 18th Avenue, 79th Street, 71st Street, 62nd Street, 55th Street, 50th Street, Fort Hamilton Parkway, 9th Avenue: 12 screeches, on such a short line. A drop in the bucket if you consider the entire subway, and all the trains. The whole caboodle. And kit. The System. Transit. One small step for a man, on the Moon. 'But the moon wanes and disappears, and the night becomes understood as the blackness of death: Night gave birth by herself to Death.' Benardete's second Note, interpretation of the first shield. I need to walk, fast, plenty, to get my head together. This is the place for it, the 8 tracks and 4 island platforms, so well timed, B, F, D, N trains, I'm walking *very briskly* up one platform and down another, at random. Briskly. Very briskly. I used to take to the subway to get my head together—a three in the morning or longer, less Taoist trip—but I can't do it anymore, *I'm already in the subway,* indefinitely, I'm part of the transit system now. Here and now. Briskly. Very. Their cries. My head is clearing, like the cold Crete February sky. And tonight the Brooklyn sky is studded with stars, the end-of-March sky, I'll see it as soon as my train leaves the station. Right now, instead of the endless

screech, people off, people on, that has become my world, my
life, my being (such as it may be, or not be), here, now, me,
up, down the platforms, randomly, up, down, the way up is
the way down, to say nothing of 'you can't go twice through
the same stream.' To say *absolutely* nothing of 'let me show
you the path on which there is no coming and no going.'
Your delusion. Me, whatever I am, a flashing into the vast
phenomenal world, as Suzuki-roshi put it. A 21-year-old NYU
student traveling to discover—no! not to discover America, à
la Simon and Garfunkel, counting the cars on the New Jersey
turnpike, no, to discover what a decision is and what making
a decision means. To *make* a decision. Yes. Necessarily.
Freely. The prisoner's deed. Down to the ship. B Train again?
4 platforms 4 trains, up, down, randomly—a no-mind decision,
Just do it. Does this mean just take one without even looking,
without even thinking. Now THIS is a question. *No, this is
not what Zen means by no-mind*. It's the direct reverse, so
to speak. Absolutely free? The direct reverse? No. No-mind is
not mindless, it's full of mind. Mind-full. A dewdrop. Dogen.
Just as the entire moon is reflected in a dewdrop, a complete
awakening of truth can be experienced by the individual human
being. 'Without looking, without thinking' smacks of a being-is-
nothing decision, the zero degree of freedom *and of necessity*.
A Chinese-menu decision. I need to read the other Suzuki, he's
in my bag, perfect Saturday-Night-in-Fun-City reading, *The Zen
Doctrine of No-mind*. The Dharma Eye. What train now. The N,
who needs it. The D, definitely not. Am I nostalgic for Delancey.
I'm sticking with the B. Why. Why not. I like the B.

The sky studded with stars. A train. Coltrane! Coltrane! A
beautiful clear night, end of March, 1972, I've been traveling in
the Coney Island station. Trucking, so to speak. The platforms.
The West End Line. Benardete's second Note. *Screech*, 12
screeches on such a short line. Let me just sit and look out
at the sky for a while, the night sky, Brooklyn, the train

filling, screech after screech. Just sit and look. Sit and look. Screech screech screech. Something's on my mind. What!? The Lernaean Hydra. The System. Astronomical numbers. So many heads to begin with, and if you cut one off she grows two more. Countless heads and an infinity of extremely bad breaths. A monster. I'm joking, of course, when I say that she inspired Hegel's concept of *bad infinity*, but Hegel is coming back out of my bag. A *decision*, which may also be regarded as arbitrary, to consider *thinking as such*. Now or never. Have they led me by the nose into the wilderness. 'We practice zazen like someone close to dying. There is nothing to rely on, nothing to depend on. Because you are dying you do not want anything, so you cannot be fooled by anything.' 'To sit without moving, without expecting anything, as if you were in your last moment.' Exhale, fade into emptiness.[123] The blank screen. Satori. To empty. I 'went down to the ship' to see *the whole picture*—so to speak, because '*thinking as such*' is not a picture of anything, or is at best a picture of nothing, of being is nothing. 'The system of logic is the realm of shadows, the world of simple essentialities freed from all sensuous concreteness.' Down to the ship, into the shadows, fade into emptiness. Great. Instead of emptying my mind I've filled it with B-52s, massacres, IMAGES, placard-men, and the ten-thousand screeches. 'Which may also be regarded as arbitrary.' What if I'm on the right road but going in the wrong direction. Like the traveler in Kierkegaard's story, who asks a man by the side of the road: 'Is this the road to London?' 'Yes, it is,' the man responds (I think he was a placard-man in disguise), but without telling the traveler: 'This is the road to London but you are headed away from London, you're going the wrong way.'[124]

---

123 *Not Always So*, pp. 98 and 5–6.
124 This reminds me of a cat-tail Marina Abramovic chases in her beautiful memoir *Walk Through Walls*, dedicated 'to FRIENDS and ENEMIES,' Fig Tree/Penguin, 2016, p. 185. During her long 'performance art' walk on the Great Wall in 1988, the Chinese government imposed a military escort on her and refused to let her camp on or near the Wall at night. (A possible enemy of the people?) No, she had to march, escorted, two hours to the nearest village each night and, of course, two hours back to the

Direct reverse. The West End Line, the night sky—*screech*—instead of seeing the whole picture, so to speak, I've painted myself a bad picture of the whole. I see the screeches but not the subway. I've blinded my Dharma Eye. My direct experience. I discriminate the ten-thousand things—the countless stops, starts, stations, cars, trains, lines—but I've lost sight of the *transit system*. This blindness is what Hegel calls *bad infinity*. Now or never. Definitely traveling indefinitely. What did that long rant about political songs have to do with it. It all started with KILL FOR PEACE on a placard and went on from there. Endlessly. A B-52 on the subway. Reeking. *Clinging to images*. Just ask Eteocles. Oedipus cursed and cursing. The road to London. Satori: direct experience of what is right here, right now. 'Those mirrors are empty, there is nothing. Nothing reflects, nothing can be reflected.' 'The empty mirror. If you could really understand that, there would be nothing left here for you to look for.'

Bad infinity. Hegel's distinction between true infinity and bad infinity. Now or never. Right now. *Screech*. My book, *The Science of Logic*. A recently published, hardcover edition—probably the only hardcover I have. It'll stand up to the B-Train crowd, which may be a mob in Manhattan. *Will* be a wild bunch, I'm sure. Placard-men, I'm ready. I need to go back to the beginning of the Logic, to being and nothing. But this time I need to concentrate on what *movement* is—*logical* movement, I mean. (Subway movement *as logical*, possibly.) Let's see. After saying that being and nothing are the same, that being *is* nothing, Hegel goes on to say that being and nothing 'are *not the same*, they are absolutely distinct yet equally unseparated and inseparable, and *each* immediately *vanishes in its opposite*.' They are the same—and different, i.e. not the same.

Wall each morning. She was 'exhausted before even beginning the day's journey.' Exhausted, probably pissed off, possibly riled up. One morning, she writes, 'I was so out of it when I started walking [on the Wall] that I turned left instead of right and walked four hours in the wrong direction!' Stuff happens, as Donald Rumsfeld once put it, politically. Impoliticly. Political art. The road to London.

Good. *Screech*, 36th Street, end (beginning!) of the West End Line. Sunset Park, by night. From the Brooklyn to the Hadean night, different, the same. Same subway, same system. Realm of shadows. *So many screeches and all one screech.* Yes, and no. Not two, and not one. 'Not always so.' The Dharma Eye. Yes. No. It discriminates the ten-thousand things *and* sees the ultimate reality of the whole—the reality of Buddha, reality as emptiness. Free from dualism. 'The most important teaching: not two, and not one.' *Treasury of the True Dharma Eye*. Wait, where's my *Zen Mind,* I need to read this, wait, it's on page 134:

> The big mind in which we must have confidence is not something that you can experience objectively. It is something that is always with you, always on your side. Your eyes are on your side, for you cannot see your eyes, and your eyes cannot see themselves. Eyes only see things outside, objective things. If you reflect on yourself, that self is not your true self anymore. You cannot project yourself as some objective thing to think about. The mind that is always on your side is not just your mind, it is universal mind, always the same, not different from another's mind. It is Zen mind. It is big, big mind. This mind is whatever you see. Your true mind is always with whatever you see.

Screeched right on through Pacific Street while I was reading the Roshi, the car's full but I feel OK. Another long stretch, then Manhattan Bridge Again, as Dylan didn't put it. Madmen. Neon. Now—here's Hegel's point: 'the proposition [being and nothing are the same] internally contradicts itself and thus dissolves itself.' What may be (badly) referred to as a 'unity' of being and nothing 'can only be said to be an *unrest* of simultaneous *incompatibles*, a *movement*' that Hegel calls 'becoming.' Being and nothing are 'unseparated and inseparable' but they are distinct, different, which means that they *are separated*. It's all a question of 'bringing these thoughts together,' as Hegel often puts it. I, myself, call it *abstraction*. Mark Rothko. Separating the inseparable. For Hegel *reason brings thoughts together that the understanding keeps apart.* Intellect without reason is blind and blinding. Now, let me see: in *becoming* 'being and nothing are distinct moments; becoming only occurs to the extent that they are distinguished.' But they are also the same. They *are* only as a *transition* of one into the other. They are *vanishing moments*, and their *truth* is becoming. But this isn't the end of the story. Let me read this next passage carefully, it's the *true* story of these screeches, these stops and these starts.

> The equilibrium in which coming-to-be and ceasing-to-be are poised is in the first place becoming itself. But this becoming equally collects itself in *quiescent unity*. Being and nothing are in this unity only as vanishing moments; becoming itself, however, *is* only by virtue of their being distinguished. Their vanishing is therefore the vanishing of becoming, or the vanishing of the vanishing itself. Becoming is a ceaseless unrest that collapses into a quiescent result.

Quite a mouthful. But I know where I am now, and even have an inkling of where I'm going, to discover what a decision is and what making a decision means. Discovery. Like Cristóbal Colón. Where in the world am I. That's easy, I'm in the subway, New York City. Transit System (a.k.a. Transit *Authority*). If I lose sight of this, if I fail to see *the whole picture*, which is *no picture*—which, *logically* speaking, is a picture of *vanishing moments* and of the *vanishing* of this vanishing (but it's also a *political* no-picture)—I'll be overwhelmed by a *badly infinite* stream of 'self-subsistent' screeches. Screeches 'on their own.' I'll be devastated, like the population of My Lai. Self-subsistent. On their own. A B-52 on the subway.

274

Manhattan Bridge. We've been here before. *Xasterià*. The glitters—the Brooklyn Bridge just a little way downtown, the Williamsburg Bridge quite a way uptown from here. Shall I blow it up. A fork. Spaghetti. Travelers. An outline, emptiness, and the future. 'The way up is the way down.' Same stream. We are about to enter Manhattan, end of March, 1972, Saturday night. Have fun. Have a nice ride. 'I wish y'all gook women and children a good evening.' Am I hungry. I'm not if I don't think about it. Sleepy. Hell no. Wide awake. Now—if I fail to see the *whole picture* (so to speak) I'll be the victim of a form of *logical tyranny* that Hegel calls 'bad infinity'—also know as the *progress to infinity*. (This 'progress' may well be akin to the infamous 'domino theory'—it's quite possible.) Let's see how I can explain this to myself, if I possibly or actually can. Hegel tells us that the 'antinomy' relative to finitude and infinity rests on holding fast to the *opposition* of being and nothing—i.e. to their *absolute separation*. This is the root of the *bad infinite*. In their *truth*, insofar as being and nothing, each unseparated from its other, *is*, each is *not*: they sink from their initially imagined *self-subsistence* to the status of *vanishing moments*. At this point Hegel makes a 'further remark' that I find intriguing. He says that 'the transition of being and nothing into each other... is to be understood as it is without any further elaboration of the transition *by reflection*'—i.e., by the understanding, the intellect. But this is just what the Roshi keeps telling me. *The empty mirror. Nothing reflects. Screeeeech*, Grand Street. So well timed. 'Satori' is one of the sexiest words in any language, it signifies 'sudden enlightenment' (or 'sudden awakening'). But, Roshi says, it's just direct, pure experience—'without any further elaboration.' 'Direct, pure experience' of what? I've been saying, of what's right here, right now—but *what* is right here, right now. What's right here, right now, is *transiency*, pure transition. Change and becoming. The vanishing vanishes but nothing is ever the same.

> The basic teaching of Buddhism is the teaching of transiency, or change. That everything changes is the basic truth for each existence.... We should find perfect existence through imperfect existence. We should find perfection through imperfection.[125]

Satori is *immediate* experience. But Zen experience is also mediation, it is this mind, in this *world*, here and now. In this moment, whatever 'moment' means and/or is. (As Hegel notes.) So satori is, also, the *experience* of immediacy. 'Truth only comes to be itself through the negativity of immediacy'—this is Hegel. In Zen terms, satori is a momentary (sudden) experience *of* this vanishing of the reciprocal vanishing of self and world, which are no more, or less, real than Hegel's logical being and nothing. (His '*decision* to consider *thinking as such.*') *The Zen experience of transiency is the experience of immediacy as abstraction*, as separation of the inseparable. Am I confusing Zen with Hegel's logic. Maybe so. So be it. Not two, and not one. What! Hegel is just not credible as a Buddhist monk. Why not. Just because he loved to tell jokes and play cards with his friends. No, if you look at the picture of a Kyoto monastery as our 'Empty Mirror' Dutch friend Jan describes it (a pretty wild place), my gregarious friend Hegel would have fit right in, working on his koan[126] and drinking beer with his fellow monks.

Now, putting this aside aside—*screech*, Broadway-Lafayette—let me get back to bad infinity. Which, Hegel notes, is actually not all bad. Logical 'unrest' is the source of movement and the heart of the dialectic—'the *contradiction* that impels the something out beyond itself.' For example, the point, through its concept, moves in itself and gives rise to the

---

125 *Zen Mind*, p. 102.
126 The only thing that troubles me about this picture is that Hegel might have solved the koans faster than the Master could dish them out. By the way, he really was exceptionally 'sociable and gregarious.' And an exceptionally caring husband, father, brother, and friend.

line. And the line to the plane, et cetera. The infinite turns bad when you let yourself be overwhelmed—or fascinated, which is worse—by big numbers *on their own*, i.e., just because they are big. Astronomical. By bigness as such. Big business. Shopping malls, rather than corner groceries—great. Infinite progress—wow I'm going to count to a zillion, good for me. Star-studded sky. Zillions. For Hegel this is not true infinity. But, I'd better reread this section, 'Infinity.' Read it very carefully—WATCH OUT, this next screech is *West 4th*, prime placard-man territory. Ye placard-men, I know there's no end to you. You may be five, ten, or ten thousand, I KNOW you are infinite, and—fuck you all—*I hereby declare you a true infinity*. Take that, ye placard-men. I caught you off guard with this one. No, this is a declaration you were not expecting. *Screech*, West 4th, NOT A PLACARD-MAN IN SIGHT. Not in this car. Not this time. No My Lai massacre, no B-52. But the transit system is infinite. Big, but also a *true* infinity. In a dewdrop. And so are the placard-men. Even if there's only five of you in all, in this system you're a true infinity. Just do it. Keep on truckin'. Screech after screech and all the same screech. No, not always so. Always different. Not always so. I've got my Dharma Eye on you, ye placard-men. I don't know what you're after, and I'm not after you, but—we're down here together. Somehow—I have an inkling—we're all in this together. In what. 'Down to the ship.' 'Heavy with weeping.' 'Our bodies also.' Big mind. Zen mind. No-mind. *It is time to cling to your images*. Images of the gods. Defend the City! B-52s in the subway. 'I wish y'all gook women and children a good morning.' Hegel! Help! Fuck the Saturday night fun seekers, *it is time.* 'Time Is Come Today,' as the Chambers Brothers so eloquently and magnificently, and—possibly, or impossibly—not politically, sang it, *truly infinitely*, in St. Mark's Place, with naked girls throwing flowers from the roofs of houses and of our minds, under the pouring August rain. 'Summer of Love' the publicists call it. I'd say satori summer. Direct experience, here, now. The moment, whatever 'moment' may be or mean. Let's go, fun seekers, Brooklynites in the Village, Manhattanite *genii loci*, tourists of all stars and stripes, 'our' flag, fuck you all. I'm getting my head together now, Love it or leave it. Reread this section, 'Infinity,' very carefully. The premise is this: 'In going beyond itself [the finite] thus equally rejoins itself. This *identity with itself*, the negation of negation, is affirmative being, is thus the other of the finite that is supposed to have the first negation for its determinateness; this other is the *infinite.*' This is Hegel. The negation of negation, identity with itself. The subway, a mass transit *system*. *Screech*, 34th Street, Remember me to Herald Square. A big night in Fun City, star-studded springtime, Saturday night. Down here in the subway it's really nothing special. Sure, the car is full, but in Manhattan it's always full in the evening. Looks like the usual crowd to me. No, the real Saturday night is *up there*, in the streets, the restaurants, clubs, theaters, movies, whatever, people just wandering around, aimlessly in many cases, looking at each other. In terms of *transit* it's for *taxis* that Saturday is very special, the evening and the whole night, until dawn. Cruising up and down (or down and up) (or both or neither) Manhattan at four, five in the morning, summer of 1969, I'd just turned 19, Saturday night, there were only a few of us cabbies at that hour, all of us young, Young Turks, and hungry—it reminds me now of Fishturk, Psarotourkos, better known as Psarantonis (the Elder)—cruising, catching our fares like fish. On Central Park West the traffic lights were staggered, the almost-empty street—at the right speed you could cruise from Harlem to Columbus Circle and on down 8th Avenue without stopping, watching the lights change to green right in front of you, picking up your fish. But 5th Avenue was a drag strip. Action. All the lights changed together, red to green right on down to Washington Square. *Floor it.* A taxi screech. Psarotourkos would have liked it. That was his kind of fishing. Action fishing.

Screech, 42nd Street. Fun City. The distinction between true infinity and bad infinity. Here's Hegel's point: 'The infinite is not yet really free from limitation and finitude. The main point is to distinguish the true concept of infinity from bad infinity, the infinite of reason from the infinite of the understanding. The latter is in fact a *finitized* infinite... in wanting to keep the infinite pure and aloof from the finite, the infinite is by that very fact only made finite.' 'The infinite set *over against* the finite, in a relation in which they are as qualitatively distinct others, is to be called the *bad infinite,* the infinite of the understanding, for which it has the value of the highest, the absolute truth. The understanding believes that it has attained satisfaction in the reconciliation of truth while it is in fact entangled in unreconciled, unresolved, absolute contradictions.' The infinite set *over against* the finite. Ye gods, what a tangle. *Screech,* Rockefeller Center. In Zen this is called a 'koan'—like 'the sound of one hand clapping.' The Dharma Eye. As the Roshi said, you just need to realize that one hand *is* sound. That sound and hand are separate *and* inseparable. True infinity sees the finite and the *one-sided* infinite of the understanding as *vanishing moments* of the true concept of infinity—moments of a *single process.* The single screech and the ten-thousand screeches—*in the realm of shadows,* each is equally only the moment of the other. Not two, not one. The same, different. We need, says Hegel, 'to be aware that this unity and this separation are themselves inseparable.' Wait, I want to read that again about one hand clapping—here, page 60:

> We say, 'To hear the sound of one hand clapping.' Usually, the sound of clapping is made with two hands, and we think that clapping with one hand makes no sound at all. But actually, one hand *is* sound. Even though you do not hear it, there is sound. If you clap with two hands, you can hear

the sound. But if sound did not already exist before you
clapped, you could not make the sound. Before you make
it there is sound. Because there is sound, you can make it,
and you can hear it.

Ten thousand, 'the ten-thousand things.' This is a Buddhist
expression, going back thousands of years. Instead of saying
'a zillion things' or some such (a ton, a load, a bunch, a heap,
droves, oodles, whatevers)—meaning *bad infinity*—they always
say 'the ten-thousand things.' The Native Americans—a.k.a.
Indians—used exactly the same expression. Often. I am a
damn good student, a 21-year-old NYU student, a *very careful
reader*, I renounced my student deferment, BUT they gave
me a 4-F, and fuck them all. I'm graduating in a few months,
and I HAVE A FORK. Where three roads cross. Shit, that's bad
infinity, even if the number is extremely far from astronomical,
that's not the point. What's my point. MY point. Monsters. Off
with their heads. The Lernaean Hydra. Too many screeches.
Big numbers. *Screech*, 7th Avenue. Astronomical. *Xasterià*.
Sky-studded-with-stars is a picture of a badly infinite big
number, the ten-thousand things, but 'Xasterià' the song is
true infinity. The *sky itself* is true infinity, not *set over against*
anything finite. The whole picture. Here I am, definitely
traveling indefinitely, a decision, the prisoner's deed, et cetera,
and—all these screeches, leading me by the nose into the
wilderness. Blinding my Dharma Eye. But the Dharma Eye is
not always enough. Sometimes you have to *see the sound* (as
the distressed maidens in the *Septem* put it), which, in itself,
cannot be *distinguished*. And this is Hegel's true infinity. The
understanding without reason is blind and blinding. The way
I was headed, the road to London—so many screeches and
all the same screech—*I would never have discovered what a
decision is and what making a decision means*. Not in a zillion
years. I'd have ended up right where I started, with a fork,

spaghetti (Western or not), and a being-is-nothing decision, to live with for the rest of my life. I took stock on my *brisk walk* in Coney Island. After a day and a half in the realm of shadows I was *ready* to take stock. It was high time.

Now it's time to take stock of my taking stock. 'And then went down to the ship,' the subway, satori, *the system of logic*. Screeches—stops—on the F Train, then the B, the D, now the B again. *Screech*, Columbus Circle, Dogs of God, 1492, edicts, expulsions. The ten-thousand screeches, *in my mind*. But what about all the other screeching going on. On all the *other* Fs, Bs, Ds, and *all the other trains* of the entire New York City Transit System. The A, C, E, S, Q, G, J, Z, M, L, N, R, S, Z, to say nothing of the 1, 2, 3, 4, 5, 6, 7, 9 (a.k.a. the IRT). Just think of the stops—the screeches—on the Broadway Local, the Lexington Avenue Express, the Flushing Local. Locals. Expresses. *Every day, all day, all night.* The stops never stop. Who can count them. Zillions upon zillions. What Dharma Eye can see them. What mind can discriminate them. No-mind. *No discriminating mind can discriminate bad infinity.* But Zen mind, big mind—'the mind that is always on your side'—sees the screeching as 'a flashing into the vast phenomenal world.' This mind knows that everything is in flowing change. A vanishing moment. 'To see a fish you must watch the water.' 'No one shows a child the sky.' With this mind 'I stop the sound of the murmuring brook.' With this mind, which is no-mind, I see the whole picture, 'one hand clapping,' which is *no picture* because it is *truly infinite*. In Hegel's sense of the word. Just do it, sure, OK. 'And Wilderness is Paradise enow.'[127] Don't kid yourself, neither the Zen Buddhist nor Hegel has ultimate reality, the system, just fall into their laps. It takes practice. Constancy. Zazen. The strenuous effort of the concept—of thinking in terms of the concept—Hegel says.[128] But I promised myself *my point*. Have I made it. Maybe so, but, it's slippery.

127 *The Rubaiyat of Omar Khayyam,* translated by Edward FitzGerald, XI.
128 *Hegel's Phenomenology of Spirit,* p. 35.

Screech, 72nd Street, The Dakota, 'The Chin' Gigante. Not down for the count, motherfucker. Tip-top mobsters, fuck them, I need to stick to the shadows. Let me try this. You can look at the subway in two ways. In one way it is a hyper-astronomical number of *screeches*—stops, starts, lines, trains, cars, PASSENGERS (by the way), days, nights, weeks, years, decades, and whatever. Bad infinity. In another way it is, so to speak, *the subway itself*. 'In and for itself,' as Hegel likes to put it. The New York City Transit *System*. Now, let's drop the word 'system' if we like. Hegel did like this word, but, what's in a word. Try this: if a passenger—if I, a passenger, experience each screech as self-subsistent, a.k.a. 'on its own,' then I am fucked out of my mind, badly infinitely. Hegel says so. Monkey mind. Acorns. Never mind three in the morning, I mean ten thousand a minute. *Screech*, 81st Street, the Museum upstairs is closed, but I bet there's a lot of guys and cute chicks strolling and possibly rolling around somewhere up there in the Park, despite the muggers, under the splendid star-studded end-of-March sky. The road to London. If I take the screeches this way, each on its own—which, I think, is exactly what I've been doing, up to now—I am royally, and plebeianly, fucked. I will never, ever, discover what a decision is and what making a decision means. I will have blinded my Dharma Eye. Cursed. Oedipus cursed and cursing. An unhappy ending, a bad end. But it's not too late. *Screech*, 86th Street, not a placard-man in sight this time, neither the 'pledge-of-allegiance' placard-man nor the 'approach-the-village' placard-man, or any other past or future placard-man. *Mon semblable,—mon frère!* Truly infinite. GAM, bomb, exile, the curse of Vietnam, *our* war in the defense of tyranny. In my name. Defend the City! Not just in Vietnam, not just now, but everywhere, yesterday, today, and tomorrow. A decision: What am I *myself* going to do. A question: *Am I going to decide my own fate, or am I going to be decided for by the curse of Vietnam.* Another question:

Isn't 'decide my own fate' a contradiction in terms. But—the might of the spirit. Positing contradiction in itself, enduring it, overcoming it.

End of March, 1972. Musing. How many U.S. soldiers *are* there in Vietnam now, after almost four years of Nixon, and Kissinger, of their 'Vietnamization' of the war, compared to the old days, the JFK-LBJ war. I read an article in the *Post* about this last week, I have it right here, I stuck the clipping right into *Zen Mind* to keep from losing it. The older clippings are in *Ramparts*, the newer, and/or most important ones, in *Zen Mind*. *Screech*, 96th Street, time, a river, they say. Who says. Who knows. Time is come today. The pouring rain. Stats. As usual, there are no stats on THE BOMBS, THE MASS MURDER, but one day we will be able to read about it all, down to the last ton, the last bomb, the last sliver that destroyed 'the last' life. In *our* name. There were 900 U.S. soldiers in Vietnam in 1960, 23,000 in 1964, 185,000 in 1965, 536,000 in 1968 (when I became a 'deferred student'), 'just' 335,000 in 1970 (when I 'undeferred' myself), and then just (!) 156,000 in 1971 (when I got myself four-effed). But now, this year, they say, there will be less than 24,000 U.S. soldiers, but over *one million* South Vietnamese patriotic warriors. And by next year, Nixon says, thanks to me, your President, and my friend Henry, *all our boys will be home.*[129] Joyfully reunited with their families. *Screech*, 103rd Street. A fork, a decision, *the prisoner's deed*. Why bother. When the music's over, turn off the light. 'If the doors of perception were cleansed every thing would appear to man as it is, infinite.' This war is coming to a (badly infinite) end. Fuck it, fuck the fork. I already made one decision, a damn good one, *in itself*, and so much the better if it also got me four-effed. But who *decided* all this, these MILLIONS of Vietnamese WE have killed, in our defense of tyranny. Our 'Defend the City!' fearless leaders. They decide. God bless

---

129 As I mentioned earlier, according to the official statistics there were 50 American troops in Vietnam in 1973.

Captain Vere. But have they ever looked in their mirrors and asked themselves—seriously—what a decision is and what making a decision means. Have they. Maybe so. I doubt it. I didn't even vote for them, I was too young. That's their problem, so to speak. My problem is MY decision. MY tangle of Hegel and Zen, of freedom, necessity, and *responsibility*. The war is over, long live the war. THIS is my problem. The fork. My second decision. A question—*screech*, 110th Street, the northern edge of Central Park, I like this street. A question: Is this war an end or a beginning. Is the way up the way down. If Hiroshima was the 'model'—the 'example' (as in: let this be an example)—for Korea, and Korea for Vietnam, and all of it for U.S. hegemony, a.k.a *imperialism*, well, may I ask, where is my country going. WHO decided to go this way, to take this path. We, the people, perchance. Is this OUR path. Shall I, too, decide to take it. My body also, heavy with weeping. 'Whether there be any patch left of us/ After we cross the infernal ripples.'[130] Has *my* country learned a lesson from Vietnam, such as, supporting tyranny and suppressing freedom is not a good idea. Mr. Nixon, Mr. Kissinger, have you *learned* a lesson. Hell no. You have *taught* a lesson. A lesson to the world, goddamit. I am definitely traveling indefinitely, here in Hades, the subway, the NYC Transit System, because I see, clearly, that this lesson is MY problem. MY responsibility. This is what I have learned.

The doors of perception. *Screech*, 116th Street, Columbia University, SDS, heads bashed, Weather Underground, Velvet Underground, I'm underground myself, for now, for ever, what ever. Central Park is Central Park, it's not the navel of the earth. Fun City, the USA, Delphi, Hanoi, Havana, I have nothing against navels, we all have navels, the navel is a true infinity. Wait! What ever happened to Hegel's 'true concept of infinity.' Hold your horses. I have not come to the end of this tale. Let's start again. The B Train, end of March, 1972, Coney Island to Washington Heights, damn near round midnight, but

---

130 Ezra Pound, *Homage to Sextus Propertius*, XII.

who's counting, Monk may be playing at the Village Vanguard at this very moment, or unannounced incognito at Slugs' in the Far East,[131] on East 3rd between Avenues B and C, five short blocks straight uptown from my place on Rivington. Round midnight, but at Slugs' the real players don't even show until around 2 acorns in the morning. I wish Coltrane and the whole quartet were with me in this car right now, playing. Sound! But Trane is dead. He was born in Hamlet, North Carolina, and died from liver cancer in 1967, in New York, 40 years old. Albert Ayler played at his funeral. Bach is Bach—'The Well-Tempered Clavier,' preludes and fugues in all 24 major and minor keys, *if this isn't true infinity what is*—and Monk and Coltrane are Monk and Coltrane. Damn good infinity. The same screech. *Screech*, wow, 125th Street, serendipity. No-mind, no-screech. Albert Ayler, SO FAR OUT, so far, SO far, so FAR, they fished his body out of the East River in November, 1970, a presumed suicide, possibly, or murdered, not likely, who knows. Music Is the Healing Force of the Universe. Who knows, who decides. 34 years old. Hold your horses. Let me put it this way. The screech makes no sense without the subway. The part is meaningless without the whole. And vice versa, I wonder. Yes, no question. They are inseparable. But the 'bad' habit that imprisons us consists in seeing the screech but not the system, the *transit* system. After all, the system is just one while the screeches are so outrageously many. *Badly* infinite. We love big numbers and long trips. A man on the Moon. Dogen-zenji saw the moon in a dewdrop. This is the true path, true infinity. 'If you think

---

131 For the record, it is *Slugs'* and not *Slug's*. The name derives from Gurdjieff's term for 'terrestrial three-brained beings' who go through life in a state of waking sleep, as 'slugs.' The club (or 'saloon') opened in 1964 and shut down in 1972 after the hard bop trumpeter Lee Morgan was shot and killed at the bar by his common-law wife Helen More on February 19th. I used to go there during my years on Rivington Street. It cost me less than a dollar for a whiskey, if I was thirsty. As a rule a little known musician was on the marquee, but during the night the greatest jazz musicians of all time showed up to play. This was not your 'normal' jazz club. It was also famous because getting there, and back, without getting mugged was not exactly a piece of cake, but on this score I was an expert.

you really come and go, that is your delusion.' Zen mind in the subway and the subway in Zen mind. A decision. *The prisoner's deed*. With that alone we have to do. Let me put it another way, Hegelianly: the *idea* of the subway. The subway's idea is not the direct reverse of its reality, no, its idea is its true reality. If I lose sight of this, I am lost. With my own hands, with these screeches, I dig my own personal Twin-Towers Hole in the Gulag. This babbling heap of buildings, streets, people is not the *real* city. The *ideal* city is the real, the true city. This is what Hegel means when he says that 'the finite is ideal.'

Hegel's distinction between true infinity and bad infinity. Now or never. Now: a trip to the Moon. 135th Street, no matter, I'm coming to the end of the line, again, soon. The unicorns fast asleep. Who's in the car with me. No idea. Not many. A Latin type. Dark hair and beautiful eyes. No, I'd have noticed something like that, especially if she were right next to me. Possibly, at this point. No, just a few Washington Heightsers straggling home. I am traveling. People are fascinated by big numbers *on their own*, for their own sake. The infinite set *over against* the finite. Bad infinity and true infinity—and vice versa. Sometimes we confuse them. Take the case of the commuter. Instead of the usual NYC subway let's take a look at the Lackawanna Railway. Equal time for the Jersey commuter, who is far more systematic, or systemic, or jaded, or dumbed down, or whatever, than the flighty New York infra-five-borough commuter. (Never mind Staten Island, not far from Hamlet, North Carolina.) New Jersey is hard to imagine if you happen not to live there. Like Timbuktu—what do you know about Timbuktu. Like everywhere. But let's commute. Bad and true infinity—they can be slippery. This may or may not be important. It may be totally beside any imaginable point. I can only do what I can do. Create problems. Dave Leahy's specialty. Make philosophical problems. 145th Street, I'm listening to Coltrane, the Sound, the screech is all in my mind. Satori. The screeches are *never* the same, no two screeches are exactly alike. Mechanics. Reality. Zen. SOUND. No two sounds from Coltrane's sax are ever exactly the same. Not only is 'My Favorite Things' never the same, but no two SOUNDS are ever the same. It's true infinity. Separation of the inseparable. Anyway, here's what I'm thinking. The Jersey commuter, the Lackawanna Railway, from somewhere in Jersey to Hoboken, birthplace of Frank Sinatra. Then, in Hoboken the 'true' commuter takes the Hoboken Ferry to lower Manhattan, rain or shine, hell or high water, while the 'bad' commuter takes the 'tube'—the subway under the Hudson—but let's forget about the ferry or the tube and stick to the train. Let's say that the commuter travels twenty miles to Hoboken in the morning and, of course, twenty miles home in the evening. Forty miles a day, always the very same forty miles, again and again and again. Same old grind. A bad infinity, perhaps. Well, I don't know. Set *over against* the finite, possibly. Or maybe this is his true infinity: after all, he gets to work, gets home, makes a living, mows the lawn on weekends, raises a family. But—again and again and again, always the same train, the same trip, the same 20 + 20 = 40. Now, just to create a problem, let's take both sides now, as Joni Mitchell put it. Both at once. This Jerseyite has the feeling he's not going anywhere—he gets to work, gets home, but doesn't GO anywhere. Well, 40 miles a day, 5 days a week, makes 200 miles a week, a little over 800 miles a month, and about 10,000 miles a year. Simple arithmetic. Multiplication. In ten years he travels 100,000 miles. Now, since he has a very good job on Wall Street or thereabouts, let's say he works, and commutes, for fifty years. Sooner or later he'll probably buy a bigger house farther out in Jersey and may even commute 60 miles a day or more, but, never mind that. 40 miles a day is quite enough, it adds up to 500,000 miles in his lifetime, which—I did the math—is equal to about 83 round trips to California or *20 trips around the world*. And every day he thinks: But I never GO anywhere, this commute is a bad infinity. 163rd Street, Coltrane, SOUND. But is it actually a bad infinity. Are there no Zen Buddhists in Jersey. And what if he *thinks*—well, it's also true that I'm taking 20 trips around the world. That's one way of looking at it. Now, in this case, which would be the bad infinity—the commute, the small number, or the trip around the world, the BIG number. Which one. I've been thinking about this. Or, which would be true infinity. The Roshi would probably laugh and say, Ask your friend Hegel, he's the one who makes this distinction. OK, Hegel—the first section of the Logic is 'quality,' which passes over into the second section, 'quantity,' and the bad versus true infinity distinction is in the 'quality' section. So it's not actually a question of numbers. SOUND, the end of the line, the unicorns, 168th Street. I rest my case.

What case. Am I leading *myself* by the nose into the wilderness. No, I'm just thinking. Sometimes you can make a point without knowing what it is, or without knowing that you've made it. Like Eteocles, in Benardete's second Note, which I shall now read, on the downtown B, to Coney Island. There it is, on the other side of the platform, 168th Street station, dead, nobody around, 'Night gave birth by herself to Death,' as Benardete notes in his second Note, in his interpretation of Eteocles' interpretation of the *first* of the seven shields. The downtown B just sitting there, inert, it looks like a dead worm. Have no fear, it will soon come to life. Fun seekers, placard-men, the night is still young, Saturday night in Fun City. Meanwhile, to kill some time, apart from the Jersey commuter I have another example of this sometimes slippery distinction between true and bad infinity. The cockroach. New York City—ten million people and possibly ten billion cockroaches. (Never mind the rats.) Worse than the Lernaean Hydra. If this isn't bad infinity, what is. And not just on the Lower East Side—$55 a month and it's all yours—but in Park Avenue apartments worth millions. They leap from the chandeliers. True democrats. But—I read this, it may or may not be true—I read that the cockroach is the oldest species of living creature on the face of the earth. They used to torment the dinosaurs, traipsing through their food. 200 million years ago. And they're still here, and thriving. They're the Elder Statesmen of the history of the world, and will outlive us humans for sure. No question. If this doesn't make them *truly* infinite, what does. Look! I'm on the move already, the worm is not dead. Is it a problem of 'quality' and 'quantity.' Beats me. If I ask the Jersey commuter, Where's the real quality (true infinity)? Is it the daily round trip to Hoboken or twenty trips around the world? he'll probably answer: Quality? Quality is my summer vacation. Asbury Park, the Poconos, the Boardwalk in Atlantic City. OK, he has a point. At this point I wonder what Hegel really means by 'true infinity.' SOUND, 163rd Street. SOUNDS now, no more screeches. And not 'self-subsistent' sounds, sounds 'on their own'—no! Zen sounds, one hand clapping, flashings into the vast phenomenal world. Practice, constancy, the strenuous effort of the concept. No duality. No gaining idea. The *peep-peep-peep* of blue jays on the roof during zazen. A sound that *we* make. The sound is *in* our practice. True infinity—what does Hegel mean, what's he getting at. His point. Images are rare in his writing, with 'the realm of shadows' he went way out on a limb. But Dogen-zenji—so different from Hegel, but also so very like him—was a true master of images. *Truly* a Master: just as he mastered the image he was himself mastered by it. I've read a few of his poems, and some snippets from his enormous *Treasury of the True Dharma Eye*, written in the thirteenth century. I copied this one, my favorite, on this little piece of paper, here it is—I stuck it into my *Zen Mind* to keep from losing it, along with the clipping from the *Post*, the one with the stats on our troops in Vietnam. I also have an article I came across the other day with the latest stats on murders in New York, year by year. 'Analogies,' Dogen says.

A fish swims in the ocean, and no matter how far it swims there is no end to the water. A bird flies in the sky, and no matter how far it flies there is no end to the air. However, the fish and the bird have never left their elements. When their activity is large their field is large. When their need is small their field is small. Thus, each of them totally covers its full range, and each of them totally experiences its realm. If the bird leaves the air it will die at once. If the fish leaves the water it will die at once.

Know that water is life and air is life. The bird is life and the fish is life. Life must be the bird and life must be the fish.

It is possible to illustrate this with more analogies. Practice, enlightenment, and people are like this.[132]

Quality, quantity—analogy—a whole picture, a picture of the

---

132 I quote, again, from *Moon in a Dewdrop: Writings of Master Dogen*, published in 1985. The quote is on pp. 71–72 and is from one of Dogen's most important and most famous essays, *Actualizing the Fundamental Point*. I promised to make a big effort not to talk too much about Dogen in this book, but, on the previous page, page 70, we have the passage for which he is most famous, and rightly so. Dogen was unique, a genius. I have to quote this in full—alas, this and no more. I won't even quote the one where he says, on page 71: 'Enlightenment is like the moon reflected on the water. The moon does not get wet, nor is the water broken.'

Firewood becomes ash, and it does not become firewood again. Yet, do not suppose that the ash is future and the firewood past. You should understand that firewood abides in the phenomenal expression of firewood, which fully includes past and future and is independent of past and future. Ash abides in the phenomenal expression of ash, which fully includes future and past. Just as firewood does not become firewood again after it is ash, you do not return to birth after death.

This being so, it is an established way in buddha-dharma to deny that birth turns into death. Accordingly, birth is understood as no-birth. It is an unshakable teaching in Buddha's discourse that death does not turn into birth. Accordingly, death is understood as no-death.

Birth is an expression complete this moment. Death is an expression complete this moment. They are like winter and spring. You do not call winter the beginning of spring, nor summer the end of spring.

whole. A picture of what cannot be pictured—emptiness, 'no dualism,' Zen mind, 'always on your side.' Yes! it's not the *size* of the sky that makes it truly infinite, no! True infinity is bird and sky *taken together*, bird-flying-in-sky. Separate and inseparable. On the roof. In the mind. *In no-mind.* No bird, no sky. No sky, no bird. Fish/water. Screech/subway. Trips around the world. Traipsing through their food. One solitary bird or ten-thousand birds. No end to the sky! Bird-sky, sky-bird. The true path. Analogies. The true concept of infinity. No commuter, no train. No train, no commuter. Ye gods, it's not the train set *over against* the trip, the commuter set *over against* the commute, no! It's the tripping-train, the commuting-commuter. They never leave their elements.

A decision. The prisoner's deed. SOUND, 145th Street. The train still pretty quiet, it'll start to heat up in Harlem. Round Midnight. The empty mirror. Now—I'm going to read Benardete's second Note—DAMMIT ALL, THAT'S WHAT I WENT DOWN TO THE SHIP FOR. Eteocles' decision, and mine. But— how about the other Suzuki, D.T. Suzuki, he of the hundred books. *The Zen Doctrine of No-mind* is in my bag—look! it's coming out. Here it is. DO NOT SAY that I painted myself into a true-versus-bad-infinity corner with my Jersey commuter going 20 times around the world on the Lackawanna Railway or my cockroaches older than dinosaurs, no! Just think of the think tanks. They think of everything, and 99% of what they think has a blunter point than my commuter or my cockroach. Philosophically blunter, but razor-sharp on trivial matters such as improved formulas for napalm and Agent Orange. Ballistics. Better bombs. Now, believe me, D.T. Suzuki is no Dogen, and he's not the Roshi either, he's the 'other' Suzuki as far as I'm concerned. But he makes his points and they are *acute*. I've learned a lot from him about the Dharma Eye, which, as I said, is not always enough, and which I keep bringing up because it may well be the key to my problem of *what a decision is*

and what making a decision means. The key to this tangle—
freedom, necessity, responsibility—which is not a fork but a
no-fork. GAM, bomb, exile—this is a fork. Absolutely. And a bad
infinity. A small number, just three prongs, but a bad concept of
decision. Better than a straight being-is-nothing decision, but,
bad. SOUND, 135th Street. I hate to mention this but, alas, in
Buddhism there are FIVE eyes—the physical eye, the god eye,
the wisdom eye, the dharma eye, and the Buddha eye. Yet
another tangle. But, let's try to steer clear of it, I want to focus
on the Dharma Eye, famous for its power of discrimination. As
Hegel tells us in the greatest detail imaginable, it is not just
a matter of 'bringing thoughts together,' no, they also have
to be separated, and what separates—discriminates—is the
understanding, which, therefore, is absolutely not all bad. On
the contrary, Hegel—as I noted—calls it 'the most astonishing
and mightiest of powers, or rather the absolute power.'[133]
Why he does this is a long story, which involves Death (a
democrat, as Melville put it), but, let me put it this way, in Zen
terms: You can't just shine 'the Buddha Eye of omniscience'
on anything you please, no, you're not a Buddha, even if you
are Buddha-nature. What you do have is the Dharma Eye,
but discrimination on its own is clearly not enough. On the
contrary, it can get you into Big Trouble. But I have a Big Point
here, and it has to do with the empty mirror. SOUND, 125th
Street, SOUL SOUND. I have plenty of company in the car
right now, but this is nothing, let's see what it'll be like under
Times Square. Mayhem, perhaps. Murder Incorporated, no.
Now, The Zen Doctrine of No-mind. This book is, basically,
the story of Hui-neng, the Sixth Patriarch of Zen Buddhism
in China, let's see, born 638, died 713 (approximately),
WHAT A PERSONAGE. The Jimi Hendrix of Zen. An incredible
story, which, alas, I'd better not go into now. No, it's time for
Benardete's second Note. Let's just say this: to become Sixth
Patriarch he wiped out the 'dust-wiper' school, which compared

---

133 Hegel's Phenomenology of Spirit, p. 18.

the mind to a bright mirror (so far, so good) that needed to be dusted constantly, through meditation. Zazen. Hui-neng liquidated this wiping with his famous saying 'from the first not a thing is' (as Suzuki translates it, rather awkwardly), which is the basis of his doctrine of *no-mind*. In a nutshell: if ultimate reality is *emptiness*, it doesn't need to be dusted. Fortunately, however, Hui-neng did not liquidate the idea of the mirror, which, however, for him—as we shall see, in my possibly convincing interpretation—is, by its very nature, an *empty mirror*. SOUND, 116th Street, this 'other' Suzuki says some very important things, but he sure can be convoluted. Dharma Eye. 'Discrimination,' in Chinese *fen-pieh*, in Sanskrit *vikalpa*— the original meaning of this key Buddhist term is 'to cut and divide with a knife.' Suzuki: 'analytic knowledge, discursive understanding, speculative reasoning,' depending on the sharpness of the knife. Good. The other, even more important term here is *Prajna*: intuitive knowledge, intuitive wisdom. As this Suzuki puts it,[134] 'discriminative reasoning is always based on non-discriminating Prajna; the mirror-nature of emptiness always retains its original brightness, and is never beclouded by anything outside that is reflected on it.' Very good. SOUND, 110th Street. 'How is it possible for the human mind to move from relativity to emptiness, from the ten-thousand things to the contentless mirror-nature or self-nature, or, Buddhistically expressed, from *mayoi* to *satori?*' This, for *this* Suzuki, is 'the greatest mystery not only in Buddhism but in all religion and philosophy.' This, I must say, is not Suzuki-*roshi*'s idea of 'the mystery.' (Perhaps because he's a roshi.) No, he has another idea. In his talk titled 'Emptiness' he says: 'There is no way set up for us. Each one of us must make his own true way, and when we do, that way will express the universal way. *This is the mystery.*' True understanding will come out of emptiness.

---

134 The series of quotes that follow are from *The Zen Doctrine of No-mind*, pages 56, 52, and 51. My italics.

Moment after moment we have to find our own way.[135]

The Dharma Eye, why do I keep harping on it. Make our own way—well, we do need to *see* where we're going. Or see *where we are*. In the subway, for example. The stops never stop. What Dharma Eye can see them. What mind can discriminate them. No-mind! *No discriminating mind can discriminate bad infinity.* What a decision is and what making a decision means. WATCH OUT. A Zen placard-man. Shen-hui, Hui-neng's greatest disciple. The 'other' Suzuki quotes this passage from his *Sayings*. What *blows my mind* here is not the 'mystery' but the *logic*:

> A bright mirror is set up on a high stand; its illumination reaches the ten-thousand things, and they are all reflected in it. The [old] masters were wont to consider this phenomenon most wonderful. But as far as my school is concerned it is not to be considered wonderful. Why? As to this bright mirror, its illumination reaches the ten-thousand things, and these ten-thousand things are *not* reflected in it. This is what I would declare to be most wonderful. Why? The Tathagata [a Buddha] discriminates all things with non-discriminating Prajna. If he has any discriminating mind, *do you think he could discriminate all these things?*

This is Zen logic. On one side it is self-contradictory, being is nothing, 'logical' moments, a tangle of shadows. All reflected in it, not reflected in it. Nothing. But, taking both sides at once, it *blazes* with logic. A fire in the mind. It's William Blake's 'Tyger! Tyger! burning bright/ In the forests of the night.' I read these lines over and over, in the darkness, and then, suddenly, I see everything. Satori. I open my Dharma Eye. I do NOT have the Fifth Eye, the Buddha eye of omniscience, but then again, who does. Not Hegel, not the Roshi, the best we can do is to open our Dharma Eye and see *what discrimination is and*

---

135 *Zen Mind*, p. 111.

what it means. And what it *isn't* and what it *doesn't* mean. It separates, it cuts with a knife, but it does NOT mean *seeing the ten-thousand things*. This Shen-hui was a genius, he's opened all the eyes I have. Ten-thousand things—all together, self-sufficient, *on their own*—is bad infinity. 'The most astonishing and mightiest of powers, or rather the absolute power' is the power *to discriminate, to separate*, but it doesn't mean *seeing the ten-thousand things*. No mind can do this, *and why bother*. Not even the most over-the-top tourist wants to see ten-thousand things, all at once, and *in a mirror*. It's true, without discrimination nothing is seen. Wonderful. Mighty. But what is most wonderful is *no-mind*, the 'free play of the concept.' Emptiness. Buddha mind. Reason, as Hegel sees it. If the Mind Mirror reflected all things, its glare would blind all the eyes. What is most wonderful is this: 'The mirror reflects everything coming before it *unconsciously*, with no-mind.'[136] THIS IS THE EMPTY MIRROR. 'If you could really understand that, there would be nothing left here for you to look for.'

The ten-thousand things. To make a decision, do you have to discriminate, separate, SEE ten-thousand things. No. This is *not* what a decision is and what making a decision means. Dammit all, I've learned something here. Prongs, forks. SOUNDS, I SEE the sounds now but don't hear them—103rd Street, 96th, this is 86th already. A decision? Do you think it's a great big Chinese menu—take your pick, pork shrimp beef, Group B D F like the subway? Rice, noodles, or in-between. The ten-thousand different soups! Wonton, bird's nest, shark's fin, whatever. Kit and caboodle. Chopsticks or forks, a bad infinity. Now—if I've actually discovered what a decision *is not*, good! Just keep truckin'. The true path. No coming and no going. This

---

136 *The Zen Doctrine of No-mind*, p. 73. This is the sharpest thing this Suzuki said, and it's in a footnote.

Hegel, possibly in a different context, had a great deal to say about the unconscious, and unconscious mind. See, in particular, the 'Anthropology' section of his *Philosophy of Mind*, a.k.a *Philosophy of Spirit*. For a whole book on Hegel and the unconscious, see Jon Mills, *The Unconscious Abyss*, Albany: SUNY Press, 2002.

Suzuki, the 'other' one, on his 'greatest mystery' page—it's page 52—writes about the human mind moving 'from *mayoi* to *satori*.' In a footnote he tells us that *mayoi* means '*standing on a cross-road and not knowing which way to go*.' Ye gods, a fork. A decision. The prisoner's deed. 'From *mayoi* to *satori*.' 'The greatest mystery.' I think he's making a point after all. In Zen mind, in big mind, in beginner's mind, in Buddha mind, a *true* decision is an *unconscious* decision. A decision made with no-mind. Although it was a matter of surviving on the battlefield, the samurai fought his fight in the zendo. It's not a 'pick one of the ten-thousand things.' It's not a 'here's the fork, pick a prong.' No. The mirror reflects everything coming before it *unconsciously*, with no-mind. What this actually *means*, of course, is anybody's guess. Zen is an open book, but the pages are blank. It takes practice. I'm only 21. SOUND, 81st Street. IS IT A PLACARD-MAN! Shen-hui in person? I'm not sure yet, it's hard to tell. Wriggling, the car is packed, whatever it is it's coming from the other end of the car. Let's see. It's a man. Anthropus. The answer to the riddle. And he does have a placard—or a sort-of placard. It's not as big as the other placards, not rectangular, not hanging from his neck. I can barely see it in this crowd, at the other end of the car. It looks oval-shaped from here, and he's brandishing it like a shield. He's saying something—he's wriggling through the throng, brandishing his shield, and saying something to everyone. It's the sixth placard-man, I can tell. Maybe he's not actually brandishing it, he's just pushing his way through. I wonder what he's saying. The people aren't showing much interest. Is he a Vietnam veteran, like the other five? The sixth placard-man. I still can't see what's on his placard. He doesn't seem to be asking for money, like the other placard-men. What's he doing? What's on his mind? Here he comes, he's getting close. He's wearing green army fatigues, I bet he's a Vietnam veteran like the others. The placard—it can barely be called a placard.

It's perfectly round and the pasteboard is thick. A lot like a shield. And he's not brandishing it, he's holding it very steady, with one hand. No sword in his other hand, but I can imagine one there. A samurai. BUT I DON'T SEE ANYTHING ON HIS SHIELD, no image, no device. Wait, here he comes. Dark long wavy hair and a full beard, unkempt, definitely a little older than I am, maybe five years older. He's saying END THE WAR, again and again, to everyone, turning left and right, both sides of the car, he wants to say it to everyone. END THE WAR. The placard-tide is turning, against the massacres and the B-52s. He's not shouting or yelling END THE WAR, he's soft spoken, he's just saying it, to each individual, face to face. No cap in his hand or on his head, not asking for money, he's just asking to be heard. Here, in the subway. I *knew* the placard-men were a true infinity. A bird flies in the sky, and no matter how far it flies there is no end to the air. But—nothing on his shield? Wait, here he is right in front of me. He says END THE WAR to me! To me! No, there's no image on the round circle of his shield, but—I see it now—there are two words, hand printed, very small, you have to be close up to see them. From the distance you only see an empty shield. All small letters, not the blazing capitals of the other five. Scrawled, indistinct, like a stain on an empty mirror. Two words: *winter soldier*. SOUND. Coltrane! Coltrane![137] A flashing into the vast phenomenal world. Gone. 72nd Street. He's gone.

No-mind. It's as if this car were empty, suddenly. This whole B Train, this whole subway, this entire New York City Transit System. Empty, suddenly. ARMIES. WARS. EMPTINESS. All I can think of is this, three lines of verse spoken by a dying Japanese warrior under a shower of swords:

---

137 The second track of the album *Monk's Music* (Riverside, 1957), 'Well, You Needn't,' begins with a duet—Monk's piano and Wilbur Ware's bass. Suddenly Monk *cries out* 'Coltrane! Coltrane!' and the SOUND of Coltrane's tenor sax flashes into the vast phenomenal world. 'Sheets of sound.' Monk's cry is an invitation and, at the same time, a cry of liberation. A new beginning, a new world.

Both the slayer
And the slain
Are like a dewdrop and a flash of lightning.[138]

The sixth placard-man just said—to me!—END THE WAR. *As if it were my decision to make.* The winter soldier. A war of images, a war of realities. A B-52 on the subway, and 7,658 North Vietnamese SAMs to shoot it down. Five placard-men. One image summons the next, one reality summons the next. Magic. Typhon and Zeus. Seeming and being, image and reality. Then, now, the EMPTY SHIELD—not the victory of reality over its images, no, it is *the triumph of the image.* Which is no-image. Seeming and being are now the same. Shin-hui, the Zen placard-man. I hear his voice. The winter soldier 'abides in the thought of emptiness and absolute sameness... even when his body is cut to pieces in a melee between two fiercely contending armies.' I'd better get my head together *now*, and fast, before I come to the end of this line. It seemed to be an endless line and now, suddenly, it's as long as a dewdrop. Am I going to decide my own fate—my life, my future, my *now*—or am I going to be decided for by this Curse, the curse of Vietnam. What *seemed*—an image—to be MY curse of Vietnam *is*—in reality—THE curse of Vietnam. *My image*, my seeming—but the curse is real, it is my reality, and everyone's reality. It is *our* curse, but the decision is still *mine.* Love it or leave it. *Here* I am. A *responsible* decision means responding to the curse by accepting its reality, and its reality is its image, which is expressed by its no-image, the empty shield. This tangle of freedom and necessity. Responsibility. END THE WAR, said the winter soldier. To everyone. To me!

138 Quoted in *The Zen Doctrine of No-mind*, p. 119. The last line is from the *Diamond Sutra*, Hui-neng's favorite. Suzuki goes on to quote Shen-hui: 'He who has definitely attained the experience of [Zen] mind retains his no-mindness even when his body is cut to pieces in a melee between two fiercely contending armies. He is solid as a diamond, he is firm and immovable. He abides in the thought of emptiness and absolute sameness.'

What now. On their placards the Vietnam veterans have suddenly, abruptly, dramatically, changed sides. No 'both sides now,' absolutely not, not here, not now, not this war. This is Vietnam Veterans *Against* the War, and the *Winter Soldier Investigation*, which I followed, *passionately*, last year, right at the beginning of my own Long Winter. I listened to the testimony on WBAI, Pacifica Radio. DOGS OF GOD, Columbus Circle again. Cristóbal Colón, a Man of the World. SOUND. Cracked requiem. A lot of people are getting off, but—a SWARM, they're swarming into the car. How can the sixth placard-man fend them off, with his empty shield, here, on the B Train, round midnight, Saturday, in the heart of the viscera of Manhattan. How can he speak his three words to this SWARM, one by one, face to face, END THE WAR. His demand! He's demanding A DECISION. He's demanding that I you he she they we DECIDE TO END THE WAR. This is the winter soldier. His empty shield has turned a war of images and realities into a war of decisions. Placard-men, a *true* infinity, which side are you on. Truly infinitely speaking, are you Vietnam veterans *for* or *against* the war. Demanding that WE make a decision. Who do you think we are. We're not Richard M. Nixon. We, the people. What are we to decide. SOUND, 7th Avenue. No, who ARE WE to decide. We're just the people of this country, bodies, nobodies. We can 'decide' to END THE WAR as much as we please, but what in the world does this *mean*. Being, seeming, the logic of being is nothing. Great! 'We decide' to END THE WAR. And me, what does this mean for *my* decision. My FORK, if I want to stick to this term, which Oedipus, cursed and cursing, made famous. Great. I 'decided' to END THE WAR when I was 15, back in 1965. Just ask Eugene Genovese. Ask Norman Morrison. My problem now is GAM-bomb-exile. It's a real problem, and a problem of *images*. It's a *real* problem of images, placards, and placard-men. Of *true* infinity. A problem of the relation between freedom, necessity, and responsibility—

MY responsibility. Personal responsibility. Political responsibility. Separate and inseparable. Not two, not one. The *real* problem (of *images*) is *what a decision is and what making a decision means.* END THE WAR. Right on, brother. Just do it. 'The fire is in the minds of men, not on the roofs of houses.' Zen mind. Placard-men. I gave my legs, I pledge allegiance, I approach the village, I destroy the village, I kill for peace with a B-52— and now, I am the winter soldier, with an empty shield. What more do you want of me. SOUND, Rockefeller Center, practically no one getting off and all sorts of people pushing their way in. They want Times Square, they want the Village. I wonder if the sixth placard-man changed trains at Columbus Circle. A Man of the World. This melee is no place for his message. I think it would be a good idea for him to head back uptown, take a B up to the unicorns, or even a D to the Bronx, he'd still find plenty of people to say END THE WAR to, this MOB might trample on his shield, smash it to a pulp. How come I never change direction myself, a good question, I just keep going to the end of the line. My Lai is My Lai, a B-52 is a B-52. A winter soldier. What's this! It looks like some pushin' an' shovin' goin' on. Might be some Vietnam spirit here on the subway. A miniature atrocity. The Naked City, just another one of the eight million stories. Just a little strafe those gook creeps. Perhaps a dash of Kill Kill Kill. Let's see—it's two guys yelling at each other, loud. Standing right next to me (I'm *sitting down*, of course, the privilege of an end-to-end-of-the-liner), near the door, I think we're coming into the 42nd Street station any second. No, it's one guy yelling at the other guy, in Spanish, I wonder what he's getting at. No, it's not a penny for the Old Guy. He's definitely making a point—watch out! We're *screeching* into 42nd. The door is opening. Look! The yeller pulls out a very short knife and *sticks the other guy in the ass.* Right in the cheek. He's pushing him out onto the platform, following him—to finish him off, possibly. No, I doubt it, it looks to me like a minor skirmish, just a small stabbing. No, definitely not Eteocles and Polyneices at the seventh gate, no reciprocal suicide, as Hegel put it. Fun City! Our local reality. No, no atrocities, no war crimes, no. Locally speaking, I've never heard anyone say 'we destroy the city in order to save it.' Defend the City! I haven't seen a single cop since I went down to the ship. No, no harm done. Fun City. Amigos. I'm just glad they didn't have guns this time. Saturday night specials. Junk guns—cheap, but have no fear, if your aim is good you'll do fine. With a shotgun you don't have to aim, but they're a lot less practical here on the streets and subways. Too showy. On Rivington Street these *real short knives*—pocket knives, not even switchblades—are all the rage, all the muggers have them. Fashionable. When I first moved into the neighborhood they used to point one at my neck if I took a little stroll after dark, but they never poked me, I never had more than a dime in my pocket. Later, when I drove the taxi, I deposited all my cash in the taxi garage, except for my subway token, plus a token dime. Brother have you got a dime. I taught the Rivington Street muggers a lesson we'll never forget. SOUND, Remember me to Herald Square. By the same token, New York muggers don't just have tiny knives, no, they also have gigantic knives, small, medium, and large switchblades, clubs, cleavers, bats, machetes, you name it. You can get anything you want at Alice's Restaurant.[139] But guns—guns are another matter. Guns are great. Strafe those gook creeps. Kill Kill Kill. Blood, gore, guts, and veins. Eat dead, burnt bodies. That's the spirit. Murders. Absolutely. For murders you can't beat guns, they hit the spot. I mean, clubbing people to death is hard work. Guns, or bombs. B-52s. Arc Lights, 3 times 60,000 pounds of 108 bombs. Wait, I have this little article I ripped out of the *Post* last week, it's right here in *Zen Mind*, the latest

---

139 'Kill Kill Kill. Blood, gore, guts and veins. Eat dead, burnt bodies!'—in Arlo Guthrie, *Alice's Restaurant,* 1967, monologue with ragtime guitar backing. A classic album. Political theater put to music. The refrain: 'You can get anything you want at Alice's Restaurant.'

stats on murders in New York City, year by year. Very
interesting. Let's see—1928, 404 murders, each year around
400 to 600, in 1966, 654 murders. But then, a murderous
escalation: 746, 986, 1043, 1117, and last year 1466 murders,
a record.[140] No, without guns murdering all these people would
be quite a job. In my neighborhood we have guns, and there
are guns on the subway too, I've seen them. Saturday night
specials, and not only on Saturday nights like right now. I once
saw someone get shot in the 42nd Street station. I'll never
forget it. A black guy. No shooting tonight, luckily. Not so far,
anyway. Our bodies.

Also. Heavy with weeping. Thirty-block stretch, to West
4th. The car still jam-packed, but pretty relaxed. Most of these
people are going to the Village, and the rest, home to Brooklyn.
The worst is over. END THE WAR. No, the war is not over. Just
'winding down.' We'll do better next time. We'll do IT better
next time. No more quagmires. That's the spirit. *Next time*—
that's exactly what worries me. The point. Next time, and the
time after that. Defend the City! Nail their asses to the wall.
Storm the living daylights out of them. Eat shit motherfuckers.
Eat dead, burnt bodies. But the placard-tide has turned. Has
it turned. Yes and no. Not exactly. (Was the placard-man

---

140 Records are made to be broken. The escalation continued, peaking at 2245 in
1990. Since then the numbers have been going down. Rudy Giuliani. The Iron Fist.
Michael Bloomberg. Gentrification. *Chic eateries and 5 star hotels on Rivington
Street.* I'm not nostalgic about murders (or about Rivington Street either) but, ye
gods, what have we come to. Where are we going. *Where* have all the flowers gone.
Speaking of jazz musicians, this reminds me of a little story. An episode. Me, in
Zurich, early 1980s. Wow, a Johnny Griffin concert. The *great* tenor saxophonist,
one of Monk's favorites, I'd heard him play at Slugs'. No, I didn't expect the venue
to be a Zurich version of Slugs' or the Village Vanguard either. Especially not in
that neighborhood, just off Bahnhofstrasse, the Big Bank street. No, but—surprise
surprise—it turned out to be a large conference hall, with a series of very long
tables, geometrically something like the Coney Island subway station. A slightly
raised 'platform' for the musicians at one end. Before playing (halfheartedly), Griffin,
disconcerted, turned to the audience and asked: Is this a jazz concert or a business
meeting? No one laughed. An environmental question. Alas, it wasn't much of a
concert. Then again, Sitting Bull, one of the greatest Americans of all time, did a stint
as a freak in Buffalo Bill Cody's Wild West Show. A tour of fifteen American cities.
Chic eateries. Where do we come from? Where are we going?

Michelangelo for or against the war, or just a great painter.)
The placard-men are a true infinity. A system, of images and
realities. In the subway. Why in the subway. Why not on the
street. Why in the subway goddamit. 'The system of logic is
the realm of shadows.' I don't know, maybe it's the continual
movement. Shadows never stay still. The system. 'The basic
teaching of Buddhism is the teaching of transiency.' 'Its
illumination reaches the ten-thousand things, and these ten-
thousand things are not reflected in it.' The placard-tide. VVAW.
'Vietnam Veterans Against the War' began as a placard slogan
in the staging area for the Spring Mobe demonstration in
Washington in 1967. 400,000 people mobilized against the war.
I myself—I don't like crowds. I didn't even go to Woodstock.
I've never been 'moved' by masses, mobes, noise, but by
individual faces, words, deeds. Testimony. Bearing witness.
Individual lives and individuals who put their lives on the line.
'Individual lives have been changed by this.' Last year—all of
last year, from January to December, which included my own
Long Winter, from January to June—VVAW organized what were
for me, personally, the most important events since Norman
Morrison's sacrifice in 1965. A Long March is not a stroll, as
Mao has taught us. The Winter Soldier Investigation, in Detroit,
last winter.[141] Dewey Canyon III, in Washington, last April. The
stormy VVAW Kansas City meeting last November. The Statue
of Liberty occupation last December, on December 26th, three
months ago. Strenuous efforts to come to grips with the curse
of Vietnam, by war-hardened Vietnam veterans. No, I'm not a
veteran myself, I'm just a war-hardened 4-F. I believe the sixth
placard-man is one of the 109 Vietnam veterans who testified

141 For the record, from January 31st to February 2nd, 1971.
The superb documentary film *Winter Soldier*, produced by the Winterfilm Collective
and first released in 1972, can be seen on the Internet. In fact I watched it again
yesterday, August 26th, 2015. Scott Camil plays a prominent role in the film, and in
my own discussion in the text, in which I quote from the Wikipedia articles *Vietnam
Veterans Against the War, Winter Soldier Investigation, Scott Camil*, and *William
Calley*. In a few of the quotes 'after the fact' I have changed the verb tenses to fit
into my 'end of March, 1972' narrative, without distorting the meaning in any way.

in Detroit. It's not John Kerry, the Winter Soldier leader, Kerry doesn't have long hair or a beard. Clean-shaven, clean-cut. No, definitely not him. It could actually be Scott Camil, he's all over the place and in the eye of every storm. Could be. Camil—no, no relation to the 'woman arrested naked behind the wheel: she thought she was a camel.' SOUND, West 4th. Look at them all pouring out of the car. The Red Sea has parted before them. Now, let's see. The car's half empty. Brooklynites, trolley dodgers, straggling home. Billy already in his shroud. God bless you, Brooklynites. God bless Captain Vere. Off we go. Where has the winter soldier gone, the sixth placard-man. Is he still somewhere on this B Train, headed for Brooklyn. I doubt it. Has he weathered the storm of midtown Manhattan, his placard unpulverized. Why bother! He bears the message of the empty shield, he's in the system to deliver it, and 42nd Street was not the place, no. It was the place to get stabbed in the ass. Absolutely. The place to *get stabbed in the ass*, not the place to say END THE WAR. But, what do I know. A placard-man *on my side*, but, what do I know about what these placard-men are actually doing. Who they *are* and what they *mean*. No, I know this: *they've made a decision. To be placard-men.* Yes they have. What do I know about the Winter Soldier Investigation? Pardon my Zen, but this one is an open book, and the pages are *full*. Literally. I have the whole story in my bag, stuffed into my copy of the *Ramparts* issue with Che Guevara's Bolivia diaries. All of it. Winter Soldier, Dewey Canyon, Kansas City, and the Statue of Liberty. I have the full transcript of John Kerry's testimony before the Foreign Relations Committee, chaired, with true wit, by J. William Fulbright.[142] A senator

142 A video of Kerry's testimony before the Fulbright committee, April 23rd, 1971, is also on the Internet, including remarks before and after his testimony, TAKE A LOOK, it's magnificent. Fulbright was truly the Groucho Marx of U.S. politicians. When Kerry tells him he'd been 'up most of the night' preparing his speech, which Fulbright had invited him to give 'at such short notice,' and right in the middle of Dewey Canyon III, Fulbright remarks, 'If it'd been me I'd have been dead.' Too strenuous. How sorry I am I couldn't make him a placard-man. But, he would have upstaged me. Too witty.

against the war and a veteran against the war. Defend the City! END THE WAR. Who is going to end it. I don't have to ask who Norman Morrison is, but I do have to ask who J. William Fulbright is. A U.S. senator against the war, but, what does he decide. He decides to hold lots of hearings. As for John Kerry, I don't ask. A penitent. Wounded three times, three Purple Hearts, a Silver Star, a Bronze Star, and he trashed them on the steps of the Capitol, along with 800 other veterans, and he is—or was—the Big Man of Vietnam Veterans Against the War. A spokesman, a public speaker. Scott Camil had more medals than you can shake a stick at, *more* than John Kerry. A farce, he called them. Trashed them on the steps of the Capitol. SOUND, Broadway-Lafayette. The Marquis de Lafayette, a winter soldier if ever there was one. Valley Forge, a long hard winter. Kerry *organized* the Winter Soldier Investigation, behind the scenes, but Camil *testified*—plenty. Publicly. Plenty. Trashed the whole farce on the steps of the Capitol, Friday, April 23rd, Dewey Canyon III, along with Kerry and over EIGHT HUNDRED other Vietnam veterans. A storm, a downpour of medals and ribbons. Against the War. END THE WAR. Trashed. Defend the City! What am I doing in the subway. What are they doing in the subway. Logic. The realm of shadows. Transiency. Change. What's changing. WE may change, and won't. But, WHAT is changing. This is my problem. Changing. For the better or for the worse. For better or worse. The sixth placard-man, VVAW, the empty shield. No image. No-image. From image of the curse to reality of the curse, from seeming to being. Hegel: Being, Essence, Concept. Logical moments. A tangle. Everything ends, nothing ends. Everything is, logically speaking, always there. Dasein. Existence. 'Therebeing.' 'Being

---

For what it's worth today, I have to say that Fulbright was one of the very very few United Statesian politicians in my lifetime that I've admired. An intelligent man and a serious politician. His book, *The Arrogance of Power*, New York: Random House, 1966, is well worth reading, any day. His arena was a far cry from the obscene circus we have today, whose first—and unequaled—ringmaster was Richard Nixon. Dick! Dick! I don't miss you! [Fourth stab: Trump! Trump! American carnage!]

in a certain *place*; but the idea of space is irrelevant here,' says Hegel. Shit, this is *logic*. Shadow. An image of nothingness. 'Being is nothing' is there at the beginning, in the middle, and at the end. Seeming to being—no, it's just not so simple. Benardete has a lot to say about this in his second Note, which I shall read in just a moment. On the empty shield seeming IS being, it's the triumph of the image. It all begins, middles, and ends with 'being is nothing'—logic, realm of shadows, subway. In a moment. First, I have to run through a few things in my mind. Winter Soldier, Dewey Canyon, Kansas City, Statue of Liberty. Where's the empty-placard-man now. Will I see him again. Will I see any of the other five. Are there ten-thousand others. 'Not reflected in it.' Will I see another one before I stop traveling indefinitely. Because I have to stop. I've seen for myself that the subway is endless, a no-end, a true infinity (in *some* sense). But my line will end. *This* war will end. Who decides. END THE WAR. Who decides. SOUND. Grand. So well timed. The bricks. Madmen. Neon.

So perfectly. Climb, ye madmen! Ye neon. Timed. In a nutshell: The purpose of the Winter Soldier Investigation was to show that American *policies* in Vietnam had led to war crimes, and that these crimes were the rule, not the exception. William Calley's trial for the My Lai massacre was going on at the time, and most everyone was riled up, in one way or its 'direct reverse' (as Melville put it). Exactly one year ago, approximately, on March 31st, Calley—a hero for many, a criminal for some—was sentenced to life imprisonment and hard labor. The next day, April Fools' Day, Nixon had him transferred from prison to house arrest, which is where he is now, scratching his balls, waiting for his pardon.[143] A parade

143 Nixon finished the job in 1974, and Calley was released after three and a half years of 'hard' house arrest. It seems that the American public was 100 to 1 in favor of leniency. After his sentencing the governor of Indiana asked that all state flags be flown at half-staff, while Georgia governor Jimmy Carter, outraged by the guilty verdict, instituted American Fighting Man's Day and asked Georgians to drive for a week with their lights on.

is a parade is a parade. Ticker tape. The Winter Soldiers were *extremely riled up*. Let me read this testimony, I've got a bunch of papers here, wait—this is Donald Dzagulones, 'decrying the travesty' of Calley's trial, saying:

> The U.S. had established the principle of culpability with the Nuremberg trials of the Nazis. Following those principles, we hold that if Calley is responsible so are his superiors up the chain of command—even to the president. The cause of My Lai and the brutality of the Vietnam War are rooted in the policies of our government as executed by our military commanders.

Well said. In a nutshell. Winter Soldier. A stain on an empty mirror. Manhattan Bridge in the dead of night. Artificial light, some sort of bulbs, in rows, reflecting on the water. Hades below, Hades above. The system of logic. Manhattan Bridge — Brooklyn Bridge. Same river, same deal. Just names. Outrage! Let me read this carefully, testimony of 1st Lt. William Crandell, Winter Soldier:

> We intend to tell who it was that gave us those orders; that created that policy; that set that standard of war bordering on full and final genocide. We intend to demonstrate that My Lai was no unusual occurrence, other than, perhaps, the number of victims killed all in one place, all at one time, all by one platoon of us. We intend to show that the policies of American Division, which inevitably resulted in My Lai, were the policies of other Army and Marine divisions as well. We intend to show that war crimes in Vietnam did not start in March 1968, or in the village of Son My or with one Lieutenant William Calley. We intend to indict those really responsible for My Lai, for Vietnam, for attempted genocide.

Strafe those gook creeps. I've been thinking a lot about this.
The Pequot. The B Train seems so peaceful now. This long
stretch to Pacific Street, then 36th Street, then the West
End Line. Most of the veterans who testified were not this
eloquent, they were not used to speaking in public, many were
really choked up, some of them wept. They had hard stories
to tell, ugly stories. Atrocities. Barbarity. Heart of Darkness.
Attempted genocide. Speaking of genocide, I think that the
core—the heart—of the entire Investigation was this testimony
by a Native American. He is weeping at the end, and his fellow
Winter Soldiers and the public are on their feet applauding:

> If you took the Vietnamese War, or the American war as it
> is, and compared it right to the Indian wars a hundred years
> ago, it would be the same thing. All the massacres were the
> same. When I was small I kept growing, and learning, but
> it was so much that when I watched TV and watched the
> Indians and the cavalry, I would cheer for the cavalry. That's
> how bad it was. You can take any culture, and if you look
> back into it deep they had something good. Way back they
> had it. [*applause*] And the people started getting onto the
> money bag. And that was when it all happened.
> We made treaties long ago, it was for as long as the grass
> shall grow and as long as the rivers shall flow. The way
> things are going now, one of these days the grass isn't
> gonna grow and the rivers aren't gonna flow.[144]

He's absolutely right. The Vietnamese call it 'the American
war.' Wait—here's my copy of *The Crisis* by Thomas Paine,
the first *Crisis* paper, December 1776, he wrote a series of
them. Thanks to the sixth placard-man I'm reading it again.
Thomas Paine was not highly-educated but he *was* eloquent.
Passionate. These terrific lines are where the name 'winter
soldier' comes from:

---

144 This is a word-by-word transcription from the *Winter Soldier* film.

These are the times that try men's souls. The summer
soldier and the sunshine patriot will, in this crisis, shrink
from the service of their country; but he that stands by
it now, deserves the love and thanks of man and woman.
Tyranny, like hell, is not easily conquered; yet we have this
consolation with us, that the harder the conflict, the more
glorious the triumph. What we obtain too cheap, we esteem
too lightly.

Wow, one hell of a writer, and he went on like that for pages
and pages. A Brit, he moved to America and changed sides
immediately. A convert. Revolutionary spirit. At the Fulbright
hearing John Kerry had this to say about the origin of the
name:

The term Winter Soldier is a play on words of Thomas
Paine's of 1776 when he spoke of the sunshine patriots and
sometime soldiers who deserted at Valley Forge because the
going was rough.
We who have come here to Washington have come here
because we feel we have to be winter soldiers now. We
could come back to this country, we could be quiet,
we could hold our silence, we could not tell what went
on in Vietnam, but we feel because of what threatens
this country, not the reds, but the crimes which we are
committing that threaten it, that we have to speak out.

Kerry is no Thomas Paine, but he can turn a phrase. He could
never be a placard-man. Too dour. No sense of humor. Or of
image. Fulbright would make a magnificent sixth placard-man,
he's witty and he knows his lines: 'The question before this
Committee and the Congress is really how to END THE WAR.'
'This unfortunate war in Vietnam,' as he puts it. But I'm afraid
he's too old and too busy for placards *here in the subway*,

what a shame. Then again, he still has the senate. But I don't. I can't 'take to the senate.' I'm just a soon-to-be-graduated NYU student with a decision to make, *concerned* about what a decision is and what making a decision means. A concerned citizen, so to speak. Where in the world am I. Subway! B Train! So much on my mind, I didn't even hear the one hand clapping at Pacific Street, and now we're sitting here, at 36th. It's late, the train may be tired. No, here we go now, again, into the Brooklyn night, again. West End Line. I've been traveling for a long time. I'm not tired exactly. Hungry—no, it's been less than two days, that's nothing. Practice. It may not make perfect, but it helps. I still have some apples. I wonder how many. Six placard-men. Benardete's second Note. OK, just take it easy, there's plenty of time. A sea. A tiny handful of stragglers in the car with me, true dyed-in-the-wool Brooklynites, that's for sure. The night is young. The screeches have become sounds. Good.

THE ATROCITIES. 109 winter soldiers in Detroit, and what's really on their minds is what they themselves saw and did in Vietnam. War crimes, atrocities. 'You can't just take Calley alone.' We, the people, knew something about My Lai, but Winter Soldier gives us a far bigger picture. SOUNDS on the West End Line, the quiet Brooklyn night. The *peep-peep-peep* of blue jays on the roof. Testimony. Gratuitous brutality. Indiscriminate bombing. Cutting off heads and putting them on stakes.[145] Torture. Cutting prisoners open while they're still alive. Cutting off ears to show how many people you've killed, *and then trading the ears for beers.*[146] Mass rapes. Soldiers

---

145 Today we are justifiably shocked by the 'barbarity' of ISIS, and by its decapitations in particular. Alas, American barbarity in Vietnam plays second fiddle to no one, be it ISIS, Hitler, Jack the Ripper, or Genghis Khan.

146 *Scalp hunting* redux, a great American tradition, going back to the first settlers on the perilous frontier. When I was a kid 10,000 TV shows and movies convinced me it was the Injuns who did the scalping, when actually it was the other way around. Paleface business, ever since the Pequot War. Bounties initially for the heads of murdered Indians and later just for their scalps, which were more portable in large numbers. No, not just beers. Reward money. Bounty. Scalp away, ye settlers! Kill, kill, kill. Although the colonial government in time raised the reward for adult

raping a young girl in front of her family. Murdering children for throwing stones at troops, or just 'for fun.' Murdering the old and infirm, men and women. 'Free-fire zones,' which means shooting anything that moves. Leveling villages for no good reason. Mutilating bodies. Throwing Viet Cong suspects from an aircraft after binding and gagging them with copper wire. The first public testimony about the effects of Agent Orange. First public testimony about Operation Dewey Canyon in Laos. I heard all this with my own not-cut-off ears, on WBAI, Pacifica Radio. The East Coast newspapers refused to cover the hearings at all, apart from a *New York Times* story a week later, which commented, '*this stuff happens in all wars.*' Great. But this is OUR war. I gave my legs for my country. I pledge allegiance. I approach the village. I destroy the village in order to save it. I kill for peace. The empty shield. These men are asking themselves, How is it possible that WE did these things. When did we *decide* to do all this. THIS IS THE QUESTION: Did we decide or were we decided for. Decided for, and done for. Decided or decided for. This is exactly what Winter Soldier is about—this, and the fact that the question can only be seen in retrospect. After the fact. Thanks to the *political* event, Winter Soldier Investigation. Speaking out, public testimony. Kierkegaard was quite right: Life can only be understood backwards; but it has to be lived forwards. This is a BIG problem, for the winter soldiers, and for me. Decide or decided for. Unfortunately, I won't have MY answer from Winter Soldier. I've known PLENTY all along about our policies and the atrocities they've produced. The curse of Vietnam. If this is ALL I KNOW, then I'm decided for. Done for. I'm wasting my time here in the subway.

---

scalps, lowered it for adult females, and eliminated it for indigenous children under ten, the age and gender of victims were not easily distinguished by their scalps nor checked carefully. In Vietnam no such distinctions were made. The settlers gave a name to the mutilated and bloody corpses they left in the wake of their scalping: *Redskins.* In Vietnam: Gooks. Creeps. See the fine and chilling book by Roxanne Dunbar-Ortiz, *An Indigenous Peoples' History of the United States,* Boston: Beacon Press, 2014, pp. 64–65.

SOUND SOUND SOUND SOUND SOUND, the West End Line. Coltrane! Coltrane! I need to see ALL the placard-men together, in their true infinity. This is my only hope of seeing what a decision is and what making a decision means. Of making my own decision responsibly. Still, I have plenty to learn from Winter Soldier, and from Scott Camil in particular, his whole story. He's had a lot to say for himself in the past year, starting with:

> My testimony involves burning of villages with civilians in them, the cutting off of ears, cutting off of heads, torturing of prisoners, calling in of artillery on villages for games, corpsmen killing wounded prisoners, napalm dropped on villages, women being raped, women and children being massacred... bodies shoved out of helicopters...

Like the fourth placard-man, the placard-man Michelangelo, he's definitely *lived* what he's painted. A real Vietnamese village. A true Vietnam veteran. No doubt about it. Participating in Winter Soldier led to a sea change in Camil's life. He had been brought up to believe he lived in the best country in the world, and that he had a duty to go into the military to serve this country. Called to serve, as they say. He enlisted in the Marines and entered boot camp on Parris Island three days after graduating from high school. Two days ago I dreamed I'd never finished high school, which is not true. Scott Camil dreamed about fighting in the service of his country as soon as he finished high school, and he did—he finished high school, and went to Vietnam. And fought. For four years. Burning villages and shoving *living bodies* out of helicopters. Great. The Defense of Freedom. He tells how all the soldiers were taught to believe—and did believe—that the Vietnamese were not human beings. Gooks. Gook creeps. Injuns. Niggers. All one big 'free-fire zone.' The American War. The Winter Soldier

Investigation woke him from his dream. It 'made me think, look at the big picture, and understand that the Vietnamese were humans.' 'A small step for a man.' A giant leap for Scott Camil. He had been leery of going to Detroit at all, but the experience was decisive. An awakening. The Dharma Eye. It took him a long time to open it. It takes practice. Since then he has been an *extremely* outspoken protagonist in Vietnam Veterans Against the War, taking positions far more extreme than the clean-cut clean-shaven John Kerry, who has now *left* the VVAW scene. Is Camil the sixth placard-man, I muse. Right here, right now, here, with me, in the subway. It's possible. He lives in Florida but was born in Brooklyn, four years older than I am, and right now he's *moving around*, an anti-war *activist*. Getting around. Plenty. Taking extreme positions. Is *winter soldier*, barely decipherable, on an empty shield, an extreme position. Like a stain on an empty mirror. END THE WAR—an extreme position. A demand. A decision. Whose decision. His? mine? yours? theirs? ours? A decision. Whose.

Coney Island. Soundless. End of the West End Line. Or, beginning of the West End Line. And/or. Kierkegaard: either/or. Decide. Make up your mind. Kierkegaard's nephew: neither/nor. Cracked requiem. His shroud. Already. Weeping philosophers. Zen mind: not two, and not one. Hegel, 'both/and' MY ASS, Hegel is *decisive*. Go on, stab me in the ass all you like, motherfuckers. SING SING SING SING SING. Attempted genocide. For as long as the grass shall grow and as long as the rivers shall flow. Their cries. A nocturnal stroll in the Coney Island station. 8 tracks, 4 island platforms, so well timed. B, F, D, N. The Hadean night. System of logic. My legs don't feel much like walking. Just a little. The time: night. The last night, possibly. Last night was last night, tonight is tonight. Here, now. Uptown. Downtown. NYC Transit System. Mosey on over. Truck. Travel. Stroll. Beginner's mind. The Roshi said,

In the beginner's mind there is no thought, 'I have attained
something.' All self-centered thoughts limit our vast mind.
When we have no thought of achievement, no thought
of self, we are true beginners. Then we can really learn
something.[147]

A lot happened last year, politically. I don't mean elections.
Defend the City! I mean activism. The massive big-crowd anti-
war mobes became far more pointed, more personal. My Long
Winter was a miniscule part of this. But for me it was a big
part. It was a *political* 4-F. (Sure, also personal. Not two, not
one.) Winter Soldier was a historic event. Possibly, almost no
one will ever understand this. It was not an Atrocity Exhibition,
it was *our men, my brothers, Vietnam veterans*, who stood
up, in public, and said: Atrocity. WE did it. Sons, fathers. *Who
made us do it.* How were we decided for, and why. *We are not
done for*, we are here, now, and speaking out. AGAINST it. But,
how about me. I, personally, am a Political 4-F Veteran Against
the War, not a Vietnam Veteran Against the War. I am going to
make my decision. SOUND, Bay 50th Street. On the move. So
clear, so limpid, this Brooklyn night, again, end of March, 1972.
Or is today April Fools' Day. Look! 'White jumper and white
duck trousers, each more or less soiled, dimly glimmered in the
obscure light of the bay *like a patch of discolored snow in early
April*.' Billy! I see you. I'm not in my shroud just yet.

The true path. Brooklyn night. Dewey Canyon III. SOUND
SOUND SOUND, night, at home on Rivington Street it's time for
Coltrane, or Monk, or 'The Well-Tempered Clavier.' Albert Ayler.
WNCN, Harry Fleetwood, 'Saint Mathew Passion,' possibly.
Later. Now is now. B Train. Time for Dewey Canyon. Fished
his body out of the East River in November, 1970, a presumed
suicide, possibly, or murdered, not likely, who knows. Now—at
Winter Soldier, along with the testimony about Agent Orange,
the other major *revelation* (lots of people already knew plenty

147 *Zen Mind*, p. 22.

about the *atrocities*) came from five veterans who described
their secret operations in *Laos* during Operation Dewey Canyon.
But Dewey Canyon was supposed to be in South Vietnam,
and just a few days earlier the Pentagon had denied that any
American troops had crossed the border into Laos. One more
lie for the American people. What's more, the veterans testified
that they were given meticulous orders to hide the fact that
they were American including, but not limited to, the removal
of identification from uniforms and switching to Russian
arms that were typically used by the North Vietnamese. *Two*
invasions of Laos, Dewey Canyon I and II, revealed by Winter
Soldier. What would that old stickler-for-the-rules Captain
Vere have to say about this, God bless him. Just last night,
here on the West End Line, I was reading about him and his
decisions, and Billy, decided and *done* for. SOUND SOUND
SOUND. Glimmerings. Vietnam Veterans Against the War lost
no time in organizing Dewey Canyon *III*, in our nation's capital,
from April 19th to 23rd. Momentous days. On Monday, Gold
Star Mothers (mothers of soldiers killed in the war) led more
than 1,100 veterans across the Lincoln Memorial Bridge to
the Arlington Cemetery gate; from there the veterans went
on to the Capitol, where they presented Congress with their
16-point resolution for *ending the war*. On Tuesday, 200
veterans listened to Fulbright's Committee on proposals to
END THE WAR. No, the sixth placard-man is by no means the
first person to say END THE WAR, though I do believe he's the
first—perhaps—to demand it of passengers in the New York
subway. Who, what are the placard-men. How many are there.
Who knows. Are they a true infinity. On Wednesday, more
than 50 veterans marched to the Pentagon and attempted
to turn themselves in as war criminals. On Thursday, a large
group of veterans demonstrated on the steps of the Supreme
Court, demanding to know why the Court had not ruled on the
constitutionality of the war in Vietnam. They sang 'God Bless

America' and 110 of them were arrested for disturbing the peace. Sing sing sing. SOUND SOUND, West End Line. On a number of occasions VVAW sought to tie its anti-war activism to patriotic themes, though some members (Scott Camil among them) were not enthused. Thursday was also John Kerry's Big Day at the Foreign Relations Committee—I have a photo of him here, with his Purple Hearts and Stars, well groomed, longish hair, clean-shaven, green fatigues. On Friday more than 800 veterans, one by one, threw down their medals, ribbons, discharge papers, and other war mementos, right on the steps of the Capitol. Trashed them. What the Italians call a *gran finale*. Scott Camil called his medals a *farce*. Kerry had lots to say to the Committee, Fulbright praised him for his eloquence and he wasn't wrong. It seems he 'stepped down' as VVAW leader sometime after Dewey Canyon III. Before the Kansas City meeting last November at any rate. I have the text of his 'speech' right here. Wrote it all in one night, he told Fulbright. A strenuous effort, as Hegel put it. Sure, it has some catchy lines. 'Four score and seven years ago'—no, sorry, wrong speech. Probably the catchiest is this: 'How do you ask a man to be the last man to die in Vietnam? How do you ask a man to be the last man to die for a mistake?' Here's another good one: 'Now we are told that the men who fought there must watch quietly while American lives are lost so that we can exercise the incredible arrogance of Vietnamizing the Vietnamese.' Take that, Dickhead! Our Fearless Leader. A Grand Strategy. Incredible arrogance. But it's the last lines of the speech that really concern me—worry me, in fact. Kerry says 'where America finally turned'—I don't think we're on the same page. I do not share his optimism. This is precisely why I'm here, now, with a fork in the realm of shadows. Let me reread this carefully and see how it grabs me this time, coming to the end—the beginning—of the West End Line. Sunset Park in the dead of night. Cracked requiem. Their cries.

We wish that a merciful God could wipe away our own memories of that service as easily as this administration has wiped away their memories of us. But all that they have done and all that they can do by this denial is to make more clear than ever our own determination to undertake one last mission—to search out and destroy the last vestige of this barbaric war, to pacify our own hearts, to conquer the hate and fear that have driven this country these last ten years and more. And more. And so when thirty years from now our brothers go down the street without a leg, without an arm, or a face, and small boys ask why, we will be able to say 'Vietnam' and not mean a desert, not a filthy obscene memory, but mean instead where America finally turned and where soldiers like us helped it in the turning.

I don't like this fork I'm at, but I don't like this 'where America finally turned' either. I don't buy it, I don't buy what Kerry's selling. In fact, these two dislikes of mine go together. Like SAMs and B-52s. I'm not convinced by GAMs, I'm not convinced that blowing up the Williamsburg Bridge would do any good at all, and I know that exile means a slave's life.[148] But Kerry, by 'turned,' means turned *for the better*, turned *away* from wars *in the defense of tyranny*. Dear John, what the fuck are you saying. This is easy to say, and eloquent, but show me a *grain* of truth in it. No, I don't see it, not a grain. End of the line, beginning of the line, which. No answer. Vietnam is not a Zen puzzle, it is national policy, a political decision. I am convinced it is *political karma*, and that for the rest of the world, for as long as the American Empire shall live, there will be hell to pay. Luckily I don't have my copy of *Johnny Got his Gun* in my bag now,[149] but I know the last lines by heart, and they are one HELL of a lot truer than Kerry's last lines. This

---

148 43 years later I know it for a fact.
149 By Dalton Trumbo, the greatest anti-war book of all time.

American World-War-I winter soldier who has lost his arms, his legs, and all of his face, but he's found the true path. *Masters of war*, we're ready. *To point our guns not for you but at you.*

> Put the guns in our hands and we will use them. Give us the slogans and we will turn them into realities. Sing the battle hymns and we will take them up where you left off. Not one not ten not ten thousand not a million not ten millions not a hundred millions but a billion two billions of us all the people of the world we will have the slogans and we will have the hymns and we will have the guns and we will use them and we will live. Make no mistake of it we will live. We will be alive and we will walk and talk and eat and sing and laugh and feel and love and bear our children in tranquility in security in decency in peace. You plan the wars you masters of men plan the wars and point the way and we will point the gun.

SOUND, 36th Street, under the ground. You can't say it any better than that. Dostoevsky. A fire in the minds of men. B Train, still practically nobody else in the car, Saturday night, but heading for the middle of the night, nobody headed for Manhattan at this hour. Whatever happened to Benardete's second Note, 'II. Eteocles' Interpretations of the Shields.' Hold your horses, I'm coming to it *right now*, it's why I'm here. In the transit system. First, just one word on Scott Camil, who may be but probably isn't the sixth placard-man. I happen to know that, ever since Detroit, he has been getting more and more riled up. It's quite possible that he's read *Johnny Got his Gun* recently. 'Bring the war home.' No, he hasn't joined Weather Underground, but—riled up. A sea change. 'The World Turned Upside Down,' as the Brits sang when they lost our Revolution. Last April, in Washington, as an alternative to trashing medals—and he had the longest list of them I've ever seen—he thought it might be better *to shoot the most hardcore hawks in Congress.* A fork. A decision. Let's DO something about 'this unfortunate war in Vietnam' (as Fulbright daintily put it). Fortunately—fortunately for the most hardcore hawks, at any rate—VVAW is a democratic organization. At their meetings in Kansas City last November, the veterans (it seems Kerry had already 'stepped out') discussed Camil's proposal (he named it The Phoenix Project after the original Phoenix Program operations used by the CIA to assassinate Viet Cong) and voted it down. As far as I know, there's no record of how close the vote was—no, VVAW is not the U.S. Congress. No Congressional Record. OK, before tackling Eteocles, and Benardete, for my own record let me reread this little statement of Camil's, who may be but probably isn't the sixth placard-man, which he made recently.[150] It seems he's bowed to the will of the majority, but still thinks the idea wasn't all bad.

> I did not think it was terrible at the time. My plan was that, on the last day [before the Christmas recess] we would go into the [congressional] offices we would schedule the most hardcore hawks for last—and we would shoot them all...I was serious. I felt that I spent two years killing women and children in their own fucking homes. These are the guys that fucking made the policy, and these are the guys that are responsible for it, and these are the guys that are voting to continue the fucking war when the public is against it. I felt that if we really believed in what we were doing, and if we were willing to put our lives on the line for the country over there, we should be willing to put our lives on the line for the country over here.

---

150 For the record, he made it in an interview in 1992. It's quoted in the Wikipedia articles *Vietnam Veterans Against the War* and *Scott Camil.* I've modified the verb tenses a few times.

The FBI 'monitored' Dewey Canyon III—never mind the Kansas City meetings, where FBI agents vacuumed the floors and did the dishes. But these 'rebels' were whites, nobody was murdered in his sleep like the Black Panther leader Fred Hampton in Chicago two years ago, 21 years old. In his bed, at dawn. Old enough to vote. It's a wonder the agents didn't chair the meetings themselves. We happen to know that Scott Camil has a place of honor on Nixon's 'enemies list.' 'An extremely dangerous and unstable individual whose activities must be neutralized at earliest possible time.'[151] 'Neutralize subject without delay.' Wide, wide river. Sure, Camil had some 'unfriendly fire' of his own in mind. But. But in Vietnam ALL the fire was unfriendly, *and he was there*, and fired. Plenty. But Camil's fire now, here, they say, is not 'justified.' He says, 'I do not think it was terrible at the time.' Neither do I. River of shit. 'An enemy of the people.' Stalin's term for anyone he wished to ELIMINATE. Not particularly democratic. No. Camil was brought up to believe, and believed, that the United States of America is the best country in the world. A Shining City on a Hill, a beacon to the world. He was dead wrong. Add this to his *lived* experience in Vietnam. Then Winter Soldier really opened his eyes. THIS is awakening, enlightenment, satori. *This*. He, too, has seen the puppeteers of fate. I know this. In the span of my own short life, anyone HERE who did not believe, and pledge, and *swear*, that this is the best country in the world— in the history of the world—has been considered an enemy of the people. *Denounced* as an enemy of the people. *Done* for,

---

151 December 22, 1971, J. Edgar Hoover classified memo to the FBI Jacksonville office. Other FBI memos about Camil used the word *neutralized* less ambiguously. Camil later explained, 'When you pin the government down, they'll say, well, *neutralize* just means to render useless. But if you talk to the guys in the field, they say it means to kill.' In his case, Camil was shot by FBI/DEA agents in 1974 in a drug entrapment sting, and nearly died. I myself have been out of the country for 43 years now, but the 'sting' would be less complicated today, thanks to the great American progress in anti-anti-American technology. From political bureaucracy to drones, all under the aegis of the USA Patriot Act, massively reinforced by Obama, and now named the USA Freedom Act. God bless the Land of the Free. God bless Captain Vere.

if possible. Wasted, rubbed out, erased, as an enemy of the people. But I know that this is wrong. It is the government of this country, the military of this country, that is an enemy of the people of this country. An enemy of the people of this country, and of the people of this world. Thank you, Dalton Trumbo. Point the way and we will point the gun.

As for the Williamsburg Bridge—it's a sense of political impotence, of frustration, of having a voice that is no voice. A bombing, an act of terror, and, strangely enough, it has to do with a sense of *responsibility*. A sense that being a citizen of this country means being responsible for what this country does. Anyone who thinks this is a crazy idea—well, OK, it's a free country. You can think what you want. But so can I. Camil fought in Vietnam for four years, he's experienced things, *done* things, that I haven't at all. He can't *undo* them and he knows it, but he wants to do something *now*. A sense of responsibility. A half-brother. More than half.

'Lady Liberty in distress': Occupation of the Statue of Liberty by Vietnam Veterans Against the War, 26 December 1971. Photo courtesy of VVAW.

THE SEVENTH GATE

SOUND, Pacific Street. B Train. Zuikan? Yes! Neon—at this
hour, a handful of madmen, heading for the heart of Fun City.
Climbing. So well timed. A free country. Wide, wide river.
NOW, let me say this. I once called Eteocles my half-half-half
brother, give or take a 'half' or two, because we both have
decisions to make. 'I have a fork.' 'Shall I go *myself* to the
Seventh Gate.' The prisoner's deed. But, let me say this, quite
frankly. Bluntly. Eteocles has no sense of responsibility. None.
As I see it. WHAT! you scream. Screaming—yelling—is fine,
but no guns please. I scream, you scream, we all scream. No
Saturday night specials, *please*. Small stabbings, well, OK, fine,
as long as you don't stab ME in the ass. He's King of Thebes.
He's doing his level best. He holds the helm of State, and from
the bridge pilots with sleepless eyes his country's fortunes. He
screwed his brother. He was cursed by his father—ye gods!
the haunch instead of the shoulder. He's *ready* to put his life
on the line for his country. A patriot, no question. Patriot and
king. He's responsible *for* a whole bunch of things. What an
ambiguous locution 'responsible *for*.' A double-edged sword.
Hitler, Stalin, were responsible *for* millions of murders, but
don't tell me they had a sense of responsibility. Am I too hard
on Eteocles. Perhaps. He IS responsible for the City, Thebes,

Defend the City! no, he's no shirker. He pilots with sleepless eyes, as he puts it. But if—which Heaven forbid—there is disaster, throughout the town, with threats and wailings a multitudinous swelling prelude cries on one name: 'Eteocles'! Responsibilities galore. King. Responsible for the City. And, if he and his champions fail to defend the Seven Gates, responsible *for* the disaster. Why did I say, bluntly, he has no *sense* of responsibility. I'm not sure, it just crossed my mind, popped into my head. This unfortunate war. NOW is the time for Benardete's second Note. 'II. Eteocles' Interpretations of the Shields.' Now—I'm putting all these political papers back into *Ramparts*, the Che Guevara Bolivia diaries issue, and here it is. Here's the second Note. I have a fork. No question. Absolutely. A friend of mine—a chemistry expert—once told me that if you put a fork in a glass of Coca-Cola and leave it over night (or maybe for a week or two) it will *dissolve*. Vanish. This may be true, but it's not the solution for my fork, no, I need to figure out *what a decision is and what making a decision means*. Here, now, in the transit system, the realm of shadows. I may still encounter some 'fun activism' on my path. Especially between West 4th and Columbus Circle. Gay pride. Colón again, it's always Colón. A Man of the World. Father of all Holocausts. It's late but it's Saturday. But, definitely no *crowd throng mob swarm horde* packing me in like a sardine and threatening to mash my Note. No. It's too late for that. A skirmish or two, at the most. Calling in of artillery on villages for games—no, too late. Not tonight. SAMs, B-52s—well, possibly on placards, but images on placards do not mash Notes on the *Septem*. *People* mash Notes on the *Septem*. Not tonight. Too late. Watch out! A spacetime singularity. Wide, wide river. ALL the fun seekers on the ENTIRE island of Manna-hata, once home of the Lenape, before their extinction—ALL the fun seekers seeking fun at this moment, AGAINST ALL ODDS, at ye gods know what time it is in the middle of the night, suddenly swarm into *this very car* on the B Train where I am peacefully rereading Benardete's second Note, thinking about what a decision is and what making a decision means. ALL of them at once, every last one. Deep shit. Spacetime singularity. Ask Einstein. Big number. True infinity? Or just the longest shot there is. *Smashing* me and my Note to a pulp. Focus. No more distractions. It's late. Time exists. Bodies exist. Behold. The *Manhattan* Bridge. Who decides. 'Which may also be regarded as arbitrary.' Night. The *East* River. Just names. Power. Power to the People! The way up, the way down. The true path. Night on the river, separating inseparable Hadean nights. Not two, and not one. The place, the time to take stock of the *Septem*, and of Benardete. Take stock of his first Note, since, at last, it's time for the second. I'll never forget the first time I ever saw the river and the three bridges from the B Train. It seems only yesterday, and in fact it *was* only yesterday. The placard-men. Are there any more, or any more of the same, or have I seen the last of them. It's late. But it's Saturday night. (Sunday morning actually, not that it matters.) One was a maniac scumbag. Fellow B-52 enthusiasts. Michelangelo, the My Lai man—is he *against* the war now, like the winter soldiers. Who knows. Why am I convinced the placard-men are a true infinity. No, not a conviction—no, *a way of looking at them*. The Dharma Eye. If a true infinity expresses a *concept*, as Hegel puts it, what concept do the placard-men express. Wow, a damn good question. I don't know. Possibly a Really Big One. To muse on. Ye Muses, shall I plead Socratic ignorance. Now—let me remember where I am, for a moment. Thebes, a little before dawn. Aeschylus. *Political theater*. Pigasus for President. Eteocles addresses the citizen body. He's thinking about war. An 'outlandish' and 'savage' army of Argives, led by his brother Polyneices, encamped on the dusty plain of Thebes, is about to attack the Seven Gates. Defend the City! *Una parola*, as the Italians put it, concisely. *A word*. (I've been studying Italian lately.) Easier said than done, as we say, while the Italians say it in one word: *una parola*. The Hadean night. Under Manhattan. In any event, after a long siege this will be a short war. No quagmire here. They attack the gates, we defend the gates, and *que sera sera*, as the French put it. *Coup de grâce*. The sudden way. Hui-neng. No-mind. As for the attack itself, Aeschylus liquidates it in a couple of lines. The spy anticlimactically tells the Chorus, Relax, mother's darlings, the gates have been defended, the Argives are hightailing it back across the plain, alas, at the Seventh Gate *the brothers have been reciprocally suicided* (as Hegel put it, echoed by Van Gogh[152]). *Polluting the City.* Unfortunately. This unfortunate war, as J. William Fulbright notes. Unfortunately, Eteocles makes a bad decision. It seems he has not figured out what a decision is and what making a decision means. Wide, wide river. Badly infinite? With the help of Aeschylus-cum-Benardete, can I learn from his mistake? Or, much more precisely, can I figure out *what* his mistake *is.* In the first almost-400 lines of the play we have the questions Benardete tackles in his first Note; in the second almost-400 lines we have the second Note, 'Eteocles' Interpretations of the Shields'; the whole tragedy is just over a thousand lines, and much of the last part may well be spurious. Now, let's see, what did Benardete tackle in the first Note. Three questions: the rebuked Chorus; the threefold meaning of Ares and its relation to the Curse; the dual origin of the City—sexual (divine and human) and non-sexual (serpent's tooth)—and its relation to Eteocles' decision. This sounds simple enough, but every time I read the first Note it seems to get more complicated, also because the Note itself is a *labyrinth*, Benardete keeps switching from one question to the other and to the other, and back, and forth, and back, and so forth. So well timed. SOUND. The. Bricks.

Lay. On. *Grand Street.* Quite a few fun seekers getting into the car. Fun finders actually, after their fabulous late-night dinners in Chinatown. Shrimp fished out of tanks and sweet-

---

152 No, actually by *Artaud*, in his essay on Van Gogh, *The Man Suicided by Society.*

and-soured on the spot. Then again, 'Curse' and 'decision' are
big words. Never mind 'images.' Placards. Michelangelo was
yelling 'Vietnam veteran' (for or against the war?). The maniac
scumbag had a B-52. Eteocles *rebukes* and *ridicules* the Chorus
because they cling to images, while wailing and shrieking.
As for Ares, Benardete says 'What is Ares?' is *the* question of
the *Septem*. The Curse! The Curse is the soul of the play, and
Ares is its heart. Absolutely. Eat your heart out, Aphrodite.
Make war not love. Wars and curses go together, like love and
marriage, flies and swatters, soup and a sandwich, SAMs and
B-52s. No question about it, Benardete is himself *exercised* by
the question that has exercised so much recent scholarship:
does Eteocles decide his own fate, or is his fate determined by
the curse of Oedipus. Decide, or decided for. Or in-between.
The more the merrier, take your pick, clap your hands, stamp
your feet. After all, he's *done for*, and so's his beloved brother,
whom he screwed. Done for. Reciprocally suicided. The Ghost
Dance. SOUND, Broadway/Lafayette. What a winter the
Marquis had with George Washington at Valley Forge, the
cherry tree chopped down long since, I tell you no lie. Honest
to God. A long hard winter. No, I've gotten ahead of myself.
Time exists. The play exists. The Curse of Vietnam exists. The
transit system exists. Screech by screech, sound by sound. The
'free play of the concept' also exists. I, personally, don't exist.
A flashing into the vast phenomenal world. 21-year-old NYU
student, graduating in a couple of months. Politically, however,
I do exist. For better or for worse. There's the rub. 4-F Vietnam
veteran against the war. Brooklyn/Manhattan Bridge. All names.
Three acorns in the morning, four acorns in the morning,
morning, evening, just do it. Focus. No filter. Direct experience.
Satori. Dawn is dawn. A moveable feast. Or famine. The
dawn's early light. The twilight's last gleaming. 'Our flag.'
Sunset Park. B Train. Transit system. Rebuked Chorus. Ares
and the Curse. How much freedom and how much necessity is

there in Eteocles' decision to go *himself* to the Seventh Gate. (Benardete likes the quasi-Hitchcockian word *compulsion*.) He had a bad/true infinity of alternatives. Does he have one sliver of a sense of responsibility, or none at all. Not a single one, like the tears of a cat? (No offense to cats. They may get sad, but they shed no tears.) THEN Benardete slithers—innocently—into the third question of his first Note, like a B-52 placard-man in a packed subway car. God bless him. God bless Captain Vere. God Bless America, and Kate Smith, *our* apple-pie fat lady. À la mode. We all scream. For ice cream. The dual origin of the City—sexual (divine and human) and non-sexual (serpent's tooth)—and its relation to Eteocles' decision. 'A sin sown long ago.' Eteocles 'glosses over the fatal doubleness of sexual and non-sexual generation with a single origin. In obedience to Apollo he tries to save the city "without issue." A patriotism, whether genuine or assumed, blots out that fatal doubleness in the city that he and his family particularly reveal.' Eteocles the blind patriot—this, in a nutshell, says Benardete in his *first* Note, is, in a nutshell, what Aeschylus is trying to tell us. Successfully, or not. Political theater. Let's see.

Absolutely, let's see what happens in the *second* Note. What a decision is and what making a decision means. Figuring this out is why I'm here, traveling indefinitely. Discovery, à la Cristóbal Colón. SOUND. Definitely. Bless our souls, it's West 4th, and what kettle of fish do we have. Nothing special. Roshi: 'When you give up, when you no longer want something, or when you do not try to do anything special, then you do something. When there is no gaining idea in what you do, then you do something.' Good. Nothing special. No placard-men. The true concept of infinity. The car is pretty full. Beginner's mind. Still fun seekers or tired heading-home fun finders. Who knows. Finders keepers, I'd say. People heading *out* for fun this late generally have limos or, at the least, take taxis. Other transit systems. Dikê, and I don't mean dikes, better known as lesbians, or, even better, as gay women. No, the goddess of Justice. Benardete concludes his first Note with a vibrant and severe critique of Eteocles' 'apparently complete devotion to the city.' Benardete smells a rat—a Fun City gutter rat. Big, and slimy. A *Pequod* rat, probably, from Ahab's ship. This slippery world, as Melville put it.[153] Eteocles' 'complete' devotion *splits* the City. The no-longer-wailing and no-longer-rebuked Chorus ends the play with the only glimmer of *wisdom* (definitely more *sophia* than *prajna*) we have on this bleak horizon, with its polluted and polluting reciprocal suicide (as Hegel put it). 'This grief is common to the race, but now one way and now another the City approves the path of Justice.' No, *this* is the question, posed on Polyneices' shield, at the Seventh Gate: WHAT JUSTICE? But the point we are coming to, and getting at, and which is the point of all points of this play, as I see it—its true infinity—is at the Sixth Gate, not the Seventh. Amphiaraus, the prophet who takes *being* (and—or and/or—*seeming*) a prophet seriously. Makes philosophical problems. Asks impossible questions. His shield is empty but his mind is chock-full. Of no-mind. I'm getting ahead of myself again, as usual, *leaping* ahead, almost to the end of Benardete's *second* Note. But, after all, this is the *transit* system. (What self! the Roshi says.) His placard is empty but, like the END THE WAR sixth placard-man, he himself has something to say. Here, and now, alas, I'm going to *get ahead of myself*, but, then again, WHAT SELF—we have to depend on the *spy's report* of what the prophet said, and this spy—I fear—may be a Peter Arnett *ante litteram*, as the Latins later put it. What's more, since Benardete doesn't do me the favor of translating these lines, we have to depend on Grene's translation, and Vellacott's translation, mixed, heaven help us, with my own translation. Wide, wide river. What the hell, we have thirty Hadean blocks till Herald Square. The night

---

153 Melville! 'Something in this slippery world that can hold.' *Moby Dick*, Chapter 108. He wasn't referring to Fun City rats, but to something even Bigger, Slimier, and more Hegelian.

is young. The prophet, says the spy, says, *to Polyneices*, a little before dawn:

> Is such a deed as this dear to the gods, and fair to hear and tell of, for posterity—bringing an alien army to ravage your father's city, smashing your country's gods? *What justice shall quench a mother's tears?* The earth of your father mashed to a pulp by your zealous spear—shall it be your ally?

Nutshell or not, on one side, this is what it's all about. On the other, the ruler-brother-foe side, what it's all about is what a decision is and what making a decision means. What I'm coming to and getting at. On Eteocles' side. Which is my side, since his decision is what concerns me. Polyneices, screwed, does whatever he likes, right or wrong. After all, what's right, what's wrong, when you've been royally screwed. Defend the City. Attack the City. 'Just do it.' Very Zen. Dikê. Whose side is she on. Pushin' and shovin'? Again. Please, no Saturday night specials, please. Rap, brother, rap. Work it out, somehow. Converse. Keep on truckin'. Keep up the good work, bro. I'm just about to read the second Note. Come on, this is Fun City. How about a little civil conversation in the transit system. Look at me. My monologue. My *interior* monologue, for that matter, fuck you all. Defend the City! Dig it, bros, all along the watchtower. Dylan Hendrix. Sing sing sing sing sing. *Canta che ti passa*. Dig my earth. Hendrix. Guitar! Guitar! Barefoot servants. Hendrix Dylan. Dylan Hendrix. Not two, not one. SOUND. Jimi! All the women. Sing play sing play. The hour is getting late.

Now. Both sides now. Benardete begins his second Note.

The spy tells Eteocles that Tydeus carries a shield whose insigne is the sky blazing with stars, and a full moon, 'the eye of night,' gleams in their midst. There are no words on the shield, for there is no one who could properly be thought to speak them, but Tydeus was heard to castigate the soothsayer Amphiaraus and reproach him for cowardice, since, Amphiaraus claimed, the sacrifices were still unpropitious.

The sacrifices. Norman Morrison? Not exactly. In this case, we're talking about animal guts. Entrails. The liver in particular. Haruspicy. SOUND. Herald Square. Remember me. Pushin' and shovin'. Rap, brothers, rap. Be cool now. Thanks. Sacrifices still unpropitious? Well, nothing's perfect. All this goes back to a haunch and a shoulder, to a fork, and to loving folly. That's life, as Frank Sinatra put it. Profoundly. Philosophically. Sing sing sing. *Sing.* '*The spy tells Eteocles*'—I'm coming right back to this, but, first, Benardete needs to complete his first thought in this second Note.

Eteocles, in his reply, offers an interpretation of the shield that is meant to allay the fears of the Chorus, as he apparently considers that women who are ready to fall down before statues of gods would be *a prey to false imaginings.* He declares himself to be immune to anything of the kind. He tries to show that Tydeus, who despises soothsaying, *carries a sign that might itself be a prediction.* He puts the stress, accordingly, on the night and not on the sky ('this night you speak of on his shield'), and he says that the night, not the sky, is ablaze with stars. If Tydeus is killed, the night would fall upon his eyes, a Homeric phrase that turns upside down the spy's 'eye of night.'

Well, I have a lot to say about this. Perhaps I should set the scene a little better. Why the hell not. The scene in the Note, and the scene in Thebes. The scene in Thebes is a lot easier to set. Seven gates and seven Argive Attackers/Challengers/ Champions, 'posted to each gate by lot.' I think, by picking a pebble out of a helmet, but I'm not sure. The spy tells Eteocles the name of each Challenger and describes (à la Peter Arnett) the device on his *shield*. Eteocles chooses a Defender for each Attacker, and gives a little speech describing *his* shield. Benardete goes to town on this Shield versus Shield business (in *Mad* magazine it's Spy versus Spy), and who can blame him, since *this*—well, if the Curse is the soul and Ares, the heart, then this is the *mind* of the play. So to speak. The mind of Aeschylus. Benardete's mind. Mind, *tout court*, as the French put it. *Geist*, as Hegel puts it. Spirit. Now, let me list the Attackers, in case I get confused later: Tydeus—Capaneus— Eteo*clus* (watch out, an Artaudian theater-and-its-double)— Hippomedon—Parthenopaeus—Amphiaraus—Polyneices. Perfectly linear. This will compel Benardete to make his second Note more linear than the first. To a certain extent. Benardete is *never* linear, he's a paragon of nonlinearity. No, but the second is *more* linear, relatively, because he has to follow the gates—1-2-3-4-5-6-7, he has no choice. What's more, this time he *makes his point at the end*, instead of scattering it all over the place as he does in the first Note. Then again—this second Note is pure Hitchcock. *The Lady Vanishes.* I need to *follow* Benardete and not get ahead of him. It's his story. WATCH OUT, just a little pushing, shoving, yelling, what're they yelling, fuck you bro—eat shit motherfucker—kill for peace (possibly, but I doubt it). SOUND, Coltrane! Coltrane! 42nd Street—the bros get off. Blue jays on the roof. A cry of liberation. *Peep.* So much the better. Less is more, as someone put it. Perchance to rumble on the platform. Knives, guns, whatevers. Bring the war home, baby. Fun City. I'm keeping my head down. Way down.

Rumble rumble. Be cool. Doors closing. B Train moving again. So he said, 'How about four in the morning and three in the evening?' Suit yourself. Be my guest. Taking both sides at once. Harmonizes right with wrong and rests in the balance of nature. Good, I've set both scenes at once. Two scenes, never mind this scene, here now, the transit system. Long live the Tao. Now—the car is pretty full, but I've gotten used to it. Not Note-smashing full. Some of the passengers are a little shaken up by that little rumble—the tourists, I mean. We locals—PLEASE, *bad* motherfuckers,[154] no shooting. That's all we ask. Perilous frontier. Now—I have a lot to say about this first exchange between the spy and Eteocles. I don't think Benardete would contest my thinking here. What he goes on to say does not contradict it. But my emphasis is different. (We'll discover, at the end, whether my conclusion is different from his, or not. What a decision is and what making a decision means.) After all, he only wrote this Note once, and I'm reading it for about the dozenth time in the past few months. And this time I'm reading it here, in the transit system, the realm of shadows. First, the spy. Right off the bat (I'm a bat expert), a serious problem, which Benardete—possibly—underestimates. What does the spy actually see on the shield. No question. He sees the sky at night with stars and a full moon. Period. In his speech he calls it an 'arrogant device' (Grene), an 'insolent device' (Vellacott). Why. Then, from unwarranted commentary he goes straight to *imagery*: the 'eye of night.' THIS is what he says to Eteocles, who has just finished *rebuking* and *ridiculing* the Chorus for clinging to *images*. But the moon IS not the eye of night, it just SEEMS to the spy to be the eye of night. The spy—right off the bat, out of hell—confuses being and seeming. Serious business. Deep shit. Wide river. To me, it smacks of *counterespionage*. Or, more innocently, our 'spy' is also a poet, and poets—as Plato said, repeatedly—tell many lies.

---

154 In Black slang a *'bad* motherfucker' means a 'good motherfucker'—a fine fellow, a good guy. This is extremely Hegelian.

Mythmakers. A danger to the City. Corrupting the citizen body. And mind. *Serious business.* Dead right. Dead serious. Just look at Eteocles' reply. FIRST, he says 'devices on a shield deal no one wounds.' (Vellacott goes overboard: '*pictures* can deal no wounds.') He's no prey to imaginings, false or otherwise. Not our Eteocles. He's immune to images. Reality, not image. Being, not seeming. Then, what does he, *himself*, do, *immediately*. He turns the *spy's image* upside down—like the Brits when they lost our Revolution—turning it into an *image of his own*. Never mind Tydeus and what's actually on his shield. One image to another. Image to image. No, says Eteocles, not sky but night. (The *East-West* River.) (Being is nothing, as Hegel dramatically, and logically, put it.) Then, not 'eye of night' but 'if in death night fall upon his eyes'—a line from Homer, a Big Big Liar (Plato says). But never mind Big Lies and counterespionage, I have a point to make. This Note—'II. Eteocles' Interpretations of the Shields'—is supposed to show us the *process* of Eteocles' *gradual* transformation from champion of reality to champion of the image. (A.k.a. from freedom to necessity, a.k.a. compulsion.) (A decision. The prisoner's deed.) Devices on the shields. Interpretations. Sure, the Curse is the Curse—the Curse of Oedipus, the Curse of Vietnam, either way it's deep shit. One image leads to another—freely and necessarily—and in the end we are confronted with an image we cannot deny. Prisoners of the image. Who's responsible. The prisoner's deed. A decision. What a decision is and what making a decision means. Already in his shroud. Eteocles, from the bridge pilots with sleepless eyes his country's fortunes. Compulsion. Decides his own fate. Sealed. Trained seals. Goes *himself* to the Seventh Gate. Being, seeming. For Hegel they are inseparable, the three moments of his logic are being—appearing—concept. From being to seeming—to being dead, and done for. Reciprocal suicide. GRADUALLY. Shield by shield. *Not the moment he opens his mouth*. A 'logical' moment. SOUND, Rockefeller Center. Ice-skating all night. No, I don't think so. I don't know. Round the clock. I don't know. More people off than on. Hotels. At Columbus Circle the B Train crowd will really thin out, and grow calmer. No pushin' and shovin' under Central Park West. I'm sure 'The Chin' Gigante never took the subway. *Gradually*. But RIGHT OFF THE BAT (with more than a little help from the spy) it's image versus image, a war of images. Shields, not men. Placards. Pasteboard masks. Benardete might say I'm getting carried away. Exaggerating. I raise my hands and spread out all my fingers. Has nobody noticed *the very first thing Eteocles does*. All at once, right away, not little by little. He *decides on* images. From the start. His goose is cooked before he's even plucked it. Not only is his cart before his horse, but the horse is prancing around the meadow, heading for a lost horizon. Or, maybe this is precisely the point: *images are there from the very beginning*. The placard and the man are separate and inseparable. No placard without the man and no man without the placard, and we are ALL placard-men. Or *women*, as the case may be. Or children. Or *animals*, possibly. We can't just *decide* to start with reality and deal with images later. We spend our whole life chasing our own images. I'm not sure, but I think the Roshi wouldn't disagree with this. Make your screen blank. Empty. Monkey mind. Let's see how I feel when I get to the Hitchcockian end of this Note. Eteocles a prisoner of images from the very beginning, that's what I see right now. What does this mean for our strenuous effort to figure out what a decision is and what making a decision means. This voyage of discovery. My half-half-half-brother and I. His first, almost invisible decision: 'if in death night fall upon his eyes.' An image. Image versus image. Blaming it all on the spy would be far too easy. Does this mean he's already decided for. No, I don't think so. No, that would kill the play. Aeschylus, Benardete, they don't think so. Starry Vere, God bless him, showed us how decisions come in bunches. Perhaps, most especially, in the case of men of *responsibility*, such as Captains and Kings. Blind patriots. No, we are *all* responsible for what we do. Prisoners of our deeds. This is what makes us human. Anthropus. Or animal, possibly. *Zoon politikon*. Karma. The answer to the riddle. I decide ('unconsciously') on images, from the start. From then on I chase my own images, like a cat chasing her tail. I am responsible for the war in Vietnam. I am going to make a decision. How free will it be. The empty mirror. A bright mirror is set up on a high stand, its illumination reaches the ten-thousand things, and these ten-thousand things are *not* reflected in it. What is most wonderful is this: the mirror reflects everything coming before it *unconsciously*, with no-mind. Seth Benardete is—in my own experience of him—an extraordinarily calm and understated individual. He's austere. Witty, but in a very quiet way. (Dave Leahy loves to laugh.) I don't think he'd like my bombast. OK, let me get back to his reading of the first exchange between Eteocles and the spy. Let's have a little sobriety. SOUND, 7th Avenue. Nothing special. 'The night of Tydeus' shield is literal and the eye metaphoric, while the night in Eteocles' interpretation is metaphoric and the eyes literal.' Gospel truth. But what about the spy. 007. *From Russia With Love*, even the title is subversive. *Dr. No*—Hegel's power of the negative. Benardete: 'Eye of night' is not a literal account of what the spy saw; it too is an interpretation. An *image*, I'd say.

> It might therefore be completely unmetaphoric, if the moon were regarded as a sentient being. [What would a Buddhist say.] Eteocles seems, however, to have divorced the phrase from its reference to the moon, applied it to Tydeus, and played with it as though it were simply a periphrasis for night. Eteocles, in any case, *has been forced* [all my italics] to find a meaning in Tydeus' shield that in itself it may not

bear. Even [even!] the spy's 'eye of night' goes beyond the representation, which contains nothing to inspire fear or reveal a presumptuous pride.... Eteocles, then, is guilty of over-interpretation. He imposes a 'reading' on what perhaps cannot be read.

Well, OK, but, sifting and sorting,[155] in my own reading, of the play and of the Note, I wonder whether there might not be a tad of 'under-interpretation' in Benardete. Or am I myself guilty of 'over-interpretation,' along with my half-half-half-brother. Who knows. We'll see. Being and seeming. 'The night is young,' so to speak. *Images*. From the start. The word go. On with the Note. The second Challenger.

> The shield of Capaneus, however, is the man. It shows an unprotected or naked man with a blazing torch, and golden letters proclaim, 'I shall burn the city.' Eteocles finds it easy to connect Capaneus' insigne with his boast that not even the 'strife of Zeus' could check him in his course. These words lead Eteocles to apply the description of the insigne to the lightning that Capaneus thinks so harmless.

I need to flesh this out a little. Now, the *spy* says that Capaneus *says* (in Grene's translation) that 'not even *Zeus' wrath* striking the earth before him shall be obstacle to his purpose.' Then, the *spy* goes on to say that 'the lightnings and thunderbolts he likened to the sun's warm rays at noontide.' Fair enough. Or unfair. Or not quite fair. Or not quite enough. My point is this. This time the Challenger gives us an explicit metaphor ('likened to'), but I wonder about this 'strife of Zeus'/'Zeus' wrath.' Did Capaneus actually say this, or is it a hidden metaphor cooked up by the spy (again, after his 'eye of night'). Capaneus—says the spy—is a giant, and inhumanly

---

155 Pardon this outrageous, but extremely pertinent, reference to (the English translation of) Thomas Bernhard's masterpiece novel *Correction*.

arrogant. Outlandish and savage. Yet *this* giant (unlike Tony the Chin, I'm sure) *waxes poetic*, saying 'Zeus' wrath' instead of saying, quite simply, lightnings and thunderbolts, as our poetic spy, *himself*, does. Dig it bro. I have my doubts. SOUND. Columbus Circle. India. No shit, the earth is round. The round circle of his shield. Let us not talk falsely now. Said the joker to the thief. Speak, Benardete. Illuminate. That's what I'm here for. The car is half empty.

> Whereas in the case of Tydeus, the shield's image is silent and Tydeus' words without a direct bearing on it [he's riled up at Amphiaraus], Capaneus' words, through the resemblance of man-made fire to lightning, allow or rather prompt the union of an image no longer silent with a boast that implicitly ranks fire higher than lightning.

Fire, more on the roof, possibly, than in the mind. Now, Eteocles' riposte. He has improved.

> Eteocles' hermeneutics, on his second try, have improved. He now transforms an image of something into something else without appealing to any metaphor. Tydeus has shown an image of the night sky that had to be forced to bear on what he said; but Capaneus' words refer to the Zeus of the sky and his insigne to the present siege of Thebes. Tydeus had not mentioned gods, Capaneus threatens them. The shield of Tydeus is partly bright and partly dark with nothing but cosmic gods: man and man-shaped gods have there no place. The shield of Capaneus, on the other hand, is the world of unarmed, post-Promethean man, who challenges the sun and Zeus as ineffectual. We seem to be presented, then, with two stages of, or two layers in men's understanding of the sky that overarches them, and each layer is in turn subject to a double interpretation.

A Note. This is theater. *The Theater and its Double*, Antonin Artaud. I can't resist,[156] I know this by heart, soul, and mind. 'The second phase of Creation, that of difficulty and of the Double.'

> For the theater as for culture, it remains a question of *naming and directing shadows*; and the theater, not confined to a fixed language and form, not only destroys false shadows but prepares the way for a new generation of shadows, around which assembles the true spectacle of life. [....]

> When we speak the word 'life,' it must be understood we are not referring to life as we know it from its surface of fact, but to that fragile, fluctuating center that forms can never reach. And if there is still one hellish, truly accursed thing in our time, it is our artistic dallying with forms, instead of being like victims burnt at the stake, signaling through the flames.

Ye gods, Artaud, this is important. SOUND. 72nd Street. Central Park West, prime placard-man territory. Will I meet another one. Or one of the six I've met. Michelangelo. Or the maniac scumbag *again*. The B-52! No, I hope not. How about I GAVE MY LEGS. The winter soldier. Naming and directing shadows. Pigasus. Did a police officer really eat him. Pig! Political theater. Political animals. (What does *zoon* mean? Benardete didn't ask, fortunately. This unfortunate war.) Is Eteocles artistically dallying with forms. No way. If I thought so, I'd 'reciprocally suicide' myself all by myself. His balls are on the chopping block. That fragile, fluctuating center. Give us a break. We have a Curse. We are chasing our own

---

156 I tried to resist. Reading Benardete's lines in the second Note, Artaud *leaped* out of his tomb, screaming. *The Theater and its Double*, New York: Grove Press, 1958, beautifully translated by Mary Caroline Richards, pp. 51, 12, and 13.

images. We *have* a decision to make, and goddamit we'll make it. Do or die. Or both. We have friends who help us. Melville Aeschylus Benardete. Dogen. Suzuki-roshi. The other Suzuki. Kafka Dostoevsky Artaud. Dave Leahy. You think I'm at the end—END THE WAR—but I'm just getting started. I'm 21, I'm graduating in a couple of months. I have no choice. *We must do*, says Starry Vere. 'The effect was as if the moon, emerging from eclipse, should reappear with quite another aspect than that which had gone into hiding.' What am I going to do. *Responsibly*. Free, necessary—responsible. *Politically* responsible. A cry of liberation. Personally, a flashing into the vast phenomenal world. Strike through the mask. Fun City, but *it is a city*. A country, a nation. A whole, a totality, a system. A *transit* system that, alas, is convinced it is *permanent*. Carved in stone. A *statue*. Lady Liberty. Unfortunately. For me. For Eteocles, the blind patriot. 'This unfortunate war.' But he screwed his brother. But he was cursed by their father. Then again, who wasn't. Love it or leave it. Why do I keep veering away from Benardete. His *second* Note. The keynote. Pilots with sleepless eyes his country's fortunes. Each layer subject to a double interpretation. I need to get back to Artaud. Later. I *will* get back to Artaud. Possibly. Signaling. Burnt at the stake. The Note. Subject to a double interpretation.

> The first is the sky at night with a full moon that looks on men but seems indifferent to them; but the moon wanes and disappears, and the night becomes understood as the blackness of death: Night gave birth by herself to Death (Hesiod, *Theogony* 211-213). The first interpretation can be imitated, the second can only be talked about; but, for the second layer, the view that regards lightning as harmless can only be talked about in likenesses, and only unprotected man can be shown: Capaneus' threats seem to be only talk. Eteocles, in his interpretation of this second layer, trusts that unprotected man will prove

to be exposed to the *just punishment* of heaven. Thebes' champion against Tydeus with his cosmic device was one of the Spartoi, whom 'consanguine justice,' the justice of defending his own mother, the earth, will exhort. Eteocles, then, has transferred his trust from earth to heaven, even as Tydeus' reliance on the sky has yielded to Capaneus' reliance on himself. Eteocles indicates this change when he presents the first confrontation as a matter of chance even if Ares presides over the throw of the dice, and the second confrontation between Capaneus and Polyphontes as entirely in Thebes' favor, since the good-will of Artemis and other gods seconds Polyphontes.

SOUND. 81st Street, Museum of Natural History *and* Hayden Planetarium. Dinosaurs galore, but cockroaches are older, Elder Statesmen, they tormented the terrible lizards, traipsing through their food. Today they're leaping from chandeliers on Park Avenue. But Eteocles would be more interested in the Planetarium, checking out the 'eye of night.' Difficulty and the double. The plot has *already* thickened. Plenty. Lightning—Zeus!—is *harmless*—dig *this* bad motherfucker. Naked man (Naked City) carrying a torch (Persevere and Excel!), and fuck you all. Fug God. I've got a torch. What torch. What fire. What is fire. (What does 'animal' mean?) (Kill for peace.) No, Benardete seems unconcerned. Two layers, each subject to a double interpretation. In my opinion, these are not the clearest lines he's ever written. Be patient. Zuikan? Yes! All alone in his small zendo. Zuikan? Yes! But he's building up to something, gradually, Hitchcockianly. And linearly, more or less—1-2-3-4-5-6-7. Anyway, in a nutshell, I'd put this second tête-à-tête between Eteocles and the spy this way. The *spy* says that Capaneus says that 'not even Zeus' wrath striking the earth before him shall be obstacle to his purpose. The lightnings and thunderbolts he likened to the sun's warm rays at noontide.' Eteocles responds, to the spy, that (in Grene's translation) 'I trust on him [Capaneus] will justly come the bolt that carries fire, in no way like the sun's warm rays at noontide.' Fair enough. Have no fear, there are lots of difficulties and lots more doubles further down the line. FIRE. Flames. Signaling. Flames and voices.[157] Benardete continues, with Eteo*clus*—absolutely Artaudian, as I said. While chasing my tail I seem to anticipate my own every move.[158]

> Eteoclus, the third Argive attacker, has a shield that shows
> a hoplite approaching with a scaling ladder the walls of the
> city, and he proclaims, 'Not even Ares would cast me from
> the ramparts.' Eteocles' reply of nine lines is the shortest
> of his interpretations, but it is no less significant than the
> others.

SOUND. 86th Street. No, no placard-man in sight. I met the pledge-of-allegiance man here going uptown, and the approach-the-village man going downtown. The Note.
> He seems again, as he did with Tydeus and Melanippus,
> to regard the issue between Eteoclus and another Spartos
> Megareus as a toss-up, for he concedes that Megareus

---

157 'Being more live than they, more full of flames and voices.' Ezra Pound, Canto VII.

158 I must say, this reminds me of our equally Artaudian Vietnam Veterans and former Senators John *Kerry* and Bob *Kerrey*. Veterans for-or-against the War, or both, or neither, or in-between, or what have you. The 'Vietnam War' or War in general, who knows. *Kerrey* is a highly decorated war criminal, a Navy [trained] SEALs officer who led his [trained] SEALs in the 'lesser' (compared to My Lai) massacre ('only' 21 women and children slaughtered) in the village of Thanh Phong in 1969. Ker*rey* admitted his atrocity many years later, in 2001, when/because his war crime was about to be exposed, quipping 'both sides did a lot of damage in the Vietnam War.' A parade is a parade. Is a parade. And now—2016—Kerrey has been named chair of the board of trustees of the brand new U.S.-sponsored Fulbright University of Vietnam (known as FUV) in Ho Chi Minh City. Absolutely! a place of higher learning (Persevere and Excel!) to teach the Vietnamese how to be good global-era capitalists and world capitalist citizens. (See Paul Street, 'Bob Kerrey, Fulbright University and the Neoliberal Erasure of History,' in *Z Magazine*, October 2016.) Look! a fine photo of *Kerrey* and his close buddy Secretary of State *Kerry* celebrating the opening of FUV. Shit, I wonder what J. William Fulbright would have had to say about *this*.

might be killed; but if he is not, 'he will adorn his father's house with booty,' when he seizes 'two men and the city on the shield.'

Ye gods, *TWO* men. The plot thickens. Again. Even more. Being and, or and/or, seeming. Clearly a triumph of the image.

Eteo*clus* himself does not make any boast, he leaves it to his emblem to speak for him; and what the shield shows is literally true: Ares cannot cast *this image* [all my own italics] form the ramparts. This absorption of Eteo*clus*, as it were, into his image is echoed by Eteo*cles*, who almost puts the image of the hoplite and the hoplite himself on the same level, even as the image of a city, if captured, is almost as glorious a deed as the capture of Thebes. In the first interpretation of Eteocles, the literal and the metaphoric in the image were inverted; in the second, the image suggested something else that was not an image; but now *the image becomes the equivalent of that of which it is an image.*

Wow, this is my favorite part of the whole second Note. This is really the heart of the eternal pyramids, as Melville said somewhere.[159] The core of the tangle. OK, I know, Benardete understates and I overstate, but it's MY life on the line here. My decision. Benardete *does* take himself seriously, but I take him *seriously* seriously. Here. Now. I have to get a grip on the point. *Two men and the city on the shield*. *TWO* men, and both are *placard-men*. Zuikan! I *told* you they were a *true* infinity, but what in the world do I *mean*. The placard and the man, and the man on the placard. For Eteocles, equivalent. Warriors. Samurai. Attacking Thebes. Reality-image, image-reality. Easy, easy, let's go easy. Be cool, bro. Dig it. '*The image of the city, if captured.*' Eteocles started off by playing 'image versus image'

---

159 On the next-to-last page of *Bartleby*.

with the spy, but this time he has no need of the spy, the image on the shield is quite sufficient. What's *with* Eteocles. What's on his mind. Has he never seen a device on a shield before. I saw a solitary G.I. approaching a village on a placard, but I never imagined the village on the placard was *actually* a village in Vietnam. Defend the City! Absolutely. Eteocles is King, he's *responsible for* Thebes. And he thinks he can defend it by *capturing a city on a shield.* Well, good luck. SOUND. West 96th. Cracked requiem. What has come over him. This Note is supposed to be about the *process* of his *gradual* transformation from champion of reality to champion of the image. Don't tell me that itty-bitty line about the 'eye of night' threw him for a loop. A loop-the-loop. Permanently. A loop-de-doop. The spy! Itty-bitty line, threw him off the top of a cliff, and he'll never stop falling. Pretty hard to believe. But he *has* been a prisoner of images from the word go. Absolutely. Then again, who hasn't. 'The prisoner's deed. With that alone we have to do.' What is the *decision* that decides the deed. 'His right arm shot out and Claggart dropped to the deck.' 'Diminished responsibility' it's called today. But Eteocles is responsible for the city. Completely responsible. Absolutely responsible. Politically and/and personally responsible. Sure, there's his father's curse. The question that has exercised so much recent scholarship: Does Eteocles decide his own fate, or is his fate determined by the curse of Oedipus. But what does the Curse have to do with his *going overboard* for images. Lock, stock, and barrel, so to speak. Totally thrown for a loop. Off a cliff. A loop-de-doop. Completely, and/and absolutely, losing his head. When he seizes two men and the city on the shield. What about what a decision is and what making a decision means! which is supposed to be the point of this Note. I definitely need to take stock here. But how. Buy stock, sell stock, take stock. Shares. Odd lots. I haven't got a clue. Just musing. I'm as clueless as the sky is blue. Zazen. On the roof. The *peep-peep-peep*. Wait.

A clue, possibly. Eteocles doesn't even seem to notice that the third Challenger's name is almost the same as his. Just one letter different. He takes it *completely* in his stride. Is this normal. Names were a big deal in Ancient Greece. 'Polyneices' means 'much strife,' for example, while 'Eteocles' means 'true glory.' I wonder what 'Eteo*clus*' means. He doesn't seem to care, at all, that his City is being attacked by someone—a real flesh and blood Attacker—with *nearly* his exact same name. All he cares about is capturing images on shields. I said it before and I'll say it again: no sense of responsibility. He has an 'outlandish' and 'savage' army of Attackers at his Gates, and he's supposed to be defending the City against *them*, not against their *images*. Or perhaps Eteo*clus* got under his skin *unconsciously*, with no-mind, à la Hui-neng. SOUND. 103rd Street. This would explain a lot. He's faced with a who's who of outlandish Argives and *he is not intimidated*. He doesn't pass the buck, no, the buck stops with him. Defend the City! No question. He won't be intimidated, by Singles, Doubles, Triples, or what-have-yous. This reminds me, for some reason, of the famous Abbott and Costello baseball sketch 'Who's on first?'. The first baseman's *name* is Who, so when the first one asks 'Who's on first?' the other one answers 'Yes, Who.' 'No, *who?*' 'Yes, Who's on first.' Zuikan, in his zendo, would get a kick out of this one. Eteocles says, My problem here is not *names*, it's all a question of *images*. He's not shirking his responsibility, he'll burn at the stake if need be. But will he signal through the flames. Like Norman Morrison! That is the question (which is no question). A decision. A *sense* of responsibility. By reading Benardete's *second* Note, again, and in the subway, I've been hoping to figure out what, for Eteocles, and for me, a decision is, and what making a decision means. Have I royally painted myself into a corner. It's possible. I don't know yet. Benardete is Hitchcockian. He knows—he *must* know, he knows much more about the *Septem* than I do—that Eteocles *went* *overboard* for images, *completely lost his head* for images, from the word go. But in this Note he doesn't want to say so *at the beginning*, he wants to *save it for the end*. And he has a reason. Now I see it. This Note is not about Eteocles' decision to defend the city, there's no question about that. He's King, Defend the City! is what he's there for, on that score there's nothing to decide. It's not like Kennedy, Johnson, Nixon, *deciding* to kill millions of Vietnamese in the defense of tyranny. No, Eteocles didn't *decide* to get himself cursed by his father, though he *and his brother* decided on the haunch rather than the shoulder. He definitely *did decide* to screw his brother, but this isn't the decision we're grappling with now. No—and this is what makes Benardete's Note Hitchcockian—the decision we're grappling with now—namely, the decision to go *himself* to the Seventh Gate, knowing full well that *his own brother* is at the Seventh Gate—doesn't exist yet. It won't exist until the spy tells him—later—that his own brother is at the Seventh Gate, which is exactly where Eteocles—free to go to any Gate he liked—intended to go *himself*. Possibly. SOUND. Cathedral Parkway. Some exegetes have wondered whether Eteocles actually did intend to go to the Seventh Gate, or *to any gate at all.* He 'interprets' all the shields, but perhaps he intended to do a Kissinger all along, hanging around the Oval Office, cooking up strategy, and sending *the others*, and their theaters, to the Gates. I'll get to this, possibly. For once I'll follow Benardete and not get ahead of myself. Now—only *then*, when the spy tells him that his own brother is at the Seventh Gate, will he have to make the *decision* that is the hero of this Note. My own situation is exactly the same. I can't decide what I'm going to do when I graduate from NYU in a few months until I graduate from NYU in a few months. No, I take it back, it's not exactly the same. I can *think about* my decision now, because I know what's coming, but Eteocles can't think about his decision until the spy tells him *his own brother* is at the Seventh Gate. Then

348

again, his brother is *definitely* no Kissinger, no, *he's going for a gate*, personally, *himself*, that's for sure. Personally, and politically. Great, I am graduating, definitely, tip-top, unless, of course, I'm mugged, or suicided, in the next few months, no, I *did* graduate from that miserable high school, and now *I am graduating* from NYU. The prisoner's deed. At dawn. In a few months. We don't need a spy to tell us that. Then again *again*, the point is what Eteocles and I decide to do, not what Polyneices and NYU decide to do, that's beside the point and not to the point. Then again again *again*, the situation *is* exactly the same, because *the* question—the hero of the Note— is not *what* we decide but *what a decision is* and *what making a decision means*. Freedom, necessity, responsibility. Compulsion. Forks, prongs, theaters, singles, doubles, triples. Fine, BUT—a *sense* of responsibility or, more precisely, *the* sense of responsibility. Political, personal. Not two, not one. Great. Now. After this minor aside I'd better get back to the Note, where Benardete has not quite finished with the question of the Third Gate. Almost, but not quite. He has something to say about the spy.

> The closing of the gap between the image and the imaged is subtly presented as the merging of the spy with the Argive leaders. Eteocles ends by saying [in Grene's translation, Benardete just gives the Greek] 'on with another's boasts— don't grudge me the story.'

In other words—and this really is very interesting—he no longer sees the spy as a Theban 'eye of night' poet *to be emulated*, but—say it ain't so—as a Peter Arnett embedded in, or actually *in bed with* the enemy (so to speak). Outlandishly and savagely. He is so completely *captivated* by the spy's reports that he no longer sees them as *his* reporter's reports but, rather, as coming *straight from the horse's mouth*. And, here, the 'horse' is no Trojan, no, it's the wild bunch of Argives, bunched under the command of his own brother, Polyneices. Attacking the city. Benardete concludes:

> Eteocles himself can be equally charged with confounding the reporter with the report, just as he has doubled Eteoclus, whose name is almost the double of his own.

I have one more thing to say about the doubled Eteo*clus*, placard-and-man and man-on-placard. East/West River. SOUND. 116th Street. No river, this is 116th and St. Nicholas Avenue, where it's Christmas every day. Saint Nick. Possibly. There are still quite a few people in the car, at a now absolutely and completely uncertain number of acorns in the morning. I've lost all track, and all tracks. Lost *track* 'in-and-for-itself,' as Hegel loved to put it. Night. Shadows. Three, four acorns—but how many MONKEYS, no one ever asks *how many monkeys*, why? Not two, not one, ten thousand, suit yourself. A man who kept MONKEYS, said to them, What time is it. Why ask. Night. Up there, down here. Round Midnight is long gone, for now. Dawn. Dawn dawns when it dawns. Time, what is this thing called time, as Nina Simone fantastically and beautifully put it. Where the time goes. Who knows. Who's counting. At this point. What point. Why *point*. Why not *expand*. Expanse. Great plain. Universe. Dust bowl. Fertile crescent. Quite a few people going to Harlem for some *soul* at this hour. No, just musing, no amusement, these are people straggling home. To the unicorns, possibly. The Unicorn in Captivity. Too many addicts, pushers, and muggers on the streets these days, a few years ago things weren't this bad. Things change. For the worse. I came up here with my taxi all the time. Have a cigar. Took my chances. Pimps, prostitutes, big tips. The other drivers never came, if they could possibly avoid it. Scared shitless. Wives and children. Whores, skunk pussies, buggers, queens, fairies, dopers and junkies. Like Rivington Street but more variety. Lively. Cool. Extravagant. SOUND, 125th Street. The Apollo Theater, just a short block and a half to the east. Legendary. Soul music. I prefer Slugs' in the Far East, East 3rd, just five blocks straight uptown from my place on Rivington. Stanton, Houston, 1st, 2nd, 3rd. Greatest jazz in the world. A short-lived legend. Time flies. SOUND SOUND SOUND. A few people straggling home. It used to be a Ukrainian restaurant, bar, and meeting point for drug dealers, until Jerry Schultz turned it into a jazz club in 1964. In 1966 he already had Albert Ayler, our prophet! Spirits rejoice! Now late and much lamented. Life on East 3rd Street. Schultz put it this way: 'From the time somebody would leave the door [of their taxi, if they could afford a taxi] to enter Slugs', from the taxi to the door, somebody could come and stick a knife in their ribs and say "Your money or your life." And they would empty their pockets before they could ever afford to buy a drink in the club.' Frankly, on Rivington I never heard anyone say 'Your money or your life,' it's a cliché. Or if, perchance, they did, they said it in Spanish anyway. And now Slugs' is closing, since Lee Morgan got shot at the bar about six weeks ago. February 19th, a Saturday night (Sunday morning) like tonight. But snowy. A shot heard round the Lower East Side. Lee Morgan, 33 years old, the great hard-bop trumpeter, many of us like him more than Miles Davis. No guns. PLEASE no guns. Knives. We want knives! Long, short, or in-between. This one really was a Saturday night special. What a story. What a sad story. A tragedy all around. Shot by his common-law wife, an 'older woman' (she's 46) named—watch out—Helen Moore a.k.a. More a.k.a. [Mrs.] Morgan. The Theater and its Triple. Here, again, different sources, and very different versions of the shooting. Moore was jealous that Morgan had found a new girlfriend. 'Somebody his age to play with,' as she put it. As Schultz tells it, late that Saturday night/Sunday morning (early) Moore/More/[Mrs.] Morgan confronted [Mr.]

Morgan as he stood at the bar before his last set. 'She just walked right up to him and says, "I have a gun, I'm gonna kill you." And he said, "Bitch, you don't even have any bullets for the gun"—because they kept a little pistol in his trumpet case. What happens, she goes out, gets bullets in the gun, comes back, points the gun at his heart and kills him right at the bar.' Ye gods. As gruesome as it gets. But Helen Moore/ More/Morgan's version is completely different.[160] She took a taxi down to Slugs' that Saturday night, she was talking with Morgan and the girl walked up to him and said 'I thought you wasn't supposed to be with her anymore.' And he said, 'I'm not with this bitch, I'm just telling her to leave me alone.' As she tells it: 'And about that time I hit [i.e. punched] him. And when I hit him I didn't have on my coat or nothing but I had my bag. He threw me out the club. Wintertime. And the gun fell out the bag. And I looked at it. I got up. I went to the door. I guess he had told the bouncer that I couldn't come back in. The bouncer said to me, "Miss Morgan I hate to tell you this but Lee don't want me to let you in." And I said, "Oh, I'm coming in!"' — SOUND SOUND SOUND, 163rd Street, I missed a few stops. Engrossed. Straggled home. The car is empty. — 'I guess the bouncer saw the gun because I had the gun in my hand. He said, "Yes you are." And I saw Morgan rushing over there to me and all I saw in his eyes was rage.' So she shot him. She sat in the middle of 'the pure pandemonium that broke out in a complete daze, wondering if this was a dream, or was it a nightmare?' Possibly, an abyss of dreams. Meanwhile, because of a heavy snowfall the ambulance took so long to get there that Lee Morgan bled to death. All this six weeks ago. OK, this is more of a *Rashomon* than a *Seven Against Thebes*. A tragic story. Why did it pop into my head like this. Plowmen dig my earth. At this point I could proffer an analysis of poor Helen's *decision*. In the hope that it helps me discover what a decision

160 It's in the only interview she ever gave, in February 1996, 24 years after the fact and less than a month before her own death.

is and what making a decision means. To go *himself* to the
Seventh Gate. No, never mind. Eight million stories. No no no.
One story. 'Local' news. Crime news. The news Dostoyevsky
loved so passionately. Image, reality, being or and/or seeming.
Power of the negative. Logical moments. SOUND. Washington
Heights. End of the line. Again. Never. Always. Whenever. Time
and again. What a decision is, what making a decision means.
Getting late. What hour. What self. No-hour. What mind. No-
mind. Began to howl. The wind. When.

> When, when, and whenever death closes our eyelids,
> Moving naked over Acheron
> Upon the one raft, victor and conquered together,
> Marius and Jugurtha together,
> one tangle of shadows.[161]

Silence. The dead of night. What night. Nobody here. Standing
on the platform. No time. *A note on a Note*, is that all there
is. Is that all she wrote. A dead worm. I could sure use a good
'getting-my-head-together' trip in the subway right about now.
But I'm already in the subway. Long since. Time and again.
Immer wieder, as Rilke put it. Ye gods. Night gave birth by
herself to Death. This isn't much of a station. It's empty. Just a
few people got off the old B, and now I'm all alone, like Ismael
clinging to Queequeg's coffin at the end of Moby Dick. 'And I
only am escaped alone to tell thee.' An orphan. At the Queens
end of the F Train the joint is jumping compared to this.
Jamaica—to say nothing of the Jamaica south of Cuba, where, I
imagine, it's reggae round the clock. I march up and down the
platform. The 'body' of the downtown B, doors still closed, on
the other side. Up, down, up, down. OK, 'up' is in the direction
I came from, 'down' is in the direction I'm going. Coincidentally,
or tyrannically, possibly, uptown and downtown. Sez who.
Where was Hiz Honor and his ambulance when Lee Morgan bled

---

161 Ezra Pound, *Homage to Sextus Propertius*, VI.

to death because of a couple of feet of snow on the streets. One line, two directions. Not the same direction. Names are problematic. Reality is a problem. Images seem to be *the* problem. The doors of the dead B are now open but there's no sign of life, I might as well be on the Moon. The 'eye of night' as the spy put it, thanks to his poetic license (to kill). A dead worm. Headed 'downtown.' Midtown, the Village, Brooklyn. Headed *down*. Where. Coney Island. What head! that's the tail. What tail. What head. What head/tail. What chase. What white whale. People straggling home from a big night in Washington Heights. With the unicorns. Up. Down. There's a subway map here on the platform but no clock, who cares. Do I still have an apple, or two. Or three. Or ten thousand. Who's counting. Not hungry. Who cares. I guess I'm 'convinced' that these trains have a schedule, but that no one knows what it is. A sound. Coltrane? No. The B is clearing its throat. But 200 million years ago cockroaches were traipsing through the dinosaurs' food. Did they—the cockroaches—clear their throats. What throats. Do two-inch Elder Statesmen clear their throats. No, they don't, possibly. But the subway is here for a minute, and the cockroach for a million years. What justice. No justice. The mass murder of Hiroshima. The Bay of Pigs. The jeeps rolling through the streets. The mass murder of Vietnamese. All in my name. All in my mind. On the roof. Wars of images. Let's talk about placard-men. True infinity. Possibly.

Princes kept the view. I'm on the move, on the B again. Mass murder. I keep it in mind. Reality is a problem. Images seem to be *the* problem. The Note! The Note! The car is empty. Back to Benardete's second Note. Where am I. Zuikan! Yes! One more thing about the doubled Eteo*clus*. According to some—to many—'sources' he was not one of the Seven against Thebes at all. In all the sources I've seen six of the seven match six of the *Septum*'s seven, but the seventh—actually the first—is Adrastus, not Eteoclus, who, of course, in Aeschylus is the third. The whole order is mixed up. Upset. Absolutely. In any event, most sources think that the Seven without Adrastus is like soup without a sandwich, a B-52 without a SAM. After all, Adrastus was King of Argos. He was the one that Polyneices convinced to raise the 'outlandish' and 'savage' army in the name of Justice. Dikê. No question, absolutely, Adrastus is the main man, and almost all the sources have him at the top of the list of the Seven Against Thebes. But not Aeschylus. Why. An interesting question, possibly. Aeschylus, flying in the face of all the sources I know of, assigns him a role à la Kissinger, lurking in some Wing, cooking up strategy. A fine kettle. Possibly the role Eteocles wanted, on the other side of the Walls. Out of the line of fire, so to speak. Far from Firing Line, from William F. Buckley, from God and Man at Yale, no, Huntley-Brinkley is quite close enough. Humpty Dumpty no! Out of the question. Off all the lines. In the mind. On the roof. What kettle. What fish. And who does Aeschylus send in his place. Eteoclus. Why. Possibly a tribute, *ante litteram*, to Antonin Artaud. Who knows. Signaling through the flames. Answer to the riddle. ANTHROPUS. The Note. I've been thinking. Now—I said, some time ago, that I had a lot to say about the first exchange between the spy and Eteocles, and I said it. A lot. All that BAT business. First the spy, then, in no time, Eteocles, *images right off the bat*. Out of hell. I, personally, saw Mickey Mantle hit home runs that SHOT right off his bat. Lightnings and thunderbolts. Fastballs, sliders, knuckleballs. *In a flash.* Off the bat and into the upper deck, in no time. Zeus! Post-Promethean man. Harmless. What. Who. What ever happened to Eteocles' *gradual* transformation from champion of reality to champion of the image. Good question. I *may*, possibly, have seen the end of the placard-men, but I'll never see the end of this question. I've already said a lot about it, but why didn't I say much about Capaneus' likening Zeus' lightning to the sun's warm rays at noontide? The *fire* of Zeus, the *fire* of naked post-Promethean man. Not two, not one? Ten-thousand? 'Its illumination reaches the ten-thousand things, and these ten-thousand things are *not* reflected in it. This is what I would declare to be most wonderful.' The empty mirror. Capaneus' boast. Outrageous. I barely mentioned it. Said practically nothing. Why the hell not. This, definitely, is a Double. A Theater and its Double. Both sides. At once. '*The shield of Capaneus is the man*.' Not two, not one. 'It shows an unprotected or naked man,' a.k.a. 'post-Promethean' man. The *divine fire* has already been stolen, and man has it. Meanwhile, Capaneus is armed, he 'is' the shield, which is the man, but *on* the shield—the image—the man is naked. Unarmed. *Difficulty* and the Double. Double doubled. What does this remind me of. Ye gods, the pledge-of-allegiance man. Not dressed as a soldier, *himself,* no longer a soldier, but the man on his placard is dressed *to the hilt* as a soldier. Magnificently painted image, which says SUPPORT THE TROOPS and the Dylanesque GOD IS ON OUR SIDE. All Vietnam veterans. The I-gave-my-legs man, a true patriot, his image is beyond words, fuck all spies and kings. The pledge-of allegiance man. A penny for the Old Guy. A G.I., the 'approach-the-village' man, Eteo*clus*. The Double. Thickens. What plot. Dressed as a soldier, himself. On his placard, a hoplite, not some naked hippy. A scaling ladder. A village. The City. SOUND, 163th Street. B Train. No one is in the car. What self. I think faster when the train's empty. Get more thinking done. Did Helen Moore/More/Morgan decide or was she decided for. Hard to say. The distinction is not clear-cut. 'If he has any discriminating mind, *do you think he could discriminate all these things?*' Where/what am I. Doubles. Capaneus *himself*, placard and man. What the placard says—'I shall burn the city'—and what the man says. As the spy puts it, he 'likened the lightnings and thunderbolts to the sun's warm rays at noontide.' Let's forget about the fact that the spy says that Capaneus said 'strife of Zeus' or 'Zeus' wrath,' I'm making an *other* point now. Fuck the spy. The essence/substance/gist.

Reality. A boast. This placard, definitely, explicitly, is 'a boast that implicitly ranks fire higher than lightning,' Benardete says. Frankly, for starters, I'd say it seems more explicit than implicit. Ye gods, he 'likened'—says the spy—I'd say, he boasted, he SAID that Zeus' lightning, his FIRE, is harmless, is nothing, compared to that itty-bitty flame in the torch of a naked man. A nudist. A hippy, possibly. St. Mark's Place. 'Time Is Come Today.' Woodstock. Divine fire *nothing* compared to hippy fire. Or, possibly, academic torch fire. Or, more possibly, our military fire, in our wars in the defense of tyranny. OK, I did get somewhat riled up a while back, I went so far as to say that Benardete's 'regards lightning as harmless' lines are, possibly, not the clearest lines he's ever written. ZEUS' FIRE AS HARMLESS AS THE SUN'S WARM RAYS AT NOONTIDE, ye gods, what have we come to, NOT EVEN NIXON SAYS THINGS LIKE THIS. No, he blurts stuff like 'Vietnamization' and 'kill for peace.' Benardete takes it in stride, but, I don't. The placard, and the man, and what's ON the placard. A B-52 is a B-52, on a placard, GOD ON OUR SIDE is GOD ON OUR SIDE. But Capaneus' boast, and, *even worse*, Eteocles' response—'I trust on him will justly come the bolt that carries fire, in no way like the sun's warm rays at noontide'—No, no, no, no! Come, let's away to prison.[162] River of shit. Wide, wide river. The prisoner's deed. Zeus' lightning, his fire. Post-Promethean men. McNamara, Curtis Lemay, Westmoreland—'I was participating in my own lynching, but the problem was I didn't know what I was being lynched for'—the whole band has God on their side. Ode to Joy. Nixon! Fucking God-fearer. A goddam Quaker. A prayer, a thanker. And here we have Capaneus of Argos, saying—if you've noticed—fuck you god! The naked man on my shield has a torch. Fire! Fuck the City! Who's kidding whom. Or vice versa. Who's on first. What's he saying. He's saying, Zeus' lightning is just an itty-bitty *tickle*. He's 'likening' a firing squad to aspirin for a headache. That's what he's saying, and likening,

---

162 We two alone will sing like birds i' th' cage. *Macbeth*, V, iii.

basically. WHAT fire is this, incomparably stronger than lightning. Prometheus stole fire, from Zeus, gave it to post-Promethean man, and here it is now, in a torch, on a shield. Fine. But how can Capaneus possibly claim—boast—that this tiny flame, in a torch, on a shield, is badly infinitely more powerful than *Zeus' lightning* in the sky. Ye gods, *being is nothing.* What have we come to. Hegel, logically. Atheism, actually. Seven Against Thebes. The whiteness of the whale is the blackness of the whale. Moby Dick![163] I know this by heart. I spout: 'Or is it, that as in essence whiteness is not so much a color as the visible absence of color, and at the same time the concrete of all colors; is it for these reasons that there is such a dumb blankness, full of meaning, in a wide landscape of snows—a colorless, all-color of atheism from which we shrink.' I shall burn the city! Fire in a torch, on a shield, in my name. A fork! A bomb. The Williamsburg Bridge. A boast! Zeus' lightning is *nothing*. His fire. *Nothing*. Being. Right off the bat. Nothing. Roof. Mind. Black. White. Black. Pitch black, possibly. Fire versus fire. WHAT fire versus fire. On a shield. In the sky. In the mind. On the roof. Ye gods, I need to ask Dostoevsky about this. Desperately. I have no choice. Possibly. What compels me. Sting like a bee. 'Free' association. Fine. Like birds in a cage. *Psari*. What fish. What Greek. Political autobiography. What kettle. Dostoevsky. The more the merrier. Defend the City! said the Tsar. What tsar. I'm young, but I know a lot about Dostoevsky, his books, his life. I wonder what he'd think about these placard-men. My grandfather, Harry Donishevsky, was born somewhere in Mother Russia (whose mother?) twenty-six days before Dostoevsky died. January 1881. A village. Stitching the fabric of time. History. In time. Saves nine. My grandfather shared twenty-six days with Dostoevsky. BREATHING. What we call 'I' is just a swinging door that moves when we inhale and when we exhale.[164] In history, possibly, up is up, down is down.

---

163 Chapter 42.
164 *Zen Mind*, p. 29.

East is east, west is west. Relatively speaking. Historical time, direct reverse, as Melville put it, of logical time, which is no-time. Historical events, logical moments. Not two, not one. No, not this time, possibly. Actually. Logically. Ill-logically. History, like a madman with a razor in his hand.[165] Silence. SOUND. Stops. What stops. At this point, who's counting. No time. Hiz Honor. What point. Where was He and His ambulance when Lee Morgan bled to death because of a couple of feet of snow. Defend the City! WHAT parade. 155th Street. Completely empty. Not a creature stirring. A Transit System singularity. No-time, no-mind. No man and placard. No placard and man. NO MAN. Woman. Child. Cat. Mouse. What self. *'A man of no fortune, and with a name to come.'* Where have all the flowers gone. Dostoevsky, his POLITICAL NOVEL, *Demons*, a.k.a. *The Possessed*, a.k.a *The Devils*.[166] Lembke, the provincial governor, bareheaded, watching the fire consume his provincial capital, watching his mansion go up in flames, notes: 'It's all incendiarism! It's nihilism! Whatever is burning, is nihilism.' (A major claim.) Observing a fireman on the roof, he remarks, 'He'll catch fire.' (No doubt.) He asks, logically (possibly), 'What's he doing there?' Answer: 'He's putting out the fire.' Riposte: 'Not likely. *The fire is in the minds of men, not on the roofs of houses.'* A good point! What point. What fire.[167]

---

165 'When fate was following in our tracks/ Like a madman with a razor in his hand.' Last lines of Arseniy Tarkovsky's poem *First Meetings*, quoted in Andrey Tarkovsky's film *Mirror*. See Andrey Tarkovsky, *Sculpting in Time*, London: The Bodley Head, 1986, p. 101. In the last lines of the second Note, we'll see, possibly, whether Benardete, Hitchcockianly, confuses *fate* with *history*.

166 My copy is *The Devils*, translated by David Magarshack, Penguin, 1969, see p. 513. Dostoevsky's title is actually *Demons*.

167 What fire. Speaking a while back of turkeys, Thanksgivings, goddam Puritans, *shining* cities on hills, I spent a few words on President-Elect John F Kennedy, 'beset by terror within and disorder without,' along with Ronald Reagan, his farewell speech to the nation: 'I've spoken of the shining city all my political life, but I don't know if I ever quite communicated what I saw when I did. But *in my mind* it was a tall proud city built on rocks stronger than oceans.' Kennedy, Reagan, they both had the same orgasm—let's say, à la Dostoevsky, a fire in the mind. But, ye gods, George W Bush, our Dostoyevskian President! He darn well deserves equal time. I barely mentioned *his* 'fire in the mind' in his 2005 Second Inaugural Address. Now's the time. [For a fuller account of 'W and Dostoevsky' see Justin Raimondo, http://

Dostoevsky saw fire *himself*—like the placard-man Michelangelo, he *saw* it, he *was there*—in Petersburg in 1862. Students, nihilists, *Young Russia*—an incendiary leaflet written by a twenty-year-old—*a call for total destruction.* The horror. Setting fires, devastating whole areas of the city. Fire—the peasants called it the Red Rooster. Definitely, on the roofs of houses. But ten years later, when he wrote *Demons*—his *scathing* portrait of Russian nihilism and nihilists—he says, no! it's in the minds of men. Good question. Two different fires or one fire in two different places. Pre- and post-Promethean man—no, pre-Promethean man didn't have fire. Prometheus stole it from Zeus, gave it to him, he became post-Promethean man, attacked Thebes, and dropped millions of tons of bombs on Vietnam. Roof. Mind. Two, or one. *If this isn't a Zen question, what is.* A very big and very good question. A fork. My life depends on it. Like the placard-man Michelangelo— FIRE, Typhon versus Zeus—Dostoevsky SAW ACTION. *He was the original placard-man Michelangelo*, I'd say. Saw action. His portraits. His *mock execution*, wait! *Ramparts*, I have my notes on this, I always have them with me. Dostoevsky my great-grandfather, or great-great, who's counting. Born in 1821—on October 30, like Ezra Pound in 1885. Moscow. Hailey, Idaho. I

---

original.antiwar.com/justin/2005/01/21/w-and-dostoevsky/.] W! A name. Dubya, it even *sounds* Russian. 'The ultimate goal of ending tyranny in our world.' Wow! Defend the City! 'Because we have acted in the great liberating tradition of this nation, tens of millions have achieved their freedom. And as hope kindles hope, millions more will find it. By our efforts we have lit a fire as well, *a fire in the minds of men.* It warms those who feel its power; it burns those who fight its progress. And one day this untamed fire of freedom will reach the darkest corners of the world.' Mistah Kurtz—he lives. W! A Theater, and its Double. The sun's warm rays at noontide. In no way like the sun's warm rays at noontide. Dostoevsky's nihilists thought they were agents of progress, destined by history to sweep away the old in the purifying flames of a great uprising that would be the prelude to a new world. A similar messianic sense of being on the right side of history pervades Bush's polemic: 'History has an ebb and flow of justice, but history also has a visible direction set by liberty and the author of liberty.' Strange bedfellows, W and the nihilists. Authors of liberty. Redeemers of Humanity. Worldwide revolution. Burn, baby, burn. In the mind. Where's the fire. Demons. Possessed. Devils. Justice. WHAT justice. Killers. Fanatics. Crusaders. All things considered, *perhaps* (I'm not sure) we were better off with shining cities on hills. Perilous frontiers. Turkeys.

rest my case. Mock execution. Petrashevsky Circle, the whole Circle arrested on April 22, 1849. Dostoevsky twenty-seven years old. Six months of interrogations, Tsar's secret police, day and night, jeeps rolling through the streets, Peter-and-Paul Fortress, on an island in the Neva, *a lot grimmer* than Alcatraz. Though some Greek islands are no picnics these days. No. *Thalassa! Thalassa!* as Xenophon put it.[168] *Xasterià.* December 22, Petersburg, Semenovsky Square.[169] 'It was covered with newly fallen snow and surrounded by troops formed into a square. On the edges far away stood a crowd of people looking at us; everything was silent; it was the morning of a clear wintry day, and the sun, just having risen, shone like a bright, beautiful globe on the horizon through the haze of thick clouds.' Beautiful. What's the story. WHAT action. A tangle. A tangled tangle.[170] A long/short story. Uptown/downtown, who's counting. Melville/Dostoevsky. What's the story. Closing of the frontier/last decades of the Tsars. Lenin, a train from Zurich. Alexander II freed the serfs in 1861. The Tsar-Liberator whom Dostoevsky revered, assassinated in 1881, a month after Dostoevsky died. BOMBS in the center of Petersburg. FIRE. *Narodnaya Volya. People's Will.* Populism. Long live the peasants! Down with the Tsar-Liberator! Revolutionary socialist intellectuals. Students. Terrorists. History. A razor in his hand. A mock execution. Petrashevsky Circle. Petersburg was full of circles in the 1840s—a veritable *circle of circles*, as Hegel put it—and Dostoevsky was tangled up in them. Belinsky's Circle. The Beketov Circle—Beketov, an old school friend. Then, on

---

168 400 BC, Xenophon's *Anabasis*. The Greek mercenaries struggling homewards from defeat in Persia. The leaders of the column come over the ridge of a mountain and begin shouting *Thalassa! Thalassa!* The sea! The sea! Coltrane! Coltrane! A cry of liberation. They've made it to the Black Sea.

169 My source here is *Dostoevsky. A Writer in His Time* by Joseph Frank, Princeton: Princeton University Press, 2010; see, in particular, Chapters 12 to 14. The quote, p. 175, is from the account of one of Dostoevsky's fellow prisoners, Akhsharumov. For the mock execution, see pp. 174–180; for most of my account I quote Frank directly. On the 1862 Petersburg fires see pp. 338–339.

170 Defend the City! For the record, today is November 10, 2016, Donald Trump was elected President the day before yesterday. A perilous frontier.

Fridays, the Petrashevsky Circle. A literary circle and debating club specializing in social-political questions. Petrashevsky himself—Dostoevsky's own age—was, basically, a make-love-not-war hippy. Extravagant, original. Purple haze all in my eyes. No, there was nothing secret or conspiratorial about his Fridays, just interminable debates over the merits of one or another literary-libertarian-utopian socialism. Getting on Dostoevsky's fragile nerves. Then again, this Circle did in fact harbor, unwittingly, the extremely secret and absolutely conspiratorial Speshnev Circle, devoted to *socialism-atheism-terrorism*. Defend the City! Nikolay Speshnev, who went on to become the model for Nikolay Stavrogin in *Demons,* was a close friend of Dostoevsky's, much closer than Petrashevsky. Strangely, since Speshnev was, in fact, secretly, the *guru* of genuine anarchist-nihilist hippy terrorists whom Dostoevsky despised. Meanwhile, the whole Petrashevsky Circle of Circles was rounded up and arrested, the good with the bad with the ugly. Not because of Speshnev! Who *in fact* had a BIG FIRE in the works, no, the secret police did arrest him, as an interminable Petrashevsky debater, but never discovered his secret society. SOUND. 145th Street. Someone? A few someones in the car. Stirring creatures. Doing what, going where, who knows. Straggling home to Coney Island, end of March, 1972. All these secrets, what ever happened to *Benardete's second Note.* An *open* secret. Why am I thinking about Dostoevsky. The Note! The Note! Well, hold your horses. I need to complete my thought. Chase my tale. Six months in the Peter-and-Paul Fortress, the whole Circle, a motley crew. Ironically, logically, actually, Dostoevsky's fellow prisoners—utopians, atheists, hippies, terrorists—were exactly the people he *mocked* his whole life. Despised and *mocked.* Semenovsky Square, the sun has just risen. Covered with newly fallen snow. The prisoner's deed! Ye gods, condemned to death by a firing squad. The Petrashevsky Circle. Literary circle and debating club. Fifteen prisoners. In the Square. Three at a time, Dostoevsky in the second group of three. The prisoners were given long white peasant blouses and nightcaps—their funeral shrouds. First group of three. The order was given to pull the caps of the bound men over their heads, but Petrashevsky *himself* defiantly pushed his back and stared straight at the firing squad. Ready! Aim! Extravagant, original. In his eyes. Purple haze. The suspense of waiting for the firing squad to pull the trigger lasted about a minute, and then the roll of drums was heard beating retreat. A *mock* execution. Grigoryev, in the first group next to Petrashevsky, never recovered his senses, he remained a helpless mental invalid for the rest of his life. Enemies of the people. Already in their shrouds. *Where's the fire.* A Moby Dick question. A fork. Oedipus! The Curse. The roof. The mind. No-mind. No-roof. What justice. Next stop, Siberia. Gulag. House of the Dead. Weather Underground. Subway! Logic. His shroud. Realm of shadows. Discolored snow. Captain Vere! What's going on. What am I doing here. Is Ahab Ahab? What a decision is. What making a decision means. A fork! Monkey mind. Tyrant versus tyrant. Where did it come from. Where is it going. Acorns. The Note! WHAT ever happened to Benardete. Who knows. Here he is now. He's back! He's back! Right here, at the Fourth Gate.

It was impossible to confuse the armored Capaneus with his device of an unprotected man, but it seems a smaller step to treat the image of a hoplite as a hoplite, especially since the hoplite Eteoclus is silent and the image of a hoplite speaks. The silence of the central Argive, Hippomedon, is even greater and produces greater consequences; for though he shouts, his shouts are meaningless: 'he has raised his war-cry ... enthused by Ares he revels in violence like a Bacchant.'

As the spy puts it. (In mostly my own translation, Benardete only gives the Greek.) Dostoevsky had a hard life. Melville too. Kafka! Luckily—for them, for us—they were geniuses. Not just 'fire in the mind.' Not just 'great minds.' *No-mind*. Winter soldiers. Empty mirrors. The mirror reflects everything coming before it *unconsciously*, with no-mind. Genius. Unique. Now, ready or not, Typhon! Father of all Monsters. (No, his wife Echidna stayed home.)

> His shield, moreover, contains no letters. It pictures Typhon breathing soot-laden fire through his mouth. This is the only image whose artfulness the *spy* mentions, as its bearer is the only one who strikes terror in him, for it is the first image of a god on the shields. The *spy*, in fact, becomes so filled with the scene he describes that two other gods beside Typhon are said to be present. Hippomedon is *éntheos Árei* [enthused with Ares], and his terrifying glance induces the *spy* to declare that Phobos [Terror] now glories at the city's gates.

Spy spy spy. Sing. Spy. Sing. Give us a break, goddamit. How about a smallpox-infested blanket for a change. This Peter Arnett of a spy with his 'license to kill' poetic license. This Note is '*Eteocles'* Interpretations of the Shields' but the spy always gets there first, with his *own* interpretations, images, and hallucinations. He had promised Eteocles 'clear reports.' Unvarnished truth. We destroy the village in order to save it. Grievous distortion. Great and undying chagrin. Meanwhile:

> Eteocles is forced to meet Hippomedon on his own grounds. He first says that Onka Athena, whose temple stands nearby, will keep the serpent from the nestlings. He takes the simile of the serpent from the snakes that are coiled round the rim of Hippomedon's shield; and for the first and

last time he assigns an emblematic shield to the Theban champion.

Image versus image. SOUND. 135th Street. Stir, creatures, stir. A war of images.

Hermes, the god of interpretation, brings them 'reasonably' together. Hyperbius will bear the likeness of Zeus as the hurler of lightning, and since Zeus conquered Typhon it is 'likely' that Hyperbius will conquer Hippomedon. Both men yield in importance to the images each displays, for the outcome of their contest should be in proportion to their signs. Eteo*cles* had taken the image of Eteo*clus'* shield as possessed of a certain weight in the world, but it did not prevail over its bearer, for image and image-bearer were still two. Now, however, the image of Typhon appears so powerful that only another image can match it. Hyperbius and Hippomedon are each subordinate to their tutelary devices. The devices, moreover, are almost separate from what they imitate: Zeus upon the shield, Eteocles implies, might prove to be Zeus Sotêr [Zeus the Savior]. The Chorus reinforces this implication when they sing the antistrophe. They trust that the bearer of Zeus' adversary, which is at once the malign body (*démas*) of a chthonic god and an image (*eíkasma*) hateful to gods and men, will lose his life before the gates. It is Typhon's *image* that gods and men abhor, it is his *body* that Hippomedon carries before him. Only in the *Septem* is *démas* applied to an image. What confirms that the Chorus, like Eteocles, are gradually endowing the images with a life of their own is the way in which the spy refers to Hippomedon. His 'vast frame and giant form' [Grene] — his 'tall and splendid figure' [Vellacott] — context aside, could literally be 'the tall figure and statue of Hippomedon' [Benardete]. Hippomedon loses

365

a reality that Typhon gains. None of these turns of phrase by itself is conclusive, but their cumulative effect points to their literal meaning as overshadowing their less precise and figurative sense.

A mouthful. Food for thought. The malign body of an image. A mosquito in bright light, *there* on a white wall. Its exquisite evil. The infinite intricacy of its form. *Both men yield in importance to the images each displays*. A war of realities—of men, Attackers and Defenders—has, somehow, *openly* become a war of images. How has this happened. Who/What *decided* this. What does it mean. Typhon and Zeus. Zeus is stronger, but *they had one hell of a battle*. A battle royal. No, definitely not a quagmire. War is hell. Eteocles ripostes with Zeus on a shield to Typhon on a shield. A snap decision, but a good one. No question, possibly. Tough love. *Was he supposed to respond to Typhon on a shield with an empty shield.* What would General Westmoreland say about that. Then again, in engaging in a war of images, he does have a couple of problems. The *second* problem, possibly, is that he places too much trust in Zeus' defeating Typhon. The war between Typhon and Zeus is by no means a 'pacific' war. No, it's a divine battle royal. A major melee. In retrospect, we have to say that the outcome was not self-evident. For one thing, Typhon has his reasons. And his allies. He attempts to destroy Zeus at the will of Gaia, the Great Mother, because Zeus imprisoned the Titans. In the defense of freedom or in the defense of tyranny. Who knows. A musing question. Then, the battle itself was absolutely beastly. Sorry, I mean no offense to beasts, I love beasts, especially cats, camels, and hamsters. Cockroaches—our Elder Statesmen—and rats, *not* particularly. On Park or Rivington. Fucking democrats. Tearing out sinews, hurling mountains. Extremely gruesome. It's quite true, thunderbolts are thunderbolts, Typhon doesn't have them and Zeus does. Hold

your horses. Where's the fire. In the mind. On the roof. Where.
SOUND. 125th Street. Soul sound. Rap. Sex machine. James
Brown. Rap Brown. Perking up. Time does not exist. Nina! What
is this thing called time. Bros, on the move, be cool. Harlem to
Times Square, what's the point. What point. My bro, my fellow
man. *Mon semblable*. Make your point. The Fourth Gate. Still, it
took Zeus *one hundred lightning bolts* right on top of Typhon.
Not even to kill him, 'just' to cast him into Tartarus. The Hole
under the new Twin Towers is a pinhole compared to the Abyss
of Tartarus. One hell of a battle. A whopper. The winter soldier
abides in the thought of emptiness and absolute sameness
even when his body is cut to pieces in a melee between two
fiercely contending armies. Never mind the Halls of Montezuma
and the shores of Tripoli. Never mind the Pequot Wars or
Hiroshima. This was god-versus-god even-steven combat. Let
the best god win. Then again, Eteocles is *responsible for
Thebes*, not for Tartarus. For a City, not for an Abyss. *Second*
problem, second, first, just names. East/West River. Wide/Wide
River. The *first* problem is—it seems to me—that *at this point*
Eteocles abandons 'both sides now' and *puts all his chips* (so to
speak, such as he has) on images. Defend the City! He was
supposed to be defending the city against his brother—whom
he screwed, royally—and his brother's 'outlandish' and 'savage'
Seven Against Thebes, supplied by Adrastus, even though the
Prophet strenuously advised him against it. Quite rightly.
Adrastus' *wretched and miserable decision*. This might be the
reason—or one of, or another of, the reasons—why Aeschylus
cut him out of his masterpiece, replacing him with Eteo*clus*,
who is *himself* a long story that only Artaud can explain. In any
event, abandoning both sides now and putting all his chips on
images *is, I think, a decision*, and an absolute game-changer.
Whatever a decision may be and may mean. We'll see, possibly.
Possibly a bad bet. Does he have any choice, or has he already

been decided for. Is the jig already up, as the Irish put it. Benardete, Hitchcockianly, in his second Note, has big, and surprising, things to say about this. As for my own decision, no, I want to keep going with the question of what a decision is and what making a decision means. Now, I don't want to get too far ahead of myself—or too far behind myself either, for that matter—but, I'm thinking about *'the'* question of the *Septem*. There seem to be more than one. 'What is Ares'—said Benardete—is *the* question of the *Septem*. But, then, we have the question that has exercised so much recent scholarship: Does Eteocles decide his own fate, or is his fate determined by the curse of Oedipus. Freedom and necessity in Eteocles' decision—this is *the* question. Benardete likes the word *compulsion*, as we shall see, eventually. But, now, *images* seem to be *the* question. The placard-men. *The* question 'for us' (as Hegel puts it), interpreters of Eteocles' interpretations. But what is *the* question for Eteocles' *himself*. There's no question that Eteocles is *not* interested in *the* question of what a decision is and what making a decision means, that's *my* question. Just as there's no question that he makes a bad decision, and I'm trying to learn from his mistake, which means, trying to figure out *what his mistake is*. This is exactly what Benardete is trying to do himself, in his second Note. I'd like to say this. I'm truly sorry he went *himself* to the Seventh Gate. Curse or not, there must have been some other way. I saw Thebes *myself* two summers ago, jeeps day and night. Dusty. Not a pretty town. I saw traces—bare minimal archaeological traces—of the Seven Gates, maybe not all seven, I can't remember. A dusty inland town. But, it's home. Mother Russia. The home sweet home of a long line of cursed kings. Sure, let's blame it all on Laius. It's his fault. He started it, his 'loving folly.' Shit, I'm just a 21-year-old almost-graduated NYU student, Classics, but I *know* it's not that simple. A Curse is not simple. History *itself* is not simple. Who/

What started it—not a simple question. A chaos. A chaos
started it. Start/finish—roof/mind—logic/history, NOT so simply
not two/not one. Hard to figure. There must be a *concept* here.
The whole picture. Hard to find. Hard to see. SOUND. 116th
Street. Columbia. Fire! Firing line. At Yale, God and Man. Line
of fire. Bloodbath. Whole picture. Both sides now. We cherish
our hate. You don't need a weatherman. To know which way
the wind blows.[171] SDS. Mark Rudd, underground,
aboveground, fucking the ground, suit yourself. Get sick, get
well. Hang around an inkwell. No, I don't mean simply his
going *himself* to the Seventh Gate when he knows his own
brother is there, even a child can see that this is a mistake. No,
I mean the 'line of reasoning' (so to speak) (or possibly of
unreasoning) he follows that leads him to his mistake. *The*
question. For Eteocles *himself*, what is *the* question of the
Septem. Well, at the risk of getting ahead of and behind myself
at the same time, I'd say that *the* question for Eteocles *himself*
is this: Do his placard-men constitute a true or a bad infinity.
Does he see the *whole picture*—the *transit system*—the placard
and the man—or does he set the infinite *over against* the finite.
For a man with Eteocles' responsibilities, this is truly a life-and-
death question. His life is at stake but so is the life of his City,
because pollution of the City is *deep shit*. A wide, wide river. A
Curse! No end to the Curse. His images. His bad decision. 'On,
on with the favoring wind! Let this wave of hell engulf all Laius'
kin.'[172] From Hiroshima to Vietnam *and so on. And on. Ad
infinitum. Ad astra.* Hardships. In the defense of tyranny. Bad
infinity and the true concept of infinity. Dogen expressed it in
his own way, in images. A fish in the ocean, a bird in the sky. A
fish swims in the ocean, and no matter how far it swims there

171 Dylan, 1965, obviously. 'Subterranean Homesick Blues.'
172 A free translation of lines 690–692. Eteocles laments his own bad decision
as soon as he makes it. I'll come back to this dialogue between Eteocles and
the Chorus, lines 677–719. Suddenly Eteocles is eloquent, paradoxical, and
uncharacteristically dignified. Sober—that's the word for him. Benardete does not
discuss this curious dirge.

is no end to the water. Is Eteocles swimming *right out of the ocean*, badly infinitely, with his interpretations of the shields. This is *the* question. King of Thebes. The Seven Gates. Are his placard-men showing him the true path or are they leading him by the nose into the wilderness. (Haven't I heard this before. It sounds familiar.) *The* question of images, but *what* question of images. That is *the* question, for Eteocles. 'The main point is to distinguish the true concept of infinity from bad infinity, the infinite of reason from the infinite of the understanding. The latter is in fact a *finitized* infinite... in wanting to keep the infinite pure and aloof from the finite, the infinite is by that very fact only made finite.' 'The infinite set *over against* the finite, in a relation in which they are as qualitatively distinct others, is to be called the *bad infinite* ....' 'A patriotism, whether genuine or assumed ....' The blind patriot. Chasing images, badly infinitely. SOUND. 110th Street. Tip-top. Upper West Side. Central Park. West. Upper-left corner. Bottom-right, if you're upside down. Logically speaking. All Quiet on the Western Front. The Seven Gates. History. West is West. Seven is Seven. Quiet is Quiet. Gate is Gate. Lower East Side. Standing on your head. Is Vietnam east or west! Watch out for falling dominoes. Swimming, possibly, right out of the ocean. Have no fear, no matter how far I swim I'll never swim right out of Benardete's second Note. No, I shall *follow* the Note and see where it leads me. A true—a genuine—concept of infinity. No more interruptions. PLEASE, no Saturday night specials. When, when, and whenever we get to the heart of Fun City, again. No spacetime singularities, please. Where am I. Memphis blues. Again! Stuck! Mobile. Really. The end. If the doors of perception were cleansed. No way. The true path. The Fourth Gate. Typhon versus Zeus, on the shields. Gradually endowing the images with a life of their own, *but it's been a war of images from the very beginning*. What's Benardete saying. Let's see—two doubles: the first two devices, and the second two. Both, doubles. Artaud lives. The Note.

The third and fourth devices, along with the men who bear them, seem to form as close a unit as the first and second had.

OK, Tydeus with his sky and Capaneus with his naked man; then, Eteoclus with his hoplite and Hippomedon with his Typhon.

Eteoclus' hoplite is clearly opposed to Capaneus' unprotected man, and we no longer have to do with interpretations of the cosmos but with the city, for the city now first appears in an image, whereas before it was only present in words. The city replaces the sky, just as Eteoclus' boast about Ares replaces Capaneus' boast about Zeus. The gods, however, are still in speech and not until the central episode are they manifest. They then show themselves as of two kinds, chthonic and Olympian. What was a contest between naked man and the sky (Capaneus) becomes a contest between the old and the new gods. Both Tydeus and Zeus are armed with fire, but only Zeus is of a human shape, for Typhon had a hundred snakeheads [in Hesiod]. We do not know what shape, if any, Capaneus and Eteoclus would have attributed to Zeus, as neither mentions any human or non-human trait.

SOUND, 103rd Street. Nothing special. Coltrane, 'My Favorite Things.' Monk, 'Blue Monk.'

Eteocles then trusted that the 'fire-bearing lightning' would strike Capaneus, but now it is a Zeus who sits erect that makes a missile flash in his hand. Function and being are now distinct: Zeus is no longer expected to hurl the thunderbolt. The emergence of Zeus as an anthropomorphic god accompanies the 'psychologization' of Ares, who is now embodied in Hippomedon, that is, Ares too has become anthropomorphic. Ares' incarnation was anticipated by Eteoclus' boast that not even Ares could cast him from the ramparts, as though Ares were a soldier on the side of Thebes. Ares still remains a soldier when he appears as Hippomedon, but he never again is a Theban. He becomes impartial and universal as he becomes 'human.'

No, you can't beat Benardete, he can spot a needle in a haystack a mile away. Aeschylus. The history of Greek religion. Doubles, the dual origin of Thebes. From the earth gods—some good (Gaia, Gê), some terrible (Typhon and his clan)—to the Olympians. From—but this is truly a shot in the dark, and I don't exactly endorse it, and neither does Hegel, in my opinion—*from necessity to freedom*. A Zeus (and an Ares) less 'predictable,' but 'freer' and more 'human'—whatever that means. A snake slithers, thoughtlessly and undecidedly, while an anthropus thinks and decides. Possibly. At times. Well, who knows what it's like to be a snake. Anthropo*morphic*. Maybe just a matter of shapes. Forms. In a note in this Note (note 25, page 14, I'll get there eventually) regarding Eteocles' 'degree of freedom' in his Gate-to-Gate matchmaking, Benardete notes that 'the *Septem* is the only play of Aeschylus where *anágke* [necessity] never occurs; though *bía* [force, might] in all senses is most frequent.' Whatever this may mean, I think it's quite interesting. SOUND. 96th. Stir, creatures, stir! Back to the Note:

We had seen before, in comparing the parodos with the first stasimon, that the Chorus, once forbidden to adore the statues of the gods, cease to pray to them by name, and their fear, apparently because of this, becomes more deeply settled within them. Now, however, we have a counter movement. Ares and Zeus are once more visible, Ares in the guise of Hippomedon, Zeus in a human image, and even fear [Phobos, Terror] is drawn out of the heart and becomes, at least in speech, visible as well. What further distinguishes the third and fourth layers from the first and second is the greater agreement between Argives and Thebans. The first two layers could bear a double interpretation, the third and fourth seem to point to a single meaning. Not only does Eteocles have to resist Hippomedon's emblem with another one, but he has to resist it on its own terms. He no longer indulges in transformations of the literal into the metaphoric and vice-versa, nor has he transformed an adjective ('fire-bearing') from the enemy's device to his own hopes. He now admits that the area of conflict is the city and its gods. The gods of the city are either of the earth or of the sky, either Gê, to whom Eteocles originally prayed, or Athena and Zeus. Eteocles had at first trusted Earth and her descendants (Melanippus and Megareus) to be the main bulwarks against the Argive invaders; but Hippomedon's image of Typhon, whose snake-heads inevitably remind us of the serpent's teeth from which the Spartoi sprang, forces Eteocles to abandon Earth to the enemy—Capaneus is a Giant—and rely solely on the Olympian gods. Eteocles purifies as he restricts the basis on which the city stands. Thus the war that began as a war between two cities becomes a war within a single city between its two principles. These two principles, which first appear as far apart as Typhon and Zeus, turn out in the end to be related. Eteocles and Polyneices, the offspring of an incestuous union between mother and son, mutually destroy themselves.

SOUND. 86th Street. Placard-men! Again! In my mind. The pledge-of-allegiance man. The approach-the-village man.

Reciprocally suicided, as Hegel happily put it. I now have five or six fellow passengers. Who's counting. The Note is heating up, and so am I. Reciprocal suicide. Two principles. Related. Two princes. In destroying the other, each brother destroys himself. Defend the City. The Curse. Pollution. Deep shit. Wide, wide river. An ocean whose other shore is far from the story told in the *Septem*, which, I think, is about the *origin* of a story as long as human history. Long Time Coming and a Long Time Gone, as Richard Fariña put it. The answer to the riddle. Political *history*. What logic. A tangle of questions. Polluting the City—who's responsible. Laius. Oedipus. Eteocles for screwing his brother, or his brother for not taking it lying down. For *attacking his own city* with an outlandish and savage army. Aeschylus appears to pin the responsibility on Eteocles' bad decision to go *himself* to the Seventh Gate, but—could he have done otherwise. This is *the* question, a *political* question, à la Robert McNamara, the Weeping Secretary,[173] but Aeschylus—as Benardete sees it, and I, in my own way, see it—in the *Septem* makes it a question of *images*. The interpretation of shields. Placard-men. A series of placard-men. Eteocles *himself*—never mind the spy, we can't always blame *everything* on the spy— *sets one over against the other*, badly infinitely, without seeing the whole picture. Which means without a glimmer of what he's actually doing. Not a clue. No sense of responsibility. *This is the price he pays for never asking himself what a decision is and what making a decision means.* A chain. The slavery of images. Polluting the City. 'Eteocles purifies as he restricts the basis on which the city stands.' Artaud—Van Gogh—suicided by society. What would the Pequot call it, I muse, ye muses. We almost forget that 'Eteocles purifies' refers to the war of *images on shields* that he is waging. A war of images that has

---

173 Way out of my time frame, see McNamara (*without* his band, if he actually had one) weep in Errol Morris' documentary *The Fog of War: Eleven Lessons from the Life of Robert S. McNamara*, 2003. Heraclitus was known as the weeping philosopher, for some reason I don't happen to know, but, anyway, that's another story.

already become *a war within a single city*. Defend the City!
How, if the City is at war with itself! In images. Polluting itself.
'The war within.' This expression has been used recently[174] in
reference to the 'internalization' of America's battle *within itself*
over Vietnam. The antiwar movement. Americans who oppose
this war. Some of us hate this war, and cherish our hate. Some
claim that the antiwar movement—the 'mobilizations,' large
and small—has had a real impact on our government's policy.
That it has shortened the war. Made it less terrible. I have my
doubts. Big ones. So do the winter soldiers, with their empty
shields. But we are all tangled up in images. All together.
All tangled up together. *This* war within—it, too, perhaps, a
reciprocal suicide. A pyre. The Curse. The City Polluted. Ashes,
from which not a Phoenix but a Monster will rise. SOUND.
81st Street. Who's coming, who's going. Who's on first. Our
Presidents. Free leaders of the Free World. In images. Perilous
shinings. Closings of the frontier. Eteocles sets Zeus (the
flashing infinite) *over against* Typhon (the monstrous finite).
(So they say.) He does his best. But now the shit hits the
fan. The Fifth Gate. The Sphinx, in person, Typhon's terrible
daughter, *on a shield*. A mother's darling if ever there was
one. I'm sure that Typhon's incredibly-named wife, Echidna,
Mother of All Monsters, is incredibly fond of her little Sphinx,
who 'ate men raw' *as the spy puts it* (line 541). This spy, this
Peter Arnett *ante litteram. Did he expect her to cook them first.*
This whole Note is great, but I really adore this next part, I can
hardly wait to read it again. Benardete:

> Parthenopaeus carries the image of the Sphinx, the solution
> to whose riddle was man, Parthenopaeus who swears by
> his spear, in which he reverentially puts more trust than
> in any god, that he will sack Thebes in spite of Zeus. All
> seven attackers had jointly sworn by Ares, Enyô, and

---

174 Another reference way before its time, to *The War Within. America's Battle over
Vietnam* by Tom Wells, 1994.

Phobos either to sack the city of the Cadmeans despite the Cadmeans or to die in the attempt; but now Parthenopaeus drops the alternative of possible defeat, swears by his own power, and extends the war to include the gods. The war becomes more openly theological—Hippomedon had been silent—as it comes closer to being fratricidal. *Amphiaraus will soon predict his own conversion into a Theban oracle,* and Parthenopaeus now carries an image that, though inimical to the Thebans, is not alien, as Typhon was, to them. The body (*démas*) of the Sphinx in high relief tramples a Theban underfoot, '*so that most spears are cast against this man.*' 'Against this man' is more simply related to the sculpted Theban than to Parthenopaeus, as if the image were the more important to the defense of Thebes. Perhaps, however, *the ambiguity is deliberate* [I underlined this],[175] and 'against this man' means either the image or the image-bearer depending on the interpreter. Eteocles, at any rate, sees the greater threat in the Sphinx. Aktor, he says, will not allow the beast to enter 'within our gates'—a phrase exactly describing the internalization of the war [lines 200/201, rebuking the Chorus]—but the Sphinx, overwhelmed by blows beneath the city's walls, *will reproach her bearer.* The Sphinx lives. She tries to enter the city under her own power and, when foiled, will speak. The Sphinx is in such high relief that *she seems to be not wholly nailed down.* If the images of Typhon and Zeus overshadowed their bearers, they still had not yet become so animate that they moved and spoke. Eteocles considers the Sphinx to constitute a present danger to Thebes. He does not argue that as Zeus conquered Typhon, so Oedipus conquered the Sphinx, and hence the emblem augurs well for Aktor as Hippomedon's emblem did for Aktor's brother Hyperbius.

---

175 For the record, there are *no italics at all* in Benardete's Notes. The italics in my text all correspond to my own underlining of passages on these pages I've been poring over for some 45 years now.

B Train, end of March, 1972. SOUND. 72nd Street. This unfortunate war. J. William Fulbright, what a great placard-man he'd make. A Theban oracle. Conversion. In Greece, two summers ago, I not only saw the sanctuary of Amphiaraus *myself*, I spent the night there. A day, a night, another day. Thinking about the *Septem.* Just think, that was before Benardete's Notes and before Zen. But not before Dave Leahy's Greek Tragedy course. How I wish I could take it again! And again! He gives it every year. Always different, always the same. The same Tragedies, there aren't any new ones. It's called The Amphiareion of Oropos, about 25 miles north of Athens and due east of Thebes. What a beautiful place! A lush green forest in the hills, just a couple of miles from the sea—the South Evian Gulf, to be exact. Lush. Direct reverse of dusty Thebes. Absolutely nobody around. No jeeps, no cars, no people. A sacred spring for drinking and bathing. A sanctuary. Oracular responses, healing, and, especially, the interpretation of dreams. I was supposedly hitchhiking, but doing a lot more hiking than hitching. I walked forever to get there. It was worth it. Thinking about the *Septem*. For a day, a night, another day. Theban oracle. What's the story. As one famous story goes—many sources, many versions—Amphiaraus was not killed *himself* at the Sixth Gate. No, after the debacle he took off like a shot, in his chariot, with his empty shield, heading due east, with a wild bunch of riled up Thebans hot on his heels. But Zeus loves his Prophets, he threw his thunderbolt and the earth opened to swallow him, chariot and all. Empty shield and all. In the hills, just a couple of miles from the sea. From Argive attacker to Theban oracle. Interpretation of dreams. The Note! The Sphinx. I'm reading this part very very slowly. What a story. And it's all images on shields. Benardete completes his thought:

The Sphinx has to be destroyed again. Her destruction by a mere mortal no longer suffices. Whether the mention of Oedipus would have reminded Eteocles of his father's curse, or the Sphinx as an image has lost none of its terror—the satyr-play was devoted to her—Eteocles has so far entered into the world of signs that from now on signs alone will seem real to him. *The image finally usurps the place of the thing imagined*.

Ye gods, this Benardete is truly the Coltrane of Aeschylus exegetes. The image finally *usurps* the place of the thing imagined. Ye gods what have we come to. Where are we headed. Where are we. Hades. System of logic. Realm of shadows. Their cries. Cracked requiem. Dharma Eye. Blind patriot. Blinded to the system, the transit, the whole. Picture? Motion picture. Eteocles' transit system—his 'whole picture'—has moved, from the possibility of a good infinity of placard-men to the actuality of a bad infinity of placards, which have usurped the place of men. He shall pay the price. Unfortunately. No free lunch. He's shifted the scene, badly infinitely. The prisoner's deed. Meanwhile, I have a few questions. Benardete! you sure make your point, but— at this point, aren't *you* confounding the reporter with the report. *You* said so yourself: 'Eteocles himself can be equally charged with confounding the reporter with the report.' The spy, Eteocles—but now *you* seem to be doing it. Birds do it, bees do it. Who's on first. *Who* says—perhaps deliberately ambiguously—'most spears are cast against this man.' It's the spy again, in his 'clear report.' No, we can't blame *everything* on the spy, even if we *can* blame him for one hell of a lot. Absolutely. It's always the spy, with his poetic license to kill, who gets Eteocles into trouble. Digs him a deeper and deeper hole. But then, *you* write: 'the *Sphinx* will reproach her bearer.' Sez who. The way you write it, it looks like the Sphinx *herself* says it—'I'll reproach my bearer'—but no, it's Eteocles, in person, chasing Doubles again—chasing the *spy's image* of/ and the *image on the shield*. Believe me, I'll get back to/at this in the end, possibly. Otherwise, after the end. No, it's not just Eteocles chasing his own images. It's not just the chain: Shield (image) — Interpretation — Defender — Shield, and so forth. No, it's: the spy's interpretation ('clear report') — Eteocles' interpretation of the spy's interpretation — Defender — spy's next interpretation, and so forth. There are no shields, they've all been *usurped*. What 'thing imagined'! The mirror is empty. A cry of shadow. Wait! I see Artaud, signaling through the flames. '*The ambiguity is deliberate*': the placard and the man. Take your pick. Image or man. As You Like It, theatrically speaking. Deliberately ambiguous. A decision. 'My' placard-men in the subway *have decided* to be placard-men, *themselves*. But what do Eteocles' placard-men decide? Nothing. Decided for. Not a thing. What's more, the placards have usurped the men. What does Eteocles, *himself*, decide? If anything, he decides *not to think* about what a decision is and what making a decision means. In-and-for itself a bad decision. Infinitely bad, and/or badly infinite. Because in *this theater* the Double is not *identical* to what it doubles. This is *difficulty* and the Double, the second phase of Creation. In this case, I'd say, the *political* phase, the Defend the City! phase. Ye gods, he's King of Thebes. The *Septem* is *political* theater. Eteocles makes *political* decisions, *about* images. In images. In and out of images. This unfortunate war is real, unfortunately. The savage and outlandish Seven are real. Real, *and* real images, unfortunately, for Eteocles. Politically, personally, not two, not one. History. Logic. Responsibility. A decision. The spy. Not the spy. Everything. Nothing. Being is nothing. Am I contradicting myself, possibly. Has the spy thrown me for a loop-de-doop. Possibly. 'For the power of life, and still more the might of the spirit, consists precisely in positing contradiction in itself, enduring it, and overcoming it.' Political phase. Not 'over against' a *pure* imagery phase, no, *there's no such thing as a pure image.* No. Images may be there *from the word go,* but a 'pure world of images' is imaginary. No, not *una parola,* as the Italians put it. Easier said than done. No. Forget it. Completely. It doesn't exist. There's no image without an imaginer. No deed without a doer. No theater without an actor. What's real is their *relation.* Relatedness. A Sphinx on a shield! Aktor, a toss-up! says Eteocles. *Has to be destroyed again.* Political theater. Second phase of creation. A war of images—this unfortunate war—but the City is clearly in the foreground. Defend! Attack! Reciprocally suicide! Eteocles! A decision. My decision, too, is a political decision, which—not-two-not-one—is a personal decision. In images. Placard-men, placards and men, true and bad infinities. Decide, decided for. What's more, at the Fifth Gate we have yet another 'coincidence,' possibly. A serendipity, as Benardete might, would, and will say. Ye gods, just think! This actor, Eteocles' fifth Defender, is named Aktor. He's the brother of Hyperbius, the fourth Defender. One brother for My Lai (but, was Michelangelo *for* or *against* it), one brother for the B-52. Typhon. Sphinx. Defend the City! Images. Shadows. *The King* does what's necessary. BUT WHAT AM I DOING. Wow, a good question. Freely, necessarily, responsibly. Placard and man. No, the *Septem* is absolutely not an action play, a Spaghetti Western, it is an *actor's* play. Placard-men. Eteocles' 'free choice' of a Defender to *set against* Parthenopaeus and 'his' Sphinx is an Aktor. No question, bros. Keep on truckin'. My Lai and a B-52. Soup and a sandwich. This time, the whole lunch. Free? No such thing. B-52, SAM, and Uncle Sam *himself.* Flesh and blood. In person. Politically. Personally. Responsible for. The Fifth Gate. Kit and caboodle. Fare thee well. Hail and farewell. Ave atque vale. The senate and people of Rome. 59th Street, sailed right through it. Cristóbal Colón. A Man of the World. Dogs of God. Poets and sailors.[176] Father of all

---

176 Italy, a country of *poeti e navigatori,* so they say/said. Actually, 'saints, poets, and sailors,' but never mind the saints.

Holocausts. *Even speaking their name was prohibited.* The SOUND is fading to a whisper. Blue jays on the roof. Traveling to a place beyond both noise and sound, possibly. What a decision is and what making a decision means. This, clearly, is not Eteocles' problem. It's my problem. Not his? A loaded question. Don't ask. No, Eteocles has lots of problems. But— fortunately and/or unfortunately—not this one. Just like Starry Vere. It seems that Captains and Kings just *make* decisions, they don't ask what a decision is and what making a decision means. As I'm doing. Speak then to me! Eteocles. With all your problems. Suddenly, here comes a whopper. A genuine Moby Dick. *Being* and *seeming*. The heart of the eternal pyramids. Double. Or nothing. Or so it seems. Place your bets. The chips are down. The Note:

> After the appearance of the anthropomorphic Zeus, the spy tells Eteocles that the fifth attacker is the beautiful Parthenopaeus, whose savage spirit belies his name. Neither his beauty nor his name reveals the truth about him. Appearances are deceptive, and their meaning cannot be directly read. Parthenopaeus undermines the basis of Eteocles' previous interpretations, for if seeming is unconnected with being, there is no way of knowing the true significance of the shields. Parthenopaeus thus prepares for the soothsayer Amphiaraus as the sixth attacker, whose shield bears no device.

No image. The circle of his shield. The empty shield. At this point Benardete gives line 592 in Greek: 'For he wants not to seem *áristos*, but to be.' Frankly, I think he could have set the scene a little better. He quotes this line from the most eloquent, sober, and interesting of the spy's reports. For once, the tale is calm. Dignified. The spy seems to revere Amphiaraus, the Prophet who 'reveres the gods,' as the spy puts it, *himself*. He quotes him credibly, no loop-de-doops. No eyes of night. No *images* of his own. He seems to have lost his poetic license. Two quotes. In the first, Amphiaraus attacks Tydeus: 'Murderer! High priest of bloodshed! Awakener of avenging spirits! Adrastus' infamous advisor in this unfortunate war.'[177] No, no Kill for Peace. In the second, Amphiaraus attacks Polyneices, the screwed bro. The spy says, for example, that Amphiaraus says 'What justice shall quench a mother's tears?' and, just this once, we believe him. Implicitly. Explicitly. Eteocles and I. A credible quote. And, after the quote, a sober description: 'Holding motionless his brazen shield. *No sign is on its circle*.' For this sign-loving image-loving spy, this sure boosts his credibility. No, he didn't make this up. Not even a metaphor. Followed by this *great* line, which Benardete quotes: 'For he wants not to seem *áristos*, but to be.' What a shame. The spy has lost his head. Again! Carried away. Again. Thrown and throwing for a loop, possibly. No, not with one of his usual imaginings but, this time, with his *own thinking*. Not with no-mind but *mindlessly*, he decides to consider thinking as such. Suddenly inspired by Hegel, possibly. An anti-illumination. He couldn't resist. He spouts—in my own modest opinion, the opinion of a 21-year-old Ancient Greek student— *the* line of the *Septem*, the crucial line. *And* I have a big problem with it. Big! It *seems* to be and *is* a perfectly Peter Arnettean line. A genuine 'we destroy the village in order to save it' line, give or take grievous distortions. Its translation is wildly problematic. What a *shame* Benardete doesn't give *his* translation. But that's not the point. What point. Probably not this one. This time I may be guilty of 'confounding,' *myself*. No, not exactly of confounding the reporter with the report. No, let's say of confounding the tragedian with the tragedy. This is Aeschylus' play. HE invented this spy. Be WE spy on the spy, in-and-for himself, in-and-for ourselves, as Hegel puts it. Benardete spies on him, I spy on Benardete, I scream, you scream, the

---

177 OK, my translation is an itty-bit free.

more the merrier, we all scream. This spy wants, needs, and deserves to be spied on. But I've really led myself by the nose into the wilderness this time. Goddam spy. In any event, it's a great line. In itself. Its translation is wildly problematic. And Benardete 'decided'—possibly 'unconsciously'—not to help me. Now, when I really need him. Monday I might go look for him in his broom closet and tell him, sincerely, you didn't help me with this one, now when I really need it. No, I won't do that, Benardete always helps me, he'll help me forever. In his own way. On his own terms. *Pazienza*, as the Italians say. I'm doing my best, myself. With what I have. And don't have. I have Grene: 'He is best not at seeming to be such but being so.' Vellacott: 'For he cares not to seem the bravest, but to be.' I like Grene's, I think this is what Aeschylus *means* to say, but Grene takes serious liberties with the Greek. As I see it, as literally as I can: 'For not to seem the best/bravest/noblest [*áristos*], but to be he wants'—the verb is at the end. (Grene omits it altogether, and he does something very tricky with *áristos.*) Let's say: For he wants not to seem *áristos*, but to be [it?]. What concerns him is not seeming *áristos* but being [*áristos*] [possibly *sous rature*, as Derrida puts it]. *Áristos*—as in 'aristocracy'—is itself a big and tricky word, but it's the least of my problems here. It's the spy again! The spy, it's always the spy. SOUND. 7th Avenue. Creatures. Creatures stirring. Stirring creatures. Off on. On off. Fare us well. Nothing special. Coltrane, 'My Favorite Things.' Monk, 'Blue Monk.' Albert Ayler, 'Spirits Rejoice.'[178] Eternal pyramids. Just keep on playing the records. No need! Here now always. Jazz is not needy. It's the spy who 'needs' to give us this 'clear report' of what Amphiaraus said, along with his *own* savagely and outlandishly one-line out-of-line editorial comment. It's true, with good reason, I don't trust this spy any farther than I can throw him. Or than he can throw me. To say the least. With good

---

178 'i was standing and the earth was not there/ i have risen/ a spirit passing through,' Albert Ayler is said to have said.

reason. Just for starters—*áristos*. *Eteocles* quite rightly calls
Amphiaraus 'wise, just, good, and holy' (Grene) — 'modest,
brave, upright, and pious' (Vellacott) — while his Wild Bunch
of fellow Attackers are savage and outlandish, 'loud-mouthed,
blaspheming, boastful.' Why—as the spy says he says—would
Amphiaraus say he's better—nobler—than they are. There's
no comparison. It's like Benardete going into a kindergarten
and saying, to the four-year-olds, in Ancient Greek, 'I'm the
best Plato-scholar here.' It makes no sense. Or Hegel, in the
Essex Street market, telling my butcher 'Das System der Logik
ist das Reich der Schatten.' No, they don't speak the same
language. *Áristos* is *áristos*, it's not savage and outlandish.
The spy is raving, again. But—what is Amphiaraus/Aeschylus
getting at here. Who knows. *That's* the problem. Not to seem
but to be. I muse. Just taking a cheap shot at 'seeming'—
appearances are deceptive. Shades of Starry Vere. Watch out
for your *Handsome Sailor*, your picture of innocence, plotting
a new Great Mutiny right here in your City. It can't possibly be
that simple. It wasn't that simple in Melville, and it can't be
in Aeschylus either. No, it isn't that simple at all. 'The empty
mirror. If you could really understand that, there would be
nothing left here for you to look for.' Let's see how Benardete
handles this.

It might seem, then, that Amphiaraus' refusal to carry
a device would have the effect of shifting the play from
dokeîn [seeming] to *eînai* [being], so that the two became
indistinguishable. Eteocles had begun with a contrast,
though he seems unaware of it, between the soothsayer
Tiresias and himself. He must manage the tiller of the
ship of state with his eyes open and awake, but the blind
Tiresias manages birds of augury with his ears and wits.
The conclusions of each seem appropriate to their trust
in either sight or hearing. Tiresias, in spite of Eteocles'

elaborate praise, can only report that the Argives have held a nocturnal council and will attack the city; while Eteocles has sent out scouts and spies, one of whom soon returns to report on the exact dispositions of the enemy. And yet Eteocles ends up by accepting as true the visions that came to him when asleep. (709—711).

Benardete doesn't even quote these lines, he just refers to them. Let me see, I like Vellacott's translation here: 'This rage was kindled by the curse of Oedipus. How true a prophet is that figure of my dreams who comes each night to apportion our inheritance!' SOUND. Rockefeller Center. Stirring. I can't believe they're still ice-skating. I never skate, I'd fall over immediately. I can't even ride a bicycle. No balance. Nothing special. No, this time it's Benardete who's gotten ahead of himself. Way ahead. He's jumped right into Eteocles 'sober' dialogue with the Chorus (lines 677–719), in which he regrets and laments his bad decision to go *himself* to the Seventh Gate, to be reciprocally suicided with his brother. Regrets it instantly, as soon as he makes it. The sudden way. Suddenly, after a long procession of placards, a dirge. No, Benardete jumps around, he's a paragon of nonlinearity (not the only one!), but I find his Great Leap Forward here a little strange. Sudden, and absolutely momentary: he beats an *immediate* retreat to the Sixth Gate, the empty shield. What's on his mind. Who knows. But it's a good place for me to take stock, since in the rest of this second Note Benardete *really makes his point*. He gives *his* interpretation of 'Eteocles' interpretations of the shields'— namely, of his *decision* to go *himself* to the Seventh Gate. So— now or never—I have to be ready to give *my* interpretation of *his* (Hitchcockian) interpretation, in the hope that this will be *decisive* for my *decision*. Which will be 'unconscious.' My *responsible* decision, be it or seem it good or bad. The point! A decision I can live, and eventually die, with. No-mind. The empty shield. What concerns me is—guess what—what a decision is and what making a decision means. All this time in the subway, traveling, the transit system. *I've discovered what really concerns me.* Personally. Politically. Not two, not one. I'm *concerned* about being-is-nothing *decisions*. My fork. My spaghetti. No no no no, PLEASE no Chinese-menu decisions. I LOVE Chinese food, especially the sweet-and-sour shrimp at the foot of the 'Manhattan' Bridge, so-called, randomly. I have to do better. I need to. Something *áristos*. Decide *something*—no! decide *in a way* that I can live with for the rest of my life. A way that shows me *I had a glimmer* of what a decision is and what making a decision means. Yes, I'm *concerned*. But being-is-nothing never goes away. It is a logical *moment*. In logical time. Beginning-middle-end of Hegel's Logic. No escaping it. No love it or leave it. The vanishing of vanishing. *Freely releases* itself. This self-liberation. Being is nothing. No 'way of living outside the jurisdiction of the Court,' as Joseph K. put it, ill-logically. He also said—tragically, facetiously—'but I mean the *real* courts, not the ones in the attics.' But the attic courts are—are *and* seem to be—the real courts. The mosquito. The B-52. The realm of shadows. The system of logic. That's The Trial. As Hegel might have said, nothing escapes except escaping itself. Release. Liberation. A big release, as Tuli put it, beyond words. Killing for peace. A curious dirge. Liberation. Ask Eteocles. 'The idea *freely releases* itself, absolutely certain of itself and internally at rest.' Being-is-nothing is the beginning, but also the end—and the middle (essence, seeming, semblance)—of the science of logic. A logical *moment*. Like death, like birth. 'Birth is an expression complete this moment. Death is an expression complete this moment. They are like winter and spring. You do not call winter the beginning of spring, nor summer the end of spring.' Satori. Logic. No-mind. A decision. Freedom, necessity. The zero degree of freedom is the zero degree of necessity. Being-is-nothing. A problem. Absolutely.

No-problem. Just a moment. Absolutely. Let's get ahead of ourselves. The slant of the rest of the Note is: what *leads to* Eteocles' decision. (Freedom, necessity. Benardete's word is *compulsion*.) The End. Of the Note, and of what concerns me. But Eteocles is my brother—half-half-half, more or less, who's counting—and I'm genuinely concerned abut him. I care about him. A bad decision. Definitely. No question. Nothing good about it. Absolutely nothing. Being is nothing. Bad. My own may be bad too. Not as bad as his—he's a king—but, bad. Not good, possibly. A King, responsible for the City. But I, too, am responsible. For this unfortunate war. SOUND. Coming into the 42nd Street station. Just don't stab ME in the ass. The car is full. Look! A lot of people getting off, a lot of people getting on. Fun City! We're under 6th Avenue. Hadean night. The realm of shadows. Up there, in the Manna-hata darkness, Times Square is a long block west, and Grand Central a long block east. The streets are full of wild young cabbies, fishing for fares, like Psarotourkos, better known as Psarantonis (the Elder). The true concept of infinity. Saturday night specials. Pushin' and shovin'. No, nothin' special. Never mind. Be cool. Monkey mind. No-mind. A fire in the mind. I've been thinking about this. Is chasing our own images an example of monkey mind? Like a cat chasing her tail, possibly. I actually don't know what it's like to be a cat. Chasing her tail may be equivalent to our reading the *Science of Logic*. No, monkeys don't chase their tails, I'm sure. I think. Who knows. Not the point. No, chasing images—your *own* images—is more like chasing *tales* than chasing *tails*. Possibly. With Eteocles and the spy I'm not quite sure. An *inside* narrative, possibly. Oops, he just stepped out! Johnny Got His Gun. Burn, baby, burn. 'You plan the wars you masters of men plan the wars and point the way and we will point the gun.' Newark, Detroit, Watts. The more the merrier. A fire in the mind, as Dostoevsky put it. Not on the roof. Just do it. This unfortunate war. Liberation! Monkey mind? Zen mind? a.k.a.

big mind. Dostoevsky, Melville, Kafka, no, not fire in the mind, not great minds, no. No-mind. Empty mirrors. Most wonderful. 'Unconsciously'—what in the world does this *mean*. These ten-thousand things are *not* reflected in it. The Note. The point. Anthropus, the answer to the *riddle*. Human being. Human mind and spirit. The might of the spirit. Contradiction. In itself. The City. Responsibility. Tangled up in images. For Eteocles, I'd say 'badly infinitely' tangled. *Himself* to the Seventh Gate. I am here to figure out my own tangle. I want to look at Eteocles' 'dirge' for a moment. 'Bring me my greaves!' Line 676, a controversial line, which Benardete does not discuss. The spy has just this minute 'reported' that his brother, Polyneices, is at the Seventh Gate. Which is absolutely no surprise, since this whole Attack is Polyneices' idea, and doing, and Thebes only *has* Seven Gates, so, at this point, where else can he go. Polyneices is no Kissinger, that's not his role. But Eteocles *decides* to go *himself* to the Seventh Gate to reciprocally suicide himself with his brother, polluting the City. Which is what this Note is all about. And, in a sense—a big one—what these two days in the realm of shadows are about. The placard-men! Can I possibly meet another one, or one of the six I've met before. A penny for the Old Guy. The car is nearly full. Amazing. Amusing. Sing, ye Muses! as Homer put it. Poets tell many lies, as Plato put it. Classics. Midtown. Middle of the night. After the spy's 'report' what's the first word out of Eteocles' mouth. THE CURSE. First word out of his mouth: The Curse. The race of Oedipus. Then, instantly, his bad decision. We'll see what Benardete has to say about *this.* Eteocles' last words in this speech [to an attendant]: 'Run, bring me my greaves, to protect me against spear and stone.' But this poses a question that has *not* exercised Benardete but that does exercise me, and the Chorus. The question of *Eteocles' fork*. He *does* have a fork. But apart from this line about the 'greaves' Aeschylus presents it as an *unconscious* fork. For us. For

Eteocles. In-and-for-itself, as Hegel puts it. Eteocles has to
send an attendant to run off and get him his armor. His shield
too, I presume. Any old shield. Never mind the image.
Eteocles, the Great Imaginer, 'past the care' of images. Positing
contradiction in itself, enduring it, and overcoming it. What
about it, Benardete. The greaves—glorified shin-guards—are
the *first* pieces of armor to be put on, *before* the body-armor.
The other six Defenders are already fully armed. We get the
idea that *he didn't intend to go to any Gate at all.* The Oval
Office. A fork. SOUND. 34th Street. Peep peep. Blue jays on the
roof. Car still pretty full. Pretty quiet. Herald Square.
Remember me! Remember me! I, long gone, remember me.
No, Eteocles only 'remembers' he *has a fork* when/because he's
told, by the spy, that *his own brother* is at the Seventh Gate.
All of a sudden, as if from a dream, he wakes up and *decides*,
on the spot, to go *himself* to the Seventh Gate. I have a fork!
he muses. Polyneices gets the Seventh Gate *by lot*, by chance,
he picks a pebble out of a helmet (possibly). But Eteocles has a
fork, where three roads cross. He can *not go* to any Gate. He
can move his Defenders around and go himself to *another*
Gate. (I'll grant you this wouldn't be so easy, since the
Champions on both sides have become placard-men. The
image has *usurped* the reality.) Or, he can go *himself* to the
Seventh Gate. The Curse. Satori. A bad decision. *Politically*, for
starters. No sense of responsibility. Defend the City! Pollute the
City! Fun City! Fuck the City! Eteocles! Waiting for his greaves,
and the rest of his armor, I presume—any old shield, with any
old image—he has a very interesting dialogue with the Chorus,
which Benardete barely refers to. His 'dirge.' *Already in his
shroud*. Firing line. For real. No mock execution. The maidens,
of course, clutch at the first—or, possibly, the second—prong,
hugging it for all they're worth. 'Go not you, go not, to the
Seventh Gate!' But Eteocles' mind is made up. *He has decided*,
so to speak. What's his reasoning. 'It is the gods that drive this

matter on. Since it is so—on, on with the favoring wind, this wave of hell that has engulfed for its share the race of Laius, whom Phoebus has so hated.' The gods, ye gods, poor Eteocles. 'We are already past the care of gods. For them our death is the worthy offering. Why then delay, fawning upon our doom?'[179] Can you call this reasoning? What would Hegel call it. I'm not sure. I've gotten ahead of the story for the last time. Now I'm going to follow the Note right to its Hitchcockian end. On with another's boasts—don't grudge me the story! Where was I. 'Eteocles ends up by accepting as true the visions that came to him when asleep.'

What prepared the way for his acceptance has been the insignia of the enemy and his interpretation of them, which paradoxically find their culmination in Amphiaraus' empty shield. Amphiaraus interprets Polyneices' name to mean exactly what it says [poly-neices, much strife]. The counter example of Parthenopaeus has no weight for either him or Eteocles. Seeming is being and being seeming, for Amphiaraus, in predicting his own death and the failure of the expedition as a whole, testifies to the truth of Eteocles' interpretations. [Unconsciously. What does Amphiaraus know about Eteocles' interpretations! The spy can't possibly be giving clear reports to both sides.] What up to now had been only likely become inevitable meanings. Signs have become fates. The arbitrary order in which the attackers appeared—they obtained their posts by lot—became necessary once Eteocles decided to match the Theban champions in light of his own interpretations of the Argive shields; and whatever degree of freedom he had in matching them before Hippomedon, disappears as soon as he believes it fitting that the image of Typhon should be opposed to that of Zeus. That confrontation thrusts

179 I have—mostly—followed Grene's translation. The lines are 689–692 and 703–705.

Eteocles into a world where gods as the representatives of men impose a compulsion on them, and which, confirmed by Amphiaraus as true, prevents Eteocles from later distinguishing his own will from the gods'. Amphiaraus' acceptance of his prophesied death becomes the model for Eteocles' own acceptance. What the Chorus calls his 'desire' and 'longing' he calls a god and a father's curse. Not that what he says is false and what the Chorus says true, but that anthropomorphic gods 'are' as much inside ('enthused by Ares') as outside a man ('Zeus, standing erect'). They are as much to be seen in statues as sensed in the heart. They are as much of the body as of the soul.

This is the heart/soul of Benardete's argument/analysis, and the foundation of his Hitchcockian conclusion. (I'm just two paragraphs from the end of the Note. A long one, then a short one.) I have been profoundly influenced by this part of the Note: *the empty shield as triumph of the image*. 'Signs have become fates.' This is not self-evident. It's Benardete. What's more, it's ambiguous: I know what signs are, but what are fates? Isn't Eteocles' chasing his own images the heart/soul of the *Septem* (and of the second Note)? Isn't this what's 'special' about it (them)? (*Septem* and Note.) The Tragedy is the Triumph of the Chase over Eteocles, and over the City, since he *is* the King of Thebes. Shades of Ahab and Moby Dick. Discolored snow. Early April. End of March, 1972. Chasing his own tail, tales, images, whatevers. Names. Just names. Float like a butterfly, sting like a bee. And they call it *free association*. Free. How free. If the ground zero of freedom is *the ground zero of necessity*, who's responsible. Who's on first. The *Septem* is a tragedy, and the tragic is *a decision*. The prisoner's deed. A *bad* decision, no question about that. What. An invisible fork. An 'unconscious' decision. I've put all the Zen I've practiced these last nine months, since my F-4, into this.

Becoming. Big mind. The vanishing of vanishing. What does it mean that Amphiaraus' empty shield 'means' a *triumph of the image*. Dogen-zenji, Suzuki-roshi, the other Suzuki, Hui-neng, Shen-hui the Zen placard-man, have been helping me with this. No, no mystery. Logic. Zen. The realm of shadows. That's why I'm here. Still here. But—*signs have become fates*. Ye gods! SOUND. West 4th Street. Under the West Village, again. A placard-man! Now or never, possibly. A Michelangelo. A B-52. A true infinity. Someone new. A seventh man. A seventh placard. No, no shadow of a placard-man, or placard, or man. The eternal silence of these infinite spaces terrifies me, as Pascal once put it.[180] *Everyone is staggering out of the car.* An emptying singularity! A letter from emptiness, as Suzuki-roshi puts it. Up there—the NYU Classics Department. When it rains I usually/sometimes take the F Train, West 4th, corner of 6th Avenue, then just a few blocks east, right through Washington Square Park, to Waverly Place. I dig the Washington Square Arch, built to celebrate the centennial of George Washington's inauguration as President in 1789. I always read the inscription: 'Let us raise a standard to which the wise and honest can repair. The event is in the hand of God.' In the hand of God. Decided for by the gods. Is this what Benardete means by 'fate'? Signs have become fates. I still think the best [*áristos*] inscription would have been: 'I cannot tell a lie. I chopped it down.' Defend the City! Great moments in American history. The Classics Department. Waverly Place. Rickety elevator to the fourth floor.[181] Benardete might be up there in his broom closet this very minute. I'm raving. I'm losing my acorns. Saturday night. Dead of night. Sunday morning, actually. On Monday I'll be there myself. Talking with Dave Leahy. Waverly Place, Classics Department. It seems like

---

180 *Pensée 206*. Epigraph to Thomas Bernhard's novel *Gargoyles*.
181 Or was it the second floor? Or the third? I cannot tell a lie, I don't remember which floor it was, though I sure remember the rickety elevator. I even remember the elevator *man*. Anthropus! In those days elevators had men (and women possibly, though I don't remember seeing one myself), not buttons.

another world. Night journey. The Hadean night. The Noter and the Note. In his teaching and his writing Benardete famously insists: Stick to the text. Eschew the image. See what the text actually says. Suddenly, there's no one in the car. A strange image and strange prisoners.[182] Flowers gone. Where. History. Hitchcock in the offing. No fear. Speak! Favors. Nor hate. Signs. Have become fates. What are fates. What do 'fates' mean. Do Eteocles and Amphiaraus *decide* that signs have become fates, or does Benardete. Or Aeschylus. Frankly, I put my money on Benardete. 'Fate' sounds ancient, but it also smacks of the modern. Of mystery. The empty shield. Seeming is being and being, seeming. Good. But is that the whole story. I haven't been here in Hades for a day, a night, another day, almost all of another night, just to *endorse* Benardete's 'Eteocles' Interpretations of the Shields.' No, and not just to *interpret* Benardete's 'Eteocles' Interpretations of the Shields' either. No! I have to figure out the 'inevitable meanings' (as Benardete Melvilleanly puts it) of these interpretations. Their dumb blankness, full of meaning. In a wide landscape of snows. Semenovsky Square. The compulsion. Because I have a fork. And because Eteocles has *become* ('the vanishing of vanishing') my half-half-brother. Half, halfs, the more the merrier. *What about* what a decision is and what making a decision means? Eteocles *never asks himself this question*, but isn't THIS what all these 'interpretations of the shields' is all about. Otherwise, where's the Tragedy. The Curse is there from *before* the beginning. Images are there from the *very* beginning, from the moment the *spy* opens his mouth. The Great Imaginers, Eteocles and his spy. Mutt and Jeff, possibly. Abbott and Costello, probably. But *what the Tragedy is all about is the triumph of the image*, which drives Eteocles to his tragic—bad— decision. Done for. Compulsion. In the *Septem* Aeschylus shows us what *decided for* means. As he sees it. An *example* of what 'decided for' means. *Billy Budd* is another example. Logico-

---

182 Plato's *Republic*, right at the beginning of Book VII.

political examples, I'd say. SOUND. Broadway/Lafayette. The Marquis de Lafayette. In the thick of it. Our side! their side! his side! Revolution. Turning the Brits upside down. Winter soldier. Summer soldier. Universal soldier. *Qu'un sang impur/ Abreuve nos sillons!* Winter, spring, summer or fall/ All you have to do is call.[183] Valley Forge. Emptying. Empty. Emptied. Zen emptiness, like a quantum void. Nothing reflects. The mirrors are empty. Benardete says 'the gods ... impose a compulsion' but, at the end, of the Note, he says it's the chain of images, the empty shield, the *triumph of images*—I could almost say the *hegemony* of images[184]—that 'constitutes the compulsion.' I'm getting dangerously ahead of myself. Too many clues kill the suspense. Kill the chicken before it's hatched. Kill for peace. Tragically. Let's back up. 'Amphiaraus... testifies to the truth of Eteocles' interpretations.' Logically, personally-politically, or in-between? (Not *literally*, that's for sure.) I think this is a fair question. And the spy, what, never mind the spy! 'Eteocles decided to match the Theban champions in light of his own interpretations of the Argive shields,' but it's all based on the *spy's clear reports*. We destroy the village in order to save it. A grievous distortion. I want to create problems, make philosophical problems, like my friend Dave Leahy. Not only philosophical. I need to talk to him about all this.[185] A question. Political problems, there's no need to create them, they're just *there*, badly infinitely. Both sides, at once? Whole picture? *In politics a 'whole picture' doesn't exist.* This is the essence of the political. It's badly infinite. It's 'the infinite set *over against* the finite, in a relation in which they are as qualitatively distinct others.' SirYesSir, the political, 'entangled in unreconciled, unresolved, absolute contradictions.' Political responsibility! The prisoner's deed. Eteocles. King of Thebes. Seven Against Thebes. Inside narrative. Outside narrative. Johnny Got His

---

183 Carole King, 'You've Got a Friend,' 1971.
184 Gramsci! That's all I need right now.
185 How I miss him! How I wish he could read this, and talk with me about it.

Gun. Where's the fire. What fire. Just one more eminently fair question. *More* than eminently fair. *One* more fair one: What does Hegel *mean* by 'the true concept of infinity'? One plus one: Is it a 'purely' logical concept, or also/at the same time a 'political' concept? Not two, not one. *WHAT is reflected, unconsciously, in the empty mirror?* WHAT is a 'whole picture'? A transit *system*? A *political* animal? What what what. WHOSE delusion? 'If you think you really come and go, that is your delusion.' For now, let's just say that Eteocles' 'bad infinity' *has everything to do with his never asking himself what a decision is and what making a decision means.* For now. But it's also true that I'm coming to the end of my line. SUBway, end of March, 1972. The hour is getting late. What is this thing called time. Logical time, political time. My time, your time, our time. High time. Low time. When the music's over. Any day now. Any way now. Released. From what. Going where. From Hades. Relief. Confusion. Too much. 'Free' association. The system of logic. A cry of shadow. SUBway. A SOUND. Grand Street. Neon. Bricks lay. Madmen climb. Bless my soul. A placard, and a man. Together. Separate. Inseparable. A tired man. He slumps like an amoeba on the seat. The empty car. His placard upright on the floor. Across from me. Like the shield of a Homeric hero, planted in the earth after the battle. What self. No one else in the car. No one left. Or right. Or up or down. In this car, not a single soul straggling home to Brooklyn. But us. In this car. I can't speak for the whole train. System. Train. Car. Transit. Mind. No-mind. A fire. Wait! His placard, I know this image, a great photo, a famous photo. *The seventh placard-man.* I'm speaking to him. Right now! He's not going anywhere. Until he gets off, somewhere. His stop. Hoarse from a long silence.[186] Speak! I speak. To him.

---

186 *Chi per lungo silenzio parea fioco*, Dante, *Inferno*, 1, 63.

— A great photo. Lady Liberty in distress. Were you there
yourself last December?
— Yes, I was. The day after Christmas. Liberty Island. Liberty
Enlightening the World. Vietnam Veterans Against the War,
fifteen of us.
— It really was fantastic. Occupying the Statue of Liberty.
Flying the flag upside down from her crown, signaling distress.
Great political theater. Fantastic.
— SirYesYes, we served our country. I was in Nam, for three
years. Marines. I was at Winter Soldier. Dewey Canyon. Kansas
City. Spent some time with my Indian brothers and sisters
during the Alcatraz Occupation. Then, the Statue of Liberty.
Don't know what to do next. That's my problem.
— You know Scott Camil then.
— Sure. A main man. A little crazy, but good. Riled up. Plenty.
— Seen him lately?
— Nope. Not since Kansas City I guess.
— I guess he did go a little crazy.
— Just a little, maybe. Shooting the hardcore hawks, as he
put it. Don't know. Right on, you dig. The idea wasn't all bad.
Anyway, we did some real plain speaking in Kansas City, a
good meeting, got our heads together. The problem was—the
problem is—what do we do now?
— A good thing they didn't neutralize you. I heard that half the
FBI was there.
— Damn straight. Scumbags. Enemies of the people. Camil
really was pretty wild.
— *Maybe* I saw him here in the subway a few hours ago, I can't
be sure. I listened to Winter Soldier on WBAI, every minute of
it, but I haven't seen any photos. The *Times* did exactly one
article, with that 'this stuff happens in all wars' shit—
— Motherfuckers! Shit-eating shit-serving motherfuckers!
— Not a single photo.
— Camil here in the subway. Who knows. Anything's possible.

The subway's a big place.

— A transit system. Infinite, in some sense.

— You haven't been to Nam yourself?

— Nope. Student. NYU. Ancient Greek. Graduating in a few months. 4-F.

— 4-F. No shit.

— They decided I'd be a peril for the soldiers. Our soldiers. Military shrinks. I weighed eighty-six pounds at the time. Be prepared, as the Boy Scouts put it. When were you in Nam?

— Called to serve, 1965 to 68, height of the frolic. Semper fidelis. Parris Island, then Nam. FTA. Fun Travel Adventure. Fuck The Army. I was twenty years old.

— You were a big crowd back then.

— Goddam us all, over half a million shit-eating fucked-in-the-ass motherfuckers, the most fucked people in the history of this country.

— Along with the Indians and the Blacks.

— Dig it, *plenty* of Blacks in Nam, and some Indians too. All of us fucked together. Dupes. Nitwits. Bozos. Stooges. Fucking shit-eaters. SirYesSir. Fighting Johnson's war, McNamara's war.

— In the defense of tyranny.

— Sure as shit.

— Fragging, deserting, brigs, AWOLs, smoking dope, shooting heroin, a real funfest. When the cucumber's up your ass.

— A high old time. G.I. Joes. Fucking grunts. Sure, we fragged an officer from time to time, put him to bed with a live grenade up his ass. Fortunately. The least we could do for our country.

— This unfortunate war, Fulbright calls it.

— At that hearing, the Blathering Kerry hearing. I was there, but the Fearless Leader was Kerry. Unfortunately.

— He's stepped down, I hear. After his Dewey Canyon performance.

— Dig that motherfucker, he just stepped out. Fortunately. Unfortunately he'll be back. In some shape or form. Not that it matters. For me what matters is what I do *myself*.

— Right on, my man. I'm with you. What I do *myself*. I'm thinking about it right now, then I'll do it.

— Shit, doing it and *then* thinking about it would be revolutionary, too bad it's deep shit.

— A river of shit, a wide, wide river. Too bad. Vietnam and our Native Americans, that's what I think about all the time. A perilous frontier, like a mirror reflecting on both sides. But what do I do about it, shit, I don't do shit.

— I learned in Nam that it's a lot easier to do than to think. It's also the best way to fuck your neighbor and yourself.

— A hard lesson.

— Dig the river! Dig it! Day, night, night, day, best part of the trip. Dig the lights on the water. Some sort of bulbs in rows, reflecting on the water.

— My man, why do they call this one the Manhattan Bridge and that one the Brooklyn Bridge, I just don't get it. East River, but from Brooklyn it's West. Same river, same deal.

— Just names, I guess. I never thought about it.

— Names, sure, but I think it's also a question of the power to *give* the names. Politics. Arbitrary decisions. Dirty business. Tyrant versus tyrant.

— Defense of tyranny?

— You dig. And nobody even thinks about it. When did you go to Alcatraz?

— I went twice, the first was just before Winter Soldier, for Thanksgiving.

— Nooo shit.

— No, not *for*, I mean *against* Thanksgiving. For Unthanksgiving.[187]

— Celebrating genocide, it really riles me up. Thanksgiving my ass! Giving thanks for an extermination. A holocaust.

— The Pequot. Burned alive.

---

187 The first official Unthanksgiving Day, a.k.a. The Indigenous People's Sunrise Gathering, celebrating the Alcatraz occupation (November 20, 1969 to June 11, 1971) was in 1975. Still going strong today. As is the National Day of Mourning in New England, celebrated since 1970.

— Even speaking their name was prohibited. A great holiday. Exterminate, then thank. Dig it, two Unthanksgivings ago the Indians painted Plymouth Rock red and celebrated the first annual National Day of Mourning. Fucking parades! In New York we celebrate our heroes for burning, bombing, exterminating millions of Vietnamese, young, old, women, children, what the fuck, I hardly know what to fucking think. Why does this country do it? What do I do *myself?*

— Be cool now, man. When the cucumber's up your ass. You said so yourself.

— They had a hard time on Alcatraz, nineteen long months.

— It was no picnic, but it was a great thing in the history of the country. Our *Native* Americans, students, whole families, many of the leaders were women. Our brothers and our sisters. Great people. We palefaces, how we fucked them! From the word go. Pioneers. It must be in our blood.

— Goddam Puritans. Shining Cities on Hills.

— A great land, the land of the free. After Vietnam we'll be fucking someone else, in some new way—

— Less blood maybe, but more tyranny—

— You dig. But, after Alcatraz I really believe that things will get better for our Native Americans, they won't stop fighting, they've been doormats for our dirty feet for long enough. On Alcatraz they wanted to build a cultural center with Native American Studies, an American Indian spiritual center, an ecology center, a museum. Sure, they got their asses kicked in the end, but I think it's the start of a turn for the better.[188]

— Where America finally turned, as your friend Kerry put it that day.

---

188 The Alcatraz Occupation sparked a surge in Indian rights activism in the following years: The Trail of Broken Treaties, the Bureau of Indian Affairs Occupation, the Longest Walk, culminating in the Wounded Knee incident in 1973. Kicked in the ass again, some dead and wounded that time, but it did attract a lot of attention. Marlon Brando! Have things gotten better for the Native Americans since then? I honestly don't know. I hope so. As we saw, the Pequot have made an amazing comeback. Then again, a parade is a parade is a parade.

— *Fuck* Kerry, he just stepped out. Other things to do. Blathering fearlessly. Shit-serving.

— After Unthanksgiving you went a second time.

— I'll tell you the story. At Winter Soldier I got to know this Indian—

— Shit, a main man! The one I heard on the radio. WBAI. The one who cried at the end of his testimony, with all the other veterans on their feet applauding. I'll never forget what he said, about cowboys and Indians, about treaties long ago, for as long as the grass shall grow and as long as the rivers shall flow, and now, one of these days the grass isn't gonna grow and the rivers aren't gonna flow.

— You have a *bad* motherfucking memory, my man.

— So they say. I put elephants to shame. I can remember the page number of quotes from all Kierkegaard's books, like my friend Dave Leahy. The American war in Vietnam, the Indian wars a hundred years ago.

— An incredible person. A friend. We went to the Alcatraz Occupation together. A man of few words and so much to say.

— Did you talk about the Ghost Dance?

— Right on, he told me a lot I didn't know. Surprised me. Political things, you dig. 1889, 1890, the politics of the end of the world. All Indians must dance, here, there, everywhere, keep on dancing. The circle dance, to reunite the living with the spirits of the dead. Warrior ghosts who will drive the white colonists off the land and bring peace, prosperity, and unity to the tribes. Put on your ghost shirts and fight! Bullets can't touch you! Have no fear! Dance! They danced until they dropped. They did nothing *but* dance. Dance dance dance. Nothing else.

— Right on. Danced all the way to Wounded Knee.

— Cocksucking ghost shirts. A massacre. But my friend has a point to make. A *political* point. The Ghost Dance was a Last Dance. A sexy name but a goddam cop-out. Dance dance

dance. Desperation and despair. Passiveness. A cop-out. Took it lying down. Fucked in the ass. The white men will soon disappear! With the next greening of the grass the ancestors will return and fight *for* us! So they surrendered without a real fight. Dancing ghosts. Took it lying down. My friend told me, the Winter Soldier Indian refuses to cop out, he fights, fights back, with dignity, with decision.

— Did you talk about Chief Seattle? A main man, a true prophet. 'What will happen when the secret corners of the forest are heavy with the scent of many men? When the view of the ripe hills is blotted by talking wires? It will be the end of living, and the beginning of survival.'

—Be cool bad motherfucker, my own memory isn't half bad. Dig it, I know this by heart. 'And when the last red man shall have perished from the earth and his memory among white men shall have become a myth, these shores shall swarm with the invisible dead of my tribe, and when your children's children shall think themselves alone in the field, the store, the shop, upon the highway or in the silence of the woods they will not be alone. In all the earth there is no place dedicated to solitude. At night, when the streets of your cities and villages shall be silent and you think them deserted, they will throng with the returning hosts that once filled and still love this beautiful land. The white man will never be alone. Let him be just and deal kindly with my people, for the dead are not altogether powerless.'

— This could be the dead millions in Vietnam. Fought, and died. We killed them. Let him be just. You have a great photo on your placard, a famous photo.

— I managed to make a blow-up and turn it into this poster.

— The head of the statue with the flag you flew upside down from her crown as a signal of distress. Her upraised arm, just up to the elbow. And your statement, in capital letters: WHAT JUSTICE?

— My statement, my question. Our question.

— The fifteen of you.

— All the winter soldiers. The people everywhere who are against this war. Including those of us who fought it—fought in it, and now fight against it. As best we can.

— You put Lady Liberty and Lady Justice together in one image. A good idea. Two great ladies. With liberty and justice for all.

— Cocksucking whores! Liberty, Justice, I can't take it anymore. Freedom Freedom Freedom. It reminds me of the Ghost Dance. A cop-out. Empty words. Dance dance dance. Gives me the fucking shits. Broad stripes and bright stars. Bombs bursting in air.

— Perilous fight.

— I guess the immigrants at the turn of the century got a kick out of the Statue of Liberty, the land of the free—

— When my grandfather arrived from Russia I don't think he gave a shit about statues, he had other things on his mind. Survival, for example. First survival, then the beginning of living.

— Wretched refuse. Huddled masses yearning to breathe free. Nice poem. But what about the asses this free land kicks! Injuns, niggers, gooks, fuck you all! I get so fucking riled up. I saw the Vietnamese people fighting for justice, and I fought them, killed them. So we went up there in her crown, fifteen of us, and flew the flag upside down. Distress. Cry freedom! Freedom to do what? To exterminate all the brutes? WHAT JUSTICE? This is my question. My message.

— Raising the torch, passing the torch. In the statues of Lady Justice the Lady is blindfolded, justice is blind. This is supposed to mean impartiality, but I think it's a permanent distress signal.

— You're sharp as a tack, motherfucker.

— I do my best. NYU Classics Department. I have good teachers. You know, your photo reminds me of an even more famous one, Malcolm Browne's Burning Monk, in Saigon, back in 1963. A necessary photo. A fire in my mind and on my roof. We don't have any photo of Norman Morrison, burning under McNamara's window. But we don't need one. Norman Morrison is always with me. My life would make no sense without him. His sacrifice.

— It's the Eddie Adams photo that's always with me. My experience. February first, 1968. I was in Saigon myself at the time, thinking I'd served just about enough. The hand-cuffed Viet Cong prisoner getting his brains blown out in the street by the Chief of the South Vietnam National Police. Dig it, the Chief of Police of the puppets we're fighting for. The people I, *myself*, was fighting for.

— What a terrible thing, all of it. Where did it all come from? *Where is it going?*

— What did I do, *myself*? Where are *we* going?

— The war against Vietnam is almost over, almost all our soldiers have left, after we've dropped another zillion tons of bombs everyone can call it a day. Then what?

— Then what, Lady Liberty! Liberty lighting the world. Liberty and cocksucking justice for all. No, for me Justice is no Lady. A slut, that's what she is. A whore. A hooker. On her better days.

— Double-dealing. A double-edged sword. An enemy of the people.

— Tiger Cages! I saw them myself. Our South Vietnamese puppets keep their prisoners in Tiger Cages. Torture them, kill them. At our bidding, of course. A lot of women too. What justice? One woman who got out alive told it like it is. I heard her. *When the government is an enemy of the people, the prisoners are the patriots.* That's what she said. A message for our Black brothers in prison here. Prisoners, and lucky to be alive.

— Fred Hampton wasn't so lucky. Murdered in his sleep, twenty-one years old. Chicago Police. FBI. In his bed, at dawn. Neutralized. In the land of the free it's open season on Panthers. Bros. Tiger Cages. They drop all these bombs to defend torture over there, while they lock up and kill the bros here at home. The defense of tyranny. The war on freedom. The American War. I guess it wouldn't have been a good idea to bomb the Statue of Liberty. Bad taste. Wrong message. Statues don't kill people, I guess.

— Maybe not, I'm not so sure. Anyway, the occupation was a good move. Clean. Clear. A sharp image. A clear message: We can no longer tolerate the war in Southeast Asia. Mr. Nixon, you set the date for leaving Vietnam and we'll give you your Statue back.

— Just think, thousands of disappointed tourists, the day after Christmas.

— A damn shame. Distress all around. A lot of people heard us, those two days we were there. We came out with clenched fists raised and our heads held high.

— Two days. I've been riding the subway for two days now myself. A day, a night, another day, almost another night.

— No shit. A prisoner of the subway. Two days straight, that's a pretty long time.

— I'm thinking about something. Studying the transit system. The screeches were driving me a little crazy, but then they calmed down. Turned from screeches into sounds. Music. Jazz. 'Blue Monk.' 'My Favorite Things.' 'Spirits Rejoice.'

— I hate these motherfucking screeches, they remind me of Nam. Sudden. Violent. Endless. There must be some other way.

— I think so too. I hadn't said a single word in two days, until you got on at Grand. With your placard. I live around there, on Rivington.

— Rivington! A fucked-up place.

— Sure, a perilous frontier. Not a silk-stocking district. Wait, I take that back, I talked to a cute chick, very possibly an NYU student. On the F, from West 4th as far as York Street, she lives there, near the Navy Yard.

— That's pretty far from Rivington.

— Dig it. Smooth as a silk stocking. We talked about Melville and Kleist, *Billy Budd* and *Michael Kohlhass*. She quoted Kleist right at me, off the bat, a pretty smart chick. 'You can make me mount the scaffold, but I can get you where it hurts.' Michael Kohlhass. 'He sure has a great sense of justice,' I said, and she came right back at me with 'better to be a dog than a man, if I'm to be kicked around!' Smart. Cute. Too bad she got off at York Street. Not that it matters. Kleist-quoting chicks are rare birds on Rivington Street.

— So many people in the subway. Forget the stars in the sky, they're more like the grains of sand. Too many, it makes my head spin sometimes.

— Absolutely. The stars in the sky are a true infinity, a whole picture. You're absolutely right. Grains of sand. You spend a lot of time in the subway yourself, I imagine. What's it like being a placard-man?

— A what?

— Sorry, I call you placard-men. Vietnam veterans in the subway, with placards, making statements, I'd say. Speaking your piece. Your message. For-the-war, against-the-war, in-between, sometimes it's hard to say. Ambiguity. Deliberate or not. You're the seventh placard-man I've met. The Seventh Gate. WHAT JUSTICE? Thebes of the Seven Gates.

— *Bad* motherfucker, what seventh placard-man?

— You don't know the other six?

— *What* placard-men?

— A whole picture. A true infinity. A transit *system*. Even if you don't know one another, I see all of you together.

—*Who* are these placard-men? So-called. As you call them. Call us, I guess.

— A good guess. Good, I'll tell you. Not who you are, but what you are. Or appear to be. I only know what I see. An uncertain reality.[189] Apart from you, I can only speak for the placards, not for the men. I've only spoken with *you*.

— Speak, my man. Speak then to me.

— The train! We're slowing down. Not screeching yet—

— Pacific Street. I love these two long stretches on the B, my train. My turf. The Bridge, whatever it's named. Grand to Pacific, Pacific to Sunset Park.

— And vice versa. Underground. Very quiet. I've done the West End Line quite a few times the past two days. Elevated. Beautiful. Glimmering. Pretty noisy. Thirteen screeches from Sunset Park to Coney Island. But who's counting.

— Noise is relative. You've never been to Nam. You dig, compared to Nam the Fourth of July is a lullaby.

— The *peep-peep-peep* of blue jays on the roof.

— I hate those fucking firecrackers.

— Flower power. Make love not war. Fucking fireworks, why can't they have the sky-show without the goddam explosions?

— Same river, same deal.

— Touché, as the fencers say. Wide, wide river.

— East/West River. Darkness and light. Bangs and sparkles. You'd really dig Nam. It's a permanent Independence Day.

— A genuine blockbuster. An *Apocalypse Now*.[190]

— Not later. Right here right now.

— Placard-men. Right here, right now. Not loud. Not loquacious. The first is the I GAVE MY LEGS man. In a wheelchair! F Train. His placard hanging from his neck by a string, with an exquisite drawing of the legs he lost in Vietnam—lower legs, below the knee, with feet—and his message: I GAVE MY LEGS FOR MY COUNTRY. In capital letters, just like your WHAT JUSTICE?

---

189 If you like, see Bernard d'Espagnat, *Reality and the Physicist: Knowledge, duration and the quantum world*. Original title: *Une incertaine réalité*, 'An uncertain reality.' A very important book for me. Ilya Prigogine, even more important! For example, *The End of Certainty. Time, chaos, and the new laws of nature*. It's all placard-man theory.

190 Sorry, I'm chasing images.

— In a wheelchair, in the subway. Strange. A strange image.
— Absolutely. A strange prisoner. I bet he stepped on a mine.
Theirs or ours, unfriendly or friendly, so to speak. Dig it, he's
holding out his cap, asking for money, I give him a quarter
myself. For thirty red cents, my token, I can ride the subway
forever. First placard-man. In a wheelchair. Why's he in the
subway? It doesn't make sense. Right under Rockefeller Center.
Shit, why not up there *at* Rockefeller Center? He could make
millions up there. What's his point? He didn't say a single word.
Do you think he's for or against the war?
— I see what you mean. It's hard to say.
— Placard-men. Placards and men. And placard-men. I met the
second placard-man on the B, under 86th Street, heading up
to Washington Heights. A lot to say for himself. In images, not
in words. On his placard he has a magnificently painted image
of a soldier in full dress uniform saluting the American flag, his
right hand on his heart. It's the Pledge of Allegiance, remember
me! We recited that motherfucker in school every cocksucking
morning.
— I cannot tell a lie. I didn't mind it at the time.
— You chopped it down, motherfucker!
— Right again, that was another time. Then, next time, the
fire. This time, right now—WHAT FIRE? What time?
— In the mind or on the roof. Fire. Now, dig this placard, two
captions, top and bottom. Capital letters. Above the Pledge,
SUPPORT THE TROOPS. Below, GOD IS ON OUR SIDE. A Bob
Dylan fan. The man says 'Vietnam veteran,' that's all. He's
asking for money. I gave him a penny, for old Guy Fawkes, who
tried to blow up the House of Lords.
— Holy shit, *what* whole picture? My fellow placard-man, you're
riling me up. I'm a veteran *against* the war.
— Right on. But some people against the war say support our
boys anyway. It sounds like a contradiction to me. Then again,
the *whole* picture is a *big* picture. The way up is the way down.

Remember me. The plot thickens. Plenty!

— What's next.

— You're musing already. I met the third placard-man under 86th again, heading downtown. Central Park West, good placard-man territory, I bet you frequent it yourself.

— I go where the wind blows, I don't need a weatherman.

— Where the wind blows in the subway, you mean. This Hadean region. The realm of shadows. Like Kafka's Hunter Gracchus. His ship has no rudder, and it is driven by the wind that blows in the nethermost regions of death.

— I think *death* is a strong word for the subway. An exaggeration.

— I joy that Death is this Democrat, Melville said. Not referring to LBJ, JFK, or FDR for that matter. Possibly to Andrew Jackson, who knows. Anyway, *transit system* is the right word. 86th Street again, serendipity. The man, cap in hand, says 'Vietnam veteran' just like the second one, but dig this placard. The image is of one solitary G.I. approaching a village: the G.I., a path through roughly sketched vegetation on both sides, and a village of huts. That's it. Presumably in Vietnam, but the drawing is so stereotyped that the village, the huts, could be just about anywhere. His caption is THE DEFENSE OF FREEDOM. You were there yourself, tell me what's on his mind. Why is he approaching the village? Do you think he's just stopping by to say something like I wish y'all gook women and children a good morning, how'r y'all doin' today?

— Witty motherfucker, we went to some great tea parties in those villages. DEFENSE OF FREEDOM tea parties. Tripping through the tea leaves. Enough bullshitting, who's next? Don't grudge me the story.

— Dig it, this one will make you feel right at home. Under the Village now, West 4th, the B heading uptown. I call him the placard-man Michelangelo, a main man, I wish you could see his placard. Blow your mind. All this, exquisitely painted, almost too much to take in. On the upper left, an army helicopter breathing smoke and fire. In the center, further down, not just one crudely drawn solitary G.I. approaching a village but a *wild bunch of individual G.I.s*—tiny but so vividly depicted, each one with his own body, his own face, the hand of a real artist. Incredible. I can see it in their eyes that they are *storming* the village, not 'approaching' it. On the upper right, a Vietnamese village—wow. Take a good look. Stereotyped? *This is Vietnam*, right here on the B Train. Not 'huts' but beautifully built little houses with thatched roofs and the lushest greenery in the world all around them, and the placard-artist shows us all this. Amazing, in a nutshell, a real Vietnamese village. I can imagine the children, the women, the old and infirm, huddled in corners in these homes, terrified. This placard-man has seen this. The image. The caption, at the bottom, tops it off: WE DESTROY THE VILLAGE IN ORDER TO SAVE IT. With a placard like this who needs a man! Anyway, he's *yelling* 'Vietnam veteran' like a hot dog vendor at Yankee Stadium. Waving his hat in people's faces.

— You're right, I wish I could see this for myself. *How I wish I'd never been there myself.* HueyCobra attack helicopter. Chinook copter to unload *us*, the most fucked people in the history of this country. G.I. Joes. Shit-eating bozos. What a picture. Believe me, I prefer the image to the reality.

— I keep wondering, is the placard-man Michelangelo a Vietnam veteran *for* or *against* the war. All I know for sure is that he's a truly great painter, and *he saw what he painted.*

— He was there. He saw it for himself.

— For or against the war?

— Shit. A damn good question. I was a gung-ho idiot myself in the beginning. A lot of grunts really *dig* that massacre shit. Can't tell the war from a high school football game.

— *Yelling* 'Vietnam veteran'—I swear, I couldn't tell if he was crying with joy or angry as hell.

— I wish I knew. Maybe we'll meet him again some day. Who's next?

— The fifth placard-man is the nightmare of the group. I wish I could just forget them both, the man *and* the placard. Scumbag and image. But nothing else these past two days has been *so motherfucking real*.

— A real scumbag and a real image. Speak!

— Credible or incredible, coming back from Coney Island, under West 4th again—a fucking *bat out of hell. A B-52 in the subway!*

— *Nooo shit!*

— It's beyond words, goddamit. A *picture* of My Lai is one thing, but, holy shit, this placard is *really real*. Can't describe it. The image is *graphic*, so goddam well drawn, the work of a born draftsman. Vivid black on white. A *B-52 bomber* seen from below, like a huge bat with outstretched wings, filling the whole breadth of the placard. A B-52 mass murderer. In the car *with me*, all the way to 34th Street. And the captions! At the top, KILL FOR PEACE, the Fugs' great anti-war song, my favorite. At the bottom, WELCOME FELLOW B-52 ENTHUSIAST! But the nightmare isn't *just* the placard, or the man, *it's what's happening in the car*. My fellow travelers. The sunless dead, this joyless region. *Maniac scumbags!* Going wild. Ecstasy. Unqualified devotion. True love. *Adoration*. For the placard, for the man. A scumbag chorus screaming Kill for Peace! All we needed was some BOMB HANOI! BOMB HANOI!

— I don't know what to say. Such a far cry from my placard, and my message.

— A B-52 in the subway. Transit system. A change of tune. Let me tell you about the sixth placard-man. The one I saw tonight, round midnight. Under 81st Street, heading downtown. A Winter Soldier! Possibly Scott Camil, we don't know. Here's the story. Dig it. The empty placard. The round circle of his shield. The car's packed, he's wriggling his way through. His placard is smaller than the others, and round. It's like a shield. From the distance I'd say an empty shield. Here he comes. He's not asking for money, a penny for the old Guy, no, he's saying END THE WAR to everyone in the car. Saying it softly. Not yelling. Asking to be heard. Here he is. He says END THE WAR to me. *To me!* I was right, there's no image on his shield, just two words, small letters, no caps, hand printed, very small. Like a stain on an empty mirror. Two words: *winter soldier*. Gone. He's gone. On to the next car.

— I wonder who he might be. He sounds too calm to be Camil. Restrained.

— Yes, calm. Soft spoken. Saying end the war to everyone in the subway.

— Easier said than done.

— *Una parola*, the Italians say. A word. These are the six placard-men I've met. Plus you, the seventh.

— It's like a chain.

— How do you mean?

— I mean, one leads to the other, all the way down the line. Linked. We're all connected.

— I don't think I see it. Connection. All Vietnam veterans, obviously. Is that what you mean?

— No, I mean a chain. A sequence. I don't think I can pin it down. What sequence? Not from veterans for to veterans against the war. As you tell it, only the B-52 man is definitely for, and the winter soldiers definitely against. I think the first four are placard-men because they're still trying to figure the war out. Figure themselves out. I think maybe we are all trying to decide what to do now. About ourselves. The war—we did what we did, we do what we can. Our problem is deciding what to do about ourselves. Now. Maybe that's the connection. If we could really understand that, there would be nothing left here for us to look for.

— Do you think you might know any of these guys?

— I might know the winter soldier, but we can't be sure he's a Detroit Winter Soldier. A lot of people feel they have to be winter soldiers now.

— The empty-placard-man was wearing green army fatigues, but, you're right, a lot of people wear green army fatigues these days. He might not even be a Vietnam veteran at all. Maybe he decided to go to prison. Maybe he's a war-hardened 4-F like me. Trying to decide what to do about *myself*.

— I don't actually know what the connection is, but I can see it. A dim glimmer.

— I keep on wondering how many placard-men there are, all together. Ten, a hundred, a thousand, ten-thousand. Or just the seven I've met.

— Beats me. I haven't even seen any of the six you saw.

— Never seen a single one. Don't know a single one. How did you guys become placard-men? How? Why? What do you really want down here in the subway?

— I can only speak for myself. A few weeks ago, a couple of months after the Statue of Liberty, I got riled up as all hell. Again. The war goes on, the bombing gets worse. This Vietnamization *shit*. The grunts coming home to roost. People start to forget about all the killing going on. In our name. By our hand. Nixon. Shit-server in Chief. Motherfucker. I got riled up and decided to make this placard, as you call it. To make a statement, as you said.

— In the subway?

— Why the hell not, you're right, the *transit system*. There's plenty of transit in the streets, but no system. The subway has a logic. Trains, cars, stops, starts, off, on, down, up, back, forth. A whole picture.

— Not just names, like the Brooklyn/Manhattan Bridge. No time either, no street time. Timeless, or just subway time. Logical time. One hand clapping. The subway must have a schedule but I'm sure nobody knows it.

— No, there's a reality down here you don't have in the streets. An uncertain reality, but there's some sort of completeness to it all. A parallel reality where everything's in flowing change.

— Bright shadows on dark water.[191] Flashings into the vast phenomenal world. Zen. The empty mirror. Nothing exists but momentarily in its present form and color. Before the rain stops we hear a bird. In Japan in the spring we eat cucumbers.[192]

— It's Zen to me. Transit. The hungry ghosts of Vietnam, haunting the jungle with their souls screaming. North Vietnamese soldiers lost on the fields of battle. Unburied.[193] Not unwept. The subway. Speak! A hearing. For flowing change you can't beat the subway. It has a logic you just can't find in the street.

— Shit, my man, you're telling me why I've been here in Hades myself for the past two days.

— B-52s, BUFFs, Big Ugly Flying Fucks. Whispering death. Called to serve. What worries me is that our Fearless Leaders will find a way to make them invisible. Some day they won't even whisper. Even now, people right here, in the streets and subways of New York, are starting not to notice all this bombing going on. As you said, the screeches are becoming sounds.

— Never thought of that. A strange image after all. Shit, after all this, if we look at the whole picture we still have no idea what the placard-men are, why they're here, in the subway, what they really want. What *you* want, *mon frère*. Many are riled up, but few are in the subway with placards.

— I want to read you something. Ever read Mark Twain?

— Sure. *Tow Sawyer. Huckleberry Finn.*

— Let me tell you this. Mark Twain was a *bad* motherfucker. Even his kid stuff isn't bad. But I want to read you a few lines from his War Prayer—these three pages I've had in my pocket

---

191 A parallel Venice, for example: the shadow-city reflected on the canals. The finite is ideal.

192 *Zen Mind*, p. 138.

193 See *The Sorrow of War. A Novel of North Vietnam*, written by the winter soldier Bao Ninh in 1991. New York: Riverhead Books, 1993. A superb book.

at all times, ever since I was in Nam. You have your placard-
men, I have my War Prayer.

— Fair enough.

— He wrote this in 1905, as a response to both the Spanish-
American War and the subsequent Philippine-American War.
Two old wars of ours in the defense of tyranny, as you put it,
quite rightly. No B-52s, this was before the Wright brothers—
two years after Kitty Hawk actually, their first innocent jaunt.
But old Uncle Sam was already approaching, and destroying,
plenty of villages. Here, there.

— Philippines, Pequot, My Lai. I know about the massacre
of the Moros. Nine hundred men, women, children, trapped
like rats in the bowl of an extinct volcano. Our hero General
Leonard Wood, scourge of the Apaches and the Cuban
Insurrectos. His brave soldiers raining their bullets down into
the crater until *not one single Moro was left alive.* Fearless
Leader Teddy Roosevelt commended him for the *brilliant feat of
arms.* For *upholding the honor of the American flag.*

— O say does that star-spangled banner yet wave. Mark Twain
spent the last ten years of his life fighting against the U.S.
occupation of the Philippines. He was a member of the Anti-
Imperialist League. Just listen to this Prayer. It wasn't published
until 1923. Twain—Uncle Sam Clemens to be exact, born in
Hannibal, Missouri in 1835, he died in 1910—said 'only dead
men can tell the truth in this world. It can be published after I
am dead.' So be it. Dead, buried. Not a hungry ghost. Listen.
Blind patriots and religious fanatics, praying for the suffering
and destruction of their enemies. 1905. Good old days. Bad old
days. *These* days, bad motherfucker. 'An aged stranger.' 'If you
would beseech a blessing upon yourself, beware! lest without
intent *you invoke a curse upon a neighbor.*' A war prayer.[194]

---

194 The italics are passages underlined by the seventh placard-man. J. William
Fulbright quotes just a little less than I do in *The Arrogance of Power*, pp. 137–138.
The Fulbright quote further down is on p. 138. I've always said Fulbright would have
made a great placard-man.

O Lord our Father, our young patriots, idols of our hearts,
go forth to battle—be Thou near them! With them—in
spirit—we also go forth from the sweet peace of our beloved
firesides to smite the foe. O Lord our God, help us to tear
their soldiers to bloody shreds with our shells; help us
to cover their smiling fields with the pale forms of their
patriotic dead; help us to drown the thunder of the guns
with the shrieks of their wounded, writhing in pain; help us
to lay waste their humble homes with a hurricane of fire;
help us to wring the hearts of their unoffending widows
with unavailing grief; help us to turn them out roofless with
their little children to wander unfriended the wastes of their
desolate land in rags and hunger and thirst, sports of the
sun flames of summer and the icy winds of winter, broken
in spirit, worn with travail, imploring Thee for the refuge
of the grave and denied it—for our sakes who adore Thee,
Lord, blast their hopes, blight their lives, protract their bitter
pilgrimage, make heavy their steps, water their way with
their tears, *stain the white snow with the blood of their
wounded feet!* We ask it, in the spirit of love, of Him Who is
the Source of Love, and Who is the ever-faithful refuge and
friend of all that are sore and beset and seek His aid with
humble and contrite hearts. Amen.

Ye have prayed it; if ye still desire it, speak! The messenger
of the Most High waits.

It was believed afterward that the man was a lunatic,
because there was no sense in what he said.

— It chills my blood.
— At Dewey Canyon, when we were trashing our medals on
the steps of the Capitol, one of my fellow veterans said an
anti-war prayer, a very short one. He said, I pray that time will

forgive me and my brothers for what we did. A decent prayer, but it cuts both ways. Three ways. Forgive us, the pawns in their game, for what we did. Forgive our country for what it did—and is doing, this minute—to Vietnam. And forgive our country for what it's done to us, who went, and fought, and killed. Millions. And were killed. For what it's done to everyone who refused to go, refused to fight, or fought right here in our streets. Who refuse to swallow lines like 'where America finally turned.' Vietnam is the beginning of the shitstorm, not the end. Unless we can turn things around. But how? Fulbright, back in 1966, talked about that fatal presumption, that overextension of power and mission, which has brought to ruin great nations in the past. The process has hardly begun, he said. I find this eminently questionable. A long story. 1966, hardly begun *in Vietnam*. But I agree with him when he says—six years ago— that Vietnam can be a crucial, a decisive turning-point—*for the worse*. He wrote, and this is prophetic: If the war goes on and expands, if that fatal process continues to accelerate until America becomes what she is not now and never has been—a seeker after unlimited power and empire, the leader of a global counter-revolution—then Vietnam will have had a mighty and tragic fallout indeed.

— Is not now and never has been?

— Dig it. I don't agree. But when I went to Nam in 1965, I thought so myself.

— This unfortunate war.

— That's an understatement. A decent prayer. It cuts three ways, but—*I pray that time will forgive.* I have a big problem with this. Time forgives? No, I don't buy it. Men, women, children can forgive, in and out of time. But time itself cannot forgive. I think this is why I'm a placard-man. The Statue of Liberty in distress, in the subway, with a message: WHAT JUSTICE? When I'm in the subway I'm outside time. Time does not forgive—not me, not my country, for what it's done to

Vietnam, and to me. War crimes! A War Prayer. I spent three years in Vietnam. Fighting. I don't know your story, your war-hardened 4-F, but I respect you. There are many ways to fight a war, and to fight against a war. Hard fights. Will we ever be able to forgive what our country has done to Vietnam? I don't know. But there's a forgiveness that's even harder. *They used us.* We, the people, the young people of this country. Used us. Grunts, blacks, workers, students. Will we ever be able to forgive our country for this? For making us the pawns in their game. Their game, ours, whose, we are the country, after all. Here, in the subway, under Brooklyn, not long before dawn, *we are the country.* Me, with my tired placard. You—ye gods know what you're doing here. The pawns, the sinew in their game. We, the young men, and women, our sisters, of this country, with our blood and flesh, our minds and hearts. What have they done to our spirits? Whatever we do now, and for the rest of our lives, will we ever be able to forgive? We won't quit, we'll do what we can, we'll decide to do something, I wish I knew what. Dance dance dance, fuck the Ghost Dance. We'll fight. We, *ourselves*, will fight. Somehow.

— Right here, right now, the war is not over. Minimum troops, maximum bombs. B-52s going wild. Blood blood blood, shedders and shed. Forgive the country that made us all victims? All of us together. Victims.

— Hard to say. Can we ever forgive? Forgiveness is the supreme sacrifice. Can we make it? It may also be the ultimate liberation. *Self*-liberation.

Screech. He's gone. What justice? Winter soldier doubled. Seventh placard-man. End of March, 1972. 36th Street. Brooklyn. Two long stretches together, in the realm of shadows. In logical time. Grand to Pacific, from neon madmen to an ocean on the other side of the world. Digging the names, Manhattan/Brooklyn Bridge, East/West River. Pacific to 36th. Long motherfucking stretches. Express, at all times. No stops.

Placard-men. He must live in Sunset Park. Beautiful! I'm sure it's not just a name. For once. I hope. The sunset *is there*. At sunset. Seventh placard-man. Fare thee well, my brother, what more can I say. I muse. Again. Dawn dawns when it dawns. Not just names. No name. No fortune. No name to come. And set my oar up, that I swung mid fellows. Facing the sunless dead and this joyless region.[195] You do not call winter the beginning of spring, nor summer the end of spring. Are the *screeches* back? No problem. Nothing special. Coltrane. Sheets of sound! Spirits rejoice! Dig it, bro. Alone again. No. A decision. What a decision is and what making a decision means. Never alone. Contradiction. Self-liberation. The might of the spirit.

---

195 Just once I'd like to quote a whole little piece of Canto I, just to give you an idea of what it's all about, and of where the poetics of The Empty Shield comes from. Here. Ezra Pound.

But thou, O King, I bid remember me, unwept, unburied,
Heap up mine arms, be tomb by sea-bord, and inscribed:
A man of no fortune, and with a name to come.
And set my oar up, that I swung mid fellows.
And Anticlea came, whom I beat off, and then Tiresias Theban,
Holding his golden wand, knew me, and spoke first:
A second time? why? man of ill star.
Facing the sunless dead and this joyless region?

Pound, Homer, Odyssey. In time. The Trojan War. An unfortunate war. Chasing my own images? I rest my case.

THE GATELESS GATE
a decision

Mu-mon-kan, literally 'no-gate-barrier,' is a Zen classic by the Chinese master Ekai, also called Mumon (1183–1260).[196] His introduction begins:

> Zen has no gates. The purpose of Buddha's words is to enlighten others. Therefore Zen should be gateless.
> Now, how does one pass through this gateless gate?

Years from now, the events—the people, the sky, the land, Vietnam, that war—it will all be unreal. Be unreal, seem unreal. Just names. History. Past events. Old pictures. That will be bad. This placard-man, the other six, the no others or ten-thousand others—the dead, three or four million, fifty thousand—they all say, together, no! It's flesh and blood real. Real fire. In the mind. On the roof. Wherever. Eteocles, the spy, Aeschylus, Benardete—another reality. Also real. Not exactly the same as the fields and the people of Vietnam, and *our* war in the defense of tyranny. Norman Morrison knows this. The placard-men know this. *Our* bombs know this. All the dead know this. What do the living know? Screech, sound, West End Line. Brooklyn, end of March, 1972. What. WHAT JUSTICE. What

---

196 See *Zen Flesh, Zen Bones*, pp. 89–131.

freedom. What necessity. Responsibility. Liberation.[197] Self-liberation. Forgiveness. The supreme sacrifice.

Yet another reality. The subway. Almost two full days now. Do I have any apples? Let's take a look. Yes! We have no bananas.[198] Two apples. I'm hungry. Suddenly I remember that I'm someone who has had rice. Thirsty. I have some water. I've had water, and I'm drinking some right now. Brooklyn. It's dark outside, but not for too much longer. I can feel it. A glimmer. Eat slowly. I've learned this. I won't devour this apple in three big bites. Slowly. One little bite at a time. Now, one apple. Another apple, later. Sooner or later. Night. Day. *The Hour of the Wolf*—I saw that film, at NYU, the Contemporary Cinema course. Tedious. Pathological. Bergman. Extremely gruesome. Demons. Insomnia. Real or imaginary strangers. Attacked by demons. Original title, extremely gruesome, *The Maneaters*. Who needs it. I nibble. The hour between night and dawn. When most people die, when sleep is deepest, when nightmares are most real. When the sleepless are haunted by their deepest fears. When ghosts and demons are most powerful. The hour of the wolf is also the hour when most children are born. Sez Bergman. *Compulsion*, sez Benardete. The night journey that ends, and begins, in shadow. Contradiction. The might of the spirit. Nibble nibble. It's time. Subway time. The sunless dead. Time. For what a decision is and what making a decision means. Not now-or-never-time. My time. Our time. Let's take it. Take time. Along the watchtower. Night time. Brooklyn night. Not for long. The emptiness singularity! There's absolutely no one in the car. Myself. What self. Maybe this B Train is *full of people* heading for Coney

197 Saigon was liberated on April 30, 1975, the end of the American War. Liberation. Self-liberation. I was here in Venice, it was the greatest celebration in my 45 years here. Greater than the two World Cups our football team won. Everyone took to the streets—women and men of all ages, children, truly great old Venetian ladies, boys diving off the Rialto Bridge until dawn. The Great Spring Victory. A cry of liberation. 198 I adore this song. No, it's not the Marx Brothers, Karl Marx, or Woody Allen. It was composed for a Broadway show in 1922, and first sung by Eddie Cantor. 'Yes! We have no bananas.' Dig the lyrics, bro. They don't sing songs like this anymore.

Island in the hour before dawn. Full, every single car, except this one. Empty. It's possible. The transit system is a strange system. A strange image and strange prisoners, as Plato put it. A mouthful. Forgiveness. The supreme sacrifice. I need to think about this. It's a new idea for me. I think I understand Norman Morrison's sacrifice. His wife explained it so well. A message. 'Norman wanted to tell people this is how it feels to be burned, as we are burning people—men, women, civilians—every day. Individual lives have been changed by this. I think it has been worth it.' The supreme sacrifice. Forgiveness, says the seventh placard-man. Message—this is the placard-man. Messages, from I GAVE MY LEGS to WHAT JUSTICE? But the seventh *placard* says nothing about forgiving this country. Land of the free. Home of the brave. Not only for the atrocities perpetrated in Vietnam, but for the atrocity of *using us* to perpetrate them. The atrocity of playing their game with our lives. *With my life*, that's for sure. Fork fork fork, I have a fork. Shit-shoveling motherfucking fork. Shoved up my ass. Life, a cucumber. One day it's in your hand, the next day it's up your ass.[199] Before the rain stops we hear a bird. Transiency. Transit. Control. 'To give your sheep or cow a large, spacious meadow is the way to control him.'[200] No, 'forgiveness is the supreme sacrifice' is not on the placard. WHAT JUSTICE? is on the placard. That's the message. The *placard's* message. But the last *man* speaks, to me, about forgiveness. The supreme sacrifice. The man's message. But, aren't they inseparable, placard and man? Not two, not one. The whole picture. The B Train is making its way through this Line of serried screeches like an icebreaker through the polar floes. East/West River. At the Poles it's not just names. At the North Pole everything is south, and at the

---

199 A friend of mine in 1968, a young Black Panther, from Chicago, 18 years old like me, told me this. He wasn't wrong.
200 *Zen Mind*, p. 32. 'So it is with people: first let them do what they want, and watch them. This is the best policy.' I have tried to do this with my placard-men. 'The best way to control people is to encourage them to be mischievous.' Suzuki-roshi. In Japan in the spring we eat cucumbers. Ali! Ali! Float like a butterfly, sting like a bee.

South Pole it's all north. Everywhere you look. However you look at it. Even if you stand on your head. This emptiness singularity! The placard-men. Coltrane! Sheets of sound! The *whole* picture. The seven placard-men are a whole picture. *A true concept of infinity*. The existence, possibly, of ten or ten-thousand others does not change this. Not a single whit, jot, or iota. But also the placard-and-man is a whole picture. The not-two-not-one placard and man. The separation of the inseparable. Abstraction. I may not *know* the man's tale but he has it. He knows it. Serendipity. Time. Place. The last man *told* me his tale. Forgiveness. The supreme sacrifice. His whole picture. Placard and man. But each placard-man is a whole picture, even if I don't see it. Each one has a tale and chases his tail, like a cat. A true infinity. Doubled. Difficulty and the double. Tale and tail. Placard and man, placards and men, the placard-men all together. *Compulsion*, says Benardete—he's about to say it now, at last. The Note! The Note! Where's the Note! I only have two paragraphs to go. A long perfectly linear one. Then the last. End of the tale. Tip of the tail. Short, Hitchcockian, nonlinear. A decision. Compulsion. The prisoner's deed. Wait! I raise my hands and spread out all my fingers. The courts in the attics. A question. A fair question. Are the placard-men free or necessary? Or both, or neither, and/or in-between? A question of naming and directing shadows.[201] Did I, myself, 'direct' the placard-men? 'Control' them, like the Roshi's sheep or cows? Wait. Did I 'determine' their order and what/who they are, placards and men? Myself. Did I *decide for* them? 'Compel' them? Dare you suggest that I *invented* them! Myself. How dare you! Benardete may be right, about being chained inhabitants of Plato's cave, but the prisoners don't *invent* the shadows on the wall, no! They're all real. Puppeteers, puppets, prisoners. Prisoners watching the shadows of the puppeteers'

---

201 As Artaud put it, *Theater and its Double*, p. 12: 'For the theater as for culture, it remains a question of naming and directing shadows; and the theater, not confined to a fixed language and form, not only destroys false shadows but prepares the way for a new generation of shadows, around which assembles the true spectacle of life.'

puppets. The gall! I invented the shadows! That wasn't Artaud's point at all. Or Hegel's either. The placard-men appeared in the cars, and I was in the cars where they appeared. Eteocles *sets* the shields/placards, *and men*, placard-men, one over against the other, *badly infinitely*. 'The infinite set *over against* the finite, in a relation in which they are as qualitatively distinct others, is to be called the *bad infinite*.' BUT I DON'T. They just *appear*. Logically. Improbably. Probably. Fine! Cockroaches leap from chandeliers. I raise my hands again, I'm getting riled up. All these false accusations. Eteocles never even *dreams* of the whole picture. He just does it. Badly. Compulsion, as Benardete puts it. Possibly. He *makes* a decision but *never asks* what a decision is and what making a decision means. As Aeschylus, Benardete, and I do. I, myself, *decide for* the placard-men in this subway, end of March, 1972? How dare you! I'm just a 21-year-old NYU almost-graduated student, with a goddam fork. It's true, *I did play Eteocles and the spy with the seventh placard-man*. This is true. Difficulty and the double. Clear reports. The seventh, Winter Soldier, among other things, *himself* a double of the sixth, the empty-placard man, winter soldier, in some sense. A triple. I, myself, am, in a sense of some sort, a winter soldier. That's why I'm here. Did I invent myself! How dare you. FBI! Are you out to 'neutralize' the last iota of sense, meaning, and, possibly, sanity in the subway? Here and now. Such a dumb blankness, full of meaning, in a wide landscape of snows. Semenovsky Square. Right now. When? What is this thing called time. The hour of the wolf. History. End of March, 1972. OK, I admit it, I did play Eteocles and the spy with the seventh placard-man. Speak! Serendipity. I got my chance. Speak! I spoke. To him. Clear reports. I spoke, he spoke, we spoke. I scream, you scream. We all scream. Pie à la mode. A big scoop please. Invented him, ye gods. Placard and man. They came right into this emptiness singularity at Grand Street, on their own. What self. Appeared. They disappeared in Sunset Park. Dawn dawns. When. It dawns. I told him the tale of the six placards. Tale of which he is, truly infinitely, the tail. A tail chasing its tale, I'd say. Tale of the six placards, and placard-men, if not—no, if not of the men. Themselves. They're placard-men! What self? Only the seventh, the last, abstracted the man and the placard. Inseparable. Separated. Leaving the placard-man intact. Perfectly, completely, absolutely. Intact. I'm not George Washington *myself*, but I tell you no lies. A chain, he said. The prisoner's deed. First Gate. Eye of night. Night falls upon his eyes. Geneva, 1954, the 17th parallel. In two years, free elections for y'all gook motherfuckers, and fuck you all. Second gate. A naked hippy claiming that the divine fire of Zeus is nothing compared to hippy fire. The task of building a new government on a perilous frontier, as JFK put it, eloquently. Ye gods, he likened Zeus' lightnings and thunderbolts to the sun's warm rays at noontide. Eteocles accuses him of pure invention. Raving. *Buona notte*. Forget it. Who's next. Third Gate. Watch out, Eteocles, it's Eteo*clus!* Deeper shit, but, not up to your neck yet. A hoplite, with a ladder. Shit—as LBJ put it—we can handle this. Let's get our hands dirty. Just a little. No problem. Not too big. We'll wipe out the hoplite on the shield and the hoplite on the ground, in one fell swoop. The image, definitely. Wiped out. Done for. On the ground. You bet! Why the hell not. Just do it. *Una parola*, as the Italians say. However. The plot thickens. A penny for the old Guy. Fourth Gate. My fellow Americans, as Lyndon liked to drawl it, Texanly.[202] I'll grant you this. The situation is a little more serious than we imagined. McNamara, and his Band, best and brightest, tell me that the placards are about to boil over. People, it seems, are setting themselves on fire under his windows. Typhon *on their shield*, Father of all Monsters. No problem, sez Eteocles, we have Zeus

---

202 How can you not love a man who just happened to be named LBJ—Lyndon Baines Johnson—born in Stonewall, Texas—who therefore renamed his wife 'Lady Bird' Johnson, named his daughters Lynda Bird Johnson and Luci Baines Johnson, and his dog Little Beagle Johnson. Sure, all just names. LBJs. What's in a name. But, you have to hand it to him, he took names seriously. My president. Why the hell not. Roses have thorns.

on our shield. Over half a *million* of our troops in Vietnam, in a strenuous effort to exterminate these goddam brutes. Creeps. Apocalypse now and fuck you all, redux. They *say*. But, who *thinks?* Is any *thinking* going on? How about 'the decision to consider thinking as such'? How about a goldfish splashing joyfully in the middle of a desert. At this point, possibly, thinking has been prohibited. Like spitting in the subway. Have a cigar! Smoke smoke smoke.[203] Don't grudge me the story. Fifth Gate. Ye gods what a melee. The gang's all here. The Ghost of Christmas Past. The more the merrier. We have the Sphinx, in person and politically. We have the major, serious, no-shit philosophical question of *being and seeming*. We have Nixon, we have Kissinger, what more could we want. Vietnamization! Bombing galore! We have 'the beautiful Parthenopaeus, whose savage spirit belies his name.' Even though, by the way, as the spy did not note, and Benardete did not note, but as I now note, his name does not mean *virgin* (*parthénos*) but *seemingly virginal*. Another double! The question of seeming versus being is *itself* doubled, and no one notes it. But it's a great story. Overexposure. On a pinhead. Parthenopaeus was the son of Atalanta by either her husband Hippomenes, or by Meleager, or by Ares, depending, of course, on the source. His mother left him—*exposed* him—on Mount Parthenius ('virginal') to keep from *exposing* the fact that she *herself* was no longer virgin, hence the name 'seemingly-virginal.' Naturally, he was rescued by a shepherd. Sixth Gate, the empty shield. Not seeming *áristos* but being, whatever in the world this means. Personally. Politically. The war within. If only we could understand it all our troubles wouldn't only *seem* so far away, they would actually *be* so far away. Possibly. As

---

203 No reference to *Havana* cigars. Right now we are beyond partisans and partisan politics. Trump is president-elect. Castro died last week. Muhammad Ali, Fidel Castro—with Dave Leahy, I've lost the whole trio of my ideal readers. Their sense of humor! How I miss them.

the Beatles might have put it. Yesterday. A shadow hanging over me. Yesterday, today, and tomorrow, as Sofia Loren did in fact put it, memorably. Troubles. It looks as though they're here to stay. Who knows. In any event, a winter soldier. Two winter soldiers, in some sense. END THE WAR. WHAT JUSTICE? Oral. Written. Speech. Phenomena. West End Line. Hour of the Wolf. Supreme sacrifice. Forgiveness. The Note! The Note! WHERE'S THE NOTE? That's what I should put on my placard. Or, possibly, WHAT NOTE? Or how about WHY THE NOTE? Shit, a good caption. But what would my image be. No idea. A drawing of BILLY IN THE DARBIES,[204] possibly. But I can't draw—can't draw it, can't draw shit. Can't draw, period. If I draw a cat it looks like a dog. My tree looks like a house. My head, like a horse's ass. What's more, the scene is imaginary—doubly, triply, the more the merrier imaginary. Billy before dawn, waiting for his hanging. Just a poem. A rude utterance from another foretopman gifted with an artless poetic temperament, as some sailors are, Melville notes. On a placard? Ye gods, the second Note. Where. Have all the flowers. Gone. When. Will they. Ever. Learn. The system of logic. Is. The realm of shadows. Chasing our own images. That's what it's all about. Young girls have picked them. Every one. The Note, Aeschylus, Dylan, Melville, these two days in the subway. Memphis Blues. Again. Being a citizen of this country I have an image of this country. Not just one image, but many. Images. I can't catch them. Any of them. That's why I'm here. FORK FORK FORK, DEAD HORSE OF A FORK. That's what I should put on my placard: a fork and a dead horse. A fork beating a dead horse. A dead horse beating a fork. A decision. Thinking. Imagining. An idea just pops into my head. Fine. No problem. The problem is that then I start to chase it. Like a cat chasing her tail. OK. But, then, this idea I'm chasing

---

204 This is the title of the 'artless ballad' at the end of *Billy Budd*. April 19, 1891. A last word. I think it is supremely great poetry. We'll meet it again: the last verses of the ballad are the last lines on this Empty Shield. By the way, 'darbies' is an archaic word for handcuffs.

leads me to another idea. And I chase it. From one idea, another. Another. Another again. Free association. How free? What association. A chain. New Jersey Turnpike. Counting the cars. Look for America.[205] Placards. Images. Men. Reality? What reality. An uncertain reality. A necessary reality? Clear reports. Separate and inseparable. Not placards and men but *placard-men*. There's no other way of putting it. What decision. A chain. The prisoner's deed! Wait. Bless my soul. The B has stopped. Completely. I'm in the Coney Island station. An emptiness singularity. Surfin' Safari.[206] Ride the wave, baby! I've ridden it to the end of its line.

Where have all the flowers gone. The answer to the riddle. Who are all these people, I muse. In the illusory emptiness of the Coney Island station. My fellow human beings. *Hypocrites lecteurs! Mes semblables!* Brothers, sisters, 'all' these people— well, a dozen or two maybe, but who's counting. Yes! We have no bananas. Some heading for the exit, heading home. Coney Islanders. Saturday night, Sunday morning. Great film. Albert Finney. Black-and-white. Fun finders. Found fun. Others headed for the 8 tracks and 4 island platforms—ye gods, early risers. Morning seekers. I take it back, *these* people are not my *semblables* at all, getting up before dawn to *go somewhere*. On the subway. At dawn I go to bed. Myself. Normally. What self. Do placard-men get up at dawn, in Coney Island, breakfast on Coney Island hot dogs, and then head for the subway for a day of placard-manning? I don't know. I didn't ask. Is a placard-man about to appear right now. Right here. One of the first six I've met—the seventh definitely not, he just went to bed—or, possibly, a new one. I'm happy with my seven, like the Seven Gates of Thebes, but, who's counting. Zen should be gateless. It's not like Che's two, three, many Vietnams.[207] One, ten, or

---

205 Simon & Garfunkel, 'America,' 1968.
206 Beach Boys, 1962.
207 'How close and bright would the future appear if two, three, many Vietnams flowered on the face of the globe, with their quota of death and immense tragedies, with their daily heroism, with their repeated blows against imperialism, obliging it

ten-thousand placard-men, that's not what counts. No, what counts is the whole picture. The true concept of infinity. I'm heading for the toilet. I haven't taken a piss in a dog's age. I drank all my water, all that conversation made me thirsty. What a Lucky Jim, I conversed with the seventh placard-man. Plenty. Conversation. From Grand Street to Sunset Park. I'm refilling my water bottle, it's empty. I still have an apple. It, too, has its fate. If indeed we are Russian serfs to Fate, as Melville put it, somewhere.[208] Pasteboard masks. But, I wonder, who are the puppeteers of fate? A good question for Benardete. Everything's so calm here in the station It's a good feeling. Let's see what the 8 tracks and 4 island platforms have to say for themselves. I mosey on over. Now, how does one pass through this gateless gate? On the F Train, of course. No question about it. The way up, the way down. I'm on the F. In the car. The path on which there is no coming and no going. Silence. Illusory emptiness. Sit. Still. Suddenly, the doors close. Action! Traveling. The F is on the move. Like in the old days, the threes in the morning. The Tao. Acorns. Monkeys. Do we chase our images with monkey mind or with big mind? A big question. A monkey question. A gateless gate, possibly. Taking both sides at once. Get ready for a lot of stops. Screeches, sounds. Elevated, as far as Ditmas Avenue. They have pretty names on the F. Neptune Avenue. Kings Highway. Bay Parkway. Prospect Park. Park Slope. Avenue I. What self! Avenue X! I love this one. X marks the spot. Great! There's another guy in the car. No more emptiness singularity. An early riser. Strange creatures. Stirring. I wonder if he had a hot dog for breakfast. A flat gray light outside the car. More night than day, but

---

to disperse its forces under the lash of the growing hate of the people of the world!'
See 'Vietnam and the World Struggle for Freedom,' Che's last public message 'from somewhere in the world' (possibly Bolivia), in *Che Guevara Speaks*, New York: Grove Press, 1967, p. 159. Che was referring not to finite numbers but to the true concept of infinity.
208 *Pierre*, Book VII, V: 'If indeed our actions are all foreordained, and we are Russian serfs to Fate; if invisible devils do titter at us when we most nobly strive; if Life be a cheating dream... and all things are allowable and unpunishable to man...'

dawn is not far off. What's on my mind. THINKING THINKING THINKING. FORK FORK FORK. Oedipus just *came* to the fork, *appeared* at the fork. *He never thought about it.* Never thought about the fork. Speak then to me! Fork! Who *gave me* this fork. What Chinese menu *stuck me* with this fork. This unHegelian fixed idea. It's what he calls *begrifflos*. Conceptless. It's not in the Logic. A decision. In the Logic, at the beginning, we have the *decision* to consider thinking as such. At the end, free release: 'this *next decision* of the pure idea to determine itself as external idea,' 'as the externality of space and time.' No forks here. What fork? *What do the placard-men decide?* They decide to be placard-men! Message-messengers. They *are* what a decision is and what making a decision means. Are, and seem to be. A true concept of infinity. Eteocles!!! You're the problem. You *have* the problem and you *are* the problem. Do your placard-men constitute a true or a bad infinity? This is *the* question for you. And *the* question for the *Septem*, since *you are the Septem.* And you never even ask it! You never say to yourself, Eteocles! What is a decision and what does making a decision mean? No! You *miserably* set one placard-man over against the other, unHegelianly. Badly infinitely. Tyrant versus tyrant. You mutually suicide yourself, *and* you pollute the City. The Note! The Note! At last. It's time for the Hitchcockian unhappy ending of the second Note. *Compulsion*. High time. The Ladies. Liberty, Justice. One vanishes, the other is a whore. Tis a pity. *Pazienza*, as the Italians put it. Blue Note, Blue Monk. Albert Ayler. He played at Coltrane's funeral in 1967. In November 1970 he went missing for three weeks, then they found his body floating in the East River, a presumed suicide, possibly, or murdered, not likely, who knows. Some say he took the Statue of Liberty ferry and jumped off as it neared Liberty Island. Depressed. They say he smashed one of his saxophones over his television set. 'I don't have any freedom,' possibly. Suicided, possibly. The answer to the riddle. Here it is, again, the second Note. 'Eteocles' Interpretations of

the Shields.' Where am I. *The* question of the *Septem*. What/
Who is Ares? *The* the question. That has exercised so much
recent scholarship. Does Eteocles *decide* his own *fate*, or is
his fate determined by the curse of Oedipus? So, Benardete.
As we have seen. What's *more*, as I, *myself*, have seen, in
nuts and bolts, *the* the the question: He decides to go *himself*
to the Seventh Gate for his reciprocal suicide, polluting the
City. *Why? How* does he come to make this bad, despicable,
disgraceful, and unfortunate decision? The chain. The prisoner's
deed. How free and how necessary is his miserable *decision*,
which he makes *himself*. How free and how necessary will
my own miserable decision be? Which I am about to make.
Myself. With the help of these Notes. Especially the second
Note. On a pinhead, that's the point. Freedom and necessity
are separate and inseparable. Being-is-nothing never goes
away. The point of the *Septem*, as Benardete sees it, *is that
chasing images can lead to a river of shit*, as the Fugs put it.
That's the point. Especially when there's an *evil* motherfucker
of a decision to be made. Be careful! Temporarily like Eteocles
can mean permanently like Eteocles. A good point. A decision.
Eteocles' interpretations of the shields. Interpretations. A chain
of images. Playing. A play. Theater and its Double. Eteocles
and the spy. The empty shield. 'Amphiaraus ... testifies to
the truth of Eteocles' interpretations.' Fair enough. 'Gods as
the representatives of men impose a *compulsion* on them.'
Compulsion? 'Signs have become *fates*.' What/Who are fates?
(Asks Melville. *Ask* Melville.) I've been convinced, all along,
that the Note is all about Eteocles' *decision*. Chasing images.
But *compulsion* is not the same—at all—as the inseparability of
freedom and necessity. The Lady Vanishes. Let's see. Let's take
a good look. At Benardete's crack in the Liberty Bell. Where am
I. Where am I going.

The next-to-last paragraph of the second Note. Glimmering.
A dim glimmer, more dawn than night. Old mole! A worthy

pioneer![209] A Ghost! Of Hamlet's father. 'What?' 'I am thy
father's spirit.' Benardete. The specter of your broom closet!
The next-to-last paragraph. Dig it. Be cool. Let's take our time.

Eteocles and the Argive champions between them have
reestablished the presence of the gods that Eteocles
had at the start ordered the Chorus to forsake; but their
reappearance is no longer solely as statues. They are
now vividly present as defenders and attackers (Zeus and
Typhon), who only have to move and speak to become the
principals in the war. It is the work of Polyneices' shield.
His emblem is twofold: a woman soberly leads an armed
warrior, and she claims to be Dikê, as the letters say: 'I
shall bring back this man from exile and he shall occupy his
ancestral city and home.' For the first time we have a god
who speaks and moves. Eteocles had to attribute motion
and speech to the Sphinx, which by itself needed its bearer
to approach the city; but now the scene is so complete in
itself that 'this man' refers at once to Polyneices and his
double on the shield. The phrase is not ambiguous as it was
on Parthenopaeus' shield, whose interpretation depended on
the interpreter. Here it means the same person regardless
of whether the image or the imaged is meant. On Tydeus'
shield there was no man, on Capaneus' a man who could
not be Capaneus, but on Eteoclus' shield Eteoclus himself
was shown, though he still remained distinct from the
image. On Hippomedon's shield in turn, a god was shown,
whose relation to the bearer had to be supplied; and on
Parthenopaeus' shield, though its meaning is unmistakable,
Parthenopaeus himself does not appear—only the image
and not the image-bearer belongs to Thebes; but now
god and man come together in a single image, and their
relation to the city is completely spelled out. The ultimate
manifestation of the gods among men is the *enérgeia*, the

---

209 *Hamlet*, I, iii.

being-at-work, of the anthropomorphic goddess Justice. And Eteocles accepts it as it shows itself. He does not have to discover or bring out a latent meaning in it. 'If the daughter of Zeus, the maiden Dikê,' he says, 'were present in his deeds and wits, then perhaps this [what the letters say] would be.' He does not distinguish between the image of Dikê and Dikê herself, but only claims that if Dikê backs Polyneices, she is falsely named; but that of course does not differ from Polyneices' claim. It is no longer two gods of different principles but one and the same god whom both sides lay claim to. The dual origin of the city is nothing but the duality of justice and the city, whose coincidence Eteocles affirms, Polyneices denies, and Antigone questions: 'now one way and now another the city approves the path of justice.' It is this duality that Antigone calls 'last of the gods.'

SirNoSir, no rain on *this* parade. No smoke, no mirrors. A clear report. Screech! Sheets of sound! X marks the spot. Avenue X. Stirring creatures. Early risers, probably. Improbably, all-nighters. Coney-Island-fun-finders staggering home to ye gods know where. Borough Park, Rivington Street, Times Square, Trump Tower.[210] Aeschylus and Benardete. Spy versus spy. Completely spelled out. A Great Lady. Deeds and wits. The prisoner's deed. I think this is the clearest paragraph in the Note. In both Notes. Dawn dawns when it dawns. The Prophet berates Polyneices, a little before dawn: What justice shall quench a mother's tears. Polluting the City. Brothers. The Curse. Their mother is also their father's mother. Not a Great Lady but a Grand Mother. Identity and the Double. *The ambiguity was not deliberate.* A fork. Oedipus appeared at *a fork*. He never *thought* about it. He decided *nothing*. Being is

---

210 *Sorry*, this is out of line. We have no right to pull our presidents' legs. George Washington and his cherry tree, OK, but Trump Tower didn't open until 1983. Fifty-eight stories in the Naked City. Way off the time-line. What is this thing called time, as Nina Simone so unforgettably sang it.

nothing. What-so-ever. Logic. No-*one*, no-*body*, decided that
being is nothing. No-mind. Big mind. It's just part of the whole.
Realm of shadows. Buddha mind. The might of the spirit.
Beginning, middle, end of the decision to consider thinking
as such. System of logic. Defend the City! What City. What
about the City. A big question, a monkey question. Cradle of
democracy. Jeeps rolling through the streets. Night and day.
And night. Day. Islands. The sea blue crystal. Island prisons.
Cut crystal. Special police. *Now one way and now another the
city approves the path of justice.* A *big* line in the *Septem*.
A *Plato* line, actually. The *Republic*. Battle Hymn. Mine eyes.
Trampling out the vintage. A monkey line. A big monkey line
these days, end of March, 1972. 137 Rivington Street, unlocked
building (!!!), railroad flat, third floor, on the back, the door on
the left. The whole picture: 4 floors, 4 landings, on each floor
2 front flats, parallel and identical, and 2 back flats, parallel
and identical. Mirror images. Double-8. 16 identical parallel
mirror-image flats. 8 front flats on the Rivington Street side,
8 back flats (mine, for example) on the elementary school
playground side. Wait! This reminds me of something. The
Coney Island station! 4 island platforms, 8 tracks, 16 rails,
parallel identical. Same deal. It never occurred to me. Until
this very moment. Maybe they were designed by the same
person. History. Chasing images. Swear! Swear! said the
Ghost. I swear. It never occurred to me. *Geist*. Spirit. Acorns.
A big monkey line. For me, *myself*, my line. And it is *non*linear.
End of the linear line. Logic, ethics, politics. Benardete. Fate,
history, confusion. Possibly. Here comes the last paragraph,
and a short one to boot. *Gran finale*. He's about to get
suddenly, strangely, Hitchcockianly nonlinear *himself*. Why the
hell not. The physical world—nature—is nonlinear. Cats are
nonlinear. Hegel's logic is nonlinear. Ye gods know what ethics
and politics are. Linear? No way. Like a madman with a razor?
Quite possibly. This unfortunate war. Wait! A question. I raise

my hand. Seventh Gate. A clear report. I ask you, Benardete, what ever happened to the spy? He just stepped out? There's no sign of him. Whatsoever. None. Signs have become fates, you say, but, *who* are the puppeteers of fate? Invisible devils, tittering? Interpretations, but, interpretations of *what? Of the clear reports.* Without the spy there's nothing to interpret. Polyneices' shield. Eteocles accepts it *as it shows itself*. To whom? To the spy, who else! Or perhaps he read about it in the *New York Times*, a truly, utterly, absolutely reliable source. Unlike the spy. At dawn. No, believe me, it's the spy, *it is always the spy*. Seventh Gate. The spy makes the most chilling of his reports, to Eteocles, and you don't note it in the Note, Benardete. 'Your own, your very brother. Hear how he *curses* the *city* and what *fate* he invokes on her.'[211] The spy reports. Big words. Curse. City. Fate. This is what *the spy* reports to Eteocles, who is about to *make the decision* of his life. And death. *Himself*, to the Seventh Gate. Personally. Politically. The spy goes on and on, chillingly. *The spy says* that Polyneices 'prays that once his feet are set upon the walls, once he is proclaimed conqueror of this land, once he has cried paean of triumph in its overthrow, he may then close in fight with you and killing may find his death beside your corpse.' Strong stuff. Famous last words. Read it in the *Times?* Hell no. *Who knows what the spy may be inventing this time.* In fact, just this once the spy ends his report with a dab of modesty. Just this once he covers his ass, so to speak. Somewhat. 'These are the *signs*. But you *yourself* determine whom to send. You shall not find a fault in my report: but you determine how to steer the state.' What, me, grievous distortion? Who's *Mad*. Who's on first. This actually reminds me of some politicians we have today, I can't quite remember which ones. 'Mr. President, that's how I see it, but, of course, it's up to you. You decide.' 'Thanks a bunch, Mr. Secretary. The buck stops here. It's right here in my pocket.' 'He shouts and calls the gods of his race and of his fatherland

---

211 I'm following Grene on this, he's done a good job.

to witness his prayers—a very violent Polyneices.' *This* is what the spy reports to Eteocles. Who immediately decides, *himself*, to go to the Seventh Gate. Himself. At dawn. Mac! Henry! Bring me my greaves. It's the *spy's* report. He *might* have phrased it differently. He might have said, 'Dig it, chief, the river's wide, the shit's deep, let's have a short beer.' Lured to safety. My favorite clipping! *Offer of Beer Cools Off Prospective Suicide.* But, that was in the *Post*. Eteocles is a King, he reads the *Times*. Truly, utterly, absolutely reliable. Authoritative. The newspaper of record. Reciprocal suicide. By all means! Be my guest. First door on the left. *The* door on the left. Third floor. On the back, on the elementary school playground side. What a melee at 8 in the morning. But I sleep fine. After all, why dream? With all this reality, why dream?

SirYesSir, come to think of it I have a few more things to say about this next-to-last paragraph. With its 'pacific' end to the war of images. WHAT JUSTICE? The play—the war—suddenly shifts from logic to politics, shadow to substance, image to reality. WHOSE JUSTICE? *What ever happened to the war of images?* What, on this mortal coil, ever happened to Eteocles' decision? The prisoner's deed. Benardete. A single image: duality and the city. Eteocles! All of a sudden, *l'état c'est toi!* What ever happened to your *decision?* The hero of the play. Tragedy, or farce. All of a sudden, Eteocles sez: Dikê is just what the King-Captain-President *does*. What, me decide? as Alfred E. Neuman might well have put it. Well. Decide? Hell no, *we must do*, as Sudden Vere did in fact put it. Badly. Do what? *Do justice!* A Great Lady. No question. Hugs and kisses. I wonder who's Kissinger now. Who's on first. *Do justice* to the City. Pollute it. *Do justice*. To what! To the City. Just as we *do justice* to a T-bone steak? Absolutely. Same deal. My fellow Americans, let us *do justice* to our Thanksgiving turkey. Stuffed. Delicious. Devoured. To the last morsel. The last drop of old blood, and fire. Let's *do justice* to a *big* slice of Mom's apple pie. À la mode. We scream. Devouring. Every last crumb, savage, gook. Creep. Yummy. It crawled into my hand, honest. Goddam brutes. Fug you all. Polyneices: Dikê is what I, screwed by my own brother, unjustly exiled, *say* it is. *Do* justice to the City. Pollute it. Defend the City! Last of the gods. In the end it's only the Chorus—the virgins/women/maidens/whatevers, previously rebuked—who cling to the image of a just decision. What have we come to. The maidens. Virgins, possibly. The in-betweens. Where are we. *Who* says 'now one way and now another the city approves the path of justice'? Benardete makes it *seem* like it's Antigone, the grievously distorted sister. But it's not true! It's the Chorus, their big dirge, at the very end of the play. The maidens/virgins. Even Antigone is upstaged. Outdone. Ye gods. Upstaging Antigone. Isn't this a strange, *Realpolitik* conclusion to a play about *chasing images*. About *Eteocles*. And the spy. Tyrant versus tyrant. *Chasing*, like a cat, her tail, their tale. Eteocles, with a little help from the spy. Much more than a little. Badly infinitely chasing his own images. All the way, linearly or nonlinearly, to his doom. A play *about his decision.* Decide. Decided for. How? Why? Who? What? (Never mind *when*. In the subway we're on logical time.) Free? Necessary? Responsible? Irresponsible? All of the above. Not a single one of the above. *Ché pasa.* What's up. What's down. Done for. End of the line, and I don't mean Coney Island. Or Washington Heights. Or Jamaica, and I don't mean the one south of Cuba. At least, in *some* sense, my *trains* are linear. This transit system. But the placard-men aren't. Stop, screech, sheets of sound, start again, keep going, end of the line, way up, way down. What could be simpler. The placard-men! Flesh, blood, mind, spirit. Complexity. The 'direct reverse,' as Melville put it, of simple. 'Of a saint.' Of mysterious. Of Vere's shrouded privacy. Of Claggart's discourse on being and seeming. *Although it was a matter of surviving on the battlefield, the samurai fought his fight in the zendo.* We quote, Aeschylus: Now one way and now another the city approves

the path of justice. Is this the best Aeschylus, *himself*, can do?
What self. Suddenly: exit the logic of shadow and image, to
enter the city of substance and power. Is this the message of
the empty shield? I don't think so. No. Decisively. Possibly. I
have my doubts. Does Benardete? Master of Ancient Political
Theory. Possible, impossible. A good/bad question. 'Duality
and the city.' Next-to-last paragraph of his second Note. Clues,
foreshadowing a surprise ending, a Hitchcockian reversal of
the reversal. Foreshadowed. Foretold. Foretelling. I have my
doubts. Broom closets. *Bring the war home!* I cherish my hate.
Compulsion—no, literally, not Hitchcock.[212] *Frantic*, that's ol'
Hitch. *The Lady Vanishes*. Hitch. What justice? Lady Liberty
shoots her Muse an amusing question. Mortal coil. Planet Earth.
Satori. The Brooklyn light is awakening. This has been a long
trip. 'The sea-reach of the Thames stretched before us like the
beginning of an interminable waterway. In the offing the sea
and the sky were welded together without a joint, and in the
luminous space the tanned sails of the barges drifting up with
the tide seemed to stand still in red clusters of canvas sharply
peaked, with gleams of varnished spirits.' How I wish I could
write like that. No, this one isn't Melville. It's Conrad, again.
At sunset. Exterminate all the brutes. The fork! Fuck my fork?
GAM/bomb/exile. A question. *Una parola*. It's not quite so easy.
But I'm getting there. I'll fuck it yet. Look! Outside. Inside.
Glimmering. Billy! Brooklyn Blues. Again. 'White jumper and
white duck trousers, each more or less soiled, dimly glimmered
in the obscure light of the bay like a patch of discolored snow
in early April lingering at some upland cave's black mouth.'
Blues, whites, who's counting. What Note. What am I noting.
Or notting, 'the absolute power,' the negative. Or knotting,
logical knots, knotting the not. A net of logical categories
knotted here and there, as Hegel notes, not 'the ten-thousand
things.' Science. The prisoner's deed. Aeschylus. The question
that has exercised so much recent scholarship. I'm exhausted

---

212 It's Richard Fleisher, unquestionably Hitchcockian.

now. Traveling. End of the line, this line, whatever line. Linear.
Nonlinear. Subway. No joke. Two days. Unbroken. Welcome to
the end of Benardete's line. The second Note. Tell it like it is.
Tell it like it is? What it is. What is it. Tell it. Fate. History. Logic.
It's just a note. What's this? An empty shield. A note on a note.
A note, itself. My note, myself, what self, on what war. This war.
Unfortunately. Against Vietnam. Against the possibility for the
people of this world to live in *peace and freedom*, as Eldridge
Cleaver put it, at his party.[213] Two, three, many Vietnams.
Flowered. Young girls have picked them. Every one. To live
in the possibility of not being decided for by the government
and the power elite of the United States of America. *Now
or never.* The point. Why I am here. Not just now, but *ever*.
The root and the branch. A stand. What stand. What pathetic
motherfucking stand. Who am I kidding. No, I'm not kidding.
Not kidding *myself*. Or you. A stand, my decision. This is why I
am here. *Alas*, a fork. *Eat with your hands*, motherfucker. Fuck
forks. Chopsticks! But I love turkey. Except on Thanksgiving.
Stuffing happens. Even speaking their name was prohibited.
Last paragraph of the second Note. Let's reverse the reversal,
double the double, and give tragedy its due. If possible. I can't
get ahead of myself this time. Welcome to the end of the line.
Speak, Benardete.

> The action in these seven pairs of speeches consists in the
> interaction between the effect each shield has on Eteocles'
> interpretation and the effect each interpretation of Eteocles
> has on the succeeding shield. Eteocles' interpretations are
> so evocative that they transform the discrete series of: the
> first shield, its interpretation, and the Theban champion:

---

213 It was a pretty wild party, if anyone—I doubt it—is still interested. Cleaver was—
somewhere, in some sense—the Peace and Freedom party candidate for president
in 1968. I was too young (18) to vote for him, but—as I mentioned—I heard his
speech that time, at NYU, Washington Square, his NIXON IS A MOTHERFUCKER
HUMPHREY IS A MOTHERFUCKER, *tout court* and vice versa, time and again, that's
all she wrote.

the second shield, its interpretation, and Theban champion: and so on, into an unbroken succession of: the first shield and hence its interpretation and hence Theban champion and hence the next shield and hence the next interpretation and hence the next Theban champion, and so on. Eteocles becomes so gripped by the images he hears about and so much enters into their spirit that he seems capable of summoning the next image through his interpretation of the previous image. He no sooner opposes Zeus to Typhon than Parthenopaeus challenges Zeus. Eteocles is a citizen of Plato's cave, whose chained inhabitants compete for prizes in divining the sequence of shadows cast on the wall. It is the consistency of image and interpretation when put together and in order that constitutes the compulsion in Eteocles' choice. His serendipity proves to be his fate.

Hold my peace. Speak my piece. Our peace. His piece. Easy piece. If you think I'll take this lying down you haven't been traveling with me for the past two days. F Train, B Train, a quick jaunt on the D, the B again, the F again, THE END. Screeches, sounds. Placard-men. Sheets of sound! Blue Monk! Coltrane! Has this whole journey been about *mis*reading this Note? Not at all. It's about fucking a fork and making a decision. Making? Yes and no. Both, neither. *And* in-between. Entropy. Thermodynamics. Order to disorder. Running out of gas. The creation of the universe. The birth of physics. The theory of nothing. Of being is nothing. Quantum void. Traveling. Original emptiness of the mind. Logic. *Non*linear. Hegel's science of logic. Making, being made. Decide, decided for. Separate and inseparable. Justice. Great Lady. Blind Justice. Impartial. Takes no parts. Whose side? *You can't win people over if they're already on your side. Im*possible. Whole picture. Blind-*folded*, not *blinded*. A fundamental, and decisive, distinction. What makes it? Let's hold our horses. Control our sheep and cows. Benardete! What's up. What's down. What you're saying here, *possibly*, is that 'these seven pairs of speeches,' in Thebes, *transform a simple series of coincidental images into a true infinity in the realm of shadows.* Hegelianly speaking. That could be one way of looking at it. Yes? You agree, possibly. The subway is not Thebes. Logic is not history. Fate! What in the world is fate? It's not logic. No. History, maybe. An unbroken succession of images and interpretations. The history of Thebes. The history of a Curse. The history of a War God. Consistency. Hiroshima, Korea, Vietnam. Is this what you mean by fate? As in the lines 'When fate was following in our tracks/ like a madman with a razor in his hand.' Battle hymn of the subway. No? That's not what you mean? What! You mean *compulsion?* The Great Ladies. You've bartered Lady Liberty for Lady Justice? Possibly. Who's Kissing-'er now, I wonder. Hitchcock. *The Lady Vanishes.* Reverse the reversal. Just when we were all expecting Justice to vanish, no! It's Lady Liberty. Vanished. Compulsion. Fucked the separation and inseparability of freedom and necessity. Pawns in their game. Wait, Ben, let's back up a moment. (May I call you Ben?) A couple of questions. I raise my hand. The same old questions. Wasn't this a play—a tragedy—about Eteocles' decision to go *himself* to the Seventh Gate? His tragically *bad* decision. Bad for *him*, himself, you say. But, after all, Thebes won the war! Ye gods, the dominoes have been effaced. California hasn't turned red. No misery, terror, death. On our shores. In our subways. But the Curse, Ben! Kid us not! They won the war but lost the curse—I mean, did *not lose* the curse, *the curse abides.*[214] The 17th parallel, Ben! Practically no more of our boys in Vietnam,[215] but, the Curse! Abides? A polite way of putting it.

214 As *The Big Lebowski* later put it, in a manner of speaking, dude.
215 By the way, on March 29, 1973, the last of 'our boys' left Vietnam. After the Lottery there weren't so many anyway. Just a zillion tons of 'our bombs.' The 'Kill for Peace' bombing just about ended that tale. The old old story. 44 years later. 'Last of the gods,' as Antigone did put it, herself, during the dirge, referring to Eris, the Great Lady of Strife. Dissension. Dissent. 'The highest form of patriotism.'

A big-time major understatement, politically speaking. As I, *myself*, see it. My decision. With all this 'consistency of image and interpretation' haven't you *rubbed out* Eteocles' *decision?* Mafia sì, Mafia no. Frank Costello. No, not Abbott's partner, Lou. On, possibly, first. No, Frank took it from The Chin. From the hip. No? No no no. *Your* 'interpretation of Eteocles' interpretation of the shields' is perfectly linear, you say. It's *my* interpretation of *your* 'interpretation of Eteocles' interpretation of the shields' that is chaotically nonlinear. You say. That's the problem. You say? Just a moment. Wait. Second of the 'couple of questions.' The spy? I spy. An amusing question. Seven pairs of speeches. Shield and interpretation. *Eteocles'* interpretation. Of what? *Of what the spy tells him.* The point of the pinhead. Fuck the Postmodern, or pre- or post- Postmodern. It's always the spy. *It's what we see.*[216] We see what the spy tells us. Peter Arnett. A grievous distortion. Clear reports. By all means, and meanings. Let's destroy the village! Let's save it! Aeschylus had it all in his pen, or in whatever it was he wrote his tragedies with. Dig it. That's it. Ben! Shield and interpretation. The spy! Not *even* of what the spy *sees*, but of his poetic-license-to-kill *interpretation* of what he sees. 'These seven pairs of speeches'—Ben, it's the spy. First, if not last. OK, I did play the spy and Eteocles with the seventh placard-man. I—spy—spoke first, in fact. Speak! I said. *To myself. My* serendipity. I spoke. To him. The *whole* picture. Or a sliver of it, wholly. And here you are, Ben, seven *pairs* of speeches. Who's Eteocles talking to? His mother? His aunt? His cousin? His cat? A fair question. It's the spy! What ever happened to the spy? The source. A *source* who is, *himself*, a terrifyingly bad infinity of sources. A genuine motherfucking *resource*. A shaft. A mine. A *New York Times* multiplied by ten thousand. Dig it. Deep shit. Dig it. Fuck it. This *unfortunate* war.

---

216 See, if you like, the film *Manhunter*. (No! not Bergman's *Maneater*.) It's highly educational, I learned a lot. 'Reflections, mirrors, images.' Iron Butterfly. *Seeing.* 'What we see.'

Along the watchtower. Barefoot servants. 'His serendipity proves to be his fate.' Ye gods, Ben, a *beautiful* line. Unforgettable. Compelling. Eteocles' decision. The spy. Chasing images. *My* decision. Dawn dawns. Screech, sound, Avenue I. What self. Brooklyn glimmers, faintly. The placard-men, Ben! 'The realm of shadows.' An *image* in the Science of Logic. A rare bird. Hegel wasn't big on images. Eteocles *so gripped by the images. He hears about. So much enters into their spirit.* Absolutely, sweet Marie. This is what it's all about. The *Septem*. The second Note has been perfectly linear. To this point. Of the pinhead. 'Eteocles' interpretations of the shields.' Alas, *my* interpretation of 'Eteocles' interpretations of the shields' has *not* been linear. The spy, the fucker. Yes, no, inside, out, it's been downright *non*linear. Why? Because the placard-men are nonlinear. They are actual figures in the realm of shadows. Inseparable. Placards and men. All I do is watch them, when they appear. I *spy*. No compulsion. They are absolutely free to appear, or not, to me. But, in themselves, they are not free to exist or not, *they do exist.* All together. A true concept of infinity. A decision? They decide to be, and seem, placard-men. Fate, Ben? I don't see it. They have a history. A serendipity, possibly. But, fate? What is this thing called fate? Nina Simone doesn't sing about this. From fork to fate, led by the nose into the wilderness. Possibly. Gripped by images. The second Note, Ben. Beautiful. Linear. Hitchcockian. Clues. Pairs of speeches. Suspense. Gripping. A Note *about* being gripped by images. The End. This is the end, my only friend, the end. The end, Ben, and what do you do? *You grip us with an image.* An image in words, not on a placard or a shield, but, absolutely, an image. A surprising image, a surprise ending, which overwhelms the reality you've gripped us with in the Note. A reversal. Hitch the *non*linear, Ben! The Note turned upside down. Inside out. The sudden way. From a chain of images to *chained inhabitants*. Open the roof to the rain! Welcome to Plato's Cave. What an end, my friend. The prisoner's deed. The compulsion in Eteocles' decision. Forks have become fates. How did you do it, Ben? Who saw it coming. We spent a whole semester in a two-semester course, Ancient Political Theory, doing most—somewhat most—of the *first* book of Plato's *Republic*. The beginning! You started at the beginning, and practically finished there too. A long trip on a short line. Nonlinearly. Feedback loops. Zigzags. I'll never forget it. 18th Avenue. Still elevated. *That* was Hitchcock! Suspense. Reversal. Inside out. What's the *Republic* about? It's a long and winding effort to answer the question: What is justice? Socrates agrees to discuss it with his friends, but, right off the bat, he asks WHAT JUSTICE? What does justice *mean?* We need to define it before we can discuss it. Easier said than done. *Una parola.* So, at the very beginning, Cephalus, the old man, says, well, we might define it as truthfulness and repayment of anything that we have received. Socrates ripostes, well, for example, let's say we were given weapons by a friend, of sound mind, who then went mad and reclaimed them. So Cephalus immediately reverses himself, admitting it would not be just to give them back. Then our young friend Thrasymachus suggests— rather forcefully—that justice is nothing other than what is advantageous to the stronger. Might makes right, to put it bluntly. *Chi comanda fa legge*, the Italians say. A position with a long and disreputable history. Socrates, of course, does not take this lying down. And so it goes. Ye gods, muses Socrates, this is going to be a long trip. The ten books of Plato's *Republic*. And what do you do, Ben, at the end of your short Note? Do you begin at the beginning, by any chance? Hell no. Suddenly you *leap* straight to the end. (Relatively speaking. It's Book VII.) The *chained inhabitants*. Compulsion. A *beautiful*, absolutely memorable line: His serendipity proves to be his fate. The End. A strange image and strange prisoners. So, Ben, this is what a decision is and what making a decision means.

This is Eteocles' tragedy. Aeschylus' tragedy. My tragedy. The placard-men. A stain on an empty mirror. The prisoner's deed. A decision! Swiftly! Propelled by these huge black wings I am already a white speck on the horizon. A beautiful sight. At dawn. The end. A glimmering speck on the horizon.

A wildcat did growl. In his shroud. Underground again. Adios elevation. Hades. Sunless dead. Weather Underground. Whether. Or not. Or both. Which way the wind blows. Show and tell. Church Avenue. Borough Park. The *sub*way. The true path. No coming and no going. A patch of discolored snow. *What a decision is and what making a decision means.* An apple? Maybe. Maybe not. The puppeteers of fate. A haunch. A hunch. A curse. GAM/bomb/exile. Defend the City! I've been thinking about something Suzuki-roshi said. The original emptiness of the mind. 'It is absolutely necessary for everyone to believe in nothing. But I do not mean voidness. There is something, but that something is something that is always prepared for taking some particular form, *and it has some rules, or theory, or truth in its activity.* This is called Buddha nature, or Buddha himself.'[217] This is Hegel's realm of shadows, the world of simple essentialities freed from all sensuous concreteness. Some rules, or theory, or truth. Thinking as such. The concept, the activity of the concept. In Japan in the spring we eat cucumbers. In New York they're up our asses all year round. Possibly. Probably. It depends. On you, on us. Possibly. The power elite! Misery, terror, death. A democrat. Cockroaches, dinosaurs, chandeliers. True concept of infinity. In Buddha nature, in the activity of the concept, *there is no compulsion.* This is the only thing I'm sure of. Traipsing through their food. Freedom and necessity are separate *and* inseparable. Hades. The sunless dead. The subway. A decision. Defend the City! Neighbors. Travelers. Ends. *Taking* responsibility. From *out* that shadow?[218] Leaving Hades behind? Going where. Coming.

217 *Zen Mind*, p. 117.
218 'And my soul from out that shadow that lies floating on the floor/ Shall be

444

Into our own. Going. Out of our minds. True path. System of
logic. Gateless gate. Creatures stirring. Believe it or not there
are quite a few of us in the car. Hegel! Where's my *Science of
Logic*. Have no fear, it's coming back out of my bag. Here! Now!
F Train, end of March, 1972. A curse. This unfortunate war.
That's what it's all about. Young girls have picked them. Every
one. Norman Morrison. Being, seeming. Saigon, The Burning
Monk, 1963, photo by Malcolm Browne. Take a look. I may not
know where I'm going but I do know where I am. Where, if not
who. What self! *Taking* responsibility. Suddenly, I'm enjoying
the ride. Too bad I won't be seeing the Manhattan/Brooklyn
Bridge again, this is the F. My train. Rutgers Tube, under the
East/West River. *High* over the Gowanus Canal. Infinite murk.
I wonder if they'll have chic eateries and 5-star hotels along
this canal some day. Possibly. Who knows. Let's take it easy.
Chill out. Keep an eye on the nether darkness. Traveling. Let's
fuck a fork and make a decision. Why the hell not. Wait—*fuck*
a fork and *make* a decision? *Wasn't the point of the decision a
prong of the fork?* Let's get back to the beginning. This is the
end. The *sub*way. The night journey. That ends in shadow. Ends
and begins. Begins and ends. The true path. No coming. No
going. In his shroud. Semenovsky Square. A mock execution.
Revolutionaries! Free release.[219]

A wildcat. Growl. A beginning. *Sub*way. Science of Logic.
The decision to consider thinking as such. With What Must the
Science Begin? The Empty Shield. Right now! Let's begin this
tale. Placard-men. A fork. What! *Begin* now? After all this. Isn't
it time for *The End?* (What is this thing called time?) What!
Am I, myself, about to pull a Joseph K./THE END on myself?
'Am I to show now that not even a year's trial has taught me
anything?'[220] Are people to say of me after I am gone that at

---

lifted—nevermore!' Quoth Edgar Allan Poe, *The Raven*.
219 End of the Logic: 'The idea *freely releases* itself, absolutely certain of itself
and internally at rest.' No, the prisoners in Semenovsky Square were not exactly
'internally at rest,' or absolutely certain of themselves either. They were much too
busy confusing history and fate.
220 Let's say a three-years' trial, possibly. Three stabs at an Empty Shield: June–

the beginning of my case I wanted to finish it, and at the end of it I wanted to begin it again?'[221] No, I don't think so. Suddenly, for some unknown reason, I feel happy about my End. This trip. Tip of this tail, end of a tale. The sunless dead. Down to the ship. A decision. What a decision is and what making a decision means. True infinity. Bad infinity. The cockroach. The Jersey commuter. A good laugh. *Right now.* Screech. Sound. Fort Hamilton Parkway. I *did* sing 'River of Shit' in the subway! Under the tip-top Upper West Side. OK, I sang real soft. Sang it to myself, I guess. But I did it! Fuck the fork. Sing sing sing. I can't sing shit. But I did! I can sing just about as well as I can draw BILLY IN THE DARBIES. No problem. No worry. Just do it. Surviving on the battlefield. The samurai. The zendo. A question. *Have I been chasing the placard-men or have they been chasing me?* Who knows. The mirror is empty. Shen-hui, the Zen placard-man.

> A bright mirror is set up on a high stand; its illumination reaches the ten-thousand things, and they are all reflected in it. The [old] masters were wont to consider this phenomenon most wonderful. But as far as my school is concerned it is not to be considered wonderful. Why? As to this bright mirror, its illumination reaches the ten-thousand things, and these ten-thousand things are *not* reflected in it. This is what I would declare to be most wonderful. Why? The Tathagata discriminates all things with non-discriminating Prajna. If he has any discriminating mind, *do you think he could discriminate all these things?*

Satori. Just got it. Get it? Direct experience. Beyond words. Like Tuli. Kill for peace. Christmas bombing. War within. Winter

---

221 Franz Kafka, *The Trial*, translated by Willa and Edwin Muir, New York: Schocken Books, 1968, p. 226. Last chapter: THE END.

soldier. Shall we *discriminate* each and every inch and iota of these Lines, F, B, D, one and all, the more the merrier. Hell no! It's the system, stupid! Transit system. Whole picture. Placards and men. 'The basic teaching of Buddhism is the teaching of transiency.' The mirror reflects everything coming before it unconsciously, with no-mind. Whatever in the world this means. Free release! We, too, have weapons. We have mind, and we have no-mind. What more do we want. Beyond words. Whatever in the world this *means*. Let's see. Let's ask Hegel. Bad infinity. True concept of infinity. Ye goddam Puritans, your Cities on Hills, here and now *let's begin this tale*. At last. Again! Here, in the subway. Here, on Rivington Street. Here, with my cat.[222] 'This next decision.' Wait! Whether I've been chasing the placard-men or they've been chasing me *makes absolutely no difference*. Whatsoever. This is what it's like to be a cat. The secret. She chases her tail and/because her tail chases her. Obviously a question of freedom and necessity. Never mind responsibility. A tangle. Look! The chaser is, and seems to be, the chased. Like a schnapps to a beer, as the Danes used to say.[223] Chaser and chased. Chasing tails. ART ART, it's an ART. I have something to say. Again. I raise my hands and spread out all my fingers. Again. Listen! Suddenly, it's Mark Rothko, *my painter*.[224] A tail to tell. He said, at the end of his life, 'the dark is always at the top.' But I'm thinking of this, from 1947: 'I do not believe that there was ever a question of being abstract or representational. It is really a matter of ending this silence and solitude, of breathing and stretching one's arms again.'[225] This is not Hegelian in the least. Just as Kafka is never Hegelian, in the least. BUT—Rothko and Kafka are truly infinite. Never mind cockroaches tormenting dinosaurs and leaping from chandeliers. Never mind commuters taking trips

---

222 In Venice. Right now.
223 In the 1970s, in my direct experience.
224 Years later, Wolfango Intelisano became *my painter*, my brother, my friend. The Empty Shield is dedicated to his struggle and to his memory.
225 'The Romantics Were Prompted,' from *Possibilities* 1 (Winter 1947/48).

around the world. Hegel alone can *tell* us, somewhat, what truly infinite *means*. By *means* I mean *does*. The prisoner's deed. A decision. What is to be done. The mourners carried chains at Dostoyevsky's funeral, lest we forget that he had been a prisoner and an exile. Fuck forks. I call Rothko's last paintings the 'horizon paintings.' Possibly a misnomer. No more rectangles, magically interacting, truly infinitely. Unity and separation that are themselves inseparable, as Hegel put it. No. The prisoner's deed. Now, at the end, the canvas is broken in half, cut in two, horizontally. Disconnected. Eyeless night above, dawnless dawn (gray, or blue) below. A decision? No-mind. Somehow—inexplicably—an *absolutely* true concept of infinity. Beyond intellect, beyond words. Nothing to think about, nothing to decide. Possibly, *beyond thinking as such*. The *next* decision. Free release. What did I, *myself*, say a few stops ago? (A few hundred, a few thousand, who's counting.) The blank screen. To empty. To see *the whole picture,* because *'thinking as such'* is not a picture of anything, or is at best a picture of nothing, of being is nothing. What! Seeing the whole picture, or painting myself a bad picture of the whole. Swear! Swear! said the Ghost. Old mole! Worthy pioneer! Rothko! Horizon paintings. In one fell swoop, his personal and pictorial negation of freedom and necessity *together*. Logically. Hegelianly. Absolute. Magic. Death. An extremely gruesome suicide, two years ago. Rothko, without greaves. No, it wasn't 'signs have become fates.' Not in the least. It was THE END. Period. ART. (Life? What is this thing called life, as Nina Simone didn't sing it.) In his studio uptown, on East 69th Street. It wasn't 'reciprocal suicide' either, as Hegel put it. Eteocles and Polyneices. Mark Rothko did not pollute the city. But he saddened the city. Saddened me. I've felt much more alone on Rivington Street since then. Felt pain. I see Allen Ginsberg pretty often, while I'm walking to or from school. He's always wandering around wearing these high rubber boots. I wonder what's on his mind.[226] 'The dark is always at the top,' Rothko said. Propelled by these huge black wings I am already a white speck on the horizon. In the late 50s Rothko's studio was in an old YMCA building at 222 Bowery, between Prince and Spring, just a few blocks due west of my railroad flat. Sometimes, when I walk to school, instead of heading due north to Houston I go due west to the Bowery, to walk past that building and think about Rothko. A neighbor. A traveler. An end. Art. Abstraction. Separation of the inseparable. Endlessly. Breathing and stretching his arms again.

A decision. What's my point? Have I been pulling my own leg, *myself*, again. The point. Eteocles! *Have you been chasing your placard-men or have they been chasing you?* Good question. You're no cat. No, you're a King, and a Tyrant. Self-sufficient. Just like your pal, the spy. Pals, tyrants, and tyrant *versus* tyrant. Alfred E. Neuman. Democracy! Defend the City! A brother-fucker. A curse-shoveler. A new frontier. An old frontier. Any motherfucking frontier. A frontiersman. So to speak. Beyond words. This is Greek Tragedy. *The true concept of infinity. Your* placard-men. *This* is the point. If there is one. If not a point, how about an edge? An edge isn't half bad. It may be a point in time. But, logically, no, not in time. Timeless. A logical point, *in logical time.* So to speak. *Sub*way. Screech. Sound. Prospect Park. Eteocles! You *have* the problem and you *are* the problem. Logic. The problem of infinity. *Bad infinity.* A double-edged problem. Two-sided, like a reversible jacket. On one side, if Hegel says it's bad it must be *bad.* On the other, from start to finish *it never goes away.* Just like being-is-nothing. Same deal. (Never mind the East-

---

226 Why these rubber boots on the Lower East Side? No idea. Born in Newark, died in the East Village in 1997. 'The best minds of my generation destroyed by madness, starving hysterical naked.' In flashes, great poetry. I met him here in Venice a short time before his death. He was hawking a rehashed book, at a wild price—a benefit, at a plush Venetian event. Frankly, we met in the toilet—serendipity—pissing side by side. As Zen as you like it. That's the fact. We spoke for a minute. Nothing special. I didn't ask him about the rubber boots he always wore, that time. No point. They'd have been more useful in Venice.

West River, that's another deal.) No, it's not like a *bad cold*. Shit, you say, I'll get over it in a week, or possibly in seven days. No, I think it's like what the bros (Hegelianly) call a *bad* motherfucker. A *good* ol' guy. It's not the true concept of infinity, but it does have logic *on its side*. Intellect! The Elder Statesman of the history of the world, logically speaking. The understanding. 'The most astonishing and mightiest of powers, or rather the absolute power.' The power to separate. Badly infinitely. The power of the negative. No, not a bad cold. The power of *death*. A democrat, said Melville, joyfully. Emperors and kings, beggars and paupers, together. *Big* business. The prisoner's deed. Wait. Let's start. Again. Sunless dead. Down to the ship. Fork. Prongs. GAM/bomb/exile. Take your pick. Eteocles!!! I want to say this. *Your mirror is not empty*. Hell no. You've been playing with your placard-men like a cat with mice—with a *chain* of mice. *Chained mice*, apparently. An ugly image, ugly prisoners. Compulsion? Perhaps, in the end, Benardete isn't all wrong. No question, you've been playing with the spy. Or—direct reverse!—the spy has been playing with you. Or both, or neither. So much the worse. The more the merrier. Fuck you both. Be that as it may, all I know for sure is that your mirror is not empty. In itself. And *because you did nothing to empty it*. Such as, for example, by asking what a decision is and what making a decision means. *King* of Thebes. *Yourself* to the Seventh Gate. Great. You *set* image versus image and never even *dream* of the whole picture. You, your spy, your *great imaginations*. Tyrannically—Defend the City!—you *set* prong versus prong, and never even *imagine* the fork. The City! Yes, we have no spaghetti! JUST EAT IT, with your prongs. Without a fork! An unfortunate war. Eteocles! You decide without deciding. Tyrant! You can't tell a decision from a horse's ass. *This is tyranny, not compulsion*. Disaster, not fate. History? Could be. Or catastrophe. Who knows. A King! No sense of responsibility. It never occurs to you to ask—yourself— *what are all these prongs doing here without a fork?* It never crosses your mind. These goddam clear reports. These seven gates. These ten-thousand bright-mirror things. Prong after prong. Prong *versus* prong. *Bring me my greaves!* Great! You pull a rabbit out of a hat and call it a decision. From tragedy to farce. Chasing your placard-men, your placard-men chasing you. Freedom, necessity, logic. What decision! *Bad* infinity. Shadows! A catless cat with a chain of chained mice. Bad news. Be my guest, take your shadows for a walk. Like dogs. On a leash. *Wie ein Hund!*[227] What does *Aeschylus* have to say about this!

The infinite *set over against* the finite in a relation in which they are as qualitatively distinct others. The fork as qualitatively distinct from its prongs. Ye gods, this is *not good*. Not good for you, Eteocles. Not good for the City. *Screeech*. Park Slope. What a pretty name. A lot worse than a *bad* cold. Good only for Aeschylus and his tragedy. Very good! A great tragedy. I told you bad infinity wasn't all bad. Entangled in unreconciled, unresolved, absolute contradictions. Even worse than not good. *The fork has vanished.* If this isn't Hitchcock, what is. Logically speaking, a tragedy. No, not the might of the spirit—positing, enduring, overcoming contradiction. In yourself. No. I'd call it a mess. A *pasticcio*, as the Italians put it. A huge Alberto Sordi dish of spaghetti—without a fork![228] Serious business. Unfit for a King. A mess! Let's start again. One hand clapping. The hour is getting late. Or early. East/West River. For example: 'bad infinity' is not just big numbers but also 'I have a fork.' Chinese menu. 'Where three roads cross' is bad infinity, even if the numbers are far from astronomical. Eteocles! You don't see the *transit system.* You hear the ten-thousand screeches—the points—but brutally ignore the line. A King! Defend the City! Prongs? *Where's your fork!* Starry Vere!

---

227 Joseph K., last line of *The Trial.* '*Like a dog!* he said; it was as if the shame of it must outlive him.'

228 *With* a fork, see the film *Un americano a Roma,* 1954.

We must *do*. Clear reports. Decide! About a forkless tangled unreconciled unresolved absolute dish of prongs. A fork may be bad infinity but it's not all bad. It's *a chance* to bring your thoughts together. Eteocles! You never ask what a decision is and what making a decision means. BUT I DO. What, me worry? Shit, I worry plenty. Did you mistake me for Alfred E. Neuman. A 21-year-old not-even-graduated NYU student. At least I'm 4-F, fuck you all! I put my little life on the line for it. Hunger. Determination. Decision.[229] My political autobiography. 'Being is nothing' I can handle, as best I can. It never goes away. Neither does bad infinity, it's not like a bad cold. Lasts a week, or seven days. What's more, a bad cold is not *necessary* but bad infinity is. True infinity *needs* bad infinity. The concept *needs* abstraction. 'In the *necessity* of the concept.' Freedom *means nothing* without necessity. Is nothing. Seems nothing. Bad infinity is not a dead end, it's a *live* end. The bad infinity of screech, stop, start again, gives us the terms of a contradiction that cries out for completion. A contradiction that *needs* to be developed until its ultimate consequences are exposed in true infinity. Needs. Necessity. Suddenly, a bright curtain of rain. Out of nowhere. And now, dazzling sunlight. At the end of the Logic Hegel refers to the progressive expansion of the content of thought as an enrichment that proceeds 'in the *necessity* of the concept.' But on the same page he calls the concept the *supremely free*.[230] Fork, prongs, infinity. A decision. The plot is thick. Relation. Non-relation. Different differences. *True* logical differing is a differing not *from another* but *from itself*. Self-reference. Self-differing. It's not the differing of the understanding—a cat is not a dog. No, it's the cat's logical *self*-differing. Her chasing her tail. Abstraction. Separation of the inseparable.

---

229 Thanks to that decision I am still here, alive, today. In Venice.
230 To be precise, for Hegel the *concept* is *free*; the *idea*—the concept in its full self-realization—is the *supremely free*.

Cracked requiem. One hand clapping. Time for my decision.
What is this thing called time. The true concept of infinity. *Bad*
infinity. Holding fast to the *opposition* of being and nothing.
Their absolute separation, self-subsistence, unrelatedness.
Non-relation. This is not Rothko's 'horizon paintings.'
Disconnectedness is not unrelatedness. No! Rothko *gives us
the fork as such,* somehow without giving us the prongs. Pure
abstraction. Absolute abstraction. Contradiction. Not the power
of the intellect but the might of the spirit.

> In the pinioned figure, arrived at the yard-end, to the
> wonder of all no motion was apparent, none save that
> created by the slow roll of the hull in moderate weather, so
> majestic in a great ship ponderously cannoned.

His death—his gruesome suicide—unfortunately. This
unfortunate war. Logical unrest, the source of movement and
the heart of the dialectic—the *contradiction* that impels the
something out beyond itself. Eteocles and his spy. The spy and
his Eteocles. Logical tyrants. Thebes! Its chain. Compulsion.
The chained inhabitants. A chain of chained mice. A catless
cat. The dazzle. The placards have nothing to do with the men.
A chain. Taking the shadows for a walk. Pairs of speeches. A
King, a spy. Whatever they cook up. *Images*. Seven prongs
badly infinite. Forkless. Boiling over. The placard *unrelated* to
the man. The fork *unrelated* to the prongs. Now what?

> The hull, deliberately recovering from the periodic roll to
> leeward, was just regaining an even keel when the last
> signal, a preconcerted dumb one, was given.

Eteocles *makes* his decision. So-called. *Makes*, in a manner of
speaking. He goes, *himself*, to the Seventh Gate. Decides to
go. *Does*. Goes. A blind-patriot decision. Or compulsive. Can

Ben be right, but in the wrong way? I wish I knew. *What if it's no decision at all.* Two days ago I moseyed on over to the Delancey Street station. 'I have a fork.' Has it vanished? Look! *The Gowanus Canal.* Crept right up on me, like a cat. Suddenly. Like a bright curtain of rain. At dawn. A dazzle. The light! The sudden way. Soaring! High, above the infinite murk. Look! To the east. To the heart of Brooklyn.

> At the same moment it chanced that the vapory fleece hanging low in the East was shot through with a soft glory as of the fleece of the Lamb of God seen in mystical vision, and simultaneously therewith, watched by the wedged mass of upturned faces, Billy ascended; and ascending, took the full rose of dawn.

The heart of a Brooklyn I don't even know except from the subway. Dawn dawns. Already gone. A moment. In logical time. Transit system. Hades. Realm of shadows. Sunless dead. *Screech away.* Carroll Street. *Sub*way. This joyless region. A whitish dazzle of fog.[231] The prisoner's deed. A decision. Don't grudge me the story.

We've come this far. How far? Who knows. THE DECISION GODDAMIT, WHAT HAPPENED TO THE DECISION. Eteocles' decision, my decision. Your decision, our decision. Cats', dogs', birds', bees' decisions. Bats. Mosquitos. The prisoner's deed. We must DO. Sunless. My fellow passengers. Everyone is sitting, I note. At dawn. Almost all the seats taken. The car is mostly empty. How *full* is the car? Half full? One third full? One quarter full? But I mean rush-hour FULL. Times Square FULL.

---

231 The light in the subway—underground, un-elevated—always reminded me of Kafka's 'whitish dazzle of fog.' Joseph K.'s first interrogation, in the Court in the attics (p. 46).

> Here K. was interrupted by a shriek from the end of the hall; he peered from beneath his hand to see what was happening, for the reek of the room and the dim light together made a whitish dazzle of fog. It was the washer-woman, whom K. had recognized as a potential cause of disturbance from the moment of her entrance. Whether she was at fault or not, no one could tell.

Packed. Sardines. Pole-grabbers, strap-hangers, and wish-me-luckers, writhing in the void. Extreme sports. A seat on the subway is a joy forever. It takes luck, skill, or circumstance. In my case, circumstance: I'm an end-of-the-liner, I always have a seat. Actually, I should say a *beginning*-of-the-liner, but no one ever puts it that way, why not? Traveling end-to-end, or beginning-to-beginning, or end-to-beginning, or beginning-to-end. Who can say. Just words. This is *not* what I mean by a fork. Anyway, it takes stamina. All this traveling, back, forth, forth, back, just imagine if I'd been grabbing poles or hanging from straps, or worse, all this time. What would Billy Budd, what would Benardete have to say about that! Unimaginable. I could never have done them justice, such as I have. Or haven't. I've tried. Crushed like a sardine, writhing in the void, for two days and nights. I don't even want to think about it. It's not in the Logic. No, it has nothing to do with the decision to consider *thinking as such*. Or with the decision of the pure idea to determine itself as external idea either? I hope not! Free release—absolutely free, sez Zappa—the *externality of space and time*. Nature. The subway? No! The subway is the realm of shadows. What about the street? SOUND SCREECH Bergen Street, that was a short stretch. Now we have a long one to Jay, then another long one to York. Near the Navy Yard. The true path, no coming and no going. Why does the *supremely free* make the *supreme sacrifice* of *freely releasing itself into nature?* Good question. How can supreme freedom *express itself*—express its *freedom*—if not by *freely sacrificing itself?* By freely sacrificing its freedom. Necessarily? A *necessary* sacrifice? What else could it DO. A decision. I raise my hands and spread out all my fingers! A question: What is a decision, and what does making a decision mean? It's hard to say. It takes practice. Training. Mediation. Meditation. The zendo. Travel. The sword of no-mind. HEGEL GODDAMIT. Let's ask him.

Bless my soul, here he is now! Here, now, at dawn in the realm of shadows. Speak! He says: Logically speaking, it's a question of freedom and necessity. Their relation. Separated and inseparable. Contradiction. As we noted, he says (he remembers everything!), speaking of being-is-nothing decisions we said there's a *bare minimum* of freedom in 'I decide to brush my teeth' or 'From this day forth the official language of this Banana Republic will be Swedish.' But it's the zero degree. Well, OK, you say, so it must be the *maximum* degree of *necessity*, but you're completely wrong! *Mein Gott* how wrong you are! *The ground zero of freedom is the ground zero of necessity.* This is what practically no one notes! This, for example, is what Eteocles does *not* note. His problem isn't his lack of freedom, *mein Gott*, no! It's his lack of necessity. Didn't Benardete note, in a note to his second Note, that the *Septem* is the only play of Aeschylus where *anágke* never occurs. See what I mean! This is why a question like 'what a decision is and what making a decision means' is so tricky. You wonder—Is my decision *free?*—but that's not the point. Is it *necessary?* That's not the point either! What matters is the *relation*. And this, logically speaking, is tricky. Read my book, *Wissenschaft der Logik*. It's a long one, my longest. Some people think it's a journey from the zero degree of freedom to the supremely free, and this isn't wrong. But then they think, it must also make its merry way from absolute necessity to no necessity at all, and this is pure unadulterated *Scheiß*. Deep *Scheiß*. A river of *Scheiß*. Freedom, necessity, it's all about the *relation*. *Mensch*, it's complicated, this isn't kindergarten stuff. Let's see if I can explain it. You haven't got a beer by any chance? — Ye gods, I'm raving. New York Transit System, end of March, 1972, Hegel, *himself*, asking me, *myself*, if I've got a beer. Yes! We have no bananas. — No beer. *Pazienza*. Let's see what I wrote at the end of my big book, four pages from the end, where I try to say, in a pretty big nutshell, what I mean by a *system of totality*—my journey in the realm of shadows from 'being is nothing' (simplicity, immediacy) through the many forms ('the determinateness that was the result') in which immediacy is mediated. Just remember this: it's all freedom and necessity *together*, always the same *and always different.* Together! Like SAMs and B-52s. The relation! Complexity. Difficulty and the Double. Not for kindergarteners, no! No one shows a child the sky. Now, where am I? Look! I wrote this:[232]

> We have shown that the determinateness that was a result is itself, by virtue of the form of simplicity into which it has withdrawn, *a fresh beginning*; as this beginning is distinguished from its predecessor precisely by that determinateness, cognition rolls onwards from content to content....
> In the absolute method *the concept maintains itself in its otherness.* ....
>
> This *expansion* may be regarded as the moment of content... the universal is *communicated* to the wealth of content. But the relationship also has its second, negative or dialectic side. The enrichment proceeds in the *necessity* of the concept, it is held by it, and each determination is a reflection-into-self. Each new stage of *going forward*... is also a withdrawal inwards, and the greater *extension* is equally a *higher intensity*. The richest is therefore the most concrete and most *subjective*, and that which withdraws itself into the simplest depth is the mightiest and most all-embracing. The highest, most concentrated point is the *pure personality* that, solely through the absolute dialectic that is its nature, no less *embraces and holds everything within itself*, because it makes itself *the supremely free*—the simplicity that is the first immediacy and universality.

---

232 This is Miller one hundred percent, zero di Giovanni. I transcribed it myself three years ago, for the ending of The Empty Shield.

It is in this manner that each step of the *advance* in the process... while getting further away from the indeterminate beginning is also *getting back nearer to it*.... The method, *which thus winds itself into a circle* .....

Mein junge Freund, I know, the last three pages get even trickier—the circle is a circle of circles, truth only comes to be itself through the negativity of immediacy, I know, it's been a hard ride all the way. The next decision. 'The idea *freely releases* itself, absolutely certain of itself and internally at rest. Thanks to this freedom, the *form of its determinateness* is just as absolutely free—the *externality of space and time* absolutely existing for itself without subjectivity.' The supremely free that supremely freely sacrifices its freedom, *completing its self-liberation* in the science of spirit. Logically speaking, supreme freedom and supreme necessity, together. 'Without subjectivity'—but, *mein Kind*, you, *yourself*, need to figure out what a decision is and what making a decision means. Subjectively. Personally politically. As for me, *myself*—I need a beer.

Gone! He's gone. What a thirsty ghost. The Sorrow of War.[233] The *necessity* of the concept. I think I see what he means. Possibly. As the Roshi said, it must have some rules, theory, truth in its activity. In the Logic as a system of thought-determinations, the concept has 'the capacity to *determine* itself, that is, to give itself a content, and to give it as a *necessary content*.' The concept, which is *free*, has—or rather *is*—its own necessity. Pretty tricky. 'The enrichment proceeds in the *necessity* of the concept.' I can't get this line out of my head. There's no escape. The *freedom* of self-realization is equally a higher *necessity*. Just as being *is* nothing, freedom *is* necessity. The greater extension, a higher intensity. *Pure*

233 See, again, Bao Ninh's Novel of North Vietnam. Hungry ghosts. The Jungle of Screaming Souls.

personality—the supremely free, because absolutely necessary. But, ye gods, A DECISION! HEGEL! You were just about to tell me, possibly, what a decision is and what making a decision means, and you stepped out for a beer. 'Tell me'—no. Give me a few clues. Help me figure it out *for myself.*

SOUND SCREECH. Jay Street. Wow! He's back! Here he is again. Dead philosophers must have their own secret ways of getting beers.[234] Purity, body, and flavor. Of going and coming with no-going and no-coming. After all, as Dogen-zenji said, death is an expression complete this moment. Death does not turn into birth. Accordingly, death is understood as no-death. You do not call winter the beginning of spring. Here he goes again.

Mensch! What a decision is and what making a decision means. This question complicates things. Let's take the fork and the prongs. There are no chopsticks in my philosophy, and nobody eats spaghetti with their hands, not even Alberto Sordi. You're quite right, Eteocles has prongs but he's lost his fork. His placard-men are badly infinite. *Jawoll.* Bad infinity. Excellent, *mein junge Freund.* Jersey commuters, cockroaches leaping from chandeliers. Never mind trips around the world, what matters is Atlantic City in the summer. The crunch crunch crunch of cockroaches under your feet when you walk around your flat, but they're the Elder Statesmen of our *Weltgeschichte.* Absolutely! The history of the world. Good infinity, bad infinity, another tricky question. GAM/bomb/exile. YOU HAVE A FORK. Bad! Necessary! Good! Deep *Scheiß.* Supreme freedom. — HEGEL! Hold your horses, they're prancing around the meadow. — Prance, prance, it's the best way to control them. Never beat a dead horse, it's a waste of time and energy. A fork may be bad infinity but it's not all bad, you said so yourself. The sunless dead! You've figured out, *yourself*, that Eteocles has lost his fork, if he ever had one. If he ever knew he had one. Or, even if he never had one, he

---

234 I *don't* mean by trading ears for them.

lost it. Lost it! Is this good, bad, or ugly? So be it. He and his spy have badly infinitely cooked up a BIG POT OF PRONGS and LOST THE FORK. Rules, theory, truth, *Auf Wiedersehen meine Lieben!* Goodbye my sweethearts goodbye. King and Spy of Thebes, and they don't even know what an *image* is. Images are TYRANTS, if they get out of control they'll *usurp everything*, as your friend Benardete notes, in his Note. We have placards, we have men, and we have placard-men. Relations, *mein junge Freund*. LOGIC, goddamit. MY logic. True infinity! Read my book! Prongs, *Mensch!* Their images run wild and boil over. They think their mice are *chained*, but *mein Gott* how wrong they are! The mice are absolutely free and snapping at their balls. Tyranny! Your country's specialty these days, all these wars in the defense of tyranny. Specialty of the house. Defend the City! Eteocles puts all his chips on images, without even knowing it—without ever *thinking* about it—and they boil over and usurp everything. Reciprocal suicide, I said so *myself*. Pollute the City. Bring me my greaves. Past the care of gods. What sort of logic is this! A dirge. Can you call this reasoning? A DECISION. What decision! What fork! A fork is not like a *bad* cold, *nein*, it's a *bad* motherfucker.[235] How can Eteocles ask himself what a decision is and what making a decision means if he's lost his fork! Thrown it out the window. Shat on it, he and his spy *together*. A fistful of prongs, and *buona notte*. Forget it! A snowball in hell. *Let this be a lesson to you*, *mein junge Freund*. You have a fork! Rejoice! Sing 'An die Freude'! It's heroic. Catchy. 'Joy, beautiful spark of the gods, daughter from Elysium.' Sing sing sing. Sing *I have a fork!* Don't *worry* about bad infinity, you *need* it, badly! Eteocles' placard-men are badly infinite, his so-called 'empty shield' is swarming with shadows. Teeming. Bursting at the seams. Empty your shield *yourself*, my young friend. No one will do it for you. *Your* placard-men, *together*, are a true infinity. You have a fork! So *ask yourself*, *yourself*, what a decision is and what making a decision means.

---

235 I told you this was extremely Hegelian.

Never stop asking! Never ever stop![236] I, *myself*, can't tell
you. If only I had a beer I could put this a little better, but, let
me put it this way: True infinity *takes* the finite as such—the
fork—and the totality of finite moments—the prongs, the ten-
thousand things, as Buddhists and Indians put it—*together*.
Separated, and inseparable. Forget about whole *pictures*, they'll
just give you grief. Pictures, images—*Mensch!* we're talking
about logic. Thinking as such, not picture-thinking. Realm of
shadows, as I, myself, so poetically put it. No tyrants here,
no compulsion. Where freedom is necessity. Where shadows
end in endless shadow. *Mein Gott!* You still want to know: How
do a fork and its prongs *together* become a decision? Free,
necessary, responsible. 'Become'? You mean, the vanishing of
vanishing? Being is nothing never goes away. *Mensch!* A beer!
I need a beer! Long-dead German philosophers need beers.
Avoid dead horses, *mein junge Freund,* and never forget that
you, *yourself*, have a fork. Take a stab at it, and *Viel Glück!*

Gone again. *Viel Glück.* Of no fortune. A name to come.
Auf Wiedersehen, see you again. Sometime. Someplace.
This unfortunate war. Lots of luck. Break a leg. The train has
stopped. F Train, end of March, 1972. No sound, no screech.
York Street, of all places. Near the Navy Yard. I bet Hegel has
gone off to look for that chick, in the dawn's early light. Kleist!
Have no fear, my dear Hegel, she'll tell it like it is. To you! long
dead, and still looking for beers. On/off the New York subway.
'Magic, which does not create but summons.'[237] WHAT JUSTICE?
Forgiveness, the supreme sacrifice, the seventh placard-man
said, to me, *myself*. A mouthful. A supreme mouthful. Great

---

236 A confession: In 1972—end of March, end of June, LOVE IT OR LEAVE IT—I *did
not ask myself what a decision is and what making a decision means.* I 'just did it'?
Decided? Much later, I started *wondering*: How did I come to make that decision?
How did I get here, where I've been ever since? *I can't remember ever actually
deciding anything.* I do remember that I didn't feel particularly free. The prisoner's
deed. Philosophy begins in wonder. Over the years I've wondered about this more
and more. I started asking, *and I've never stopped.*
237 Kafka, *Diaries 1914-1923*, p. 195. I might add (*Diaries 1910-1913*, p. 233), 'Even if
no salvation should come, I want to be worthy of it at every moment.'

sense of justice. *Michael Kohlhass.* 'Better to be a dog than a man, if I'm to be kicked around!' What joy! I have a fork. Hegel! 'Yet whoever claims that nothing exists that carries in itself a contradiction in the form of an identity of opposites is at the same time requiring *that nothing living shall exist*. For the power of life, and still more the might of the spirit, consists precisely in positing contradiction in itself, enduring it, and overcoming it.' He also said, somewhere: 'I am the struggle between the extremes of finitude and infinity. I am not one of the fighters locked in battle, but both, and I am the struggle itself. I am fire and water.' He says these things often. He also said, 'reciprocal suicide.' No Manhattan/Brooklyn Bridge over the East/West River, no. This is the F. My train, so to speak. Get ready for *a very long stretch*, under Brooklyn, under the East/West River in the invisible unknowable Rutgers Tube, all the way to under East Broadway. Henry Rutgers, Revolutionary War hero, with *two* streets named after him on the Lower East Side—Henry Street and Rutgers Street—to say nothing of his Tube under the East/West River. The subway, the street. Hadean darkness. Dawn's early light, and not so early, lots of people digging into their cornflakes already, and Hegel looking for beers. But Hegel is *on logical time*, for him any and all times are time to look for a beer. Some people breakfast at 7, some at noon, but the breakfasters at 7 do not breakfast at noon, and vice versa. At last, a genuine Kierkegaardian either/or. Let's fry some fish, I have fish to fry.

Why are the placard-men in the subway and not on the street? Ask Hegel. It's obvious! The subway is the realm of shadows, and the placard-men are a true infinity. Logically speaking. The system of logic. What do they decide? They decide to be placard-men, and here they are. But 'logically speaking' is not the only manner of speaking we have. How about 'personally speaking'? How about 'politically speaking'? How about personally-politically and politically-personally speaking? Whispering. Muttering. Shouting. Yelling 'Vietnam veteran'! Screaming BOMB HANOI! Logic! As Kafka didn't quite put it, eminently unHegelianly, 'The subway is doubtless unshakable, but it cannot withstand a man who wants to go on living.'[238] The first decision, thinking as such. The second decision: 'freely releases itself... externality of space and time... without subjectivity.' I haven't finished with this. Just a moment, I'll be back. 'The negativity of immediacy.' Mediation. Meditation!

> Sit without moving, without expecting anything, as if you were in your last moment. Moment after moment you feel your last instant.
> Calmness of mind is beyond the end of your exhalation. If you exhale smoothly, without even trying to exhale, you are entering into the complete perfect calmness of your mind. *You do not exist anymore....* If you are still alive, naturally you will inhale again. 'Oh, I'm still alive! Fortunately or unfortunately!' Then you start to exhale and fade into emptiness.[239]

This unfortunate war! The curse of Vietnam. Seven placard-men in the subway, or ten-thousand placard-men in the subway. All Vietnam veterans. For the war, against the war, in-between. Winter soldiers, summer soldiers. Winter, spring, summer or fall/ All you have to do is call. *The war in the subway?* Kid me not. Pure unadulterated *Scheiß*. Deep *Scheiß*. A river of *Scheiß*. An amigo stabbed in the ass. A very minor skirmish. The war in the subway, in a manner of speaking. A placard-man manner. Logically speaking. But the war *itself?* Strafing. Burning villages. Hell no! The war is in the street. Sure, Newark, Detroit, Watts. Plus the *war within*, a major war.

---

238 They didn't have subways in Prague at the time. So he said, '*Logic* is doubtless unshakable... ' Last page of *The Trial*.
239 *Not Always So*, pp. 5–6.

But the placard-man war is not in the subway, it's in Vietnam.
The American War in Vietnam, in the defense of tyranny. The
millions of Vietnamese killed, most of them women, children,
the elderly. The zillion tons of bombs, the mines, which will
go on exploding forever. On the roof. In the mind. Forever
and ever. Better to maim than to kill, say the brass, and their
band. Forever. Logic is doubtless unshakable. WHAT LOGIC?
Shit, ten-thousand placard-men, I'm sure plenty of them have
WHAT LOGIC? on their placards, truly infinitely. Or not? WHAT
LOGIC? The logic of the subway? But the subway IS logic. It's
the street that's illogical. The American street. The streets of
Vietnam, such as they are. The American War. The American
carnage. When when when will someone stand up and say:
This American carnage stops right here and stops right now.[240]
Someone—I mean some *President*. Of the United States. We
the people can say it all we like. We winter soldiers say it all
the time, in the subway, on the street. Fuck free-fire zones.
Fuck B-52s. Fuck napalm and Agent Orange. Fuck ears for
beers. Fuck the carnage of Empire, of Imperialism, of Tyranny.
Watch out for the chickens coming home to roost. Beware!
Chickens can be dangerous birds, especially when they feel
humiliated and there are zillions of them. Coming home to
roost. Deep shit. A decision. What do WE DECIDE? 'In the

---

240 Trump! I enjoyed your speech, your Inaugural Address, January 20, 2017. After
perilous frontiers, shining cities on hills, fires in minds, it was time for some plain
speaking. Let me quote this, for posterity. Lest we forget!

A nation exists to serve its citizens. Americans want great schools for their
children, safe neighborhoods for their families, and good jobs for themselves.
These are just and reasonable demands of righteous people and a righteous
public.

But for too many of our citizens, a different reality exists: mothers and children
trapped in poverty in our inner cities; rusted out factories scattered like
tombstones across the landscape of our nation; an education system flush
with cash, but which leaves our young and beautiful students deprived of all
knowledge; and the crime and gangs and the drugs that have stolen too many
lives and robbed our country of so much unrealized potential.

This American carnage stops right here and stops right now.

Trump! I also loved your immortal line (referring to Vladimir Putin): 'There are a lot
of killers. We've got a lot of killers. What, do you think our country's so innocent?'

end/ The love you take/ Is equal to the love/ You make.'[241] WE DECIDE!—another placard plenty of placard-men must have. Logically speaking. We decide to be placard-men. We decide to end the war! *Viel Glück!* Gone again. Spirits rejoice! I have a fork! A decision. To make. Free, necessary, responsible. That I can live with for the rest of my life.

A *logical* decision? WHAT LOGIC? Is there one logic of the subway and another logic of the street? A logic of logic and a logic of the City and of history? A logical logic and a political logic, one timeless and the other in time? A logic of *pure personality* and a logic of the externality of space and time, *without subjectivity.* A *logic* of nature? WHAT LOGIC? Can we call it logic? Nature, the *unfree.* Is *nature* the street, or is it on the subway, somehow? Where's the decision? On the street or in the subway? Does a decision *mean nothing* without logic? And by *logic* I mean *Hegel's* logic. Great, I said fish to fry, but this is a Moby Dick to roast! Which takes a *bad* motherfucker of an oven. Which I don't have. But, then again, who does. OK my friends, young, old, in-between, I'm back: here comes my last stab at the last page of Hegel's Logic. (My last stab for this trip anyway.) One last *little* stab. Last paragraph, just before the *decision* of the pure idea to determine itself as external idea.

> The idea, in positing itself as the absolute *unity* of the pure concept and its reality and thus collecting itself in the immediacy of being, is the *totality* in this form — nature. This determination, however, is nothing that *has become,* is not a *transition*... The pure idea into which the determinateness or reality of the concept is itself raised into concept is rather an *absolute liberation*... In this freedom, there is no transition that takes place; the simple being to which the idea determines itself remains perfectly transparent to it: it is the idea that in its determination abides with itself. The transition is to be grasped,

---

241 The Beatles, 'The End,' 1969.

therefore, in the sense that the idea *freely releases* itself, absolutely certain of itself and internally at rest. Thanks to this freedom, the *form of its determinateness* is just as absolutely free—the *externality of space and time* absolutely existing for itself *without subjectivity*.

Hegel! What a trip! In two pages, from *pure personality* and the *supremely free* to a *self-liberation* in which the supremely free freely releases itself into—into what? Let's face it—into the *supremely unfree*. Logically speaking. Necessity. Nature, with its mountain streams, trees, meadows, volcanos, tornados, and hurricanes, and which *decides nothing*. But on the street we decide lots of things. With or without logic? Unfree and irresponsibly? Personally/politically. Hegel! What are you saying, exactly. If 'being is nothing' is the ground zero of freedom does that make it the 110th floor of necessity? No! Your Logic as a journey from maximum to minimum necessity is pure unadulterated *Scheiß*, you said so yourself, in no uncertain terms, I'd say. Logically speaking. But, Hegel, WHY, exactly, does the supremely free—no, not *become* externality without subjectivity, no, it *freely releases itself* into absolute unfreedom. WHY? You don't really say, and now you're the devil knows where, looking for beers. *Pazienza.* I can only guess. Let me guess. I guess, only *if you're fully free* can you decide not to be it. Decide to be a slave. But who on this mortal coil is fully free? And if you were, would you call your free release self-liberation? I'd call it *self-sacrifice*. A big one. Ask Norman Morrison! The supreme sacrifice. Forgiveness? Let me guess again. You're *fully free* when you *truly ask* what a decision is and what making a decision means. Endlessly. The night journey that begins *and ends* in shadow. The subway, permanently. But I have a fork! Spirits rejoice! But shadows have no forks, there's no such thing as a shadow fork. The true path. Watch out! I'm trying again. No coming, no going.

Another fish, to fry.

Freedom and necessity—the *relation. Mensch*, it's complicated. But if you—if I!—*confuse logic with practice*—with politics, history, ethics—goddamit the whole kettle of fish *will boil over*. Badly. Badly infinitely, logically speaking. Practically speaking, a wide, wide river. If I say 'the ground zero of freedom is the ground zero of necessity' in his *logic*, Hegel will pat me on the back and, possibly, grab me a beer. But if I refer it to politics, even the chickens will laugh (as the Italians put it). The first rule of politics is: zero freedom equals absolute necessity. Everyone knows it! Birds, bees, educated fleas. In the political world—in *political autobiography*—the ground zero of freedom is indeed the 110th floor of necessity, and the tower is *built to last*. There is *absolutely no ground* for a decision. We need to build the ground *right under our feet*, ourselves, in and through the strenuous effort of asking *what a decision is and what making a decision means*. Never ever stop asking, Hegel told me, *himself*. Speaking *logically. Scheiß*, river of *Scheiß*, but I'm speaking *practically* now. Politically. Responsibly. Personally/politically. Never ever stop asking! Great, but what about *crossing* the river of shit. Decide, or decided for. A decision. Spirits rejoice! Let me repeat myself! One last time, possibly. The same question, again: WHY does the supremely free freely release itself into externality, supremely *sacrificing* itself? Why? *Mein Gott*, it's pure Zen! Ask the Roshi, ask Dogen-zenji. It's no-mind. A bright mirror. All reflected in it, not reflected in it. The empty shield. 'When there is no gaining idea in what you do, then you do something.' No thought, no idea of gaining, of attaining. This is supreme freedom. And supreme necessity. Hegel is ON the subway but Zen IS the subway. The supreme sacrifice? I don't know. I know that if my shield is not empty, I *need* to empty it. The strenuous effort of the concept—of thinking in and through the concept—is the supreme discipline not only of thinking but of doing. I *know* this, *unconsciously, with no-mind.* The prisoner's deed. I *spoke* with the seventh-placard-man.

— Forgive the country that made us all victims? All of us together. Victims.
— Hard to say. Can we ever forgive? Forgiveness is the supreme sacrifice. Can we make it? It may also be the ultimate liberation. *Self*-liberation.

A heroic idea. WHAT JUSTICE? I've been thinking, Hegel's logic, this journey in the subway, is an *unimaginable* tangle of logic and practice. Of logic, politics, and history. Of the Sorrow of War. *It has no image.* No placard, man, or placard-man. Fate, compulsion, I really don't know. The tyranny of images. The true path. I know where my country is coming from, and greatly fear for where it is going. I know I don't want to go there along with it, a submissive fellow traveler. Can I forgive it for what it's done in its war against life and freedom in Vietnam? And for its 'next decisions,' its future wars in the defense of tyranny? No, I can't. I'm not the seventh placard-man, not a placard-man at all, not a true infinity. Perhaps they can make the supreme placard-man sacrifice, I can't. Won't. 'You plan the wars you masters of men plan the wars and point the way and we will point the gun.' That's how I feel right now.[242] I'm not a hero. There is no Hegelian hero. No shadow hero. A decision. The prisoner's deed. How do a fork and its prongs *together* become a decision? True infinity *takes* the finite as such—the fork—and the totality of finite moments—the prongs—*together*. Separated, and inseparable.

---

242 For the record, it's how I feel today. More than ever. 45 years and so many wars later. I won't list them. Jimmy Carter on the American War in Vietnam: 'The destruction was mutual.' What a despicable thing to say. Madeleine Albright on sanctions in Iraq that killed half a million children: 'We think the price is worth it.' How about 'rusted out factories scattered like tombstones across the landscape of our nation.' Take your pick. Chopsticks. A Chinese menu. The carnage stops right here and stops right now!

HEGEL! *In the subway*. Get yourself a beer. Do I still have an apple? The supreme freedom to sacrifice its freedom *thanks* to its freedom. A true thanker. A decision. Absolutely! What joy, I have a fork. I have traveled. This long journey in the realm of shadows. There is no Hegelian hero. The *Mensch* is cursed. 'From out that shadow.' Not 'logical decision' (of which we have only two examples) but compulsive freedom of choice. 'From out that shadow' our ultimate destination is exemplified by Eteocles, 'an inhabitant of Plato's cave... whose serendipity proves to be his fate.' A decision. Street, subway, SEEING the way does not mean FOLLOWING the way. Necessarily. The true path, no coming, no going. Here, possibly, Hegel and Zen part ways. Possibly. Logic, a matter of mind; Zen, of no-mind. Possibly. It's very complicated. Anyway, no happy ending. No victory. *Whatever* I, *myself*, decide, will not be self-liberation, it will be *defeat*. Spirits rejoice. A presumed suicide, possibly, or murdered, not likely, who knows. Some say he took the Statue of Liberty ferry and jumped off as it neared Liberty Island. Beyond the fork, spirits rejoice. Defeat. No Hegelian hero. The realm of shadows. SCREECH SOUND SCREECH, East Broadway. I wonder what's up, up there on East Broadway. On the street, practically, and illogically, speaking. East Broadway and Grand, to be precise, where the neon climbs. The madman climbs. We climb. Broome, with its beautiful buildings, is one block north, but, when the light is right, Grand has a gleam all its own. A gleaming glimmer. Gently throbbing. Logically speaking? Ask Hegel, if you like.

I'd like to. But the F is relentless. Life goes on, so to speak. Life, death, in-between. Logic, illogic. Freedom and unfreedom. Necessary, and unnecessary. Just as well. 'On, on with the favoring wind! Let this wave of hell engulf all Laius' kin.' The curse. *Viel Glück!* This unfortunate war. An apple. Has its fate. Why? Why not? Why? Logic in the world of practice. WHAT JUSTICE? WE DECIDE! WHAT LOGIC? I do have one apple left.

But who are the puppeteers of fate? Placards, men, placard-men. The system of logic is the realm of shadows. An idea just pops into my head. Fine. No problem. The problem is that then I start to chase it. Like a cat chasing her tail. OK. But, then, this idea I'm chasing leads me to another idea. And I chase it. From one idea, another. Another. Another again. A chain. Reality? What reality. An uncertain reality. A decision. What a decision is and what making a decision means. WHAT FORK? Never ever stop asking. The supreme sacrifice. You *ask forgiveness* for your sacrifice, because you *cannot forgive*, you cannot *make* the supreme sacrifice. WHAT FREEDOM? If my shield is not empty, I *need* to empty it. 'Analogies,' Dogen says. 'Practice, enlightenment, and people are like this.' The political *world,* the logical *world*—wait! WHAT LOGICAL WORLD? WORLD means time, history, the City, Defend the City! A logical *world?* Hegel! *Your* koan. Are you puzzled? Listen to Dogen-zenji:

> A fish swims in the ocean, and no matter how far it swims there is no end to the water. A bird flies in the sky, and no matter how far it flies there is no end to the air. However, the fish and the bird have never left their elements. When their activity is large their field is large. When their need is small their field is small. Thus, each of them totally covers its full range, and each of them totally experiences its realm. If the bird leaves the air it will die at once. If the fish leaves the water it will die at once.

Ask, ask, never ever stop asking. The City is our *world*, logic is our *element.* Be it the element of mind or of no-mind, so be it. What self! Zuikan? Yes! Hegel! You said so yourself! The street! The sea! The sky! Nothing has *become*, there is no *transition*. So how do we get there? Great! Absolute liberation! Free release! Logical, illogical, or neither/nor? I have an idea! I raise my hands and spread out all my fingers! One last time.

A friend of mine gave me this idea, an artist, a great artist. A political artist. *Abstract* art, separation of the inseparable. Hegel! No becoming, no transition. Pray tell, how do we get there? I'll never stop asking, but here's an answer. Here, now: ART. No *system* will get us there. 'System'—of logic, 'the transit system'—means putting together, uniting, *giving form*. The system—the realm of shadows—*is there*, exists. Form exists. Mind exists. But so does no-mind. How does one pass through this gateless gate? My friend said,

> FORM! I work day and night to create FORM. Form, and matter; shadow, and substance. I work all the time, I never stop, I'm a samurai fighting his fight in the zendo. Then, when I finally GET IT, I LET IT GO. I SMASH IT TO A PULP. This is art.

He stretched out his arm, his hand almost in a fist—not clenched, a gentle fist—FORM—then, suddenly, he opened his hand, decisively, and let the invisible bird fly up, high into the sky. Coltrane! Coltrane! Zen has no gates! A pulp! Smashed. Let it go. I call this a decision that is no-decision. Chained mice. The tyranny of images. Free release. EMPTY THE MIRROR, let *my* placard-men *go*. They *are* the decision. My decision. This is the message of the empty shield. Zuikan? Yes! What self, say I, the happy messenger. Nothing reflects, nothing can be reflected. 'The empty mirror. If you could really understand that, there would be nothing left here for you to look for.'

The Pequot.
Sacrifice.
Norman Morrison.

From out this shadow.
The zendo.
Never stop asking.

OK, with an ad in the *Village Voice* I should be able to get maybe $500 for the contract on my apartment, with a few decent pieces of furniture thrown in. I have a little over a thousand dollars saved from my nights driving the taxi. I know a guy who sells very cheap plane tickets to Europe. I have good friends in London, with a cottage in Sussex, where I can spend next summer, reading Hegel's Logic. [As I in fact did.] Ezra Pound in Venice. May he live so long. [He died on 1 November 1972.] Beyond the fork.

SOUND. Blue jays on the roof.
Coltrane! Coltrane!

A decision? Be my guest. 'He just stepped out.'
The prisoner's deed. With that alone we have to do.
'Forward! Into the slave's life.'

This last screech was Delancey. My stop.

Just ease these darbies at the wrist, and roll me over fair,
I am sleepy and the oozy weeds about me twist.

EPILOGUE: *political autobiography*

I had remarkable conversations with my grandfather. I went to Atlantic City to see him every few months when I was at NYU. The last time, of course, was in June, 1972. I told him I was unhappy with life in the United States—with the political life, which he knew. Vietnam. Injustice. I said I had decided to *try* to do something about it, not accept it passively. 'When you were unhappy with life in the Old Country you *did* something.' 'To accept it was to die,' he said. 'But what will you do?' he asked. I said I wanted to write a book that would change people's minds, make even just a few people see things differently. It's the only political action I can believe in. 'If you believe in it, do it,' he said. 'To have any chance of doing it I have to get outside of this life. I have to move back to the Old Country.' 'It will take a long time,' he said. 'Yes, I think so.' He said, 'I think it will be a very long book.' Unfortunately, this was our last conversation.

from *separation of the inseparable* (1977)

I saw the slow leaves falling,
(they are bright and swirl,
like snow in an old man's eyes),
drifting, swirling, falling,

until I became a plain white bird,
high, nearly still,
in a dream,
high and alone and blind
above the sea you had left behind.

POSTSCRIPT: *a palimpsest*

I decided to write The Empty Shield after my trip to the U.S. Consulate in Milan on June 15, 2014. Its 'future consequences.' FORM. First, in a single afternoon, I wrote 'An Enemy of the People.' There was a lovely gentle rain in Venice that afternoon, without it I could never have completed the story.

I was riled up. I knew that the cucumber was up my ass. The 'American War,' right here, right now. Strafing. Bombing of villages. Ears for beers. Obama's anti-anti-American technology, from drones to political bureaucracy. Not as blunt as Trump's but no less insidious. What ever happened to LOVE IT OR LEAVE IT? 'It just stepped out.' Amerika! It's everywhere. 'Hi, I'm Patrick. How'r y'all cocksucking commies doin' today? Ready or not, we'll fuck you all! Patriot Act. USA Freedom Act. Homeland Security will fuck you. The State Department will fuck you. The IRS will fuck you. Your mom's apple pie will fuck you. Freedom! Fuck you! Have a good day!'

Why oh why do they hate us, and knock down our Towers?

For the record, from when I ASKED FOR IT (so to speak) until my 'expatriation' was 'approved' by the U.S. government, I went through twenty-two months of 'misery, terror, and death.' Hillary! Make war not love! Kerry! Winter soldier! The IRS! No-bullshit fuck-you threats. Big time. It turned out that I owed them $3,200 for the previous six years—not *per* year, but for all six together. Ye gods I nearly bankrupted the country. If I hadn't found Steve, the expatriation lawyer, they'd be playing cat and chained mouse with me to this day. Steve told them (*not* in these very words), 'After twenty-two months, still no Certificate of Loss of Nationality. Expatriation! Law of the land! He should have had it within 90 days. Time's up. USA Freedom-To-Fuck-You Act. Fuck him or free him. Take your pick. A decision. Chinese menu. Beat him to death with your chopsticks, if you think it's worth it.' I got my Certificate *the next day*. Express Courier. From Milan. My cat rejoiced. The tension had been terrible. Vicious. Killing.

Why? Why all this horror?

Steve taught me some interesting things about American history. Everyone knows the Revolutionaries were riled up about taxation without representation, but they were also protesting the English doctrine of 'perpetual allegiance.' The Brits denied their subjects 'the natural right of expatriating themselves' and the Revolutionaries were riled up about this too. UN-AMERICAN, they screamed, and the states wrote the right into their laws. In 1868 the U.S. Congress enacted legislation declaring that 'expatriation is a natural and inherent right of all people.' They said so in no uncertain terms. Steve sent me this document, it's the LAW OF THIS GREAT LAND: 'Any declaration, instruction, opinion, order, or decision of any officers of this government which denies, restricts, impairs, or questions the right of expatriation, is hereby declared inconsistent with the fundamental principles of this government.' So they say. Spirits rejoice!

Even in my Postscript I've gotten off the track, traipsing off into the wilderness. My subject: *a palimpsest.* Make your point, dude.

OK, I'll do my best. Let me just preface it a little. I first got the idea for The Empty Shield when I took Dave Leahy's Greek

Tragedy course in the winter of 1969, but I really got it, bad, when Benardete gave me those two Notes. Believe me, I've never gotten over that, and never will. But the placard-men in the subway as a reality parallel to the Seven against Thebes? This hit me when I took the subway out to Brooklyn in the winter of 1986 or '87 to visit Dave. What a great idea! But how to make it into a story? Easier said than done. I thought about it a lot, but never *really* tried to *do* it. Until that trip to Milan. That grilling. Section Chief. Slimy shit-server. June. First, I wrote 'An Enemy of the People,' in a single afternoon. The next day, I got out my two translations of the *Septem*, Benardete's Notes, my many notes on Benardete's Notes, and a ton of notes on the so-called Vietnam War. I sat in the courtyard in front of my house, with my cat, Gilda, every afternoon all afternoon for two weeks. THINKING HARD. Making TONS of notes. A decision! Now or never! I'm going to *discover the relation* between the seven placard-men in the subway and the Seven against Thebes NOW. Or never. Cristóbal Colón. Believe me, it wasn't easy. No no no no, I didn't *invent* the placard-men, I *discovered* them. Mind and no-mind. Practice. Constancy. Transiency. Drawing *many* pictures of placards and shields. I did it. I discovered the relation, *noted* it, and started writing. Took a stab at it. I was doing fine. July to December, 2014. I'd already made it right up to the Sixth Gate! Then my first stab got stabbed. An ugly gash. Slimy motherfuckers. Six months and no Certificate of Loss of Nationality, and a BIG threat from the IRS. Big! January to June 2015, IRS full time. 24/7. New York tax lawyer. Bad time. Very bad. Horror. The silence of the Shield.

A palimpsest. June, again. Starting again by *doing it all over again*. From the very beginning. Rethinking and reliving it. All of it. Dead horse, awake! *Una parola*. Big changes. The first stab had *some* Zen, but not that much. Jan the Dutchman and his empty mirror. Second stab, *lots* of Zen. Lots and lots. The Roshi. Dogen-zenji. It made quite a difference. Still, from June to October I barely made it to the Seventh Gate. Political songs, they sure surprised me. How in the world did they get onto my Shield?

October 2015, the second stab stabbed, and very nearly *stabbed to death.* Still no Certificate and the SHIT was DEEP. 90 days. 22 months. Whatever happened to 'expatriation is a natural and inherent right of all people.' Scumbags. The LAW OF THIS GREAT LAND. I was ready to declare war, burn some villages *myself* (WHAT villages?), but Steve's cool head prevailed. His savvy. The end of October—freedom! A *Certified* Enemy of the People. My cat rejoiced, my mother rejoiced, my friends rejoiced. Free, but at what cost. The Shield and I both mortally wounded. Second silence of the Shield, *for eleven months.* Nervous breakdown. Physical breakdown. Panic attacks. Terror attacks. So be it. A long time.

September 2016: start *all over again.* Third stab. Read it all again, over and over. Rethink it, relive it, revive the dead horse. The might of the spirit. Rewrite *wildly.* A palimpsest. After all, the American War is the American War. My Lai is My Lai. A B-52 is a B-52. A winter soldier is a winter soldier. Monk is Monk. Coltrane! The Seventh Gate. *Free association.* Suddenly, *I speak with the seventh placard-man.* Wolfango! Palimpsest. Free it all up. Let it go. Smash it to a pulp! Coltrane! Coltrane! An invitation. A cry of liberation. Sheets of sound. EMPTY the shield. Good! The Gateless Gate. Wolfango's really helping me now. But my health is breaking down. A bad illness. Mouth, throat. Really bad. January 2017, just twenty pages from the end of the Shield. Stab *stabbed.* Too sick. Doctors, hospitals, biopsies, ugly words. Silence, again. Painful silence. In May—give it a stab. No, not possible. It's June again! Stab it! Suddenly, the sword of Zen mind! Every page a surprise. *To empty*, the Roshi says, means to have direct, pure experience. Satori. Hegel, *himself*, in the subway. The sudden way. No-mind. I never *imagined* such a thing.

When you give up, when you no longer want something, or when you do not try to do anything special, then you do something. When there is no gaining idea in what you do, then you do something.

'An artist friend of mine,' on the first and last page. Wolfango Intelisano. I met him in Sicily in 1986 and we immediately became friends for life. Political art. Abstract art. Brothers. Palimpsests. Do it over and over and over. Never stop asking. FORM. Form is form. There's nothing trickier in Zen than the relation between form and emptiness. A *bad* motherfucker. One of the *baddest*. There's a BIG story here. In a nutshell (*Zen Mind*, p. 41):

> [The sutra] says 'Form is emptiness and emptiness is form.' But if you attach to that statement, you are liable to be involved in dualistic ideas: here is you, form, and here is emptiness, which you are trying to realize through your form. So 'form is emptiness and emptiness is form' is still dualistic. But fortunately, our teaching goes on to say, 'Form is form and emptiness is emptiness.' Here there is no dualism.

Form is form and emptiness is emptiness. Wolfango had a word for it: *spappolare*. Smash it to a pulp. I see his gesture, here, now. His arm, his hand, the invisible bird *released*. Freedom *is* necessity. 'You do not call winter the beginning of spring, nor summer the end of spring.' *The responsibility of art.* Mind that is no-mind. A decision that is no-decision.

Venice, 15 June 2017

ACKNOWLEDGMENT

Gilda, my Zen cat, and I wrote this book together in ferocious solitude. With the book finished at last, the struggle to find a publisher was long and hard. Then came the equally long and amazingly complicated struggle to get permissions for the passages quoted. On this difficult voyage I have had two companions: my old friend David Webb of Staffordshire University, and my new magical friend Anthony Rudolf of the now permanently dormant Menard Press. Anthony, for me you have been like Joseph K.'s lawyer in *The Trial*, who 'lifts his client on his shoulders from the start and carries him bodily without once letting him down until the verdict is reached, and even beyond it.' *Merci mon ami! mon frère!*

BIOGRAPHY

Giacomo Donis, born in 1950 in the USA, living in Venice, Italy since 1972, made and sold thousands of beautiful inexpensive earrings for ten years to survive and then prosper, before forging ahead into the slave's life: thirty years translating philosophers, marxists, and art critics. *The Empty Shield* is his first book, to be followed by its companion volume, *An Abyss of Dreams: Tails of the Night of the World.*